HEIRS TO THE KINGDOM

Part Four

QUEEN OF THE VIOLET ISLE

Robin John Morgan

www.heirstothekingdom.com

First published in 2014 by Violet Circle Publishing
Print ISBN 978-1-910299-03-6
Digital ISBN 978-1-1910299-13-5

Cover Illustration
Concept and design, Robin John Morgan.
'The head of the Wolf' By J. M. Bailey.

All characters and scenarios in this publication are fictitious, any resemblance to real persons, living or dead, is purely coincidental.

British Library Cataloguing in Publication Data.
A catalogue record for this book is available from the British Library.

Violet Circle Publishing, Manchester, UK.

www.violetcirclepublishing.co.uk

For the dream that became my future.

Iona Jade.

Life.
Circle.
Line.

Green Circle of Life,
White Circle of Knowledge,
Whitelines of Time.

The coming of Violetline.
To unite everything into the minds of all.
Creating unity and harmony as one.

(The equation of Runestone Sapphire.)

I knew how much the old man had grown to love me, I too felt the same way, I saw so much of him in my husband Robert, and watching him in pain and dying was the most awful thing I think I will ever have to endure.

I will never forget that one day though, it was only hours before he would leave us forever, I had sat most of the night with him and had fallen asleep. I woke with a start in the early hours, and I sat back quickly and opened my eyes. Jake was awake and smiling, his dark brown eyes sparkled as he looked at me.

"I was right Jessie Love, I knew it all along." He gave a soft chuckle, and I smiled as I stroked his soft white hair back from his face. He had not looked this happy since before the tree had fallen on him.

"What are you right about Jake?" He looked up from the pillow and grinned at me.

"I was right about young Robbie, I always knew, and now I know for sure." He gave a cough as if he was using the last of his strength, and I worried he was using too much of his energy. Jake forced out the cough so he could speak. "Jessie he will do great things, he has been blessed in ways you may never understand, I have left him the Mere for it is a sacred place, he was made there Jessie love. You and my Rob did a wonderful thing that night; you have saved the line of the high lord, and my grandson will ensure its survival."

Jake seemed to chuckle as he slipped off into a dream, and for three hours his eyes seemed to wander the ceiling as if he was watching some other world, it was almost dawn when he spoke again, he just turned and looked at me and gave me that smile he always had for me.

"Oh Jessie love, you take care of my boy and young Robbie, watch him for he is what I have given my life preparing for. I love you Jessie, you have been the daughter I always wanted, take care my sweet." Jake smiled as he closed his eyes and I lost him to the other realm. He did not even give me enough time to tell him how much I loved him. I have never forgotten my father in law, I learned so much from him in the time he was around me. There is not a day since he left, I have not thought of him.

(The lost diary of Jessica Lox. Recovered by Runestone)

CHAPTER ONE.

THE FIGHTING SPIRIT OF LOXLEY

Robert John Loxley was young; he was seventeen, and had been restless at home not knowing what to do with his life. He was a new line and the future of a world that had been torn apart with the attack of the fatal virus the Red Death, twenty-six years earlier. The world that was known, had crumbled and the ways of the old past had been the only way to survive in a country that had become a hostile and wild place.

The power of nature had taken back what was hers, and the land had become a green mass of decay. It had taken a long time for groups to recover and bring about a new way of life, and as communities grew up, some looked to the old ways of what was now called 'the old ways of modern man.' Others like the community he lived in at Loxley had found a new way of living, a way of life that centred on the land and used little of the past to survive. Here the laws of the old woodsmen had come back, and the new communities looked to skills that had been feared lost from hundreds of years past.

Just before his seventeenth birthday Robbie had been told of his heritage and destiny, he had struggled to cope as one man rose to power to try to take over the country. With the girl, he had loved all his life, he had set off with a group of friends to try and stop the evil that was sweeping the land. Robbie was of the true line of Loxley, and without understanding at first why he had such skills with a long bow, he soon realised that what everyone had told him was true. He was the true ancestor of the man of Loxley himself, it was hard to believe but now he could see it. Robert John Loxley was indeed the hooded man returned.

Robbie had finally married Runestone on her birthday, which was also the first day of Samhain, the celebration in their Earth Faith of the woodsman's New Year, and the coming of winter and the ending of the days of light. He had returned from victory with the Specialists, and had planned the defence of York, it was hard work and he had spent a lot of time away from home out on the wild moor.

On the late afternoon of December 21st, he had returned, and with Runestone they led the vigil in the old stone circle above the stockade, and celebrated the winter solstice and the going down of the sun on the shortest day of the year.

Rune had smiled with joy as they headed back to the Mere in the darkness, and placed a fat heavy log on the fire to banish the darkness, and celebrated with wine and ale. It was a time of family, and together they decorated the house with fresh holly and mistletoe, and Rune laughed with delight as Robbie carried in a large potted pine to decorate with small decorations made of woven straw, and biscuits hung on red ribbon. The tree was topped with an elaborately made five pointed star of silver, which was their first ever Yule gift as a couple, and made by Jade's skilled hand. All round the house candles burned, casting a warm flickering glow across everything, as the house rang to the sound of Rune, as she giggled with happiness while she prepared the meal for all the family who would be arriving shortly.

Happiness in the Lox households ran high in the air, as the start of the calendar New Year came closer. Even with war in the air, happiness was about to visit the home of the hooded man again.

The stockade of Loxley was set back from the road; it was not the easiest of places to find, set high in the moors on the border of Derbyshire and Yorkshire. It was even harder to find after a week of heavy snow, especially after the clock had ticked one hour into the start of New Year's Day, and the year of 2039.

At one hour past midnight in a glade filled with soft snow, the sound of a small baby's cries echoed through the bare snow dressed trees, and around the ancient woodland that surrounded Robbie's Mere, and the house of the Lord Loxley and his wife Runestone. As if they all knew, the few animals that scratched in the snow for food stopped, and all raised their heads and looked in the direction of the wooden house. It was a sacred time when a power of the sight of the future was delivered by Stephanie and Jessica into the world.

The house rang with cheers, laughter, and the ringing of glasses of celebration, and somehow in the world of the woodland that was asleep for the winter, life seemed to tread round the trees, and bring tidings to all of a new addition to the noble line of Loxley.

The glade was silent as the large fluffy snowflakes glistened as they fell from the sky. The glass doors banged, as a group of cloaked figures came out of the house laughing and joking, and hurried through the deep snow, leaving a wide furrow as they rushed through the cold night air. Happy voices echoed through the dark of the empty woodland, and the group came through the trees and into the glade of the large silent Sacred Oak. There were giggles from Rune and Jade, as they all gathered around in a circle below the oldest tree in the area, their breath flowed white as they laughed, and Robbie raised his arm and pulled the shivering Rune close, as he looked with happy sparkling eyes at his father and uncle. John Lox beamed as he looked at Robbie. "You are the lord of this land; it should be you."

Robbie nodded and smiled. "You are her grandfather; her father is not here. This Uncle John is your duty." John beamed as his eyes glistened with tears, and he turned and gave a bow to the Sacred Oak, and raised the small bundle wrapped in blankets high in the air. Rune wiped a tear from her eye as Robbie pulled her close, Jade snuggled into Rowan, and he smiled with red glowing cheeks as he drew her close to him, his eyes glittered in the moonlight reflected off the white snow all around. The voice of John Lox boomed into the quiet night as his love and his pride magnified it.

"Hear me my lord of the forests and all creation. Hear me a proud man of Loxley as I offer you my praise for the birth of my granddaughter. She is our future and the prize of my house, take her into your realm and protect her, show your love to her for she will be known as Jessica Sapphire Lox."

He held her high in the air as the woodland fell calm, and Rune's eyes flickered violet as the breeze lifted and blew around the glade. She smiled as she felt the presence of her grandfather, as his spirit blew into the glade of the Sacred Oak. The snow swirled around John and then fell; everything was still as John turned and gave a huge smile to Robbie. "Thank you, Robbie Lad."

Robert Lox pulled his brother into a huge hug. "Come on now John, it's bloody freezing out here let's get her back to her mum." John nodded the happiest smile on his face Robbie had ever seen; they turned and began to walk back.

Robbie pulled Rune back for a second and pulled her into his arms, his hand ran across the small lump in her stomach and she smiled. Jade giggled as she threw a huge snowball at Rowan, which bounced off his head covering him in snow, she screamed as she turned and flew into the trees, as he raced behind her sweeping snow into his hands.

Robbie looked down at Rune's bright happy face. "It will be my turn next; I will offer up two to our lord." She leaned forward and kissed him softly, as he beamed with delight.

"At least it will be warmer." She shivered in his arms and he smiled, as her eyes danced with happiness and shone bright in the darkness.

"Come on let's get back and get warm." They turned and ran laughing through the snow, to catch up with the happiest pair of brothers Loxley had ever known. Robert and John laughed as they hurried back to the house, Rune screamed and giggled as the snowball just missed her, and she ran laughing into the glade and across to the gate. She looked back her face beaming as Robbie ran up laughing. Jade screamed as Rowan rolled her in the snow, and laughing hysterically, she ran for her life and followed Rune into the house.

Set back in the darkness of the trees, a tall stag turned and walked slowly into the darkness, it was a very happy time for the Lox family. The birth of Jessica

Sapphire to Alice on the first day of the year, had given them all hope in such an uncertain time. That night at the house and all the following day there had been a long line of visitors, and Robert and John Lox had laughed and smiled, as they proudly introduced everyone to the first of the next generation of the Lox family. Out of a dark time, wonder and light had been brought to their lives, and now all eyes were on Runestone as she carried the next of the line of Loxley, and the heir to the hooded realm. As all brightness fades, it was only months before the long finger of darkness, clouded the skies over Loxley.

Robbie stood by the window as Rune slept deeply behind him, it had been two weeks since the funeral, the snow had gone as the happy month slipped past, and February turned to rain and sunshine. Life in the stockade had been busy, as Robbie had waited for the attack that had not arrived. March had approached bleak, and then the rain had lifted and although there were cold spells, it was dry.

Dry enough to open the gates and roll out the cannons... Robbie closed his eyes and tried to force back the tears as he remembered the pain of that day, why had he let him go? It was a question he had asked himself a thousand times over the past week. He stared out at the darkened Mere, with the moon casting white lines on the water, his eyes looked dark and sunken, and his face was as white as the snow had been, it was rough with the lack of a razor, as he looked across the Mere, knowing behind the trees and down the lane at the Lox farm, his mother lay quietly crying in her bed alone.

She had blamed him, and she was right too, her screams of anger pounded through his head as they carried the broken body of his father back into the glade. Robbie looked down and clenched his fists as the tears came again to his eyes. He shook with the pain of losing a father, but he had also lost his mother on the very same day.

Two warm slender arms came round him from behind, and he turned and forced his head into her shoulder. "Robbie you cannot go on like this, you have to stop tearing yourself apart."

She held him tight as the pain shook deep inside him. There was nothing that Rune could do, she stood and held him close, in hope he would release the overwhelming pain she felt boiling up inside him. Rune felt real fear inside her, she was almost six months pregnant and Robbie was falling apart. The death of his father up on the moors on lookout duty, had utterly destroyed him, and she could not seem to get through to him, as the light inside him died with the break down between his mother and himself.

Jessie had snapped at the sight of her son crying across the body of his father, she had pulled him off and flung him in her grief across the floor, screaming at him and blaming him for the death of his father. Rowan had tried to calm her, but the grief that had flowed out of Jessie in a rage was powerful. It only ended when Rune who could not stand Robbie being hurt any more, snapped her fingers and Jessie collapsed on the ground.

As Robert Lox, had been lowered into the ground at the side of his father Jake, Jessie had turned and slapped Robbie's face, he had stood there silent as she walked away and borne the brunt of his pain with dignity, now alone in the dark hours and out of sight, Robbie had started to crumble. He spoke to no one and saw no one, he spent his day locked in his office as Rowan assumed command of the war that now raged on the moors. Rune had been the only person Robbie would see, she curled around him night after night and held him hoping she could find a way to pull the pain from him. Robbie had resisted and he now was consumed with the blame of the loss of his father.

For Rune, it had felt like the longest winter ever. In early November, the Specialists had moved out onto the moors of Yorkshire, they had built the observation platform, and in shifts they had taken turns leading the woodsmen out on patrols. The moors were open, cold, and hostile; they spread out their men into every available clump of trees and had established a long line of communication.

York had been cleared of its women and children, and now as the start of the war approached; the city had been filled with woodsmen from all over the north. Rafe and Robbie had joined Harry with Blades and the Bandit outfit, and they had sprung attacks with their portable catapults every night, pounding the black city for all it was worth to keep Mordred busy behind his gates. Woodsmen right up the country attacked the high walls of Mason, and tried to create as much havoc as possible to hold back the vast army and prevent it from facing the lines of Loxley on the moors. They faced overwhelming odds and holding them at bay was their only real chance of wearing them down.

Robbie had hoped that by the time the gates opened, they would have inflicted enough damage to hold back the tide of the massive black army that would sweep south, and crush York on its way to Loxley.

Robbie had returned home exhausted after three months away on the moors, he had sat on the steps at the farm and his father had been worried to see his boy look so white and weak. Robbie had refused to let his father out of the Stockade, and had argued with him in the yard, but finally his father had convinced him to have three days at home with Rune and rest. Robert Lox took command on the moors in the cabin of the observation post, he saw the cleverness of his sons plan to create havoc, and he watched as they continued to strike. No one saw the day coming when the gates swung back, and an army of thousands swarmed out into the wild open moor.

News came fast to the house, and Robbie had jumped out of bed, but by the time he was dressed and Rune had opened the window of shimmering violet it had been too late. Mordred had used his guns and pounded the camp. Many woodsmen died on that day, Rune sat at her table as she saw Robbie arrive, and as the cannons began again, she had used her powers and turned all the land in a circle for a mile around the guns into a swamp. The guns sunk deep into the softening ground, and were silenced, but it was too late to save Robert Lox.

Rune pulled him from the window and walked him slowly over to the bed. "You must sleep Rob; you have not slept in a week, please don't do this, Iona and Halbert will soon be here and I need you." The tears ran as she lowered him to the bed and pulled the covers over him. Robbie lay back and Rune looked down at him and softly kissed him, he blinked as if coming out of a dream, but Rune clicked her fingers, and before he realised, he was in a very deep sleep. She sat back and smiled as she pushed her hand on his chest and it glowed with a deep violet light, Rune closed her eyes.

"Hear me Maddy, I have finally done it, please come to me."

"I hear you Runestone I am coming."

It was just over an hour later when Madeleine arrived at the house; Rune threw her arms around her and cried. "Oh Maddy, thank you for coming, I am not sure I can take any more." Maddy pulled her close and held her tight in her arms.

"Come on Rune my love, don't break on me now, we are almost there." She squeezed Rune tightly and Rune shook with her pain. "If you want, I can pull all the pain out of you while I am here." Rune gave a quiet giggle.

"Oh Maddy, just help him and I will be fine."

Robbie lay still in a deep sleep in the bed as Maddy walked into the room; she smiled as she looked at him. "He is pale Rune; I see what you mean." Maddy undid her cloak, and then stood at the end of the bed, she winked at Rune and then she focused on Robbie, Rune stood back and watched as Maddy's pale watery blue eyes began to glow with a deep blue light.

Robbie seemed to lurch slightly on the bed as he raised and fell. Wisps of smoke rose slowly out of his chest, and Rune gasped at the hideous smoky face that came up out of him. It was almost black and grimaced with an evil smile as it fought to stay inside him. Blue light flooded the room as Maddy pushed all of her power at Robbie, and the black smoky face snarled at her as she dragged it up out of him. It snapped away from his chest and fought as it rose into the air, it spun around in the air as Maddy controlled it and slowly it floated over to her, she opened her mouth and sucked hard as the smoky cloud was drawn inside her.

Maddy snapped her mouth shut, and staggered back against the back of Rune's dressing table chair. Rune moved quickly toward her, but Maddy lifted a hand and slipped round to the front of the chair and sat down.

"Stay back Rune, you do not want this near the children, leave me a while, I will be fine soon." A tear ran from her eyes as she breathed hard and composed herself, Rune felt the tears in her eyes as she saw the strength of the pain that had been trapped inside him, and she looked to the bed where Robbie seemed to have relaxed more under the sheets and his face seemed less drawn.

Maddy came down the stairs an hour later, as Rune sat by the fire waiting. "He will be fine now. Oh, I tell you Rune that was a whole load of pain, it has never taken this long to absorb a feeling from just one person, no wonder you have been so worried." She looked at the relieved looking Rune and she touched her cheek. "You should talk to Jess; none of you can go on like this, not when there is so much love being destroyed. Help them heal it Runestone, they need each other."

Rune gave a weak smile. "I will try; she just ignores me when I see her." Her eyes glistened.

"If you want, I will try and get close enough to her to pull it out of her." Rune nodded.

"No, I think it should come from me Maddy, thanks for helping him." Maddy gave a soft smile.

"We all love you both, all of us are here Rune, don't forget us." Rune stood up and pulled Maddy into her arms and squeezed her. "I will tell you one thing Rune; Hearne help the poor bugger I hit with this lot." Maddy kissed Rune as she left and walked on to the glade where her horse stood waiting, Rune waved goodbye and closed the door, she felt exhausted as she held her huge tummy and walked slowly up the stairs to bed.

Robbie slept until well past dinnertime, Rune was up by mid-morning and took the small horse and trap to the farm; John Lox smiled as Rune lowered herself out of the cart. "Hello Rune love." She smiled as he crossed the yard toward her.

"Hi John, is Jess about I need to talk to her?" John looked worried. He cast his eyes toward the large greenhouses as he scratched his head.

"Are you sure that is wise Rune, she is still not herself you know? We all took it hard, but she has taken it worse than any." Rune looked him in his dark brown concerned eyes.

"I doubt she has taken it worse than Rob, I need her to help him or I tell you John, I am afraid he will do something daft and we all will lose him too." John nodded as the tears ran down her face, and he pulled her into his big arms.

"Hey Rune love, come on don't cry now, I tell you what, I will try and talk to her again for you."

Rune looked down as she wiped her eyes. "No John, this is for me to do, Jess will talk to me today, and if have to use force I will." John looked very worried.

"I don't think that would be right in your condition, come on love and have a cup of tea and calm down a bit first, you cannot go upsetting yourself like this, it's not good for the babies." Rune pulled back a look of determination on her face.

"I need them talking, that will do my babies a world of good and Hearne help her she will bloody well talk to me today." Rune turned as the greenhouse door slid shut, Jess looked across, and seeing Rune; she turned to walk to the orchard, Rune moved off, and John watched with a very concerned look on his face.

"Jess wait, we have to talk." Jess ignored her and carried on walking, "JESS STOP!" Rune's eyes began to glow purple, Jess spun round a look of shock on her face, her eyes burned with anger as she stared back. Rune waddled up toward her, and her eyes flowed back to lilac as Jess shook herself.

"How dare you use your powers on me, who the hell do you think you are?" Her eyes glared brighter as she stared back down at Rune from the high step. Her hair hung loose, and her clothes lacked their usual neatness, she looked pale, but there was a fire in the eyes and stare of Jess, and the atmosphere around her rose to one of almost electric.

Rune stopped and looked at the angry eyes of Jess. Her own face bore the grim look of determination, she showed the power of her line as she gritted her teeth determined to have her say in the defence of her husband. "I am your daughter, and in case you haven't noticed, I have two of your grandchildren inside me."

Jess looked down at the large belly of Rune and began to turn. "Leave me alone I have nothing to say." She began to move toward the path that led round the greenhouse to the orchards, Rune screamed at the top of her voice and began to follow her.

"WELL, I HAVE LOADS, so stand still, shut up and listen to me... don't even think of leaving Jess, because I will freeze you to the spot if that is what it takes." Jess stopped and turned back to look at Rune, whose eyes streamed with tears. Her voice softened as the emotion she had held so deep inside flowed to the surface. "He loves you and he needs you, your son is falling apart blaming himself and wishing he could trade places, because if it hadn't been Robert, you can sure as hell have guaranteed it would have been Robbie."

Jess looked down at the fire in Rune's eyes, for all of the power she contained, the pain, fear, and worry, were very visibly mixed with Rune's anger. "IS THAT WHAT YOU WANT JESS? DO YOU WANT ROBERT BACK AND ROBBIE DEAD? My grandfather is Hearne he can do that if you want it, because I am telling you now, what is sat in my house is not the father I want for my children."

Rune collapsed on her knees and she wept as her own pain flowed out of her, and Jess silently stared at her. "You cannot blame him; Rob did everything to protect the father he loved. Robert was not the sort of man who would turn his back on his family or see his people suffer. He would have been by his son's side everyday if it hadn't been for Robbie holding him back here."

Rune looked up as the tears made bright pools of violets across the floor, Jess stood frozen just staring at her. "Sooner or later Robert would have gone to war to protect his people and you know it? No one is safe, we are all facing death every day in hope that enough of us will live to keep Loxley going in the future. There has not been a day that like you, I have lived with the fear of losing the man I love, but like his father he is duty bound to his people." John ran down the yard as Rune shook violently and sobbed on the ground. He pulled her into his arms, and held her tight as the pain flowed out of her. John looked at his sister as she stared at Rune weeping deep bitter sobs into his arms.

"This aint bloody right Jess, you got to fix this. Rob would be ashamed of all of us tearing his family apart like we are." John turned and lifted Rune into his arms as Beth came out of the kitchen door and ran to Rune, her own tears flowed at the sight of Rune's grief, as she helped John get her to the horse and trap.

John sat her carefully in the trap, and climbed up by her side as Beth leaned over and hugged her. John drove Rune back up the long lane, and into the woodland track that led to the glade of the Mere. Jess turned, and walked quietly away into her orchard.

He helped Rune out of the trap, and walked her slowly up to the door. "Are you sure you will be alright, I got to admit, I don't like leaving you alone like this Rune love." She gave a smile as she sniffled.

"I will be fine John thanks; Rob is here I will not be alone." He nodded and looked saddened.

"I am sorry about all this Rune, honestly I have screamed at her, but she loved him as you do Robbie, it will just take time that is all, so please do not think too badly of her. You know she is a kind loving person, it's just hard for her at the moment, she will come round you will see."

Rune shook her head. "I know John." She gave him a soft smile. "Thanks."

"Now if you are sure you will be fine?" Rune nodded. He gave her a smile. "Alright love I will be off, but listen, if it gets too bad, me and Beth are here for you love. Any time day or night... You know if it gets too much just knock on the door."

Rune smiled and pulled him into a hug. "Thanks John."

"Alright then, I will be off, just don't forget... Knock."

Rune watched as the tall large muscular frame of John Lox walked up to the trees, he looked back and waved as he headed into the tree line and Rune waved back as she slid back the glass doors and walked into the house.

Robbie was still in bed asleep as Rune came into the room, she felt exhausted and it was not long before she slipped up the covers and climbed in bed beside him. Rune snuggled up to him and held him tight, he moved in his sleep, and slid closer. Rune gave a soft smile and held him tight.

The black army paced through the heather in a long line like a sea of black. The wall appeared in front of them, as a swarm of arrows came at them, Rafe screamed his orders as more boards lifted covered in heather and from behind them, more arrows flew into the midst of the black army. Soldiers in black fell in a pile before the carefully concealed barricades of the woodland soldiers, the idea had come from Robbie who had been looking at ways to hide men out in the open, but keep them safe. Rafe had put it in to good practice, and now as the black army walked through what it thought was just low heather, they found that out of the ground a whole hooded army could just spring up.

Thick boards covered in dry heather lay across sunken trenches. One woodsman controlled the boards, and the bowmen hid underneath, as the army approached the boards went up protecting the vulnerable men out in the open, and the bowmen let fly with deadly accuracy. Rafe had lost two men to date, and had managed to wipe out several hundred of the black army as they surged forward in large groups. Hawk and Saff worked with Fish and Big John in a large pine forest, and they too were holding back the large army with a thousand woodsmen hidden in the trees.

Mordred had finally come out from behind his walls, and yet he was just five miles from his city, and had not gained in the whole of the week. The woodsmen fought hard and used the little cover they had, Jade had scored high as she had snuck round behind all the troops and single handily killed six of Mordred's Generals. Crystal now hunted with Melanie and Jaz, they swung round wide of the battle, looking for those groups that were trying to take a wide arc and catch the woodsmen from behind. She would spring out of the trees and let fly with an arrow, and the whole group would freeze, she worked wide on the western borders as the bandits now covered the eastern border, so far Mordred could not get a single man through.

Rowan watched from the rebuilt observation post with a large pair of binoculars. Jade watched from his side, Harry and Blades had teamed up with Todd and Woody, and now with Hornet and Amethyst, they worked the northern lines behind the black army. They helped direct the woodsmen from the north into better positions that squeezed the black army from the rear, they had seen a lot of combat and Harry was pleased to see that the well toned Amethyst was as good with a pole and sword as she was with a bow. Woody was a worry, as he kept falling down holes or getting stuck in the mire. Harry noticed it happened a lot around Amethyst, whereas Todd was a brutal fighter and twice they had been taken unawares, and it had been his swift reactions alongside Blades, which had saved their lives.

The black army was being held in place, but Rowan was under no illusion, he knew there was far more to come, and Mordred was just testing the lines. The field Headquarters had been set half a mile behind Rowan, where ten thousand men rested and prepared, as Skip and Treen worked with Scarlet and Phillip. Rune had scanned the moors and discovered a large cave below it; Robbie had wasted no time in using the techniques of Rose in Scotland, and the cave now served as a safe place to store arms, and run the command and control centre in the field. It had proved very useful in the snow of the winter, and provided all the troops with a welcome rest out of the biting wind.

All the officers in the Specialists now had two of the best officers of the woodsmen from all over the area working side by side to train with them. Rowan knew at some point Robbie would call all the Specialists out of the field for strike missions; he wanted to make sure it left no weak points in their defence of York. At any given time, a Specialist could be replaced with a fully briefed and trained officer.

Malcolm Prosper kept all his black city rebels together, Steph and Smokes had put them through their paces in Loxley Woods, with a little assistance from Joe, and they now formed a night strike squad. Dressed in their long black hooded cloaks, and black pants and tops, they had hit the rear of the camps with explosive arrows, doing their best to take out all the officers of the young soldiers. The young boys would flee in fear only to be rounded up by Crystal, or the bandits and then shipped back out of the conflict away to the camps outside Loxley. They were fed, and disarmed and promised protection if they refused to fight, many had collapsed with relief at finding out the posters Robbie had placed all over the Black City had been true. Within a week, ten thousand had already surrendered to Loxley.

As April arrived, a stale mate had now been reached, Mordred had screamed with rage killing four of his generals, as he found his victory of wiping out York in a day was now a two-week campaign of no movement. The woodsmen were dug in and going nowhere, without their cannons they faced a well organised and very well trained fighting force. Where there was no cover, they had built their own, and Fuse with his books on combat, found more and more ways to keep the troops protected and out of sight of their enemy. Megan had learned a great deal from Fuse about explosives, and over the winter she had come up with the Striker Arrow. It was a slender dynamite arrow that could be used with greater accuracy to hit one man and explode killing five, for the Specialists and the Night Strikers; it became their favourite tool very quickly, especially when faced with overwhelming numbers. The striker arrow evened the odds up considerably, and at least made it a much fairer fight.

Rune opened her eyes as she felt his hand from behind slowly move across her tummy. She closed them again and gave a small smile, as he pulled closer. Slowly his hand moved round and round and then it moved. She felt him stiffen as he held her, her tummy moved again, and she felt the excitement come from him. She gave a little giggle, and rolled over on to her back and opened her eyes and looked into the dark eyes of the man she loved. "Hi gorgeous."

He smiled at her as he looked down. "Hey beautiful." Rune slid her arms up round his neck and pulled him down to her, Robbie kissed her slowly and she felt the warmth of her life returning. Tears formed as she hugged him hard and she wept.

"Oh Rob I have been so frightened and alone, you went inside yourself and I thought I had lost you."

He slid his hands round her and pulled her close. "I am here Rune; I will never leave you. I am sorry, I just got lost for a while." He raised himself up and looked down into the bright sapphire blue eyes that sparkled like pools of crystal with her tears. "Don't cry now, come on now." He kissed her softly and she smiled back up at him.

"I do love you Rob." He gave her a smile as his eyes gave a twinkle; it was the first in three weeks

"I love you too." They lay arm in arm together as the sun shone the bright rays of spring down on the glade of Robbie's Mere. The trees were uncurling their leaves, and the grass was growing, the cherry trees around the lake were opening the first of their flowers, and like bright fluffy cushions of white and pink, they reflected in the calm surface of the Mere.

Robbie had lost a lot of weight; he had barely eaten in over a week, and he had a hunger that would even rival Big John, as Rune piled his plate high. She smiled as she looked down at him; she had to admit she preferred him clean shaven. "Do you have to go straight back out there? I have been so lonely can we not have a little time here together?"

He looked up and smiled. "It is my job to be there Rune, I will see Rowan and then go to York. I have to get back up to date, I have lost valuable time and need to get things back where they were." He got up from the table and slid his arms round her. "I will be back tonight, and we can spend it alone, I promise."

Rune nodded and smiled. "Alright, I will watch from my table, please be careful I have just got you back, I do not want to ever go through that again." She kissed him softly and waved her hand as the window opened behind him. He gave her a smile as he passed through into the deep dry heather of the moors of Yorkshire.

He walked up the hill dressed in all sage green, his longer hair and cloak billowed in the breeze behind him, the golden sword glinted in the sunlight as the guard snapped to attention beside Rowan and Jade. "My Lord." Rowan and Jade spun round and the smile broke across Rowan's face as Robbie walked up the hill towards them. Jade flew down and leapt screaming into his arms, and Robbie smiled as he felt the love of his sister embrace him.

"Oh Robbie, I have missed you. How are you and how is Rune? Oh, Rowan and me have been so worried about you, and we have been stuck here and could not get back to see how you were. Oh Robbie I missed you I was so worried." Robbie smiled at Rowan as he held Jade close, and she hung from him in a tight embrace.

"It is nice to see you, I have missed you too Pebbles." He gave her a kiss on the side of the cheek, and she slipped down smiling her beaming radiant smile of happiness. Rowan pulled him into a hug and patted his back.

"I have missed you; it's not an adventure without you." Robbie smiled.

"Thanks Rowan, I needed the time. You covered well for me." Rowan slapped his back.

"It's what brothers are for." Robbie nodded, and together they walked to the top of the hill and Robbie looked out on the scene across the moors. Rowan filled him in on what had been happening, Robbie looked down his scope and surveyed the front lines, smoke rose in the air toward the black city, the night strikes had hit them hard, and the black army had lost many men.

"He will not wait much longer Rowan; he has a large army of talent in there waiting. He has worked out our tactics and now he will start to grow confident, it will soon be time to change tack, as he brings forth some of his bigger fighters. Prepare all the men; Rune is now ready to begin her side of our operation."

The two men stood side by side at the top of the hill, the sun shone behind them and all the woodsmen for miles could see that the hooded man and his general were behind them watching, the word spread as the men looked back and saw their symbol of hope.

Crystal smiled as she looked across the moor through her telescope, she handed it over to Mel. "We have our leader back, and not a moment too soon, come on let's go and find Harry and tell him the news." She pulled her horse round beside Jasper and smiled. With a large grin, he kicked his heels into the horse and the three of them rode at high speed out of the trees and into the deep heather, Robbie watched the white figure on her shining white horse with her two companions ride across the moor in the far distance.

"Shouldn't we get Crystal something green to wear?" Jade gave a chuckle.

"Are you kidding? When the black army see bright white coming towards them, they run like hell, the cold arm of Miss Frosty Knickers there terrifies them, she has become one of our secret weapons. I dressed Saff in all white last week, and the soldiers bolted before she was within half a mile of them."

Robbie gave a chuckle, it was smart thinking, and exactly what he would expect from Jade, he lifted his arm around her. "I've missed you sis."

Harry heaved on Woody's arm as he pulled him out of yet another hole filled with watery slush. "Whoa man your karma is jangled; you need to like get your vibes together dude." Blades tittered with Todd, as Woody squelched on to the solid earth, the ground gave a long loud sucking pop, and Hornet grinned at Amethyst.

Wilson Allwood, or Woody to his friends, was a tall and somewhat gangly member of the bandits led by Ox. Harry had warmed very quickly to the quiet animal loving and very good-natured man, he seemed a little on the shy side but that had never worried Harry, who enjoyed talking for hours about his cosmic thoughts of the world. Woody seemed to look to the moment and didn't really focus on the big things in life; Harry felt it only right to educate the man in the spectral happenings of the cosmos. It helped that Woody was the only one who was too polite not to listen. Woody went everywhere with his sheep dog Bess, back in Cumbria he had been a shepherd, and now out in the wild world he clung to his dog and his long crooked staff, as his only link to the home and the mother he had loved.

He was thirty-nine and still very single. It was not really his fault, he just found women unnerved him, and whenever one seemed to show interest, he would panic and find it impossible to talk, and usually he had some sort of accident. It did not help that Amethyst was incredibly beautiful, and she happened to spend most of her day in the group a few feet away from Woody. She found him very endearing and wanted to mother him, her radiant smile of white teeth usually ended up with her having to lift him up off the floor, which just seemed to make things worse. Hornet seemed the only one who did not frighten the life out of him, and Woody tended to keep close to Harry or her.

Bess licked his boots as he jumped up and smiled, Harry patted his back. "Hey dude, focus man or we will be out here like forever. You need to think happy vibes man it will help boost your karma and bring a peaceful and mellow flow to your aura." Woody nodded even though he had not understood a word Harry had just said. Blades and Todd giggled in the heather up in front.

Amethyst stood up and watched the horizon as the white clad figure of Crystal rode towards them; she gave a wave and Crystal spotted them and turned course toward them. The group stood and watched as the three horses rode up to them. Crystal slid down and pulled her sister into her arms. "We have good news, Robbie is back." The whole group beamed and Harry nodded with happiness.

"Cool man, he was like off there in an uncosmic land, man my vibes is glowing knowing he is fine." Jasper patted him on the back and pulled him into a hug.

"Harry you old maniac I've missed you how is life in the wilds of North York?" Harry beamed with delight.

"Hey man, I am like here and happenin, my vibes is all back and my karma is flowing." Jaz gave him a smile; somewhere at some point, the man who communicated with the spirit world had reached an understanding with Harry, the man who feared spirits more than any. They were as alike as chalk and cheese, and yet somehow a bond of deep fondness had grown between them.

Jasper had told Harry he knew where all the spare karma in the world was kept; he had made Harry swear to secrecy and had told him he could top up his Karma whenever he needed it. Jett and Jade had roared with laughter in the woodland as they had watched Harry's respect of Jasper grow. Jasper had felt a little guilty about the jokes he had played on Harry at Dunnottar, and felt he should somehow make up for it. Up until that point whenever Jasper had appeared, Harry had run away kissing his pendant and searching his pockets for his purple tinted glasses, which contained hooded magic to keep the green evils at bay.

Woody talked softly to the horses as he led them over to the group, and all of them mounted up and prepared to ride back to the headquarters and make their reports, smoke rose in the distance to the east, as the sun headed across the sky towards the west. It would soon be dark and they had a long ride ahead of them.

Rafe sat back in the heather and opened his thick green mud splattered cloak. Jett smiled as she slid on to his knee and he pulled the cloak around them. She shivered as he pulled her close. "Oh Wolfie I can't wait to get home for a few days." He smiled as her black eyes looked up into his and she gave him a huge smile.

"Oh I could sleep for a month." She gave him a shrewd look.

"Yeah right... Two months out here in the cold... You will be in bed, but believe me babe, we aint doing no sleeping."

He gave a long chuckle as he slid his head down on to hers to keep lower than the cool wind. "Saff will be here soon."

Sapphire had always been told she had power more than most; she had after all been destined to be the centre of the Circle of Knowledge. It had been one twist of fate that had brought Rune to the centre of both circles, and now they had merged and become the one circle of the wheel of Runestone.

Rune had spent a lot of time with Sapphire over the past December, and Rune had given her more training in the powers she contained. Like all centres, Saff had the power of passage, and Rune taught her how to open windows like hers, and bring people through. It had proved a useful tool as Sapphire now could help Rune move large numbers around the battlefield; it gave the woodsman a very good element of surprise and attack. Saff opened circular windows of shimmering blue that seemed to pulsate as they hung in the air; it had confused quite a few of them at first, who were all used to the arched windows of violet that Rune preferred.

Rafe sat quietly having had his new commander take over his watch on the very front of the lines, Jett felt warm in his arms as they quietly talked. The soldiers looked back and smiled, they would miss the wild couple that led by example, and screamed and howled in the night to frighten the enemy. Rafe and Jett commanded a lot of respect on the front lines, everyone knew they were part of the hooded man's Specialists, but more than that they respected the couple who although wild at times, really cared for their troops. Rafe knew every man's first name and whether or not they were married or had children, he always talked to the troops and asked after their families, apart from Robbie and Rowan, he was the most respected man in the woodland forces.

The blue window opened just in front of them, and Jett leapt up into the arms of Sapphire. She smiled as she pulled her close. "Hey cous you missed me?" She held Jett close as she smiled at Rafe. "You two ready for some well earned time off...? Come on we are all meeting at York and then heading on to Loxley." Jett whooped with delight and waved to the troops.

"See you soon guy's, keep your heads down and no fighting till I am back, I won't have you lot having all the fun." She beamed a smile at the happy faces in the heather.

"Bye Lady Jett." They all waved as she went into the window, Rafe gave a smile and waved at his men.

"See you soon guys, howl at them for me." The whole platoon threw back their heads.

"Ow ...Ooooh!!!" Rafe laughed loud as he stepped into the blue window, and passed into the large assembly room at York. Bear pulled him into a vice like grip as he came through smiling and caked in mud. It was a happy reunion for a group of friends who had not been together since Christmas.

There was laughter and cheers and Rune smiled as she watched through her table. She loved them all and missed them dearly, and she felt a little sadness at not being there with them. Her eyes sparkled as she opened the window and Robbie came through flanked by Rowan and Jade, the level of happiness rose as 'Gov,' rose loudly into the air and Robbie smiled as they all embraced him.

She watched and felt a few tears as he smiled; he looked pale, tired, and worn. Seeing him surrounded by his friends brought some joy to her heart, she knew it was what he needed to fulfil the recovery of his loss, and bring him back to the man of power he was. She stood up from the table, as she now knew they were all safe and walked quietly up to the bedroom to change. Saff would bring them all back to Loxley and she now prepared for the night alone with him.

Rune sat on the bed in the quiet house and looked at her fat tummy, she smiled. She was life and was not far from bringing the first of her own lives into the world. It was early April, and soon it would be Robbie's Birthday, and then as the month of May slipped quietly away and late June came, she would head to Iona and bring forth the Queen of Fae, and her brother who would be the heir to Robbie and the line of Loxley would follow her. They moved inside her and she knew they could feel her thinking of them; Rune gave a smile as she rubbed her tummy.

"Be patient Iona and Hal, your time will be here soon enough." Rune gave a giggle as her spirits lifted, he would be home in a few hours and they would be together again, if only for a short time.

Rune dressed in all violet and hummed as she combed back her long flowing red hair, she braided it back and clipped the ruby encrusted butterfly hairpin into the back of her braids. She smiled happily in the mirror as she rose to go and prepare for his home coming meal. She gave a soft giggle as she looked at her tummy. "Daddy is going to need feeding up now; he will need all the strength he can get when you both arrive." She giggled as she walked to the stairs and headed down to the living room, she gasped as she saw the lone figure at the open glass door. "Jess!"

Jess looked at her with her pale hazel eyes and the tears formed as she looked at the floor. Rune walked slowly over to the sad looking figure and without a word, she slid her arms around her and pulled her close. Rune stood quietly as Jess sobbed huge tears of grief into her arms; she rested her head on Jess's shoulder. "It's alright; I know the pain you hold. Let it out Jess."

Jess shook with the pain that flowed out of her. Maddy watched with tears in her eyes from the gate, Rune gave her a soft smile and Maddy understood the thank you. Rune pulled Jess round and walked her into the kitchen; Maddy followed and put a pot on to boil, as Jess went to speak, but Rune lifted a finger to her lips and touched hers. "What is done is done Jess, it's in the past. Robbie needs you, and you believe it or not need him. You have a son who is his father, you need now to heal the wounds between you and make Robert proud of both of you."

Jess nodded and looked up with tear filled eyes. "I am so sorry Runestone." Rune smiled and pulled her into a hug.

"I know... I tell you what Jess; I am amazed I did not drop your grandkids off on the farmyard floor." Jess gave a slight giggle.

"Its ok, John is good with the sheep." Rune started to giggle and Jess started to laugh. Maddy set two hot cups down on the table. "I have missed you so much Runestone."

Rune smiled at Jess. "I missed you too mum." Her eyes sparkled as she smiled at her daughter in law and nodded. Maddy blew her nose a lot louder than expected, Rune and Jess burst into laughter, Maddy gave one of her very rare smiles, and Rune leaned over and kissed her cheek.

CHAPTER TWO

THE RETURN OF THE SPECIALISTS

The window of Sapphire's opened at the side of the Village Hall, and the happy smiling faces of the Specialists came wandering out. It had been a long winter and they had spent little time together, so the noise levels were higher than normal. John had a thirst and the bar in the hotel beckoned. Jett taunted him as they walked laughing and joking to the front doors of the hotel that had been built only in the previous summer, and the doorman looked a little dubious at the mud covered members of the group.

The commander insignia on Rafe's cloak was enough to tell him these were the men of the frontline, and he stepped back quickly, and opened the doors as the rowdy party entered. Rowan looked back at Robbie. "They will want you with them Robbie, it has been some time since we were all together."

He smiled at Rowan. "I know it's just... I am not ready for this Rowan, I still need some time, I want to get back to Rune, this has been harder on her than any and I would like to make it up to her."

Rowan understood and patted him softly on the back. "Alright Robbie, take your time... we are all happy to see you back in the fold again, I will see you tomorrow for our first meeting."

Rowan stood by the door and watched as Robbie made his way up the track toward the top of the village street; passing people bowed, spotting the sage green cloak and the wolf head crest, and Robbie gave a smile and nodded back politely. Steph sat in her yard amongst the clothes rails as Robbie walked past, his mind on many things, she gave him a smile and he smiled more out of habit than anything, as his brain woke and he realised who she was. "Sorry Steph, I was miles away." She got up out of the chair and came across to the garden wall.

"I take it everyone is back on leave?" Robbie nodded.

"They need the break before I call them back for Specialist activity."

"We are going to be brought back then? I thought for a minute our days were over." Robbie leaned on the wall as he turned to her.

"Why would you think that? I would never break up the Specialists."

Steph shrugged. "I am not sure really Rob, I guess with Rune being out of action

and Alice being so busy with the little one... And you know... Your dad. I thought
you would be spending more time here; the group have been spread around
a lot over the winter." Robbie could see what she meant; but he had not really
considered it, in his mind there was no doubt that the team would remain around
him. Not only were they the best, they were also his closest circle of friends and
family.

"I will never break the team up; I just needed them to show everyone the ropes
before I pulled them back to do other work."

Steph leaned over the wall, and put her arm on his shoulder. "I know it has been
hard Rob, no one expected Jess to go for you the way she did. She does love you
Rob, just give her time, try to imagine a world without Rune, you may understand
her better."

He nodded; Steph had a great way of gently pressing the point. "I could not
survive without Rune, I understand my mum, but I just don't understand why she
could just give up on me, when I know she would welcome Billy back tomorrow."
Steph slipped over the wall and sat by his side, she looked down the busy street of
the village as she spoke.

"Jess loved Billy and he betrayed her and her family, she is blinded by her love
for him Rob. She has always seen him as weak and vulnerable, because when she
found him, he was. Jess will always see Billy as the victim she saved; you are the
strong one, the one with the power of your dad." She gave a long sigh and turned
to him; her bright green eyes were filled with concern.

"You are the lord and the force behind Loxley. You alone have become the
symbol of hope that has gone around this country, and always returned and
brought most of us through. Rob think about all we have done together, you have
led us always and we have only lost three. Have you any idea how incredible that
is...? Your mum has seen the concern you placed on the safety of your men,
but you lost your father through no accident of your own, the one time she sees
you slip, it cost her the most important thing in her life... I do not agree with her
behaviour and she knows it, I bloody well told her how I feel, but I do understand
as a woman how hard it hit her to have lost her husband and see you fall in her
esteem at the same time."

"I would have given anything to have been the one who was there when the
cannons fired. I would trade places anytime." Steph put an arm around him and
pulled him close.

"I know Rob, but you know what? And this may sound cruel, I am glad it was
not you, horrible as it sounds, I am glad. You and Rune are the future of Loxley
and the woodland realm, and when push comes to shove, every one of us would
lay down our lives to ensure that you two come through. Jess is isolated and does
not always see the bigger picture. Your dad understood the risks, and he did see
the full view of all of this. He knew you needed to rest and he knew the danger,

and if you bring him back do you know what he would say?"

Robbie shook his head. "No what?"

"He would grip you firmly by the shoulders and say, I am glad you lived." Steph nodded as she spoke. "He would Rob, because Robert understood like all of us that his sacrifice has probably saved the community, he spent all his life protecting."

He knew she was right and he looked out across the village as he imagined his dad. He swallowed hard as he felt the tears in the back of his eyes. "I miss him."

Steph squeezed him hard. "We all do Rob, he was a good man, but every day I see him in this village. He stands before me in a younger version, but he has one hell of a lot of Robert in him, and I know from years of talk with him that he was as proud as hell of the man he called son. Honour him Rob and be like him."

Robbie turned and looked at her as the tears ran from her eyes. "I am afraid Steph." She pulled him closer and held him tight.

"We all are Rob, even your dad was. Just remember that no matter how worried or concerned he was, he never showed it outside the house. Robert always said to me, I will not let the buggers think for a moment I can't whip them." She gave a soft giggle. "I really respected him Rob, and you know what? I hold you as high as I did him, you still have a lot to learn, but it is all in there, in times of need Robert will show through."

He pulled back and wiped his eyes on his sleeve, and he nodded. "I know, he is a hard act to follow Steph, I really am not sure I can fill his shoes."

"Well, My Lord, I think, and I certainly know for a fact he thought you already are." She gave him a smile and he gave a little smile back. "Go home to Rune and hold her in your arms for a while, you will find all the healing you need is right there. She loves you Rob, pull her close instead of pushing her away, I know my daughter, and she will give you all the strength you need."

"Thanks Steph, I know you are right, you have helped me a lot."

She gave him a grin. "I am always right and full of wisdom, why do you think the group call me Mother?" He gave a little laugh as she beamed at him. "I am always here for you Rob." He nodded. "Go on get home and hug your wife." Steph swung her legs back over the wall into her yard, and Robbie walked down the road, she watched as he turned at the bottom of the street and headed for the shortcut, between the storehouses, and across the fields to the far end of the lane and the back of Robbie's Mere.

Jett beamed as she stared across the table at Big John. The Specialists gathered round in a big circle as Rafe placed the large jug of ale down on the table, he slid the two full tankards across to each of them, and Jett gave a howl of a laugh. "Ok big guy, this has been a long time coming, prepare to leave a broken man." Big John's blue eyes twinkled as he ran his hand back over his bald head and smiled.

"Little lady I have the capacity, you don't have a chance, but I admire your pluck girl, let's do it."

Jett gave a cackle as she lifted her tankard with John and the contest began as they started to drink, the group cheered as they both matched each other and slammed their tankards down empty on the table. Jett and John beamed at each other as Rafe refilled them, everyone watched as they lifted them up and cleared them easily. Jade screamed with delight as Jett smashed her tankard down on the table slightly ahead of John. He laughed as he rammed the tankard to the table. Fish stood behind John and rubbed his shoulders, and Jade howled with delight as they lifted their next tankard. Drop for drop they matched each other, and Jett's eyes glistened as she impressed everyone. She was so thin compared to John who after all did have a reputation for being able to enjoy a mug or two.

The pace slowed as the tenth tankard was placed before them, John had a bright glow of red about him, and Rafe was sure that small flashes of blue kept emitting from Jett's eyes. She slurred a little as she continued to taunt John, who in all honesty was greatly impressed. Meg looked at Bear who was laughing loudly. "Isn't this stuff made by that woodsman who makes Harry's tonic?"

Bear gave a hearty smile. "This is the strongest ale in the north, they will have more than a headache in the morning, three glasses of this and I am out for the day, and I am no stranger to a drop of good brew."

Jett laughed hysterically as she slammed down her tankard, she wobbled in her seat as Jade helped to steady her. "Yew want more, big yon." John was swooning a little as Fish held him square on the seat, his eyes seemed clouded as he tried to focus on the slightly leaning Jett. He slowly slid his hand forward as Rafe pushed the tankard into his hand. Jett now wore a fixed smile, and missed the tankard and had to really focus to get her hand close to it.

They reached their fourteenth tankard and they both now struggled, as they pulled the tankards to their mouths, which were now much closer to the table. Jett took a deep breath and began to slowly drink; she stopped as she gave a huge belch and started to laugh. John forced the drink down, taking his time as Jett began again. The group all laughed as they watched, Jett had really impressed them, John was struggling which amazed everyone, and all of them had thought it was bravado on Jett's part. John emptied his tankard and dropped it on to the table; he fell back in his chair and gasped with relief. Fish yelled and everyone cheered him.

Jett was struggling there was no doubt about it, but she was determined to beat him, and she forced the drink down as her eyes flickered a deep violet to blue. As she placed the empty tankard down on the table, the noise was deafening as the group more out of surprise than anything roared and jumped around.

Jett's head was almost level with the table, she squinted to try to keep John in sight, and she wore a permanent smile. John breathed deeply as the room spun before him, Rafe chuckled, as he looked at the pair staying upright more out of will power, he looked at Jett and then John. "More?"

John leaned over the table and wobbled in front of a Jett who was swaying from side to side. "More... or draw." He had to focus hard to get the words out, and Jett gave a huge smile.

"Hood enuff hab you?" Her eyes seemed to be moving around independently of each other, John stared back at her, although he was actually looking past her swaying shoulder.

"Lots finisssh, ebon." Jett slid a shaky hand across the table to John, it swayed around and he found it hard to get hold of. Rafe took both hands and placed them together and shouted. "Draw."

The whole group of Specialists erupted into the air and the noise shook the whole hotel, they all danced with delight, Rafe gave a wolf howl and looked down. John and Jett had both slid under the table where they lay out cold. Fourteen pints of Joe's ale was enough to sedate an elephant, Rafe knew tomorrow was going to be hard on little Jett Amber.

Jett hung over his shoulder like a limp rag doll, as he pushed the key in the door of number six the high street. He carried her up the stairs, and slipped off her golden spiked heeled boots, slowly he undressed her and slid her under the covers, and he laid her on her side and pulled the pillows up behind her.

Rafe slid the biggest bowl he could find at the side of the bed and chuckled. He really admired her spirit, he had been sure she would lose to the thirst of Big John, but the grit and determination of Jett Amber had shown through again. He felt exhausted as he slid in beside her; it had been a tough three months out on the moors and the feeling of clean soft sheets was heaven. His sleep was deep if not short; the sounds of retching soon woke him.

The worn face of a hard year showed on Robbie as he walked round the side of the Mere. The sun shone and the new pale green of the leaves seemed to lift his spirits, the daffodils had faded and now the long stems wilted to the floor as the ferns and the grass greened up and looked lush. The white petals of the apples and cherry blossom floated down like soft snow as he felt the sense of deep calm flow from the wood into his soul. He had missed the feel of leaves above his head, and he watched as the birds fluttered happily through the trees to build their nests. Pigeons cooed in the deeper wood, and the starlings and blue tits chatted happily around him.

He walked lost in thought with his hands in his pockets, and wove slowly down the path that he knew so well he did not need to look. He came out in front of the glade and the long stretch of water he had just walked round, the surface of the Mere was like glass, as it reflected the sun and the trees round the bank, he took a deep breath and breathed in the fresh clean air. He loved this place, it stood for the world he wanted to create and protect, this place was Rune and the happiness he found with her, he stared out across the water and felt the calmness grow inside him. The silent figure of Lord Loxley stood alone for some time facing the water lost in thought.

"Robbie?"

The moment was long before he realised he was not alone and he turned. Jessica Lox stood looking lost and awkward as she stared at her son. He looked at her and felt the pain resurface as the tears came to his eyes. "Mum." Jessie stepped forward and pulled him into her arms, she held him like she was never going to let go, as she cried with the pain of what she saw in her son. Robbie pulled his arms around her and they stood silent as both of them wept into each other's arms.

Rune watched with Maddy from the gate as her tears flowed, Maddy sniffled as she smiled to see a mother reunite with her son.

Jess clung to Robbie as he wept and let the grief of his loss out. "I am sorry Mum... it should have been me." Her hazel eyes streamed as she was caught in the trap of knowing she would have lost one of them. She loved them both, how could she choose, but for a time she had lost them both anyway.

"I miss him Rob, but I miss you too, will you ever forgive me?"

His eyes were red as he looked up at her. "I love you mum." Jess pulled him close and felt the joy of her son in her arms again. They stood close at the side of the Mere as the sun shone down and they talked quietly, Rune watched from the seats outside the glass doors with Maddy, she gave a smile knowing the healing had started, and she hoped that soon her Robbie would be returned back to his full self. Maddy watched as Rune's eyes never left him. "You did a good thing Runestone."

Rune never moved as she watched him walk with his mother round the edge of the water. "I need him Maddy, I cannot be without him, as I am the centre of the wheel, he is my centre. Robbie is the life I bring to everything."

The day slipped past, and Robbie and Jess walked back to the house. Rune hugged them both and felt the whole spirit of the glade lift, they all sat down to a meal, and Rune smiled as she watched Jess and Robbie laugh and talk with Maddy. She left them talking as she washed the plates and placed them carefully to dry in the rack by the sink. She turned and saw Jess as she stood in the doorway. Jess walked across the kitchen and pulled Rune into her arms. "Thank you... I lost sight of everything; you made it all clear at the farm. I am so sorry Rune for putting you through that, I hope one day you will forgive me my stupidity."

Rune smiled at Jess. "I love him Jess, and yes I will fight for him, even against you. I learned that from Robert and you, both of you fought together for all of us and for these people, I will do the same."

Jess nodded. "My Rob admired and respected you Rune. He loved the way you supported his son; he was proud of you both for what you had done for this community. I am too; I will always feel the pain of what I put you through."

"We belong to the line of Loxley Jess, heal yourself, there is still a battle going on out there and Robbie will need two women who can fight behind him. Be at peace in your heart, there is no rift between us. Stand by my side and give Robbie the support he needs. He is now the future of Loxley."

Jess gave her a squeeze. "Oh Rune I feel like I am learning all over again and it surprises me who my new teacher is." Rune gave a giggle.

"I am the centre of my circle, jump in and join in the madness." Jess gave a soft chuckle and kissed her on the head.

"I am so happy Robbie chose you. Steph I love, when she is not shouting at me, thank Hearne it was not bloody Agatha Patterdale, I think I would have killed her."

The two of them laughed as they came back into the room, Jess looked down at Rune's belly. "It's not long now; I bet you are so excited."

Rune's eyes sparkled as she beamed a huge smile at Robbie; she saw the happiness in his eyes as he gave a bright smile. "I want her and her brother so badly Jess; I cannot tell you how much joy there is trapped inside me." Jess looked at the pair of them and remembered the same look on Roberts face; it was one of her happiest times.

Jess sat with Rune, Maddy, and her son, and they talked of the children to come, and the plans they had for the future of Loxley, it was past midnight when Rune finally slipped back into bed and curled round Robbie, she gave a long sigh and snuggled into him, life was finally returning to normal.

It was Saturday morning and school was out for the weekend. The children of Loxley had two days of freedom from Miss Maggs and her teaching staff, yet the school now had another use. The Specialists gathered in what was now the school hall and sat around waiting for Rowan and Robbie.

John looked very pale sat next to an even paler looking Jett. He slid his arm round her shoulder as his head hung low next to hers. Woody sat with Hornet and Flash; Mel smiled as she looked at him, stood next to the bronzed toned figure of Amethyst. She gave him a smile, and he blushed and put his head down, spilling his coffee. Amethyst whispered in Mel's ear. "Cute isn't he? I tell you Mel, I don't know what it is, but he makes me feel all motherly." She gave a soft giggle, and Mel tittered.

Meg sat with Alice and Blades as they whispered about Todd, Alice nudged Blades who smiled a wide smile and blushed a little. "You are a sly one, fancy hiding him in the woods, he is a dish." Meg chuckled as the colour in Blades face deepened.

"Honest Alice we are just mates that's all, we work well together, he likes how I fight."

Alice gave a giggle. "You want to drop the weapons and have a fight with him, I tell you girl, if it wasn't for Bear, I would have a roll around with him." Blades giggled and shyly looked over at Todd who smiled.

"Oh don't Alice, you are wicked." Alice gave her a wink.

"Yeah, it's about time you learnt to be." Meg gave a gasp and a long giggle as the door opened and Rowan and Jade came in.

"Good morning." Rowan smiled as John and Jett visibly shrunk in their seats. Robbie came in smiling with Rune; he walked to the end of the small hall, and sat on the desk and gave everyone a big smile as Rune sat in the chair at his side. The group all pulled their chairs round and sat in a large circle as they looked up at Robbie. He sat and smiled at all of them and they all smiled back at him. "Good morning Specialists. It is nice to have you home again; it has been some time since we were all gathered together. Loxley had need of your skills elsewhere, so as of today we will stay together, I want you out in the trees and back to full skills; we have a lot of work to do."

They all smiled as they looked around at each other, a sense of excitement filled the air. Robbie leaned back as Rune smiled up at him. "Right before we begin, you all know that Keith has finally been named, Harry in his wisdom has bestowed upon him the honour of calling him Hawk. He also informs me that our new arrival to our ranks has the ability to be cunning in the field of battle, so for those of you who have not met our new fighting partner of Blades, Todd sat at the back there will now be known as Fox."

A few of the group had not yet had the pleasure, and looked and gave him a welcome. Todd smiled rather shyly as Robbie continued. "Megan you all know for her sterling work behind the walls with our honoured fallen comrade Lee Sherman. Her father is the leader of our Night Striker team and Megan will be acting as liaison between the two. I have also been, informed she has learned a trick or two off Fuse. Meg I am told by our esteemed wild man Harry, tends to sing like a bird when she walks in the woods." He gave her a smile as she blushed and looked down as everyone smiled.

"Megan will be awarded her name in honour as such, and from now Megan, you will use the name Jay." She looked up surprised and Rune gave her a big smile, Robbie looked down at Alice and gave her a huge grin. "I am delighted to see the return of one of our best bowmen, welcome home Pigeon." The group all exploded with clapping as Alice beamed a huge smile and stood up and bowed. Robbie laughed as Jett and John almost sunk through the floor.

"Pigeon will enhance our bow cover ability, but will be only a part time member as she has the care of my niece. For those of you who have not seen the wonder of my new household member, shame on you she is delightful and maybe one day Jessica Sapphire will be a part of our team." Alice gave Robbie a huge smile and her eyes sparkled. He clapped his hands together. "Last but not least, Lady Jett

Amber."

Jett tried to look up, but her head felt much too heavy.

"Our Wolf man seems to think you have dropped through the net, and looking at you this morning it is hard to place your name, but considering the two tattoos you carry, Harry thought Sting, would be somewhat appropriate, so there you all have it." Jett gave a weak smile from under her fringe as her head pounded; every one smiled and felt a little sorry for her, she had impressed the whole group matching Big John.

"Ok team, we have been out in the field working and passing on our skills. I want to see what all of you have learned and I want all of you out on the range this afternoon, I want bow skills back up to full power. We have a long battle coming and I want that to be handled by Fuse. He is still a very important part of this team, but as you can see by his absence today, his gift truly is tactics. He will remain beside Scarlet who has requested to stay in the field and help. A new troop of a thousand Caerleon men will be arriving tomorrow and going straight into the field. I realise Commander Rafe will be missed by his howling front line, but I want all of you here to begin a new campaign."

Sapphire looked up at Robbie. "What you got in mind Gov?" Rune smiled as Robbie nodded. Harry gave a big beaming smile next to Maggs.

"From this moment my Specialists we have only one aim and one aim alone. We seek out and make Mordred's life a living hell, he will slide out from under some northern rock at some point, and when he does, I intend to draw his dark evil ass out of my brother. When I do my beautiful wife here will send his black soul into a place he will never be able to return from." They all looked at Rune who gave a sweet smile; they were impressed there was no doubt, but also they still had the memory of Dunnottar. Robbie had a tall order in mind; he smiled as he sat back against the desk.

"Mordred will be my task; the mayhem will be up to all of you. Loxley will be threatened as long as Mordred is around, so we must locate him and soon. We know he has been to London, and we know he has been to Dunnottar. I think he will be making regular visits to the Black City, but I am not totally convinced he is there all the time. If he is moving around, we now need to find out where and how, and in between I want to create as much trouble for the black army as possible. The Night Strikers are doing well; we can do a lot better. I want all of you as sharp as you can get, this will be the biggest task we have had to date; the people of the woodland realm are looking to us, so let's not disappoint them."

The group rose from their seats as Rowan came over to Robbie's side, Jade organised the group ready to head for the range, and Skip looked at Robbie and smiled. "You have taller orders every time we meet; we have done everything to get word on Mordred and drawn a blank. Robbie what makes you think you can get information on him when others cannot?"

Robbie smiled and rested a hand on his shoulder. "Skip my good friend that is easy, I will sit on his doorstep and watch where his advisors go. I am quite sure his General's get their orders from somewhere. If we watch them, we will find him. Stealth my friend it is what we do and what we will use."

Skip gave him a smile. "You are right of course, it is simple really, and so simple I had not noticed."

"Let's go and do a little shooting, the practice will help."

Saturday was a rest day for the bowmen of Loxley and so the range was always quiet, Robbie now intended to use these times to train his own team, but also to show the people of Loxley the true skills of the Specialists. He saw the effect in Dunnottar of a well run display, and he now felt that a repeat performance at Loxley could help boost everyone. Many of the woodmen were on a valued day off and did tend to head for the market, if they were not with their wives, they were looking for girlfriends, and Loxley market place was the focal point for the whole area. The group assembled and Robbie walked on to the range, down at the far end, three young bowmen practiced their shooting. Robbie watched as Rowan briefed the group, Alice came up by his side and smiled as she saw him watching the young bowman.

"He is talented Alice, look at the way he holds himself, his knees are a little weak, but he will be a very fine bowman indeed."

Alice gave him a big smile. "He has been here every Saturday since you gave him the bow." Robbie gave a short laugh.

"Is that brave little Jimmy from my gatepost?" Rune slipped her hand into Robbie's as she watched.

"I spoke to his mum some time back in the cheese shop, he has practiced for two hours every night after work and school, you are his idle Rob, he wants to grow up to be your best man." It was touching for Robbie as he watched little Jimmy Perkins with the rowan wood bow Robbie had given him. He thought back to the night when he had thought how brave he had been at having his hood pinned to the gatepost by Robbie's arrow.

"I think he is in need of instruction." Robbie walked down the field slowly with Rune on his arm and Alice at his side, Jimmy lifted his bow at the one hundred and fifty meter point and aimed. He released his arrow and it hit just outside the ring of the bull. "I feel Master Perkins you need to improve your stance; I think you will find you will hit nearer your mark."

Jimmy spun round and looked fearful, he recognised his Lord of Loxley and he and his two friends dropped to one knee. "My Lord Loxley."

"How does my young bowman fair these days, I see you have been following my command?" Jimmy glanced up at Robbie and looked back at the floor.

"I have My Lord, I practice every day."

Robbie went down on one knee and looked at the white face of Jimmy. "Tell me Jimmy, do you still want to be a bowman in my service?"

"Yes and no My Lord." Rune and Alice smiled at the politeness of little Jimmy.

"Yes and no, how can you mean both master woodsmen?"

Jimmy looked right into the eyes of his lord. "I need to be better than a bowman My Lord, so I can join the Specialists." Rune gave a giggle as Robbie smiled.

"A Specialist eh...you set yourself a high bar to jump at my small friend, they are the cream of Loxley and not easy to match."

"I know My Lord, I really am trying harder."

"Tell me Jimmy, have you ever met them or seen them in action?"

Jimmy's eyes widened as he looked into Robbie's eyes. "No My Lord, but I have heard every tale that has ever been told about them many times, and I write them all down so I will not forget."

Robbie smiled and squeezed his small shoulder. "My loyal member of Loxley, you will be rewarded for your efforts; I have not seen such devotion to my house as I have in you. How would you like to be my special guest for a day's training with the Specialists of Loxley? It will certainly give you plenty to write about."

Jimmy looked overcome; he could not believe his ears. "My Lord I have no words to tell you how proud that would make me."

"Then I think my young woodsman, we should give you the chance to earn your pride. Come on I will introduce you." A young woman slipped under the fence and ran across the grass.

"Jimmy what have I told you about bothering the bowmen, come on... I am sorry sir and miss; I tell him over and over not to bother folks who are training."

Robbie stood up and she stopped in her tracks as his crest showed on his cloak, the crossed black and white arrow told her instantly who she addressed, she gave an instant curtsy. "My Lord and Lady forgive me, my son means no harm, he wants to be a bowman of Loxley and he can be a pest, please do not be displeased with him."

Rune turned to the young woman and gave her a smile. "Jimmy is known to us my dear lady, you must be aware that his bow was given to him by my husband?"

"Yes My Lady, but I thought he was boasting."

"Jimmy has a favoured spot with his lord and we have asked him if he would like to be our guest at our training session, he has shown some remarkable talent with his bow, would you mind if we allowed him to join us for the afternoon?"

"My Lady, you are the first lady of Loxley, you have not to ask my permission."

"You are his mother and it would not be right if we did not ask your approval." Jimmy's mother seemed a little more than surprised as she looked up at Robbie and Rune stood with Alice.

"My Lord and Ladies, for my son I know it would be a dream come true, I would not be able to thank you enough, for I know how devoted he is to you both.

If it will not inconvenience you, I would feel honour to know my son has such company, I am but on the market, I help on the yarn stall on Saturdays, it helps pay the rent."

Robbie looked over to the market where a crippled woodsman stood, on crutches watching. "Is that your husband who stands with crutches?"

"Yes My Lord, he was injured in the attack at Hathersage."

"He has fought for Loxley in my service, and what does he do now?"

"He carves figures and motifs on the market My Lord." Robbie walked past her and across the grass toward the woodsman; he climbed over the wooden fence and approached the man. The man could not bow but lowered his head.

"My Lord of Loxley." Robbie looked at the smashed leg and then over his shoulder at the wooden carved figures and motifs.

"Woodsman Perkins, I am told you received your injuries in my service, I see you have a talent for wood."

"Thank you, My Lord, and yes, I served in the attack that saved the black force from attacking last year."

"I am looking for a man of wood craft; tell me would you be interested in extra work for the community? I require men who know how to carve with care, and your work here does you great justice."

Woodsman Perkins nodded. "My Lord, I admit I could use the work, times have been hard on the market of late, but my leg slows me down and most will not hire me."

Robbie looked at him and smiled. "I am not most; I am looking for skill, not pace. Would a little extra work help, it will pay well?"

"If My Lord is sure about the time span, I would be most grateful."

Robbie slipped out his hand. "Good, it's agreed then. I have a training session to run, which I have invited your son to join for the day; we have had the approval of your good wife. I shall return him at the end and we shall talk." Robbie shook his hand and with a big smile he jumped back over the fence, and left the woodsman lost for words with a big smile on his face. Robbie called Jimmy over as he walked up the field and with his arm on his shoulder; he walked to the Specialists who were now all sat on the benches waiting for Robbie.

"Everybody, this young man is Jimmy, he wants to grow up to be a Specialist, and I have invited him to join us for the day. He is brave, and good with a bow as well I feel as being very loyal to all of you, Harry I believe for today we should name him."

Jimmy beamed with delight as he looked in awe at the group. "Hey man with eyes that big and filled with cosmic vibes, I would say call him saucers dude." Jimmy could not believe it; Mad Harry had given him his own nickname. Robbie looked down and winked.

"Saucers it is." The group all gave a smile as Harry came up and shook his hand.

"You're Mad Harry?"

"Hey saucers it's like totally cosmic and very happenin to meet you, your vibes is glowing man." Harry gave Saucers the official tour as Robbie and Rowan began to get organised.

"This man, is the very cosmic and stinging Hornet, if she like goes for her boots, run. We have a very cool Lady Sting with her sword of cosmic ability, and Crystal who can give like a real frosty reception. These happening dudes, are Hawk, he can see for miles man, Fox whoa this dude goes to ground like no one man, and Jaz he does things I can't talk about man. These totally cosmic ladies are Maddy, she can blue you out man, Mel who can totally talk to birdies. Whoa man that is cosmic and Una, and she is the queen of the holly pole. This is the well fed Big John." Saucers was lost he was so delighted and his eyes just got wider as Harry showed him round.

"Whoa man this is Woody; he is real cool with the animals, that there is like Bess. This is Flash baby, she has like red evils that will toast you, and Skip, this guy can fight man and he is like totally good with a pen. Bear, man he can hug, here we have the very happenin Pebbles, she is one of my favourites, this is Mother and Smokes, these totally hot chicks are Saff, cool bow woman and Amethyst, she has like babe power. Whoa this guy can breathe under water for like ages, Fish. I like this one too she is cute, this is Treen she like can make you think uncosmic things, and beside her is another new member, this is Jay, she can totally sing like a birdie man. Here we have my own baby girl Blades, with a very cosmic guy indeed."

"Oh wow you are Wolfie" Saucers looked like he was about to explode as the wolf man knelt down and growled at him. Jimmy's face burst with delight, Harry turned and introduced Rowan, Jimmy again almost exploded.

"Hey man last but not least the only two able bow women in Loxley, Lady Alice, but I call her pigeon, and Lady Runestone Loxley, the hooded dude's totally awesome wife." Rune crouched down.

"I believe Harry we have already met, welcome to the Specialists Jimmy."

"My Lady, I cannot believe I just met Wolfie and Rowan." Rune chuckled.

"I take it you admire Our General and his Commander, well if that is the case, I think a lesson with each will be a good place to start."

Jimmy took his place with great pride in the line on the range. Jay, Hornet, Blades, Fox and Flash lined up with Jimmy in the middle. Rowan walked down the line and checked on everyone's stance, Saucers got a few extra pointers.

They took their shots as some of the others walked up to their side, and increased the line. Saucers squealed with delight as his shot under instruction was nearer the bull. Robbie sat back with Rune and Alice as they watched the Specialists at work. Word ran round the market, and as planned by Robbie he saw the crowds start to gather at the fence. Saucers improved with each shot.

Wolfie crouched down by his side. "Ok little Saucers, listen carefully and I will give you a secret of the Specialists." Rune smiled with Robbie as they leaned forward to listen. "What you must do is summon the power of your arrow, Lord Loxley thinks his arrows, and he is smarter than all of us, which is why he is the best. I growl em, I think you should try."

Saucers lifted his bow and sighted his arrow, Wolfie made a growl behind him as Rune giggled. Saucers aimed and. "Grrrrr...." His arrow shot down the range with pace and landed just on the edge of the centre of the bull. He screamed with delight as he turned to Wolfie. "It works, look it works Wolfie."

Rune and Alice laughed as Wolfie gave a huge smile. "See my young apprentice, a growl will always win the day." All the Specialists threw back their heads and looked to the sky. "Ow Ooooh...!"

Alice and Rune screamed with laughter, as Saucers threw back his head and howled like a Wolfe. The crowed all cheered and Jimmy beamed from head to foot as he turned and looked back at Robbie who bowed and clapped at young Jimmy. For the delight of the crowd came the final finally. Alice, Rune, Hawk, Rowan and Saff lined up as Robbie joined the line to great applause.

They stood at the three hundred meter mark and drew their arrows. The crowd watched with breath held as in complete synchronicity they lifted their bows and took aim. Six arrows all flew together and there was a deep resounding thud, as all six entered their mark. Robbie looked at his rivals. "Who is up for the title?" They all smiled as he walked backwards.

The crowd went silent as at three fifty meters they all aimed. Six arrows split as their next shots hit. Rune gave a giggle as Robbie nodded. They all moved back and the crowd looked in amazement. Six bows rose. Six bows fired. Saff and Hawk hit, but their arrows didn't split; they dropped out as the group took five paces back. Four bows rose as the group all giggled. Rowan took off the feathers but his arrow didn't split, the crowd all sympathised. Rune and Alice giggled as they walked back five more paces.

Alice shot first followed by Rune; Alice sheared the arrow and Rune's split right down the core. She shook her head as Rune and Robbie walked back five more paces. "Well Mrs Loxley, you have improved I am worried."

"You should be Mr Loxley, I want your title." Robbie fired and his arrow, which slipped right down the core, even the Specialists now held their breath as secretly they all wanted Rune to win. She fired and her arrow hit her last but only scored it, a moan came from the crowd. Robbie winked as he walked back another five paces. Rune stood at the side of Rowan as Robbie, almost now at the fence pulled his string back.

"Growl for me Saucers." Saucers was almost passing out he had held his breath for so long. He looked in awe at the target and back at Robbie and as loud as he could he growled.

"Grrrrrrrrr...."

The arrow flew from Robbie's bow at an enormous speed. It hit the target like a thunderbolt, and the arrows that were spliced into the bull exploded out as his arrow sunk deep into the thick straw. The crowd and Jimmy went wild, he jumped in the air and screamed with Alice and Jade and they all laughed in amazement, Robbie bowed to the crowd, and walked over to Rune who giggled as she slipped her arms around him. "You are such a show off. I will beat you one day." She kissed him softly.

He winked. "Got to give the home crowd a little more than the others." He turned to Saucers. "Go collect that arrow and save it, it was your growl that gave me a little extra edge." Saucers ran down the range and heaved on the arrow; he came back up the range and carried it as if it was the heirloom of his household. Robbie turned to the group. "Ok girls you know the routine let the blades fly." Jett still looked pale as she slipped off her jacket and winked at Blades.

"Hey girl it's your home crowd." All the Specialists moved to their seats, as the display began. Jett pulled Harry's swords and rubbed them together, Saucers squeezed between Wolfie and Rune. She gave him a big smile.

"You will see now how we got the name Specialists." Blades spun her swords in her hands as she bowed to Jett; the clash of steel came quickly. Headache or not, Jett still gave the performance of a lifetime, the blades whirled through the air in a blur, and the crowd were silent with awe. The group were all heroes for their exploits around the country, but this was the first time that the people of Loxley really got to see the real reason why. Jett and Blades whooped and screamed louder than ever, they fought faster than they ever had, and the display was unbelievable. Even the Specialists had not seen them fight with such daring and skill. Blades shot high into the air somersaulting and back flipping, and never once could she throw off the spinning whooping advances of Jett. Finally, Jett gave the signal and Blades vaulted high in the air and came down to the floor behind Jett landing in the splits. She bowed forward as Jett spun round and gave a curtsy to her, she then rushed forward panting and pulled Blades into a huge hug, they turned and bowed to the crowd as the people of Loxley went wild.

Jasper and Woody walked up with long staffs; Una bowed to Flash. The pole fighting began in earnest as each pair began with speed and agility, Robbie leaned forward and watched Woody, he had heard from Harry he could be a bit accident prone, but with his shepherds' staff in his hand he was as Harry had said, quite cosmic. The group separated as they fought and soon it was hard to know who was fighting who, as with great speed and blurred poles they swapped and changed fighting partners. Flash broke her pole apart and stepped into the middle; Rune was concerned and leaned forward with Robbie. She giggled loudly in the centre as three poles hurled at her and she deflected them all, there was no doubt Flash was the queen of pole fighting. She looked so vulnerable and partially blinded in the sun, yet with her mirrored glasses on, she flowed like water and her glasses glinted in every direction. Jaz counted out loud and they all stepped back as Flash spun in the centre and then came to a halt.

"That was fun." Her small voice echoed as the crowd cheered wildly, and the group gave a bow. For the grand finale Rowan, John, Jade, and Robbie came up as Wolfie passed apples into the crowd.

"Ok everyone, throw them one at a time and as fast and as high as possible. Keep them over the range so we don't lose any eyes." The apples flew through the air and with speed unknown the competition began, John was out first followed by Rowan, but to Robbie's surprise Jade was like lightening and kept good pace with him, Jett screamed with delight as Rune and Alice screamed for Robbie, it was a draw and Alice knew how to decide. She gave two apples to Big John as Robbie stuck an arrow in the ground by his foot. He winked at Jade.

John hurled the apples with all his might into the air, they shot up like bullets and with lightening reaction Robbie fired his first arrow and stooped for his second, he loaded and fired as the first apple split and then the second apple tore into two pieces. Jade stood looking stunned, he gave her a smile, she bowed out and the crowd roared. Saucers stood silent and just stared with adoration in his eyes, Rowan patted his back. "Now you see why he is the hooded man." Saucers nodded unable to speak. He was as happy as a person could be when Robbie walked him back to the market stalls, Jimmy clutched Robbie's arrow tightly in his hand. His mum bowed and smiled as Jimmy ran up talking wildly about his day. She pulled him close and smiled at the Lord of Loxley. Robbie gave Jimmy a wink as he moved to the next stall to speak to his father. "Woodsman Perkins, I have lost men from my Specialists and men in the fields of York, who have paid a high price for us all at Loxley. I want to place a monument to those who have fallen outside the Village Hall. I have always felt it would be fitting to carve something out of the wood of the land, we live and die by the laws of the woodland; I feel it would be a great tribute."

"My Lord you would honour every life of every soldier and woodsman with such a tribute, and I would consider it an honour to do the work." Robbie smiled.

"I think a bowman would be nice, it is the symbol of this community, I have a large fat trunk of Oak at the farm, which could be delivered to you, so you may work at home if that would be convenient?"

"It would help me My Lord; I find it hard walking far."

"I will make the arrangements and leave you to work out what would be the best pose from the timber. Thank you, would you require payment up front? I have forty gold pieces here, just in case you need more tools for the Job." Woodsman Perkins, eyes widened as he felt the soft cloth bag in his hand.

"My Lord this is too much." Robbie patted his shoulder.

"Take your time and do me a good job, there is no price too much for a brave man's life." Robbie gave him a bow and waved at Jimmy as he slid under the fence and walked back up the range to the smiling Rune. Jimmy's mum threw herself into her husband's shocked arms.

It was the ninth day of April 2039, and the Specialists of Loxley gave a clear and strong signal to everyone gathered that they were back. They were faster, and sharper and greatly advanced in their skills. Exactly one year to the day, they had set out from Loxley as a small party and met up with Rowan in the woods. None of them would have known at that time how the group would have grown.

Rune sat at home and looked at her diary, she read the page that detailed the cave of Harry's and the coming of the sword of truth, and she sat back in Robbie's chair by his desk and remembered that day. She gave a smile as he came up the stair with a drink for her, he sat down at the desk and she slid her diary round for him to see, he chuckled as he saw how much detail of the day she had included, including how nice and tight his pants were. Jett's eyes in her head, Alice losing it with Harry over his map it was all there and he gave a long smile as he looked up at her. "I did not realise you had kept such detail. It's nice Alice came back today of all days, I have missed her bow beside us."

Rune got up out of her chair and came round; she slid on to his knee and smiled. "It seems like so long ago, and yet it is exactly one year today. There was just ten of us Rob, we lost Billy to their side and Eric and Martin have been lost., and today seven of us now form the heart of those first Specialists, if we include those who have been lost we have had thirty nine Specialists to date."

Robbie looked into her bright blue eyes. "Forty, my dad was a Specialist for a while." She smiled and kissed him.

"I am sorry, yes forty how could I forget one of our most important?" He pulled her close.

"It has grown hasn't it? From just ten it is hard to believe."

"I don't think it is really, look at the man they follow, I am surprised we do not have more."

He gave her a kiss and she snuggled down on his lap as he rocked her gently. "I am so happy Robbie."

"Me too."

"I missed you, I am so happy you and Jess have made up, it was horrible not having you hold me when I needed you too. I was so afraid you would do something stupid and hurt yourself. I don't want you ever to leave my side again."

He held her tight and kissed her neck softly. "Oh God Rob, My goose bumps."

"I know." He smiled as she giggled.

CHAPTER THREE

BLACK BIRDS & MAGGS REAL TALENT

The Black Lord walked briskly down the corridor. "I want everything possible doing for the General, he served my mother well at Tintagel and now he has come here to oversee the battle, I do not want this one lacking as the rest have been, let it be known that I favour him highly." The young assistant ran along the side of Mordred as he walked at great pace, he seized the large black doorknobs, and with a twist, he pushed them open, the doors swung back, and entered with a smile on his face.

"Ivor my friend it is good to see you." The tall giant of a man turned, and the assistant gasped in shock. General Ivor Walter's was well known in Tintagel; he was a cruel and sadistic beast of a man that had risen to power from the ranks of the early Cutter Brigades. To most, he was known as the bone crusher, his favourite display of command was to take those who displeased him and with his bare hands, he would kill them. He inflicted death by squeezing their head until the bones shattered and splintered in his hands, it was a terrible sight to behold, and he smiled happily whilst his victim screamed in agony, as their skull would move inwards pressing onto the brain before that final moment of splitting.

He had driven the Cutters to their height of terror by picking out the most evil and vicious men from Mason's forces, and training them into the most ruthless of killers. He felt nothing for no one, his only pleasure was the pleasure of pain and he encouraged his men to take prisoners so he would have sport after his evening meal. He was almost seven feet tall and his shoulders expanded out wide at his side; he wore all black robes and looked like a giant and terrifying monk. His head was bald and he bore the scars of many battles that mapped his head in white and bright pink lines, some places on his head were so scared that it looked like wound up string.

One of the fiercest battles he had ever fought had almost been his last, and now he wore a black patch across his left eye to hide the mutilated eye socket below; his left ear was also missing. It had been pure luck he had lived, as his opponent had left him for dead on the edge of the Cheddar Gorge, the red haired warrior with the golden sword still prowled his dreams, and he would drink heavily at night to mask the pain in his soul. General Ivor Walters, was probably the only man to survive the young twenty two year old Scarlet of Caerleon. He had made the mistake of attacking the town where one of her friend's, mother had lived, and she had been visiting at the time. Walters who was just a Captain in the Cutters at the time led the attack into the town; the warrior with the red hair had not been very forgiving.

Wounded he had escaped into the fields, but when Scarlet found her friend slaughtered with her mother she had tracked him and on the edge of the high cliff, and she had fought with a force that still to this day amazed him. Bleeding and half dead, she had pushed with her boot and he had rolled over the edge, head first he had crashed at high speed into a tree growing out of the wall, and his life although almost expired had been saved. The memory of Scarlet his only true adversary remained, he respected her, for she had with pure skill beaten him. Everyone else he hated, and felt no remorse or guilt when he killed them, simply put he was cold to the bone.

Ivor looked down with his cold eye at the smiling lord in all black. "Le Fey, I am here, show me what you want and I will start." Mordred beamed a cool smile.

"Oh Ivor, take a seat, let us talk and join me in a glass of vintage claret, I know you like your reds." The comment seemed to sting a little as if he thought Mordred was referring to something past, he glared through his eye as Mordred poured out the claret. "I have problems here Ivor; my Generals are getting nowhere; they have been out over a week and not moved an inch; I need you to show them what war really is. I need a man here who can crush and strangle his enemy."

Ivor tipped the contents of the glass down his throat in one gulp. His right hand remained always on his sword. "I am here am I not? Just show me and I will start, I presume you have maps and the placements of the enemy?"

Mordred nodded. "Be patient Ivor, you have just arrived, there is no need to rush I would like to sit and talk a while."

Ivor lifted his cloak off the chair. "Talk to her, and then take her for all I care. I came here to do a job, when it's done, I will go back to my own place, I have things to finish." He walked with a slight limp towards the door and Mordred laughed as he hobbled out in a rush.

He smiled at his assistant. "Wine?" His black eyes seemed to glow with delight. "Make yourself at home, we shall talk instead." She shuddered as a long cold tingle ran down her spine. Fear sat behind her eyes. "What was your name again?"

"Nadia sir."

He passed her a glass as she backed slowly to the fireplace. "That means hope if I am right, how wonderful, I certainly have very high ones."

The staff below put their heads down and worked harder as the screams from the drawing room wailed louder and louder, and bangs and smashes could be heard in between the sick laughter of Lord William.

The Operations room was on the very bottom floor of the black palace. The centre of the room like Loxley had a large map on which small coloured blocks had been placed. Young women with papers in their hands pushed the blocks on long sticks as they moved. It seemed only the green blocks were moving; most of the red were stationary. Colonel Franklin stood on the high platform and looked down surrounded by his captain's as they watched the Loxley woodsmen move across the moor. To the west of the moor, a long line of green moved slowly east, and more woodsmen piled in across the front of York and to the north. Woodsmen were now closing in behind. Rowan and Robbie had managed to create a thirty mile square, defended by woodsmen that had boxed the forces of Mordred completely in.

They had used every device they could think of, from boards covered with heather to long rows of sharp wooden poles, which shot up from the ground and speared the soldiers as they ran into them. Pits had been dug filled with spikes, which the soldiers fell into, and then there was Rune, who would channel through Sapphire and create wide cracks in the earth that would swallow hundreds of men and close again, crushing all those inside. Cannons were no use; as soon as they came out of the gates, they sunk into deep mires that just appeared.

Stealth and observation was helping the woodsmen hold them all back. For the Generals of the black army it was a nightmare, twenty in the first week had seen the Black blade of Dunnottar, as the anger of the lord had risen higher and higher, he had lashed out and slaughtered most of the seasoned officers.

The two doors smashed open and bright light flooded into the room. The entire room jumped with shock, fear was high and nerves were already frayed. The huge dark figure of General Walters stood framed in both doors, he glared round the room and then across at the map. He limped, his heavy foot clumping on the stone floor towards the table, a young woman bowed and he slapped her across the face. She flew like a broken puppet across the room and smashed into cupboards that contained the paperwork, she slid, her neck broken and skull cracked to the floor. "Get out of my way bitch."

The General was not a man to be crossed or inconvenienced, his eye worked quickly across the map as he took in every detail of the battle plan. He glanced up at Franklin. "You... Tell me what all these are and hurry, I have a war to win." He looked down, and stared as his eye ran down from York and centred on Loxley, he smiled for the first time since his arrival. "Blow up my home will you boy?"

It was mid-morning and Sunday. Spring had arrived and the sunlight streamed across the glade of Robbie's Mere. Robbie took a deep breath as he opened his eyes buried deep under the bedding, his arm felt warm around Rune. The scent of fresh cherries and the soft silky hair caressed his nose; he felt a jolt in the palm of his hand and Rune giggled. "She knows you are awake and wants to shake hands," her tummy gave another little jump and she giggled. He softly rubbed her tummy as he smiled, she had only ten more weeks and then he would see his two children. Robbie slid up the bed and stroked back the long red hair that glistened with golden streaks. He leaned over and kissed the side of her neck; she gave a soft giggle and rolled back. He looked down on the soft white face, and the brightest sapphire blue eyes he had ever seen.

"Hey beautiful."

Rune gave a smile. "Hi gorgeous," he leaned down and kissed her. The bed jumped and she giggled.

"I think they are hungry?" Robbie stretched his arms as he yawned.

"Yeah, me too."

Rune sat smiling at the small table out in the sun on the top of the front steps; she wore her lilac bed coat that just about made it round her tummy. She smiled as the birds sang in the trees and the breeze blew softly across the Mere. The last few days had seen such a change in her life compared to the past three weeks. She gave a long restful sigh and lifted her cup of Jasmine tea to her lips.

Robbie came out and placed the cooked breakfast down in front of her. She gave him a big smile as he sat down with his; he winked as he cut through his eggs. Jade had bought a few chickens for a corner of her garden and she was delighted to find that they had begun to lay. Rune looked down at yet more eggs, Robbie grinned as he shovelled his own up and began to chew. She looked at him with a slight smile. "Aren't you getting sick of seeing eggs? Honestly Robbie it feels like it is all we seem to eat now."

"Jade is overrun; I thought you liked a fried egg in the morning?"

"Oh Rob I do, it's just we had scrambled on toast for supper last night. I sliced loads of hard boiled ones, in with the woodland salad we had for tea last night, we even took egg sandwiches to the range for dinner yesterday. I feel like it is all I have eaten in weeks, I am sorry I love it when you cook breakfast, but I just do not think I can eat another egg."

"I will swap you." He lifted her four eggs off the plate and then gave her his bacon and winked, she gave a giggle as he shovelled yet more fried egg into his mouth. It was nice to be alone in an empty house and enjoy just being together.

After breakfast they went back into the house, Robbie sat at his desk with the sun streaming in through the window, with his feet up on the polished surface. Rune curled up on his lap as he read her the story of the Crimson Pirate. He made all the voices as he read, and she giggled as he made high-pitched funny ones for the ladies.

Steph stood at the bottom of the stairs with Smokes, and tried not to laugh as they listened to Robbie read aloud and Rune giggled. "Oh save me, save me from this brute of a man my lord, save me before he robs me of my honour."

Robbie coughed as his voice went a little too high and it caught his throat, Rune squealed with laughter, and she gave him a big smile and kissed him. "Will you read like this to Iona and Hal?"

He stroked back her hair from her bright happy face. "Every night as we tuck them in bed." Robbie saw the shadow on the wall as Steph's green eyes appeared by the base of the rail. "Hey Mum, hey Dad, go on get it over with." Smokes appeared with a beaming smile.

"Wow man you are good, I thought you had a room full of people acting out a play." Rune giggled as her dad leaned over and kissed her. "Hey princess."

"Don't be mean Dad, I love Robbie reading to me, it reminds me of you when I was little." Smokes gave a smile.

"Wow you remember that?" She nodded.

"It's one of my earliest memories, and you too made all the funny voices, I remember."

Steph slipped her arm round Smokes as she saw the memory pass through his eyes. Smokes looked at Robbie, and somehow Robbie seemed to know the conversation was going back to business. "Rob... I have been talking to Harry." He smiled, Rune turned to look at him as he spun the spare chair round sat on it and then leaned on the back of it facing Robbie. "Are you still serious about us attacking Mordred in the black palace?"

Robbie felt a little apprehensive. Smokes he trusted, but Harry had some very odd ideas about life, and he looked with suspicion at Smokes as Rune turned to look at him. "Well, we are not sure he is there, but if he is and that's the only place to get him, yes I would consider looking at it."

"Cool... we have been talking with Harry and Maggs, and we think we have an idea that could give you a faster way in and out."

"OK... I am listening.... I am nervous, but I am listening." Smokes nodded and gave a smile.

"Cool, Harry and we have wondered if you have ever thought of using bikes."

"What?"

"Bikes Robbie, you know... brum, brum?"

Robbie looked more worried, as did Rune who frowned at her dad. "Robbie can't ride a bike dad."

He shrugged. "I know Princess, but hell Harry and me are two of the best, and your mum and Maggs are a pretty close second, the four of us have ridden every dirt track in the country. Maggs is wild with wheels under her, Blades, Jade and Todd are pretty, good that is seven riders and seven passengers, and fourteen should do the job we reckon."

"Won't they hear us coming? Harry does have some pretty loud bikes."

"Well yeah, but we will run diversions, we thought of blowing up that grate, and making the hole bigger. We could then run up on to their ramparts and up the steps, and straight off the wall into the palace, I could put you right in Mordred's lap without you having to get off the bike, you just whack him and it's like split time."

"That is all well and good Smokes, but have you thought of how you will get out with thousands of soldiers shooting at your bikes?"

"Robbie chill a mo, we can run along the top of the wall, hell it's four times wider than the bikes."

"And about a hundred foot high."

"Well that's not a problem, just boost the springs a bit and we can jump."

"WHAT...? You and Harry are stark raving bonkers." Rune did not want to, but she looked at Robbie's look of total surprise and burst out laughing. She kissed him on the cheek.

"Oh you are funny at times."

"Funny, Rune have you heard what your dad and my completely bonkers uncle are planning? It's insane, Harry will have me wearing wings and flapping as he rides off the wall." Steph burst out laughing as she leaned on the rail, Robbie looked up at her.

"Steph please tell me you are not considering this? I thought you were at least sane enough to notice the madness." He looked back at Smokes. "I thought Harry didn't do birdie stuff?"

Smokes gave a shrewd smile. "Hey man this aint birdie, we are now talking bikes."

"Smokes I love you, but have you been sharing Harry's nerve medicine? Bikes do not fly; only Harry after those funny mushrooms at Joes thinks he can fly. Seriously, this has to be the wildest plan he has ever come up with, believe me when I tell you my uncle is lovely, and I adore him, but understand he is as mad as a March hare."

Steph chuckled and looked at Robbie. "The thing is Rob, Harry didn't come up with this plan...I did."

Robbie felt that the world of sanity had just crashed around his head. Steph who was the rock of intelligence and the queen of science seemed to have gone biker chick on him and regressed to her teen years. Madness was exploding around him. Smokes smiled at her with pride.

She was flattered and winked at him. Robbie stared at Rune who was happy, and chirpy and smiling. "What?" She kissed him.

"This could work you know." His bottom lip hit his chest, the circle was complete, and the whole of the Lane family had gone mad in the night without him noticing. Rune beamed up at her mum and dad, all three turned to him smiling. He was right, insanity had struck Loxley.

It was an hour later when Smokes walked at Robbie's side through the woods towards Rowan's, Steph and Rune still giggled as they walked behind talking quietly. Smokes put his arm on Robbie's shoulder and he noticed the long fringe of black leather hanging from under his arm. "Look what I am saying is this, just watch and let us show you what bikes can really do, honestly Rob man, they can do much more than people realise. Just watch and let us show you, I tell you man you will be surprised."

Through the trees, Robbie heard the loud whining of an engine as a bike set off. They came round the side of the house, where Rowan sat watching the small figure in all black leather, with a black crash helmet and mirrored visor, with small blond curls sticking out, run round the spare land at the bottom of Jade's garden. Some sort of assault course had been built, and he watched as Jade jumped up on to logs, and ran across a narrow beam ten foot in the air and then jumped off, landed and ran off down the bottom of the garden where a large ramp had been set up. She disappeared out of view and with a loud gunning of the engine; he heard the bike head for the ramp. "Drink?" Robbie turned and took one.

"Cheers Pebbles." He took a sip as the bike appeared at the top of the ramp and sailed through the air, Robbie looked back at Pebbles who smiled at him.

"She is good, isn't she?"

"Eh...?" The bike landed with a soft thump and raced up the garden towards them, it slid to a halt as the engine gunned loudly. Her arms came up and slid up the helmet, Maggs beamed with delight as she hung the helmet on the handle bar and shook her wild hair full of feathers and beads. She killed the engine as Harry came up smiling with Todd and Blades.

"Oh wow, that was pure cosmic and oh so groovy. Harry babes that was orgasmic." Rune pushed his glass away from his lip in fear he would drown, as Robbie stared in disbelief, Harry winked at him.

"Oh wow man she is wild, I tell you dude, she is the queen of cosmic in leather. Oh whoa she got my number." He raised his eyebrows several times, but Robbie could not quite find the words to respond.

Maggs smiled with long front teeth as she cradled his face in her hands. "Oh Robbie sweetheart, I got a real wild feeling if you like get my vibes?" She gave him a long slow wink. Robbie suddenly felt very unnerved; Maggs gave him a big squeeze. "You want to like have a totally cosmic ride with me; I will show you just how I unjangle my vibes."

Jade and Rune sniggered behind him; Robbie slowly raised his glass. "I think I will have this first Maggs."

She winked again. "Ok Robbie baby, but if you feel the need for speed, you got my number... groovy boy." Rune and Jade exploded into laughter as they stepped quickly into the house; Robbie turned and looked at Rowan, he gave a shrug.

Robbie watched as Blades and Todd tinkered with the row of machines, Jade ran out with a helmet and squealed as she jumped on to the bright red metal machine, she jumped down on the pedal and the engine roared. Robbie had seen Jade ride on many occasions; she had torn down the village making everyone jump and rode back pulling wheelies, he knew she was capable. Blades and Todd both jumped on to a bike each. Robbie had never really thought about Blades, he supposed that in the years that Harry had been visiting his daughter, he must have shown her how to ride. Robbie knew there were three bikes in the barn at her old house; he had just thought they were Harry's.

He sat on the log pile next to Rowan, he felt safe knowing there was someone else who was a simple and logical being as he was. "Have you heard what they are planning?"

Rowan nodded as he watched Jade come up the ramp and fly through the air. "I must admit Robbie, at first I was not so sure, I have little knowledge of these machines, but I have watched what Steph, Smokes, and Harry can do, and I have to say Maggs has a talent I would never have spotted." He turned and looked at him. "They could well have a point."

Robbie felt the surprise creep over him, in all the time he had known Rowan; he had always admired his sense of good logic. He admired the way Rowan would look at something and then pull it apart to see how it all fitted; he had never once seen Rowan rush into a plan. "You really are serious?"

"To be honest Robbie these machines move fast, they are faster than horses, and they seem to jump with ease, I think we could get in so fast that by the time they realised we might have the time we need. These things climb stairs which is not easy on a horse."

Robbie sat back and watched as the three riders jumped, climbed and ran along the thin beam, Rune sat down beside him. "I can open a window from my table, two feet off the top of the wall, it will bring you out level with the top of the escarpment, and I can put you on the wall level with the palace. Rob you can be in and out before they understand what is happening. Think about it." Steph watched as he looked at her, she knew he trusted Rune more than any other person alive.

"Be completely honest with me Rune, I will not risk the lives of these people unless you are one hundred percent sure this can be done. Can they really pull this off?"

Rune smiled as she saw the absolute faith in her glow in his eyes, she leaned forward and kissed him very slowly. "Robbie they can do this, so have some faith, they have planned this for some time." She smiled at him. "Thank you, Rob."

He smiled. "What for?"

"Loving me enough to ask me." She smiled and her blue eyes sparkled as he smiled back.

"Alright Steph, we meet tonight at my house and you show me everything you have on this. It is up to you to convince me, if your plan holds water, we will do it.

Hearne help me I am as mad as my uncle."

Steph smiled as Smokes slipped his arm round her. "Right Rob you are on."

It was later that night in the office at the top of Robbie's house, that Steph looked up from a very detailed presentation with plans and drawings and charts. The whole group of Specialists looked at each other as Steph smiled. Robbie got out of his seat next to Rune and walked to the front. "Thanks Mother." She gave him a big smile. He winked and turned to the group. "Ok all of you those are the plans. We have only seven bikes capable of doing this so Harry, Maggs, Mother, Smokes, Pebbles, Blades and Fox are in. I am obviously going and so is Rowan, for this one job, the five other places will be volunteers only; the rest of you will be back up."

Maddy and Sting stepped forward together, Jett giggled at Maddy. Maddy looked up. "I am not a lover of these machines but you will need my bow in there just in case." Wolfie was already at Stings side; Flash had jumped forward holding Woody's hand. Flash giggled.

"I want to ride with Maggs."

Robbie nodded. "Alright everyone thanks, the rest of you will be supported by the Night Stalkers, and they have more knowledge of the black city than any of us. Let's get prepared we will go tomorrow night just after dark, Saff hold back a minute while you and Rune coordinate the windows. Mel, I need you to call up a friend." Mel stopped and gave Robbie a strange look.

A black cloud flowed over the city of London. Screams echoed from the top of the pale town house, across from the crumbled decay of the palace of Westminster. The sky turned black and the clouds swirled in the air, Lance knelt by the bed and held the hand of his stepmother as she screamed and wailed in agony. "She is coming just hold on, Grandmother will be here soon."

Dana Knox held her stomach and clenched her teeth tight, the pain was overwhelming, and she pushed her head back into the pillow and screamed with all her might as the contraction felt like a hot knife slicing through her stomach. Lance screwed up his eyes, she squeezed so hard on his hand it almost broke his fingers. Her face was red and covered with sweat as she panted and gasped in between screams. He leaned over and wiped her face tenderly; she gave him a smile and nodded unable to speak. He smiled at her. "You are brave Dana; I can see why my dad loved you. She will be here soon, and then things will be fine." Dana clenched her teeth as she felt the next bout starting.

Out in the street below, the guards looked up in fear as the screams of pain rang down from the rooftop and rattled in their ears. They shuffled at the door uneasy on their duty, they knew her time had come and they knew what that meant. The

Dark One would soon arrive, it was not a prospect they were looking forward to, they had enjoyed being away from Tintagel and watching over their new mistress. Dana was hard there was no doubt, but she did not kill or beat you up if she felt in a bad mood, after being at Tintagel for ten years, her screams of displeasure were nothing. The cloud thickened above them and they both stepped back into the doorway, as the light seemed to be drawn out of the air as darkness descended, both guards shivered with fear.

Lance smiled down as the light outside the window faded, he wiped her face. "She is here now, and it will all be fine." Dana gave a weakened smile; the pain had robbed her of all of her strength.

The doors on the balcony burst open, and the dark feathered figure stood cold and pale looking; she let the thinnest of smiles wash on to her lips as she stepped into the room. The temperature seemed to fall and the breath from Dana's exhausted mouth turned white as she panted, clinging to the hand of her Stepson Lance. Morgan le Fey had waited for a long time for this, she had known that the child from the Hargreaves woman had power; she had just known all along that she would be a disappointment. She gave a long smile at Lance; her cold voice fell dead to the floor. "Lance my darling; it is time for you to meet your sister." She looked at Dana, who wore a look of fear, Lance looked down at her.

"Soon over now Mum." Morgan smirked as she saw the bond between them, maybe the woman should live, she had not considered that. She had been good for the boy and given him instruction in the manner of his father. She lifted the bedclothes and looked between the legs of the woman; Lance looked away to hide his embarrassment. Morgan slid her arm under the sheets and Dana winced. She felt a strange tingling sensation as Morgan began to speak words she did not understand. Her body relaxed as the pain left her and she felt the strength run back into her. Morgan smiled a cold unfeeling smile. "Push down hard and it will be done."

Dana closed her eyes and gave one almighty push, she strained hard, and then felt movement, and she gasped for air as she thrust down with all that she had, Morgan le Fey gave a hideous cackle and the pain left Dana as she collapsed gasping for air. The Dark One continued her mutterings, and then Dana heard the cry of her child; Morgan lifted the blood-covered child above the sheets and smiled at Dana.

"She has great power my child, you have done well, and Mason will be pleased when I tell him." She held up the child and inspected it, and then quickly she wrapped it in a blanket and gave the child to its mother while she attended to the rest of the job. Morgan looked down on the mother and child, as Lance leaned over to see his new sister. "So, what are you to name her? Mason told me you had both named her, he would not say what?"

Dana looked exhausted and looked up from the bed. "Your son wanted her to be called Raven, I chose the name Merle." The Dark One smiled.

"Child, I had no idea you knew of the bonds in my house. Merle is the sign of the black bird and you call her Raven. You have honoured my house; I underestimated your commitment to my son. You will rest now and I will send others to care for you, when you are stronger, I shall return and we can talk. Lance take care of your mother, she is precious. There are things I must do now she has come, we must prepare for her properly and make sure all is correct."

The Dark One lifted the afterbirth wrapped in cloth, turned and flew through the doors over the balcony and was gone. Lightning struck from high in the air and the thunder roared across the sky. The night sky over London stayed black and the lightening flashed through the night.

Hearne looked to the sky from the top of Hearne's rock and stretched out his hands. "Life has been given without our consent, this child is not written on the table of life, we demand a life from you in payment black queen. Restore the balance to the lines of time." Lightening bounced down from the skies, as a scream and a cackle broke through the clouds, the lord of creation was being defied. His anger rose quickly as he looked to the heavens, but a violet hand touched his shoulder softly and he looked down into the violet eyes of his Daughter of the Woods.

The slender violet figure of Runestone Sapphire glowed brightly as she smiled at her Green Lord and Grandfather of creation. "I am life and the balance is mine to hold, I have chosen the life I will have, let the Raven live, I will bring you the life to restore."

Hearne smiled and took her hand. "You are life my dearest daughter, and so like the grandmother who brought gifts to you. I will hold the balance for a short time, work quickly my child and return the balance, we live on the edge of dreams, we cannot afford to tip the balance for long."

"Fear not grandfather, we have chosen to use the things they treasure as the tool of their destruction, and tomorrow fire will be fought with fire." She smiled as the lord embraced her.

"Oh you have grown in power my daughter, you are already stronger than we expected and the life you bring to the Violet Isle will increase your power tenfold. Stay close to your bowman and follow his steps from the table, she does not control all of the lines of time, there are some whites, black will never taint, they are within him. When light passes through them they are violet."

Rune smiled. "I love him as deeply my father of the woods." The Green Lord smiled.

"It was not seen, but it has brought me joy to watch the one who I hold so precious to me blossom beside him. Go now and prepare and I will hold the line together until you return."

Rune bowed to her lord, and turned, she faded as she crossed the top of the rock and the Green Lord stood and looked to the heavens.

Rune sat up in bed as Robbie watched, her eyes faded back to normal; she gave him a sweet smile. "Your Lord is happy, to see you have begun healing. Robbie the wife of Mason gave birth to a girl tonight; she will be Raven, the black bird of her line. We must now move swiftly with our plans, if you face Mordred remember you must think of me if you feel he is gaining power, there are lines that work to our favour, even in the black city." Robbie nodded as he listened carefully.

It was a busy day as Robbie sat with Steph and ran over the plans again. Word was in from the Night Stalkers that Mordred had been seen in the city, and so Robbie gave the approval to put the plan into action. Half his group moved out early to liaise with Malcolm Prosper, Bear commanded the second group as Harry and Todd, made all the last minute adjustments to the bikes. Mel stood in the centre of the glade and lifting her gold eagle's talon pendant she threw back her head and screeched into the air. Robbie sat with Rowan on the steps as a huge bird flew down from the sky and landed on the stump of an old tree. Mel gave a big smile to the bird and bowed. "Hello my queen, I have missed you."

The large Eagle of Callanish gave a long slow bow of respect to her. Mel walked closer to her and held out her hand, the bird seemed to nibble it in an affectionate way. Robbie watched captivated by the sight, the eagle was a huge bird, he had not realised how big the eagles of the island grew. Mel had no fear at all, as she softly spoke to the bird, which nodded its head from side to side. She smiled and then softly stroked its head, she stepped back and bowed; the eagle gave her a regal bow and then swept its wings wide and lifted into the air.

Mel shaded her eyes as she stood and watched the huge bird rise up into the sky, she gave a little chuckle of excitement and then with a beaming smile, she walked back up the glade to the small gate at the front of the garden. Mel looked across at Rune as she came down the path. "It is arranged, we will have our eyes in the sky."

Robbie looked back as Rune nodded and smiled. "I will be watching you Rob at all times, Mel will track you through the bird and if you get into trouble Saff will be there so I can always channel through her to help." She gave him a warm smile. "I will feel more relaxed knowing you are safe." He gave her a nod and looked back up at Mel who now looked up at the skies and the small black dot that flew high above Loxley.

As the afternoon slowly crept in, Smokes organised the building of a ramp. The idea was that the bikes would need momentum as they came out of Rune's window and over the high wall; Robbie felt his stomach churn every time he looked at it. The idea of blowing a big hole in the wall had been scrapped, it would be simpler and help the element of surprise if they came out of the air, over the wall and landed on the ramparts.

From the ramparts, they were just twenty feet from the Black Palace, and so it would be closer than having to ride through the city and the barracks to reach their objective. Rune pointed out this would give less time for Mordred to prepare, his apartments were on the top floor and so they knew that as long as they got there ahead of the guards, they could all hold off an attack whilst Mordred was dealt with.

Smokes seemed to be in command of the bikes, and so Robbie had to sit back and place his faith in his father in law, and hope he had got it all right. He ate very little tea as his stomach twisted and turned, he was not familiar with bikes, and it affected his confidence. Rune pulled him close as he checked his dagger and sword. "Be careful my darling, remember the white lines flow through both of us. I will be here watching and waiting." She kissed him softly and he pulled her close.

The sun began to slip down in the sky as the time approached, Harry had topped the fuel, which was moonshine based, and the bikes all sat in a long row waiting. The riders all wore leather as they waited for their passengers, Todd had fitted extra swords and arrow quivers to the backs of the seats, and now they all sat waiting for Robbie to appear with the others.

Maddy slipped on behind Smokes, as Rowan joined an excited and giggling Pebbles. Woody held on tightly to Harry as Wolfie slipped in behind Fox. Blades chuckled as Sting took her seat behind her. Robbie walked down the line to Steph as Flash giggled at the front of the row behind Maggs. He took a deep breath as Steph kicked down hard and the bike fired up, somehow this was not his idea of woodsman craft.

The bikes shot off down the glade as the shimmering window of violet opened at the top of the ramp. Robbie held tight and closed his eyes, he knew he was not going to enjoy this. Maggs and Flash screamed with delight as they hit the ramp, and the bike shot into the air and disappeared through the violet window. Rune watched with Mel as all the bikes disappeared, and then she turned and went down to her table to watch, as her eyes grew bright with violet and the mist in her table swirled.

Bear and Malcolm placed the last of the explosives in the tunnel grate at the south of the city, Jay worked quickly as she fitted the fuse and unrolled it a length. "How quickly do you want it to go off?" Bear glanced at the wide expanse of land to where all of the Night Stalkers stood waiting in the trees. The Specialists lined the walls, with their backs flat against it.

"Can you give us two minutes?" Jay nodded and pulled the fuse through her fingers as she had been taught, she pulled out her knife and cut the fuse. Bear and Malcolm ran along the side of the wall as Jay lit the fuse and followed. The Specialists all loaded their bows and prepared to light their fuses.

The wall shook as the flash lit the whole valley, with hoods up the Specialists waited. The explosion was ear splitting and the ground moved below their feet as dust fell from above. Concrete and stone blasted into the air, soldiers screamed as they were tossed off the wall and the empty houses inside the walls were rained on with large heavy chunks of concrete, which smashed through the roofs and crashed through the walls. The Specialists lit their arrows and moved like the wind, before the soldiers realised what was happening, fizzing arrows shot into the air as all the guards ramparts felt the steel of a Loxley arrow bite into their stonework. They flowed over the rubble of the wall as explosions left right and centre lifted more stone and soldiers into the air.

Bells rang all over the city as soldiers poured out of their buildings and tents. Father Warren stood alone in the tower of the church and watched the chaos as it rained down on the black city. Hawk was swift with his bow beside Saff, and any soldier who recovered in time to stand, was hit and fell back to the floor. The Specialists moved up to the roofline, with the advantage of high ground, the Night Stalkers flowed through the streets. Explosions lifted into the air as every target marked by Malcolm was hit. They moved quickly through the city bringing death with them, they headed for the wall where the barracks started, it already bore the repair scars of their previous visit, and they intended to leave it with a great deal more.

All eyes looked south as the soldiers ran to defend the barracks; no one noticed the violet light that twinkled in the air two feet above the wall near the top rampart. With a scream and a howl, the first bike burst out of nowhere and the five guards who stood leaning against the wall happy to be so far away from the fight jumped. They separated fast as the bike landed with a skid and shot toward them. Two bright white gleaming poles came out of the side of the rider, and as the bike ploughed into them, they spun and whirled as a high pitched little voice screamed with laughter. They had no idea they had been hit and just sunk to their knees as the bike hurtled past across the top of the rampart and headed to the far end and the steps.

The second and third bikes were right behind as the fourth landed, and the others sailed through the air as the violet window closed behind them. Fox and Blades screeched to a halt spinning their bikes, and gunning the engines loudly, they turned and headed on to the west wall, which many months ago Robbie and the crew had run along. Wolfie stood up as did Sting, they had their bows loaded as the bikes hurtled at a terrific speed at the few soldiers who had turned and were starting to make their way back. Fox flicked on the bright headlamp and blinded them as he sped towards them, Wolfie and Sting fired their bows. Maggs was now halfway down the steps heading into the compound; Harry with Woody was not far behind. Flash slipped around Maggs and now sat in front of her on the fuel tank, her glasses were deep in her pocket as her eyes began to flicker red.

Thousands of soldiers rushed with their arms down to the market end of the city, none of them noticed as two bikes hit the floor far up the compound behind them. Smokes slowed at the corner of the middle and south wall; Steph spun the bike with Robbie holding on for his life. Smokes winked at Steph. "You ready baby?" She blew him a kiss as she gunned the engine, Robbie noticed as Maddy slid her arms right round Smokes. Before he could do the same the back wheels of the bikes screamed on the floor as smoke rose into Robbie's nose. The two bikes leapt forward, and at break neck speed, they flew back along the wide walkway that they had just come down. Robbie screamed as he realised what was happening and the bikes lifted into the air and crossed the twenty foot gap toward the Black Palace.

Both bikes crashed through the wooden rails, skidded on the wooden balcony and then crashed through the glass windows. They shot across the room and as Robbie looked up, he saw Smokes crash through the wooden door that led out into the corridor. "Load your bow." Steph screamed as she followed her husband. Robbie pulled an arrow and fumbled as he fitted it. Smokes shot up on to the stairs at the end of the corridor as Maddy released her arrow. It was just an ordinary arrow and the guard at the top shot back as the two bikes tore upwards. Steph handled the bike with skill, and she screamed with delight as she caught a glimpse of her husband's face as he spun at the top of the stairs and raced down the next corridor.

A guard ran out of a doorway, and forcing his feet down hard into the pedals Robbie stood up in a flash and fired, the guard leapt backwards with the arrow in his chest as Steph whooped and cheered like Jett. He was getting use to the bike, and now loaded quickly, his eyes watched carefully, as Steph swung the bike on to another flight of stairs. He saw the face of cold white with black dead eyes looking down, and in a beat of a single heartbeat, Robbie lifted the bow and fired. Mordred jumped back as the arrow flew past and hit the ceiling above where it vibrated in the beam. He was here and Robbie felt the calmness of his destiny flow over him, he reached for another arrow and saw the hilt of his sword and dagger both glowed white from the centre of the moonstones.

Both bikes burst on to the landing as Mordred ran down to the end of the corridor, Steph took the lead and gave chase, Maddy spun round on the seat and pressed her back up against Smokes, she drew a long white arrow out of her other quiver. The soldiers at the far end of the corridor spilled out, as Maddy pulled back on the string. "Move it Smokes!" She released the arrow as the wheels spun and the bike shot off down the long corridor at high speed. Flames erupted in the midst of the troops and engulfed the whole top half of the corridor; soldier's screams were snuffed out as the flames drew them into a deadly embrace.

Steph skidded on the carpet as Robbie looked at the door, she turned the bike to face the oncoming Smokes and with the engine running, she pulled out her bow and fitted an arrow to the string. Robbie slipped off as Smokes came to his side with a huge smile on his face.

"Not too shabby man." Both bike engines ran as Smokes, and Robbie stood either side of the door, Maddy and Steph watched with bows up and loaded. Smokes looked at the door and counted to three; they both turned and kicked with all their might, and jumped back out of sight as the doors exploded open. A long silver spear came through the gap and stuck in the wall, it glinted as it shuddered. Smokes gave a smile from the side of the door. "If you kill him, can I have that? Whoa man that is some spear." Smokes looked round quick and spotted the black cloth heading for the window; he pulled up his bow and fired. The arrow hit the window frame and Mordred stopped in his tracks as Robbie rolled round the doorframe and looked into his dark frightened eyes. He drew the Sword of Destiny out of it sheath, and as he lifted it up two claw like arms slipped out just above the hilt, Destiny felt the moment was looming.

"We have unfinished business Dark Boy, give me my brother back."

The fuses fizzed as Sting and Wolfie took aim, the bikes slowed a little as the two explosive arrows headed for the large glass window of the guardroom. On the market side of the guardroom, soldiers fled on to the ramparts, and ran as fast as they could away from the room where all the controls to the lights and speakers were situated. It lifted off the wall and chased the screaming guards, as the concrete flew down from the high wall and crushed the swarming masses below.

Rowan now stood on a clear rampart with his bow next to Pebbles, as they looked on the black palace, the flash from the exploding guard room illuminated everywhere as all the flood lights went out. The walls danced with the flickering lights of the flames; Pebbles bike chugged with its engine running on its stand as the two woodsmen watched. Rowan looked down at the bike of Maggs, which flew down the centre of the huge barracks and grounds. "Pull your hood sweetheart." He pulled on his hood as he heard the wail from the little voice in the distance.

"Hey boys can we all play?" Tents, flagpoles, and fencing ignited and ran in a line with the wide band of white light, as Maggs with Flash sat up front raced down the plain. The heat burned the soil and the grass, as everything in the barracks was engulfed. The Night Stalkers faded and the Specialist retreated, as the guards all turned and looked at the light of the sun coming towards them. Like a tide of fire, Sting and Wolfie watched the flames devour everything in a line that cleared the floor of everything. All that was left behind the bike was a wide trail of ash. Blades turned the bike and headed back to the black palace with Fox behind her. They raced back along the empty wall, in the direction of Rowan and Pebbles.

The gates of the barracks were twenty feet tall and four inches thick. They were made from the hardest oak; they were wide open and smouldering as Maggs skidded the bike to a halt. She lifted her mirrored visor and wiped the sweat from her face as she looked at the devastation created by Flash. There was nothing left but smouldering soot and dust, and it was chilling to see and witness. Maggs had lived all her life in the pursuit of peace; she had not so much as killed a spider, now twice as her family and friends had been forced to survive against a force that wanted to kill them all, she had joined the Specialists at Canterbury and now at the Black City.

Maggs had loved Harry all her life; she had met him at sixteen and been with him for most of his young life. She had come close to losing him, and now as she reached thirty-seven she had him back. In all of the time she had known the kind, gentle and loving man that he was, she had never understood the gossip of how brutal he could be with his swords. As she sat on her bike with the engine running and looked at little Flash, she began to see the bigger picture of how their life and their world was at risk. She was saddened by it, but she knew that the devastation she had helped create was just a small amount of what was being amassed to crush Loxley. She did not feel happy about the death, but she understood the reason behind doing it. Maggs turned the bike and looked back up the long wide stretch of black sooty floor; there was a green line where Flash had opened her eyes, and from the line to the black palace far away in the distance, the grass still grew green. It seemed surreal to her.

Harry and Woody raced up to her side as he spun the bike in a skid, and Woody franticly snatched and grabbed at Harry, as he slid sideways towards the floor. Harry raised his visor. "Hey chicken, whoa baby girl, that was some sunshine man, it was like cosmic and very happenin."

Maggs gave a weak smile, as she dropped her visor, and revved the engine.

Robbie would need them back up at the top, and she had promised Rune she would not leave him alone for long. Pulling a wheelie with Flash screaming with joy she set off. Woody climbed back on the bike, and gripped Harry with both hands as he set off behind her.

Blades and Fox came skidding to a halt behind Rowan. They looked at the palace where the shadow of Mordred stood frozen in the window, the smashed rails hung loose where Smokes and Steph had crashed over lower down. The two bikes revved across the long empty plain and Rowan peered through the darkness, as the two headlights bobbed over the surface of the soot towards them. "It's now up to Robbie, stay sharp and let's seal this place, we still have an army of the dead to deal with if Robbie cannot stop the Dark Lord."

Rowan watched as Maggs and Harry hit the steps halfway down the long plain. They would come up the ramparts and back on to the wall; he glanced up at the window and caught the shape of the figure that had just drawn a sword. There was nothing to do now but watch and wait. "Keep your engines running, I want Robbie out of here as quick as possible when this is done?" Blades and Fox nodded;

Pebbles was too busy watching the windows above her. Rune's eyes blazed violet as she watched the figures in the windows through the eyes of her sister. Mel's eyes flickered blue as she gazed down from the eyes of her eagle and watched as Harry and Maggs came up the steps and along the high ramparts towards Rowan and Pebbles. The eagle swooped out of the sky and sat on the roof of the guardroom, it watched level with the windows as Mordred raised the Black Blade of Dunnottar. Mel held her breath as Rune connected with her; she now watched with her heart pounding as the shadow of Robbie disappeared as he walked towards his destiny.

CHAPTER FOUR

THE RULE OF A LORD

Rune sat at her table and watched the shadows behind the windows through the eyes of the eagle. Mel's eyes flickered bright blue as she focused herself on the large bird, whilst Rune with a nervous heart focused into Mel. Violet light spilled out on to the table, her thin white fingers held the side firmly as she felt the worry of a wife of a fighter for the first time.

The sword of destiny gleamed in the dim room; the power contained within the blade gave out an aura that filled the walls with a bright glowing light. Robbie watched with his dark focused eyes, as he felt himself relax and prepare, the dark figure before him stared back with hatred and venom. This time he was fresh and felt much stronger, Mordred seemed to sense it as he backed away from the window and drew out the Black Blade of Dunnottar. Robbie felt the almost shiver like tremble in the hilt of his sword; he knew that Destiny wanted the conflict. Mordred looked at the sword.

"You are a fool to come back Bow Boy, your so called brother is now trapped forever and will not fight his way out again, you now face only me alone. You have no friends to help you this time."

Robbie drew the dagger of Victor Thornson out of the sheath with his left hand and held it up with the Sword of Destiny. "I have all the friends I need here to face you Mordred." He gave a smile as his eyes sparkled at the white face and black eyes of his opponent. Mordred moved slowly face to face with about twelve feet between him and Robbie. Robbie shadowed him as he noticed the door to his right; he was not going to let Mordred run into Smokes and Steph in the corridor. He took a step forward and Mordred stepped back, his eyes glanced at the closed wooden door and he backed quickly towards it.

"What's wrong Dark Boy; have you no taunts about killing kings and fighting worthier men for me tonight? You seemed full of yourself last time, your boasts and bragging all gone now you are alone without your staff to club me from behind?"

The dark black eyes scowled with hate at him as they looked to the long golden dagger, and the golden sword in his hands. Mordred drew a long ornate silver dagger out of his belt and held it up in his left hand. He gave a smirk. "I need no servant to help me, you will die and your soldiers will be crushed. Then woodchopper I will personally slice up your witch."

Robbie smiled. "It's amazing how much we have in common really, I have sliced your brother and slaughtered countless numbers of your men, and then yes Dark Boy I intend to use my bright golden sword to dispatch the rest of your evil and vile family to a realm so dark even they will not find each other."

Mordred spat on the floor as his hand shook with rage; Robbie smiled his eyes never leaving the hateful stare of Mordred. He watched the anger build inside him, and Robbie tensed feeling the moment coming. Mordred screamed loudly and lifted his black sword. "My line will live longer than Loxley, Bow Boy."

Rune gasped as she saw the shadowy figure lunge across the room towards Robbie, who she could not see for the wall. Her heart pounded hard inside her chest as her hands gripped harder into the cool surface of her table.

Destiny rose gleaming in the hand of its master, the golden blade struck with vengeance and the ring of steel echoed around the room, sparks flew as the blades slid together, and Robbie twisted his wrist bringing more power to the blade as he forced Mordred backward. Both of the blades screamed in pain as the hate for each other flowed out, the silver dagger shone in the air as it sliced towards Mordred, and with a flick of his wrist the dagger of Thornson struck hard on the blade and Mordred's hand jumped back with the force, he stepped back quickly as Robbie swung Destiny round with speed and brute power.

The blow was a heavy crashing blow, and Mordred felt his arm shudder with the impact, again he stepped back and defended. Robbie had faced him once and he knew this time he would not give him the chance to strike a return.

The table at the side of Mordred flew across the room and smashed, as Mordred kicked out at it. Rune sat at her table, flinched as she heard the crash; she felt the cold grip on her heart, as she was unable to see what was happening for the wall. Robbie spun round with the gleaming blade that glowed on the dark boy's face, and he brought the sword down with a crashing slicing sweep. Mordred squealed out in pain as a gash opened up on his left arm, and the blood flowed out to the floor. He thrust the sword out wildly and Robbie pulled back as the sword just missed slicing his chest. Rune gasped as she saw him move quickly out of the way across the window, and then Robbie responded with another crashing blow on the staggering panicked Mordred. She had to breathe out as she had been holding her breath too long; she looked at Mel who had eyes filled with bright blue light. "I am not sure I can watch this, if I have another scare like that one, I am quite sure I will give birth here."

Mel chuckled. "I will watch if you want and warn you if you are needed." Rune shook her head and swallowed deeply. The two figures fought across the light of the window, and Rune watched as she saw Robbie pound yet more blows onto

Mordred, she knew she had to watch; she wanted to know what was happening even though it raised huge fears inside her. The dark shape of Mordred in the light through the window backed away from Robbie.

A tall wicker chair sat silent beside him and quickly he rushed behind it. His arm stung with the pain of the golden blade, and he felt the fear of the power of Gwendolyn in his arm. He pushed the chair forward as Robbie calmly stepped sideways to keep the dark opponent in view. "You are losing your nerve dark boy. I thought you were a killer of kings and saw me as no sport?"

Robbie wiped the sweat from his brow as he watched the black clad Billy, which contained the dark lord of old's essence step back behind the chair. Robbie tensed, as he knew what was coming, and as Mordred raised his foot and the basket chair shot forward, Robbie lifted his blade, and stepped sideward, letting the chair fly past and smash through the window as Mordred flew at him waving the Black Blade of Dunnottar.

Rune jumped and screamed out, as the chair crashed through the window and bounced across the balcony and over the rail. Rowan watched as it hit the floor eight levels below and smashed on the stone. Guards moved toward the doors of the black palace, he patted Pebbles on the shoulder as he looked down and the clash of steel rung inside on the top floor.

Sting, Wolfie, Fox, Blades and Pebbles pulled their bowstrings with Rowan, and sent a hail of arrows on the guards below. They ducked and ran for cover, as they looked up in the darkness to try to see where the bowmen were. Mordred crashed and swung at Robbie with all his power, Robbie side stepped and walked as he twisted and stretched, his blade flowing with rhythm through the air as he blocked the dark lord with skill and great ease. Mordred screamed with hate and rage at Robbie, whom he thought was not really doing much to fight back. The sweat ran down the nose of the white face containing the black evil eyes, but Robbie just smiled and waited for his moment, he had learned much the last time that they fought.

The black sword wailed each time it felt the touch of the sword made by Gwendolyn. Robbie watched as the blade grew duller and blacker, he knew his sword was soaking up the power of the White Circle that had been mixed with evil into the blade, he felt Destiny growing stronger in his hand and he knew soon the time to strike would be upon him. Mordred swung wildly but still with great strength, as Robbie blocked the shots and felt the vibrations run down his arm. He cursed, spat, and raged with his fury, as he could not seem to get Robbie to stop smiling as he calmly absorbed every shot, and stepped casually out of the way.

The moment arrived, as with a flash across his eyes the Sword of Destiny began to swing with purpose. The blade came up in a blur before Mordred, and he staggered a little as the force of the blow from Robbie almost lifted him off his feet. His opponent was calm and struck with skill; Mordred felt more fear stir inside him, as the golden dagger swiped round and kissed the black blade. It was the softest touch of the dagger on his sword, but it hit his heart with a chill as the voice of Gwendolyn laughed in his head. His whole arm shook as if the blade wanted to get away and be free of the dagger, adding to the fear he was now feeling surging up inside him

Mordred stepped back against the tall smashed window, his eyes now wide as Robbie came at him with thundering blows, he hit the low wall, and fell sprawling out of the window, onto the broken glass outside on the balcony. Robbie leaned through and continued to pound him. Mordred crawled quickly across the glass to free himself of the onslaught; he clawed at the railing dragging himself to his feet, and looked out at the ramparts. He looked across at the row of bowmen and then glanced up at the eagle with violet eyes, he now knew he was alone and the Violet Witch was watching him, he turned quickly as Robbie climbed through the window.

The Bowman of Loxley stood tall and proud, Destiny sparkled with radiance and light like it never had before, the moonstone on the dagger grew brighter knowing the time of its own destiny was coming. The calm face and eyes that burned with life and justice, stood before Mordred who was trapped on the long balcony. He turned to the rail as Jett Amber walked round the wall and pulled up her bow, she wagged a finger like Flash would do, he had nowhere to run and turned and faced the true power of Lord Loxley.

Rune watched half filled with hope and half filled with fear, she held her breath as Robbie stared at the dark figure with wild eyes. "Your time has come spawn of the Dark One, face me like a man and die."

Mordred lifted the dagger and threw it with all his might, Rune jumped on her seat as Robbie swung up the blade and hit it away like an annoying fly. It glinted as it flew through the air, the small hand snapped around it, and Pebbles pulled it out of the air, and smiled as she looked down on the very well crafted dagger.

Mordred gripped his sword with both hands; he lifted it into the air and screamed with all his terrified might, and lunged at Robbie. The power of the blades meeting was awesome, sparks flashed into the air as both blades screamed a violent and loud scream of death, as they met with hatred in pain. Robbie still holding the dagger pushed his feet firmly into the floor as the heavy blows rained down and sideways at him. His wrists shuddered with the power, Billy had never been weak, and now Robbie absorbed the power of Billy, being wielded by Mordred. He cut up, and sliced back, and threw the balance of the black blade. Now Robbie seized his opportunity, and he flew at Mordred stepping into him as he brought Destiny slicing across, Mordred twisted badly to stop the shot, and he staggered as Robbie lifted the blade with all of his strength, and brought the dagger around and onto the black blade.

Mordred gave a terrifying scream, and red light exploded out of his eyes,

Robbie was shocked and jumped back as Mordred thrashed with his free arm to pull backward. He brought up a leg and Robbie felt it connect with his hip, he staggered back with the force, and Mordred pulled away from the blade screaming. Rune had risen to her feet and clenched hard on the table, her heart was pounding with fear and joy. "Yes," she had gasped as she had risen from her chair, willing all of her love and her power to Robbie. She flopped back down in the seat as they broke apart, and Mel raised a hand to her shoulder.

Mordred shook like a frightened rabbit, somewhere deep down inside had squeezed hard on his heart as he felt the cold icy feel of the taste of Excalibur, and Mordred felt something he had not felt in a thousand years. His last memory had been as King Arthur had gripped him with a powerful arm as he hung impaled on Mordred's lance. With the power of a king who stood for all that was good, he had pulled Mordred toward him, and slid the sword of power through him, it now felt the same as he stared not knowing what the dagger contained. The eyes of the bowman stared at him, and Robbie lifted the dagger as he gripped his hood and pulled it up over his head. Mordred stared into the darkness that had been the bowman's face, and all he saw was the brightness of the eyes. He knew it was the way of the woodsman to pronounce sentence of death from under a hood, and he waited for the words he knew would come.

"Stand up spawn of evil, your time is here." Robbie's voice was as cold and hard as the blade he now held, and Mordred slowly rose clutching the sword and faced the Lord of Loxley. Rowan shuddered as he felt the power of Robbie; his bow was ready and waiting as he watched his lord face a deadly enemy. Robbie bowed to Mordred, as was custom at a woodsman's hearing. "Your time is here, prepare to return to the darkness from whence you came."

Mordred seemed to shake as the bowman came at him with great speed. Rune leapt up at her table with a scream, as she watched Robbie whose wrist now glowed blue with a bright bracelet, swinging the blade of the Sword of Destiny across the path of his enemy. Mordred blocked but his arm snapped up with the force as Robbie turned and brought his shoulder crashing into the dark son of Morgan le Fey. Mordred flew backward crashing and sprawling on to the floor, and the Black Blade of Dunnottar swung free from his hand.

A small laugh gasped from Rune as her eyes flowed with more violet than ever before. Mordred scrambled as he fell backward stretching and twisting for his sword, and as his back crashed onto the glass and splintered wood on the floor, he felt his hand just touch the hilt.

In one last huge effort, he snatched at the handle and gasped with relief as he turned and looked up at the hooded figure. The scream of pain was heart stopping, and rang and bounced off the walls, as a heavy long suede laced black boot crunched down hard on his hand. Robbie threw all of his force into his leg, and pinned the hand holding the sword to the floor, Mordred screamed and thrashed as the bones shattered, and Robbie wasted no time.

The golden dagger plunged into the hilt of the black blade, and Mordred's screams of terror rang into the air, red light exploded out of his eyes as his whole body shook in a violent fit. The sound of fair voices rose into the air, as white light exploded all around Robbie. The Specialists covered their eyes as the light filled the whole of the city, and Mordred's cries and wails for his mother were drowned by the voices of the people of Fae, as they took the power of their old queen back to the land of the Violet Isle. The arm gave one last huge shudder and fell limp, Robbie knew Mordred was pulled out of Billy, and held prisoner in the knife of Victor Thornson.

He stepped back and tears ran down Rune's cheeks as she saw he was safe, he looked at the figure curled crying on the floor like a baby, he reached down, and picked up the now golden sword from Dunnottar, and threw it behind him. The moonstone on the dagger glowed and pulsed in its sheath on the belt of Lord Loxley, Rune went very still as she watched Robbie pull the sword to the huddled figure on the floor. She drew a long breath and held it, as Robbie looked down at him and spoke. "Billy?"

She held her breath as she watched, Robbie had promised to kill him, her hands wrung together with nervousness as the figure on the floor twitched in pain cradling a broken hand. Rune gasped a breath as the blonde hair flicked as he moved his head, and the two bright blue eyes she knew so well, looked into the eyes of a man he once called brother.

Robbie looked down into the eyes he had grown up with and he raised the Sword of Destiny to his chin; he lifted the head of Billy up into the light. Billy blinked. "Kill me for god's sake Rob and get this over with." He shut his eyes tight and waited. Pebbles gasped and Rowan clutched her by the shoulder and pulled her back, he nodded at her, this was Robbie's moment and no one would interfere.

Robbie slid the sword back an inch, his eyes held the betrayal of a man he once called brother, and stared darkly down on Billy. Billy opened his eyes and glanced at the tip of the gleaming sword, he looked up at Robbie, and he saw the rage and pain of the one he had hurt so deeply.

"DO IT!" He screamed, as he shook on the floor. "I BETRAYED YOU, AND DESERVE THIS. DO IT FOR THE BETRAYAL OF A BROTHER YOU ONCE LOVED. OH FOR GODS SAKE ROB JUST GET THIS OVER WITH, WHAT ARE YOU WAITING FOR, YOU KNOW YOU WANT TO? JUST KILL ME!"

His voice fell frightened and weak as Robbie just stared coldly down at him. "Please Rob, hurry my courage is running out; please spare me the humiliation, even though I deserve it. For the love you once held just kill me and end this." Rune felt the emotion tearing at Robbie inside him, she wanted so desperately to be there with him, all she could do was stand and watch each pain filled moment as the tears ran down her cheeks with the feeling she felt inside him.

Robbie glared at the frightened face of Billy. His emotions boiled and ran wild inside him; he swallowed down hard and looked Billy right in the eye. His voice was strained and yet low. "I should kill you for the pain you have caused to those that I love; you are right Billy you do deserve to die." Billy closed his eyes and took one last long breath of life.

Robbie pulled back the sword and bent down to the shaking huddled figure. He seized Billy roughly by the scruff of his shirt, and dragged him to his feet slamming him into the wall. Billy opened his eyes with the fear and surprise, Robbie glared at him face to face, his nose almost touching Billy's, his anger rose quickly and he spoke through clenched teeth, as Billy shook against the wall, his eyes wide.

"You are a brother no more to me Billy. You will never look on a mother who gave you her love and her care again. Your daughter will never know the look, sound, or touch of her father, for she is under my protection now. I will take from you everything you took from those that loved you, and I will leave you empty and with nothing."

Billy shook more violently as the full meaning of the words resounded inside him. Tears welled in his eyes as he looked with pain at Robbie. Robbie released him and stepping back he lifted his sword to Billy's chest, and turned and looked across at the others. His voice was loud and all could hear him. "I am the Lord of all Loxley, and under the law that we live by and the woodsman's code, I have the power to grant life or death. I give life to this man solely for the memory of a once true brother." He turned and scowled at Billy. "Although you do not deserve it."

The tears flowed on to Billy's cheeks, he flattened against the wall and was utterly defeated, and Robbie raised his voice. "I order you to leave this place and leave here the names of Knox and Loxley behind. You are from this moment banished from Loxley for as long as your miserable life remains, go now and do what you can to atone for the evil you have brought to my realm and the good people that live there."

Billy fell to his knees. "Kill me, for God's sake do not set me adrift to suffer. Please Robbie for the sake of what we once were as brothers I beg you kill me."

Robbie turned and looked at the weak shaking mass on the floor. "I have given you my last, now go." Robbie slid the Sword of Destiny into its sheath and climbed through the window into the room that was once the living quarters of Mordred. He strode across the room, as Steph stood by the door watching pale and frightened. Robbie strode right past her and sat on the bike as it chugged on its stand, Steph looked at the weak face of Billy who stared lost through the window as his arm dripped blood on to the floor, and he cradled it to his chest. She turned, and hurried, and jumped on the bike.

"Keep your bow handy Robbie, we are not clear yet." She gunned the engine kicked up the stand, and the bike roared forward, Smokes shot off behind her. The two bikes rattled down the stairs, but the sound of the bikes was too much and the soldiers fled.

At the broken doors, Steph revved the engine and the bike picked up yet more pace. The Specialists watched as the two bikes shot out from the doors and across the balcony and lifted into the air across the gap and on to the ramparts. Steph's handle bar scuffed the wall, and bright sparks shot off as the bike wobbled. "Sorry," she screamed over the engine.

Steph and Smokes skidded the bikes round. Billy's tear filled blue eyes met with Robbie's as he watched from the smashed window above, he was broken and Robbie knew it, he pulled his hood forward and the bikes revved off and then returned to where Rowan with the rest of the group waited. They shot down the ramparts as Rowan lit the fuse and aimed at the rubble that was left from the guardhouse. The arrow hit, and exploded and lowered the pile, and the seven bikes lifted into the air as a bright violet window opened up in front of them, the eagle was through first.

Maggs and Pebbles screamed with delight as the violet window opened above the mere and the bikes shot out across the water, and came down with a thud on the grass. The seven bikes came up the glade fast as Rune came out with Mel to the top of the steps. They grumbled to a halt, in a straight line in front of the gate, as Rune came down the steps, the Specialists bounced off the bikes with joy. Maggs still screamed with Jade and Jett, and Harry threw his arms round Smokes and Steph. Robbie looked up at Steph and she smiled as she pulled him into a hug. "You planned a good maneuverer Steph and you executed it with skill, congratulations this is your victory, you deserve it." He gave her a huge smile as everyone nodded and patted her on the back. It was hugs and smiles all around as Robbie turned to the pale face and concerned eyes of Rune.

She came forward and pulled him softly into her arms. "Are you alright? I cannot imagine how hard that must have been." She leaned back and held her face close, as he looked into her bright blue eyes.

"I could not kill him Rune. I know I should have done, but when it came to the crunch.... He is my brother and I still love him." She saw his lip tremble slightly and pulled him close.

"For what it is worth Rob, I am glad you didn't, you must always follow your instincts, they have never been wrong, you have given him the choices, if he throws it in your face you have no need to worry, I will kill him myself." Robbie held her in his arms and pushed his head into her shoulder, he was just glad it was over and he was back with her at home. She kissed the side of his cheek as the party atmosphere exploded, as the blue circular window opened and the rest of the Specialists flowed out.

The party raged in the glade biker style, from somewhere on the bikes of which Robbie was not sure where, many bottles of Joe's wine appeared. Robbie leaned on the door and smiled as the bikes rode round the glade with the other Specialists all now wanting to have a ride. He felt a weight seem to lift, Mordred was dealt with, and tucked for the moment in his belt, and the long months of Billy in his mind seemed now to have gone. Right or wrong he was not sure, but at the decisive moment, the boy he had known since he was seven years old was at least alive and free in the world. It was up to Billy now to do what he could and face his own inner demons

Rune slid her arms around him from behind and pushed her head onto his shoulder. "We still have one more task to do before bed; do you want to help me?"

He turned and pulled her close. "What do we have left to do before bed?" She gave him a smile, and kissed him on the nose.

"I have to take care of the evil my very brave husband dealt with tonight."

Robbie realised he had completely forgotten the knife in his belt, he went to pull it out, and Rune caught his hand. "I would prefer you remain Mordred free Rob. No one can touch that now or else he will be able to enter into them, let me deal with it." Rune took him by the hand and led him into the kitchen. On the table was a long crystal tube and a pair of large metal tongs. Rune gently lifted the dagger and dropped it into the tube; she placed the lid on and then waved her hand across it, and the top glowed violet. She gave him a big smile and waved her hand opening a window. Robbie followed her through and found himself stood at the top of Hearne's rock. The Green Lord stood smiling and gave a low bow to Robbie.

"You have done well my Bowman; in both things tonight, you used good judgement and showed mighty character. I think my young sapling has begun to grow tall." Robbie gave a bow.

"You honour me My Lord, I am glad I have returned my party safe and unharmed."

"Do not underestimate your own valour my Bowman, you have faced trials and overcome a great deal this evening. I watched with pride, and now you have taken a great threat from this world. You will be honoured by many for this task."

Rune came up to her lord and her eyes flickered as she smiled to him. "I am Life and the lines of time require a life do they not? It is black but it will bring back the balance."

The high lord placed his hand on her shoulder. "You have great faith in your bowman to promise a life he had not yet caught." She gave a little giggle.

"I know things my father of the woods, and I knew in my heart that he would be victorious." Hearne gave a small chuckle as Robbie smiled.

"Faith in the heart is very important, this life will restore the balance of the lines of time, and you too my little flower of the woods have blossomed with the life that you hold. Go in peace and be together for a short time, we still have much work to do; I need to help my guardian, as we now look to the coming of a queen. Enjoy this time together we soon will be very busy. Fear not for I shall deal with this life of no value." Hearne waved his hand and they found themselves alone in the woods, Robbie walked with her hand in his through the quietness of the night's trees.

Her eyes sparkled as she looked at him. "What?" She smiled.

"You made me think of your father tonight, you really reminded me of him."

"I did how?"

"You only took the life that was necessary; you only kill if you have to."

Robbie stared into the trees ahead. "It's funny really, I felt like he was with me."

"He was Robbie." He stopped and turned to her.

"Could you see him?" Excitement, grew in his eyes, she nodded.

"Oh yes I could see him. He held a golden sword and he dealt out justice with a fair hand. He had the power of authority and command." She smiled and slid her arms round him. "You have no idea how like him you are."

He gave her a smile and let out a deep sigh. "I miss him Rune." She kissed him softly.

"I know you do, but he is there in your heart Rob, you carry him every moment of the day. His love will always be with you; open yourself to him and you will be surprised how much of Robert Lox tumbles out."

Robbie smiled at her with her bright shining eyes. "That is a nice thought Runestone."

She started to giggle and he looked at her and felt the smile grow on his own face "What?"

She gave another little giggle. "Just promise one thing Rob."

"What's that?"

"Never call me Runey Love."

He kissed her and chuckled. "I promise," and smiling arm in arm, they turned and walked into the trees towards the sound of motorbikes and the wild screaming of Jett and Jade... or was it Maggs and Steph?

It was a long night of celebration in the Glade of Robbie's Mere. Jett and Blades lay passed out in the chairs with happy smiles on their faces, as Rafe lifted Jett up on to his shoulder and Harry lifted Blades. Robbie watched as the last of the Specialists staggered singing into the dark, and Rowan ran with Jade sat screaming on his shoulders, and he pulled the door closed and headed up the stairs for bed. He slid under the sheet to the soft warm body of Rune. He slid his arm round under her tummy and she smiled as he held her in the dark.

He felt strange inside. He knew somewhere out there in the quiet lonesome dark was a huddled figure with long blonde hair and bright blue eyes. Down on the farm fast asleep in her cot was the figure of a small child with long curly white hair and two huge beautiful blue eyes. Jessica Sapphire would grow up never knowing her true father, and he was not sure if it was right or wrong.

"You were right, go to sleep Robbie." The bed softly shook as she giggled and rolled over. He looked at her pale face and her huge bright sparkling eyes in the darkness lit only by the moon.

"How can you be so sure, Rune? Have I the right to make that decision for little Jessie? I was angry and upset."

She stroked the hair back from his face and looked into his dark eyes. "Billy can never return here Rob, you are lucky Jade didn't put an arrow in him, she wanted to. Bear or John would tear him apart and what about your mum? Do you really want to put her through the pain of seeing him again? You made the right choice Rob, if you do not believe me talk to Alice. I have never thought he deserved to die, I always thought he was put in a trap he could never get out of. Tonight, you released him from everything that held him a prisoner; you did the only thing that was right to do. I respected and admired you for what you did tonight; I know you truly are the hooded man who stands for the weak and the oppressed. It showed in your treatment of Billy."

Rune leaned forward and kissed him softly. "You need sleep, you will see tomorrow." Rune curled round him and he lay in the dark softly stroking her hair until the sleep took him to the land of dreams, and a small boy with long brown hair and blue eyes ran around shouting and laughing, as a small girl with bright violet eyes looked up and called him daddy.

The woodland grew quiet and all the animals sensed the darkness flowing around them, they scurried home to the safety of their burrows and nests. The High Lord of creation and the green world stood with the moon behind him and called into the night. "By the Whitelines of time and the powers you hold I summon you return on wings, the life I hold will balance the lines, come now and receive what has been taken, Goddess of the Moon you are summoned to me."

A ripple ran over the moon and a silvery blue light sped down from the sky. Like a shooting star, it shot through the woods and circled around Hearne's rock, it shimmered before the High Lord and formed into a shapely figure dressed in the palest of blue with long flowing wavy golden hair. The slate grey eyes sparkled as she smiled and bowed to the high lord. Her long cloak of silvery blue feathers glistened as if moonlight itself. "My Lord it has been many moons since we last met."

Hearne gave a smile as his limbs creaked and he embraced her. "Rhiannon my shimmering pearl of wonder how glad I am to hold you again."

She gave a smile of shimmering radiance. "I have missed you my old teacher, I see you have the balance for me to take to the end of all realms, his black soul will do well there in the darkness."

His long twig like fingers ran through the long golden hair as he held her tenderly. "You have the speed I need to out run her; she will come after you my precious angel of the night time light."

"I have done it before; you know I will only be caught if I allow it." She gave a smile and he nodded as he thought of Pwhyll.

"I have a favour to ask of my greatest student, I feel you know of what I ask for my granddaughter and her children?"

"You know the rule my teacher, as I do not agree with your life for a life rule; I know you will not agree with the rule of my line. They cannot enter the crystal castle of light for they are of this realm not mine." She gave him a soft happy smile. "He has asked too and I have already told him. Rayne will return to his family for a short time when the new Queen of Fae comes to this realm. He loves her still and I cannot let him suffer as he has."

The eyes of the high lord sparkled. "You always did have a way of pleasing me my child of light; I see the light of your eyes in the Runestone at times and wonder if you and your sister both shared the same qualities."

"I miss her too my teacher, and yet I saw her in the life of Opal many times, Runestone carries her in those sapphire eyes there is no doubt. I will look upon them and tell you when we next meet."

Rhiannon took the crystal cylinder from her lord and teacher, and with a smile she blew him a kiss. She spun on the spot and her figure broke into light, and like a rocket she shot into the air. The high lord stood and watched, the darkness in the woods deepened as a thick line of black streaked into the sky behind her. The laughter of a line of the moon echoed back through the air as the darkness trailed her. The high lord knew that Mordred would now never return to the realm of the living earth, the Dark One was no match for a moon goddess of light.

He smiled as sadness filled him, he turned and walked back over the lonely rock and thought of the time at the beginning of the earth realm, where a young woman of shimmering white and red had come to him, and together they had created the beginning of the lines of life. He gave a long sigh like the swishing of a falling tree, and watched the dust crystals she left on his rock home shimmer in the moonlight; they reminded him of her eyes. "Eve," he mumbled to himself as he smiled and walked to the cave.

Robbie woke very late; it was already midday, when he stretched at the side of Rune, he rubbed his eyes as he slowly sat up and turned to look down on her fast asleep. Rune was curled in a little ball; her hands round her tummy as if protecting the precious contents. He grabbed the new shirt and slid it on as he walked to the stairs and came down yawning. It was a little time later when he walked down to the mere, his violet shirt bright in the weak afternoon sun. Alice stood quiet and watched the water; somehow, he had expected her to come up and see him.

Robbie passed her a cup as she turned to see him; she gave a weak smile and her pale blue eyes met with Robbie's. "Mickie told me Mordred was dead." She looked at the cup as it steamed in her hand. Robbie watched his cousin fight with the mixed emotions inside her. She slowly looked up at Robbie; he could see the question coming. "Is Billy..."

"Alive, I did not kill him Alice, I pulled the black soul of Mordred out of him, but he was alive when I left him, didn't Bear tell you?"

She looked a little embarrassed. "I didn't wait; I just came straight up here, I knew you had promised if you had the shot, and I thought..."

"I didn't have my bow Alice; I had a sword, so I didn't think it counted." She nodded and looked back down at her cup; Robbie slid his arm round her as he looked out across the mere. "Do you think I was right or wrong? Be honest with me Alice." She took a sip of her cup and slid her arm round him.

"I am glad he is alive Rob; I know I wished him dead, but when I heard and I thought you had killed him, I don't know, I just had to come and find out from you." He nodded.

"I can understand that, I will not lie to you Alice, he will never walk on Loxley soil again, I will never allow it, and if he does he will be killed. I did not pardon him; I banished him from the realm." He looked down at her as she looked into the cup as she drank.

"I understand that Rob, you have no choice."

"I am the lord of this realm I have a choice, Alice. I chose to expel him because of the pain and the hurt he caused to you and my mother. You both mean much to me and he used his position to undermine and hurt both of you, he will never receive a pardon for that alone. I do understand the pressure that was placed on him, but again Billy knew one word with John and we would have been the family we were. Billy knew that we would have protected him. He had a choice and he chose to waste it. He will not walk this soil again for that one reason alone."

"I know it seems strange but now I have little Jessie... He is her father Rob and it means something. I have no idea how to explain it to you but at the castle in Scotland, that last time I saw him, I knew he would never see his child, and I thought this is the last time I will ever see him again. He was caught in a trap he wanted to get free of and I do think he was trying to do the right thing. She poured that foul one into him before he had a chance." She took a sip of her drink and then looked up at Robbie. "I don't know Rob, I just think if he had been given a little more time, he would have let me go, in his strange way at that castle he was trying to protect me from her and save his child, am I making sense to you?"

Robbie turned to face her and his voice was soft and gentle as he took her hand in his. "Alice, I loved him too. I pulled a sword to his throat and I froze, you will never know the hate I felt at Caerleon, but when it came down to it and I looked him in the eye as he begged for death, I could not kill my own brother. All the evil and nasty things meant nothing compared to those close happy moments we shared as children. Billy is a part of me as I am he. If I killed him, I would be killing a part of me that meant something; I know you are the only person who might just understand that."

Alice nodded and gave a soft smile as two tears ran from her cheeks. "I thought I was the only one, but I am not. Thanks Rob, just knowing we feel the same means a lot to me." Robbie wiped her eyes with his finger.

"For all his faults, he loved us both Alice. I saw that in his eyes, it is up to you how you raise his child; only you can decide what to tell her when she is old enough to understand. I will be by your side always and little Jessie Sapphire will always have the protection of her uncle as I have always had John's. We are Loxley and that is what we do for each other, I will always be here for you Alice." Robbie pulled her close with his arm as she quietly sobbed, and he watched across the Mere standing with his cousin, who had always felt more like his sister. He loved her she was special.

Rune gave a soft smile from the bedroom window as she looked down on the glade and saw him holding her close and talking softly to her. She saw the love between them and felt happy to know they were finally talking about Billy. They could heal each other together.

Once again, the Specialists had proven themselves; their daring and talents had brought chaos to the black city. General Walters had been asleep with several empty bottles beside him out on the moors. Stealth and the woodsman's way had proven itself, and the addition of four crazy bikers had helped. It was something that the black army had never expected, and it had been enough to give the edge to Robbie as he had come out with the greatest prize of all.

The removal of Mordred had lifted the woodland world, and it gave hope to the woodsmen who pushed forward in their fight to contain the masses who still greatly outnumbered them. The Dark One now had to re think her strategy as all her hopes now lay in her grandson Lance, General Walters raged with his fury for two days about the black city. He looked out across the battlefield at the army before him and he knew that he faced for the first time in his life an enemy who had equal ambition to win him. The Cutters had always won by fear and surprise, and now he found his own tools being used against him, now he had no time to waste, he had to return to the ways of old that he knew well.

The huge monster of the general turned to his messenger, and handed him the note. "Get this to Tintagel as quickly as possible. I want all my legions up here as fast as possible; let's see how our woodsmen fight against the Tenth Legion. I also think it is time our mistress got her son out of his box." The general lifted his binoculars up to his eyes and looked across the moorland, as the messenger saluted and turned away. General Franklin and General Jarrod walked slowly back from the observation point; Franklin looked at his colleague. "The Tenth Legion is nothing more than a bunch of cut throats and rabble, they are evil and vicious, I want nothing to do with them, I am a soldier not a thug."

Jarrod nodded as he walked. "He is under pressure, the only reason he still has command is because he was out here and not in the city, and this is the first time his reputation has been tarnished. I think our new general has just realised that what we have been saying for months about the skill of these men is right. I saw what they did at Dunnottar and I warned them not to underestimate them, it looks now my friend like they might just start to listen to reason."

"Can she really bring him back after all this time?" Franklin looked a little sickened.

Jarrod knew more about her than any, he had served at Tintagel for many years; he looked at his friend and gave a scared almost worried look. "She brought the Dark Prince back, and he had been dead for a hell of a lot longer." Franklin looked sicker and he shuddered.

The large dark figure looked across the moors as he swept from left to right, his heart gave a slight flutter as there in the far distance he caught the glint of gold, and he turned back to see what it was. High on the hill in the morning sun was a warrior in red, the long golden sword hung from her belt and her hair, which was the brightest of reds, shimmered in the sun. Scarlet lowered her telescope and smiled.

"Well, well look who has crawled out of his hole, I wondered when they would think of bringing him to meet me, it's time for a change of tactics I think." She handed the scope to Phillip who lifted it to his eye and focused on the large general far in the distance.

"Maybe my dear we can get you his other ear as a keepsake." He looked back at her and smiled.

General Walters felt the cold twinge of fear for the second time in his life. He faced the only enemy he had ever respected; he swallowed deeply as he gazed at her glowing brightly in the sunlight. He knew his long life had now come to its moment of destiny; years of carving men down who were unworthy of him had taken its toll, now he knew he truly had the greatest fight of his life. Now was the time to lay his nightmares to rest, and put an end to the scarlet clad warrior of Caerleon.

CHAPTER FIVE

THE NEW FELLOWSHIP

The attack on the Black City brought a lull in the conflict, Flash and Maggs had single handily wiped out a very large amount of the dark forces that had been barracked in the city. Those that had survived had seen an awesome power used against them, it was chilling and now fear was at a higher level than ever. The disappearance of Mordred the Dark Lord of the city created many rumours about the true power of the hooded Specialists. There was talk of ghosts and spirits as young minds ran wild, the daily reminder was right in front of them, in a wide band of black ash that ran from the market gates, to the middle of the long barracks. Many of the soldiers feared to walk on the burned earth that still contained the ashes of soldiers they once knew.

The sight of General Walters on the battlefield had alerted Scarlet, who knew his tactics better than any; she had spent ten years defending Bristol and Scarlet knew every aspect of the general's game plan. She moved quickly back to Loxley to talk with Robbie, where she arranged a new battle plan for the coming weeks. Sat in the office above his house, Scarlet filled him in on the detail of the man everyone feared the most. Robbie listened as Scarlet recounted the story of the brutal attacks of the Tenth Legion of the Cutter Brigade, they were the group that began the tree hangings and the slaughter of children, they were all woodsmen of a fashion, the only difference being they painted their faces red, with eyes of black when they went into combat.

The Tenth Legion had no rules of conduct, they killed for fun and maimed and tortured for sport, Scarlet spoke with reverence about them, as she did not underestimate their abilities as fighters, she still carried the scars of one or two of her encounters with them. Robbie knew that Scarlet was a warrior of the highest calibre, and when she gave a warning, he took her very seriously. Scarlet expected a twelve to fourteen day gap in the hostilities, and then she warned of the surprise attacks all the way along the lines of the woodsmen, she revised her plans with Robbie, and returned to the cave on the front line to work with Fuse.

The removal of Mordred had a lifting effect on the green army, in York, the celebrations had been high, as in Loxley, a new feeling of hope was in the air and the view of the hooded man had risen higher than ever before. The following day at the Village Hall, everyone had stopped as he walked in and given him a round of applause. Most of the staff had shaken his hand as he made his way to the office at the back. The next ten days would bring him a chance to rest and spend that all-important time alone with Rune and his family.

Robbie spent a lot more time on the farm working with Jess and Beth to sort out the working schedule, replacing his dad was not easy, but with Alice and Big John available to him, he found that he could spend time with his mum and work out who would do what. Rune helped a lot, she had the power of life, and so it was easy for her to simply walk through one of the field's unseen, and by the time she left, the crops were the biggest and freshest you would find anywhere.

Jess now assumed overall control of the farm, Martin's widow Hanna, who had shown great skill at her management practice with the pickling operation, became a full time assistant to Jess, and slowly the farm reorganised, and Loxley was able to slip back into normality. Robbie's most annoying factor was Ernest Wicks. Ernest was the undersecretary of the Fellowship of the Bowmen; he constantly popped up wherever Robbie was and pestered him about the future of the fellowship.

Ernest was becoming a real nuisance, and so finally Robbie arranged a meeting of the leaders of the fellowship at his house to try to get the man to leave him alone. He had so much to do and frankly, he found it irritating to be constantly told his father had died and needed to be replaced. Ernest had been very upset that the venue had been moved to Robbie's Mere, Robbie had not really cared, he knew Skip had enough on his plate with the war and he politely informed Ernest, it was there or not at all. Ernest grudgingly agreed.

Robbie stood at the window looking into the sun as it slowly set, Rune sat at his desk reading some of the papers. "Wow Rob, you have made some sweeping changes here."

He turned and looked down at her bright blue eyes as they sparkled up the room at him. "I have put the right people in who deserve to be there, they are after all the ones who know and defend Loxley, and we shall see what our undersecretary thinks." Robbie turned as the farm cart pulled up, and he saw them all getting down and walking toward the gate, he knocked on the window and Jess looked up and smiled.

Robbie had laid out a long table in the centre of the room, Rune and he sat at one end, all of the others supplied with hot drinks and cakes sat down and waited for Ernest, who sorted through his papers to settle. He read his notes, his horn-rimmed glasses on the tip of his nose, and his thin white hair was combed back in a quaff. It was easy to see from his clothes which all bore the lines of a hot iron that this was a man who was organised and a stickler for the rules, Robbie somehow felt a conflict looming.

Ernest gave a cough. "Seeing as our lord is new to these sorts of meetings, should I chair?" Robbie shrugged and sat back as he winked at his mum, she gave him a smile. "Good evening most honourable members of the Fellowship of the Bowmen of Loxley." They all grunted a quick hello and John Lox smiled. "I am saddened at the loss of our most esteemed and beloved Grand Master, and offer my deepest sympathies to his widow and family." Jess and Robbie nodded; Rune smiled as she felt that Robbie was being very tolerant of a man, he found most irritating.

"In my role as undersecretary of the Bowmen of Loxley, I feel it is my place to suggest and discuss the future of this institution, and I would like to table a recommendation that we the assembled take a vote to select a new leader, and a replacement for our previous High Master who has disappeared without notice. Will any one second my motion?" He looked over the top of his glasses.

John Lox raised his arm. "If it means we can get on with things, yes."

Ernest gave a polite nod. "Thank you esteemed Master of Arms; I appreciate your support on this. Right onto the business of the motion and its full and proper contents."

Robbie slid forward in his chair. "I thought that was already agreed, have you not said we should replace our missing members?"

"I am sorry My Lord, but we must all agree the correct wording of such things, it is very important that young Jane over there has a full and correct notation of the meeting." Robbie leaned over in his chair, to view the young woman sat almost out of sight at the end of the room near his desk writing. He gave her a wave and she blushed.

"Jane is it? Why are you sat all the way over there? Would it not be easier if you sat at the table and rested your pad on it instead of your knee? Come down here and have a drink and some cake, do not be a stranger here, Rune and myself welcome all of our guests."

Ernest coughed. "My Lord, Jane is here only to take notation, she is not here to partake or socialise with us, we have things to discuss that are far more important than where she sits."

"I am glad then you feel it's unimportant Ernie, I would be happier if a guest in my house sat at my table, and so I feel that she should... Please Jane, come down here you will hear what is said much better." She gave a smile, and lifted her papers and came to the table and sat down. Robbie looked across to her. "Have you met my wife and first lady of Loxley? This is my good lady Runestone."

Rune gave a smile at the girl who looked positively shocked at the lord of the community being so informal with her, Rune smiled at her. "Welcome to our home, it's nice to have you amongst us."

"Thank you, My Lord and Lady, I am honoured." Ernest scowled at her and she quickly put her head down and focused on her papers.

He shuffled his papers to bring the attention back. "My Lord please, may we proceed? We have a protocol of these meetings to follow." Robbie waved him to continue.

"As undersecretary to the Grand Master, I would gladly be willing to offer my services in the interim period until a suitable candidate can be named and selected in the appropriate way, I would however like to also submit my name to those who would be offered to the board to be included in the short list."

Rune looked at him and smiled. "How will a new candidate be selected, and who selects them, if you do not mind me asking?"

"A very good question my good lady, we the board select candidates and then we discuss their suitability at which point we then take a vote." He gave a large smile at her, which was to some degree a little creepy.

Robbie leaned back in his chair, and stretched. "Thank Hearne for that, I thought this was going to go on for hours." Jane gave a little titter, as did Jess and Steph. Robbie lifted a piece of paper from his pile and looked round the table. "I have been looking very carefully at who has done what for the fellowship, and I have made a short list of those who I as the Lord of Loxley feel has made a very full contribution to this community." Robbie looked down the table at his mother.

"Mum I know for a fact that dad discussed everything with you and Len, I think dad will be hard to replace but you knew what he wanted for Loxley better than any, it seems only natural you should replace him as the new Grand Master."

Ernest looked shocked and stared at Robbie, Jess was very surprised but she smiled a warm and loving smile at him. Rune and Steph beamed with delight, and Dave Williams and John who sat with Joe chuckled. Ernest was for a moment lost for words. He gave a cough.

"My Lord, I understand your loyalty to your family, but Mrs Loxley is a woman, and as a far as I can recall, there has never been a woman as Grand Master before. It is not something that has been done."

Robbie sat back for a second as the room went silent. He leaned forward in his chair. "Ernie, correct me at all if I am wrong, but wasn't the fellowship which has now spread across the whole of this country, set up and founded by a single woman? Has Marion of Blidworth and wife to the first hooded man slipped from your mind?"

"Well My Lord that was different." He smirked at Robbie. "I mean she set this up in order to prepare for the return, since that time we have always had the head of the Loxley family as our leader, the land owner and farm owner have run this fellowship."

Robbie nodded. "You are quite right Ernie, which was a point I had completely forgotten. Congratulations Mum, you are the second female Grand Master in the history of the Loxley Fellowship... I take it no one here disagrees?"

Ernest shook his head. "My Lord your father has just passed away and you are the natural heir."

"Thank you for reminding me about my father Ernest, I can assure you I have not forgotten. As for the heir, you are right, looking at the will of my father I have seen he has passed on all he owns to my mother until she feels she will pass it on to myself, and my wife. I loved my father because he was a kind and fair man, and as I have seen he has as always done what is right for the people of this community. My mother is the landowner and farm manager of Loxley Farm Estates, so therefore she is the rightful candidate for Grand Master, so once again as your lord I would ask you all to support her as I will."

Joe gave a smile. "I second."

Dave rose slightly from his seat. "Third." Rune looked round the table.

"Any objections?" She looked right at Ernest as her eyes flickered with violet, he slumped in his seat, and she smiled. "Congratulations Jess." Everyone beamed a big smile. Robbie shuffled his papers.

"Right, that will leave the High Mistress position vacant; I would like to suggest that we use someone who has shown courage and dedication beyond the call of duty, including a near fatal wound in her service to Loxley. I think Lady Jade Opal should fill the position; do I hear any objections?"

Joe gave a hearty laugh. "God knows why, but I will second you Rob lad, she will liven the meetings up that's for sure."

Rune gave a giggle, "any objections?" Everyone smiled at her. "Ok Jade it is, right Rob who is next?" She gave him a big smile.

"We all miss Leenard, and I do not want to replace him yet. I would however think he should have a temporary cover for him, and I know in the past he would receive a lot of information and discuss it with Pete. So I feel he would be the ideal man to cover, he has a good working relationship and when Leenard returns, I think the transition will be smooth."

Steph gave a big smile. "Oh Robbie, he would be so proud to, he gave a lot to my father and assisted him a great deal before he was captured. It would mean a lot to him to be involved again."

"He has a lot to offer this community and I think it is a wise choice, I take it no one objects?" Every one nodded happily. "Alright then, I have asked them to attend later so Ernest can swear them in for us, Mum you will be first and then take over... Right, that just leaves one Able Bowman. As you all are aware that my good lady here is now the first Lady of Loxley and as Lord she will be by my side always." He gave her a big smile as her eyes danced with delight; everyone in the room except Ernest smiled. "I would like you all to consider John Styles. He has proven beyond doubt to me he is a very loyal defender of this realm and protector of his Lord and Lady. His devotion to this community should be recognised, and I think he will be honoured by this position, do you all agree?"

Steph slapped the table, as did Jess. "Here, here!" Dave, John and Joe all nodded and Rune gave a resounding, "Definitely" He smiled.

"Good, well unless Ernest has any other business, I think we should retire below and wait for our new arrivals, they should be here shortly." Ernest looked bitterly disappointed as he shuffled his papers.

The group all got up and began talking. Ernest looked up at Robbie who stopped and looked down at him; Ernest gave a long sigh as Rune stopped at the end of the table with Jane and looked back. Ernest stood up and offered his hand to Robbie.

"I am sorry My Lord, but I feel strongly that a new broom has taken over from that of your father. I have served the Fellowship for twenty years; I feel it is time for me to also step down." Rune watched as Robbie took his hand.

"I am sorry to hear that Ernie, you have served this community well, if I cannot change your mind, I will have no choice but to find a replacement. However, if you feel this strongly, I will accept your decision, I would however suggest this. I am going to change things, I will not deny it, and I feel it is time to review all the laws of the woodsmen to bring them in line with the changes that will come in our future. You are I believe a very well versed expert in the field of the constitution of the fellowship?"

Ernest nodded. "I am My Lord, I have studied it in great depth, I am surprised that you are aware."

"I understand that you feel I have a casual approach to affairs Ernie, in many ways I do, but believe me when I say that I am the true son of Robert Jake Loxley, and I will not dishonour his name. I work hard behind the scenes and I know who is loyal to Loxley, I think you would best serve your lord in the new position of Constitutional Advisor to the fellowship, I would offer it to you if you would accept it."

Ernest gave a proud smile. "I have underestimated you My Lord, forgive me. It would be an honour and a privilege to serve in such a role; it is one I would enjoy a great deal. Yes, I would accept."

Robbie shook his hand. "Good, that is all sorted then." He gave Rune a smile as he walked to the stairs and he looked at Jane who looked back at him nervously. Robbie stopped. "Jane, tell me how long have you worked alongside Ernest here?" She blushed deeply.

"My Lord, I have spent about five years as his volunteer."

"So... You know his job quite well then?"

"I suppose so My Lord."

"Great." He smiled at Rune and offered his hand to Jane. "You will be the new undersecretary then?" She almost dropped her papers she looked so shocked.

"My Lord... I would love to." He gave her a smile and took Rune by the arm as she walked down the stairs.

"Great... I think I am getting the hang of this fellowship stuff... Oh and by the way Jane, in my house it's Robbie and Rune, we do not stand on formality at home."

Pete stood with a huge smile on his face as Robbie and Rune came down the stairs to the living room, Steph and Jess gave him huge hugs as Dave, Joe, and John patted his back and shook his hand. Robbie smiled as he approached him. "Oh Rob I am honoured, you have no idea how much this means to me." Robbie pulled him into a hug and squeezed him tight.

"You have earned this Pete; you have paid a high price in the past to protect everyone here, and it has not been unnoticed." Rune gave him a huge hug as Robbie headed for the kitchen; Jess was filling the big coffee pot as he walked in. She gave him a big happy smile.

"You would have made him very proud tonight Rob. You took charge in the same way he did, I watched the son of the man I married tonight and he made me very proud."

"I always wanted him to be proud of me; he will be a hard act to follow. He was my hero you know, I wanted to grow up just like him."

Jess pulled him into her arms and she kissed him on the cheek. "You have my word Rob, you have."

"I love you mum." She squeezed him hard.

"I love you too sweetheart".

The arrival of Jade was heard by all, she swept across the room and into Joe's arms, he looked as happy as she was to see him, and despite all of his complaints about her noise, it was clear to see how much he cared about her. Jade adored Joe, he was her hero and she held him in great esteem. Joe was given the task of breaking the news to her and she looked terrified and sat with a bump on the chair. "You are joking?" Joe laughed as he shook his head.

"No Jade love."

She gave a smile and her eyes danced under her long curly fringe, Jade leapt up into Rowan's arms with delight, and he beamed as he held her close. John Styles arrived last with Alice, looking nervous as he was escorted up the stairs to the office where Robbie now waited sat at his desk with Rune. John sat down in front of Robbie his face was almost white. "Is everything alright Robbie, I have not done something wrong have I?" Being called before the Fellowship was a serious situation and John was very nervous. "It's not about our little drinking competition is it? I know we were a bit rowdy but we meant no harm."

Robbie leaned on to the desk. "I will not tell a lie John, we have a serious problem and I need to speak seriously with you." The colour drained from John's already white face.

"Robbie tell me what's wrong and I will fix it if I can."

"John my wife is now the first lady of Loxley, that leaves me in a serious position,

as I need to find someone fast to replace her as one of the Able Bowmen. She is
unguarded and I fear for her.”

He looked serious and a little relieved as he nodded. John thought for a moment
and rubbed his chin. “Well to be honest Robbie, I would say Rafe or Keith is your
best men, they are good with a bow and very loyal to all of us.”

Robbie nodded his head as he thought. “Yes... I can see what you’re saying,
I knew John you would be the man to ask, you have good eyes and ears in this
community, although Rafe is new to the stockade, he will need to be resident
longer, come to think of it so is Keith.”

John waved a finger. “No... Keith was born here Robbie he qualifies.”

Rune started to giggle. “Oh John, do not listen to him, he is playing with you,
we brought you here tonight because both of us think the only man for the job is
you.”

It was a rare moment when John was lost for words; Robbie reached across the
desk and patted his arm. “John your devotion to Rune and myself deserves so
much more than a bowman’s white arrow. Rune and I had no hesitation in putting
your name forward and the whole of the fellowship agree with us. What do you
say? Will you fill the role of Able Bowman next to Alice and us?”

He looked stunned and tears welled in his eyes as he smiled. “I would be proud
as hell to stand by you both, I would consider it the highest honour ever paid to
me. I love both of you and that’s no mystery, it has been my honour to help you
both this last year.”

Rune gave a sniffle and stood up; John rose from his chair as Rune hugged
him. “I am so pleased John, and you honour all of Loxley with your loyalty to this
family, you deserve this more than any.” He was lost for words; Robbie pulled him
into a hug and gave him a huge pat on the back.

“Congratulations my good friend.” Robbie stepped back and handed him the
new patch of the wolf head with one black and one white crossed arrow on it. John
stared at it and wiped the tears from his face.

“I wish Matty was here to see this, he would have laughed his ass off.”

Rune smiled at John. “He can see John, and he is happy to know you have been
honoured for your service to us, I would say he is very proud of his friend.”

John gave a nod and smiled through his glistening eyes. “Thank you, My Lady, it
is nice to know.”

The group assembled and the swearing in took place in the living room of
Robbie’s house. Robbie swore in his mother, as the lord and hooded man
returned it was his duty, he gave a small titter as he drew Destiny out of its sheath,
the old sword of the hooded man was in the office back at the hall, and as Ernest
pointed out, constitutionally it was to be the sword of the hooded man that was
used. Technically Robbie was now the hooded man and so Destiny was the
sword to use, the fact it was the sister to Excalibur also made it a more convincing

argument.

Robbie placed the Sword of Destiny on her head and she swore her oath to the fellowship. She smiled at her son all the time, and when it was over, he winked at her. "Kinda freaky isn't it? Now you know how I felt at the wedding." She gave a giggle as she lifted the sword off him and turned to swear in Jade.

Jade knelt on the floor with a beaming smile, and with a pride never seen in her before, she gave her oath loud and clear, Steph wiped the tears from her eyes as she watched, and Rune slipped her arm round Robbie with a happy smile on her face. Pete gave his oath with tremendous authority, and John beamed with honour as he swore his solemn oath to Jess. Robbie raised a glass stood on the rug with a coat of arms on it, and everyone raised theirs. "The Fellowship of the Bowmen of Loxley," they all repeated and drank to its future.

It was a long happy night as they all sat around talking, and toward midnight, Steph looked up at Robbie as they sat in a large wide circle around the room. "So what now for us all Rob? You must have something in mind."

He sat and looked round at all the face's looking his way; Rune was curled on his knee and looked up at him. "We need to stop the black army; I can only see one way forward... I will return to Kirklees Priory and recover the documents of Leenard. I think now is the time to start looking for our king, with a king on the throne no army will march against his supporters."

Steph nodded, as did all the others. "Well Rob it's the one thing that will keep the walls of York upright and that has to be good news for Loxley."

"Come and see me tomorrow and we will start to prepare Steph, I think it will be a good run out for the Specialists as well." Pete nodded and gave him a smile.

"We can let Harry visit his ancestor again, he will be delighted." Everyone started to laugh as Robbie pulled Rune close.

"Remember the garden and that hidden corner." Her eyes sparkled and she chuckled.

"Oh yes I still have the goose bumps."

It was early morning when Robbie woke up. He opened his eyes and blinked at the bright light flowing into the room, as the sun came over the top of the house. Rune lay warm and curled at his side, her head on his chest. He lay still feeling the heat that radiated through his body from her, and looked down at the mass of red hair that covered him. Somewhere, under all that hair was Rune, fast asleep and filled with contentment. He slid his arms round her soft warm skin and held her as he lay back in the soft pillows, and just enjoyed the quiet of the moment. He softly fingered her silky hair, as he absently minded drifted around with his thoughts, he didn't feel her move at first; he slowly came out of his dream world as he felt her hand on his shoulder.

Robbie watched as Rune traced her finger round the 'R' shaped scar on his shoulder, where the arrow had come through from the time in Scotland. Her bright blue eyes gazed at the long pink line on the top of his shoulder, from his fight with Mordred. She looked up at him through her tangle of shimmering hair. "We are both lucky you are still here; you came very close last year to losing your life." She slid up to him and he saw the concern in her eyes melt as she lowered her face close to his and she gave him a long slow kiss. Her eyes danced as she sat up on top of him. "Hi gorgeous, Happy Birthday." Rune burst into a huge and happy smile as he sat up and pulled her close. She giggled into his neck as she squeezed him tight. "I got presents... you want to have them now or after we eat?" He gave her a tickle and she squirmed and giggled.

"Now." Rune squealed with laughter, and fell back as she fought off his tickles, and crawled across the bed. She opened the door of the large wardrobe, and pulled out a long thin package wrapped neatly in green paper, she sat back on the bed and watched as he opened it, excitement jumped out from her eyes.

Robbie unrolled the blue velvet cloth to find a golden dagger in a new leather sheath. The handle was the shape of a hooded figure, but as he looked, he saw that under the hood were two Sapphires that glinted like hidden eyes. It reminded him very much of those first encounters with the hooded white lady, it was made with great skill and as he slid it out and looked at it, he saw it was a miniature replica of Destiny. Rune fidgeted on the bed as she watched. "Bobby made it for me, he is good, isn't he? I thought because yours had to leave with Hearne after you drew Mordred into it, you would need a replacement. Bobby says you will have a miniature me with you always now."

Robbie was lost for words as the dagger glinted across his face. It was beautiful and he loved the idea of the hooded Rune on the hilt of the dagger. "Rune this is so beautiful." She beamed as he looked up and pulled her close, she gave another excited giggle as she leaned over the bed and pulled a long flat green wrapped gift out.

"This is very special; you cannot show this to anyone Robbie." He carefully undid the ribbon and opened the paper, inside was a large purple leather bound book. Robbie turned it over to look at the gold letters on the front. Rune gave a squeak. "Judy found an old book binding machine in the upstairs of her shop, Harry fixed it and she has printed this out especially for you." Robbie read the golden letters set deep into the purple leather of the front. 'The Bowman of Loxley.' He looked up at her as she beamed at him. "Open it."

Robbie opened the book and read the print on the first inside page.

The Bowman of Loxley
Jan 2038-Jan 2039
The account of the man I love
By
Runestone Sapphire Lane Loxley

He was lost for words as he opened the page and looked at the chapters, it was all there in front of him, every thought and feeling from the moment he crossed the yard with hot scones to the killing of Mason Knox. A whole year of his life from the point of view of the woman he loved. There was nothing he could say; she pulled him close and giggled. "I knew you would like it." She gave him a huge kiss. "Happy eighteenth birthday Rob."

"Rune this is amazing, I am utterly lost for words." She slid the book off him and opened it; she quickly flicked through the pages, and found what she was looking for. She gave a giggle.

"I was so frightened as I started to run, his hand was tight in mine, but I must admit the terror flowed through me. There could have been Cutters anywhere and if they had fired, either of us could have been killed. Robbie twisted as we hurtled with speed toward the old stump down the steep bank, I saw his bright deep sparkling eyes and in a flash, he turned to the stump, opened his arms and caught me. I felt his warm arms around me and felt his breath blow across my face as he panted. I knew then this was the man I would spend the rest of my life with, and I pushed myself forward and felt his arms come around me. Somehow, I no longer cared about the Cutters or Joe's cabin, or Billy and Jade above me, I could just see Robbie, he was all that I wanted and I knew in that moment I would never leave his side again."

She smiled as she closed the book. "You were sexy as hell that day." She gave a giggle and he started to laugh.

"You were as white as a ghost when I snatched you into my arms, I was so glad you were safe, my biggest fear was you would get hurt and I would lose you."

"My biggest fear was Melissa, I watched her flirt with you a thousand times, she was a right vulture."

He started to giggle and nodded at the sudden look of hatred that crossed her face, "She never had a chance Rune, I saw two bright blue eyes look through the gap in your mum's gate many years before, and I knew then I would always belong to Runestone Sapphire."

She gave an almost shy smile like she had when he had first taken her out. "Really Rob?"

He pulled her into his arms and she nuzzled into him. "I have loved you for as long as I can remember, and you will be forever the only one for me Runestone."

She squeezed him tightly.

"I am so happy Robbie, sometimes it scares me. I could never be without you."

He stroked her hair down her back. "You won't be... This is a very special present Rune, thank you it means more to me than I can say."

She gave a soft giggle. "I am starving, let's go and get breakfast." She kissed his cheek and giggled as she slid off the bed and pulled on her robe.

The day was a happy day for Robbie, Alice swung from him as she squeezed him and wished him happy birthday. She gave him a new compass as his old one had cracked glass from his time in the cave, Jess held him for an age. He got several lace up tops and a new pair of badly needed suede boots, she also handed him the watch his dad always kept in his pocket.

It had been the pocket watch of Jake Loxley and then his dads, he knew how much it meant to his dad and he filled up as he looked down on it, with the golden stag stood proudly on a background of engraved mountains of silver. He had seen his father check the time a million times in his life; it was a picture he would never forget. Rune smiled as she watched with tears in her eyes, and Jess pulled him back and held him tight. "Happy Birthday sweetheart."

Rags gave Robbie a small heavy cloth moneybag she had made herself. It was embroidered with the wolf's head and two crossed arrows; she blushed a little as she wished him happy birthday; Robbie checked the coast was clear and gave her a soft kiss on the cheek. She blushed as he stood up. "I am married now Rags, it's cheeks only from now on... this is really nice of you, thanks."

The afternoon was spent round the village; it had been a long time since they had walked together down the main street. Rune had him dressed in his best blue pants and top and he wore his long deep violet cloak. Rune had a long violet dress and her cloak with the golden coat of arms on it. They laughed and talked as they walked slowly, and everyone nodded and bowed as they passed them. Rune was now heavily pregnant with only around nine weeks to go, and everyone smiled as they watched the happy couple pass by.

Alice Kirk ran out of her shop with a bag of fresh baked scones and handed them to Robbie, she asked about a million questions and he laughed as she left. "Thanks to Alice and her scones you got archery lessons, and I got the girl of my dreams." They chuckled as they arrived at Steph's house. Steph was out in the yard as always, and gave a big smile as they entered.

They went inside, and through the front room into the kitchen. Jade and Jett screamed with delight. "SURPRISE!!!" All of the Specialists raised their glasses "HAPPY BIRTHDAY GOV." Jess and Alice smiled as Rune beamed with delight.

"It's not as big as a wedding, but got you." She gave him a huge kiss.

The Lord of Loxley was now eighteen years old, and had reached that time of coming of age. The last year of his life had been hard, and he had faced untold dangers and perils, and fought for the freedom of the green world. In many ways, it had taken its toll, but it had also made him the man he now was. Robbie had grown a little taller and he had filled out more, he was stronger and fitter than he had ever been; and he carried a look of his father and had the stature of all the line of Loxley. It was easy to see that in years to come, he would have the power and influence attributed to his father.

Although his face was now thinner and often carried the stubble of a day without shaving, he had lost some of the boyishness about him, and he like Rowan, now looked like the lords they had become. Around the stockade they were greatly admired, and shown a great deal of respect. They were often seen side by side, and they carried a powerful presence between them. Robbie was now seen as the leader of the community, and many people approached him and asked his advice. There had been a few occasions, when neighbours fell out and it had been Robbie and Rowan, side by side who had resolved the issues; there were not many who would argue with the high lord and his kinsman.

There had been a lull on the moors for ten days, and Robbie knew that soon something would happen, the words of Scarlet had stayed with him, and he now felt the time was coming to bring the Night Stalkers and the Specialists into a protective role. He placed watchmen all down the south with fast riders, the Cutters had to come from Tintagel and if they came over land, he would know.

Out on the coast near Scarborough, Alfie and the bandits kept watch for boats coming into the harbour, it was mid-afternoon on the twenty fifth day of April, when the first reports started to arrive. Rowan was sat in the chair opposite Skip as Robbie looked down at a map of the Kirklees area; he wanted to go to the Priory so that he and Steph could recover the documents, to begin the search for the true heir to the kingdom. Robbie looked up as a very dirty Jennifer Watson came in after knocking.

"Begging your pardon My Lord, I have important news from Captain Silvers." Robbie offered her three brass bits but she waved her hand. "I gets paid proper from Miss Rags My Lord." She nodded and bowed as she stepped back toward the door. In a flash, she was gone and Rowan gave a small laugh.

"Miss Rags, is it? She has gone up in the world since she came to Loxley."

Robbie chuckled as he opened the letter and looked down to read it. "I knew it; they have come up through North Wales and are heading up through Old Manchester. They will try to wind round above Huddersfield, and attack the rear of our lines at York. Right Skip let's see who we have and what can be done, we have about two days to prepare."

Skip walked to the door and opened it, he shouted into the busy hall "Treen, Mabel, Patsy, I want everything we have on Huddersfield right across to York. I want to know who we have there, how many there are and the names of all the commanders." He turned and winked at Robbie, Rowan gave a smile as he rocked the chair off its back legs on to all four, and lifted the letter off the desk to read it.

It took forty minutes to gather all the information that they needed, Robbie and Rowan scoured the maps and looked at the terrain, Loxley was well protected, and if the Cutters deviated towards Loxley, they would have plenty of warning. All the northern border of Loxley was guarded day and night as was the west and east, nothing would get past without being spotted.

Robbie looked up at Treen. "Let all of your family know to gather the Specialists at the mere tonight at six, we have a little work to do and then we will move to the west to await our guests. Tell Scarlet what is going on and let her know now is the time to move to the next phase of our defence, she will know what I mean." He looked up at Skip and Rowan. "Let's prepare, the Black City will empty in two days as this Cutter group try to blind side us."

It was all hands on deck as Rowan, and Robbie rode to the Mere. Alice, Bear, Harry with Blades, Todd, Hornet and Woody joined them as they rode down the Sacred Wood Road towards the Mere. Jett, Rafe and Jade were already waiting as they rode into the glade. It was late afternoon when all the Specialists were gathered on the grass outside Robbie's house. Rune slid her arm in Robbie's. "Can I come? I would love to see the Priory again." She gave him a smile. "It has special memories for us."

"I am not sure Rune; it could have enemies all around it, what if we are attacked?"

"Robbie I can open a window anywhere, first sign of trouble I will want all of us out of there, it's not like we are going to be there for long is it?" He looked unsure but the look on her face was too much for him and he smiled.

"Alright, but stay close to my side, and if there is even a hint of trouble you come right back here where I know you are safe." She gave a big smile and pulled him into a hug.

"Oh Goodie, it will be wonderful to look upon that corner again." She turned and headed into the house for her cloak. Once the whole of the Specialists were assembled, Sapphire opened a window and they all passed through into the overgrown gardens of the Priory at Kirklees. Pebbles and Rowan were first out followed by Wolfie and Sting; they shot round the place as the others took up defensive positions around the whole priory to ensure it was secure.

Rune came through with Big John, who now acted as her personal protection; Robbie watched with a smile as he saw his team move like shadows into the trees and seal the whole place. They had become the very best, and it now showed in the way all of them moved. Even Maggs, who had spent some time with Blades and Hornet at Joe's place, now disappeared with as much skill as Pebbles. Robbie walked with Rowan and Harry round to the old grave under the trees of the first hooded man, Robbie stopped in his tracks as he saw the desecration, Rune gasped with shock, Harry moaned several feet behind them.

"Whoa man I knew it, that's why my karma has been jangled for a year, he thinks it was me and sent like the green evils after me, that's why my life man has been so not cosmic, his uncosmic monsters have been after me man."

The trees had been torn out of the ground, and the stone that had covered the grave of Robyn in the Hood lay smashed on the ground. The metal rails were bent and twisted, and there was a huge hole and a splintered old coffin. Bones were strewn across the floor all over the overgrown garden and Harry gave a big shudder as he realised there was a long old bone beneath his boot; he jumped back with a squeak. "Urghhhh!"

Robbie felt sick; he knelt down as he lifted the few bones around his feet and gathered them together. He placed them together neatly and looked to his side as the black clad figure of Harry came down beside him. "He is the first of our family Harry, look what they have done to him, he is everything that Loxley is."

Harry lifted his arm around Robbie. "Hey Robbie man, you just mellow a while, I will help put things back as they should be man. This aint right man, uncosmic things have happened dude and there will be vibe jangling all over for this one man. Hey don't get upset, let your old Uncle Harry take care of him."

Rune watched with a smile as the tenderness of Harry comforted Robbie. It was odd in a way because Harry feared the dead, and yet his love of his nephew was such that he helped Robbie collect all the bones off the floor. Rune and Rowan, both gave a small chuckle, to see Harry close his eyes and chant to himself as he lifted each bone with only the tips of his fingers. Eyes shut and mumbling, he carried each bone at arm's length to the graveside and stacked them all up neatly.

Robbie stood in the hole and took off his cloak. He laid it in what was left of the coffin and placed the bones carefully inside; he folded the cloak of the hooded man over the bones of his ancestor. Harry and Robbie pushed the soil back in on top of the grave and placed the pieces of stone on the top.

Rune knelt down as they stepped back and she touched the soil. A long shoot grew out of the earth and branched sideways; Robbie watched as a large oak tree grew before him to mark the final resting place of his ancestor. He smiled at Rune, as Harry looked at the tree as the leaves unrolled and gave a gasp. "Whoa man that is totally freaky and cosmic." He looked down and froze.

A white mist flowed round the tree and shimmered in front of him, his eyes opened wide, and his jaw dropped as he took a step back. "Whoa man uncosmic things are like totally happenin, it's like time I split dudes."

It was too late; a hooded figure in white came out of the tree and rose before Harry. Harry snapped his eyes shut and put his fingers in his ears, and began to chant rapidly, he opened one eye and peaked, the figure bowed and he snapped it shut and began to chant faster as he shook from head to foot. "Whoa dudes and cosmic beings bless my vibes and make me happenin. Give my karma vibes of white, stop the uncosmic beings in the night." Harry chanted loudly over and over, and opened his eyes and the white figure lowered their hood, he swooned, and Robbie and Rowan both leaned over to grab him.

Holding Harry under each of his arms, Rowan and Robbie bowed to the white figure, Harry slid forward as they bowed, and his nose almost touched the misty figure, he squealed as they pulled him back. "Harry you are safe here, no harm will come to you, chill out and listen." Robbie patted him on the back.

Rune moved close to Robbie's side, as Harry sagged, his eyes fixed with fear on the misty figure of Gwendolyn White Circle. She looked older than the last time they had seen her, and she was no longer able to appear solid, she smiled and her voice echoed as though it was distant. "Greetings woodsman of my line, I am touched at the care and respect you pay to my grandnephew and the start of your own line. Your return has corrected the desecration of a site held in reverence by the people of the Fae."

Harry hung trembling between Robbie and Rowan. "Hey dudet it wasn't me lets like be peaceful and happenin about this."

Gwendolyn turned to Harry, who began to tremble much quicker and swallowed hard. "Greetings Harold of Loxley, You have fear of your family which troubles me, have no fear here you are safe with your kin of the past and the present."

"Whoa! No offence like, but you aint like real cosmic lady, you is dead, your vibes have like split forever man."

Robbie couldn't help but smile, talking to the dead was Jasper territory, and Harry had no concept of it. Gwendolyn smiled at him.

"I know a great deal of you Harold of Loxley. You are true to your heart and a fierce protector of your kin. I have watched many of your deeds, and seen those you have sent to other realms, as they whisper your name when passing my realm. Rest peacefully Harold of Loxley, for your deeds have been through loyalty to those you protect, you have no reason to fear those who were listed to meet and die by your hand in the early days of creation."

Harry's eyes grew wider and wider, his voice was almost a whisper. "There's a list? Oh whoa man I knew it, now the uncosmic monsters can talk to everyone I killed and get them to join in the hunt for me, I am so cosmic toast, there is nowhere for me to like run to." His legs buckled, and Robbie and Rowan felt the jolt of his weight on their arms. Robbie strained as Gwendolyn smiled at him.

"The time of the new queen is close; beware of those who hide behind words, for their deeds will be more deadly than a sword or an arrow. There are dark deeds behind hidden doors Bowman, protect the children and prepare, for things done can be undone, even unnatural things." Robbie swallowed hard at the seriousness of her words, Harry moaned in despair.

"My life is over; unnatural happenings will find me and chomp on me." With a pitiful moan it all became too much and he passed out, Robbie and Rowan released him, and he slumped to the floor, as Gwendolyn turned to face Rowan.

"Rowan is the tree of protection given to all by the Green Lord, you have lived up to your name well in the defence of my kin, my time here is short, but know this Rowan of the Green Realm, your name amongst the Fae is spoken with high praise, and I thank you for all you have done in your lords service." She hurriedly turned to face Rune.

"My Lady of the Woods, prepare for your time on the Violet Isle, but be wary of what hides on the rocks, when at your safest, there will always be danger. Heed well these words and we will meet on the roads of my world one day, go swiftly for danger moves against you as I speak. Farewell my family and loyal supporters may the blessings of the White Circle shine around you."

The misty figure began to fade, and Harry moaned on the floor, Robbie felt a pressing need rise deep inside himself. "We must move and quickly."

The Old priory had been smashed and destroyed even more than the first time they came. It was obvious that someone had been searching the place and most of the church was now wrecked. The pews lay in pieces and all the windows were smashed. Robbie ran up to the old stone altar, which was still intact, his gamble had paid off as even the army of Knox had not had the faith to smash an altar. Rowan and the still shaky Harry lifted the stone top off, and Robbie reached inside and smiled as he pulled a big polythene bag out filled with the precious documents, they needed to trace the line of the king. He stuffed it into his shirt and the altar stone was replaced.

"Right let's get the hell out of here." They came down to the doors as a whistle sounded, the Specialists had company, Robbie turned to Rune. "Pull all the team back here and open a window."

Rune nodded and her eyes began to flicker with violet. Purple light rose up the walls of the old church as she protected the whole site, the violet window rose out of the floor surrounded by flowering violets. Hornet, Woody, Amethyst and Blades came down the corridor, Pebbles and Alice stood guard with their bows as the others appeared out of the trees. Hawk and Jaz joined Pebbles and Alice as they fired at the black vests in the tree line. Robbie slipped out an arrow and fitted it to the string, he aimed out of the window as Maggs, Crystal, Una and Maddy came across the lawn. Rowan came up at his side as he watched Mel with Flash and Jay back slowly towards them shooting into the trees.

They fired across the path of the retreating girls who realised they had cover and turned and ran, Bear came out of the trees slicing at two unexpecting black clad soldiers, Skip followed his sword gleaming in the sun with a red line of blood running down it. The Specialists flew into the protection of the church, as Wolfie and Sting came last. Robbie and Rowan stood either side of the doors with Hawk and Saff behind them; they fired past Wolfie and Sting at the soldiers coming up behind them. Sting shot through the doors and Harry and John pushed them closed and wedged them. Everyone shot through the violet window and as the window closed, the doors crashed open and a large group of soldiers piled in. They stopped and looked round confused, the church was empty, a tall soldier in black shivered, as he looked round.

"Glad he is not here, that hooded man has unnatural powers, see they have vanished into thin air, I am telling you guys, these Specialist aint human." The whole group looked round with fear in their eyes and shuddered.

Harry sat on the grass with Jaz looking pale; Jaz patted his back and gave a chuckle. "You have shown bravery beyond the call of duty my friend, I am proud of you."

"Whoa dude my vibes was jangled and wangled, it aint cosmic man, you should stay down and under man, I aint happenin when you come back like that. Oh, man I done bad things, and my karma has gone like totally tilted." He hung his head down and breathed deeply, as Jaz smiled.

"Chill out and absorb the power of Loxley my friend, it will unwangle those unhappenin vibes."

Harry nodded as Rune smiled at Harry; she pulled Robbie close and smiled, he pulled the bag out of his shirt and tossed it over to Steph. "You have a new task Mother, I want Rune and you to start sifting through all of this and find me an heir, we have to move quickly now to find this legion. I want you to stay here and help Rune."

Rune pulled him closer. "Be careful Rob."

He gave her a soft kiss and smiled. "I have a date with some violet eyes, believe me I will not be risking it."

She gave a soft giggle. "I know, I found your letters."

"How many?"

"Two more."

He kissed her. "You need to keep looking." She giggled.

CHAPTER SIX

THE COLD FACE OF REALITY

General Walters sat behind the highly polished desk and looked with his one good eye at the small black clad figure in front of him. The bishop gave a small smile as he stood behind the silent figure, his eyes watched from the lined face of a man who had served his lord over his life of many years. The grey hair was almost completely gone. "I can assure you General, they do not call him Shadow for nothing."

Walters grunted as he thought about the proposition being put before him by the churchman. He eyed the small dark figure with curiosity. "He doesn't speak at all?"

"Nothing you would understand, he will not speak our language, and he uses only his native tongue, although he understands every word that you say." Walters eyed him suspiciously.

The black clad warrior was barely five-foot tall. His dark green eyes remained fixed as he stared at the foot of the desk, he was not muscular looking, and yet he carried a sense of power. The eye of the General followed him from his proud eyes down to the black sash like belt, which had the long thin sword of his house pushed into it, across his back was a short thin black bow and a holster of thin black arrows. His feet had on small soft black shoes; the General scowled at him. "You know what I want you to do?"

The small silent figure bowed; his eyes fixed on the general at all times. The bishop smiled, he knew the general was afraid and needed to muster his power against the realm of the woodsmen. "He has been instructed thoroughly; you have no fear. He will slip like a shadow behind the hooded man's lines, and no one will even notice him. He has proved very useful to us on a number of occasions." There was a look of conceit about the elderly Bishop

The large general looked at the tall grey haired old bishop. "The Church has used his service before, it surprises me Bishop that you would need such tactics, I am a godless man and have taken life without care, but you are a man of the cloth, I am a little intrigued that you would consider such notions."

The bishop's smile faded as he shuffled a little on the spot. "These are times

of doubt and uncertainly my dear General, none of us want the old practices of
before to return. This Earth Faith is godless and embraces rituals that we know are
not civilised, we eradicated it before and we will again. There can only be room
on the throne for a God fearing king who will support the church. Heaven knows
what heathen they will bring forth as a pretender."

General Walters understood the bishop, he had been around men of power long
enough to know how the game worked. He nodded as he pulled open the draw in
his large polished desk, and he lifted the black cloth bag out and tossed it on to the
desk. "A thousand now and two when the job is done."

The bishop smiled and leaned forward; his hand slid the weighty bag across the
table as he gave a satisfied smirk. "It will be done; you shall have her head as soon
as the task is completed."

He turned and walked across the room to the large polished doors. "Come
Shadow. It's been a pleasure General; I will contact you when we have what you
require." The small black figure bowed, turned, and walked five paces behind
the Church leader; the door closed quietly as the general sat back in his chair and
pondered his deal.

He had no trust of the church at all; he had no trust of anyone, he closed his eye,
and a long sigh emitted from the general as the pictures rose to his mind of the
young red clad warrior. She had to be removed from the equation before he could
really get ahead with his campaign, he was no fool and he already knew she would
be changing her plans as he thought of her. Scarlet of Caerleon had proven to be
his only weakness in a life of force and power, she had to die and die soon.

It was dim in the trees as the Saddleworth Constables watched them below.
Word had come quickly from Loxley, and they now spread along the edge of the
reservoir, high on the bank below the trees and made note of the group of dirty
and scruffy looking Tenth Legion of the Cutters. Captain Patrick Smith's long
pale face observed, as the group sat on the bank and drew the water into their
canteens. It was a disturbing sight to see the black clad warriors with red vests, and
an assortment of weapons, including long bows.

All of them were big men with huge arms; the word 'Brutes' came to mind as he
watched. Their hair was plaited in long thin dreadlocks and looked matted and
unwashed, their faces were quite frightening at first, but having spent at least an
hour watching them, he could see it was makeup of some kind and he now viewed
them with a curious manner. The Cutters had painted their eyelids and round
their eyes black, the rest of their faces were a deep pillar-box red. They looked like
wild devils, and he could understand how easy it would be to put terror into the
hearts of young women and children. He had known they were coming, and yet he
still had taken a deep gasp when they arrived.

They began to stand up and move around on the grassy bank as they organised, one very large and scarred Cutter seemed to be the leader, and he barked orders as they formed into three groups. The order was given and they began to move out across the bank on to the pathway and they headed north up to the bridge and through the trees, that would lead up to the moors and Huddersfield.

The whole troop stayed low and quiet until they had cleared the area, and then Captain Smith turned to the young corporal, he handed him a letter that had all the notes he had quietly given to his Sergeant as he watched. "Get this down there and quickly to the girl, Lord Robert has not much time to prepare."

The young soldier saluted, and clutching the letter tight in his hand he ran down the high steep bank through the trees, and headed down the path toward the top of the large wall that held back the millions of gallons of water.

He sprinted for all he was worth across the top of the dam and down the steep path to the old road that led to Blades Cottage. The blonde girl sat on the bench by the door, and watched as he came running down the lane round the trees. She stood up and smiled as he came gasping toward her holding up the letter. "You want to take it easy mate; you will give yourself a heart attack running like that."

He fell to his knees drawing in as much air as possible, as he gasped and faced the smooth road. "Tell the Lord.... He has not got.... much time." He looked up as the sweat ran down his face.

Rags patted his cheek. "You aint got too much if you keep running like that mate." She gave him a smile and nodded. "Robbie knows, but I will let him know." Rags pulled on the saddle of her trusty mount Bags and she swung herself up with a smile. She gave him a wink. "Maybe I will see ya again cute cheeks." She gave a giggle. "See ya." The young soldier gave a bright smile as she turned the horse and with a grip of her heels, Bags bounded off down the road back towards the dam. The young corporal stood with a smile on his face and watched as Rags and Bags bounded away onto the other side of the moors that would take her to Robbie's Mere. He gave a cough and took a long breath, and wiped his face on his red cloak. Rags raced up into dry grass and heather and headed for the tree line east, she knew how important it was to get ahead now and report the information to Robbie.

Robbie and Rowan looked down at the map with Malcolm Prosper; Robbie looked up at them both. "I think they will go for the fastest route, they will have to be on foot, and these guys use stealth as we do, horses or vehicles will create too much noise, so I would think their best route would possibly be to come round the southern edge of Huddersfield. Let's face it; there are too many wild gangs there so they will want to avoid it. Leeds is out since the men of Settle have taken it back and are reinforcing the area, no I will bet my last bit they will come through Old

Wakefield to Garforth, and then head northeast to ruined Tadcaster."

Rowan looked down and studied the map. "Ok Robbie, we have a long line of men from Knottingley right up to Whetherby, that whole area from Tadcaster back is swarming with woodsmen as we have got all the men on standby in that area, we are not short of fighters, we have men in Leeds who could come up behind them, the only question is where do you want them hit?"

Malcolm placed his finger on the map. "The large crossroads just down from Bramhan." He looked up at Robbie. "It's part of the old motorway network, they will choose to use the fastest route and that way is the fastest. It's a straight line on solid road, it's also banked high so even in the dark we will see them coming without being spotted. This has got to be the perfect place for an ambush."

He was not entirely sure, Rowan gave a nod as his finger traced escape routes, and most of them had woodsmen already in place. He gave a nod to Robbie who looked back down at the map. "Alright Malcolm I get the feeling you know this place well, as soon as Rags gets here, I will know for definite if I am right, if I am I will trust your judgement and we will prepare." Malcolm gave a wide smile and Robbie winked. "Ok let's see who has arrived yet, we need to be ready as soon as the word comes, I want to be in place at least a day before they arrive."

Rags bounded across the back of Saddleworth moor, and headed over Bleaklow in the direction of Derwent Water. She had taken the short cut over the moor many times and knew it so well; she could spot the boggy areas long in advance. Bags strained down on the dry peat to get good purchase, he was the fastest horse that the postie's had, and he was sure footed always. She rode like the wind low in the saddle with her head down, her blonde hair now streamed behind her, as did the long dark blue cloak with the Loxley crest on it. Saff gave a smile as she looked out across the wide empty moorland and saw her, Rags lifted her hand and waved and moved Bags toward her, she came galloping up at high speed as Saff opened her blue round window, and with a beaming smile Rags burst into it and disappeared. Saff turned on her horse and rode through and the window closed behind her.

Jay threw her arms around her dad, it had been a few weeks since she had seen him, on the few occasions she had managed to get home he had been out on duty. Jay spent more and more time with Ruby staying in Robbie's old room and sharing with her. With Lucy and Blades just up the lane and Alice next door, she had suddenly found she had more friends than ever before.

Jess was wonderful with her, and she had become very fond of Beth and John. She had fitted in with the Specialists very fast, and her willingness to learn new skills made her popular with the others. She did not boast or show off, but would simply ask advice and then practice as much as she could until she had mastered her task. She carried and used the bow and quiver of Lee Sherman; Keith had given her the quiver after seeing his dads bow on her shoulder after the fight in the

Black City. Jay in her short time had become very close to the kindly old master of the woods, and she carried his bow with great pride.

Rags came flying up the track and on to the glade, and as Bags slid to a stop, she swept in one fluid movement off the saddle and down on to the floor. Rags rushed past Jay and her father, and ran through the gate and up to the glass doors. She banged on the wooden frame and Robbie poked his head out of the kitchen. "Hey Robbie I got what you wanted, them funny looking soldiers said you need to move fast time is short. Them red faced buggers left the water at Dovestones about just over an hour ago, they is going up towards Huddersfield."

He gave her a large smile as he walked down the room toward her; Rags puckered her lips and winked, he gave a chuckle, and he kissed his finger and pressed it softly on to her lips. "I only have lips for my wife now."

She gave a giggle as she handed over the letter. "A girls gotta try Hoodie Boy." She gave a laugh as she turned, "See ya lusty lips," she ran down the path and through the gate and vaulted up onto Bags, and brought him round slowly. Robbie leaned out of the door.

"Hey Rags, let the team know, we meet here in three hours." She waved as she rode off up the glade and back on the track to the old forest road. Robbie opened the letter and read as Rowan, and Malcolm stood on the steps and waited, Jay smiled as she stood with her arm round her dad, Robbie nodded to himself as he read. He looked up and handed the letter to Rowan. "Ok we got our work cut out; there are a hundred and twenty of them split into three groups." He turned and walked down the path. "Ok Malcolm, get your men ready. Saff, Hawk, they are on foot on the pass above the old dam heading toward Huddersfield, pick up their trail and follow them, let Rune know when you spot them and she will follow them from the table."

Saff nodded and turned and waved her hand, opening a window, Keith shouldered his bow with a smile. "We will find them, have no fear." Both of them shot through on to the base of the moors, the trail was easy to see, the Tenth Legion were a large group who knew little fear, they no longer worried about leaving tracks or being seen.

Over to the east of Loxley woodlands, the carriage came to a halt on the edge of the woodland road. The bishop turned to his quiet companion. "You know what to do? Meet me at the abbey when it is done." Shadow nodded and lifted his small black bag, the door opened and he jumped out and quickly ran into the trees. The bishop gave a smile and sat back in his seat; the carriage lurched forward. Scarlet of Caerleon now was the target of the small deadly assassin, General Walters wanted her out of the picture, and then the small assassin would be free to carry out his other task. He had never failed the church yet, and the man responsible for the damage caused to their Cathedral, and the sudden heart attack of their Arch Bishop would then pay for his crimes against the church. He smiled in his carriage as it rocked from side to side making its way slowly down the old cracked stone road.

Robbie sat at his desk making the final preparations for his plans; Rune gave him a smile as she came up the stairs and crossed the room to his desk as he sat back in the chair. She sat on his lap and curled close, he pulled her close as she gave him a kiss and he smiled. "You watch yourself Rob, these are powerful fighters." He gave her a squeeze.

"I promised I would take less risks and I have; believe me Rune I am not underestimating these Cutters. I want to keep everyone under cover and use bows, the swords won't go in until I am sure they can handle it, I will also have the Night Stalkers with me, if we can deal with them in a crossfire, I will be happy with that. Keep your eyes on Scarlet for me, I think any time now the black army will change their strategy, Scarlet is aware of the new plans, but just to be on the safe side watch out for her."

She cuddled up to him her head on his shoulder. "I will be watching from the table, every moment."

There were a few hours to go before the Specialists assembled, and he took the time out with Rune. He sat alone in his office with her and just enjoyed the feeling of having her close. It felt strange in many ways because he was used to having her by his side, and recently she would sit watching from her table. He had always tried to keep her from harm's way, and yet now he found he missed her when he was out in the trees. Her bow at his side throughout all of the times he had faced the enemy had given him the comfort of knowing he had cover at all times.

The Specialists began to arrive all armed and ready, they sat on the steps in the garden and laughed and joked, as Rowan briefed them on the task at hand. The Night Stalkers, who now made a force of two hundred bowmen from the Black City, stood around watching the Specialists. Malcolm Prosper with his force of black clad woodsmen had begun to build quite a reputation for the group, they had all shown some extreme bravery, and had made some very daring raids on the enemy camps, but even the Night Stalkers bowed to a superior force, and they viewed the Specialists with reverence.

Once Rowan had given them the details, the Specialists wandered around and spoke to the Night Stalkers, Jade and Blades were very keen on the weaponry they used, as they all had quite an armoury of extra weapons stashed in their belts. Smokes now carried the long silver spear that he had recovered from Mordred, he had been taking extra lessons with Flash to improve his pole fighting skills, the spear could be used for both jobs of pole fighting and if needs be throwing, although some how he did not want it out of his sight.

Jade now carried the long silver dagger of Mordred's in a new sheath she had made for her belt, it's jewel encrusted handle glowed at her side. Jay sat with Big John and Wolfie, as Sting spun her sword and loosened up, she now wore the green cloak of Caerleon and it had surprised a few to see she now had commanders' bars on her cloak. Scarlet had given her daughter a rank, and she now had the same authority as Wolfie, which in the field gave them extra respect.

Crystal was not happy about wearing woodsman attire, but her all white did show a little in the trees, she now wore a long green shawl like poncho with a silver belt over her white, and the cloak of a Loxley Bowman. The rest of the group wore full field attire, and it seemed strange to see the graceful and very lady like figure of Maddy in trousers and a long waistcoat of brown, her cloak carried the stone circle of Morbihan, as did Treen's. Alley had laughed on her visit from Good Hope, and pulled her mother up who had always done everything in her power to stop her wearing pants.

The Night Stalkers all found the group to be very warm and friendly, and soon they were talking and joking and admiring each other's weapons. Robbie smiled from the steps as he stood with Rune and watched. The Night Stalkers who had noticed his arrival all turned and bowed, he gave a smile as the Specialists all turned wondering what was happening. He laughed as he came down the steps and winked at Jett. "I could get use to that; you lot look at the respect given to the lord of this realm." Rune giggled at his side as he walked out on to the glade.

Wolfie gave a long sweeping bow. "My dearest Lord Robert of Loxley, you honour us as we follow." The Specialists gave a hearty laugh as he stood up with eyes twinkling and Robbie gave him a short bow.

"Commander, your wit as ever is as sharp as your teeth." The Night Stalkers had suddenly had one of their questions answered; they now knew which one was the wolf man, and they viewed him with great reverence. It was a happy smiling group that lined up on the grass and waited for Saff and Hawk to return. Rune's eyes flickered at Robbie's side. "She is on her way." A few seconds later the blue pulsating circle appeared in front of them, Robbie turned and pulled Rune close, she gave him a huge hug and kissed him. "I will be watching, if you need me, I will appear."

"See you soon." Steph smiled as she pulled Rune back from him, and he walked with his men into the circle of light. Steph felt a little odd as she saw Smokes go through with Jade and Rowan, she was not going, her task now was to translate the strange code that Leenard had made his notes in, and then pull together all the facts that would reveal who was the heir to the kingdom.

It was midafternoon, and the long stretch of empty road covered in leaves, and bits of weed stretched before Robbie's eyes. He looked up at the high bank on either side and the cover was perfect. It would be at least a day to wait so he started to get organised, he wanted adequate protection; the Cutter Brigade had bows, so he knew just lying in wait could be difficult. The team went to work moving earth as they dug bunkers along the top of the high banks, having some protection made a lot of sense to Rowan who walked along the line, making sure that from the road none of their work could be seen. The Tenth Legion was well known and not easily fooled; Hawk and Saff took the look out positions in the edge of the wood, as Robbie placed his men evenly along the cutting, and placed two Night Stalkers between each of them.

He felt nervous, Robbie knew he was now evenly matched, and stealth and surprise had to be the way to work. If they came into the trees, he knew his men would have a rough fight on their hands; Rowan sensed his apprehension and patted his arm. "We will be fine Robbie, we are making good preparation and the team know this is the hardest competition we have ever faced."

Robbie looked up at the bank from the road. "We are asking a lot of them this time Rowan, it's not like facing young boys or trained soldiers. These Cutters are wilder than anything we have ever faced; they will not play by the rules of combat." Rowan gave his shoulder a squeeze.

"I have told them all the restraints are off for this one, they know what to expect. Never forget we also have Rune watching in, relax a bit my brother, we will give them a fight worthy of the measure of Loxley."

The evening seemed to draw out longer as Maggs wandered with Rags down the line handing out hot bowls of a thick meaty stew; Robbie sat with his back to a large tree, peering out into the distance with his telescope. Smoke rose on the horizon, and he smiled to himself, he knew they would not be able to resist attacking somewhere. He leaned back and gave a sigh, as he missed Rune, there had been so many nights when they sat and talked together on look out.

"Hi gorgeous, I feel you."

He gave a little giggle. *"I was thinking of you."* A circle of violets sprung up through the grass around him and he smiled.

"See my love I am there with you." He felt warmth slowly pass into him, he could feel her presence deep inside him and he relaxed and closed his eyes.

Pictures of her flowed into his mind and he rested feeling his concerns flow away.

"I am with you always Robbie, can you feel me as I float up from your heart."

"Oh Rune, I hate being without you."

The violet figure of his beloved rose up from the floor and smiled at him. "I am the Lady of the Woods and you are sat in the trees, I am with you, never forget that." She sat down and curled on his lap. Just feeling her was enough as his head slipped to her shoulder; Rune pulled him close and held him tightly. "I was missing you too, it's alright having mum with me, but I want to be here with you."

She gave a little giggle. "It's odd Robbie, I am sat at home weeks from giving birth and yet look, when I appear I show no signs of the life I carry, I miss looking at it." Robbie looked down at her slender waist, she was right it did seem odd. He softly stroked her flat tummy and she smiled. "I can feel it at home it's really strange, they are moving inside me as you stroke them, it's like they sense you." He gave a smile and as he looked up at her bright shining violet eyes, she leaned forward and kissed him.

"Corr you two even get to snog in the spirit world, you aint half lucky bleeders."

Rune gave a giggle as she looked up at Rags with a steaming bowl of stew for Robbie. "I am the luckiest woman alive Rags."

"You got that right girl." Rags gave a beaming smile as Robbie took the bowl of stew off her. He gave her a large grin.

"Yet we never seem to have any privacy." Rags gave a chuckle.

"I got your hint Gov." She blew him a kiss and ran back into the trees laughing, "See ya."

Rune sat and giggled as Robbie ate his stew. She curled back round him when he had finished and as the sun went down; he sat and watched with her in his arms. He noticed how every so often her eyes would flicker, and he knew she was scanning the area to make sure no one was around. It was very late when Robbie closed his eyes and drifted into sleep, the night passed in safety, and as dawn approached, the silent violet covered figure stood up slowly and blew him a kiss. Rune faded away and left him sat with a blanket wrapped round him. Jade smiled from the trees as she silently sat and watched him as the sun rose slowly in the sky.

The group were busy when Robbie woke from the deepest sleep he had had for some time, he felt strong and refreshed and somehow, he knew Rune had used a little of her power to help him sleep. Half the group ate in the trees as half stayed by their posts. The Night Stalkers were getting used to being around the Specialists, and some of the personalities of the group were starting to show. There was a happy mood, and they all laughed and joked with each other, the camp felt more relaxed as they all had settled into their places and were just preparing themselves for the day to come.

Scarlet stood high on her hill and looked out across the moors; she was no fool and had brought extra troops up from York. Far in the distance she could see the black army organising, something was about to happen. She gave Phillip a wink. "Get them ready." Phillip turned and ran down the hill to the commanders who all stood waiting for their orders, two young women with green and red flags walked up to the top of the hill and stood either side of Scarlet.

"Right girls you know the routine, I bark you wave." The girls looked a little sheepish at the tall red clad warrior; Scarlet had a fierce reputation, she patted both girls on the back. "You will be fine. Right let's get ready for the biggest game of chess I have ever played. We shall soon find out what old fatty one ear has got up his sleeve." She gave a soft giggle as she lifted the telescope to her eye.

"Send the signal girls here he comes." Both girls raised the flags and the message was sent across the battlefield. The commanders in the deep heather ran along their lines preparing, as huge pits opened and woodsmen behind high boards decorated with heather lifted the portable catapults up and sat them on top of the long poles slid across the pits. The black army came across the moors in a long line, there was a host of at least twenty thousand, and they flattened the ground as they passed over it. All the plant life was crushed and pushed deeply into the damp peat.

They were at least a mile off when the catapults started to fire. Hundreds of tiny balloons made from the intestines of the slaughtered animals flew through the air filled with moonshine. It was Joe's best, and most of the men could not understand as they all landed over a thousand yards away and exploded on to the heather. Scarlet watched and smiled as the bowmen passed her heading to behind the catapults, they carried arrows packed with wadding and formed a long line. The black army kept on coming, building up speed as they began to run into the tall heather, their long spears were pointing forward and their swordsmen closely followed.

Commander Haughton gave the signal and five hundred yards in front of the woodsmen, long sharpened wooden poles came up out the ground to waist height, they were decorated in heather, and at first, they were not easily noticed. The roar of the black army rose into the air as they now came at a fast run toward them.

Commander Haughton walked down the back of his line as the men raised their bows. "Hold them arrows lads and lasses; if you have to do something howl for commander Rafe, I feel his spirit is here with us." Howls erupted along the lines as the bowmen smiled; nerves seemed to lesson as they all thought of their flesh tearing leader.

The noisy hoard in black came up the bluff like a steamroller at great pace, they had not noticed the waist high long wooden spikes, and it was too late for any of them to stop, the hoard pushed forward with huge force, and those at the front had nowhere to go. The screams rose into the air as Scarlet gave the order, and the flags shot into the air. Two thousand flaming arrows lifted into the air, and the moonshine soaked grass and heather at the rear of the army erupted into a fierce and roaring blaze.

Commander Haughton screamed with all his might as the front line unleashed their arrows with pinpoint accuracy, black vests screamed and fell backwards with the force. The black army was caught between the roaring inferno behind them, and a hail of arrows coming over a wall of sharpened spikes. They were trapped and boxed in as the arrows rained down on them, screams and wails rose into the air as more moonshine filled balloons lifted into the air and rained down exploding on them. The flames were moving quickly and the black army was now in a wild panic.

If they came forward the archers got them, if they ran back into the flames they were covered in alcohol, and they knew they would die. Bodies hung impaled on the spikes, and the men crouched behind them had nowhere to go, the flames were now moving towards them, fanned by the sudden rising wind that Rune had brought to the moors. It ran through the alcohol soaked grass toward the line of spikes, and as it caught hold of the soldiers at the back, they ran blindly with panic and their fellow soldiers burst into flame as they touched. It was chaos as Scarlet watched down her scope, she knew a second wave would come and now she had the weapon of fear on her battlefield. The sight of thousands of dead soldiers would slow down any more coming that way, she looked to the sides of the moor where she had another two thousand woodsmen hidden under boards.

The large host gathered at the rear came forward and then split, half moved east as the others went west. Scarlet smiled as she looked down the scope. "Get ready girls, old Fatty One ear is becoming very predictable." She looked to her right. "It is Claire isn't it?" The small red haired girl nodded. "Alright Claire you get ready." Scarlet's eyes flickered red. *"Rune darling are you watching?"*

Rune sat at her table her eyes flowing with violet as the images from the battlefield spun in the violet cloud above her table. Steph sat quietly and watched nervously. *"I hear you Scarlet, I am ready, just say when."*

Scarlet turned to Claire. "Alright let them know." Claire raised her flags and sent the message, Ox stood with Commander Wilkes, he gave him a pat on the shoulder of the Commander. "Let's light em Wilkie."

The black army thundered forward towards them as the white cloud rose up from below the heather. A thick white swirling mist blew into the invading army; the commander gave the signal and as the black army ran through the blinding mist, a thousand fizzing arrows shot into the air, all the woodsmen dropped into the heather. Ox stood momentarily alone, Commander Wilkes leapt up grabbed him and dragged him down into the heather as the first explosion erupted into the air.

Deep inside the white mists, there was chaos, as soldiers ran deafened and blinded by the flashes and the spraying sharp shards of the heather. The sound of a thousand dynamite arrows exploding was incredible, light flashed through the mist like a strobe, as soldiers were blown off their feet and torn apart. The air was filled with the moans and screams of soldiers who were blown to the floor wounded badly. The mist swirled around them and muffled everything, blind and disorientated, the soldiers staggered around and out into the open. They met the onslaught of the woodsmen who came at them from nowhere with swords and bows, unable to hear and blinded they fell quickly as Ox, his bandits and the woodsmen made short work of them.

As the black army headed west towards the trees, another thousand woodsman waited hidden as the ground opened up into a thick wide mire, the men fell screaming into the watery peat like mud, which sucked at their legs and pulled at them. They sunk quickly thrashing about to get out, and the ground squelched as they went under. Those who had enough time to stop on the edge and offer their hand to those in the mire, found woodsmen's arrows picking them out and they fell into the mire, dragging others with them.

General Walters screamed red in the face, as he watched twenty thousand of his men just disappear and fall before his eyes, he lifted his binoculars and saw Scarlet, she waved and pointed to the girl at her side. General Walters watched as the flags waved, the code reader watched through a telescope on a tripod, and wrote the message quickly. He turned white and looked up at the General.

"She knows our code sir." He stood shaking with a piece of paper in his hand. The angry general snatched it out of his hand and he recoiled away in fear. The general lifted the paper to his good eye and read.

"Hey Walters you one eared fat old slug, you better try harder I am kicking your ass. How about we sort this out just the two of us, I could use the other ear for my wall, it looks uneven."

He lifted his binoculars where Scarlet stood waving and laughing with the two flag girls. His rage exploded as he screwed the paper tight in his clenched fist, and stormed off the platform throwing the note to the ground. Walters hit and killed two of his own guards as he stormed into his tent. General Franklin stooped down and picked up the discarded note and smiled, he passed it to General Jarrod who read it and looked up at his fellow officer.

"Well I never, it was Scarlet that did that to him?" He looked at Franklin who smiled.

"I do kind of like her... I mean I know she is the enemy, but you have to admire the woman who did that to him, the woman has pluck there is no doubt." He gave a wide smile and Jarrod chuckled as the message coder gave a big grin.

The smoke drifted, and the mist cleared and in amongst the twenty thousand dead of the black army, a violet figure walked alone, General Franklin watched as the sky was darkening. Rune raised her hands into the air, and the woodsmen in the front lines went down on one knee and bent their heads low.

General Jarrod watched Rune as she threw back her head speaking out her charms and from each of the dead soldiers of the black army, small white lights floated up, and they streamed into the sky in long lines heading into the clouds and out of sight. Franklin watched fascinated. "What the hell is she doing?"

General Jarrod watched as a tear formed in his eye.

"She is sending the souls of our men into the other realm where the Dark Mistress cannot get them and use them to raise the dead, and make them fight again." Franklin pulled down his binoculars in surprise.

"Can she do that?" Jarrod smiled and nodded.

"She can, she is the Violet Witch... Bless her, whatever they may say about her, she has done right by those men out there." It warmed his heart knowing the Dark One would not be able to corrupt and control his dead men, General Jarrod watched her closely and he saw the tears in her eyes as she looked upon his own dead soldiers. She was beautiful, kind and showing huge compassion to his men, and he felt the first doubts of his command rise up inside him after twenty five years of service.

Conflict in him rose quickly, she was his enemy, and yet as he watched the delicate and gentle girl walk through and wave her hand, so his men sunk into the ground, he felt for the first time in his life he had encountered something that meant more in his life than his job or status. Rune taught General Jarrod the true meaning of humanity, and he felt utterly ashamed, he left the field of combat shortly after, and sat on his bed in his tent with pictures of a very beautiful but heartbroken face in his head.

He felt a great sense of shame rise inside him for all he had done in his part to destroy the woodland people. He had witnessed the evil and torture that had been put on the people of the woodland; he had seen the slaughtered women and hanging bodies for years. It had always been easy to ignore it and look the other way, telling himself it was what happened in war. Never once had he thought of his enemy as real people, the gentleness and kindness shown to his men by the enemy overwhelmed him. Rune's tear filled eyes haunted his mind, after a lifetime of inflicting the evil of his Dark Mistress, and suddenly he felt it was too much.

He was overwhelmed with guilt as he raised the gun to his head, he felt the barrel push into his temple, and his finger moved on to the trigger, he closed his eyes and pulled the trigger, it gave a loud click. Jarrod let out a big sigh of disappointment and opened his eyes. He jumped in fright as he saw the violet figure stood before him. Rune smiled and took her finger off the firing hammer, she crouched down before him and he saw the life and love in her eyes that sparkled before him. "I am life, and I do not think yours should be wasted so easily."

He swallowed deeply as he looked her in the face. "My dear lady, I have commanded evil, I am ashamed of what I have done to your people." She smiled at him.

"You have seen wisdom after a long life, and yet now you wish to end it, would that not be the most evil thing to do when understanding has finally come to you? You feel the guilt of your life, and yet you will do nothing to undo the harm you have done?"

He was completely captivated by her and her words. "What can I do one man against so many?"

Rune took his hand in hers and opened the palm, she looked up at him. "You do not believe one man can bring hope and make a change for the better of everyone?" A small violet flower appeared in his hand and burst into bloom. "One man can change the world, and one man will. You should watch and listen to my hooded man; he will bring great changes for the better of everyone. Go to Caernarfon there is a sage there who will need the help of a strong man, talk to him for he will lead many back to the green world. Throw away your uniform and feel the freedom of the trees above your head, end your life in peace and at peace my Dear General."

Two tears ran down his cheeks as he looked on the face of love and compassion, he felt utterly worthless before her, and yet she gave him a strange hope. He nodded to her and she wiped his tears from his eyes and smiled. "Your men have found peace and are happy to be free of the fear and darkness that controlled them; they have entered the realm of my father of creation and they are happy, she will not find them. You will be protected from her if you leave here before dawn." Rune waved her hand across the general and he glowed violet for a moment.

"Will I see you again my violet lady." Rune gave a little giggle and she pulled her hand from her pocket and placed a blue butterfly in his other hand.

"Give this to the Sage, he will know who sent you and that you are true to him. Help him and we will meet again for I am the lady of the woodland realm, and I walk where all life is spared." Rune faded away and left the General alone in the tent sat on his bed, he gazed in wonder at the small blue butterfly and then looked at the half cocked pistol on his bed. The small plant in his hand opened more blooms and he smiled as he looked at it.

As dusk approached, General Jarrod slipped the small plant into his cup and wrapped it carefully in his small pack. He lifted his long black hoodless cloak with his general crest on it and saw underneath was a hooded Lincoln green cloak. He gave a small laugh at the cleverness of the violet lady, a green hooded cloak would get him safely south and across to Wales. The light faded as the general pulled himself on to his horse and headed slowly out of the camp. He rode in a wide arc until he came to the east side of the deep woodland realm; he stopped his horse and threw his black cloak to the ground, he was no longer General Jarrod; from now on, he would simply be Martin Jarrod a man of peace. He swung the green cloak on to his shoulders and pulled up the hood. Martin Jarrod rode into the dark wood and down the long track south. He was fifty years old and grey haired, and yet inside he suddenly felt he was twenty again and chuckled as he rode away.

As the General rode south down the eastern side of the country, the word came up the line to Robbie that the Cutters were heading up the road toward him, and the Specialists pulled themselves into position ready. Down each side of the wide road, they waited for Robbie's arrow, which would be the signal to strike.

Robbie slid down in the undergrowth and looked down his line of men and women; they were as prepared as they could be. The clump of marching feet, echoed off the leaf and grass strewn stone down the road, he looked across at Rowan three feet away in the trees, and Rowan nodded and smiled. Robbie nodded as he fitted the arrow to his string, his heart raced, this would be a hard fight. The noise grew louder they were still a hundred yards away as two hundred feet pounded the stone of the old road. He took a deep breath and raised his bow ready. *"I am here with you my love, have no fear I will not leave you."*

A strong sense of calm washed over him and he smiled feeling her presence all around him. *"I love you Runestone"*

"I love you too Rob."

The long line came into view, he gasped when he saw them with their scruffy black clothes and long black cloaks. Their faces were red and vile looking, a huge brute of a man led them along the road and he knew that he was in command. Robbie pulled him into his sights and followed until he knew the whole line was in striking distance. Robbie pulled back on the string, and with a mighty heave, the arrow released from the string. The speed of the arrow was amazing as it shot silently through the air, the arrow hit the leader in the chest, and such was the power it went straight into his heart, and the brute fell instantly to the ground dead.

The others floundered, but it was too late, as arrows rained from both sides of the road, the Cutters were exposed out in the open with no cover, they fell as panic took them, and by the time they had made a decision of what to do, it was too late. The Tenth Legion fell to the wrath of Loxley, three or four broke from the road on to the banking and Sting with Blades exploded out of the floor.

Sting came fast and screaming, her sword came up slicing and two Cutters fell dead, as she spun on her heel to see Blades make two fast and fatal swipes of her blade, the other two fell limp to the floor, they looked around at the piled up dead with violet and white arrows sticking out of them. The Tenth Legion was no more and Jett looked across at Blades in disbelief.

"Is that it? I thought we had a fight on our hands?" Blades shrugged and looked up at Robbie as he came down the bank with Rowan. Jett looked up. "What's going on Robbie, I thought this was going to be a tough one?" She kicked the body below her over and looked at him; she looked over to Blades who was looking at him.

"He was quite cute, well he would have been if his face wasn't red." Blades nodded and Robbie spun round and looked at the dead Cutter, he somehow knew before he saw him properly. He crouched down and looked at the young face of the boy painted with a red face. He looked up at Rowan.

"He isn't a seasoned fighter, we have been hoodwinked, this is not the Tenth Legion these are young boys." Rowan crouched down and inspected the young face of the dead boy as Robbie walked out into the road to look at the others.

Robbie moved fast calling everyone down to the road, Saff ran up by his side. Robbie looked worried "Harry, Blades, Todd, Woody, and Amethyst protect Scarlet GO!"

Saff opened a window and without words, they shot through into the camp headquarters. Robbie turned to the Night Stalkers and Malcolm. "Get your men to Ox they will attack tonight go." Saff clicked her fingers and the window shimmered, they all ran through at high speed. Robbie looked at his team of Specialists. "These were a decoy to draw us off the scent; they will attack in three groups tonight, centre, east and west, time is not on our side, Rune is looking for them and as soon as she finds them we will be coming right out behind them. You will have your fight Sting don't you worry, stay sharp and watch each other; I consider all of you as precious. Bows keep those swords covered."

The whole group nodded. "Yes Gov!"

Saff's eyes burned bright blue. "Rune has found them." She clicked her finger and Robbie drew Destiny out of its sheath.

"Let's move." He turned and led his men into the window and through into the deep woodlands of the west side of the Yorkshire moors. The Tenth Legion was one hundred yards in front creeping up the high bank to where the woodsmen of Loxley were camped.

Blades ran along the path toward the observation post to warn Scarlet, as the others checked the perimeter of the headquarters. The small figure in black had not heard her she was so silent, Blades slowed as she suddenly realised what she was watching. She crouched low as she recognised the movements that reminded her so much of her great grandfather and grandmother. Blades knew the work of a Japanese assassin; one from the age of five had trained her, as had her mother. She sped up quietly as the figure crept silently through the dark towards the tall red clad warrior that watched out through the darkness. The arm of Shadow lifted to his bow, and Blades shot up the path at high speed, and vaulted up into the air. She came down like a wild cat in front of Shadow, and he jumped back, dropped his bow and brought his hands up in defence.

Blades was ready and prepared, as Scarlet jumped with the sudden movement and turned round. The dark eyes burned at her through the black face hood, Blades had the stance her arms raised waiting to see if he would go for a sword, he did not. Shadow walked carefully, his eyes on Blades to a more even part of the ground and rubbed his feet into the soil. His arms were ready for her to attack, Blades inched forward slightly and she spoke. It was a strange language and Scarlet did not recognise it, the assassin gave a short bow and answered. Scarlet watched confused, had he said, "Hey?"

Blades bounced like a cat, and her legs came up with speed as she spun round and her arms swung out as she gave a scream of aggression. It was fast and furious, and the assassin moved just as quickly blocking her legs and arms at high speed, Scarlet watched in awe. Never in her life had she seen such skilled and almost poetic unarmed combat. Arms shot up and stiffened as other arms connected with power. As quick as Blades hit she was already moving with her other arm and so was the assassin. It was like a slow motion film, which was being watched at double speed, as arms connected legs lifted, and kicked and blocked, Scarlet had never witnessed anything remotely like it, it was as if the two of them were thinking and reacting in a single moment to each other. It almost had the grace of a dance to it, yet in the eyes of Blades there was a hatred and aggression that burned with utter malice.

They moved like the trees as if blown by the wind, the fighting was pure and they both flowed like water into each other, Blades was unbelievably fast as was the black clad figure. Blades wailed out grunts and screams, as she fought, not unlike Jett when she used her sword, he back flipped out of her way but Blades kept coming. She fought with precision and skill kicking and punching with speed and accuracy, he spun and lunged at her, and she shot into the air like a missile and flipped over him hitting him in the back and he stumbled over.

She planted her feet square, and brought her hands back into the stance as he turned, she spun into the air screaming and brought her leg up with lightning speed, it hit the assassin on the chin, Scarlet saw the spit and blood fly, and cringed with the ferocious impact, and he flew backwards his arms flailing to regain balance, she did not stop. Blades shot at him kicking and hitting him, she showed no mercy at all, as she attacked with a power that surprised Scarlet. The assassin staggered the shots impacting on him constantly, as Blades screamed and wailed with every shot and punch.

He fell to the floor and she came over him lifting her foot for the kill, it came down to him like a falling hammer and as it reached his throat, it stopped. He gasped and lay back and relaxed, breathing heavily. Blades eyes burned with a fire Scarlet had never seen before, she spoke his language again as she stared down at him. He nodded to her and she relaxed and stepped back and bowed.

"Speak English you are defeated." Scarlet started to walk towards the panting Blades and she raised her arm, Scarlet stopped and watched. The small black clad figure sat up and pulled his mask off, Scarlet saw the black hair streaked with grey and the lines of age on his face. He turned to Blades who watched him as she gathered her breath and the sweat ran down her face. "Niko?"

Blades nodded. "My grandmother."

The small Japanese fighter smiled and nodded. "Yew has her eyes."

"As well as her fighting skills." Blades panted and he nodded.

"Yew fight good." Blades nodded and stood up straight and relaxed.

"I new your farther Rocs." Blades gave a slight giggle.

"He is here just down the way." She pointed.

"I lost... No Honour." He nodded and Blades understood him. Scarlet watched with horror as he sat up, and got on his knees and bowed to Blades. He drew out his long sword and turned it upon himself. He pushed it hard inside himself and stirred the blade. Scarlet could not believe the sight before her.

Blades screamed as he contorted his face with pain and then smiled, she came at him like a flash of light, and in one fluid movement; she drew one of her long swords and swiped across his back taking his head clean off.

Scarlet pulled her hands to her mouth as she watched Blades bow to the slumped headless figure. Blades pulled the long sword from his grip and cleaned it on his robes. She took two steps back, and bowed as she slid the long sword back into the sheath and tucked it in her belt. She turned and looked up at Scarlet. "It is the way of his people, he died with honour, and you lived." Blades bowed, turned, and walked away down the path to find her father.

Scarlet stood lost for words as she watched the young figure of Blades walk quietly away. She had witnessed a controlled form of anger, which had been devastating, and now Blades walked down the path as if it had been a dance. All she could do was watch in utter disbelief, yet she felt huge admiration.

Harry sat in the headquarters when Blades walked in. "Todd, Scarlet is fine but needs some help." He nodded to her and walked outside. The headquarters was very busy as Phillip and Fuse now looked at charts trying to find the weak spots where the Cutters might target. Blades went down on her knees and pulled the Samurai sword from her belt, she raised it in front of her on flat open palms before Harry. "Father I have avenged the life you swore to my mother, Niko has honour again."

Harry's eyes widened as he looked at the sword with the red tassels hanging from it, he knew the sword instantly. He jumped to his feet with surprise. "Whoa baby Blades girl what you done? That is your Grandmother's."

Blades looked up with tears in her eyes. "You swore to my mother you would kill him if you ever found him. He was here tonight; the church sent him to kill Scarlet and Robbie. I fought him and won, he committed hara-kiri when he lost. I return to you the sword you swore to return to my mother's line."

Harry fell to his knees and tears flowed as he snatched her into his arms. "Whoa baby girl, you have made me totally cosmically happy, your vibes is true to your mum." He hugged her close and wailed into her as everyone stared at them. Fuse was the only one who really understood what was going on.

Blades grandmother had died at the hands of the assassin because she was teaching the martial arts taught to her by her own samurai father to women, Blades mother had sworn to Niko as she died, she would be avenged and would have honour in death. When Blades mother had been taken ill she had asked Harry to complete the task in honour of her own mother. Harry had sworn to her he would, he searched for two years but no one had heard of or seen the small Japanese assassin. Harry had spoken many times, of how bad he felt. He had always thought he had let Mary down and it had brought him a lot of pain.

Blades had now recovered the honour of her family, and recovered a family heirloom; the sword was a thousand years old, and had been passed down the family line. Harry kissed Blades as he smiled; he took the sword and handed it back to her. "You won the honour for your family, it is yours Kate, and this belongs in your line, not mine. I love you Katie baby girl."

Harry spoke quietly, and seriously and straight to his daughter. She looked into the bright dark tear filled eyes of her father and he smiled. "I loved your mother; she was very precious to me. I love you because you are so like her and not like me. I could never be without you Kate, you are my life now."

Blades burst back into tears and flung herself at him, he held her tight and squeezed her hard as he rocked her. "I love you dad."

It was a rare and very special moment of understanding between a father and his daughter; it was only heard by Amethyst who watched with tears in her own eyes. She wiped her eyes as she stood up and walked out leaving the proud parent and his daughter alone to have some privacy.

Scarlet was rarely shaken, she was a warrior who had seen and done many things, she recounted the story to the others later that night in the headquarters, and she spoke with great respect about the way in which Blades had fought, but also the honour and respect she had shown to her opponent. She praised Blades highly for the skill she had used without a weapon. It had profoundly affected her and Scarlet still felt her insides turn slightly. Amethyst sat and listened, she said nothing of the story or conversation she had heard, that she felt belonged only in Blades family.

Blades sat cross legged on top of the hill in the dark for several hours, she had tears quietly running down her cheeks, the pictures of her mother ran through her thoughts, Harry had helped her overcome the loss of her mother, but without that last promise being fulfilled she had always felt like there was no settling. Now she had finally put an end to the life she had held in Saddleworth. Katherine Fields was over now, she was Katherine Stephanie Loxley.

Her life was good in the stockade but she had always felt half of her was left at the side of the grave in the small church in Saddleworth, Blades now knew that her promise was fulfilled, and it was now time to look forward into her future; she rose out of the heather and walked slowly down the path back to the Headquarters. Todd stood by the door leaning on the wall sharpening his knife on a small oilstone, she gave him a smile as she walked up to him, he gave her a grin as she came forward.

"You feeling better now?" Blades pulled him towards her and kissed him passionately, his knife and oilstone fell to the floor as his arms lifted and pulled her closer. It was a long kiss and when she pulled back, she was all smiles.

"I have wanted to do that for ages." He gave her a huge smile and swallowed hard.

"Yeah, me too." He pulled her back and kissed her again. Amethyst leaned on the other side of the door and smiled making sure Harry stayed well out of the way inside the Headquarters. Blades and Todd disappeared to be alone in the deep heather.

Harry sat smiling lost in his own little universe of cosmic memories. A slender girl with long black hair and bright blue eyes laughed as he got up off the floor for the tenth time. She bowed dressed in all black with a black woven canvass belt, she flicked up her leg and he saw stars again. She giggled as she knelt at his side and sat him back up. He laughed and then passed out.

The dark complexioned girl had screamed with laughter as he opened one eye and smiled at her. Mary had been a very special part of his life; he had forgotten for a while how special she had been. Raising Blades alone had not been easy, he had not felt parenting come easily to him, and he felt a little relaxed about it now as he thought of Mary. He realised that Blades, had already been given the best parenting by a mother that had loved her deeply. Kate was very like her mum, or she would be if she stopped bleaching her hair. He gave a soft giggle to himself.

CHAPTER SEVEN

THE TRUE FIGHT BEGINS

Darkness had come quickly, and now the trees were black shadows with the faint light of the moon, up in front the snapping of twigs came back to Robbie's ears, as he strained to hear the slightest noise. The warm breeze crossed his face, moving the leaves either side of the small saplings he crouched behind, and the bright eyes of his team shone all around him as he waited. He stared into the dark and at the rise to the small ridge above; the moon came out from behind a cloud, and faint traces of silver light painted the bark of the trees.

Robbie waited by the side of Sapphire for Rune to fill her in on what she knew. Her eyes glowed bright blue as she communicated with her, it seemed odd to Robbie who had sat by Rune hundreds of times watching her eyes flow violet, the fact that Sapphire's burned blue seemed somehow not normal.

She turned and smiled at him as the colour faded and her eyes returned to normal. "There are sixty of them straight ahead heading for the woodsmen camped down by the stream." He gave her a nod and then rapidly gave the hand signals, the light had faded fast, and he knew the moon would not give that much light, they had to be spotted and stopped as quickly as possible.

Robbie and Rowan with Pebbles and Jay led the way flanked by Bear, Skip, Sting, Wolfie, and Big John; they quickly shot up the hill as they led the party. Maddy, Mel, Treen, Maggs, Rags, Fish, Hornet, and Crystal, followed bringing up the bow support. Jaz and Una came level with Robbie on his far right, as Flash and Smokes with his long silver spear covered their far left. They moved quickly and silently into the trees right behind the Tenth Legion of Cutters, Robbie loaded his bow and prepared as he slowed the pace, up ahead he could sense them, but in the dark it was hard. *"Talk to me Rune where are they?"*

"You are almost on top of them, if you cannot see them Robbie stop they have gone to ground."

"It's so dark Rune I cannot see a thing."

"All of you raise your bows and get ready."

The word went quickly round, and everybody took cover and prepared as they brought their bows up in the dark woodland. From nowhere there was a blinding flash of light, and a huge ball of fire exploded above the trees and lit the whole wood.

The figures were just twenty feet in front, and working their way forward, they slowed and looked up into the roof of the trees. Robbie released his arrow, the others followed as their arrows left their bows, and as they went to reload the light went out and screams of pain came through the dark towards them. Robbie looked to his left. "Flash link to your cousins we need eyes in the dark."

He saw Saff's eyes flicker, and she turned to him. "Shoot ahead." She looked alarmed, his reflex action was instant, his bow came up and he pulled back on the string as a huge Cutter came out of the darkness. Robbie fired and the arrow went straight into the Cutter, as Sting leapt over Robbie's head her sword glowing in the pale moonlight. The Cutter sprawled backwards as others appeared out of the darkness.

The sword of Destiny came out, as Pebbles faded from view, Rowan drew Honour; it was like a dam being blown as waves of red-faced screaming Cutters appeared out of the darkness. Robbie sliced hard at one, and hit a second heading for Saff, Keith lunged across her, and hit the Cutter hard, as Bear and Skip came storming through. Robbie sidestepped a Cutter, as he brought up his sword and the huge man lunged wildly and hit Wolfie face on, the two of them rolled in the dirt backwards in the trees, as fire exploded again in the air lighting the scene. The noise suddenly felt much louder in the light, as the Cutters and Specialists clashed with brutal force.

Saff and Jay were side by side crouched on the ground either side of a large Beech tree, they loaded and fired trying to keep the mass off Robbie and the group. Cutters poured at the central group, and came bounding through toward the back where the group of bows covered the swordsmen.

A giant fist came up and Saff sprawled backwards blood exploding from her nose, her bow flew into the air, as the Cutter ploughed on through after the bowmen to the rear. Crystal spun with speed firing across the others with her silver bow, and the Cutter turned white as the arrow hit him; he hit a tree and exploded into a million pieces making Maggs jump out of her skin with shock. The noise was deafening as the Specialists fought hard, and the screams of their opponents rang out above the trees so loudly it was hard to hear Sting who was spinning with two very able Cutters. Wolfie rolled around on the floor with a man twice his size, as they held daggers in their right hands and fended off each other with their left.

The large Cutter rolled over on to Wolfie his heavy weight forcing Wolfie into the dirt, he pushed against the grim looking smiling Cutter with all his strength as he tried to force himself up. The knife of the Cutter came lower and he saw it glint a few inches above his shoulder, Wolfie started to growl loudly as he summoned his strength. His head came up off the floor like a striking snake, and he sunk his teeth deep into the Cutters nose, Rags recoiled with Maggs as she saw the ferocity with which he rose snarling like a wild dog. He hung shaking and tearing at the face of his opponent, as blood sprayed out from between them. The large brutal Cutter howled in fear and pain and as he rolled over on to his back Wolfie clamped his jaw tight and tore with all his might.

Maggs almost fainted as she saw the nose of the Cutter come away between Wolfie's teeth, and Wolfie leapt back snatching up his sword and sliced at the Cutter who screamed wildly on the floor. The man went limp as Wolfie fell back against the tree and spat out the nose on the ground at his side, he was covered in blood and gasped for breath as he took a moment to gather himself.

A long slice ran through his shirt and the blood ran freely underneath, he pulled it apart and checked it. It was not deep, it looked worse than it was. Fish was firing as he began to move slowly forward to get better shots; these men were real brutes and took two or three arrows before they fell.

Flash was spinning until one Cutter got just in range and with a mighty smash, his punch, lifted her into the air and she hit the tree behind her and slithered down to the floor. Fish, placed his arrow firmly in his throat as Hornet struck fast with a second, he crumpled and fell.

Five Cutters bounded toward the archers and Maddy spun bringing up her white bow. Flames erupted as her arrow left the string and a huge fireball engulfed the Cutters coming at them, they staggered screaming and fell to the floor falling over themselves and rolling in a pile.

Green eyes darted through the wood cutting and slicing as they went, Skip belted down on a brutal looking man who already had six scars across his face. He swung the blade of Justice round adding a seventh, and the Cutter screamed his last scream as Skip with ferocity sliced back across the throat of the huge man, who fell backward and gurgling to the floor. Bear had his match and had sheathed his sword as he fist fought with a Cutter who was larger; his fists pounded into the face of the man as he lifted him off his feet and sent him flying into the trees. Rowan was now back to back with Robbie as they fought five.

Jay's arrows came swift and it was four, sweat rolled down his face in the warm night as Destiny glowed bright, and smashed and swiped across their opponents. Robbie was right, this was the fight of their lives, as they used all of their skills against a force that knew no fear, and fought with strength and power. He felt exhausted and will power alone kept him fighting as the power thundering down on him was four times that of Mordred's. Rowan grunted as he swung with all his might, Sting wailed with five around her as Wolfie came out of the dark to her side; she beamed a smile as she saw his blood covered mouth.

"Hey honey pie, you been feasting again?"

"Don't be nosey." He laughed aloud as he swung with power into the Cutter in front of him. Arrows came out of the dark taking two off them, as Wolfie and Sting now swung and twisted side by side.

It was a brutal desperate fight, as Jay bobbed from one side of the tree to the other. Saff lay out cold on the floor far behind her, as she loaded and walked slowly firing at anything within range of a sword. She felt scared, and yet she hung in trying to protect Saff and help the others. Maddy spun round as she looked behind at the forty more Cutters coming out of the dark behind them and up the ridge, reinforcements were coming and already the group were tired. She screamed at the top of her voice over the screams and yells and clashing of swords. "Crystal over here!"

Her arrow leapt out of her bow flying in flame at the large approaching group, she was fast to load another as Crystal's bow sent a thin silver arrow at speed into the trees. Maddy's hit first and half a dozen stumbled as they ignited, the silver arrow hit the leader spraying frost into the air and as he grunted and twisted, the men behind became rigid and fell to the floor; they shattered on impact as Mel swung round fast and picked off the others.

Robbie came flying past with Rowan to protect the women, and with his sword high he waded into the advancing group; Keith sprinted past leaping into the air and kicking one full in the face as he sliced at another. Big John covered in blood sunk his sword deep and then ran towards the new group, as Pebbles cleaned up around him. The new group came flying past the women with their arrows, and Fish was smashed to the floor by a long pole his head taking a huge smack. It was overwhelming as more Cutters poured into the clearing. The Cutters were increasing, as the Specialists fought as their group tightened. Mel now swung round with her sword, as did Maddy. Una and Jaz worked side-by-side battering anything in their path with their long wooden poles.

Smokes spun his long silver lance a blur, as he hit stabbed and smacked anything in black; Bear was fierce and swung the mighty axe and sword with huge power as he screamed into the faces of his opponents. Robbie and Rowan fought their way back to the group. Jay was now with the others as she saw Hornet fall to the floor, and as she tried to stretch towards her to grab her, a huge metal studied boot came up into her face. She shot back into the air her eyes exploding in white light as she felt the hard floor crash into her back.

Treen's eyes glowed a bright vivid orange as the man in front of Skip raised his sword and stood still, Skip lunged with power and the man slumped. Her eyes turned to the man fighting Robbie and he fell to his knees as Robbie's sword leapt round. A huge Cutter grabbed Maddy hard by the waist and flung her into the trees, she crashed into the thick growth and disappeared into the large ferns, he came thundering over a dagger in his hands. Maddy felt dizzy and her vision was blurred, she shook her head and blinked as the huge man came down on her smiling; he grabbed her two arms in his huge hand, and pushed them hard against the soil as he pulled at her pants, tearing them off, and then loosened his own.

Maddy suddenly understood his intention. "God man it's been years, I hope you have what it takes, I am not easily satisfied." He grunted looking confused, Maddy opened her legs wide and smiled. "Oh please I have forgotten what it feels like." He stared down at her lost for words unsure of what to do now, as a tear ran from her eye. The Cutter stared as the black evil looking wisp of a cloud rose from her chest where the tear had dripped off her chin. His eyes opened wider as it floated toward him and a contorted ugly face appeared in its midst, he gasped with shock, and it shot into his open mouth and was gone.

The huge brute of a man with his trousers half down fell back in the ferns and looked suddenly very distressed. Maddy sat up and looked between his legs. "Stress can do that, it happens a lot when you are under pressure." She nodded sympathetically as he looked down with sad eyes. "Although, there is not much to boast about to begin with, is there now?" He looked up at her as she stood up and fastened her cloak round her naked lower half, and she looked sadly down at him. "It was never meant to be was it?" He burst into tears as she walked away and left him sat crying and sobbing in the deep fern.

Maddy wiped the blood from the side of her face and picked up her long white bow, she smiled as she looked back and heard the wails of grief coming from behind the trees. "Thanks Robbie, you saved me from hell."

Cutters lay dead everywhere and the Specialists had quite a few casualties, they fought hard and with all they had, they were winning the fight but their strength was waning and Robbie knew it. They would not last much longer under the overwhelming force without severe casualties. He clenched his teeth as Destiny came thundering round taking two heads clean off in one swipe. "Rune I need you." He glanced round, as he saw how widely spread out the group were, in the midst of the fight, they were drifting apart.

Bright violet light exploded into the wood as Rune came up through the floor, her eyes burned with rage as she spun round pointing her finger; Cutters flew back into the air with horrific pace, smashing into the trees. A window behind her opened and Harry and Blades followed by Scarlet and Fox came bounding out screaming. Woody tripped as he ran out and fell flat on his face, his pole flying into the face of an oncoming Cutter, the arm of Amethyst shot up with a golden knife into the Cutters stomach, and he squealed with shock.

She blew him a kiss as she threw him back with huge force on to the floor. She bent down as she helped Woody to his feet. "You alright?" Her violet eyes shone with smouldering concern.

He went beetroot and swallowed. "I... err... missed... err... the ...err... you know.... Root thingy and fell." She smiled a white and beautiful smile.

"Be careful Woody and please watch yourself." He turned and stumbled and grabbed his staff off the floor, and quickly jumped up again. He turned back to see the smiling goddess that was Amethyst.

"I err...yep... err... thanks." He turned and ran like hell into the fight as Amethyst laughed.

Rune spun round lifting Cutter after Cutter off the floor and tossing them into the trees, they knew they were beat and fled into the darkness, Harry roared with Blades after them and screams came out of the darkness as limbs fell. Woody ran with Fox and Hawk after them.

Robbie and Rowan sat together their heads down trying to regulate their breathing, they were tired, cut, and bloody, Robbie noticed Rowan's hand tremble as he dropped his sword, and he raised his arm and patted him on the back. "You fought well my brother."

Rowan lifted his hands to his face and held them there for a moment as he panted. "Robbie, that is the most frightened I have ever been, I thought for a moment I was lost." Pebbles slid down over his shoulders and kissed his neck, he pulled her round on to his lap and gave her a huge squeeze, she wrapped herself around him and they sat silently hugging each other.

Robbie rose shakily to his feet as he looked around at the carnage. Bodies lay everywhere, sniffles and tears came from the far side of the wood in amongst the high bracken, Rune's violet figure walked smiling toward him as Robbie stared at the sound of crying. She nodded her head to the far side of the clearing. "That one met Maddy."

He had seen the effects of her sadness ability at Dunnottar; it made him shudder, as he knew the man would feel worse and at some point just go off and kill himself. Sting came up her sword dragging behind her with one arm round Wolfie, they both looked exhausted as they flopped quietly on to the ground. The fact she was quiet was a sign of how hard the fight had been.

Maggs sat with Jay as she wiped her face and held her up; she was going to have a very black eye. Amethyst attended to Fish who lay quite still and smiled at her as she bandaged him up. "Looks like I am becoming your full time nurse James." He grinned at her as she smiled back.

"Great isn't it?" She gave a loud chuckle.

"It's not unpleasant."

Bear had a long gash on his leg and Treen bound it as she sat next to Skip. Una cradled a moaning Flash in her arms, as Crystal sat with a very dizzy and disoriented Hornet. Mel wiped the cut on Maddy's head. "I don't mind them being a little rough in bed but god Mel, that one was as rough as they get, what the hell was he thinking? I never did attract the right types."

Mel gave a titter as she wiped the cut clean. "I bet he made Harry look more attractive?" Maddy giggled.

"I can do weird; I am just not sure about freaky." Mel giggled loudly as she looked at the smile on her sister's face.

Rune slid close to him and held him tight, she seemed to glow around him and he felt the strength return. It was nice to feel her in his arms and know the worst was over; more than two thirds of the Tenth Legion lay dead on the floor all over the woods. Robbie gave a long sigh, "Come on let's get this lot back home. Saff can bring Harry and the others back." Rune opened her window and slowly everyone rose from the floor, and began to walk towards the window and home. John and Skip helped the injured girls and once again, it looked like Robbie's house would become a hospital.

Keith wove through the trees his keen eyes scanning the floor as he went. Harry, and Blades followed closely and Fox and Woody came up the rear, the Cutters were heading north and they were moving swiftly, silently they followed keeping up a good pace.

Steph ran down the path into Smokes arms and kissed him, she finally relaxed knowing he was safe. The others walked slowly into the house and collapsed; Rune came up from her basement and supervised the injured to the bedrooms. It was a busy night as they organised food and cleaned up the less wounded. Most of them had bruises and cuts from the savage fighting, Jett insisted on Wolfie washing his mouth thoroughly before she would even come close to him.

The others giggled as she checked his teeth for bits of Cutter skin, when she was happy he was Cutter free, she gave him a long slow and passionate kiss, the others all whistled and a wolf howl came from the kitchen, Jett burst into laughter and broke apart. The fun had begun and the group who were now happy to be over that particular hurdle slipped back into their normal fun loving behaviour.

It was the early hours of the morning, when Robbie slid into bed beside Rune. He had some very large bruises on his back, and he moaned as he lay back on the cold sheets. He stretched out his arm and Rune slid over to his side, she smiled as she snuggled into him and his arm came around her as he gasped a sigh of relief. "We did it." Rune watched as he slipped exhausted into sleep, and she was grateful he had returned to her safe. She lay by his side for a long time before she finally drifted off herself into a deep contented sleep, her biggest worry was over and the Specialists had stood the brutal measure of the Tenth Legion, Just.

Hawk stopped in the dark, and looked down at the tracks that had separated, it was just before dawn. He looked up at Blades and Fox. "What do you think?" Blades scanned the floor her face close to the tracks; she sat back as Fox examined them. She looked at him.

"These are the same boots yet I think they were made earlier." Fox nodded in agreement as Hawk watched them both.

"What are you saying...? A smaller group who left the fight before the others made the tracks that goes off?" Blades looked across at Fox and then back to Hawk, she nodded.

"That's what the tracks say Hawk." He sat back and looked at Woody and Harry.

Harry shrugged. "Hey man, my baby girl here was trained by the best. Her vibes are cool and happening, you saw her track Robbie dude in the dark and his foot prints aint radical if you like catch me."

Hawk looked at the floor. "Ok so a small group left first, at least an hour before the others, and then the main group left to escape, so what are you saying they have missed their trail and should have gone that way after the first group?"

Blades shrugged. "I can only tell you what the ground says Hawk. I have no wish to understand the Cutters, I would rather they were dead." He gave a long sigh and sat in the grass.

"What do we do now?" Hawk looked at the floor.

"The first trail is older I can follow that easily, the main group is bigger, but they have no care of their trail so any of us can follow them. I guess it boils down to the facts, that ahead of us is about fifteen of the Tenth Legion, and down there somewhere are two with over an hour's head start. We either split up or stay together and go after the larger group."

Hawk looked down the long trail into the woods. "I am not keen on us splitting up, I say we head after the larger group, it will be harder to reform a Tenth Legion with two. Fifteen is already a large enough group to reform, they are not much further ahead and I would guess they will stop for a break soon it is almost dawn." Fox and Woody nodded and Blades agreed, they stood up and prepared to follow the main group.

As dawn came over the trees, they came to the camp in a small clearing. There were sixteen Cutters left from the full legion of two hundred, four guards were placed and the rest bedded down. The group watched from deep in the cover of the trees, Blades suggested they wait until the majority were asleep, so they sat back, and rested and waited. Two hours passed dawn as the sun rose and warmed the day, and the group moved off, Harry and Blades led into deep cover as Hawk watched with his bow ready, Blades slipped her long sword of her grandmothers out from her belt as she slipped quietly in behind the guard. He blinked and it was over, she withdrew the long blade and wiped it on his shirt as she lowered him to the ground.

Harry used his long silver dagger; he was fast and silent as the guard slipped away from him. Blades signalled across the glade to him, as they swept round for the other two. Within a minute they had gone the same way, the clearing was now unprotected as the group loaded their bows from all sides and waited for the signal. They all bobbed down as one sat up on the grass, he was a large scruffy mound of a man with long shaggy hair and rough stubble, he got up and walked to the edge of the glade half-awake, and half-asleep, he scratched his head as he moved to the trees and unbuttoned his trouser front. He looked down as he peed into the grass and yawned, as he lifted his eyes, he stared straight into the eyes of the green clad hooded figure that was holding a loaded bow pointing at him. Hawk smiled and nudged his bow down. "Shake." The Cutter did and the arrow came at him, he turned and screamed and the arrow hit, as two sat up in the glade and looked, two arrows came from nowhere and they slammed back into the ground. More Cutters rose and fell before they could get to their feet, as arrows came from every direction hitting them. There was nothing that the Cutters could do and within just a few minutes, the group stood and surveyed the last of the Tenth Legion laid out and dead in the glade. The Specialist had finished the job for Loxley.

The group made their way, back towards the lines of the woodsmen of York, it had been a long night and they felt exhausted. They walked quietly back down the trail to the clearing, where the bodies of the dead lay all over the place, it was gone noon as they looked round the woodland and the last of the Tenth Legion.

Robbie woke with a long stretch, he groaned as the pains and aches from the night before woke with him. Rune made a little squeaking noise as she stretched her head under the covers; Robbie lifted them up and smiled as two bright blue eyes looked at him. "Hey beautiful, how are all three of you?"

She gave a huge smile. "We are wonderful gorgeous." Rune slid up the bed and came out from under the covers beaming a huge smile and kissed him. He lay back in the pillow as the midafternoon sun streamed in through the window, and Rune curled around him. There was a quiet tap on the door and it opened, Steph popped her head in and smiled.

"Rune I have just spoken to Scarlet; Keith has just got back to her camp. They tracked and killed the rest of the Cutters." Robbie smiled.

"That is great news." Steph looked worried.

"Robbie, Rune, Saff is not with them and they want to get back here." Rune yawned and rubbed her eyes.

"I have not spoken to her, I was so busy last night with the injured girls I did not get a chance to see her, it's not a problem I will open a window for them and bring them back here."

"Rune, I cannot get hold of her, and I am sure she did not come back here with them last night. I don't remember seeing her at all."

Rune frowned and looked worried; her eyes turned instantly purple. Robbie watched as they flickered and little flashes crossed her cheeks. She opened her eyes. "I can feel her but I cannot get her to talk to me." Rune swayed a little and brought her hand to her head, her eyes cleared and she looked up at Robbie. "She is east of here and I think she has been drugged or something, I feel the effects when I try to contact her."

Steph suddenly looked frightened; Robbie turned to her. "You go and make a drink and something to eat for them; they have been out all night they must be exhausted, Rune open a window and bring them through. Let's get down and see if your table has any answers."

Steph disappeared as the two of them got dressed and Robbie looked across at her. "Say nothing until we know for definite what the hell is going on." She nodded as she came out of the room with him. As they entered the top of the steps to Rune's table Robbie saw the violet curtain appear at the gate. He flew down the steps to catch up with Rune who was already sat at her table, and violet mist was swirling round as she focused her powers. He sat down and watched as the window rose in the air and pictures began to clear.

Saff lay on a long heavy wooden table, her head lay to one side and her eyes were black from the force that had been smashed into her face. Her right cheek was blackened down to her mouth and she had blood on her face from her nosebleed. She was strapped by her wrists and feet to the table and completely naked, as two old monks with large magnifying glasses inspected every aspect of her body.

Robbie felt embarrassed and sickened as he watched. Rune gave little gasps as she saw them consult a very old book. The moment she saw it she knew what they had in mind, her kind had seen this many times before in the past. Tears rolled from her eyes as she watched the humiliating inspection and she was just grateful Sapphire was not awake to witness the inspection of a witch finder.

Robbie looked across the table at her. "What is this Rune, what is happening to Saff?"

The picture faded back into the table and her eyes cleared. She wiped the tears from her eyes and looked up at him. "You remember when you said on the boat coming back from Canterbury, we would have to fight the Church and the Knox Empire?" He nodded. "Well Rob it seems the Church has taken its time to find a weapon it can use, and now they have looked deep into the past to find the right tool to attack us with. Those two monks are using the book of the Witchfinder General."

The moment of what Rune had just spoken impacted on him. Everyone, of the Earth Faith, knew of the dark times for women when the witch finders would drag women in to court, and accuse them of devil worship and witchcraft. They were always found guilty and there was only one punishment, death by burning at the stake. "Rune that was hundreds of years ago, no one today believes in that nonsense it was proven that it was just the church using whatever it could to maintain control of the people. They could not get away with it if they tried."

He saw her shiver. "I hope not Rob, because I am known all over as The Violet

Witch, and I will be top of their list you can bet your last bit. Rob the church lost a lot of its power during the age of modern man when everyone was educated, in this country today many are ignorant because the children of the people have all had to work to run their land and survive. You heard my father and Sister Mary; you can spot the lines of those who hold titles just by talking to their children. Loxley and York are the only two places I know of that have schools open every day, and we have only had a school for six months. This country is now filled with people who are forced to think the ways of these people who seize their opportunities and dominate them. Knox and the Church have done that, remember Bob and Stan, how they wore the uniform of Knox because their families were threatened? That was what it was like back in the times of the Witchfinders, it has gone full circle and they are using whatever they can to defeat you."

"I will not let that happen Rune; they will not hurt mine or any other families in the woodland world with this rubbish. They have no right to tell my people who they can worship."

"It is not that simple Rob, even you have been wise enough to use the weapon of fear against your enemy. For me this is the most frightening, because we all know where this leads."

He looked at the pale frightened face of Rune, he knew she was right but it was so hard to believe something so out of date and proven as foolish could be used again. He looked up at Rune his eyes almost pleaded with her. "Find her Rune so I can go and get her." Rune gave a nod and a soft smile.

"I will have no fear, as the drugs wear off, I will be able to pinpoint her exactly. I have an idea and I need to speak to someone Rob just give me a moment." Robbie felt his heart race as Rune's eyes went violet; he sat feeling nervous as he watched her.

Father Warren sat at his desk reading; he would stop and scribble with his nib on the roll of paper, and then place the book down carefully and lift another as he researched the history of Colum Cille. The violet light surrounded him and he stood up as Rune appeared before him and smiled. "Hello father of Cille, I have missed our chats and must speak with you on a matter of great urgency." He could see the concern in her eyes, and he gave a slight nod.

"My Lady of the Woods I am honoured you have visited me in such difficult times. I would help in any way I can." Rune took a long breath.

"What do you know of the Witchfinders?" He seemed a little surprised at the question.

"It was mass hysteria that got out of control and those evil men who wore the collar of my church brutalised and victimised women; they were proven to be nothing more than overzealous thugs who used the church to gain control of the masses. It is all clearly documented; it could never happen again I am pleased to say."

Rune gave a smile and looked down. "But Father it is happening today." He blanched.

"My Lady that cannot be possible, no one in their right mind would use witchcraft as a tool again."

"I am saddened to say that at this time my cousin lies imprisoned and is being inspected using the book of old. I fear she will be tried and sentenced, she must be defended and I need a man of the church to aid her. I cannot go, they will do to me as they are to her, I am actually known in these parts as the Violet Witch. Can you help her for me?"

Father Warren saw her concern and pain. "I will do what I can, I will defend her to the best of my ability, but my dear lady if they have brought back the rules of old you know she will have little chance. She will be judged long before she goes into a court room."

Rune nodded. "She will be on sacred ground; I cannot as my line orders take the life of another on it. I will look at ways to free her without harm but it may take time, she will need someone near her to know she is safe and we are trying to help her. She has been drugged; I think they know she can be controlled easily. I have Alfie waiting in the trees outside the gates; he will bring you through the passage to Loxley. I am still trying to find out exactly where she is; when I do, I will take you to her."

Father Warren nodded at her and felt a deep sadness to know the church would go back to such ways. It was with a very heavy heart that he looked at Rune. "I will prepare, I have many books that might help, I promise I will do what I can for your family."

Rune smiled as her eyes filled with tears. "Thank you, Father, you are a good man with a good heart, my house will owe you a great debt if you can help her." Rune turned and faded into the wall, and the Father turned back to his desk and closed his books. At the back of the room, he had a secret door and he opened it and placed all the work of his research inside. He pushed the desk in front of it and turned to his bookcases, taking a small bag from under a table; he packed a few items of clothing and then placed a few books inside.

Father Warren walked out into the daylight of an almost empty city. With his black hat on and his walking stick, he walked to the gates and out onto the long road that led west away from the city towards the moors. It had been many years since he had ventured so far from the church now locked safely behind him, and he turned and looked at the long line of trees that led south towards Lincoln. His face was pale from many years of attending his church and writing his notes, the dark rings under his eyes from hours of study until late into the night seemed darker in the sunlight. He gave a smile, and stepped off the road and walked across the wide band of blackened earth towards the trees.

Rune opened her eyes and smiled at Robbie. "Help is coming for her; she will not be alone for long. We have friends in the church as well; I just hope Warren can help her."

Robbie gave a smile, of course why had he not thought of him, he was a churchman of good reputation in the Knox camp. "You did well Runestone, you concentrate on finding her and I will talk with Hawk, he loves her Rune we must get her back, we had better let Mel know as well."

Saff moaned as she came into a hazed state of awakening, she felt the cold hand on her thigh and her eyes snapped open as she screamed. The monk jumped back as her eyes flared bright blue as she pulled on the straps that held her to the table. Rune contacted her. *"Hear me Sapphire for I am Runestone and centre of your circle."* Her mind felt hazy and she found it hard to concentrate as the men touched her where they should not. Fear rose quickly inside her.

"Rune help me, where am I? Why are they doing this?" She began to cry. *"Rune they are touching me."*

"Sapphire please relax and focus on me, I keep losing you and I need to find out where you are."

"Oh Rune, I am scared, help me."

"Concentrate my sweet sister I am with you; I will not leave you. Help is coming."

"What is happening to me Rune, Oh Rune help they are touching me and hurting me?"

She screamed in pain as they made their examination. Her eyes flared wildly and the room lit up with the brightest blue light, the table began to vibrate as a surge of power she did not know she had, flowed to the surface, a tall monk in brown smashed his fist into her face, and she fell back limp to the table.

Una watched as Rune looked up with tears flowing from her eyes. She folded her arms on her table and sobbed, Una put her arms around her and gave her a squeeze; everyone had been hit with the force and power of Sapphire, Rune had found her and now the table burned into life as the pictures of her prison came into view.

The town on the bank of the river Humber had been taken over by Mason Knox. He had devoted a lot of time in building a huge new Abbey and grounds filled with large outbuildings, so that the church could bring together all of its nation in praise. This was now the centre of the new Church of England, and it was here deep down in the cellar that Sapphire screamed in pain. The monks had what they had come for; on the very inside of Saff's upper thigh was a mole, it was described in the notes as to have the image of a black dog on it, this was proof she was a child of the hounds of Satan. Saff did not have a hope.

She was lifted from the table, and thrown into a small cell, the medic pushed in the needle, and smiled, she would sleep until needed and her powers would be controlled, Rune watched with Una from her table as she relived the past in her own lifetime. Her worst nightmare now played out in front of her as she felt the pain of two hundred thousand women of the past resurface inside her. The pictures on Rune's table swirled and they changed to a long corridor where a man in long purple robes walked toward a highly polished door at the end of the corridor, he carried a set of papers in his hand.

He was in his mid sixties, and yet he seemed to be quite energetic as his white hair bounced in the breeze from his speed. He walked straight in through the door to the older figure of a man who seemed to have great power in his stance, as he stood by the window gazing out into the courtyard, he turned as the bishop entered. The bishop raised the papers in his hand. "What is this rubbish, Andrew? Are you seriously telling me you aim to try a witch?" He looked at the man by the window with disbelief in his eyes.

The figure of Andrew turned; the very Reverend Andrew Holmes was now the most senior bishop in Britain. The old archbishop had died of heart failure and he was tipped to replace him. He looked coldly at Bishop John Stevens. "You have not misunderstood my intent John, we have her below undergoing examination... By the way have you met our benefactor?"

Bishop Stevens turned and looked round the room, Rune and Una gave a gasp as they watched, and saw the cold blue eyes and long white hair of Mason Knox as he bowed a slight nod and smiled to Bishop Stevens. The bishop looked even more shocked than Rune to see him. "My Lord Knox you must excuse me I had not seen you there."

"How are you Stevens? I have heard you are writing again."

"I am My Lord, excuse me for asking, but we had heard that you had been killed, and yet I see you here. It has given me quite a surprise."

"Yes, there is much gossip in the woodland world, you must not believe everything you hear, as you can see, I am very much alive and feeling remarkably well, I have a new daughter, can you believe it an old dog like me?" His smile was cold and the bishop shivered.

"I must ask you to excuse me My Lord, I had no idea that you were busy with the bishop, and I made an unwelcome intrusion. If you would excuse me, I shall return later with my business for the good bishop." He gave a bow, and turned and walked back to the door, Mason turned back to Bishop Holmes

"Will he be a problem?" Andrew Stevens gave a smile.

"John is a reformer, he always was. He is a good man, but only one in twelve. The others will vote as I tell them, she will burn in Lincoln have no worries My Lord." Mason gave a big smile.

"Oh Good, I suppose you could soon replace him if needs be, which reminds me where is your little oriental? I have not seen him since my arrival."

Bishop Holmes stared out of the window. "He is off on a small errand for me."

Mason patted his back. "Remind me my good friend not to anger you; I would hate to live in fear of the shadows." The bishop gave a smile.

"I feel My Lord you are safe enough; I would hate to live in fear of a visit from your mother."

Mason gave a hearty laugh. "I fear the wife more." Both of them stood by the window and gave a good chuckle as the gates of the compound opened and more carts rolled in.

Rune's head turned slowly as the pictures faded on her table, she looked paler than she ever had. Una put an arm around her and pulled her close. "Shall I tell him, or will you?" Rune gave a small blink as if coming out of her thoughts.

"I will have to be the one to bring Saff out; I do not want Robbie running off after him again. We need her out and fast Una, this is not a job for the Specialists that place is a fortress. If we kill on sacred ground it will work against the magic, I cannot risk that." Una understood the rules of her line better than most; she gave Rune a gentle squeeze and kissed the top of her head.

"You will not be alone." Rune smiled a little relief came to her heart.

"Thanks Una, the church terrifies me."

It was late evening when a violet window opened in the trees down the road from the new grey looking abbey. Una looked out across the plain at the ugly concrete poured replica of an old cathedral, surrounded by the large buildings and walls that made up the monastery, and living quarters of the clergy. She smiled at Farther Warren. "Good luck Father, may your god and our lord be with you, and Sapphire." She pulled him into a big hug, which startled him a little. "Thank you, Father this means a great deal to all of us."

He gave her a smile as he looked into her worried and troubled violet eyes. "I will do all I can, get yourself back and safe, you are in more danger than I think you realise." She nodded and stepped back through the window, and Father Warren walked down the grassy hillside toward the road that led to the tall wooden gates of the abbey.

Bishop John Stevens stood in his room as he prepared to leave for the courtroom in the bottom of the building; he gathered up his papers and looked at the young vicar who handed him his cloak. "Thank you, Simon, I cannot believe they are going to go through with this, Mason Knox is more powerful than even I thought. I have underestimated him greatly Simon, and this is such bad news for the church, the Lord works in mysterious ways my dear boy, and I have no idea at the moment what he plans for us all."

The young Simon gave a smile. "You have the authority, you will convince them of this madness, I have faith sir." John Stevens gave a smile.

"I hope so my boy I really do." He turned and walked out of the room and down the long corridor to the stairs.

Sapphire sat alone in the dark small cell and shivered, she had put on the white gown, and she stared unable to focus toward the wall, her mind was cloudy and her eyes kept coming in and out of focus, the sounds all around her seemed slow and loud. She swayed on the bed not finding it easy to stay upright.

She was vaguely aware of the door opening and the dark figure that examined her. "Sapphire can you hear me? I am a friend, I was sent here by Runestone."

Her eyes moved as the name meant something to her, her face felt great pain as a tear ran down her cheek; her voice was quiet from sore lips and a dry throat as she grabbed the arm of the man trying to steady her. "Help me please?"

Father Warren pulled her close into his arms and held her, her head flopped on his shoulder and to Sapphire; it was the nicest thing to happen since she had arrived. Her vision blurred but she felt the warmth and safety of the arms around her. Tears ran from her eyes as her mind spun. "I need Rune, find her."

CHAPTER EIGHT

THE TEST OF FAITHS

The courtroom of the church was deep below the building. A long bench of dark polished wood ran high up on the platform, where the Church Council of twelve sat with stern faces, dressed in a sombre black with white collars. All of them looked down on the rest of the room with their looks of unemotional cold concern. On the long bench below three young monks shuffled their papers, as a robust old and poker faced looking monk with a baldhead, looked down through old round glasses at the documents in his hand. The seats behind that led in long rows back were empty, from the balcony a few young vicars watched down. Simon felt nervous for his hero and mentor Bishop Stevens, as he clutched the edge of the rail.

Sapphire sat slumped next to three other women, all of whom seemed to be in a trance. Their hair hung lank and they had the blackened faces from the large vicious monk that now sat at their sides. Saff swayed a little and he grabbed her roughly and slammed her back into the seat, her arms were tied behind her back and she struggled to remain upright.

Mel wept with Rune and Una as they sat at the table of Runestone in Loxley, and watched the scene that brought terror to their hearts. Keith sat frozen and pale beside Robbie who squeezed his shoulder. It was a frightening scene to behold as the door opened and the rushed figure of Father Warren raced down to the front benches and bowed. He made his way to the opposite end of the lower long bench as the old monk scowled at him, he laid out his books and papers and looked up at the bench, he nodded.

Bishop Andrew Stevens banged the gavel hard and everyone looked up as the four accused were dragged up on to their feet. Saff swayed, her eyes rolling in her head, Keith lowered his head into his folded arms and gritted his teeth. Bishop Holmes looked down with arrogance at Father Warren. "I believe Father you have requested a word before we begin?"

"Yes my Lord Bishop, I am here today to represent Lady Sapphire Tor of Callanish; can you tell me by what right she was brought to you? Under the laws of this land and this church, evidence must be produced to support the arrest of a member of the nobility of which my client is listed."

He looked down angrily at the father, his anger showed in his voice. "She was seen making lights appear in the woods."

"Thank you, My Lord Bishop, and have you a statement or witness to reinforce these allegations against her?"

"We have the statement made before myself, you will find it contained with the paperwork you have just been given." Father Warren shuffled though the papers on his desk and lifted one up and read it, he looked back up at the stern looking council of twelve who all but one gave him stern disapproving looks.

"This My Lord is the statement of a Captain Bonesmith, who states I saw her make lights in the woods. With all due respect My Lord it hardly clarifies the lady's behaviour. Did she strike a match or a flint to make a fire? Which as we all know constitutes light. This Captain is lacking in detail, which I argue is not sufficient for a warrant of a lady of such standing by the laws of this Church." Bishop Stevens gave a soft smile as he watched Father Warren; Bishop Holmes seemed even more angered.

"The man stood before me, a God fearing Christian and told me of how she waved her hand and lights appeared."

"Yet My Lord, his statement does not mention any arm waving, and I would add that this God fearing Christian is also a man of a long list of convictions from the past, which include murder, torture and rape. These are hardly the qualities of a God fearing man I would suggest."

Bishop Holmes, leaned forward in his chair, his voice was raised slightly. "The man is a reformed Christian, and he stood before a bishop and made a full and true statement."

"With respect My Lord, he is a captain in the notorious Tenth Legion of Cutters, who I might add have no need for introduction as their reputation speaks volumes. I would suggest this court would be better served if it brought to trial such godless heathens, and I would state that all charges against Lady Sapphire are thrown out on such thin evidence, and this whole process of dark ages oppression be discarded before it harms the church for a second time in its history."

Bishop Holmes banged his gavel down hard on the block. His voice exploded as his face reddened with anger. "I will not have this disrespect in my courtroom, how dare you stand below me and call into question policies that I as the head of this church have chosen to undertake."

Father Warren stared with his dark eyes at the bishop who was raging with anger; he looked down the long line of the council of twelve and spoke quietly. "My Lords, please I beg you, this road from the past is well documented, do not repeat the sins of our past, our lord taught compassion and love, do not stray from that path a second time, it will mark the downfall of us all. I beg you in the name of our saviour reconsider this action and release all these innocent women."

Bishop Holmes looked down on the father as he begged. "We have heard your views, now be seated as we hear the evidence against your client witch." Father Warren collapsed into the seat. He shook his head in despair, as the old monk rose up, and viewed him with even more distaste. Bishop Holmes looked down at the stern looking monk.

"Brother Argus what have you to report, apart from the statement given by the captain?"

The large bald monk coughed, and cleared his gruff voice, and then he bowed to the bench. "Using the text of the Witchfinder General of old, we carried out a full and thorough examination of the accused, we looked externally and internally and we found that she had a mole on this inside of her upper right thigh."

Keith leaned back from the table tears in his eyes and Robbie pulled him into a close embrace. "Have no fear she will come back to us; I will not let them harm her. She needs you to be brave for her my friend, have courage." Keith wept on Robbie's shoulder and Rowan patted him gently on the back. Rune saw the look of hatred in Rowan's eyes as he watched the court scene unfold in the window above her table. She wiped the tears from her own eyes as Mel wept into Una's shoulder.

Brother Argus continued with his testimony. "I gave the mole a vigorous investigation with a large magnifying glass, and clearly saw that it had the black shape of a dog on it. The book clearly states that this is known as the mark of the hounds of hell and is a clear sign that the accused is in league with Satan."

Father Warren was on his feet. "My Lord this is medieval rubbish, the Witchfinder General was proven to be a vicious and insane man who hated women. All of this text was discarded by the church hundreds of years ago, this cannot be used as serious evidence, a mole is simply a blemish of the skin I would suggest half the clergy in this land have a mole somewhere upon their person. Are you suggesting that we prosecute and burn them as well?"

Bishop Stevens looked down and gave a large smile as Bishop Holmes recoiled from the bench. He banged down hard with his gavel. "Silence! I will not have outbursts of such blatant provocation in this court, you hold your tongue until addressed Father, you are walking a thin line with me."

Father Warren sat down and put his head in his hands, he could not believe with his own ears what was happening.

"Have you anything more to add Brother Argus?"

The monk looked back up at the bench and smiled. "Yes My Lord... During our investigation of her internally she made the table shake."

Father Warren leapt up again. "She was strapped to a table, whilst you pushed instruments inside her, of course the table shook. You caused her great pain and she screamed and cried and shook with fear, I would suggest brother if I did the same to you the table would shake a lot more than that poor slender tortured girl up there did."

The gavel banged several times as the bishop slammed it down on the block. "I will not have your repeated outbursts interfering with the proceedings Father, one more and you will be thrown out."

"My Lord, please you cannot accept this as credible evidence, look at her, look at the blood on the front of her gown, she was indecently violated by your prosecutor and she has suffered wounds as a result. Please My Lord, I beg you, stop this madness now, there is no evidence of witchcraft or devil worship here. Please in the name of God I ask you to stop this barbaric persecution of these women." He stared into the eyes of the bishop, his voice dropped. "No true man of the cloth would do this My Lord, this is not Christian activity. Please I beg you as a man who has served the love of our lord all his life, release these women and stop this madness."

Bishop Holmes looked upon the pleading face of Father Warren, with cold empty eyes. "Have you a summing up speech prepared? We shall hear from Brother Argus and then you will have your final say on this matter before we consider the evidence."

Brother Argus faced the bench. He stood with a swollen chest and a look of pride on his face. He cleared his throat, and gave a slight smile as he looked to the bench. "My Lords, as you know I have dedicated my life to the fight of evil? I have studied the texts deeper than any, and I have seldom come across a case more worthy of this court, which proves to me beyond doubt that these women are marked by the devil himself. I strongly advise you find them guilty of the charges of witchcraft and devil worship and destroy them in the name of our lord. It is written as we all know in our good book; thou shall not suffer a witch to live." Brother Argus turned with a look of hatred and distaste at Saff and pointed an accusing finger as he screamed out the text of the holy book.

He sat down and smiled smugly as eleven of the men in the council of twelve nodded in agreement. Father Warren had known all along it was pointless to try, but he had given his best shot. He rose to his feet as Bishop Stevens watched him with keen eyes. "My Lords of the council, I see before me people of different faiths and I see injustice. I have dedicated my life to the research and study of St Columba and his work that understood the need for tolerance. He too gave his life in the study of our lord and saviour Jesus Christ, and he wrote extensively on the subject of the need to understand the faiths of others. His work, which you all know was testimony to the lifestyle of Pagan and Christian worshipping side by side. Today we see no greater example of his work, as both faiths are strong in this country, I beg you to cease this path of persecution, and follow the lead of our lord who taught us the true meaning of tolerance and compassion. The evidence is weak and the charges are outdated, please my lords in the name of our father release these women and turn off this road of evil."

He sat down in his seat and gavel the banged. "We will now consider." The council of twelve rose from their seats and walked off behind the bench through the door at the back. Father Warren poured a glass of water and carried it up to the box where Sapphire stood dazed and confused not knowing what was happening. The Monk on guard looked sternly at him; Father Warren gave him a look that blazed with fire.

"I will give her this and you will not stop me. Even our lord was given a drink on his road with the cross to Calvary." The monk nodded and stepped back as Father Warren sat slowly down, as he lowered her to the seat. Sapphire's eyes tried to focus but rolled back.

He held her gently and brought the glass to her lips. "Drink My Lady Sapphire it will ease your throat." Her eyes seemed to focus just for a moment as she greedily drank down the liquid that cooled her burning insides. She gave a weak smile and the tears came to his eyes. "I am sorry My Lady I have tried."

Sapphire fought hard inside to keep her mind clear, it was Rune's, voice that spoke from her lips. "Thank you, Father, we have seen what you have done for us, we are indebted to you, she was not alone and that matters to us." He gently leaned her back to the seat and stood up. Father Warren looked at the brutal looking monk. "When you are judged before your God, your actions today will dam you; I hope you can live with that, these are innocent lives you are destroying."

He brushed roughly past the monk and walked back to his seat to await the decision. It was not long before the council came back, but he had not expected a long wait. The council walked with emotionless faces along the row to their seats, they sat and Bishop Holmes looked up as Saff was dragged to her feet with the other women. The bishop looked up at them.

"You have been found guilty of the crimes of devil worship and witchcraft, and as is written in our laws of the church you will have one final chance to renounce your evil ways and be spared. Will you all turn from the path of sin and embrace the Lord Christ as your saviour?" Two of the women fell to their knees and screamed.

"We will, save us Oh Lord." Sapphire swayed unaware of what was really happening. The rough Monk shook her and slapped her face.

"Listen to the Bishop, will you renounce Satan and follow Christ." Sapphire's eyes rolled in her head as she tried her hardest to focus through the haze of her mind.

"Who? I do not know of him."

"Satan! Will you turn from his ways to the ways of good?" He patted her face rapidly and she blinked.

"I know not of who you speak." The monk turned with a solemn face and gave a nod to the bishop. The hammer banged.

"Lady Sapphire of Callanish, and Mary Taylor of Ashburn, you have failed to renounce Satan, and as a result you will be taken from here to the place prepared. At midday on May first you shall be burned at the stake for your crimes against the good people of this land." The gavel banged loudly as Father Warren shook his head in his hands. "Take them away." Bishop Holmes stood up and smiled as he faced the other members of the council. They all shook his hand except Bishop Stevens who came down from the bench and walked across to Father Warren who was packing his notes into his bag.

"Father I am sorry, please do not think that all of us on the council feel as the head of our church does. I voted in your favour and I am very sorry that they have chosen not to listen to the only man in this room who speaks sense." He shook Father Warren's hand.

"I have heard of you Bishop and read many of your papers; I fear many of your council have not." He shook his head as he looked into the eyes of the elderly Bishop. "This is wrong My Lord Bishop, this goes against everything our faith is supposed to believe in. I am sorry but today I did not speak to men of the church, I spoke with men who crave power and glory. No true man of God would torture and burn women for having a different faith, there has been only one crime here today and it was committed by those who are supposed to be our guides in this faith."

Bishop Stevens smiled at him. "You will find no argument with me; will you not dine with me Father? I know you have great understanding of the pagan faith, which I must admit I do not. I would like nothing more than to be enlightened in their customs."

Father Warren looked saddened. "I would like nothing more My Lord Bishop, but I have my Lady Sapphire to attend to and then I must leave to inform her family, maybe we could meet somewhere other than this place and have the conversation at a later date?" Bishop Stevens gave him a kindly smile.

"You are probably right; you have faced a mighty opponent today it may be prudent to leave quickly. I will ensure your lady is cared for better have no fear. I will look forward to our next meeting Father. I am very sorry your faith shone in this room today and it gave me great hope."

Mel hugged Keith as they wept in each other's arms. Rune leaned into her table and watched as Father Warren spoke with Bishop Stevens. An idea was forming in her mind and Robbie knew something was going on; he looked at her as she watched with interest.

"What?" Rune's eyes moved across to him, burning bright with purple light.

"She will not burn; I will not allow it. You cannot enter that site it is too fortified; promise me you will let me handle this one?"

Robbie leaned back in his chair. "I am not sure Rune; it could be dangerous."

She smiled and gave him a wink. "For a woodsman yes, but not for a witch, especially a violet one."

Una nodded at Robbie who looked very unsure, he looked into the bright violet eyes of Rune. "It is sacred land; you especially cannot take life there."

Rune nodded back at him. "That is why it must be me who brings her home, we cannot risk spilling the blood of the church, we already have enough enemies." Robbie nodded at her.

"I will watch and leave you to do this, but if there is trouble, I will be by your side... Know this Rune, when Bishop Holmes comes out of his hole on to my land, he will die by the hand of a woodsman lord."

She saw the fire in his eyes and she knew he would do it. Bishop Holmes was now as big a threat to the woodland realm as the Knox Empire, and she knew Robbie would stop him. She had watched him carefully through the trial and she had seen his anger grow. Rune knew well enough not to talk him out of it, and she was not going to try. "Alright Rob, just not on sacred soil, and I will help you stop this man." He nodded and Una saw the understanding between them.

Sapphire shook violently as she held the hot drink to her lips. Bishop Stevens looked up at the monk who guarded her. "This is a Lady of the realm, how dare you treat her this way, I want hot water and soap and clean clothes now. Bring extra blankets, and some hot food, this is disgraceful." He turned to the blackened face of Sapphire as she shivered violently and sipped from the cup. "I am very sorry for this Lady Sapphire; I will do everything in my power to make your stay here more comfortable."

Sapphire nodded; her head was clearing a little as the drugs wore off. She was in a great deal of pain and shook with the cold. Bishop Stevens took off his cloak and wrapped it around her shoulders; she nodded gratefully and pulled it closer to her. She noticed the blood where her legs, met and tears formed in her eyes as she remembered the pain and humiliation of her ordeal, the kindly Bishop held her hand. "I will try everything in my power to get you out of here, but it will not be easy." Saff nodded.

"Do not try, Runestone will come for me, I will be safe when she arrives, just keep those needles away from me, they confuse my thoughts." He gave her a nod

"I take it this stone woman is the one they call the Violet Witch?"

"She is no witch that is the mother of Knox. She is love, and kindness and the leader of my line; you will never meet a more caring woman. They call her witch because she has power from a faith they do not understand." She shivered as the guard returned with blankets. The elderly Bishop took them and wrapped them around her.

"If this violet woman comes here, they will imprison her with you, they fear your people, as they have not found a way to control them. The faith in the hooded man is strong and not easily broken."

"He is the symbol of Hearne to our people, they will never break their faith in him, and they should leave us alone to live in peace as we always have. We do not want this war, but you had all better listen because you cannot and will not win it. The faith of the woodland realm is stronger than you think; we will fight to the last man to defend our faith and our lives."

The bishop nodded. "It has been the history of man to fight for survival, but this country is leaderless and there will be many fights until someone gains full control."

Saff took a large gulp of the hot tea. "A new king will come to the throne, and he will be of the true lines, the bowman will place him as the prophecy has told, I hope you are wiser than your friends and aid the true king of this land?"

"I promise you this Lady Sapphire, if what you say is right and you can prove he is of the true line, I will fight at your side to place him on the throne." Sapphire gave the first proper smile since she had been captured, the bishop saw her beauty and he smiled with her, he gave her a nod and patted her hand.

"You will be cared for I will see to it. When your violet lady comes tell her, she has some support in the church, it's not just Father Warren who is her supporter." Saff gave a nod as the bishop rose up and walked through the door. The guard appeared with a clean robe and a large bowl of hot water and soap; he placed it beside her and put two towels on the bed.

"Food will be a while; I will ensure no one disturbs your wash My Lady." He gave her a bow and left. The feeling of water and soap was wonderful, Sapphire had been violated and as she washed herself, she felt a little of herself come back. It was like washing away the dirt of them, and she gritted her teeth as she still felt the pain and dried herself down.

She pulled on her robe and pulled the cloak of the bishop around her. Saff sat alone in the corner on the bed with her knees drawn up to her face wrapped in the blankets to try to get warm. She knew that Rune would come and she focused her mind to get it as clear as possible.

Rune sat at her table and Robbie sat beside her, he watched as her eyes flowed out with violet light and the pictures appeared above the table. Rune nodded to Una, "Be ready to come when I say." They both watched the pictures as they cleared, in the study of the old man in his chair.

The bishop sat in his study by the fire, the oil lamp burned dimly in the corner casting a faint circle of light into the room. The fire crackled and spat as he rested in thought, the rain streaked down the leaded windows, set in amongst the walls lined with bookcases and a collection of texts that dated back over a hundred years. Their matching spines formed bars of deep dull colours, on the shelves in the fire light. He was warm and cosy sat in the chair with his glass of mead served up in a glass of the finest crystal. He dozed and woke with a start as the room filled with the faint glow of lilac. He had wondered if she would visit and he looked up at the Violet Witch. "I thought you would come for your family member, you have made a grave error coming here, and this is not a safe place for you to be."

Rune walked across the room, she shimmered with violet light. "I have no fear of you Bishop Steven's; you have not the power to harm me." She smiled as she sat and faced him from the other chair.

"Your cousin is it? Has been tried by the Christian courts and found guilty of witchcraft and devil worship, there is little I can do to save her." Rune nodded.

"I understand, but have no worry, she will not die; I will return her to her family long before they can harm her. I feel it strange that your faith allows you to persecute those of another, this is not the first time women who are little more than Midwives, and users of herbal medicines have been killed by your people. Why will your church not strive to understand what we believe?" She watched the bishop closely as she spoke, she could see his faith strong inside him, and she also saw the conflict, as he had been the only one to vote in favour of Sapphire.

He leaned forward in his seat. "You will never understand these people my violet lady for your people have no understanding of the values of the church that have existed for thousands of years. I would hope that you realise that there are many of us who follow the path of your good Father Warren, and try not to let our faith blind us to others, it is unfortunate that there are some in power that do not."

Rune gave a soft smile. "I understand your faith more than you realise, I know of your lord, he was known to my grandfather, who spoke with him on many occasions, he understood the realm of the green people and he bore them no ill will. I find it hard to understand why people who follow him share a different opinion to that of their lord." This was a revelation that the bishop found hard to believe.

"Your lines have documented these things? They can be read as text?"

Rune gave a soft giggle. "We have no use of books from that time we feel they can be misleading as only one view can be seen. We have tables that show us those times so we may judge for ourselves. I have seen these meetings with my own eyes, and so therefore I can tell you that the meetings with the lord of the green wood happened. You are very welcome to visit Loxley and my home and see for yourself, it would be a good chance for you to have understanding of something you know little of."

He gave her a smile, she seemed so young to him, and yet he could see the great understanding she carried inside her, he felt almost jealous that one so young could hold such wisdom, when it had taken him all his life to come to the point where now at the age of sixty-four he finally had the insight to life. "And what is it my dear violet lady that I have little understanding of? I have spent a life in study."

"Yet my Lord Bishop, you know nothing of the Earth Faith you call witchcraft.

I am not a witch, I use the term as a bad name for those with dark powers, I am a force of the natural world, with a power inherited from my line. I do not make spells to increase my powers, it flows through me as it has from birth, and the people around me treat me as an equal, not a goddess. My faith has no gods who are worshipped."

He thought about her words, he had never studied her faith in any depth for there was little written about it. "Enlighten me My Lady, and show me the errors of the ways of my faith."

Rune smiled at him. "The way of the Earth Faith is exactly that, we see the Earth as one and we are at one with it. We can see the life of everything very clearly; the creator for us has made every tree, flower and stone. Life was bestowed on everything he created by the Mother of all life."

"Then they are your gods whom you worship are they not?"

"There is no god in our realm, and no statue to place on an altar to pray before, for we believe that our Green Lord is the guide from one realm to another. We give thanks to him for he helps us by guiding us through our lives and into the next realm. I feel you do the same yet your God is a supreme hidden being, My Lord Hearne has appeared before many in his long life." She kept eye contact for the whole time she talked and she could see he was interested; this was probably the first time he had ever been able to discuss the Earth Faith openly.

"Unlike your faith we do not use water to welcome new life, but we are similar in so much as we hold up new life and offer it to the world to welcome it into the realm. The spirit of the land passes through it and the touch of the green life tells us they are accepted into the realm of our people. Is that not the same as your baptism?" He gave a nod, and she saw that he was now beginning to see that Rune knew a great deal more of the Christian faith than he did hers.

"We live a free life uninhibited for we are at ease with the natural world. Our faith allows us to do what we want as long as we harm no others, all of us are held responsible for our own actions, and we take that responsibility seriously and we have the woodsman law to enforce those who do step out of our code. Unlike your people, we are sex tolerant; to us it is not dirty or sinful. We have a mature and more understanding view, we hold love as the highest power in our realm, and surely a physical expression of that love, no matter what the gender is a pure and wonderful thing? If two people love each other deeply and wish to express that love, what right have we to judge them? They should be free to do so."

The bishop raised an eyebrow, he knew his church felt great concern in this area, and there was many who were still convinced it was sinful.

"We have marriage but it is not enforced under the laws of our faith. If two people wish to stand before the community and state their commitment to each other, we are all happy to listen and celebrate that commitment. From that day, they will live as one and from that union will come life and the future of the community. We have few children born out of wedlock, and few of the couples that make the commitment freely separate. Our way of life promotes unity and togetherness, and we all stand side by side in the struggle through life. Your faith is not so much different."

He smiled at Rune as she made great sense to him and he now began to see that in many ways there were great similarities. Rune leaned forward in her chair as she thought.

"You see My Lord Bishop; it is our belief that how we live will be reflected back to us in the lives that we live. If we do good and kind things, we believe our life will be filled with goodness and kindness. A life of evil will only bring ruin and destruction. We have no fear of death for to us it is rebirth into a different realm. We understand and honour the circle of life; the symbols of death in our faith are also the symbols of life renewed, such as the lilac bloom, which was feared by your people as a flower of ill omen."

Rune gave a soft smile. "We do not fear the dead; we honour them and celebrate their life. In my faith we try to spare life and only kill in need, we take life to eat and we take life to protect our community, we will not be enslaved for any other reason than a difference of faith. No faith should be expected to endure oppression, rape or torture, our community bond is strong and we will fight to the last to save what we hold to be precious."

The bishop nodded as she spoke, she was saying the words he had heard many times over the years in relation to Christianity. Here was a woman who was branded a witch, and yet as he sat and listened, she made a good case for her people. Rune gave him a smile as she felt the process of understanding growing inside him. "You call me Devil Worshiper, but this is something I have no knowledge of because it is a part of your faith and not mine. I celebrate life and all that is good in the world, I have no God that lives below the ground and tortures and hurts people's spirits. There is a realm; we do not speak of where bad things can happen, maybe this is where your devil lives; for it is a place I have sent people not of my faith who have inflicted evil on my realm. There is nothing in that realm we would give praise to. Christians have killed my people in the past for worshipping your devil, but the children of the Earth Faith have no interest in your gods, and they would most certainly not bow down to one of your deities."

The bishop now understood Rune perfectly, he knew that Sapphire was innocent, and yet he had allowed her to be taken and sentenced to death for devil worship. Rune breathed a long sigh. "The people of my realm live in peace and at one with the earth. Is it so wrong to look at the sun and say a thank you for shining and helping all your crops grow? You call that heathen, yet I call it respectful. I understand that there can be many faiths built to celebrate the lives of those who have stood out for their deeds in the past; I accept that they are seen as supreme in those faiths, yet I do not attack them for a belief and slaughter their race in the name of Earth. Tell me Lord Bishop which one of us is right?"

He gave a chuckle as he looked upon the smiling violet figure of Rune. "I must admit my violet lady you have indeed given me a great deal to think about, your argument is very well constructed and it has enlightened me greatly."

She gave him a sweet smile at knowing she had at least given him the chance to see both sides of the argument. "I hope you see my Lord Bishop, we are not that much different, which is why I must free my cousin from your cells. If you look close enough you will see that even the dates of our calendars are similar. I celebrate the Solstice of winter and burn a log on the fire to bring light into the world; I give gifts of food and enjoy the time of my family. You celebrate the coming of your lord under the light of a star and burn a Yule log and give gifts. Samhain is the end of our summer and the start of the winter, for us it is the end of our growing year, we light fires to light the world and know that the realms we believe in are close together, and our lost ones spirits are close. You call it All Saints and believe your saints walk amongst you." He smiled as she spoke. "Lughnasadh is our thanks giving of food, which your faith calls, harvest. Imbolc to my people is the bringing of light at the end of the winter; I believe you call it candle mass?" She gave a giggle as he chuckled.

"I do not think I need to go on, I have proven that my faith has a good understanding of yours, my purpose here tonight was to prove to you that many of your people lack tolerance, and they need someone who is of a more balanced point of view to guide them back to what is seen as the Christian ideals. I know you believe in compassion and tolerance as well as forgiveness and acceptance. I hope you will lead them back to the path of the way of your lord, for even my people could see he was a man of high honour and was respected by us. I will leave you now to free my cousin; there will be no bloodshed by my people, so stay here and think of my visit to you tonight."

He gave her a nod as Rune gave a short curtsy, she turned and he looked up at her. "What is your true name? I cannot call you the violet lady."

"I must admit I prefer it to witch. I have many names my Lord Bishop; some call me the Lady of the Woods. To my family I am Runestone Sapphire first lady of Loxley. My true name is Mother for I am Nature personified in human form; I was once called daughter of Eve. For Eve is the giver of life, as I believe your faith agrees?"

He looked at her in wonder and he gave her a smile, she was the first in many years to teach him anything, and yet the lesson she gave him was on the subject he was supposed to be the authority on. It was a lesson well learned and he stood up and gave her a bow. "I have learned much my Lady Runestone Sapphire, tonight you have taught me that which I have preached for many years and yet have not learned myself."

Her eyes sparkled as she looked at him "And what is that my Lord Bishop?"

"We must be more tolerant and remain open minded enough to continue to learn. I am thankful for the lesson and wish you and your people well. Please extend my regards to your cousin, I could do very little for her but I believe it has made the last of her time here a little more comfortable."

"I saw your tenderness toward my cousin and it was noted as we are all grateful my Lord Bishop. I have enjoyed the chance to talk to an open mind, good luck my Lord Bishop, and know that the hooded man has been angered by your leader, Sapphire is his cousin also, he will not rule for long as I am powerless to prevent his revenge." Rune faded from sight, and the violet light that had lit his room left with her, and he felt cold and alone without her presence in the room. He sat back down in his chair and crossed his legs as he stared into the fire his mind filled with thought.

He was one man alone in a council of twelve and yet somehow he felt hope. Was it not one man alone who was trying to reunite the country and halt the destruction of the green world? One man could make a difference and he needed now to find a way to implement change. The death of Bishop Holmes was probably going to be a blessing in disguise.

His mind wandered to the moment earlier that evening when he had questioned the way of the lord. He now found he had contact with the world of the green realm and a chance to build a bridge, they knew of the line of the true king, Robert of Loxley had been right in the Cathedral at Canterbury. It was a strange way in which he had been guided to the path of truth; he gave a chuckle as he stared at the bright flickering flames. "You do work in mysterious ways My Lord."

Sapphire felt the warmth of Rune flow into her and she knew she was coming for her, she gasped with relief as she pulled down the blankets. The violet figure rose out of the floor, and before Rune could speak, she felt the gasping sobbing body of Sapphire wrap around her. Rune pulled her close as she shook with fear and her tears. "It's alright my sweet cousin I am here; I have come to take you home to Keith and your mother."

Saff could not speak as the emotions coursed through her; she clung tightly to Rune and sobbed. Rune waved a hand and the violet window appeared behind her. Una came out and smiled. "Go with Una Sapphire, she will take you home, your condemner approaches and I will have words with him."

Saff's eyes opened wide. "No Rune, they will take you in my place." Rune gave her a gentle smile.

"I am in Loxley Sapphire; they cannot harm or take me. I will see this man who leads the church and convince him he is wrong, now go with Una there is little time." Una pulled Sapphire into a hug and then they stepped through the window and it closed.

Bishop Andrew Holmes walked down the corridor toward the interrogation room and cells. He strode with confidence and arrogance as he talked to the

Brother Argus and five of the council. "John was always too soft; he probably has her a feather bed and a lady in waiting by now." They all laughed as they came through the doors into the room with the wooden table with straps, the trolley filled with shiny silver instruments stood quietly at its side.

Bishop Holmes looked at the door in the centre of the room. "Ok let's see what he has done for his lady." They tittered as the old monk walked to the door. The violet figure of Rune came right through the wooden panels and seized the old monk by the throat. He jumped back with surprise and fear, as his eyes opened wider. All the other stepped back afraid of the bright violet shimmering figure. "What the hell is this?" Holmes screamed as he looked at Rune.

Sapphire stood in the room with the table of Runestone held in Keith's arms as well as her mothers. She watched with Rowan, Robbie, and Una as the pictures floated above the table. Rune's eyes burned with anger as she slowly turned to the white faced Bishop. "You trap the innocent and call them witch. There is only one witch, and neither you nor your army of Knox has the power to destroy her.

Sapphire is free with her family; it appears the witch you seek is violet and I am here before you to show you what you really face." She pushed hard and the gasping monk flew back to the table, as Rune's eyes burned brighter.

The whole group gasped and stepped backward as the straps pulled tight on the old monk and he shrieked faced down on the table. One of the council moved toward him and Rune clicked her fingers, he flew back against the wall. "Your friend needs a lesson on his skills."

Holmes looked at Rune defiance in his eyes. "This is a sacred place you cannot spill blood here."

The old monk shook violently as his trousers tore down the back. "He will not die; but he will wish to as he understands the true meaning of violation. Fear not Bishop he will live, but he will walk a little slower from now on." Rune's fingers clicked loudly.

The whole group tensed as the instrument entered the old monk; his screams showered the air as he writhed in pain. The instrument suddenly shot open and louder screams bellowed into the room, the group clenched in fear and disgust at the sight and pain flowing out of the old monk. "See how the table shakes Bishop? I think I have found you another witch." Rune glared at the bishop who now looked very pale.

Rowan and Robbie tittered as they watched, even Keith laughed and Saff gave a small smile. Una leaned forward and stared closely,

"I would never have thought one could open that wide." Rowan's shoulders shook at the side of Robbie's; Mel gave a little titter at Una who was engrossed. "It's not funny look; you could drop a whole lemon in there." Robbie and Rowan exploded into fits and even Sapphire started to giggle.

Rune stared at Bishop Holmes. "There are no witches or devil worshipers in my realm; I am the power of life. In my realm, they call me Lady of the Woods; I believe your faith call me Eve." His eyes widened as she faced him head on looking fierce as the old monk whimpered and sobbed face down on the table. "I bring life to this world and hold sway over all. I am no witch but violet is my colour, for it is the symbol of death and rebirth into other realms. Know that for every woman you torture and burn, three close to you will be taken from this world by my hand, starting with your six sons and daughters."

The brightness of the violet light and the immense power that came from Rune was in itself terrifying; Robbie once again watched the fearsome power of nature that held a cold edge; he shuddered at her cold words. "A new king will come to this realm and end the power of Knox; you would be wise to distance your church or it will fall with him. The hooded man is not pleased with your treatment of his cousin, and you will pay for what you have done, your little shadow can no longer protect you as he too failed the measure of Loxley."

She raised a hand and all of them shrunk back and closed their eyes in fear. The old monk screamed as the instrument opened a little wider. "Lead your people in their true faith and preach tolerance and compassion as your lord did in his time, and we will not meet again Andrew Holmes. My Lord of Loxley has despatched Knox once and he will do it again, and if that witch of a mother returns him, he will suffer the same fate. You have not the power to fight me, so heed my words carefully. Your torturer here needs assistance; he seems to have reached his peak." The instrument snapped shut and the old monk slumped to the table with a whimper; the long silver instrument was still deep inside him. Rune faded, and the violet in the room left them in the cold light of the interrogation room.

Rune opened her eyes and the purple light faded as her bright blue eyes shone round the room. Sapphire ran to her and threw her arms round her; Rune gave a smile as she pulled her close. "Oh, Runestone, I was so afraid thank you."

"You are my family and I love you Sapphire, I am sorry you had to go through that, I would think it will be some time before old Brother Argus uses his tools." Sapphire gave a small giggle.

"I can't believe you just did that to him." She gave another loud giggle. Rune gave a little giggle as well.

"I must admit I saw the thing and just thought he might enjoy it." Rowan and Keith smiled as Saff gave another longer giggle into Rune's shoulder. Mel started giggling

"It certainly put a tear or two in his eyes, you should have taken lemons." Rowan and Keith slid on to the wall in fits as Mel looked round and Una burst into laughter. Rune looked at them all unsure of the joke, as Robbie howled with others. She smiled and kissed Saff on the cheek.

The shocked group looked at the monk as he moaned on the table. Bishop Andrews looked at them. "Well don't just stand there pull it out." The council member looked sickly.

"What, me?"

Bishop Andrews was angry as he looked back at the old monk. "Oh for God's sake." He grabbed the long steel instrument and heaved it out, the monk screamed even louder than before and the table vibrated, as he shook in pain.

Saff had a long hot bath at Rune's house. Rune sat on a stool at her side and washed her hair for her, they talked quietly and Rune began the process of healing. She sat in Rune's robe at the dressing table as Rune brushed her hair and pulled it into a ponytail. She rubbed some of Alice's cream gently on to her face, which was now black as coal, and Sapphire put on one of Rune's long green dresses. Rune smiled and gave her a hug and kissed the only part of her cheek that was not black. As they walked to the door, Sapphire stopped and looked at Rune, she seemed nervous and afraid.

"You don't think it has damaged me do you... You know... There... Children?" Rune felt her fear and smiled, she placed her hand gently at the base of her tummy and her hand glowed violet, she gave her a smile. Tears welled in Saff's eyes. "I want children one day." Rune pulled her close.

"You are fine my sweet cousin, have no fear. You need to heal but all is well trust me, you will have what your heart desires." Sapphire squeezed her hard.

"Thank you, Rune, I was so afraid I know Keith one day wants to settle, and I want it to be with me."

Rune kissed her softly on the nose. "You have all the time in the world, heal yourself Sapphire and then you will see."

Father Warren looked up the stairs as Rune came down with Sapphire; he gave her a big smile and bowed. "I am more than happy to see you My Lady."

Sapphire came down and put her arms around him, her memory was coming clearer and now she put a face to the kindness she had been given in that awful place. The voice as he begged for her life came to her memory, and she clung to him as if he was her oldest friend as her tears streamed. Father Warren smiled at Rune who wiped her eyes, he sat with Sapphire, Mel and Keith for some time and talked quietly, Robbie sat in the kitchen with Rune, as Una washed out her cup. Father Warren came in.

"My Lord Loxley it is nice to meet again, you have a beautiful home." Robbie smiled.

"Come Father, sit with us, and please in my home I am just Robbie. You must stay with us for a few days and enjoy your time away from the city. We have some very beautiful woodland; I would be pleased to walk you through it."

"My lord... Robbie, I could not inconvenience you, I know you are a busy man."

Rune patted his hand. "You fought hard for the cousin of my lord tonight; it would be our pleasure to repay the kindness and honour you showed to Sapphire. Please Father we insist." He gave a smile

"I must admit I heard much of the wonders of Loxley from Lee, and I hear Little Megan is here in the stockade, I would very much like to see her and her father, they were like family before the end."

Robbie smiled. "Little Megan is upstairs, she took quite a blow to the head yesterday, she is here recovering, I am sure she would not mind if you looked in on her, she would enjoy the company."

"I would like that very much, if it is alright yes, I will go and sit with her, I have sat with her many times through her life as she suffered sickness, it will be nice to do so again."

Rune smiled as he left the room with Una, to administer to one of his flock. "You know Rob the church in Hathersage is the only building still standing, it would be nice for Father Warren to be closer to those he has served and he will only be eight miles away. He will need the use of my father's books to finish his research, and he will be safer here than in an empty black city. Maybe you should talk to him, we have a high Christian population here as well as our Earth Faith members and he administers to both."

He gave a chuckle; she could always give a convincing argument. "I will talk with him tomorrow as we walk in the woods."

Rune gave a smile and opened the biscuit jar; her eyes twinkled as she pulled out a small letter with the seal of Lord Loxley on it. "Oh Goodie, another one." She giggled as she gave him a look of pure love.

CHAPTER NINE

THE START OF SUMMER

It was early Saturday morning when Robbie rolled over and opened his eyes. His nose almost touched hers and she smiled, her bright blue eyes danced with delight. "What?" She pulled the letter in her hand up from under the covers. He gave her a smile. "I think I am getting better at writing them don't you?" She gave him a long slow passionate kiss. "Yep, I am definitely getting better." She giggled with delight as she sat up on top of him. He rubbed her tummy and smiled at her. "Not much longer."

Rune smiled down at him. "It's May first tomorrow, it will be the May parade, do we have a May Queen? I thought somehow I would be more involved." Robbie stretched and lifted his head to kiss her tummy. It moved and she giggled.

"I think Beth has handled most of it this year, mum has been busy and what with the farm and you know Dad, she took it on with some of the other women, I think she asked if you would be a judge, I know Jade is. It's the duty of all the ladies of Loxley.

"Oh is it and what might I ask My Lord will you be doing?" He gave her a grin.

"I will be winning the best wife in the woodland competition."

"Oh you can be so smooth at times." She giggled as she leaned over and kissed him; he pulled her close and gave her a long kiss on the neck. "Ohhhhh God Rob."

Everyone sat in the garden round the table eating breakfast. It looked a little like a panda party, and Robbie smiled as he looked down from the balcony. The top of Maddy's forehead was now black, one side of Fish's face was black, and Ruby and Meg had huge black eyes, as did Saff and Judy. It was Saturday, which meant Specialist training. Robbie pulled on his shirt and leaned over the bed where Rune was lying and smiling. "Come on Mrs Loxley we have a school to open." She pulled him down into another long kiss.

"Don't know about wife, you must be miles ahead in the loving husband race." Her eyes sparkled as she giggled. "I love you Robbie."

"I love you too Runestone Sapphire." He gave her a kiss and stood up, she smiled on the bed as he left the room, and she stretched as contentment washed all over her. The Specialists were in high spirits when Robbie and Rune walked in with Beth. They scurried laughing to their seats and all sat down. Robbie leant on the desk and smiled.

"You have all done Loxley proud my Specialists. I am very pleased to see all of you here today, some of you are somewhat knocked about, but you are alive because the people around you acted like a true team. It was a hard fight and one that was always going to test us. All of you passed that test and I am very relieved and immensely proud of you."

The group all looked around at each other and smiled. "I have a little something for all of you because all of you are heroes to the people of Loxley. I know you all have the pendants given you by Rune, and I know how proud you all are of them. I have noticed how they are all tucked safely down the front of your tunics, I feel you should all have the honour of being recognised for your services to this realm and so I have had these made for you." Robbie held up a silver pin of the letter 'S'. "I hope you will wear them with pride and accept the credit you have earned." Rune walked slowly round and handed each of them the silver pin. Closer inspection revealed a twisted branch of Oak that formed the letter, they were very well made and it was some of Jade's finest work. All of them smiled as they received their pin, and they nodded their thanks to Robbie.

He straightened on the desk. "As you know we have an award for acts of extreme bravery. It is known as the golden bow, six have been given in the time of the bowman fellowship and I have for some time spoken with the head of the council as I did with my father. I know all of you have acted well beyond the level of others, but you are after all Specialists. However there have been two instances where I feel that the acts of bravery have gone beyond even the level set for a Specialist, and so after much discussion, I am pleased to say that I feel an award is warranted. I had a word a minute ago and the fellowship has agreed with me."

Robbie pulled the bright golden bow from his pocket. "To face an enemy is one thing, to face a highly skilled enemy unarmed is another? To protect a leader at all costs and save them from certain death is remarkable. Then after all that to lead a team into the woods in total darkness, and track them and help in the cleaning up operation is well beyond what is even expected of a Specialist, and yet my dear Blades on this and many other occasions you have shown bravery beyond your years. As your lord I am honoured and proud to award you this."

Everyone roared with approval as Blades stood up and turned beetroot. Harry and Maggs screamed as she came forward, and looked up into Robbie's smiling face. "You have proven yourself so much Kate since you joined us. You really have earned this the hard way." Robbie placed the bow in her hand and she looked down with tears in her eyes, it was the highest honour a bowman could receive, Robbie turned her round to face the happy cheering crowd. Blades beamed at the group who all pulled her into their arms and gave her huge hugs, it was several minutes before the whole group settled and John helped her pin on the award.

Robbie smiled. "Our second recipient almost lost their life in their struggle to save a half dead drowning lord, I wanted to make this award some time ago but events conspired against me, I have seen unexpected bravery in all of you, but none more so than in the person who has faced desperate circumstances and come through with true courage. Sapphire I owe you my life, I feel you have shown such bravery in my service, you deserve this and more."

Mel screamed and snatched her into her arms as Keith hugged her from the other side, the group went wild and cheered for her as she nervously stood up and came forward. Robbie gave her a huge hug. "Thanks Saff, my children will know their father thanks to you."

Saff cried in his arms. "I am lost for words, I love you and Rune, and you have done as much for me Robbie." He kissed her cheek and spoke very quietly.

"No one should endure the pain you have in my service. I am proud of whom you have become and I am sorry for the pain you have suffered." She wept as he gave her the golden bow. Rune wept and pulled her tightly into a hug. The whole group looked at Robbie and nodded with approval, he smiled at them, they knew the pain she had gone through and they all respected him for acknowledging it. Saff sat down and Keith helped her pin on the golden bow. He gave her a kiss on her cheek and she smiled at him, as he spoke quietly to her.

"Alright my Specialists, today you will have different duties than normal. As you all know tonight, we begin the celebration of Beltane, there will be fires lit around the town and celebrations of dancing and song as we welcome the start of summer. Tomorrow, we will choose our May Queen and then she will be paraded around the town, we need a bower making for the cart and there are Maypoles to erect. My Aunt Beth is here with a long list of things we need to finish for tomorrow so today there will be no practice; I want you all to help prepare Loxley for the celebration. Some of our men will be coming back from the moors for a break, so let's make it a good one for them."

The day was long and busy, and the whole group seemed to be in a new happy state of mind as they threw themselves into the work, by late evening the fires were lit and roaring into the sky. Robbie and Rune walked round the town with bright smiling faces as everyone smiled and bowed as they past.

Jade came leaping over the fire, and Rune giggled as she hopped about. "God that was hot." She patted her bum as it smoked. Leaping through the fire was traditional to bring good fortune into the summer, as was hanging a piece of flowering hawthorn or rowan above the door. The whole community was celebrating and small posies of spring flowers hung on every house, it was late when they returned home with Father Warren who had really enjoyed himself, Rune sat in the carriage as they came down the lane and filled him in on the custom of welcoming the sun to the land.

The following morning Rune rose early with Robbie, it would be a busy day for the Lord and his first lady. They stood by the Mere, and together they cast two violet flowering posies on to the surface of the mere. They stood facing each other and kissed, as Father Warren watched from the steps with Una. "They have blessed the water spirits and paid homage to the realm of Fae, see the rings of Rowan hanging in the tree, it is believed that if you look through the rings at dusk you will see the spirits of the people of Fae. Rune's first child will be the new queen of Fae"

Father Warren looked stunned. "Is Rune of the line of Gwendolyn? I had no idea."

Una gave him a big smile. "Actually, it is Robbie who has descended by direct descent from Bridget sister of Column Cille, and Rune is the joining of the Whitelines and Green Circle. My mother was Gwendolyn White Circle."

He looked down the glade at the two of them holding each other close and suddenly he realised that his research had led him right to the point where he was faced with the rest of the story.

"It has long been spoken that a way would be found to bring all three powers together, but it was destined never to happen, this is unbelievable. I am looking at the start of the Violet Line."

Una gave a small chuckle. "Are you going to take your place in our church? You will see the coming of the queen of your realm they have already named her. Can you guess what she will be called?"

He shrugged. "Bridget that has the meaning of high one."

"She will be Violet Stone, named after her realm, you see the symbol around Robbie's neck, Runestone is the writer of runes, and on the day his daughter is born it will become the symbol of Iona, Life, Circle, Line. It will mark the age of dreams and a new line of power."

Father Warren's voice was almost a whisper. "I have read about this since I was a young man, and now it stands before me in the flesh." Una chuckled.

"Hang around with us father and you will see many myths and legends come alive."

The day's festivities began; the entire town placed small tables at their gates filled with cakes and sweets. Anne and Alice Kirk outdid themselves with their display. All the tables had sprigs of Hawthorn and spring flowers on them. Rune, Jade and Beth stood in a line with Jess, Alice and Kate. The women of the family

Lox, they all wore their finest clothes and golden crested cloaks and Steph sat opposite with her pad and sketched quickly. Robbie smiled at the wonder of her pencil. "I hope you do two, those are the women I love the most and I want a copy." Steph smiled as she sketched, and her hand moved rapidly. The May queens were all sat in small carts decorated with flowers and they paraded past the women of Loxley who had the difficult task of choosing the May queen for the day.

Lucy beamed with pride looking beautiful in white satin and decorated in flowers as Rags pulled her sister past with high honour, and Maggs cheered from the crowd as she passed. The judges consulted awarding points for dress and carts and design, and it was a close competition.

Rags bit her nails as Bobby held her other hand, they had spent all of their free time for two weeks constructing a cart and making the dress. Rags was not good with a needle and worried it would let her sister down, Bobby had ended up doing the sewing as he was a little better, and Rags hammered the cart together. Jess stood in front of the group and read out the points. Lisa Wild had scored a record-breaking twenty-one points, no one ever got more than eighteen. Rags shrugged and patted Lucy on the shoulder.

"Never mind sis."

Jess carried on down the list with eighteen and a seventeen and she reached the bottom. "Lucy and the Loxley postal service cart twenty two points." She gave a huge smile as the Specialists went wild in the crowd, and jumped about hugging each other. Rags burst into tears and Bobby gave her a huge hug, Lucy danced with delight her face bright and happy.

Rune smiled as she slid the May Queen green sash of Loxley over Lucy, she gave her a massive hug. "That was some cart, you owe Bobby big time." Lucy giggled.

"Rags did it; Bobby made the dress because Rags stitches were too big." Lucy gave a twirl and the Specialists thundered forward to lift her in the air and carry her to the farm ready for the procession.

The procession rolled on to Hawthorn lane. Big John Styles wearing a stag's head banged on the huge drum strapped to his belly. Jett screamed across the lane. "Hey John try hitting the drum it's not as loud as your belly."

He laughed under his mask as the Specialists screamed with laughter and Jett held her sides as she went red in the face laughing. Harry and Maggs wore jester's hats and bright clothes of coloured ribbons, they shook large tambourines covered in ribbon with bells that jangled, and carried buckets of sweets for the children to delve into; they danced wildly round making all the children laugh. Jade rolled around with Jett as she screamed across the road. "Hey Harry is that you're vibes or your tambourine jangling?" Harry and Maggs were having the time of their lives as they danced and fooled around up the street with the children handing out the sweets.

Robbie gave a sad smile as he saw his mother walk out leading the cart in her wolves head clothes. She tapped the huge rowan pole on the ground as she walked to scare away the bad spirits and leave only the good for the summer season. Robbie had watched his dad do this for years and now knew that was the past; his head came forward as the memory was painful. Rune pulled her arm round him; she knew he felt the responsibility of his father's death. Jess walked past and she understood her son, Joe sat on the seat of the cart as he drove, although you would not know it was Joe, he was covered in a costume of sticks and leaves. This was the green man leading the way for the new queen of May, this was the symbol of fertility to the land, Joe made a bow from the cart to Rune; she gave a smile and bowed back.

Lucy sat high up in a bower of flowers, and waved and smiled to everyone with pride and joy, her face beamed delight as the other contestants sat below her along the sides of the cart and threw flower petals into the air. The procession passed by and Rune pulled Robbie close. "Are you alright?" She wiped a tear away with her thumb.

"I just saw mum and realised it should have been him, he loved doing the parades, I am sorry Rune I never expected it." She pulled him close and Steph watched from a few feet away.

"It's alright Rob; I understand how much you miss him. Today is a day when the spirits are close, believe me Rob he is here with all of us, he has not missed it." She held him tight and kissed him softly. He pulled her tight and felt her love, he knew she was right and felt a little relief as he thought of his father's happy face. He would be here and smiling and laughing, Rune was right.

"Thanks Rune... I love you."

"I love you too Robbie... Come on let's follow the parade and then tell your mum how great she has done. She will be missing him as well." He nodded and lifted his face to two bright blue loving eyes, she smiled and her cheeks rose on her pale face. She was so beautiful and he loved her, he smiled back.

The parade went around the whole town and came back to the market where the celebrations began. The market stalls were decorated in flowers and Maddy, Mel, Una, Treen and Saff had worked for half the night preparing the food. Harry pulled off the covers of the ale stall, and with Todd and Woody as assistants, the beer flowed. The firing range was now a huge dance area with four brightly decorated May poles, and the band on the stage built by Bear, Skip and John stomped into a tune, and men and women ran on to the field laughing and joking and danced the day away. Harry and Maggs who had sampled a great deal of ale danced and jigged with wild energy, and everyone laughed as the bells on their hats jangled loudly, or was that Maggs jewellery or Harry's vibes, it was hard to tell.

Just after midday, the band stopped playing and the town gathered on the field in front of the stage. Robbie came up the steps with Rune; his long green cloak flowed behind him as he stood before the community to give the May Day address to the people. He looked at the happy smiling faces; there were a considerable amount more than there ever had been in the past. All the traders and farmers and many soldiers of the green army stood holding the hands of their loved ones and family. Rune gave his hand a soft squeeze and he smiled. "My dearest members of this small community, I am so pleased to see all of you come together in these times of doubt and concern. This day is the celebration of new life as we prepare for the summer and the harvest of our crops. It is also a time when we celebrate the union of man and woman, who for us symbolise our creator and the mother of all life. Today I want all of you to think about the life that surrounds you as our community is growing, and there are some who are of other faiths amongst us. Welcome them to you and embrace them into this community, for now is a time when we need to stand firmly side by side to protect a way of life that is threatened."

Robbie swallowed hard as he looked to his smiling Mother. "There is one man missing here today who all of you should remember with honour. At this time, the spirits of our loved ones are close to us, and I know he is here with all of you today. He was a great man who helped build this community, and no one has fought harder over the years to protect you. Remember my father, Robert Jake Loxley and honour him."

The crowd bowed their heads and in unison they all spoke his name aloud. "Robert Jake Loxley." Jess bowed her head and brought her hankie to her eyes. Rune stepped up and raised her arms.

"May our lord of the green lands and creator of all things show favour to our fields and our lives. May he watch over us as we fight and guide us through the uncertainty of our futures? Hearne protect us all."

The crowd responded. "Hearne protect us all." Rune smiled as the crowd all bowed to Robbie and herself and broke apart. The band burst back into tune and Rune pulled Robbie close. "He would have liked that."

May Day was also a celebration of love, Beltane was known as a festival to celebrate fertility, and it was not unusual for couples to disappear for long periods of time. Robbie smiled as he saw Dave take Mel in his arms and kiss her as they danced together. He also noticed that Fish and Amethyst were nowhere to be found, it was also surprising that Blades and Todd had gone suddenly missing. Rags and Bobby were also absent. Rune giggled as John Lox came down the path red faced.

"Bloody barn is full, and that Bobby he aint no apprentice." He gave a huge grin. "I tell you Runestone that bloody barn is responsible for more kids round here than any other spot." Robbie giggled with Rune as John gave a hearty smile. He suddenly hugged them both with his huge bear like arms. "I love you two you know that? I am glad to see you smiling together, scared the hell out of me for a bit back there. Nice having you back Rob lad, I was saying to our Rob just the other day how proud of you I am."

Robbie looked up at his uncle. "What do you mean John you were saying to dad?"

John gave him a smile. "He is here Rob I feel him, I cannot explain what it is but I am working away or worried about something and then it happens. I sense him, aye that is it, I sense him. I get that presence like when he was here, and I know my eldest brother is watching over me. I knew he would, he loved me our Rob did. So when I feel him I talk to him and fill him in on stuff just like I used to, when I am done he goes away." John smiled at Robbie. "If you feel him Robbie talk to him, never forget he loved you, and if you are missing him, well don't you think he is missing you? Be open to him lad and talk to him, our Rob would like that, ask Rune here she knows. I felt him stood by her side a few times in March when things were tough." John patted Robbie's shoulder. "Go and get drunk lad like the rest of em. Let some steam off it will do you good." He smiled and walked off in search of Beth, Rune watched him as he stared out across the field.

"Do you think John is right Rune, or does he just miss him as much as me?"

"I think John has a point, he was right about him being close when I saw your mum, I felt him that day all around me. I feel them quicker than others, and yes Rob I have felt him many times."

Robbie turned to her his dark eyes fixed on hers. "Why has he not been to see me?"

Rune gave his hand a soft squeeze. "I think he knew you were not ready yet, when the time is right you will feel him. He loved you Rob, if you feel him tell him how much you love him he will like that." Robbie nodded

"I will."

The evening cooled and Robbie stood on the field with Rune moving softly to the music. Her head rested on his shoulder and he felt at ease, everyone smiled at the couple in their finest clothes and gold crested cloaks stood swaying. Rune was huge now as the twins came close to birth, and yet he held her gently and she smiled with happiness in his arms. Harry and Maggs lay passed out together under the beer table, Blades came down the path smiling holding hands with Todd. It had been a long happy day, and the people of Loxley went home with hope in their hearts and smiles on their faces.

Robbie stood by the mere as the sun gently slid in the sky, the deep red ball reflected in the clear waters. His thoughts were of his father as he remembered how Rowan had talked of remembering everything he could. He smiled as the pictures rushed into his mind; Rune sat on the balcony of her bedroom and watched him stood alone watching the water. She looked down at the gate at the end of the path. "He is ready now Robert go to him he needs you."

He stood his hands in his pockets his bright eyes fixed on some point ahead of him, and his mind lost in thought. The faint breeze lifted his hair and he felt it, a tear welled in his eyes. "I miss you dad, I never told you how much I loved you." The breeze blew gently past him. "Iona and Hal will come soon; will you see them?" Again, his hair gently lifted as the tears dripped off his cheeks. "I never said goodbye, or told you how proud I was to be your son. You were my hero dad I hope one day I will be like you."

Rune watched with tears in her eyes as the pale figure beside Robbie lifted an arm to his shoulder. Robbie felt the warmth in his heart and looked into the water, and for just a second through his tears he saw the tall proud figure of a father beside him. "Be proud of me dad, I love you." He blinked the tears away and the water showed him alone on the bank of the mere, John was right, Robert Lox as ever was watching over his family. Robbie stood for a long time filled with the warmth of the love of his family; Rune sat and watched him with the same love in her heart. As the darkness fell, he turned and walked back up the glade towards the house, Rune was waiting with her loving smile to welcome him back into her arms.

There was no witch burning in Lincoln on May Day. The four large bonfires were lit as part of the celebration of May first, and the church provided food and wine. Bishop Andrew Holmes walked through the remains of the ancient city with his council of twelve and greeted everyone wishing them well. His turn of face sickened the Lord Stevens as he saw him for the hypocrite he really was, and it turned his stomach to think this was the man who would lead the church. He was glad to be able to give his goodbyes as he headed back to his rooms and left the council to get into the two carriages and leave.

A little after midnight, in several coaches, they headed back to the Abbey down the long cleared road and came round the bend as the horses slowed, a tree had uprooted itself and fallen across blocking their path, they were a mile from the abbey. Bishop Holmes hung out of the window. "How far are we from the abbey?"

"I reckon bout a mile My Lord." The driver moved in his seat unsure of what to do. "I could run and get help My Lord if you don't mind the wait." Bishop Holmes opened the door and stepped out; he looked at the huge up rooted tree.

"It's not far, I suppose we could walk, wait here and we will send someone back." He stood impatiently waiting as the others climbed down and joined him on the road. After some time of manoeuvring round the large tree, all of them were on the other side, and set off at a slow walk down the road to the abbey. It was a warm evening, and the moon was high and bright, and the group began to enjoy their stroll as they talked. The abbey was in sight and the tall grey spire was lit by the moon as they came round the corner to the long straight road, which put them a quarter of a mile from the gates.

A single figure in white with a long pale blue cloak and a blue hood up above her head stood with a bow, a long red-feathered arrow was held in the string. The party drew to a halt, and Bishop Holmes looked at the silent figure stood fifty feet in front of him. "What do you want? We are men of the church and carry nothing of value."

A faint trace of blue flickered under the hood. "I have no use of valuables; I seek those who torture and victimise women in the name of their religion. I seek the eleven who feel they are above all others and can hide behind their God as they judge and condemn the innocent."

The men behind the bishop shuffled nervously as Sapphire spoke. Bishop Holmes raised his open palms. "We are men of the church and carry no weapons, and we are defenceless."

Sapphire gave a small burst of laughter. "I think not Bishop, you may not have a sword at your side but the way you think is a weapon, your thoughts bring death and your schemes change the course of men. Your little dark warrior was sent on your bidding, you carry no sword and yet people die before you."

The bishop took a step forward. "Lady Tor, you will not be permitted to take the life of a defenceless man of the cloth, it is against your woodland laws, why have you come here, is it just your anger at me for your humiliation?"

"I have come for your souls witch hunters." Bishop Holmes jumped back as blue light spilled from under the hood. The arrow came fast and pierced his heart; he fell dead to the floor as Sapphire loaded her second, the group panicked and turned to run, from out of the trees other figures appeared in hoods, it took just a minute and the eleven members of the church council fell dead with the red feathered arrows of the Tenth Legion in their black hearts. There was a flicker of blue light in the trees and the hooded figures rushed into it, in a flash, it was gone. The blue window opened behind Steph's house and the group came out, Saff looked up and smiled. "Thank you my sisters."

Maddy and Una gave her a hug; Mel kissed her cheek, as did Treen. Steph pulled her close and held her tight for a moment. "Rune will know." Saff nodded. Jade and Jett both gave her a huge squeeze, Crystal smiled at Amethyst.

"Let's put the kettle on." They smiled at Saff and the whole group walked talking up the yard into Steph's house. A little while later, they all sat around Steph's table talking. Rune lay in bed next to Robbie with her eyes flickering as he slept. Steph felt her first.

"Hear me sisters for I am Runestone and centre of your circle. Your loyalty to your sister is strong, I will support it and not speak of this to the hooded man, it

was not sacred ground and so you are safe within the realm of our powers. These men were defenceless, they carried no weapons, the red arrows may cover your trail and I hope so for this could bring great trouble to the hooded realm. I will watch from my table and see what becomes of it. We all love you Sapphire, see the bond you have with your sisters of the circle. Sleep well my sisters and speak of this to no one."

Jett smiled. "Told you Rune would be cool about it, she is one of us."

Rune smiled as she curled around Robbie and snuggled into him. There would be no more witch-hunts, and she had to give Sapphire her due she was smart. The red arrows of the Cutters would with hope drive a wedge between the church and Mason Knox. There was only one senior member of the council left, and Rune knew he was at least open minded enough to lead the church back to the road of faith and compassion. Bishop John Stevens had a lot of work to do, and Rune could only hope he would cope with the mammoth task that now faced him.

The days of rest for the Specialist were welcomed. They spent their time with Robbie in the woods of Robbie's Mere, Rune was happy to see him in the trees, and to have him close. The faces of the team that had been so badly bruised seemed to fade back to normal and the hearts and spirits lifted as they began to work alongside the Night Stalkers and the Bandits, and create more trouble than ever before for the big one eared general of the black city.

Father Warren returned to the black city with Ox and a few of his men. They packed up the church, and loaded the cart, and then made the long journey to Hathersage. It took a week of repair, but soon the old church was open again and the Christian and Earth Faith population returned to the church to worship under the guidance of Father Warren. He seemed like a man renewed on the occasions when Robbie and Rune visited. The move had benefited him greatly, and he smiled more and even had a little colour in his cheeks. The local community embraced him and he was often a guest for a meal in the houses of his parishioners. Father Warren felt a greater sense of belonging than he had ever done, and he continued his research of the faith of Column Cille with the help of Rune and her grandfather's good stock of books.

Robbie often stood at the graveside of Little John on his visits; he was another reminder of the hooded family that lived in these parts. He felt a strong bond with the area now, the past and present had somehow spliced into one and it was his family history. The restless boy had gone and now Robbie was the man who would fill his father's shoes.

Robbie as his grandfather and his father had done, would now lead the next chapter of the history of Loxley, and one day so would his son. Rune slid her arm around him as he gazed at the white stone under the large Yew tree. "What you thinking?" He gave a long contented sigh.

"I feel my family has come a long way Rune, somehow it feels like we have a lot further to go yet. One day my son will replace me and so on. I wonder if there will be a time when one of my future family looks down at my cloak and my sword and panics like hell as I did." She gave a little giggle.

"Your face was funny; you were as white as a ghost as you sat next to the glass case and I told you of the sage green fabric. We seemed so young then, and I loved you so much. It's hard to believe we had just been dating a few weeks and we were about to run off and change the world. If they look on your things, and they are like you, then they will not have to worry. You have done well Rob, look at how much you have achieved in just a year. I think if they have your blood in their veins they will be fine."

"I hope so Rune, I must admit it has not come easily."

"But you did it anyway, that is the sign of a true man of Loxley. That is Robert Jake Lox; you are so like him now." She kissed his cheek and smiling she walked back to the doors of the church.

The figure of a young man of power stood quietly under the yew tree. His long brown wavy hair reached the base of his back and blew in the breeze. The golden sword glistened by his side as the sage green cloak flapped in the summer breeze. He turned with eyes as bright as the stars and looked up the graveyard to the church; the sun glinted off two diamond eyes on the pendant almost hidden in the laces of his shirt. He was a lord of power and it showed, but more importantly, he was also the son of a mighty man.

The war of the moors raged on. Loxley still held their ground and the black army pushed hard against them. General Walters made a relentless series of attacks never letting the pressure lift once. As darkness fell over Loxley, they retaliated taking the pressure off the front lines as the Night Stalkers brought surprise and fear into the ranks of the black army. There were also many nights when soldiers would stand silently watching, only to see the fearsome group of the Specialists, come out of the dark with a fierce attack. Jade and Sapphire worked as a pair fading away and sneaking into the camps, it was now commonplace for tents, and wagons to suddenly erupt into massive explosions. The bandits played their role as they would sit quietly in the deep heather and send a volley of fizzing arrows into the midst of those soldiers preparing for their dawn assault on the front lines.

Robbie had taken a small group, rather than a large army to face Mason Knox in those early days as he made a stand for the realm of the woodman. The use of stealth in small numbers had overcome many of the problems of fighting Mason. He now used it again to his advantage; fast hard surprise attacks of small groups repeatedly wore away the vast numbers of the black army. Mason's mother, the Dark One just after the birth of his daughter Raven, had brought Mason Knox, back to life.

Faced with the problems of losing Mordred he now found his work to rebuild
the south of the country slowing down as he and Lance had to find a way of
stopping the high loss of men in the north. Fighting small unpredictable groups
seemed impossible, and so he began to plan a massive assault on a scale never
known. York would be crushed on its way to Loxley. On the twenty-fifth day of
May, he sat at the table in his manner house with Lance and he rolled out a sheet
of blank paper. Maps and the positions of the woodsmen surrounded them, and
now he looked at what boats he had and how many soldiers he had in the south.
He would bring together the forces of the Dragon and the Raven and he intended
to start at York, and clear the land south until not a tree or stick was left. The end
of Loxley and its meddlesome hooded man had begun.

Ben Winters was fourteen and an orphan; he made his living selling firewood
in the busy market of Caernarfon. He would spend days in the woods picking up
old branches and then bundle them up and carry them down through the high
rocky wood and into the town. It was hard work and although only small he was
strong, he had been doing very well and had managed to raise enough money to
buy a pair of new boots and a new green cloak, and some of the other boys noticed
it.

Ben had wandered into the woods, which he knew better than any, one mid-
morning and found a group of six boys collecting his wood. They had beaten him
badly and told him to stay clear this was their patch now. Cut and sore he lifted his
tent and moved higher up the mountain, to the steep rocky edges. Here amongst
the high woodland where very few wandered, he found a bountiful supply of dead
timber and began the long process of stacking it ready for the market. It was now
late May and he had a good load, and wandered into the highest and most remote
areas to look for just a little more before making his journey down to the market.
The woods here were dense and there were many saplings growing, he moved
quietly along until he saw smoke waft into the air from the clearing under the large
cliff wall. It looked like rain and he had thought of sheltering there, Ben warily
peered through the trees.

The hooded figure sat by the fire cooking in a blackened pan. He was dressed
in all green from head to foot as his head bent down whilst he stirred the pot. The
figure lifted his head and looked right at him; Ben gasped and stepped back into
the trees. "Are you hungry boy...? Join me I have plenty."

The face was white, it was almost bark like and two bright piercing eyes shone
through it from under the hood. Ben stepped through the trees and looked at the
man sat cross-legged before his fire. He wore a long hooded coat and tunic with
a long waistcoat and pants of a woodsman. They were all sage green, on his head

below his hood was a bandana of sage green and his hands had finger less green gloves. That was normal, what frightened him had been the fine mask of birch bark that hid the top of his face. All that could be seen was the mouth and the chin of white stubble, it smiled. "Have no fear boy, I will not harm you. Come and share the food of the woodland, you look like a good meal will benefit you." Ben looked at the face and the mask.

"Are you him? The one they talk about down in the town. Are you the Sage who sees things others cannot?"

He gave a smile as he stirred the pan. "I saw you long before you arrived, I live here alone and sometimes people have asked my advice. I can dream and see things that have not yet come to pass. As for Sage, I have no real name to speak of, so if you wish I will accept the name if it makes you feel at ease. Come eat and have no fear, I am for life not death." Ben was hungry and his stomach growled, nervously he came forward as the Sage spooned out a steaming bowl; he pulled a fork from his belt and lifted it up to the boy. "Here eat it whilst it is hot, it will nourish you." Ben took the bowl and sat by the fire, he watched as the Sage tore a large chunk from a loaf and passed it to him.

"What is wrong with your face?"

"It shows the scars of a past life which no one should see; I hide it and remain acceptable... eat my friend your wood pile is safe."

Ben gave a gasp. "You know this?"

"I was lower down this morning and saw your other friends, they have headed off to the market with little, I have watched you at your labour many times, and you work hard for such a small boy. It is commendable that you work rather than steal, you hold true to the ways of the woodsman. I like that, unlike your friends who steal the work of others, they will not last long at the toil and return to stealing from pockets as they have in the past." Ben shovelled in the hot stew, he was starving he had not eaten in many days and it gave him the pleasure of feeling his stomach fill.

"Slow down my young friend, it is good to have a full stomach, just not one with an ache in it. We have plenty and when it runs low, the lord Hearne will provide more." He gave a smile as the young boy ate and enjoyed the break from isolation and his young company. He watched as Ben slowed and chewed his food and dipped his bread in the gravy. "So my young friend, do you have a name or should I call you sticks? I wear all sage green and they call me Sage, you carry sticks should that be your name?"

"I am sorry; my name is Ben, Ben Winters."

The Sage nodded. "It is nice to meet with you Ben Winters, tell me where are your family?" Ben looked up through the steam of his stew.

"The Cutters took them." The Sage lowered his head as if in pain.

"I am sorry to hear this my friend; they have done much evil in this world. I now feel the pain in the world all around me, and they have caused most of it."

Ben ate as he watched his curious companion, who seemed for a time lost in thought, he chewed on the bread as the Sage slowly ate and looked out into the trees, and he seemed to have an air of peace and calmness around him. Ben had known many woodsmen and they all had that calmness and feeling of being one with everything.

"What you thinking about?" The Sage seemed to come out of a dream and smiled.

"I think that you have a heavy load for your back tomorrow, I am heading into the town and will offer you my service if it pleases you. It has been long since I walked in the woods with a heavy load, it will do me good to have the exercise."

Ben smiled as he lifted his bowl and drank the gravy from the bottom. "I would like that."

The Sage smiled and sat back against the rock wall; he breathed a long sigh of contentment. "It will rain soon, if you wish to stay here under the rock where it is dry I have blankets, we can start out together at dawn and gather your load on route."

Ben gave a smile and nodded. The rain came within the hour and it was heavy, Ben had a full stomach for the first time in a long while and he lay on the blankets and was soon asleep. The Sage watched over the young boy as he lay sleeping, his long brown hair was matted and lank, his face pale, and his brown patched clothes and new boots made him smile, it reminded him very much of a young boy he had known. He lifted his bow and quiver and walked into the rain to hunt.

The little bell rang and Judith looked up and smiled. Alice shook her hood as the rain bounced on the street outside. "Oh this is awful." She held baby Jessie close under her cloak. "It was sunny when I left the farm."

Judith came from behind the counter and held out her arms. "Could I hold her for a minute?"

Alice gave a big smile. "Of course, you can, you do realise she is your neice."

Judith smiled as she lifted the small child into her arms. She looked at the bright blue eyes and curly blond hair, she was so like her father and yet Judy thought it better not to mention it. "She is so beautiful Alice."

Alice gave a smile as she saw Judy hold the small child close. In many ways she had no family now, Little Jessie was her only family link. Alice watched as Judy smiled and spoke quietly to the small child, who looked up at her with wide bright eyes. Alice made a warm drink while Judy enjoyed some time with her little niece. She sat down in the window on the soft chair beside her, Judy looked up at Alice. "You know she will have power? We all have."

Alice nodded. "Rune has told me she will have the gift of sight."

"It is strong in her I can feel it." She looked up at Alice and smiled. "She has no dark power in her, she will only work for the good of others, and I know we are of that line, but not all of us were dark."

Alice seemed to understand her. "I know Judy; I too saw it in him in the end." Judy nodded.

"I miss him, he was really good to me, and the others were horrible."

Alice understood Judy more than the others did. Billy was good to Judy and in many ways; he had always been good to Alice. Billy did have the ability to be very kind; it was something that had given him great conflict. In her last meeting with Billy, she had seen how hard he was trying to do the right thing, and she was no longer angry with him. Alice placed a soft hand on Judy's. "Robbie let him live Judy; he is free of all of it now like you are, he will find peace now."

Judy gave a soft smile and nodded. "I know it is daft but I worry about him, I am so glad I have you to talk to, I am not sure anyone else would understand, he is still my brother no one sees that."

"I know him better than most Judy, believe me wherever he is he will be alright. He was trained in Loxley and has the skills of the best. He was also pretty good looking; I am sure there is some woman out there being very well looked after." She gave Judy a wink and she smiled at Alice.

"Yeah, our Billy will be fine, won't he?" She gave Jessica a smile as she tickled her under her chin and her bright blue eyes sparkled. "Hey little Jessica, I am your Aunt Judy, how about that then we are family."

Alice sat smiling drinking her tea as the rain poured onto the cobbled street of the village. She stared at the rain-streaked window and moments of a gentle boy with long curly blond hair slipped through her thoughts. She remembered the long nights of love making and talking in the straw of the barn. She had loved him so much it still hurt at times, and she knew inside secretly she loved him still. He was the father of her child. Jessica was the child she had always dreamed she would have with him and it meant something.

CHAPTER TEN

THE LOYAL STICK TOGETHER

Robbie looked down at the long table that ran down the centre of his office in the loft of his home; he leaned over Steph's shoulder as she waded through the huge pile of papers, all written in strange runes. By the side of each sheet was a translation that had taken weeks of work.

"Rob this is fantastic." Steph had never seemed more excited than she had been in recent days. "Look at this, Arthur Pendragon married Guinevere Leodegrance on May first 388 in Cameliard." Her eyes sparkled as she looked at him and Rune. "It's fantastic; I have the whole line here, their son was Gawain, and he married Jennifer of Hope, they had a son called Kyle who married Poppy Meadows, they had two children Aron and Louisa."

Robbie gave a smile at her excitement. "You will have to draw this into a family tree for the wall in the village hall."

Steph gave a gasp. "It will have to be a big wall Rob; I have forty generations of Pendragon already."

He had to ask the one question that Steph did not really want to answer. "So have you any idea of who the heir is and how I can find him?" She looked disappointedly at the papers.

"Not yet, that's the bit which is giving me the trouble. I have traced the line all the way to a William Peter Pendragon who was born in Glastonbury in April 1936. He married, but I have not translated that particular paper yet, there is still a lot of searching to do, I know he died during the red death. I have something here that talks of his death, it just mentions the seventh of May and refers to a wife and son but it has no mention of their names."

Robbie shrugged. "Well at least we are getting nearer, all we need now is a date of fifty to sixty six and you will be closer." Rune looked at him strangely.

"Why those dates?"

He gave her a smile. "I would assume that he would have been somewhere between twenty to thirty when he had children, most people are roughly in that age group and he was born in thirty six." Rune gave a nod and looked back down at the papers on the long table.

"Wow look at this Bridget Violet of Iona had a son called Ninian who married Erin of Iona, and had two children Gwynfor and Gwendolyn. Gwynfor married Filomena of Callanish and they moved south." Rune's eyes sparkled as she looked at Robbie. "Their daughter was Fiona of Loxley... Wow Rob it's really true, it is all here, look at this, it is a copy of the book in the Village Hall, her son Robert married Marion of Blidworth. Their son was Robert Gwyn Loxley, and he married Lillian of Hope. You are of the line of Fae there really is no doubt."

Rune, wandered round the table lifting sheets and giggling as happily as her mother. "Look here is granddad and Gwendolyn; oh and here he is again with Opal and look it's me. Runestone Sapphire, Rimmer Lane, born October 31st 2022 in Avon. Wow look it's my birth certificate, I never even knew I had one."

Steph sat back and smiled as she watched Rune comb over the papers she had not yet translated, Rune just picked them up and read them without realising she was reading the secret code of her grandfather. Steph had spent weeks working with his notebook to get each word out of the code and placed in the right order.

Rune looked up and smiled. "Here is you and dad getting married at Caerleon, Oh and look here is Scarlet and Phillips wedding certificate. Hey look at this a piece of old parchment with the marriage of Tor and Melanie."

Steph gave a huge smile. "Oh great give it here, I promised her if I found it I would let her see it."

Robbie looked at the old piece of paper. "How do you read this Rune? It is all strange symbols." He looked up at her.

"Is it?" He nodded to her. Rune looked down at the old runic letters.

"I forget sometimes I am Runestone, I look at them and they are just like normal words to me, granddad must have known the power of the line would give me the ability to read all symbols, which is why he coded it all and taught mum how to use his cipher. It gave him the security of knowing that we would carry on his work." She gave a sweet smile to Robbie, and kissed him on the end of his nose and giggled.

The ancient castle town of Caernarfon had changed very little since the coming of the red death. Many in the town had died but those in the surrounding countryside had somehow managed to escape. What had once been a Celtic cultural area had very quickly adapted to the woodsman's ways, and it was now a busy little market town where country living people would come regularly to swap or barter goods.

With the Sage at his side, he hoisted the large bundle of twigs on their backs and set off down the mountain pass toward the town. It was just before dawn and it would be a long day before they returned to the shelter of the cave. Ben was now getting used to his strange new friend and talked away quite happily, the Sage smiled as he walked at the side of him, as Ben filled him in on the workings of a town he had visited many times before. It was around six in the morning when they walked into the centre of the town. The old tarmac streets were unchanged from the time of old modern man, the streetlights and traffic lights no longer worked and there were no longer any cars, most of the streets were lined with wooden stalls, and planks of wood stood on boxes as the traders and farmers set up for the day. Ben always stood next to Craig Jones the sword sharpener, he dropped his firewood and the Sage gave him a smile as he let the heavy load down next to him. "Will you be all right Ben? There are things I must do."

"Oh don't you mind him now, I always keep an eye on him." The red faced happy older man gave a huge smile.

The Sage smiled and nodded at Craig. "I thank you kindly sir, there are those who would steal his work and I worry for him, I am grateful to you." The old sword sharpener gave a smile; he knew of the Sage and knew it would not harm him to have the favour of one known for his wisdom. Ben waved as he wandered off into the back streets and began to unpack his wood and sort it into piles.

Craig smiled down. "Friend of yours, is he?" Ben nodded and smiled.

"We sort of bumped into each other on the mountain; he helped get my load down here."

Craig nodded as he pumped on the foot pedal and his grinding wheel began to spin. "Well, I will tell you this Ben boy, you will be safe with him, he has helped many in these parts and he is greatly favoured. You have a good friend there indeed if you're asking me."

Ben looked down to the small streets at the side of the castle, where the Sage had disappeared. "He is nice, I like him. He makes me feel calm and less nervous."

Sparks flew as Craig pressed a large sword blade on to his stone. It was a busy morning and by the time dinner came around Ben had made twelve brass bits. It was the most he had ever made in one day and he still had some wood for sale. The whole market was now a crowded mass of moving people and the Sage came up from the quayside and back into the crowds. The six boys who had stolen Ben's turf had very little money and they watched Ben from across the way as he sold bunch after bunch. He swapped some for a loaf and a nice big steak, and he managed to trade for a small sack filled with long green beans, he was delighted and laughed with Craig who patted him on the back whenever he made a good sale.

For all the hard work and weeks of effort it was still very little money, yet to Ben it was a fortune and it made all of the hard work worthwhile. The six boys moved into the crowd, the eldest was sixteen and he was a scruffy lad with short greasy hair and a very spotty face, they all called Slip. He was the best at picking pockets and he wove through the crowd like a true professional. His hand dropped into the deep pocket of a farmer who had sold a good amount of sheep, his reward was a bag of gold bits and Slip saw his chance at a very rewarding prize, his hand dropped quickly and came out in a flash with the black velvet bag of gold.

His wrist was caught in a sage green fingerless glove and a silver dagger swiped quickly across the back of Slips hand. "Drop it boy or lose the hand." The bright eyes stared from behind the mask of birch bark. The Sage moved the long silver dagger back to the blood sliced hand and Slip opened it, the Sage spun in a flash, and the bag of gold dropped back into the farmer's pocket.

The Sage still had a firm grip of the boy's wrist. "You come with me boy, and do not make it harder than it has to be." Slip shook with fear as the others walked away not wanting to get involved with the strange hooded figure. He was dragged down to the quayside his hand now bleeding fast and the grip on his wrist was hurting him. "You have two choices boy, you help my friend or we go and see the head woodsman and let him know of your antic's, what's it to be?"

"You can't force me to do anything."

The Sage stopped and spun round on him, the long silver dagger had appeared from nowhere. "You listen to me and you listen good boy. If I take you to the woodsmen and swear an oath I saw you steal you will have punishment far worse than what I have in mind for you. You help my friend and you will have something to put your fast little fingers to work honestly. You will get regular pay and have a second chance to sort yourself out." The dagger glinted. "So what's it to be, robber or ropes man?"

Slip shook with fear, there was something about the eyes that looked deep inside him and he felt afraid of them. He swallowed hard and stammered. "Rope... ropes... ropes man."

The Sage winked behind the face of white grained bark. "Good lad, I knew you had some brains, the man you are seeing is called Wilbur, he runs smalls boats up the coast and back, you work hard for him and you will have good food and money in your pocket. His boss Toby is a good man, mess him about and I find out, and you will wake with a slit throat one morning, you understand me?"

Slip nodded vigorously. "I will Mr, honest."

"Alright here wipe your hand and follow me." He gave him a long piece of green cloth and he quickly bound the bleeding hand as he followed the Sage to the quayside. The Sage looked down on the little boat, Terry the cabin boy was moving boxes to the cabin door.

"Is he here Terry?" The young lad looked up and smiled as he saw the Sage.

"He nipped off for a loaf."

The Sage nodded. "This is the lad I was telling him about, settle him in and find him a bunk, tell Wilbur he owes me."

Terry gave a big smile. "How much is it by now?"

The Sage gave a grin. "It's too much to remember." He looked at Slip. "Alright lad, get on board and don't forget, you have a good chance here to sort yourself out, never blow a second chance, it could be your last. Good luck now, hop it."

Slip dropped quickly down the ladder and Terry handed him a box. "Give me a lift with these, they go under the bunks, might as well help as I show you around." Slip saw the scar across the back of his hand; it looked like Terry had also been caught by the Sage. He looked up but the quayside was empty, he grabbed the box and followed Terry down the steps to the back of the boat.

Ben looked up and smiled as the Sage passed him a thick sandwich with salad and meat in it. "It's not that fresh but it will keep you topped up until later." Ben took a big bite and chewed vigorously.

"I have made more money than ever before; I should have bought you one."

The Sage patted his back and laughed. "I didn't buy it; people give me things." Ben screwed up his face.

"Why would people give you things?" The Sage sat on the curb and chewed his sandwich.

"I give them advice and knowledge which helps them in their lives, and when I am about the town, they just come and thank me. Like today, a farmer I helped with his sick pig gave me two big sandwiches off his wife's food stall. His pig is well and he will not have to slaughter it, he will sell it on the market and make a profit. I saved him money he gave these sandwiches. I have money but I find I do not have to use it."

"I have traded for bread and meat and some beans." Ben showed him the goods in an old sack. The Sage nodded.

"That is good as I have four carrots, three potatoes and two onions. We can have a good hearty stew when we get back, you need feeding up, I can see your bones almost through your shirt. Stick with me kid and we will put a little flesh on you." Ben gave a big beaming smile as he watched the strange Sage finish his sandwich.

Martin Jarrod had now wandered for just over a month. He had wound his way down from the north and cut across the country just below Winsford and into north Wales. He had crossed the wilds to the pass of Llanberis and followed it down to the lower vale that brought him round to the edge of Caernarfon. He was in thick woodland heading across to the east of the small town as he came to a high edge and looked out across the Menai Strait and the castle set in the distance. He dropped from his horse, his legs were tired from his journey in the seat, and he walked up and down stretching the cramps out. It seemed like a good place to set up camp. There were rock formations of height, and between two he tied up a canvass sheet, as protection from what looked like on coming rain. Martin sat in the afternoon sun by his fire and drank a hot cup of wild tea, he decided he would relax for the rest of the day, and then go and look for the Sage the following day. He was tired and soon rolled up in his blanket and was fast asleep.

He woke with a start as the sun fell, he had not meant to sleep so long and he sat up and rubbed his eyes. The violet figure of Rune smiled at him. "Good morning, or should I say evening my General, I take it you slept well?"

"My Lady of the Woods, you startled me." Rune gave a smile as she shimmered in the last of the day's light.

"I have watched you for some time Martin Jarrod; you seem to have lost much of the deep sadness you held at our last meeting. I am happy to see you feel the joy of the trees and the road."

He stretched his legs and smiled. "I do feel lighter of heart My Lady, and I have rested longer hours than ever before, and I have had time to sit and think about my life and my deeds." She watched the old man and could see the healing of his heart; he had fought for a month to come to terms with the life he had lived. Now he had made the choice to try, and undo some of his deeds by helping repair the damage he had played his part in. It had been a difficult time and he had not come to his decision easily, but now she saw he was on the right path and knew the time was right to set him his task.

"Listen to me Martin Jarrod, for the Lord Hearne will set you a task, you will not be unaided, for you have friends here that will assist you in this task. Wait here until the sun rises over the top of the rock behind you, when the sun is level walk around this rock, and travel east rising upwards. Your path will cross with the Sage and his young companion; I will return and speak with all of you at that time, eat a good meal and rest for you are safe and protected here."

Rune stood up and walked to the edge of the rock face, and as the sun setting over the ocean glinted in his eyes, she faded from view. He leaned back on the rock under the cover as the rain started to fall, and threw some wood on the fire, he pushed his old coffee pot into the flames to boil.

Robbie lay in bed as the sun had sunk below the mere and closed his eyes, it had felt like a long day and he was tired. He was going yet again to look at the defence of the moors the following day, and he knew that Rune was feeling nervous. She was still at her table down in the basement and he knew she would be watching to see if there would be anything she could spot. Rune's mind wandered as she watched the picture flicking through the tables violet shimmering window, it slowed as she watched her wedding day. Rune smiled as she sat alone, and watched herself give her vows to Robbie before the crowd; she chuckled as Robbie said 'yes mum.' Her eyes sparkled, she was so happy and it had been the greatest day of her life, how he managed to pull it off without her knowing she had not known but he had.

Una came down the steps with a cup of coco, she saw the happy smiling face of Rune as she watched and she gave a huge smile as she sat beside her. "You are so lucky to be able to see this again and again."

Rune smiled and leaned on her arms as Robbie slid on the ring. "I was really nervous, I wanted this so badly and then it just happened so fast Una, I thought I would mess it all up." Una leaned on to her and slid her arm round her.

"He loves you so much Rune, just look at how happy he is, and look at you with that smile. You look so happy you look like you will explode with the happiness."

Rune giggled. "I thought I would. Oh Una it is the nicest thing anyone has ever done, I love all of you for this." It came to the part where they were about to get in their seats and Rune spoke. "Freeze."

Una looked at Rune and she knew that Rune had something to say. "Una, can I trust you with a huge secret? I mean this is so big I have to be very careful who knows." Una looked a little worried.

"Rune darling, I would die before I betrayed you, you are my centre and you and Robbie have become to me as my own children would be." Rune leaned over and kissed her on the cheek.

"I know Una, we both love you as much too, but watch and you will understand."

Rune looked at the pictures of Hearne giving the blessing. "Continue." The pictures moved to Jessie Lox, who was on her knees looking surprised, Robert Lox turned to her. Rune gave the command to her table. "Full sound."

Robert Lox suddenly seemed to understand what his wife had said, and he looked very surprised. "Bloody hell Jess, are you sure?" He turned and looked round across the glade to where Robbie was kissing Rune softly. Her face was radiant with happiness as she pulled back, and Una could not help smiling.

He held her face cupped gently in his hands; her eyes danced bright sapphire blue on a sea of her lilac whites. "Oh Robbie, I want to cry I am so happy, My Lord Grandfather has given me the greatest gift ever." She pulled him into her arms and tears ran from her eyes. "You will never know of the pain I have felt knowing I would live longer than you. The thought of just one life without you let alone ten was just too much for me at times."

He smiled as he squeezed her tight and rocked her from side to side. "Now Rune I understand Opal in the glade at Caerleon, when she told me there were things in my future she could not tell me. She knew of the gift of Hearne."

Rune pulled away from him and smiled, her eyes dancing with the light from her happy tears. "It is my greatest wish come true. You will not regret this I promise."

He smiled at her happy face and wiped the violet tears from her cheeks. "Did I not tell you I would not leave you? I will love you always Runestone Sapphire Lane Loxley." She gave a bright happy giggle.

"We will live for a long time Robbie; it could be a thousand years."

"Is that all? We will just be getting to know each other." She gave a soft giggle as he pulled her back into his arms and he held her tight. "Oh Rune I feel so happy."

She turned and kissed the side of his neck. "We are the start of a new line of power now you know?"

He leaned back and looked at her. "How do you mean a new power?" She smiled and kissed his nose.

"Did you not hear the blessing; my grandfather of the realm bound us together and has brought the Green and White Circles together? He bound them forever with the white lines of time. Robbie those powers have now gone."

"I am not sure I understand, how do you mean gone?"

"All three lines are now one huge power, and they have come together in me and mixed with the love that we hold. Today is the beginning of the Violet Lines. From us all the lines that come will be a stronger power than the lines of power before." He looked as she smiled and nodded at him.

"What you mean Iona?"

"No Robbie, all of our children. They will be the new lines of the future; they are the age of dreams." She gave a big giggle. "All my children will be as powerful and protect the whole of the woodland realm and all the other realms. Rob our children will shape the dawn of awakening, we are the future of everything and we will still be around to see it."

He looked really surprised. "Wow Rune, you will have to help trim my beard if I get that old, or else I will keep falling over it." She laughed as she pulled him back into her arms.

"I have years and years to love you isn't it wonderful? Oh Rob I have never felt this happy ever."

The crowd were now up off their knees and the seats were being prepared, Rune gave him a quick kiss, "come on they are waiting and we have a wedding feast to go to."

Una watched with tears in her eyes as Rune pulled him by the hand and skipped across the grass to the seats decorated with flowers and the happy faces of their family. "Stop."

The pictures faded and the violet mist sunk to the table and spun on the surface. Una wiped her eyes and smiled. "Sorry I always cry at weddings." Rune giggled.

Una took Rune by the hand and gave her a smile. "Runestone my darling, I cannot tell you how happy I feel, it is the hardest pain all of us have had to deal with. Mel has suffered terribly over Tor, and Gwinne misses Rayne so much. I lost Kane and poor Maddy had an awful time with Maurice, although he didn't die, he got drunk. We all have suffered the one curse; even your grandfather has suffered although in all fairness it was the Dark One who caused that. Knowing Robbie has been given a line of time is wonderful, your love is so strong and so pure I have often thought of the pain and anguish it would cause you. I am happier than I ever thought I could be for you."

Rune beamed. "Secretly since Opal told me I was nature in human form, I have been so afraid because I knew I would lose him." She gave a huge smile and looked once again as if she might explode, Una started to laugh at her.

"Oh Rune my darling there is so much happiness in you I am scared you will push the babies out too soon." Rune giggled wildly as Una pulled her into a tight hug. "He is very special you know; he has a magic all around him if I do say it myself."

"He is wonderful Una; I open my eyes every morning and I see him there on the pillow at my side and I want to shout and scream I feel so happy. I have spent so long watching him and wishing for him, I guessed I never thought he would notice me. Do you know something Una?"

"What Rune darling?" Rune gave a huge smile and whispered.

"He had." Una chuckled.

"I know he told me how he fell in love with you the first time he ever saw your tiny blue eyes peeking through the gate, you were always meant to be together Rune. I saw it the moment I first saw you together." Una kissed the end of her nose. "Drink your coco before it gets cold, Jess has gone through hell to grow those." She smiled at Rune. "I am off to bed; don't stay up too late... Goodnight sweetheart."

"Night Una... Thanks." Una walked off up the steps and Rune sipped her coco and smiled to herself, happiness was hers forever.

The moonlight shone in through the large glass windows and she watched him as she carefully slid down under the covers, she moved and his arm slid out towards her. Rune snuggled up to him and felt his arm pull around her and hold her close. She laid her head on his chest and her bright eyes twinkled in the moonlight as she watched him sleep. He snored and Rune giggled.

Robbie rose early and padded around the house in bare feet with his shirt flapping, it was early and yet it was already warm as the sun climbed high into the air. With a cup in one hand and a large thick toasted slice of bread and honey in the other, he wandered out into the glory of the new summer's day. The grass felt damp between his toes from the overnight dew, he felt a strong sense of connection with Robbie's Mere and his spirits soared as he walked down to the edge of the water.

The surface of the mere was like silver glass, it mirrored the trees on the opposite bank, as the light bounced from the sun and splashed across him, it was the most beautiful he had ever seen it. He gave a long contented sigh and raised his cup to his lips, as the heron swooped across the mere and waded into the water by the reeds. It stood frozen waiting for the fish and he smiled as he took a big bite of his toast. The mere had always felt magical and yet to him on this glorious summer morning, it held more wonder than he had ever seen in it, life somehow did not feel it could get any better than this.

He turned and slowly walked back up to the house watching the trees. The small bright white haired figure clad in grey walked out from the track and on to the glade. Ruby was still some distance off and yet as she lifted her hand to wave, he knew she was giving him one of her usual beaming smiles. Robbie was very fond of her; she was now seventeen and yet she still seemed to keep her child like qualities, although she had grown in the past year, and with her rose coloured mirrored sunglasses she was becoming quite an attractive young woman. He always thought of her as a younger version of Una when they fought side by side with their long snow white hair, they did look very much like mother and daughter.

She ran down the glade smiling and he pulled her into his arms and gave her a huge hug. "Hey Flash, it's nice to see you, how are you?" She slipped her arm round him and walked up the grass toward the house.

"I am fine; I wanted to talk to you... Thanks for the new boots by the way." She looked down at the white boots he and Rune had given her for her birthday, they were very much like the ones Saff wore. It seemed odd her wearing boots now, she had always worn the silken pumps to help her spin when she fought with her pole.

"So, what can I do for my favourite cousin?" She gave a little giggle.

"You are going to the moors later today, aren't you? Alice told me she is coming up to spend the afternoon with Rune. I wondered if I could come with you, I have been missing mum and I need to talk to her." Robbie felt a twinge of sadness.

"Oh, Ruby you should have told me or Rune, you must not feel alone if you need to see your mum you should say so." She gave him a smile.

"I am not alone Robbie, I have loads of friends I live at the farm. Alice is always in the house and Judy and Kate are just across the way. I see Maggs and Harry every day, and Rags and Lucy. You know your mum; she is so lovely with me. Beth and John are just the best and Megan has become a really good friend, I like sharing a room with Megan we share make up and do each other's hair and talk about boys."

Robbie gave her a shrewd look. "You do?" She gave a giggle as she looked at him.

"Oh Robbie, I am seventeen now, I am not a baby anymore. There are some cute boys in the village." She giggled as he gave her a squeeze.

"I am glad you are happy; I hate to think of you as lonely as you were at the castle."

"Oh Robbie, I really am very happy, I love Loxley and never want to leave. It is just that I want to spend a little time with mum and dad. I know she misses us as well, and Jett and Rafe are pretty busy with the Specialists and their own house. It will just be nice to see her."

"Then you shall." He pulled her close and kissed the top of her head. Rune watched from the door as they came smiling up the glade and in through the gate,

Ruby gave Rune a big hug. There was a big difference in her, and he noticed the changes. Somehow, there was less of the baby side to her and if he was right there was a little more of a Jett like quality to her; she was definitely more grown up.

Ruby gave Una a huge hug and with Rune, they went into the kitchen. She seemed more like the others now and in a way, he felt a little disappointed. He had a particularly soft spot for Ruby, she had always felt the baby of the family, and yet now she was visibly growing into a young woman. Her hair was a lot longer and was almost at her waist, gone was the little child like bob, and he noticed that the oriental style jackets she always wore buttoned up was now open, and she had a lace up tunic of the palest blue.

He had never seen her wear any other colour than grey, she looked less fragile and had more of the build of Jett, how had she changed so much without him noticing? He gave a slight chuckle; it seemed the family of Rune would always confuse him. Laughter came from the kitchen, and Robbie looked up and saw Rune looking at him, her bright blue eyes danced, he pulled on his boots and stood up tucking in his long green shirt. "What?" She came through the door with a smile on her face.

"It seems little Ruby is growing up faster than I think you realised." Rune gave him a wink. "She thinks you are a dish." She giggled as she pulled him close and kissed him softly on the cheek.

He shook his head. "When did she grow up? I missed it, one minute she is this tiny little happy thing and now she is all hormonal like Jett. I tell you Rune your family defy all logic." She giggled.

"You are funny at times." She kissed the end of his nose. "Get used to it Rob, one day it will be your daughters."

"Not Iona, I just know she will be a good sensible girl like her dad." Rune laughed and gave him a big squeeze.

"She is not even born and she is already a princess." He gave her a stern look, and for a second, he looked just like his father.

"Too right she will be." He smiled. "It's not long now, she will be with us and I will have a son, he will be just like my dad." She nuzzled into his neck.

"I hope so Rob." Her eyes sparkled with happiness as he kissed her softly.

"I have to head off now; I will see you in a little while." She gave him a tight squeeze.

"Be careful and keep low." Rune waved her hand and the violet window opened.

Robbie lifted his cloak and bow. "Ruby I am off are you coming?" She came running out of the kitchen and grabbed her long white pole.

"See you soon Rune." She gave a high pitched chuckle. "Hey that rhymes." She kissed her quickly on the cheek, and shot past into the window behind Robbie.

It was busy in the headquarters, as they entered, Scarlet dragged Ruby into her arms and Fuse gave him a big smile as he crossed the room toward him. Robbie gave him a big hug. "How are you my old friend, I have missed you?"

Fuse looked happy. "You are growing up quickly My Lord, you have the air of your father around you. I am pleased to see you well and looking more rested than last time. Married life has done you well."

Robbie smiled. "I am blessed many times over." Fuse nodded.

"You are indeed and if I am right there will be two more blessings shortly. We are all very excited at the prospect of a young hooded man."

"I must admit my friend I am finding it harder to stay patient, I am very excited and cannot wait for the moment when I raise my heir to my lord, and ask him to welcome him to the realm." Fuse noticed how there seemed to be a bright light kindled in his eyes as he spoke.

Scarlet stood on the wooden platform with her daughter by her side as she looked out across the battlefield. Phillip had gone off to sleep having watched for most of the night. Robbie came up by their side and looked out. The mighty army of the black soldiers still pushed hard, they had been a little more successful, but that had only been because Scarlet was now reorganising the army as she took on a different battle plan. Robbie admired her warrior ways; she was without doubt an expert tactician. Every time General Walters seemed to be getting an understanding of the way in which they fought, Scarlet changed everything and used a different approach. Under her leadership, the woodsmen had held a far superior force at bay for over six months.

She smiled as she looked down the scope at the general six miles away. "Claire old fatty one ear has got out of bed. Wish him a good morning and tell him it is about time, we have been kicking his ass for four hours now. Ask him if he would like some good advice, he needs it." Robbie and Ruby giggled as a very bright smiling Claire lifted the flags and in rapid sweeping movements, she sent the signal.

Scarlet watched down the scope as the general got the message. She burst into laughter and waved. "He has quite a temper this morning, maybe it was because I blew his wine delivery up, I do not think he likes fighting sober." She looked to Claire. "Alright it's time, give Commander Wilkes the signal."

Claire waved the flags and they all watched and waited. Robbie pulled his field scope out of his pocket and pulled it out, he watched as boards lifted into the heather and from behind them, a group of bowmen sent a volley of fizzing arrows into the advancing soldiers. The boards dropped flat as the woodsmen disappeared, and large explosions lifted men into the air, as smoke and flames rapidly engulfed the heather, the soldiers in black vests staggered about and fell. Scarlet seemed satisfied.

"You seem to be holding well Scarlet?"

"For now Robbie, we know he has a hell of a lot more troops stashed away. What I don't understand is why he is holding them back? It does bother me, if I had the amount of men, he has I would have been across this field and kicked him back to the sea. Why has he not used them makes no sense, he could swamp us in a day with the fighting power he has. I am ready for it, but believe me Robbie when he does finally think of it, we will move back rapidly to the outer reaches of York. He can have this barren ground; I will want trees around me." Robbie nodded he could understand her; he would prefer to fight in the trees as a woodsman should. Scarlet looked across at him. "How is the wood coming along, I have not been to York for two months?"

"Rune has done a fine job, I must admit I have not seen it myself for a bit, but last time I was there it was wonderful, it felt very much like Loxley."

As part of the back up plans, Rune had helped restore the ancient forests that had surrounded York. A two mile thick band of dense woodland now ran across the north of the city and down the eastern and western sides to meet the existing thick band of the south. Robbie had always known that at some point they would lose ground, it made good sense to give his men ideal fighting conditions for the last big battle. The woodland was now filled with woodsmen who prepared for the last battle. Fuse had worked the retreat plans out long before the attack plans; it was something Robbie had been worried about.

Now he saw the wisdom behind the plans of Fuse and Scarlet, wide corridors were created for the retreating soldiers, which could close quickly with the heavy defence from fresh men. The battle weary front line soldiers would head back into the city whilst the ten thousand strong, army of fresh fighters would meet the black army under the trees. It was a strategy designed to cushion York right up until the very last minute, and give the woodsmen the time to try to defeat their enemy. Robbie greatly admired the mind of Fuse; he truly was a great tactician and strategist. More flag waving went across the field; Robbie understood the code often used by woodsmen, but was surprised at the messages being sent. Scarlet gave the order to move five ranks forward, and Claire sent the signal to move five sideways. He looked at Claire who smiled.

"I did not get it wrong My Lord; we can read their signals so it makes sense they can read ours. The commanders have a command book each, the signal I send tells them what manoeuvre to make. The enemy prepare for us to move one way, and we move the other. It was Commander Rafe's idea, it works really well."

Scarlet gave a little chuckle.

"It seems my daughters precious Wolfman knows a thing or two about strategy, he has proven himself worthy of the command. I thought you only gave him the post so he could afford a house for my daughter." She gave Robbie a knowing look. He smiled

"I took the advice of Rowan, he seemed to think Rafe was worthy of the position. I believe it was good advice." Scarlet laughed.

"If you say so my Lord of Loxley. I am happy she has found a man who bites back; Jett will never settle with a weak man; she is a warrior like her mother. Rafe is good for her he keeps her focused." She stared down her scope at the battle lines. "Hello what have we here.... Ruby talk to Rune we have the beastie brigade at last."

Robbie saw the flicker behind Ruby's glasses; he turned and lifted his scope. Across the far side of the plain, he saw a large column of walking corpses forming ranks. There were at least ten thousand, Scarlet moved fast. "Claire let everyone know the Coffin Boys have arrived, tell them to prepare." Scarlet turned to the row of boys stood at the bottom of the slope waiting. "Waggstaff let the commanders know the Coffin Boys are here. I want the fourth and fifth division up here pronto, tell them to bring strikers." The young boy bowed and ran like the clappers down the path, Robbie watched as she turned to Claire. "Do they know?"

"Yes miss."

"Good right let's hope Rune has a surprise for Old Fatty One Ear, I would hate for him to get the upper hand." She lifted the scope to her eye. "He seems happy, might have known a corpse was the only thing to cheer him up." Robbie gave a smile, he really respected the way Scarlet led from the front, and he loved her dry humour and chuckled as he lifted his scope and watched.

Commander Haughton walked down his line. "Alright my howling fools; it's time to meet the coffin boys. I hate to dampen your party but killing this lot is not that easy as they are dead already. We will have strikers coming soon to blow the buggers off this grass, if the coffin boys get here first use your swords and cut their arms off first."

One of the woodsmen turned round looking very pale. "Why cut their arms off sir?" Commander Haughton gave an evil chuckle as he leaned into the soldier. His face came up really close to the young woodsman who looked terrified.

"If it aint got arms, it can't strangle you can it boy?" The young woodsman swallowed very deeply, the colour was draining fast from his already white face.

"No sir." The Commander smiled.

"If that don't work you can always give it a big juicy bite like your hero does." The men began to laugh as the young woodsman smiled. Commander Haughton walked back along his line with a smile.

"Whatever you do, keep your nerve, help each other and for god's sake, don't forget to howl." He laughed aloud and shook his head. "Bloody Rafe, he has buggered my discipline right up." The men along the line prepared and smiled as the thought of Rafe lifted their spirits.

A blue light flickered behind Robbie as Saff's window opened. Rowan was through first followed by the rest of the Specialists; he came running up the hill to Robbie's side. "I hear they are letting out the elderly, what you got in mind?" Robbie passed his scope over to Rowan.

"I will wait to see what Rune does, I thought we might take the Specialists down to the men and give them a boost, this is going to be hard for them although let's keep Harry at the back." Rowan chuckled as Robbie walked off the platform and the fourth and fifth division ran past with explosive arrows.

Rafe stood with Jett behind his unit and leaned back his head. "Ow Ohhhh!!!" The men turned and smiled at Commander Rafe and Commander Jett Amber who walked down to their unit. They felt the group warm immediately; Commander Haughton gave a big smile and shook their hands. "Good timing Commanders." Rafe walked proudly down the line.

"I hear we have the coffin boys dragging their limp butts across my field; we are not having that are we boys and girls?"

"NO SIR!" Jett beamed with delight at the side of Robbie as Rafe walked up and down.

"This aint the other realm, this is my field, I bit these buggers once, what we gonna do boys and girls?"

"BITE EM AGAIN SIR!" He gave a hearty laugh.

"We certainly are my snarling fools, ok are we ready for action?"

"YES SIR!

"Well what are you waiting for show em who is boss?"

"OW OHHH!!!" Rafe waved his hands as the whole front line threw back their heads and howled. Jett giggled as he conducted his howling orchestra. Commander Haughton bowed to Robbie.

"My Lord I am pleased to see you; your visit has lifted the spirits of the men." Robbie shook his hand.

"I understand the fear of fighting the dead; I have seen similar looks in the eyes of my Specialists."

"Commander Rafe has a good way of lifting them My Lord, they will be fine now. I command good men they all make me proud."

"I am proud of everyman we have up here, I know these moors are not easy. I did my fair share of time up here over the winter, it can be a harsh place to sit and wait." Robbie watched as the Specialist walked along the line talking to the soldiers, he saw the high level of respect they were shown from the young woodsmen who lay in wait for the army of the dead to begin its move across the moors.

Rafe walked smiling back along the row of men. "Wicks how is the wife? She had the little one yet?"

"A week or two left yet sir."

"Johnson how's the leg? You seemed to have hopped back here fast, I knew it was just a splinter." The others laughed as Rafe came up to Robbie and Commander Wilkes. "Glad to see you kept them singing in tune for me Mike."

He smiled at Rafe. "You have not been forgotten; they miss you Rafe. It has done them a world of good for you to visit, and they have a tough fight coming." Rafe nodded as he looked out into the distance where a drum beat, he knew that they would soon begin to move across the moors.

"I hope our good lady can help, these are difficult to beat, and how the hell do you kill the dead?" Ruby walked forwards and looked out over the barrier.

"If all else fails, we play with sunshine."

She even looked nervous, Harry was several yards behind the lines, and he was not going to get too close until he knew Rune had done her bit. Robbie knew ten thousand were a lot for even Rune to deal with, and some would get through, he looked at Rowan. "Bring all the Specialists with swords together. I want the unit ready to move once we see Rune. I want strikers for all the bowmen, and volunteer lighters to support them. Today we go side by side with the men of Loxley."

Rowan nodded and gave the whistle; the Specialists all looked up, and knew their time for action was upon them.

The drums on the far side of the long plain began to beat louder and Robbie knew it was time. The army of the dead were marching forward. He walked forward level with the front line and pulled up his hood. "I need twelve volunteers to aid the Specialists as striker lighters who will aid them?"

Five hundred woodsmen stood up. Robbie smiled at the loyalty and he nodded. "First six to my left and first six to my right fall in behind." Robbie raised his arm. "Specialists swords to form in an arrowhead at the front, bows to strike from the rear." He walked forward and passed the front line of the troops who rose to their feet and waved their swords and cheered, as Robbie and the Specialists walked out to meet the enemy. Scarlet came running down the hill and drew her golden sword, she ran out behind Robbie.

"You are not leaving me out of this one." She smiled as she came up to his side. Robbie gave her a wink as he slowly moved forward, the swordsmen formed a wide arrow shaped formation, and he looked to his right and saw Jade, Fish, Amethyst, Bear, Big John, Hawk, Harry, Blades, and Fox. To his left the line ran back with Scarlet, Rowan, Sting, Wolfie, Smokes, Jaz and Woody. He came to a halt and turned to the wide line of bows behind him. Each of them now had a woodsman with two quivers of stinger arrows. Stingers were an invention of Megs, they were smaller and thinner sticks of dynamite, they had been designed specifically for blowing up the army of the dead.

Robbie looked at his bows. Rags, Treen, Hornet, Sapphire, Maddy, Mel, Crystal, Jay, Una, Flash, and Pigeon all stood ready with their bows loaded, he nodded to them and they all smiled. Robbie turned, and faced the oncoming army. The violet figure of Rune rose at his side. "Hi gorgeous." She smiled.

"Hey beautiful, I missed you."

Rune looked at him. "I will not get them all Rob, there are simply too many to send back all at once."

He nodded. "I know we are ready."

"Just watch that gorgeous head for me." She winked and walked forward to meet the army of the dead as it approached across the moor. Robbie watched as she raised her arms into the air and stretched them wide. Robbie screamed out his commands. "SWORDS." The air was filled with the screech of swords being drawn from their scabbards, and the swords of seventeen Specialists rose into the air.

All along the front line, the soldiers of the woodland army stood up from behind their cover. All of them watched with baited breath as Rune walked alone across the moor. The strikers of the woodland army stood ready behind the front line and Commander Haughton walked up and down the line. "Today you will fight alongside the hooded man and his Specialists, they honour you. I want to see all of you honour them with a fight worthy of the measure of Loxley. You have true heroes amongst you, be like them."

Rune glowed deep violet as she brought forth the power of the Violetlines. Either side of her a wide curtain of violet shot up from the floor as she created a wall that would capture the essence of those passing through it and send it to the other realm. The army were now moving at speed toward her and she rose into the air above them as she commanded the souls of the lives of each of the men to return. Bright lights shot into the air as some of the dead collapsed, and were trampled under the feet of the others. They hit the curtain, which burned white and hundreds of beams of light shot into the sky as the bodies of many fell and their souls rose to travel to the other realm and be at peace.

The first of those who came through roared at Robbie. "Get Ready," he screamed as Destiny rose into the air. The army of the dead thundered forward as the Specialists braced for impact. Fizzing arrows whizzed past their shoulders and the first in the line exploded as the arrows hit and their rotting bodies disintegrated.

The rest hit with impact and the battle commenced. The Specialists cleaved and hacked at the dead as they crashed into them, four woodsmen jumped the blockades, and drew out their swords, as they ran to assist the Specialists and a wave of loyalty ran down the line as Commander Haughton screamed at them. "Well, what are you waiting for? Go and bloody well help them."

A tide of green surged forward, roaring with hate as they met the oncoming army and battling sides met with venom. It was bedlam as each of them hacked and cleaved their way through to each other to stand side by side and protect each other. Arrows flew by the hundred, fizzing into the midst as the bowmen with deadly accuracy, took out the over whelming odds off the swords men. It was a hard brutal bloody fight and Robbie now flanked with Scarlet, and Rowan cleared a circle around them and struck out at anything that crossed their line.

Flashes of gold glinted in the midst a huge crowd as Sting spun on her golden heels screaming and yelling, her blade slicing at the dead as they passed her. Rafe covered left as Jet moved towards Rowan, and slowly a long straight line of swords was forming as the Specialists with some of the woodsmen brought order to the fight.

Harry and Blades worked like tornadoes, Harry was scared to death, and he chanted his mantra over and over and closed his eyes for a moment just to rest from seeing the dead in front, as his swords spun like lightening through already dead tissue. His enemy did not scream or yell out in pain they just dropped at his feet in bits as he jumped over them not daring to touch them, his pendant clasped firmly in his teeth as he chanted and mumbled.

Bear roared loudly as his axe came one way and his sword the other, he ploughed into the army and battered them down with huge force. Blades whooped and screamed as her swords moved with rapid cold precision. Amethyst who was a powerful swimmer was a surprisingly powerful swords woman. With her legs pushed firmly into the ground at the side of Fish, her strokes were like lightning and the speed of her blade hacked the army in half as they passed her. Fox held his protection to the side of Blades, and the line came forward slowly to meet level with Robbie. Big John hit out with huge power sending most he hit with the sword flying back into the advancing masses that stumbled and fell. As they got back up the fizzing arrows hit them and they burst into fragments.

Two hundred swords of Loxley now joined the Specialists as they moved forward leaving a trail of hacked devastation. Four hundred followed behind with swords and bows cleaning up and shooting between the swords taking out many before they could meet a blade. It was a terrible fight as the swords drew level with the violet curtain, and stopped five feet away. They had advanced from their own front line over two thousand yards and Philip screamed from behind as the rear guards lifted the wooden barriers and moved forward to push closer to the enemy.

The black army had made a big mistake. The dead don't think, and Robbie now realised that they just came forward waving weapons. They were not capable of holding a thought out fight, they were just fodder to be sliced down and thei numbers were irrelevant, he did not face an army that was organised or disciplined, this was just mass sword practice. The Dark One had made a big mistake and now her army of many was being slaughtered.

Not one soldier of the dead made it past the bows, and Commander Haughton bellowed at the reinforcements as they arrived and got them to dig in behind the barrier. Four feet behind the long line of firing bowmen and women, the new soldiers dug with great speed. The soft peat gave easily as they sunk their spades deep and soon a long wide trench was opening up ready for the defence of a new front line.

The battle raged for over an hour; it was the most brutal any would ever witness.

Robbie's hair hung wet and straggly from his face, as the sweat poured off him in the afternoon heat, Philip brought down a thousand swordsmen and lined them up ready along the new barrier. The signal was given and as the Specialists, and woodsmen stepped back. A new line of fresh swordsmen stepped forward, the bows fired a thick hail through the violet curtain to ease the change over and the exhausted Specialists and their brave soldiers all gasped a sigh of relief as fresh arms moved into the onslaught. They all quickly moved through the barriers as a new line of striker bowmen moved into the side of the first line of bows, and as they lifted and fired the first line stepped back and came through the barriers behind the front line.

Maggs ran round with a team of women passing out cool drinks and water. She smothered a hot sweaty frightened looking Harry with wet slippery kisses. "Oh, my big brave Harry pops, I love you to bits." He was white and very shaky but he smiled.

"Hey chicken I totally dig your vibes." Blades chuckled as she crashed on to the floor and tossed a severed hand out of the way, Harry squealed as it landed next to him. It was the final straw of the bravest day of his life, he passed out, Maggs squealed, and grasped his head and patted his cheeks. Harry moaned as he came slowly back to his tie dyed queen of loving.

Robbie sat red in the face with his head down as he gasped for air. The sweat ran off his nose and onto the blood stained crushed heather. Rowan and Jade panted at his side, everyone had cuts and bruises, some were gashed, and were getting medical attention but so far, not one man had been lost. The army of the dead were incapable of defending themselves and Robbie knew how it would lift morale for his men and weaken it for the other side.

The ice cool water flowed over his head and he moaned in delight as he lifted his head and saw the violet eyes of a smiling Rune. "Hi sweaty."

"Hey beautiful." He tilted his head back as she poured it over his face; it was heaven as it cooled the fire of his skin. Bits of his face were nicked and they stung as the water washed away the sweat, he didn't care it was enough. She leaned forward and kissed him.

"You need a bath, that is as much as you get until then, I will see you at home." She gave him a wink and faded away.

Jett sat on Rafe's lap red faced and sweaty as she kissed him slowly. She giggled as her face slipped off his. Jade was curled around Rowan exhausted; Robbie looked round at his tired team. Two young women in green walked up to Crystal and Maddy, the two exhausted women looked up as the young female woodsmen offered their hands. "Madam Madeleine of Carnac, Madam Crystal, we were honoured to have been able to fight beside you." Maddy looked shocked and smiled as she lifted her hand.

"You honoured all the Specialists with your support, thank you." The two girls beamed as they shook hands, and shouldered their bows and walked off back to their posts. Robbie smiled at the two surprised looking women. Ruby gave a giggle at Maddy's side.

Robbie gave the signal and the Specialists tooled up, there were very few left of the army of the dead and the soldiers of Loxley were now in control. They made their way in a weary line, dirty and sweaty toward the look out which was now a much longer walk. The soldiers of Rafe's platoon stood just as hot and sweaty, and patted the shoulders and saluted the Specialists as they walked back. Robbie and Rowan were last and at the top of the hill Robbie stopped, and turned and looked at all the tired happy faces.

The Specialists stood around him as he lifted his hood. "The hooded man and his Specialist were honoured to fight with such men of courage." He lifted his bow in salute to the soldiers. All the Specialists raised their hoods and lifted their bows into the sky; Commander Haughton smiled and nodded as his men beamed with pride. The window opened and they turned and left. Amethyst was first out of the window, she ran to the mere, and as she ran her sword, dagger and bow dropped with her cloak and her shirt and she dived into the cool water. She came up and screamed with delight. Jett and Jade had their boots off and had stripped to their knickers and short tops and followed, they landed in the cool lake with wild screams.

Within minutes, the mere was filled with happy cool screaming faces and Rune howled with laughter as they all cooled down and messed around. The grass was covered with weapons and clothing as they enjoyed the relief of the heat.

Robbie walked out dripping to her bright smiling face. "I am no longer sweaty." She beamed.

"No but you are soaking and I cannot run away, it's not fair." He chuckled as he lifted her up and turned to the mere. "Oh ... no Rob I am pregnant you cannot." He walked toward the screaming crowd of the Specialists. "Rob no I am fully dressed... Oh god no." He walked into the mere and she screamed as he lowered her gently into the cool water, he smiled.

"One Specialist has a bath, we all have a bath." Rune giggled as the others all screamed with laughter and splashed around in the water. "Anyway, I need protecting, look what happened last time I went swimming." Her bright eyes beamed at him and he held her close in the water. "Now we are both wet," and he kissed her softly.

CHAPTER ELEVEN

PREPARING FOR THE VIOLET ISLE

Martin Jarrod had awoken just before dawn. He built up his fire and cooked himself a good breakfast, as the sun began to show in the east and he knew it was going to be a wonderful hot dry day. He sat on the edge of the rocky outcrop and looked down over the lush green trees and castle in the mist below him in the distance. He ate slowly and enjoyed the leisure of taking his time, for twenty years, his life had lived the regimented lifestyle, and it was a thrill just to take his time over everything. He gave a long stretch and yawned; walking back to his campfire he poured a drink and cleaned his plate. He had a few hours before the sun would climb high enough in the sky to signal his departure, so he took down his small shelter and carefully packed it on to his horse.

Living the life of a soldier had robbed him of so many things, like just sitting surrounded by trees and actually being able to enjoy the colour of each leaf as the sun passed through it. The birds flew up and down from the rock face as they tended their young; he watched with keen interest as the male blackbird fluttered to the floor, and scratched the surface finding long worms to pull up. He had always thought he was living his life, and now he sat watching the wonders of nature, he realised that in many ways he had stopped living and not noticed. Years of routine and serving the army had swamped him in the toil of daily duty, and now he could see what a waste it had all been. His time had been swallowed up with his work and he somehow had started to take everything for granted, he had not really lived his life; he had merely existed in the routine of his job and career.

By the time the sun was high enough, he was wide awake and feeling more alive than he had in years. He killed the fire, and removed all visible signs of it, and climbed up on to his horse, he now faced the prospect of a new future, and in many ways a new beginning. It was time to try and undo the wrongs of his black past and he had no idea how he could face such a challenge; he just felt the bright violet light of hope inside him. He rode across the open glade and on to the path that would lead to the cliff and his future, the cliff path was wide and smooth with soft grass and he found it easy going as it rose at a gentle incline towards the high woods.

The fire was crackling and the coffee pot was steaming when Ben opened his eyes. The rain had been heavy the previous night, and he had slipped right back to the inside wall of the overhang where he was dry, he stretched under the blankets, he felt cosy on the soft bed of moss and broken bracken leaves.

"You slept sounder than an old log my friend, it is nice to know we can sleep safe around friends, it removes the uncertainty of being alone does it not?" The Sage smiled as Ben sat up and rubbed his eyes, he peered around a little dazed, which made the Sage laugh. "Maybe you slept a little too sound, I would say the five helpings of stew last night has sedated you, you must have doubled in weight you ate so much." He gave a chuckle as he held out a plate.

"If you can find the room, we have a little pork and eggs for breakfast." Ben smiled as his eyes cleared and they began to focus, he took the plate and fork and sat in the corner greedily eating the hot food. The Sage placed a hot tea beside him. "I wonder where you put it all, never have I known someone so skinny manage to cram thrice his own volume in food." He gave a soft chuckle as he walked out into the clearing and he closed his eyes as he looked up to the sun and warmed his face. A loud belch echoed under the overhang, and the Sage raised his arms. "Praise the lord of the woodland I have finally filled him." He turned to see a smiling Ben lift the cup to his mouth; he gulped down the hot drink and sat back against the wall with a happy face.

The Sage walked over and poured himself another cup, he raised the pot but Ben waved his hand; he had eaten and drunk enough. "You are talkative first thing in a morning Master Winters." Ben relaxed against the wall.

"I was tired after yesterday; it was a long day for me." The Sage took a large drink.

"It was also profitable, you worked hard for the money you took, and it was well earned my young friend." He looked back to the trees and was quiet for a moment. "We will have two visits today my friend; I feel destiny will beckon to us. I am now starting to understand that it was not by chance that we met."

He watched the tree line for a moment as if sensing something, he reminded Ben of the deer when you strayed too close to them and they froze for an instant, before running away. The Sage turned and looked at Ben sat under the rock. "We have company on horseback, I can hear him."

Ben sat still and strained his ears; he could hear nothing at all, he sat still using all his powers of concentration and he still only heard the swaying of the trees in the soft breeze. He looked up at the Sage who now walked across and squatted by the fire next to his bow. It was then that he heard it.

A horse panted in the trees, the Sage leaned the bow across his lap as the trees parted and the horse wandered into the clearing with a tall grey haired man sat on the back. Ben watched him carefully, his clothes were of quality and he did not look like a farmer. He was no woodsman for he had a dagger but no woods knife, his mustard shirt and grey pants looked well tailored, the black canvass waistcoat reminded him of the soldiers that had once passed through the town, Ben felt nervous as the Sage rose and smiled.

"Good morning General." Jarrod looked surprised as he viewed the green clad man with a white wooden mask. The General nodded.

"Good morning stranger, you appear to know of me and yet I am sorry for I know not your name. I have been sent to seek the Sage, would that be you my masked friend?" The Sage gave a bow; Ben felt he was less friendly to the General than he had been of him.

The Sage moved slowly keeping his hand firm on his bow. "I have crossed your path once or twice and know you by reputation, as for my name folk do call me by that name. I will respond if it's used."

The General pulled something from his pocket. "I have been sent to find you green friend, I was given this to pass on to you as a token of intention." He flicked something at the Sage who caught it in one hand and smiled as he looked down at it.

"This is a surprise to me; I know the source of this token. The lady gave you this personally and told you to seek me out?" The General nodded at him.

"I no longer use the term general, that time in my life is over. I am a simple traveller now; I go by my own name; I am Martin Jarrod." The Sage looked up from his hand and smiled at him.

"Then welcome Martin, come and sit by the fire and have a drink with me and my young friend, I feel we shall have more guests soon." The Sage looked down at the blue butterfly in his hand he nodded to himself and crouched down. Martin slipped off his horse and tied it to a small tree; he came over to the fire as the Sage poured another cup. He handed the butterfly back to Martin. "You should carry this with you at all times my friend; you will find it has the power of protection."

Martin took the butterfly back, he was relieved in a way, as he had looked at it many times in the past month as he had remembered the eyes of life and love that had looked upon him in the tent the night he raised the gun. She had changed him forever in that single moment; the butterfly was a precious memory.

The Sage smiled. "The lady of the woods is very beautiful is she not? Her eyes hold the key to all questions in life, that token one day will be the treasure of your house, keep it safe." The Sage handed him a cup of hot tea. "I must admit Martin Jarrod I am surprised to see you out of uniform, have you left the services of the Dark Army for good?"

Martin felt a little uncomfortable with this stranger in a mask knowing so much about him; he had walked away from that life and now wished to be anonymous. "You know a great deal about me Master Sage, I have left that life behind me now, tell me how you have so much knowledge of me for with a mask I will not know who I address. Will you not remove it so we can talk as equals?"

"I am known as the Sage, a man who has answers to many things, even those who command the armies. My mask is a necessity, for there are few who could look upon me unmasked and not feel revulsion. Trust me my friend I am true to my word and you are safe here amongst us, any man who will turn from the path you walked is a brave man. He is also a man who has been touched with violet light I think, I see your heart is clear and you strive to repair a life wasted. We are all in our way looking to help and repair the bad in this realm, you are welcome here. This small man with a large appetite is young Master Ben; he is my companion and yours if you wish to stay."

Ben gave a nod to Martin who stretched out his hand. "Hello Ben, I am pleased to meet you." Ben took his hand and gave him a smile. The Sage rose from his seat and looked to the trees

"I believe our guest arrives." Violet shimmered around the trees and Rune came out and smiled, the Sage fell to one knee. "My Lady of the Woods you honour myself and my companions with your visit." Rune glowed with bright violet as she smiled at Martin and then looked at Ben, who felt afraid and slipped back under the overhang to his bedding. Rune crouched down and looked deep inside the overhang.

"Fear not Master Winters for you are safe amongst friends. I see you have made acquaintance with my travelling friend, I am glad to see this, for my time here is short the black army moves its darkest soldiers and I will be needed shortly." She turned to the Sage who watched her carefully. "Walk with me my green friend for I have words for you and words for you all."

Rune walked slowly back to the trees with the Sage and spoke quietly to him. "You have done many things in your time for these people my green friend; I am pleased that you use your gift of foresight to the advantage of all others. I know of your line for you are a life in my realm, I would ask that you guide these companions in a task set for you by the Green Lord. Would you be willing to help the realm of the hooded man?"

The Sage kept his head slightly bowed for he knew that the lady of the woods knew of his ugliness, and even with his mask, he knew he could not hide it from her. "My Lady of the Woods, I would do anything to aid the hooded man in his task against the dark powers that crush the world I was raised to love."

She gave him a soft smile. "I see the same love of the woodland in your heart as I see in many of its realm; I find joy in knowing your love of my realm Master Sage. I have watched you for some time my green friend, hard has been your life and yet you have shown favour and kindness to all that have crossed you in need."

"It is indeed a great honour My Lady to know someone as insignificant as I have had your protection, I feel honoured by it."

"I have always watched my green friend, I know of the pain and where its source lies, I see the struggle in you to come to terms with your life, I know that the Green

Lord has watched you with interest. He will aid your road from this time have no fear."

The Sage looked up at her fair smiling face. "I hide the ugliness of myself from all, why would the Green Lord want to look at me?"

Rune smiled a soft and gentle smile. "Where some see ugliness my green friend, others can see great beauty. Wear your mask and hide if that is what you desire, there will still be a light that shines in you as it always has my friend." He felt worthless under her gaze and he lowered his head as he felt a great shame on him, how could someone so beautiful see him in the same way. "Walk me back to the others and we will talk more later, for there are many tasks destined for you if you can aid the high lord of this realm in the task he has set you." She turned and walked slowly back to the camp. Ben had crawled a little further forward and she gave him a sweet smile.

"You see Master Winters, I am not the Violet Witch that gobbles up children and tortures their souls, you must be more careful of the stories you hear. My name is Runestone, and I am wife to the hooded man and the Lady of the realm of life. I seek only good in this world and I have no appetite for children, like you I prefer stew, although I fear even I cannot eat as much as you." She giggled, as he looked completely shocked.

"How do you know that? It was dark when we got back." She gave a smile as the Sage and Martin both tittered.

"I know all things about all who live in my realm, including their capacity for stew." Ben was stunned and very impressed.

"Wow you must know loads of stuff." She laughed as she crouched down.

"I have my fair share of knowledge... My friends I must leave soon to aid the hooded man, Lord Hearne has a task that he will need great assistance with, you will not be unaided but it is very important that this task be completed within three weeks. It will not be easy but it is very important to the future events of the woodland realm, are you prepared to do your best and assist him?"

Martin looked at the Sage. "I cannot speak for my companions but I am willing as you know My Lady to make amends for the evil I have been party to. Without knowing the task, I cannot say if I can achieve it." The Sage nodded.

"I have seen glimpses of the task your lord will set us. It will not be easy, but this morning when my friend Martin rode into our camp, I felt it got easier. Can the high lord prevent news of Martin reaching the town; it will aid us greatly if there is ignorance of his status." Rune smiled.

"I see the freedom of the wilds has been good to you my green friend, your ability grows stronger by the day. It can be arranged that you arrive without word, I have the ability for that."

The Sage looked back at Martin. "Then my good lady I know this task can be done." Rune laid a hand on the arm of the Sage.

"My high lords faith in you is well founded Master Sage, it pleases me." Rune got up from the fire, and looked down upon them. "Make haste and we will meet on the road, I must leave for there is great danger in the north, I will return to you soon." Rune turned and walked across the glade to the trees, there was a bright violet shimmer as she passed through, and then the trees swayed gently in the breeze. Martin looked up at the sage.

"What is this task and in what town is it?"

The Sage gave a big smile. "It's in Tintagel; we have a prisoner to free." Martin looked dumbfounded as Ben watched lost in the conversation.

"Master Sage there is only one prisoner in there I know of, and he is in a glass box on her table. Tintagel is a fortress and impossible to just walk into, especially since the attack of the hooded man."

The Sage nodded in agreement and smiled. "It's not hard to enter if you are a general though, is it?"

Martin now began to understand all of the conversation and he smiled. "You are indeed a wise man my green friend." He nodded, as Ben looked even more confused. The Sage stood up and looked at the sun.

"Three weeks is not long, Ben pack up your kit we have a long walk ahead of us, and we have but one horse, although I do know one or two farmers." He turned quickly and lifted his cup and drained it, he shook it and lifted a green cloth bag, which was already packed. He slid the cup inside and shook out the empty coffee pot, and slid it into his bag and smiled. "I am ready when you two are." He turned and looked at the sun. "It's that way." He pointed south and smiled.

As Robbie and the Specialists fought their battle on the moors of Yorkshire against the dreaded army of the dead, the Sage with Martin and young Ben began their journey from the high pass of the woodland and down the mountain. They descended through destroyed towns and villages and made their way south, away from the small farming town towards the wild open country of Southern Wales.

The Sage seemed to guide, he watched the sun and knew the direction to head, and soon they found themselves crossing the wild rocky moors and mountain ranges of the welsh countryside. Martin seemed to find Ben good company, although Ben hardly stopped talking for most of their long days travel. It was early evening when they reached the top of the large hill and looked out across the long clear blue lake below. Martin smiled as he saw it. "I know of this place; it is the lake of mystery and sunken towns."

Ben looked up at him. "Sunken towns, how do you mean?" The Sage gave a smile to Martin, it must have been his thousandth question today; he admired the patience that Martin had shown. They began to walk slowly down the steep long hill that led down to the water's edge, Martin walked beside Ben.

"At one time this was a green valley with no water in it; there was a small town right in the bottom of this valley.

"Ben looked down in front of him at the very large and long lake. "What happened to the town it's just water down there?" Martin patted his shoulder.

"There once was a very horrible nobleman, who wanted to celebrate the birth of his son and he asked a harp player to make music at his very spectacular party. Now the harp player did not like the nobleman but he needed the money and agreed to play. He played all night and the guests ignored him and got very drunk and wild. While he was playing a voice spoke to him and said come with me, and when he turned round he saw a small blue bird."

"Wow what did he do Martin?"

"Well, he was being ignored and unhappy about it, so he left his harp behind and he followed the bird. It took him out of the town and right up to the top of that hill just over there see."

"Wow he must have been bored to walk all the way up there." Ben looked across at the very steep and high hill across the lake; the Sage gave a smile as Martin continued his story.

"Well, when he got to the top of the hill, the bird just vanished, as you can see it is a hard climb, so he lay down in the grass and had a sleep. He slept all night and when he woke in the morning and sat up, he looked down on the huge lake. The town was drowned, and gone forever; all he could see was his harp floating in the water."

"What about all the people who lived there, where did they go Martin?" Ben looked up at him with a very worried look on his face.

Martin chuckled as he put his arm across the shoulder of Ben. "They were all horrible and so they all drowned in the sunken town."

"I am not going near that water; it might be cursed." The Sage gave a loud laugh, as Ben eyed the water suspiciously.

"Fear not Master Winters we will keep a good eye on you. I will not easily allow the spirits to whisk you off." They came into the tree line at the base of the hill and walked in the cool shade of the trees, it was very quiet and peaceful as the Sage looked from side to side for signs of other life. "I think we will camp here tonight, there are tracks so I will go and find us something for a meal." His slipped his bow down and headed off into the trees. "Get a fire going Ben, I will be back shortly." Martin tied the horse to the tree and began to lift their bags off.

Rune giggled wildly as Robbie carried her dripping up the glade in his arms. Jett's screams mingled with large splashes and Jade's wild hysterics echoed behind them. She looked up at his smiling face with large bright eyes, and he smiled as he kissed her. "It has been a hard day for them; it will do them good to have some fun."

She had her arms round his neck and she kissed him softly on the cheek. "You fought with great power today Rob, I was frightened at first when I saw them, and I knew I would not be able to send all of them back."

He reached the glass doors and headed for the stairs. "I saw the fire in the eyes of the men, I knew we would all fight Rune, and I just felt we would win." She nodded.

"The sight of you does give them all faith."

"It was they who gave me the faith Rune... Come on get those wet things off and get dry." Robbie set her down, and opened the large cupboard door where a big pile of towels was stacked. He pulled several out and walked across the room as she slipped off her dress. Robbie wrapped a large bright blue towel round her and pulled her close.

He rubbed her gently to dry her and she gave him a big grin as he ensured she was warm. It was a quarter of an hour later when Rune sat brushing her long wet hair and Robbie sat rolled in his towel and rubbed his to dry it. The Specialists still screamed outside in the Mere. Her long red hair hung bright and shining down her back, as wrapped in a towel she crawled on to the bed and sat behind him.

She took the towel off him and rubbed his hair, she giggled, as it all stood on end in long spikes, "Would you like me to brush it?" He smiled, he loved it when Rune softly brushed his hair, it calmed and relaxed him. Rune watched his face in her dressing table mirror as she sat behind him and pulled her fingers through his hair removing all the knots. Robbie smiled and closed his eyes at the feel of the soft brush; his head fell forward slightly as she pulled the brush down to the tip of his long hair.

She watched him carefully in the mirror. "This war is going to get harder, isn't it?" He opened his eyes and saw her bright blue eyes watching him in the mirror.

"They want to destroy us and they have the numbers, it will not be too long before they realise and send out everything at us." She looked down at his hair as she brushed and then back up at him. He knew her well enough to know something was worrying her. She gave a soft smile.

"I do not have long now Rob." He watched her as she brushed and thought of the right words. She looked up and her eyes sparkled bright blue. "You will be there won't you?" She stopped brushing as she looked at him. "I want you with me when she comes Rob."

Robbie gave her a big smile. "Just try and stop me. I want to be the first to see those bright violet eyes that are as beautiful as her mother's." Rune broke into a huge smile and her eyes danced with delight. He turned and pulled her round into his lap. "Rune please do not worry so much; I will be there at your side and I will take your hand and we shall see our children come into the world together. I will not leave you Rune, this will be a vulnerable time for you and I want to be there and know you are alright."

Rune slid her arms round him and held him close. "It is so important to me Rob. I know you are Lord Loxley with all of your duties, and I have responsibilities as well. It's just that... Well, you are my husband now, and we will soon be a family. I guess I just want to make sure that on this one day more than any, we will be a family and be close; these are my first children Rob. This is very special for me."

He gave her a big smile as he lifted her closer. "It is important to me too Rune, I want to be there at your side all the way through." Rune smiled as he looked down at her and he slowly lowered his head to hers and gave her a soft kiss. "I love you Runestone." She snuggled into him as he held her tight.

Ben jumped as three hares landed dead at his side. "There you go young Master Winter's, I am sure we have enough there even to fill your bottomless stomach. Ben smiled as Martin pulled a long penknife out of his pocket and worked on cleaning the hares. They did not have a great deal of vegetables, but it made for a very meaty stew. The three of them sat in amongst the small circle of trees by the fire, the Sage leaned back against the trunk of the tree and stared out across the lake as he ate. Martin could see he was thinking about the task, he seemed to feel a strong connection with the Sage even though he had known him for less than a day. There was something about him; it was as if he had a strange aura of calmness around him. He noticed Martin watching him and smiled. "What's on your mind Martin?" He put his bowl down on the grass and lifted his cup as Martin watched him.

"You say we have crossed paths, and yet I do not remember anything at all of you."

The Sage nodded. "I looked very different at that time, I was not in need of a mask, you will not remember me. I see changes in you also; you have lost some of the stiffness in your attitude, I see less of a soldier and more of a man now. We all change as we go through life, the changes that happened to me gave me the ability to see and read the future. You have been given the chance to see the truth and life as the great beauty it is. We are both very lucky men my friend, we have a very important chance to do something of great value in this world."

Martin nodded in agreement; as Ben watched the two men, Martin looked up. "You must have a name; no man is born being called the Sage." The Sage gave a little chuckle.

"No, I once had the name of a man, but I chose to leave a life that was filled with pain behind me and put on the mask and become nameless. It is people who have named me, and now I just accept the name they gave me. If you do not like Sage, call me something different; I have no use of a label for the person I am. I accept a name given me by many simply because it is convenient to those who wish to talk to me."

"I like Sage; I think it really seems to fit you." Ben gave a huge smile and the Sage nodded.

"I thank you Master Winter." Ben scooped another large spoonful of stew on to his plate.

"I am not objecting Sage, I can assure you, I was curious more than anything."

"You are in the wild with two strangers; I understand that you are making sure we are who you think. I can assure you my friend you are quite safe, sleep safely tonight in the knowledge that you are protected."

The Sage stood up and stretched, he gathered the empty bowls and walked through the trees towards the edge of the lake where he crouched and washed them. The sun was slipping low and it was very quiet, only the gentle sound of the water rippling up to the shore could be heard. Most of the birds seemed to be settling and the whole place seemed to be bathed in a gentle calmness. The Sage found it restful; Ben found it creepy his eyes darted to the water's edge many times, just to make sure that the water level was the same.

As the sun died and the Sage stoked up the fire, Ben settled beside him in his blankets. The Sage with his back to the tree sat and watched the world around them; He slipped his hands into the long fluted sleeves of his coat like cloak and rested as he kept watch. Martin settled down close to the fire and talked quietly so as not to disturb Ben.

"This will not be any easy task; Tintagel is a very well defended stronghold."

The bright eyes of the Sage glowed in the dark behind his mask of birch. "You will get us in, after that let me worry about getting into her web. There is a new queen coming and we will need the old wizard to help protect her, we cannot fail; her life will depend on it."

"Why is it I feel you have been in her quarters before?"

The Sage gave a long sigh, "I have, and it was not pleasant. I must admit it is not something I am looking forward to again, she has grown in power in hiding and I fear for any who has to face her, she is more deadly than a snake." He looked down at Martin in the darkness. "The lady of the woods has something in mind; I shall not be alone in there."

"How do you mean you will not be alone? There are three of us, we will not see you enter and face her without protection."

The Sage gave a soft smile in the darkness. "Thank you my friend, but you and Ben will not protect me from her, she will kill you with a single thought. This is a task; I know has been set for me alone, I have the power of sight and for me it is some protection, you and Ben will have to cover the outside while I help free the old wizard. I am greatly reassured to know I will have you watching my back, just make me one promise Martin?"

He sat up and looked across the fire as the light of the flames danced on his white mask. "What promise I can make to you I will, what is it you ask of me?"

"The boy, promise me if anything happens to me you will care for him, he has a stout heart, and will grow to be a man of high value. Take him to Loxley and have the Lord there protect him, I know the Lord of the woodland realm will keep him safe." Martin looked at the small sleeping figure of Ben; he looked back into the shining eyes of the Sage.

"What have you seen, I have watched you and I know you have seen something of the outcome of our task. Can you not tell me, you have my solemn word the boy will be protected with my life?"

The Sage looked down and the front of his hood fell across his face. "Thank you, Martin, I have watched him for some time and his life has been hard, he deserves a chance to make himself a better man. As for our task I have seen little that will give the outcome, just call it a gut feeling I am unsure at this point if I will walk free again."

Martin rested on his arm as he watched. "You will come out, I will leave no man behind, I never have and it is not a habit I intend to start now."

Martin sat quietly lost in thought as the flame flickered and danced around the trees, it was not long before he lay back and closed his eyes. He slept deeply beside the fire as the bright eyes of the Sage stared into the dark, there was a sadness to them as the thoughts of a life once lived a long time ago cast a dullness across them. His mind echoed with the sounds of a screaming woman as she was brutally tortured and finally died across the body of her dead husband, the house burned, and the black smoke wafted into his lungs and the flames licked up higher and higher. He watched as the long white hair and the cold blue eyes of a tall man in black stared around. "FIND THAT BOY!!!"

The Sage opened his eyes with a start; he had fallen asleep and pushed his back into the tree. He felt the sweat run down behind his mask, as he looked around. The fire had died to just embers and the two figures slept quietly beside it, he leaned forward, and placed two large logs on to it and gently blew, the embers glowed bright in the dark, and flames sprang up and kissed the new wood. He sat back and pulled a cloth from his pocket, quietly the Sage got up and walked to the water's edge, he pulled off his mask and dampening the cloth in the water, he wiped his hot face. The cloth was cold and it eased the burning of his skin, he took long deep breaths to calm his inner turmoil. He put the mask back on and stood in the moonlight as he watched the white mists rolling across the top of the lake surface and into the reeds.

The Sage turned in the darkness of the early morning and walked back into the camp, he picked up his bow and turned, the dark alert eyes of Ben looked up at him. He smiled and crouched down. "Where are you going?" Ben looked frightened. He smiled and patted his shoulder.

"I feel your hunger will awaken soon and we will not have enough to keep it quiet. Go back to sleep Ben, you are safe here. I will go and hunt a meal, have no fear I will not leave you, and neither will Martin we are as one now. Go on sleep a while longer we will have a long walk today."

Ben smiled at him. "I like you and Martin; I have never had many friends to stand by me before."

He gave a smile. "Well you have two now, as do Martin and myself. Sleep now and I will provide breakfast when you wake." Ben settled back under his blankets and closed his eyes. The Sage watched for a few moments and then like a shadow he slipped without sound into the dark, Martin smiled his eyes closed as he lay quietly by the fireside. They had been three souls adrift, and it seemed that they had come together and found a bond to bind them. He agreed with the Sage, it was nice to know he had two friends to stand by him.

Two bright shining blue eyes peered up though the tangle of red and gold shimmering hair. "Oh, is that bacon I smell?" Her pale slender hands came out from under the cover, and pulled the hair apart. Rune looked up as Robbie sat on the bed with the tray of bacon, and tomatoes. There was a plate piled high with unevenly cut slices of toast and a large mug of coffee.

Her bright face beamed as she sat up and he fluffed the pillows behind her. "Good morning Beautiful, you hungry?" He gave her a big smile as she pulled the tray towards her.

"Oh I am starving." She giggled as she cut into the bacon and chewed with a look of delight on her face. "I love breakfast in bed, you spoil me." He sat down and pulled his fried eggs over. Rune lifted her toast and stabbed his egg with it.

"Hey, I love doing that." She gave a giggle as her eyes sparkled and she bit off the yellow coloured toast.

"You should be quicker; it's been weeks since I had an egg." They sat side by side in bed, and ate their breakfast as they happily talked. Rune began to plan the visit to Iona; they were now three days into June, and Rune was close to the time of the birth, she had just three weeks left, and she knew soon would be the time for her to leave Loxley. She would have the child on the island that would become her home as queen in future years.

There had been a lot of preparation behind the scenes and Gwinne on her return from her break in Loxley, had finally met with Isolde and Filomena, who would protect and care for the new Queen of Fae. Gwynfor had found a new lease of life as his kin came back to the island, and he laughed and joked with everyone. The truth was that when you live to his age you can get very bored, he had spent ten years in a cave below Stonehaven. Being back on his homeland he felt at last that everything he had spent his long life preparing for was now ending. He would welcome the new queen and pass on the information he needed to her so that he could ensure the legacy of his sister's line. He was also enjoying the feel of the breeze and the grass and sand between his toes, it had been a very long time since he had walked on his native soil. It was quite normal to see the old man stood on the grass looking down the long hill and watching the sea, as he remembered a time long since passed where he and his sister ran wild on the island. He always wore a smile.

Gwinne had become very attached to the wrinkled old man, with a very cheeky smile and eyes that danced with his mischief. She would walk along the beach with him at low tide and talk and laugh. "I remember Rayne when he was a very cheeky kid, I saw a lot of pranks behind his eyes, and you could tell he would never quite be his father. Pwhyll is a good lord, but I must admit he loves his rules, now Rayne; he was a lot like his Auntie Eve. Oh yes she was full of fun she was, we got into some trouble I can tell you. She could find ways of making me smile; she loved Rayne, played with him for hours on the beaches. You could see it between them he was her favourite and no doubt."

"He talked of her a few times, but it seemed hard for him." Gwinne saw the sadness pass before the old man's eyes.

"He took it badly when we lost her, you know I am not sure you realise how much good you did. Eleanor could not seem to reach him neither could Rhiannon. She was broken hearted as well. They were close as sisters, the Green Lord wanted to protect everyone and prevented her and Rayne from going after her; it almost broke Rayne and then along you came just when he needed love in his life." He gave Gwinne a big smile. Gwinne had never really heard the full story.

"What really happened Gwynfor?"

"Oh, it was an evil time; most of the line still will not talk of it. The Black One was growing in power and starting to play with the dark lines. Merlin went mad at her and threatened he would destroy her if she did not stop. No one knew she was carrying on in secret, she came out of the sky and took poor Opal and Gwendolyn. Then she came and stole her daughters with their tiny children, it was a wicked time, and we all thought she had killed them. Rhiannon and Eve went after her, and Rhiannon was badly wounded, Eve was killed shortly after. Poor sweet wonderful Eve, you know I look at your youngest and I see her in her eyes."

"In Amethyst?" Gwinne seemed surprised.

"She has a look of her, although Eve had sapphire blue eyes that seemed to colour violet at times, I see it strongest in Runestone. Hearne was heartbroken he had a rage like I had never seen, but he was a fool and let it get the better of him. The Black One knew he would be filled with pain and she exploited it, if he had just been calmer, he would have destroyed her. I suppose we are lucky he did not destroy the Earth, oh his anger was terrifying I hid for a year I was so scared of him."

"How could she trap the creator? It does not make sense. The Green Lord is the most powerful of all the lines."

"Well apart from Albanlin of course, but you see he is also male. I will tell you now my dear, no matter what you may hear, men can feel so deep it is something to be in awe of. I suppose we have hidden it, but a hurt man feels tremendous pain. Hearne loved Eve very deeply indeed, those two had shaped this whole planet together, she gave life to everything he made, they were closer than any I have known. The Black One was devious and tricked him and before we knew it, they were all caught. The age ended and the magic of the lines of time took on another age. He lost his chance and the age of sleep began."

"She killed your sister after she had helped free her daughters and place them into safety." The old Celt nodded as he thought of Gwendolyn.

"Una gave up a child's life to bring her back, it is such a shame that she had to give that one. The Black One took Mac as revenge for giving life back to Gwendolyn. My sister was clever, she had magic of the line of Fae that none of the others knew of, she hid it well in magical things."

"You mean the sword and the bracelet?" The Old man stopped and faced Gwinne.

"She knew that Opal was strong because of her parentage, she did not just use the sword or the bracelet, she used the hooded man's ring, but most of it she hid in the daughter of Eve. Your mother had many hidden powers that passed from her into Stephanie and then Runestone. It was one hell of a piece of very clever magic; I must admit I was never sure until I met her. I felt the love of my sister inside Runestone, and I think so did Merlin."

Gwinne thought for a moment and it all seemed now to be forming a clear picture to her. "She chose the name Sapphire to be her successor, but Sapphire did not become the centre of the circle of knowledge as had been her destiny."

Gwynfor shook his head. "Merlin knew when she was born that the power was not there, we talked for months about it. Neither of us could work out what she had done, we decided that we would wait to see if some object had been chosen that would bring the power to her, it was a puzzle I can tell you. I was at the farm the night Runestone was born, when she came out and I saw her I cried like a baby for I felt such power of my sister. We knew a complex magic had been written on her, and it was Merlin who renamed her Runestone, I named her Sapphire for I knew some of her power was now part of the line of Fae."

"He renamed her, I had no idea."

"She had always been destined to be called Rutile, which as you know was supposed to represent the beauty of the red hair of Venus and the arrows of love. They used to give it in the old days to put a sparkle in the eyes; it would have been a good name for her as she does have the qualities."

"I know she was marked, and he used it as a mark of the runes to confound the

Dark One."

"He was clever there is no doubt, I was impressed. None of us realised at the time because Runestone was safe in Avon, who would have known she would have ended up at Loxley and fall in love with the very heir of the line of Fae. I still think my sister knew more than she let on, if you ask me Gwendolyn set the whole thing up, she was a smart one that's for sure." He gave a soft chuckle and Gwinne smiled at him as they wandered off the sand and on to the soft grass.

"She gave Rune the bracelet knowing she would give it Robbie to communicate with him." The old man took a long breath and thought for a moment. "I think she must have; she knew he was the only one who could handle the sword, I think the bracelet was a little extra protection, he wears it on the hand that carries the blade so it must increase its power. I have wondered about it a lot, he is a great bowman there is no doubt, and yet without any training he has become equally as skilled with a blade. Gwendolyn was the greatest sword fighter I ever saw, for a woman of such slender build she could fight like the biggest warrior. Little Blades reminds me of her at times."

They reached the door of the small cottage and Gwinne opened the door. "Let's have a good cup of tea." Gwynfor gave a beaming smile.

"I don't suppose you have baked more of those cinnamon cookies?" Gwinne giggled.

"I have a tin full, you old rogue come on."

The two of them sat at the kitchen table for the rest of the afternoon and enjoyed talking about the lines and the heirs to the kingdom. He knew a lot about the lines of man, but he had been able to sit back and watch them all his life. Gwynfor knew far more than he ever let on, he had been a good friend to Leenard Rimmer. Gwinne knew that he could name any line of any lord or duke; she also knew his last task on this earth was to sit and talk to Robbie; she talked again about Rayne instead. He was no fool and knew of the hope that was rising inside as she tried not to hope he would be sent to see the new queen.

Gwinne loved him with all her heart and the separation at times had been unbearable. Gwynfor felt it inside her, he smiled to himself, he had felt the line of the moon preparing; he was looking forward to seeing Rhiannon. He just hoped she brought her son.

The sun shone high in the sky over the small Violet Isle, and the blue waters of the sea lapped onto the golden sands, as the tide came up and washed the footprints of the old man back into the depths of the sea. The warm breeze blew as the young woman with long flowing black hair stood by the old cross and smiled. Her gentle warm hazel coloured eyes glittered with her excitement. Soon would be the time of her queen and out of the thousands chosen she and her sister had been given the task. "Isolde...Isolde come on we have to go, we need to get back and prepare." Isolde gave a squeak of a laugh and with a little puff she was nothing but a small speck of light. It hovered and twinkled, as from behind the cross another bright blue speck of light hovered up.

"There you are come on, we have to get back and fast, we have been away too long." The two little specks of light gave a bright burst and with another little puff, they had gone. The trees in the glade of Robbie's Mere above the house beamed with a faint light and a soft giggle. Rune sat in the kitchen and smiled. She felt her guard had returned.

CHAPTER TWELVE

DIVIDED LOYALTIES AND PRESSURE

Dana Knox sat on her balcony, the small figure of Raven; lay just inside the glass doors snuggled tightly inside her crib. For two months now, she had been quite ill, as the birth of the new line to the Knox Empire had drained her of all her energy. She was drawn and pale and only now felt as if she was starting to fully recover, she stared into space across the river. The barges passed below her unnoticed with their heavy loads of scrap metals, the large mangled piles of rusted old vehicles and lampposts, a sign of a life now gone forever. The men of the Knox Empire had spent many years collecting, and now the things that had been so important to the past were piled high as scrap.

Her mind wandered, as the clock ticked slowly past and her thoughts were filled with the knowledge that the Dark One had brought Mason back to life. It was an uneasy feeling that crept around inside her, she had been broken hearted when he died, and now she had to come to terms with the thought of him being back. In all honesty, she had no idea how she felt about seeing him again it had been almost a year, as she had struggled to keep Lance going and cope with the pregnancy alone.

Her pale blue eyes shone brightly across the river and as if almost knowing, she blinked and looked down over the balcony as the long black car came up the road. She stirred as if coming back to life, the thought of being, touched by him still heavy in her thoughts. The questions of would he feel cold or warm were still unanswered inside her. She felt the cold metal of the railing against her palms, as she leaned forward and peered down at the car as it swept into the driveway. The two soldiers stood to attention as the door attendant swept out pulling his black cap down and grabbing for the long silver handle to the door.

She felt a little anxious, but also, she was surprised at the excitement that rose inside her, as the black polished door swung open and the black suited figure slid out and stood up. The hair was as white, but longer as it fell down his back. Mason Knox looked up with the cold bright blue eyes of a man of power. Her eyes met his and her heart gave a little flutter as the smile she knew so well crossed his lips. He pulled the huge bunch of red roses out from the back seat, and she felt her hands tighten on the rail as she gave her first smile in some weeks. He looked no different at all, except maybe a little younger, she had spent the last week thinking all sorts of terrible thoughts and she gave a soft laugh of coldness as she turned and walked into the apartment.

Maybe she had seen one too many horror films as a girl, how could she have thought such stupid things. She shook her head as she pulled the doors together and drew the pale curtains across the window, she turned to the trolley with the large upturned crystal glass and the bottle of Scotch, unscrewing the bright golden cap, she poured his usual measure and for a second, she felt like old times had returned, and nothing had changed. There was a soft tap on the door and she smoothed her skirt as she turned, and smiling, she approached the door. The door swung open to the sight of fifty huge red roses.

"He's got a bloody nerve." Rune scowled at Jade and Robbie. "He doesn't mind the gifts of my realm when he is trying to make amends with his woman." Jade giggled.

"I remember Rowan picking me bluebells in the woods; I thought he had brought them home to eat so I chopped them into the salad." Her bright green eyes danced under her fringe. "I didn't know they were poisonous." Rune gave a giggle and Jade put her hand to her mouth.

"Honestly Rune he was really upset, but how was I to know? No one has ever given me flowers; I always pick my own." She gave another giggle under her breath. Rune beamed a smile at her sister, as Robbie watched the pictures above the table, and Mason entered as Dana fell into his arms.

Rune saw the look on Robbie's face, and looked back at the picture hung in the air, Mason was lifting his daughter into his arms and holding her close. The dark black shiny hair was already growing fast and showed under her bonnet, as her tiny black eyes looked up at her father. Robbie felt his stomach twist, he was not sure what bothered him the most, the return of his enemy, or the fact he had a child that could very likely be the next generation of the Dark One. Mason passed his daughter back to Dana who was all smiles and she lay her gently back into the crib, she turned and he pulled her close.

Jade cringed, as Mason Knox kissed Dana his wife and his hands began to slide across her body. Rune shuddered. "End." The picture faded and she leant back in her chair. "I am not sure I want to watch him man handle her; I want to enjoy dinner." She looked across at Robbie; he was lost in his thoughts.

It was a little over an hour later when Robbie sat on the steps of the house at the front, and stared across the long lush green grass of the glade to the mere. The sound of talking and laughter, echoed from the kitchen inside as the women gathered around the table. The garden was in full bloom and everywhere he looked there were bright splashes of colour. Red hot pokers stood side by side with poppies of white, red and purple. Tall lines of hollyhock exploded their millions of brightly coloured trumpets as they rose six feet to the sky, and the geraniums in red and pinks and the deepest of violet seemed to bob in the breeze as if laughing at the tall pale scented stocks. He loved the garden of life that was tended with such love and attention by Rune.

Alice slid down at his side and handed him a tall glass of lemongrass cooler. He gave her a smile as he took it, Alice had that look on her face and he knew she wanted to talk. "Rune's garden is beautiful Rob." She lifted the glass to her lips as he nodded.

"She loves it; she spends hours out here in the day." Alice watched him, a shrewd look in her eye.

"I hear he is back." Robbie could not help the small smile, Alice cut to the chase quicker than expected.

"He is." Alice leaned forward at his side and looked down the glade.

"How do you feel about that Rob...? You know you killed him and she has brought him back again." It was a question that had preoccupied his thoughts all morning. He gave a long sigh and then took a long swig of the drink.

"It came as a surprise, but I am not sure why. I always knew she had the power to do it, I guess I expected it eventually."

Alice nodded. "You beat him once; Rune thinks it is unlikely he will be any different, you can beat him again."

"That's not what worries me Alice." She looked a little surprised.

"It's not...? I would have thought that having to fight him again would have bothered you?"

Robbie nodded. "I have improved a great deal since I fought him, so I know I can do it again. Mordred was always my greatest concern, and he is out of the picture now."

"We all thought you were worried about having to do it all again." She looked puzzled.

He shook his head. "No if he crosses my path I will fight again. What worries me is that we are under great pressure on the moors, it has been very quiet in the south; I somehow thought Lance was struggling to cope with the responsibility of filling his father's shoes." Robbie stared down the path at the nodding pansies waving in the soft breeze, his voice seemed as distant as his thoughts. "If Mason strikes from the south, we could get caught in between two huge forces, I know Loxley would not survive that, I fear for here more than I ever have."

Alice lifted her arm to him; she knew him well enough and it suddenly hit her. It was at times like this that Robbie would talk to his dad. Robert always gave him a little hope and sound advice mixed together, but Robert was no longer around to advise him. "What do think your dad would say Rob?" He dropped his head and thought for a moment, Alice watched him carefully with great care in her eyes. He turned and looked up at her and smiled.

"He would give me a speech about the genius of grandfather, and he would pat me on the shoulder and say something like. 'You worry too much lad; we are men of the north and we fight for our daily life. Bugger him; he will learn the measure of Loxley before we fall." Alice gave a little giggle.

"You sounded just like him." She looked at him and she gave a big smile. "You are very like him you know; I miss him as well Rob, but I see him in you and I feel closer to you. Think of all the advice he has ever given you; the answer is there you know? Talk to my dad Rob I think the two of you have enough of Robert between you to find the answer."

Robbie nodded. "Thanks Alice." She kissed his forehead.

"I love you Rob, come and see your niece, Rune is as broody as hell holding her. She cannot wait to see yours."

Robbie felt a little relief rise from him, Alice had pointed out the obvious and made complete sense, he slipped his arm round her and pulled her close as they walked into the living room. "I've missed you sis, it's nice having you around the place again."

She beamed a smile at him. "I miss not having you next door, it is odd isn't it, I seem to remember a very shy boy wishing he could talk to this girl he was mad about, and look at you both now. The happiest couple in Loxley."

He stopped and looked down at her bright blue eyes. "You were right as always you know? In many ways you know Alice; you were right about Billy as well. Your words about him after we rescued you, made a very big impact on how I could defeat Mordred, it was your words that spared him." She gave a soft smile and he knew she was grateful.

Rune came beaming out of the kitchen; Baby Jessie held close in her arms, she looked down at the little girl who was wide awake and watching Rune with huge bright blue eyes. He could see the care and love in Rune that radiated out of her toward the small child. Alice smiled with Robbie as her bright sapphire blue eyes, seemed to flicker with happiness. Robbie understood her excitement and happiness at knowing they too had only a short time.

With the house slowly filling up with women and baby talk, Robbie needed space to think. He shouldered his bow and walked out into the trees at the side of the house, alone in the woods he would have the space to bring together his thoughts. It felt good to be under the dense canopy of green, and his mind wandered as he walked without care, trying to puzzle out what he could do if the south decided to go to war at the same time as the north.

His feet followed the path and before he knew it, he was at the small gate in the large wall that would lead him into the old woods of Loxley. He felt a wave of peace on him as he wandered out through the gate; it had been some time since he had been in the ancient woodland. The birds were high up in the branches of the old trees and they twittered happily, the oxalis near the trunks of the trees shaded from the sun were now forming a carpet of white flowers lay across the clover shaped leaves of deep green. The pathway felt a little grown over as it had been some time since it had been used on a regular basis, and the worn dry dirt of old was now going thinner as the soft grass invaded. It was a warm day and even with the dense thatched roof of leaves above him, which kept out most of the sun's hot rays, it was still hot under the trees with a warm damp heavy atmosphere.

The open glade was just ahead and as he looked through the trees, he thought he caught a glimpse of violet; he slowed his pace and peered through the undergrowth. Without a sound he moved forward and slipped his bow off his shoulder, the glade was surrounded by holly so it was easy to get close and remain out of sight. Robbie slowly came around the edge of the holly tree, he raised his bow with the arrow fitted and looked at the figures meeting at the far end. Robbie lowered his bow, the violet shape of Rune stood speaking to a woman dressed entirely in the palest of blues, with long flowing golden hair.

Her eyes seemed to radiate warmth even though they were slate grey, she spoke softly to Rune and Robbie could not really hear the conversation. Rune nodded and embraced the woman, she faded away and Robbie pulled back out of sight. He turned quietly and began to walk away.

"You have no need to leave Lord of Loxley, my business with your wife is complete, come and speak with me, I have looked forward to meeting you." He turned around and she stood at the edge of the trees and smiled at him, Robbie gave a small bow. He was not sure why, he just felt somehow this was a person of importance and should show the manners of his and her position.

"You have me at a disadvantage My Lady, you seem to know who I am and yet I am unaware of whom you are." She came forward through the trees and smiled; he noticed the cloak of feathers and felt a little suspicious, hers was a shimmering blue, yet the only other cloak he knew like that one was black and the wearer was not to be trusted.

The woman took his arm with a happy smile. "I am the Lady of the realm of the moon my dear lord, have no fear of my cloak or its contents, I can assure you we fight the same cause."

"I mean no disrespect My Lady, feather cloaks have been something of a problem to these people, I must admit I do prefer the colour of yours." Rhiannon gave a laugh, in many ways she reminded him of Amethyst.

"It is sad My Lord Loxley, the cloak was once the property of my sister, and she was very much for the side of love and life. It once shimmered in the deepest of blues, as did the jays from which it came, the Black One corrupted it like everything she touches, and the love and happiness contained within it died."

Robbie turned and looked at her. "Your sister was Eve, mother of Opal?"
Rhiannon nodded.

"I was her half-sister of a fashion; you know something of the past lines of the lords of your realm I see." He felt a little relief that he got it right, he had not been sure, but did seem to remember a story that Rune had told him.

"I know a little, but I have to confess when it comes to Rune and all her relatives I do get a little lost."

"We have long lines, it can confuse, I must admit, although I am pleased to see you have tried to keep up." She smiled as they walked in the woods; and leaned back her head and looked up at the trees. The sun was gleaming down through it, her eyes seemed to sparkle with a faint bluish grey twinkle, she reminded him a little of Runestone. Robbie watched her understanding the love of everything around her.

"What actually happened to your sister?" Rhiannon seemed just for a moment to show the sadness in her heart.

"The Black One took her and killed her mortal body; she did it to get revenge on the Lord Creator. The Lord Hearne backed Merlin, and when he expelled Morgan le Fey from the Whitelines, she was so angry she took out her revenge on everyone. Poor Gwendolyn and Eve paid a very high price, by the time everyone had been able to work out the darkness of her magic it was too late. The age had begun to end and the rules set by us all many years ago worked against us." Robbie stopped and looked at her.

"This is what I do not understand, what are these rules, why can you all just not go to her castle and destroy her? Together all of you are more powerful than her, why does Rune have to risk my children and her life when you could all end this now?"

Rhiannon patted his arm. "I agree with you My Lord; I would love nothing better than to avenge the death of a sister I loved and miss every day that I breathe. But do not forget that this world is held by a delicate balance, and it is because of the balance of things that we must enforce rules created to keep the balance stable, much magic has been woven into the fabric of the earth, we cannot deviate from what was begun, mistakes were made all of us now see that, but alas we must watch and hope." Robbie gave a long sigh.

"She is very powerful; it frightens me to know that when my children are born Rune will be at risk, I know she will come for her. Rune has helped all of us stop her at every turn; the Dark One will seek her revenge at the moment Rune is at her weakest." He looked up at the concern in Rhiannon's eyes. "If I lose her, I really do not know how I will live without her."

She gave him a smile. "I will be beside her My Lord, I have returned to protect the new Queen of the line of Fae, and that also means her mother. I think you are also forgetting one very important thing."

He looked back at her. "What's that?"

"My dear Lord of Loxley, Runestone is part of my family. She is the great granddaughter of my sister, a sister I loved dearly. Do you think I would allow anyone to harm the line of a sister I loved so deeply, especially one I might add who is the most like her?"

Robbie felt a sense of relief, he had thought many times of the birth, knowing Rune would be open to attack; it terrified him to think of himself alone facing the Dark One. Rhiannon seemed very confident that she would be safe and it did boost his confidence a little, he was not sure of all the magic that existed. It still left him at a loss, trying to work out each family member, Rhiannon was one of the oldest of the lines and he knew that she must know of what protection would be available, if she thought Rune was safe that was enough for him.

Rhiannon seemed to sense the ease in him, she felt happy to know that a little of the heavy burden he felt had lifted. She gazed through the trees up at Hearne's Rock. "I must leave you soon My Lord to talk with my old teacher, for there are many things that have been seen and I wish to discuss them. I see that you have strengthened the guard to the south, it is a wise decision, although if I may offer you some advice, I would say look to the eastern seas. Use your time wisely for you have a little time yet, but prepare My Lord, for the greatest challenge to Loxley will soon come. Rune has good wisdom let her guide you if you need advice."

Robbie faced the soft warm face of the goddess of the moon and she smiled. "I can only give you advice, I like all the rest are prevented from intervention. This is the time for your dream My Lord, follow your heart and the love of Runestone and you will be victorious. Remember when all around you seems at its darkest, look to your side and light will glow in your world."

She gave him a bow and turned. He stood and watched as she moved quietly into the trees, the back of her long blue cloak shimmering in the sunlight. Long after she had vanished into the thick undergrowth of lush green, did he turn and make his way back to the small gate in the wall. Rune sat at the kitchen table when he arrived home; she looked up and smiled as he came into the room. Her eyes sparkled brightly as he slid his arm round her and kissed her softly on the cheek.

"I felt you in the woods, did you speak with her?" She missed nothing, which made him smile.

"Yes... We spoke; she has a lot of wisdom and I found her words useful."

"Good."

General Walters had watched as the Specialists cut down his army of the dead. The soldiers that he had meant to instill fear and panic into the other side seemed to have failed miserably. For the first time in his long career the general felt like he was losing his grip, remarks had flown around about how he was slipping, and for the first time he began to feel a desperation building within him. Scarlet of Caerleon had haunted his dreams for years, and now it appeared she was haunting his days. The general had always relied on tactics he knew would bring fear, and therefore he was able to control the situations he faced. His nights became more and more long binges of whiskey as he realised that Scarlet was controlling him. She had faced his forces so many times in the past that she knew his methods like scripture, and it had been a long time since he had faced the position of having to think up new and original battle plans.

Ivor Walters sat in his chair with a whiskey in one hand and a pencil in the other, he was under pressure and not gaining any more space for his mistress. He knew that soon he too would face her and her terrible anger. He glared at the map in hope of seeing something he had not seen in the other thousand times that he had looked at it; desperation was now starting to cloud his thoughts as the whiskey affected him. Scarlet had to be stopped and he no longer knew how he would achieve it. He swallowed yet another glass in the long days drinking, and the lines on the map began to wiggle and twist. This was to be another day of no resolution as he slid into a haunted alcohol induced slumber.

The battle across the moors continued in the absence of the senior General. Scarlet now pressed her advantage and slowly the black army had pulled backward as the gains made during the battle with the dead, now fuelled the hopes of the woodland army. Across the whole of the moor, the woodland army pushed hard and with woodsmen; now pushing from the west and the north the only place left for the black army was back towards the city at Scarborough in the east.

Scarlet and Phillip brought up more men from the rear, and the long lines of bows and strikers inflicted constant devastation on the forces of the Knox Empire. Skip based back at Loxley, Fuse in the field headquarters worked together, with Treen now filling in the role of liaison between the both of them and Scarlet. She and Scarlet had become close friends and worked together on the plans of the future, together they worked with Loxley coordinating the night strikes, and the bandit forces, which had begun to grow as others joined the renegade outfit. Robbie now carefully built up his defence of the south, and strengthened the whole of the borderlines.

The woodsmen of the north from Carlisle policed the long wall down from Newcastle and attacked any force that tried to sneak out higher up. The forces of Lancashire worked east across the moors and held a wall of force to the west of the dark forces, and York and Loxley now pushed hard towards the black city. The woodsman's army now reached a staggering sixty thousand, but they were still out matched by an army of at least twice their number.

General Franklin in the absence of General Walters, continued his fight and assumed command, the loss of General Jarrod had took some time to overcome and it had taken a little time to readjust. As the days wore on in the heat under the sun and June began, General Franklin began to find his own sense of being, and took it upon himself to plan his own attack of the green forces.

Reports were beginning to arrive that Mason Knox would shortly be assuming command of the war, and Franklin now wanted to get an advantage before the leader of the empire arrived. He sat with his own advisors and slowly he began to make his plan to crush the enemy of the black army. His biggest problem was Scarlet, and he knew he was up against one of the best, her attention to detail had held the Cutters at bay for over twelve years on the outskirts of Bristol. For General Franklin it was vital that he got her off the battlefield, in order to overcome the hurdle of the red clad warrior, he began to closely examine her tactics.

Scarlet had learned from watching Ivor Walters, and as a result, she could counter any of his moves. General Franklin now began a study of hers in hope he could use her own tactics against her. His first offensive involved the use of using wooden barriers, his troops pushed forward hidden behind them and when they had established a front line parallel to that of the woodsmen, he moved large numbers forward to hold the positions.

Two long barriers of either force now marked a wide highway that became a no-man's land between the forces. Franklin was now back in control and holding Scarlet at bay, behind the long barrier, he now had the chance to muster his own forces and he began to move troops out of the black city and dig in behind the long barriers. As each day crawled forward more of the black army came out of the gates and across the moor. Scarlet watched the build up with a keen eye and in her talks with Robbie, both of them knew that the black army was now building for the large scale attack they had always expected.

Behind the scenes, Scarlet and Phil began to build other defences. A staggered withdrawal would protect their men and the forces of Loxley if the black army came forward with great force. Scarlet's mind each day was moving away from the protection of York and more towards the protection of Loxley.

Rune was starting to feel the strain a little. Her time for birth was getting closer and she was busy watching everything from her table, and adding the final touches to her wild ring of nature that would be the last defence of York. The thick woodland was now at its fullest, and she finished it with a thick hedge of briar and wild bramble. In order to make it through to the walls of York the black army would have to hack through the thick flesh tearing barbs of the plants and then enter deep woodland filled with tall bracken and grasses and low growing shrubs. It was a woodsman's ideal fighting condition, and she knew that the forces of the green army would become invisible and strike unseen giving them a huge advantage.

Rune was now watching and guiding her party of three south, as well as keeping a constant vigil on the black walled cities of the south of England, so far there had been no sightings of any army, but she felt uneasy and had a gnawing doubt that somewhere something was happening. Her worry for Robbie increased, she saw the heavy load he carried and he was now sleeping less and less as he spent hours at his desk in the Village Hall trying to work on new plans that would help overwhelm the black army. He would come home very late and collapse into bed and when she woke in the morning, he was usually gone.

With Sapphire and Ruby, Robbie visited all of the front line forces to help lift the morale of the men. Harry was back with his small team of Woody, Blades, Todd, Hornet and Amethyst, working the eastern borders with Ox and Alfie. Their new task now was to watch the coast and see what was coming in and out of the harbours from Scarborough southward. Rowan and Jade worked with Jett and Rafe in the new woodland around York as they helped to prepare the defences if the front lines had to fall back fast. There was now a final force of twenty thousand troops based in the woods as York was becoming empty.

Brett and Sebastian strengthened the walls, and with the help of Todd and Harry they had managed to get four cannons in working order, these were now placed and prepared ready for use on the northern side of the city. The air across the whole of the woodland world became tense as the days of June dragged under a blazing sun.

The days slid past in a haze of heavy work and June crept through its second week, as the Sage and Ben with Martin Jarrod approached the wall across the top of Devon, Mason Knox set off by boat down the river Thames to make his way north with a fleet of fresh troops to aid the forces of the black city. Robbie felt the pressure growing and the clock ticking.

A Loxley woodsman had been captured in the last of many skirmishes around the eastern edges of the woodland. He was badly beaten and bruised as he was cast through the flaps of the tent, and sprawled bleeding, and numb onto the floor of the private quarters of General Walters. The General leered through his drunken haze at the green clad man before him; he looked up at the two guards and smiled for the first time in many days. It was a savage and twisted smile, which would chill the heart of many men. "Leave Me."

The two guards stepped out quickly and gave each other frightened looks, they had heard all about the ability of the bone crusher. Both of them stood with their backs to the tent flaps and flinched as the horrified screams burst from behind them. Walter's voice boomed, as he screamed in anger at the woodsman. "TELL ME?"

The screams intensified. "How do I get her? Tell me and I will end it." The screams were blood curdling and both of the guards seemed to visibly shrink as their minds painted the pictures of the cruel and evil pain being inflicted on the man of Loxley. Walter's voice rose higher. "How can I get into her camp and kill her? TELL ME."

The crunch seemed to echo as both guards shuddered and the screams came to an abrupt halt. The silence that followed seemed more chilling. "GUARDS!"

Both guards trembled as they turned and entered the tent; the body of the woodsman lay on the floor, his face was an odd shape, and the whole head looked elongated, with a wide split in the top from which leaked bright red blood and grey torn pieces of matter. The tall guard retched and turned rapidly, he passed back through the flaps where the sounds of his vomiting could be clearly heard. General Walters wiped his hands on a blood stained cloth as he turned and his one fierce eye glared at the guard.

"Clean that mess up and bring me his clothes, I have a job for you." The guard swallowed hard as he took the legs of the dead man and pulled him out of the tent, where the contents of his head dragged and slipped out on to the floor. He retched violently and looked at his colleague, who was ashen and still gagging from his vomiting. Together with great effort, they carried the corpse to the dump pits. They slid a sack on his head and undressed him, and when his clothes were collected his body was pushed unceremoniously into the pit and left to rot. The guards returned to General Walters with his things.

The battles raged around the moors as both sides tried to use smaller groups to counter the stalemate in the centre of the battlefield. The Night Strikers worked endlessly under the cover of darkness, and the Specialists although most of the time they were split up into groups, fought using every skill they had. The field headquarters was becoming more and more like home; the Specialists would meet up and laugh together inside the large cool cave before tooling up and moving on with yet more tasks and strikes at the enemy. Robbie walked in caked in mud with Rowan and Jade, having spent another six nights in the fields and moorland round York, he was exhausted and had not seen Rune in eight days.

He slumped down on the bed in a quiet corner and slid off his muddy boots, the heavy rain outside could be heard echoing around the cave and there was a soft dripping sound coming from somewhere nearby. He lay back and closed his eyes, feeling the relief of just being able to rest. A faint glow of lilac shimmered close by, and he felt her before he opened his eyes to see the two beautiful violet eyes that looked down on him. He smiled and lifted a hand to her bright smiling face. "Hey beautiful, I miss you." She gave a soft giggle as she slid beside him.

"Hi gorgeous, I miss you too." She snuggled up to him and he pulled her close, that familiar feeling of warmth that had been lacking for the past eight days, flowed through him and he relaxed with contentment. His body seemed to lose all the aches and pains of the wet and damp days, where he had sat alone in the heather or in amongst trees thinking of her as he waited to strike at the enemy. His eyes closed filled with pictures and feelings of the happiness she brought to his life, Rune curled around him and smiled at Jade who watched with Rowan from the bed opposite them. Jade gave a smile and snuggled into Rowan.

Scarlet and Ruby watched the table with Fuse as she went through her plans for the following day, Jett trudged in with Rafe both dripping having been out on the front lines with their men. Scarlet hugged Jett who seemed tired and exhausted, they both made their way to the back of the cave in search of a bed and much needed rest. Todd slipped off one bed and cuddled up against Blades, and Rafe collapsed dropping his dripping cloak and Jett slid onto the bed at his side. The rain had been endless and the moors were now a thick mire of damp soggy wet peat, it brought with it a dampness that seemed to soak into your bones, and make every task seem much harder than it had to be. The atmosphere was gloomy as the Specialists rested and slept.

Scarlet turned with Ruby as the woodsman rushed into the cave through the wooden door in the false wall across the opening. Ruby screamed snapping off her glasses as Scarlet lunged. The whole cave lit up with white light as the floor lifted and shook. The bright light had lasted a second and the boom was so loud most of them were deafened as the mist swirled and the lights went out.

Robbie coughed as he crawled out from under his bed. It was pitch black, apart from a few strands of white light, which filtered through the swirling dust and debris, and floated to the floor. His ears cleared as he heard a faint buzzing inside them and he shook his head. His ears suddenly exploded, with the sounds of moaning and cries, as his head spun and he pulled his legs from the tangled mess of the sheets and broken wood. His mouth was filled with a foul tasting grit, and he spat as he breathed in the smothering dust filled air that made him cough. He looked from left to right in the dark. "Rune.... Rune... RUNNNE!"

A violet shimmer appeared before him. "I am here Rob, I am safe." He dragged her into his arms and clutched her tight.

"Thank Hearne, what's happening Rune?" She held him close.

"Robbie, they have blown up the cave. I am looking at my table now to see how this happened and find a way to help. Saff and Keith are outside with Phil trying to get into you all." Rune moved back and waved her arm; primrose's rose into the air, and brought light to the cave and its collapsed front end. Dirty faces looked up from the floor as the Specialists looked round at each other with the woodsmen. Rune turned to face Robbie; two tears ran from her eyes. "Robbie, Scarlet is gone." She pushed herself into him as a wail came out of the darkness and Rafe dragged Jett back into his arms and held her close.

Rowan staggered to his feet, blood running down the side of his face, as he lifted the weeping Jade into his arms. Harry gasped a loud burst of tears as he saw Blades with Todd and swept her crying into his arms. Robbie felt stunned as he held the weeping Rune tight in his arms and looked upon the scene of devastation. The floor was littered with stone and injured woodsman; some staggered in shock or just sat in the deep dust with white bloodied faces. Half the table at the end of the long cave stuck out from a wall of broken fallen boulders. Red and green wooden figures were cast all over the place. Skip sat with a very dirty Treen as they wiped the cut head of a very, shaken Fuse. The long red cloak of Scarlet hung from a broken chair as he stared, unable to find the strength to move.

He gently pulled Rune back, and looked at her pale frightened tear filled face. "Rune, our people need help. Can you help them?" She nodded and wiped her eyes.

"I will do everything I can." He kissed her softly and she smiled as more tears formed in her eyes. Rune faded as he looked across to Rowan who was watching and waiting for his lord to command him. Robbie and Rowan made their way with Harry and Todd towards the wall of fallen rubble. Rune appeared outside where Saff and Keith passed rocks down to the mass of woodsmen who were busy pulling away the stones and boulders with a strong sense of urgency. Rune spoke quietly to Philip who turned and sunk his head on to her.

Inside the process was now underway as Robbie and Rowan headed the chain of pulling away whatever they could to clear a path from the inside. Treen pulled all the hurt and injured with Jade to the back of the cave, and those able all helped with the digging out operation. Robbie could see nothing but the rocks he grasped in his cut hands, and passed back to Rowan and Harry behind him. Outside more help arrived in the form of Bear and Jasper who heaved on the larger rocks and pulled them back from the entrance. Big John rolled them across the path out of the way, other larger woodsmen arrived and their combined strength began to speed up the operation.

Blades wiped the faces and cleaned the cuts of the others, as she worked side by side with Treen and Jade. Rafe sat quietly talking to the weeping Jett as he held her softly in his arms and rocked her. Her tears ran blue as her eyes flickered with the pain inside her. Robbie lifted a large rock and his heart froze with fear and grief, outside Rune looked up to the cave and her heart broke.

General Walters stood on the observation platform, and looked through his binoculars and began to laugh as he saw the smoke rising from the huge dust cloud that had just swept across the back of the bluff. Happiness rose quickly inside him and he bellowed a huge thunderous laugh that brought all his men to halt. The huge black robed figure shook with his glee as he watched and bellowed with a strained rough murderous laugh. The observation platform shook and vibrated as he stamped his feet in a hefty dance, as he bellowed and jeered and whopped with delight at knowing finally he had overcome his worst fear. He had finally done it, and outsmarted the bitch, General Ivor Walters had finally put an end to the scarlet clad warrior that had haunted his dreams since the day he had met her. It was he, who had won and vanquished her forever.

The lack of shock or full recognition of the moment suddenly registered as

Robbie lifted the rock and dropped it behind him in shock. He stared at the place where the rock had been. "Oh No... Please not her?" His voice quaked as it bounced around the inside of the cave; Rowan stared through the gloom as he saw the frozen figure of Robbie in front of him. His shoulders shook as his eyes filled with tears, and he lifted the small broken mirrored rose tinted sunglasses to his heart. A huge wailing gasp emitted from him as he placed his hand gently on the blood covered long white hair of Ruby.

Rowan came down by his side and turned him gently round, Robbie pushed his head into Rowan and wailed. A loud gasp followed by a louder wail, came over his shoulder as Harry spotted the glasses and fell to his knees. Rune stood unable to move as she felt the overwhelming power of grief surge out of Robbie inside the cave. Violet tears streamed from her eyes, as Steph came running down the path with Una and Maddy. Steph flung her arms round Rune who seemed unable to move such was the power of Robbie's grief.

Rowan lifted Robbie up from the floor and the deeply sobbing Harry, helped by Todd lifted the heavy stones off the small frail figure of his beloved Flash. Harry lifted her up into his arms and held her close as her long white hair trailed from his arms. He buried his head in her, and wailed like a man who had every good thing in his life torn from him.

Tears ran from Rafe's eyes as Jett screamed in yet more pain, and he held her shaking as the terrible pain flowed out of her. Robbie just sat with his back to the wall utterly heartbroken as he watched Harry gently place the frail broken body of Ruby on the lopsided bed. It was over an hour before the daylight poured in through the gap and Bear slid his head in to see the grief stricken scene.

Philip hugged the lifeless body of Scarlet as it was pulled from under the pile. Bear gently guided him in his grief away from the opening that was appearing, and helped him lay her on a stretcher. The crowd gasped as the entrance finally cleared and Harry stepped out holding Ruby in his arms, his face was dirty and had long streaks where his tears still flowed. Everyone stepped back as he walked out and bowed to the small brave figure that had become her own legend in the Specialists of Loxley.

Rafe walked out slowly with Jett who was even more distraught, and clung to him as she wailed with her pain. The Bedivere family had paid a high price; it was a price, which almost broke Philip, as he looked on his youngest daughter, as she was covered in the cloak of Lord Loxley.

Jett ran wailing into her father's arms and the two of them sat by the stretchers and cried in each other's arms. Robbie took Scarlet's cloak and laid it gently over her. He bowed beside Rune and looked around at everyone. His face was streaked with his tears and his voice was forced with his pain. "Never again in your lives will you meet a warrior more worthy. Scarlet of Caerleon was the very best, she was what all of us strive to be, pay your respects to the passing of a legend, and show her the honour she has earned." Everyone bowed to her as Philip looked up at Robbie and nodded. Jett looked round with tear filled red eyes.

She leaned over and lifted the red cloak of her mother, the weak sun glinted as Jett slid out the long golden sword of her mother's. "This sword has one more unfinished fight before it rests in the home of my line. I swear on her remains I will bring him down and do what she should have done at the age of twenty-two. Walters will breathe his last breath as I push this inside him." There was a fierceness in her eyes that looked like Scarlet's, and Philip knew there would be no stopping his warrior daughter, she was without doubt her mother's daughter, and everyone watching knew it.

It was late in the night when Robbie sat quietly at his desk in the office above his house. It had been a hard day and as he stared down at the small broken glasses in his hand, he felt the pain inside him. The slightly bent long white pole leaned against the wall at the side of him, his emotions swirled as yet another person close to him had been snatched away. Ruby had always been very special, from the moment he first met her at Caerleon, he had felt a closeness to her, she was in many ways in his thoughts like a younger sister and he always seemed to perceive her as being younger than she was. Ruby was seventeen, the same age as Rune and yet her small child like voice and her look of vulnerability had made him feel she was younger and should be protected. Losing her had cut deep, her never faltering faith in him and her little squeaky shouts of "I love you Robin Hood," echoed in his thoughts as a wave of sadness engulfed him. Rune came quietly up the stairs and crossed toward him.

She lifted his arms and slipped on to his knee, her eyes were filled with concern as she brushed his hair back and looked at him. "Are you going to be OK?"

Robbie sat back and gave a long sigh. "It's all going wrong Rune." She snuggled into his shoulder.

"It's been an awful day Rob, that's all." He shook his head.

"No, we really have problems now. Scarlet was the top of her game. I will not replace her as easily, no one knew Walter's as well as she did. Scarlet was the reason we were holding him back." Rune looked up and she saw the concern in his eyes, the pressure had increased tenfold on Robbie.

"What about Philip? He has been by her side all the time she has fought him."

"Phillip is a mess, he has just lost two of his family, he is taking them back to Caerleon for burial, it's up to me Rune, I am Lord of this land. I think it will be up to Rowan and me to lead the forces and try and hold them back."

Rune curled on his lap. "Isolde and Filomena will arrive tomorrow, my time is coming Rob, I can feel it." She was quiet for a moment and looked up at him "Please be with me, I want you by my side when they come."

Robbie kissed her softly on the head. "I have promised, haven't I? I want to be with you too." She smiled and snuggled into him. Robbie sat with Rune on his lap as the night slipped slowly by, and he felt torn in two. How could he just leave now when the lives of his people depended on him staying, but how could he not be there with Rune for the birth of his children. It would be a time of great danger as her powers faded for a short while. He was caught in a trap of equal pressure.

As dawn broke General Walters walked with a spring in his stride through the camp, he felt like a man renewed, he limped almost in a light way as his one eye twinkled.

The rocks from the cave had been cleared and inside woodsmen worked frantically to get the operations room back up and running. Fuse had been taken back to Loxley, and Skip now took overall control of the war effort with Rowan. The figures were back on the table and Rowan took in all the positions so he was fully updated. All around him, the clean-up operation was underway to get the woodsman army back on track. Treen came out of the back room rubbing her hair with a towel; she stood up and flicked her long flowing hair back. "Ow does this look?"

Rowan lifted his eyes as Skip chuckled. Treen beamed as her long flowing new fiery red hair fell down her back, she smiled. "I know it is not Scarlet, but ow will he know from so far away?" Rowan smiled at Treen who now wore bright red pants and a red top and cloak, she had in her belt Jett's copy of the golden Sword of Knowledge. Rowan had to admit; she did have a look of Scarlet about her.

Skip chuckled as he pulled her into his arms. "My word darling, I do think I rather like you as a red head." She gave him a smile as he kissed her softly. Treen nodded to Rowan.

"Ok let's show this one ear fatty who is boss." Skip chuckled.

"I do believe darling its old fatty one ear." She gave a giggle and arm in arm with Skip they made their way out of the Headquarters toward the top of the bluff. Claire giggled as she saw Treen with bright red hair and dressed like Scarlet.

Rowan and Skip lay on the hill in the heather and looked out through their scopes across the moor of York. General Walters was stood in his usual position as he scanned the lines. Treen and Claire walked past them lay in the grass as they watched the general, and the two girls walked up into view on the platform. Treen placed Scarlet's telescope to her eye and watched as the General scanned the moors. "Ok Claire get ready to let old fatty ear know we are back." Claire giggled as she raised her flags.

General Walters scanned past the observation post and did a retake as he swung back. The Scarlet clad warrior waved back at him, the flags went up and he read the message. "Sorry you missed me; I was having my nails filed."

He staggered back on the platform, and the binoculars crashed to the floor, a look of complete disbelief on his face. Panic rose quickly as he wailed and limped off the platform as quickly as he could, he headed for the tent hitting two guards and killing them outright as he passed. Everyone stared at the sight of the large black clad mountain of a man as he wailed. He entered the tent shaking and grabbed the bottle off the small table; both his hands shook as he poured a very large measure. Grabbing the glass with both hands, he drank the whiskey quickly, and poured another as he collapsed on the bed.

Treen and Claire howled with laughter as they watched, Rowan and Skip came up to them giggling. Rowan patted her shoulder. "Scarlet would really have appreciated that, you did wonderfully Treen." She beamed with delight

"I am appy, I really respected Scarlet, and she was a good friend to me."

Rowan turned and looked out over the moors with Skip at his side. "We need to prepare; Walters will throw everything he has at us now. Robbie must be with Rune for the birth, we have to pull together and give Robbie and Rune the time they need for their children." He lifted an arm to Skip's shoulder. "Robbie is under a great strain my friend, we must carry his load for a while, we owe him that."

Skip nodded and smiled. "Have no fear Rowan, we all stand beside you in support of our friend, he is not alone." Rowan gave a nod and with tired eyes, he looked out to the north and the gathering army of Mason Knox.

CHAPTER THIRTEEN

THE SILENCE OF A STORMS APPROACH

Robbie felt tired; he had slept very little and now dressed in all black, he prepared for his day and the funeral of two people who meant a great deal to him. Scarlet and Ruby would be led in a procession from the stables at the bottom of the compound, and make their way through the village to the farm. Philip and Jett would accompany them back to Caerleon where they would be buried. Robbie had a very heavy heart as he came down the stairs.

It was market day and Loxley was filling up as people wandered in from all over the area. Down at the gates Henry was on duty walking along the top of the observation platform, David Williams walked along the edge of the large open square outside the gates with Melanie. His men walked along the edge of the rows of people, security was high as the gatemen watched everything entering. Carts were checked and it was a rule that hoods were kept down and cloaks were worn open, and back across the shoulders. No one got in without at least ten of the guardsmen checking them over. Mel stood smiling in her straw hat as the breeze blew over the top of the slope of white stone, lined with trees that were the top of the shelf of limestone that the whole stockade of Loxley sat on.

She looked down the road that came up the slope lined with carts and slowly moving people and admired the view. The fields of green and trees broke down into the valley that housed the huge reservoir, Loxley sat high looking down on the start of Derbyshire. It was a very beautiful place and Mel began to see and understand the love she had seen in everyone about the place that they called home. She had only been in the town on and off for a year now, but somehow it was starting to feel like home, her long years of isolation had ended, and now surrounded by her sisters and her children, Mel was coming into her own. She smiled as Dave slipped his arms round her. "Not much longer now and I will have a few hours before the funeral."

Her slate grey eyes twinkled as she looked out across the green valley. "This place is so beautiful Davie; it is easy to see why all of you love it."

"It's home Mel, and I hope you feel it is your home now?" He gave her a squeeze and she smiled.

"I am happier now than I have been in a long time." She turned to him and she gave him a warm loving smile. He looked down at her as her eyes dropped a little.

"What is it?"

Her eyes lifted and she gazed with the eyes of almost grey into his. "I have to return home for a while Davie. There are things I must do to prepare for the future lines of my family, Jaz will one day be the Lord of the Isle, and with the new queen coming to the Violet Isle; I must now prepare him to replace his father." David could see the conflict in her.

"How long will you be?" She pulled him closer. "It could be some time, I am sorry."

"Will you come back to me, or are you telling me goodbye?" Mel looked up as tears formed in her eyes.

"I want to come back, but there is a curse on the isle, I must remove it for the sake of my son. The Dark One placed it there to prevent Tor from returning alive, Jaz cannot set foot on that isle again until it is lifted, and if he does he will die." She looked up into his bright blue eyes, as he watched the pain inside her. "I love you Davie and I want to come back, I really do, but without my father I am alone in this and he is her prisoner. I cannot risk my son's life."

"What about Rune? She has the power of your father's line. Mel you must talk to her."

Her head dropped. "It will not be possible. Rune will have to stay on the Violet Isle, she will be at her most vulnerable when the child comes, and Jaz must walk on the island to claim his place as the new queen is born. This is a task that can only be done now by me, we are alone in this Davie."

"Then I will come with you." She gazed up at him and smiled; she pulled his head down and kissed him softly.

"Oh Davie, you cannot, you are my love and she will kill you if you even come near the place. I have to go alone and do this, just know that I love you and I will try to come back to you, I will not leave you easily."

David Williams felt the pain of separation as he held her in his arms. Mel hung on to him tightly feeling the bitter pain return to her from the loss of her first love, and now it looked like the Dark One would rob her again.

"When will you leave?"

"I will leave with Rune tonight, I am sorry I have wanted to talk to you sooner, but it has been hard for me out on the moors and seeing so little of you recently. I did not want to spoil the happiness we have had together." David squeezed her tight in his arms and kissed the top of her head.

"You will come back; I know Rune would not desert you if you got trapped. Just be careful you are my whole world Mel, I love you." David Williams stood at the top of the long road and stared down into the valley; he held her close in his arms and felt his heart on the edge of breaking. In just a short space of time this slender woman in a battered straw hat, had changed his life forever, the happiness and joy he felt had been unbelievable. For the first time in his whole life, David had found the true meaning of living, and now the icy grip of fear touched him as he faced a future robbed of the woman he loved. The hours up until her departure became more special as he enjoyed what could be his last ever moments with Melanie.

The woodsmen of Loxley raised their hoods and placed their heads down as they leaned on their bows. From the stables right round to the farm, long lines of woodsmen lined the road. Black ribbons hung on every door in the stockade as Robbie rode out of the barracks stables on his gleaming white horse.

He sat up front draped in a long black velvet cloak with the golden crest of Loxley on it. He held the golden Sword of Destiny in his right hand upright, as his black plumed horse moved slowly forward. Jett and Philip sat behind him on their mounts and followed, Jett wore the long red cloak of her mother, with a black ribbon tacked over the golden crest of Caerleon. The two carts followed as the mournful drum beat a solemn rhythm.

Both carts were dressed in long black tasselled fabric, and each held the casket of a hero. Scarlet's came first with a long oak casket covered in red roses; the smaller white ash casket of Ruby followed dressed in the palest of pink roses. Rafe sat high with red eyes as he drove Scarlet's cart, Harry wept as he drove little Ruby's. The Specialists of Loxley walked in long black cloaks with hoods up either side of each cart, Rune in her small buggy with a weeping Jade, was followed by Steph and the Lox family and friends silently on foot.

People stopped and bowed as they passed the gates where David Williams stood holding up those who wished to enter as the funeral procession passed sadly by. As they came into Loxley Village Street, the men at arms drew their swords in salute, and held their sword hilts up to their faces as their lord led the procession past and up to the farm. The sound of the market and the busy daily activity had died away and the whole of the stockade was silent, apart from the boom of the solemn drum and the slow clatter of the hooves on the cobbled road.

It was one of the saddest days ever in Loxley; Ruby had become so well liked by everyone. Her happy smiling face was known in every shop and on the training field; she was respected by every member of the green army for her skill and gentle approach to the way she had helped train them. On the moorland Scarlet had commended huge respect, which was shown by young Claire as she walked dressed in black behind the Specialists, having requested leave from the front line to attend.

Jett stood beside Rafe as Robbie walked up. Her head hung low and her fringe covered her red eyes, she gave a loud sniffle as he got close to her and she looked up at his tears. Jett flew forward and Robbie grabbed her and squeezed her tight as she cried into his shoulder. He lowered his head to hers and talked quietly to her. Jett pulled him closer and nodded as Rune watched next to her grief stricken mother who held Phil tight in her arms. Robbie looked up at Rafe as Jett would not let go of him, as she screamed her pain and tears into his chest.

Sapphire opened the window and the royal guard of Caerleon came through. They lifted the two caskets on to their shoulders and prepared. Rafe gently pulled Jett from Robbie. "Come on sweetheart, it's time to go."

Rafe held her close as she stood beside her father and Steph, who wanted to see her sister off, the rest of the Specialists, formed a line and bowed their heads as the men of the castle of Caerleon carried Scarlet and Ruby to their final resting places. They had passed from the realm of Loxley and into the other realms under the care of their Green Lord.

Jett turned with tearful eyes and looked back at her friends as she stepped through the blue window and Sapphire followed, the window faded and Rune rested her head on Robbie's shoulder, he slipped his arm round her and pulled her close, nobody spoke as they drove to the glade of Robbie's mere. Two Figures in powder blue cloaks stood at the gate as Robbie and Rune pulled up in the buggy with Jade. Isolde and Filomena gave a short curtsy as Rune rose from the cart and walked toward them.

Robbie looked up from his desk into the watery pale blue eyes of Fuse as he rolled up the maps. "We have lost a strong tree and a very fragrant flower from the garden of Loxley my friend."

Fuse seemed to have aged more; his sad eyes looked down on his lord and friend. He gripped his shoulder. "We all feel the loss of dear friends departed, they died as they lived my friend... Defending what they loved." Robbie gave a long sigh and sat back in his seat; Fuse lifted the maps and slid them into his sling. "We could have lost far more, we are in some ways lucky Robbie."

It was something that had crossed his mind; if the assassin had got further into the cave, most of the Specialist could have been killed. Scarlet had hit him, and lunged on top of him as he had sprawled backward, the five sticks of dynamite bundled in his hand had fallen free and rolled towards the doorway as they exploded. Her bravery had saved all of their lives, she had shoved Ruby out of the way and she had been safe as she fell behind the table, but the roof fell in and she was crushed under the weight. Robbie got out of his seat and led Fuse down to the second floor; at the top of the stairs, he embraced his friend who would be heading back to the Village Hall for a few weeks whilst he recovered. Robbie, walked into the bedroom where Rune was packing a bag, she looked up and smiled.

"I am almost ready." Robbie pulled her into his arms, and he kissed her softly.

"As soon as Steph, Rafe and Jett return I will be there, Rowan and Skip will be fine for a few days. Keep safe Rune, this is going to be a difficult time, take no risks." She felt his fear inside him and pulled him close.

"I will be fine, Iona is a sacred place, and she cannot take life on the island." She pushed her head to his. "I love you Robbie."

"I love you too Runestone, please be careful I really do not trust her."

"I promise." He kissed her and then turning he lifted her bag, and walked down the stairs and out of the glass doors with his arm around her.

The group for the moors stood silently waiting. Jade was anxious to get back to Rowan, and she fidgeted at the side of Bear and Smokes. Keith and Fish sat silently talking and rose to their feet as Robbie came out on to the grass of the glade with Rune. She pulled him close, her bright eyes a deep sapphire blue and they sparkled as she squeezed him hard. "Keep your head down and be very careful." He smiled as she slowly released him and raised her hand to open her violet window.

"See you soon." He winked as he smiled and the group followed him through and on to the moors of York. Rune felt a small tug at her heart knowing he would be far away from her until he arrived on the island. Una placed an arm around her shoulder.

"It's not for long he will be fine, the others will be watching him very carefully." Rune nodded and gave a weak smile as she walked back up the glade with Una, and onto the steps of their home.

Rowan pulled Jade close as Robbie walked up to the observation platform smiling, Rowan patted his shoulder as he turned to look out across the wild moor of Yorkshire. The long rows stood at a stalemate and faced each other across the empty no man's land, which had been formed between them. Robbie felt a little surprise at the fact that the large army of Mason Knox had made no effort at all to push forward. He stood, his tired face looking out, he looked very pale and weary, the strain of recent days showed, as the death of his friends and the pressures of the war took their toll on him. His mind was with Rune and the possibility of danger to her, when she was at her most vulnerable; he felt more pressure than he had ever felt before, and inside his loyalties were starting to tear.

The face of the Lord of Loxley now bore the cuts and lines of the weight on his shoulders of a commander at war. His long sage green cloak flapped around his legs in the soft breeze, as he stood proud with his long rowan bow held upright in his right hand. The soldiers of the green army felt the tension in the air as they knew that soon the black army would make a move, the sight of their leader and symbol of hope, stood silhouetted behind gave them hope and courage. Beside him with a long flowing red cloak and long hair that whipped round in the breeze stood Treen, she lifted her arm to his shoulder as she saw the conflict and pain that mixed inside him.

"I ave spent many weeks with Scarlet, I ave planned every move by her side. You must not be of worry Robbie; we shall not let them through. Your place is not here you belong with Rune. Trust us and we will not be letting you down."

She softly squeezed his shoulder and he nodded as he turned to look at her. "Thank you Treen, I have never thought for one moment any of you would not give all of your best. The support from all of you has honoured me, I have always been proud of the people around me." She gave him a big smile.

"I will honour my friend with much bravery, Scarlet was my hero."

Robbie looked at Treen dressed in all red as she stood and faced the battlefield. He gave a smile to himself, she did have a look of Scarlet and he was impressed at the speed in which Treen had come up with idea, to fool Old General Walters into believing he had failed. It had been a very clever move and in many ways, he thought that somewhere in the other realm Scarlet would be watching and laughing. This was exactly the kind of trick she would have pulled.

Across the wild moorland both sides of the armies sat in wait for their next commands, the sun was high in the sky and the peat steamed as the water was drawn up to the warm surface. Robbie knew that soon the generals of the black army would finally reach the point he had been at in January, the gates would open and all of the soldiers would spill out and storm across at the woodland defences. Rowan came up by his side and patted his shoulder. "It's quiet for now Robbie; we are ready, have no fear." He smiled knowing he had Rowan beside him, which meant a great deal.

"It will start soon my brother; The Dark One will know when the children come. They will strike us hard at the moment Rune loses power." Rowan squeezed hard on his shoulder and turned to him.

"Robbie, you must not concern yourself, we will stand and hold them back. I know you feel the loss of Scarlet, but you are forgetting that many of us worked closely with her. Robbie, we know every move she had planned, Treen was beside her with Skip every moment of their planning. We will hold them back; you must be at Rune's side, please trust me and let me hold here for you while you protect your family. I can do this."

The slate grey eyes and chiselled features of Rowan looked tired, and yet as Robbie lifted his eyes and looked at his friend, he saw the power and assured confidence in his eyes. "I trust you Rowan above all others you know that? I am afraid for you and all of us, they will hit us very hard and we will lose many. I have lost one of my biggest weapons and it worries me."

Rowan looked at him not quite understanding him. "What weapon have you lost Robbie?"

A small tear welled in eye. "I have lost my little ray of sunshine."

It all became clear and Rowan nodded. The happy face of Ruby in the group had always lifted the spirits, and even though she was the smallest member of the group, Rowan understood that she was also the deadliest. Ruby had the ability to remove her glasses and with one bright burst of light, she could devastate a battlefield. With Ruby in the front line, it would not matter how many of the dark army came at them, Robbie had always known that Ruby would have taken a huge amount of their forces out in one wide sweep of the field. In Robbie's mind, she had been the difference between victory and defeat. Rowan patted his friend's shoulder. "I know my brother; she will be greatly missed. You must not give up hope; we still have talented people who are worth a hundred of their forces. We will not give them an easy day I can assure you." Robbie nodded and watched the heather sway, its buds of pale flower starting to show the first of its purple flowers.

The small brown hooded figure sat in amongst the leaves and watched across the long road. The long line of carts trundled along the road in the direction of the partially rebuilt gates of the black city of Stonehaven. The hood moved from left to right and nodded. On both sides of the road, the foliage of the trees moved slightly as metal tipped arrows poked through the trees. From under the cloak, a slender arm appeared and the hand rose and fell rapidly. The horses reared as the driver took the first of hundreds of arrows to fly across the road; the guards leapt up in surprise and felt the long shafts and brown-feathered arrows of the Scottish clan of Rose Macintosh.

Soldiers sprawled, caught in the cross fire, and fell from the carts to the road. The small brown-cloaked figure drew her sword, as two guards rushed from the road for cover. She screamed as she came down the bank and swung her blade with all her power. The guard had no time to draw his sword, as she swooped and sliced into him twisting round, and bringing her blade flying round into the second guard. Hooded figures came out of the trees, and ran down the bank as the clash of steel resounded around the road and carts. Soldiers in black fell and panicked at the overwhelming numbers that flowed from the trees on to them. The battle was swift as the woodsmen swarmed over the guards.

Grace Macintosh dropped her hood and viewed the scene, she wiped the sweat from her face as a taller figure approached her, the hood fell and the long black hair of her commander flowed down her back. "We have a good haul; these are explosives meant for the Dark One." Grace nodded as she looked at the two dozen carts.

"Leave the front one and take the rest, get them to my father at the jetty and take them to the cave. I will deliver this one to the Dark One personally."

The guards in black stood at the bottom of the long bridge, and paced as they watched the deep cutting, which had been cleared by the Dark One to allow her troops of the dead to move back up to the road and begin their journey south.

They turned and looked as they heard the familiar rumbling of the wheels of the carts; they prepared as they finally had something to do, and breathed a small sigh, as the boredom of their day was to be broken as they checked the carts inventory. At the top of the steep slope, a cart blazed as it began its steep roll towards them gathering speed as it came. Fear and panic rose quickly as the flaming cart thundered down the slope, the guards spilled off the bridge as the cart hit the far end and rolled at speed along the dark black bridge of stone.

The heat of the blaze was fierce as it hurtled along the long bridge and into the high black gates. The entire coastline lit up as the cartload of explosives burst into flame and exploded. The men, who had lifted themselves up on to the tall poles along the bridge, were tossed into the water as the bridge and the whole island shook under the power of the explosion. Stone and wood rained out of the sky, and the wall to the bridge collapsed into the compound pounding stone down on to the startled guards.

Through the narrow pathways now covered in green lush plant life, the small group of hooded figures slipped with speed and agility. They wove like lightening away from the viewing platform back towards what had once been the old general store of the now defeated city at Dunnottar. Angus stood watching as the group moved swiftly toward him; he stood back with the door open as the group flew inside, he quickly followed and pulled the door, then locked and bolted it.

Angus slipped across the kitchen and through the door to the cellar, he slid down the long ladder into the large empty warehouse below the old general store, and turned smiling as the group dropped their hoods and laughed. The happy faces looked to Angus as the group of women all caught their breath and relaxed. Grace beamed at her dad. "We did it."

He pulled his youngest daughter into his arms as she breathed hard. "You did well my child, come let's get back and see what else we can do to slow her progress."

Dunnottar was not having it all its way, as the spirit and determination of Rose Macintosh lived on and fought the cause of the hooded man. Many had died in the return of the Dark One and the rebuilding of the castle, many of the men had died where they sat as flames had leapt from the floor engulfing them, the few who had survived had suffered bad burns and died a few days later. With over half of the men of the Scottish Resistance movement wiped out, many of the women had come forward to take up arms in the fight. For a few months, they fought hard blocking the gates with fallen trees and attacking anything that came near the black city. As the word got back to the west coast, many who had fled lifted their arms and made their way across the mountains to join Angus Macintosh and the old grey haired veteran of William McDonald.

Grace Macintosh had worked for her father and been placed in the Lodge to ensure that Robbie and Rune were safe at all times. With the hooded man back in Loxley, she had returned to her part in the defence of the Scottish Realm. Grace now had her own trained group of women who formed an elite group who appeared and disappeared, causing chaos and destruction. The fight to clear the coast from Stonehaven down to the south still continued, Mason was convinced he was days away from victory, yet the seeds of rebellion were still germinating and starting to grow with daily strength.

Above the beach on the outskirts of the old ruined town of Breen, just down from Weston Super Mare was a large and thick woodland. Here the trees had grown tall and dense; it was hard to weave around them as they grew up to the sunlight bending inland as the breeze blew in off the sea. In the very centre, and well away from prying eyes, the trees thinned into a clearing, which contained what was left of an old and battered hut. In the days of Old Modern man, it had been used to store the tools of the old farm that had once occupied the site. Now very little remained to even suggest that the land had been used to raise cattle and grow the few crops it had, the woodland had claimed back all the space for its own and spread its thick protective canopy over all of the land.

Ben cut a hole in his stick and then inserted a thinner stick into the hole. Holding it between his hands, he rubbed quickly until a thin wisp of smoke rose from inside the hole; he pulled the dead grass together and tapped the contents of the hole on to it. He softly blew and the smoke rose quickly as the grass caught and he placed it on the floor and placed the shavings of wood beside it. The fine slices of wood caught as he placed the fine twigs on top and gently blew, flames leapt up and he leaned back and smiled as he moved larger pieces of dead wood on to the pile.

The Sage stood by the horses as they grazed on the soft new leaves of the saplings. He attached their reins to a line he had put up across two of the trees, lifted his bow, which was sat at the side of the tree and turned to the small camp and his young companion who was now building the fire up ready to cook the meal after the long walk. Ben looked up him with a dirty face. "Where are we now?"

The Sage smiled as he crouched by the fire. "This is a place Martin knows of, he grew up near here and this land was once his grandfathers, we are on the edge of the big wall; it lies five miles south of here."

Ben gave a reassured smile. "Where has Martin gone?"

The Sage looked up at the trees. "He has gone to see an old friend of his, we will need a few things to get inside the large wall and he thinks his friend can help. He will not be much longer, let's get a meal started it has been a long day, and I feel your appetite will have grown again." He smiled at Ben as he stood up and lifted his bag. "Here prepare the carrots and onions." He threw the veg in a small bag on the ground beside Ben as he lifted his pan and water bottle out of his sack.

The fire crackled and the pan bubbled softly as the small coffee pot steamed when Martin appeared in the trees at the side of the camp. The Sage sat quietly and watched with his bow across his lap, he nodded as Martin appeared with the tall large stranger. "This is Markus, have no fear he can be trusted I have known him all my life." The tall dark skinned man looked round and spotting the Sage, he gave a broad smile and nodded.

"Hi there." He dropped a large bag on the floor and gave a big smile at Ben and offered his hand. "You must be Ben? It's nice to meet you, I have heard many things about you my small friend."

Ben looked a little nervous and looked across the camp to the Sage, he gave a slight nod and Ben smiled and lifted his arm and placed his small hand in the huge palm of Markus. "I am happy to meet you Markus."

Martin crossed the camp to the Sage; he crouched down just in front of him. "Markus was once in the army but he retired with a great deal of relief, I knew he would still have some parts of his uniform left, we can use it to get back into the city." The Sage nodded as he looked at the giant figure of a man stood before him.

"We are grateful for your help Markus, thank you. Tell me if you were once with the forces of Knox why would you help us, knowing we now fight against him?"

Markus gave a deep belly laugh. "Relax my green friend, Martin told me you would be unsure. I must admit I do not blame you; I too would worry about getting help from an old enemy." He crouched down and his deep dark eyes twinkled as he spoke. "I have no love of the forces of Knox, I never did, although I am not a fool my friend, it does not take long to understand a new rising power. Only a fool would go against such overwhelming odds, and Knox had a very strong army when he first came to power. I was already a soldier from the old ways, he gave me a chance to join and save my family from the pain of others. I took his offer and was a guard in the fortress we all thought no one would ever attack. I served my time, and then was able to leave with the protection of knowing his Cutters knew me well enough to leave me alone."

The Sage nodded. "I can understand the need to protect those that you love, if the Cutters have let you be, you must have been powerful in combat."

The Sage watched the reaction of the man with tight curly white hair and a face of kindness. Markus sat back on the grass with his large happy smile. "I was head of the guardhouse, there are a few of his Cutters who tried to get above their station in the barracks, I taught them their position once in a while."

The Sage smiled at him and looked at the large muscular frame of the man, he was obviously around sixty but he still looked like a man who had more power than most. "We have good food if you wish to join us."

Martin patted the Sage on the arm as he stood up. "He will be joining us for a little longer than a meal my friend, Markus knows that place better than any, he will be a big help to us inside."

The four of them sat around the fire as the darkness drew in. Markus filled them in on the fortress of Tintagel as he ate with them. The attack of the hooded man had created a great deal of damage; most of the guard block and private quarters of Mason Knox had been swept into the sea. The large fortress that still stood on the mainland was the quarters of the Dark One, it was a four storey building on which the whole of the top floor was her living space, although it was rumoured she used very little of it choosing to stay on the western side of the floor where she worked her devious plans and spells. Most of the guards hated that side of the building; her tempers and tantrums had often cost the lives of the guards who were the closest to hand when she was angered.

A fifty-foot wall that ran along the cliff tops and round the whole emplacement surrounded the fortress itself. Just outside the wall was a market town where all the farmers and traders came regularly. It seemed that gaining entry would not be too hard as they could take a boat down part of the unprotected coastline and land in a secluded place and make their way into the town. Getting into the fortress would be Martin's job, getting into her private quarters would be tricky as it involved going through many of the guards' quarters, although Markus thought it may be possible to get access through a window up a rope if at least one of them could get into the barracks.

The Sage sat quietly listening as he sat by the fire; Ben's eyes flickered as he tried to hold off sleep. Slowly in his mind, the Sage began to formulate his plan; he patted Ben on his legs. "Come on young Master Winter's, get your head down, we will have a busy day tomorrow." Ben jumped awake and gave a tired smile at the Sage, he crawled into his blanket and settled down for the night, the Sage lifted his bow and stood up. "You two settle down, we will start early. I will take first watch." He looked into the trees as a feeling he was required alone came to his mind.

He walked through the trees and saw ahead the faint violet shimmer; he turned through the trees toward it, the Sage walked into the small clearing in amongst the dense trees as the violet figure of Rune glowed before him. He bowed with respect. "My lady of the Woods."

Rune gave a smile, as she looked at him. "You have done well to get here so fast my green friend; I am happy to see your party is growing. Have no fear of your new companion; his heart is true to you." Rune walked slowly toward him. "I see you have the start of your plan to save the guardian of the Whitelines?"

"I am beginning to put one together, I know how I will get into her rooms, I am unsure of how to open the case when I get there."

"Have no fear my green friend for I have the means." Rune pulled her hand from within her cloak and placed four small bright violet butterflies into his hand. "Place one of these on each corner of the case and then when the lid is removed, place this on my grandfather's forehead and leave. The powers of the Whitelines will take care of the rest. You must leave quickly my green friend, a great power will flow to that place, save yourself and your companions, head to the beaches and you will have aid."

The Sage looked down on the golden violet flower set next to the butterflies in his hand, they were very beautiful, he nodded as she spoke unable to lift his eyes from the golden flower. Rune moved a finger to his face and gently lifted it so that he could see her. "She will not feel your power as I do, the power of the White Circle is now within you, please do not fear the darkness Billy, it has left you forever. Robbie pulled it from you with your cousin." She smiled as she saw the fear in his eyes.

"I have tried to undo what I can, what will I do if she recognises me?"

"I will protect you through the lines you carry, rest your heart. You will do a great deal to help Robbie in this task and even though he is unaware of whom you are now, one day he will know of your efforts to help him."

Billy dropped his head. "I have been a fool and destroyed everything that mattered to me Rune. I lost a brother and the only woman I will ever love."

"The ways of the world are never fully seen, even by those who can see some of the future, the touch of Gwendolyn's sword has brought your gifts to the surface and you now have a great power. It will work for many but not always for you, your sister and your daughter are safe, be happy knowing they have your brothers protection for now. Know that there will be a time when Jessica Sapphire will seek others with her gifts. It is written you will meet one day."

Billy pulled the white mask from his face as the tears streamed from his eyes. "I did not know her name."

Rune smiled. "I know, she is very beautiful and she has soft white curly hair and the brightest blue eyes, you will know her when you see her in the future. Time has a way of softening the heart, prove to Robbie you have aided his cause and we shall see what becomes of it. Rest your heart and put away your pain Billy. Now is the time for the true man of Loxley to come to the surface, for you were raised by a true woman of Loxley and you know of her kindness, let it flow back into your heart and guide you."

Billy sniffled as he looked up and nodded. "Thanks Rune." She smiled.

"Put on your mask and return to being the green sage of the woodland again, I will watch over all of you especially the boy. I shall return now to my home for I too will soon be a mother and have things to prepare before that time. I will see you again have no worries."

He placed the mask back on to his face, and watched as she turned and walked back to the trees where she faded into the night. The Sage stood quietly on the edge of the beach and watched the sea as it rolled up the sand, memories of a past he no longer belonged to flowed through his mind. Small tears dripped from under his mask as they ran down his chin, he gave a long sigh and sat watching the darkened sea. As the night time passed into the darkness that approached dawn, he turned and walked quietly back to the campsite behind him. He faced a difficult task and now had to prepare.

Rune looked up from her table and smiled at Una and Mel. "We are almost prepared." She looked at Mel. "Fear not my sweet sister, your task is difficult but you will not be alone and you will have help. I feel our keeper of the gate has shared a life alone for too long, I will not see him or you apart for long."

Mel gave a smile as Una squeezed her arm; Rune looked at them both. "You will be together as sisters in life and the circle, which will give you the power. You know the incantation, but you must sit above Tor when you speak it. Below the very centre of the circle is his burial chamber, Mel you will need something that belonged to him, the charm will only work with a possession he once held close and gave you both a strong bond."

Mel nodded as tears came to her eyes. "I have his hat." She gave a soft chuckle through her tears. "I know it sounds daft, but it is all I have had to hold on to him, he loved it." Una pulled her close.

"I never knew, I have never understood why you wear such a scruffy thing. I just thought it was the country girl inside you." Mel gave a giggle with Rune.

"It is perfect Mel; there is a very strong bond between you through it. You must place it in the circle, and form a circle of your sisters and then speak the words. You must not break the circle; the stones will protect you. No matter what happens you must keep the circle to draw the power of violet to you."

Una and Mel both nodded. "We will be fine Rune; I will be by Mel's side throughout."

"Alright, we must prepare and leave soon; I feel my escort is getting itchy."

Rune came up the stairs with the two women, and made her way to the doors where her bag was ready waiting. Amethyst stood with Crystal by the gate, Judy and Jaz sat on the benches just outside the door. Maddy and Jay came out of the kitchen and picked up their bags as they followed Rune out on to the glade and her two waiting escorts. With a wave of her hand the window opened in a shimmer of violet, and with one last look at the glade, Rune stepped through on to the open grassy slope in Iona. The group followed her through and she smiled as Gwinne walked down the slope with a big smile to greet her.

"Rune darling?" Gwinne pulled her close into a hug; she felt the surge of apprehension that was inside Rune. "Have no fear my darling, he will be here in time."

Rune nodded as Gwinne leaned back and looked at her. "He is under a great deal of pressure; I am really worried about him."

"You relax and let me worry about him; I will make sure he is here for you."

Rune gave her a nod and Gwinne smiled.

As the sun started to slip down in the sky, the silent figure in a long red cloak knelt before the two freshly dug mounds as she wept in the Bedivere private graveyard, just outside the castle of Caerleon. Her head hung low below the red hood with her long black hair trailing damp to the floor with her tears; she raised her hand and wiped her face. Lady Jett Amber of Caerleon had been dealt a bitter blow; she took one more long look at the graves of her mother and younger sister. "I will avenge you." Her voice carried around the now silent graveyard, and there was a cold and powerful ring to her voice as she wiped the last of her tears away, she stood up, turned and walked from the small plot surrounded by the black metal railings.

Sapphire stood by the large gates and watched as the figure of a warrior not unlike her mother walked slowly down the path, she looked at the red worn eyes of Jett. "How are you?"

"Robbie will need you all back as quickly as possible, I will get my things."

Sapphire grabbed Jett by the arm. "Jett you need time, we understand honestly there is no rush." Jett pulled her arm free.

"I have cried my last tear, I need to get back and finish this." She walked off to the main doors as Saff watched quietly from the gates. Jett ran up the back stairs avoiding Steph and Rafe at the long table and headed to her mother's room.

It was just under an hour later as Jett stood before the mirror in her bedroom and pulled her long black hair back into a tight ponytail, she stood and looked at the long thigh length golden spiked heel boots and the tight red satin pants. She wore the red silk short sleeve top of her mother pulled close with her mother's wide golden belt on which hung the golden sword sheath and her mother's sword. Jett swung the long red cloak around her shoulders and looked at the golden emblem of the lion set upon a five-pointed star. She slid up the hood and stepped back to see herself, full length. There was no doubt she looked like a younger version of the warrior queen who had fought with Walters on that fateful day many years ago.

She dropped the hood, and slipped the sword of truth down her back under the cloak and fastened it across her shoulder on the thin golden belt her mother had given her for her eighteenth birthday. She nodded to herself and turned for the door, as she opened it Rafe stood opposite leaning against the wall, he was not as surprised as she thought he would have been. "Please Wolfie, do not try and stop me, I have to do this for her." He leaned off the wall.

"I never intended to, I know you well enough to know you will do this no matter what I think, I just do not see why you have to do it alone. I loved Ruby and Scarlet just as much you know?"

"I will live through this Wolfie; I need to know you will be there when I return. You understand that don't you?"

Rafe leaned forward and gripped her by the arms as he pulled her close, she resisted at first but he pulled his arms round her and held her tight. For a moment, she relaxed as she felt him close. "I will never stop loving you, and I will always be where you need me most. I love you Jett Amber warrior queen of Caerleon." For a moment her eyes closed as the pain resurfaced, she loved him more than he knew, but she needed to face the ghosts of her mother and put them to rest. Jett pulled away and walked down the corridor to the steps to the main hall. Steph looked up in surprise and caught her breath as Jett came down the steps.

"Saff it's time to leave." She turned and was equally surprised as Jett walked across the main hall. Saff nodded and waved her hand in the air.

"Should you not say goodbye to your father?"

Jett nodded as the window opened and she stepped right through into the yard of the farm at Loxley. She walked straight across the yard to the barn and walked into prepare her horse. As Steph and Rafe came through the window with Sapphire, Jett thundered past on her way to the gates. "Jett please wait!" Steph looked at the others worry on her face. "We have to stop her; she is riding to suicide."

Joe leaned off the wall as he smoked his pipe. "I would like to see you try; she is in no mood to be messed with. God help any who cross her path, she is her mother's daughter."

Rafe headed to the barn. "She will not be alone; I will not leave her. Tell Robbie I will be back as soon as she is safe." He shot through the door and into the barn.

Jett rode through the dark wood avoiding the trees and up past Hearne's Rock and headed out into the woods and trees that would bring her eventually to the Black City at the edge of the Yorkshire moors.

It was just before dawn, as Harry sat alone in the trees on watch. Ten yards behind him Blades and Fox slept curled together, and Woody was close to the small fire. Harry peered into the dark through tired eyes, his head nodded. The sound of galloping hooves came up the track at high speed, his head nodded awake and he looked up. The colour ran from his face and his legs trembled as the red clad hooded figure of Scarlet thundered past him. He raised a shaking white finger to point, but his scream stayed silent in his throat as he shook from head to foot.

A hand patted him on the shoulder. "Arrrrgh" He leapt to his feet and spun round, his face white and his eyes wide with terror. Todd gave a laugh as he stared at him in the dark.

"Harry are you Ok?" He trembled in front of him, as he looked down the track where the rider had disappeared and swallowed hard, he whispered quietly.

"Oh man this aint cosmic, she's back." Todd gave him a bright smile.

"Who is Harry?" He waved his hands in the air.

"Shush! Don't talk about em, it aint cosmic." His eyes stared down the road nervously afraid she would come back; Todd looked back down the quiet empty road. The sound of hooves came out of the dark and Harry began to tremble. "See I told you, what did you have to talk to em for? She is looking for me, they always look for me, it's Robbie's fault he made me do bad things man, oh man, it's like split time."

With eyes wide, and trembling, Harry fled into the trees and crawled under a low shrub. He curled up tight, and clenching his pendant between his teeth snapped his eyes shut, and with his fingers in his ears, he began to chant. Todd looked back into the trees as Harry disappeared unsure of what was going on. The rider in a long flowing cloak of green, and a Loxley crest thundered past before Todd had time to do anything. Blades sat up and rubbed her eyes as she looked up at him.

"What's happening?" Todd shook his head in wonder.

"God knows ask your dad? You understand him." Blades turned to where the leaves of the low growing shrub shook violently and whispered words of a chant murmured from underneath..

"Oh God what spook has he seen now?"

Todd gave a giggle. "I have no idea; he just thinks it's looking for him." He chuckled as he pushed the coffee pot into the flames. Blades gave a gasp and lay back, she smiled at Todd as he snapped large twigs and built the flames up. Worried mumbles continued to rise out from below the shrub as the leaves shook violently, Todd looked over at the twinkling eyes of Blades and both of them started to giggle.

CHAPTER FOURTEEN

THE COMING OF QUEENS

With the rising of the sun, Robbie watched alone across the fields and moors of York. The army was building behind the barricades, and he knew that somewhere in amongst the many officials he could see, one of them had the notion of a mass attack. He shuddered as the dampness still hung in the air from the peat, which had soaked over a week of rain into it. Saff came up from the headquarters with a hot drink and smiled as she passed it to him. "How are they all Saff?" She stared out across the moors.

"Everyone is coping except for Jett. Robbie, she has tooled up and gone after Walters."

He gave a long sigh and rubbed his eyes as he lifted the cup to drink. "I knew she would, can you find her?"

"I have tried over and over, but she is blocking me. Robbie, Walters is surrounded by hundreds of soldiers she does not have a chance."

"I take it my commander is not far away from her?"

"He went after her to try and stop her." Robbie nodded.

"I thought he would, he is no match for Jett, she is deadly at the best of times, I would fear for anyone who faces her hurt. I will talk to Rune she is her centre, Rune will find and protect her."

The row of tents stood two hundred yards from the tree line. Jett peered through the gap in the trees as she tried to work out which one belonged to Walters. As she leaned forward to make her run to the back of the tents, a firm hand slapped down hard on her back and gripped her hood; she felt the jerk and shot backward through the trees back on to the grass. A brown boot stepped onto her chest, as she whipped out her dagger. "If you want to commit suicide, be my guest, if you want to avenge your mother then start using your head and think like her instead of a spoilt child."

Jett stared up at the bright old face of Joe Whitmore. "How the hell did you get here?"

"I have my ways; the Green Lord values your hide young lady, so if you want to do this and do it proper then listen to me." He offered his hand and Jett took it.

"What's on your mind?"

Joe looked back through the trees. "I have sat here every day for a month updating Rune and your mother; I know the old ones routine better than he does." He winked at Jett.

She gave her first smile in two days. "I didn't know."

"There is a lot most folk don't know, your mum was a fine warrior and you have the making of the same if you would just cool that hot bloody head of yours. Right listen to me and pay attention, every morning the old bugger comes out of his tent and wanders over there into the trees." Joe pointed behind him to the edge of a very steep drop. "It stinks a bit, he drinks all night, but if you move down to the bottom of that incline, I promise you will face your man in private. Settle this quickly and then get back to Robbie, he will need you."

Jett nodded. "Thanks Joe." He gave her a smile.

"Just be the best you have ever been, he looks like a fat lazy old bugger but believe me, he really is one of the best with a sword. Do not forget he has slept the booze off, he will be sober." Jett patted his shoulder.

"One of the best is not good enough, I am the best." Joe gave a chuckle as Jett slipped backward into the trees. He picked up his bow, and quivers and waited.

Robbie trudged into the cave, he was exhausted, Treen smiled as he crossed past the table and Skip patted his shoulder. He made his way to the bed and collapsed on to it enjoying the feeling of a pillow and lying down. Rune opened her eyes and slid her arm across the bed, it was empty, she turned and looked at the soft white pillow.

"Hey beautiful, I miss you." She smiled as she closed her eyes and lay back thinking of him.

"I am alone in bed and missing you."

"I will be with you soon I promise, Saff came back last night."

"Be careful Robbie, I am so close now; I can feel them getting ready. A few more days and you will be a daddy." She gave a soft giggle.

"I can't wait; my son will be heir to Loxley and my daughter a princess."

"She could be wild like Jade."

"Not my girl, she will be beautiful and elegant like her mother, I will love her as I do you."

"I love you Robbie, when are you coming?"

"There is still a lot to sort out Rune, we have got the Headquarters running again, Rowan and Treen are doing alright on the observation deck, but I have lost Rafe and Jett and need to find them, Jett has taken the loss of her mum very badly,

I need to know she is safe before I leave. Can you talk to her, no one here can get through?"

"Has she gone after the general? I knew she would. Do not worry about Jett, I will find her, she is not alone on that side of the field; we have had eyes there for some time."

"Do we have a spy in their camp? I wish you had told me."

"Joe has been watching from the trees for some time now, Jett will not pass him easily. You feel tired."

"I am I was on watch all last night."

"You need taking care of; you do not look after yourself when I am not there."

"I am fine, I will be happier when I am with you, I hate sleeping alone."

"I miss you too, get some sleep and then come to me."

"I will. See you soon."

"Sleep well my love." Rune's eyes flowed with violet and high on the moors of Yorkshire Robbie felt an overwhelming sense of Rune within him. His body relaxed as the aches of the night left him and he slipped into a deep restful sleep.

General Ivor Walters pushed back the flaps of his tent and staggered over toward the edge of the woodland. He stood at the top of the high drop, and unbuttoned his pants. Jett squirmed in the trees as he urinated down the bank; it took longer than she thought. "Man he drinks way too much."

The General buttoned his trousers and began to turn round; from nowhere a flash of green streaked across his path, and as it passed, it gave him a huge shove. Jett smiled as she saw the large man teeter at the top of the hill and then slip backwards. He tumbled through the dirt and damp leaves grunting as he bounced off the roots of the trees. With a large splat, he landed at the bottom of the hill and Jett screwed up her face as she saw the fat general lift himself moaning from the filth of his soldiers. "Erg... that cannot be pleasant."

The general moaned as he stood up and shook himself of the foul smelling filth, he shook his hands and groaned with disgust. He lifted his head and there on the path before him was the hooded red clad warrior of his past, he jumped back with surprise. "It's not your day General; you are really up to your neck in it. I have unfinished business with you."

Ivor Walters felt fear rise in him as he looked to the top of the hill; he knew no one would come to aid him; it would be impossible to hear him all the way down here. He pulled his sword out of its sheath and trudged through the filth towards Jett.

"You haunt my nights and my days; I will be rid of you forever."

Jett pulled her mother's long golden blade and prepared. Joe watched from the trees as Walters picked up his pace and his temper rose to fever pitch. His sword came slicing down at Jett with the force of a steam hammer, Jett stepped into the path of the sword and her golden blade made a resounding clash as she swung with all her might and her anger.

The swords met with power and the clash was deafening, Walters, was startled by the force of his opponent, she had grown stronger with age. His wrist shook as the sword bounced under the force. Jett wasted no time and brought her sword, crashing back around as she twisted her wrists, and snapped the blade up fast. He lunged back as the blade swept past with overwhelming force, and just missed slicing his chest. He swallowed hard as his memory of his bitter fight many years ago flashed through his thoughts. He was determined this time not to make the same mistakes, and he raised his blade with the single resolute thought of killing his demon. Jett came quickly at him again.

His blade came up across himself and whipped back at her, she blocked as he forced his blade with all of his might towards her, he smiled as the tip sliced into the top of her arm and he saw the red blood run. Jett stepped back from the blade and shook her head; her arm hurt like hell and she cursed herself for being careless. She steadied her grip as the blood ran on to the hilt of her sword, Walter's felt joy at seeing the wound and came back at her fast, his swipes were fast, and furious as he pounded down on her using all of his huge mass to throw his weight behind the sword. Jett clenched her teeth at the sheer power exploding down on her as she fended off the heavy powerful blows of his sword. Every bone in her body shook as he pounded her backwards, it was overwhelming as she staggered and felt his power grow as he thought he had the upper hand.

She felt the tree burn into her back as she hit it, and watched the blade fly at high speed towards her; she moved quickly sideways and stumbled on the roots. Jett fell sprawling backwards as the huge monk like figure began to laugh; he felt the coming of victory as he stepped towards the rolling red figure as her sword flew into the air out of her hand. White light flashed in front of her eyes, as her head bumped on the ground, and her vision blurred for a moment. She blinked on the ground, and saw the huge dark mass before her stoop and pickup her mother's sword, the sound of her mother's voice echoed in some distant part of her mind.

"How many times do I have to tell you? Use the balance of your heels; you will never win if you have no balance. Jett you must dance with the blade, stop being a bloody tomboy, and for God's sake fight like the warrior queen you will become. Use the power of your womanhood and no man will ever win you."

Jett shook her dazed head as her sight cleared. "Sorry Mum." She saw the large figure lift her sword and laugh in a cruel and sadistic way.

"You will die on your own sword Scarlet of Caerleon."

Jett leapt to her feet, and throwing back her hood, she reached over her shoulder and pulled the bright gleaming sword of truth from its sheath. "I think not fatty."

He looked stunned. "Who the hell are you?"

Jett beamed a smile. "Something far worse than Scarlet, I am her pissed off daughter."

He began to laugh as he looked at the young girl before him. "She sends her child to face me?" His laugh boomed even louder as he raised the golden blade of Scarlet. "I will give you a lesson you will not forget child."

Jett stared with eyes of hate. "I came of my own accord, and I will be the one giving the lessons." The blade of her mother's swung as the large foul reeking figure of Ivor Walter's took the measure of it, his smile was cold and evil as he stepped a little closer. Jett slid her hand in her pocket and lifted out a dried up and shrivelled ear. She gave a smirk as she wafted it in her hand. "You got my mother's sword, but look what I have of yours? My mum wants the other for a set; it's time to pay up big boy."

Ivor Walters shuddered as he saw his ear in her hand. Jett smiled as he looked at her nervously, she came at him with the ferocity of a raging bear. She spun up on her heels and swiped across him, he jumped back as she screamed and brought his sword to block her, but before he could move, she swung wildly spinning round on her heel and swiped upwards and down slicing with all her might.

Ivor Walters screamed as his ear flicked into the air and flopped to the floor. He staggered back clutching at the side of his face; his eyes were wide as he watched her come back at him. Jett spun faster than she ever had, and screamed with a wildness that echoed around the woods. Her pain, hatred, and anger flowed to the surface and ran down her blade. Blue flickered behind her dark black eyes, and the power of her line showed its full and lethal force. Walters saw a glint in her eyes he had seen before in the eyes of another twenty two year old from Caerleon. He stepped back as he relived the force of a twenty two year old red clad warrior, who fought with skill and lethal aggression. He swiped wildly in the air as he tried to watch the blade of Jett Amber, but it was a blur of dancing rainbows, and only her screams, and whoops told him it was coming back.

Joe gasped from the top of the hill as he watched Jett spin like the wind and pound the large brutal general with shot after shot, she was just a blur as her blade glowed, and her hair lifted behind her head. Like the wind of a hurricane, she blew across the floor towards him and he blinked as her sword hit without him realising it. Slices appeared in his clothes as she screamed and swung with pinpoint accuracy, and he staggered away from her a wild look of panic in his eyes. His face was cut with hundreds of tiny nicks as Jett picked slowly away at the man who had robbed her of her mother and sister.

The attack was unrelenting and savage as the red clad warrior of Caerleon lived up to the reputation of her hero and mother. Her temper flared with a power unseen before, Ivor Walters crashed to his knees as Jett cut up with a mighty slice and screamed at him. "HOW DARE YOU RAISE MY MOTHERS SWORD AT ME!"

The sword with his hand still holding tight, shot into the air and he screamed with almighty pain, Jett spun to a halt her eyes burning bright blue with her fury, as she faced the man who ordered her mother and sisters death. The sword landed with a thump and he looked away from Jett to the golden sword with his hand still holding it tight.

Walter's looked back into the blood-splattered face of hatred and power. He clutched his bleeding stump to his chest as he shook with more fear than he had ever known. Jett faced him filled with fury; her eyes were wild and terrifying. She spoke through gritted teeth to control her wild flowing emotions as she twitched. "All your life you have brought fear to others, now face me and know the true fear of life. Know now your life will end shortly, and you will have paid for the evil you have done to my family and friends; know the name of Jett Amber Bedivere, for your life is now mine."

The huge figure of the feared General Ivor Walter's shook like a small child, as he faced a far more frightening figure than he ever had witnessed. The true power of a warrior queen stood before him and it terrified him. Joe watched with respect and shuddered as Jett screamed and drove the sword into Ivor Walters up to the hilt. The glistening blade came out through his back and sparkled in the light. He shuddered and looked into the eyes of his death; they were Jett black and flashed with deep blue light. She held the sword firm and shook with anger, his final gasp of fear left him and his head flopped to his chest. She pulled back hard on the sword and the large figured collapsed in the dirt.

Jett trembled as she stepped back and looked at the dead general. She took a deep breath to calm herself and turned as she walked back to the ear on the floor and picked it up. She returned to the body and kicked it over; Walter's lay with his eyes wide open a look of frozen horrified fear on his face. She pulled the dried up ear out of her pocket and placed it on his chest with his other ear, then turned and looked up towards Joe, he nodded as he saw the tears in her eyes.

Jett slipped the sword of truth back into its sheath and walked to where her mother's sword lay on the ground. Clenching her teeth, she pulled the firm grip of the dead hand off the hilt and dropped it. Jett slid the sword into its long golden sheath and turned. Rafe stepped out from behind the tree; he rested his bow against it and opened his arms.

She stood and shook as her tears ran down her face, he walked up and pulled her close as she wept long and bitter sobs into his shoulder. "Oh Wolfie, what will I do without her?" Jett's real grief flowed out and Rafe shouldered it, he held her tight as Joe kept watch and let the fear and the pain flow out of her with her tears.

Rune and Gwinne sat in the kitchen of the cottage just down from the Abbey; they felt the fear and pain that flowed through Jett as she struggled to come to terms with the loss of her mother. The power and rage that had flowed from Jett as she opened her true feelings to fight had for a moment overpowered the whole circle before Rune blocked them out. Now only Gwinne and Rune felt the true extent of Jett's pain.

It was some time before she quietened in Rafe's arms, he held on to her close, and kissed her head and she looked up at him. He lifted his cloak and wiped the tears and blood off her face. "Now Jett Amber My Queen, you live a life that will make her proud."

Jett nodded her eyes red and swollen, and she sniffed. "Take me home Wolfie."

He slid his arm around her and holding her close, he walked away from the corpse of the general and into the trees. Silently they worked their way away from the enemy and headed back toward the moors and the woodland defences. Joe sat in his trees and watched the enemy as they prepared for another day of combat.

It was two days before the body of General Walter's, was discovered. The troops who found him quaked with fear at the sight of both his ears on his chest, and the look of disfigured horror on his blue face. No one would touch him until General Franklin came down to inspect the body, the sight of both his ears told him straight away who had been responsible, he knew Scarlet of Caerleon had taken his first and the sight of it confirmed to him she had come for him. What worried him was the fact that he had watched Scarlet for the whole time on the observation platform directing the battle. It bothered him as he tried to work out how she could be in two places at once. It was a riddle never to be solved.

It was a very pale and tired Jett that came back into camp with Rafe. He found a quiet spot at the back of the cave and she curled in a tight ball and fell asleep. Rafe talked quietly to Robbie and Rowan as he described what he had seen. He was a man of immense bravery and yet when he confessed how frightened he had been, it surprised Rowan a lot. Rafe spoke of the power and terror of Jett as she fought, he was frightened of it but he held her so much higher in his esteem. It was the bravest and most brutal fight, he had ever witnessed, and he was the flesh tearing Specialist. It painted a sobering picture for Robbie and Rowan.

Jett slept until late into the night and as she woke beside Rafe it was Robbie she saw sat beside her in a chair, he was doing the internal watch with Skip, and he sat at the back with his bow on his knee and watched over her so Rafe who was refusing to sleep got to settle. He gave her a smile. "Welcome back, you had me worried." She sat up slowly so as not to disturb Rafe, and gave him a small smile. She glanced at the bandage below her sliced top and stretched her arm; she winced and gave a small moan.

"I am sorry; it felt important I did that." Robbie nodded.

"I am sure most of us agree, but you are one of us Jett, and we stand beside each other always. I would have stood beside you and protected you, but you cannot go running off alone and expect us not to worry, we all love you Jett and we feel your pain with you." She lifted her head.

"I love all of you too... You do all know that, don't you Robbie?"

"We know, and I am glad now to know that you know. You are never alone Jett in the Specialists we stand, fall, and fight side by side, that is why we are the Specialists."

She nodded and leaned off the bed and gave him a hug. "Thanks Robbie."

"There is coffee and hot stew over there, go on and get something to eat, I have covered your rota. Take the day with Rafe tomorrow and build up your strength again; we have a big fight coming." Robbie watched as Jett walked up to the end of the cave and poured out two coffees. Skip had a quiet word and Robbie smiled as he saw him embrace her.

It had been a long day of organisation as Gwinne sat back at her kitchen table. Rune was staying at the Abbey, and there were many new guests who would arrive to pay homage to their new queen, so Gwinne had moved out to the farm cottage across the fields. It was a large five bedroomed house and she had plenty of space for her daughters and sisters, and of course, there was Jaz, Judy, and Megan.

Her day had started sat with Rune, as she felt the pains of Jett. It had been a hard moment for her as Scarlet was her sister and she too felt the pains of her loss. She had tried to get busy and keep her mind from wandering back to her sister. All of the beds had been made and the whole house cleaned and prepared, and as the hour struck midnight she collapsed with a hot coffee by the kitchen table and breathed a long relaxed sigh of relief. Crystal and Amethyst dozed in the chairs in the front room and despite being told several times, neither of them had risen to go up to bed. The lamp was low and a warm glow filled the small compact kitchen as she stared out of the window at nothing in particular. Her thoughts had turned to Scarlet, she had been in isolation for so long now, and yet she did feel glad she had spent those few precious days in Loxley with Rune. She had spent many hours with Steph and Scarlet and she had been able to catch up and enjoy the feeling of her sisters again. Losing her so soon after had been a bitter blow, and she had wept several times alone in the house.

The tide washed under a full moon up across the soft white sand of the beach, and round the rugged rock of the coastline. It was a warm night with a soft breeze that kissed the sparse trees softly and stroked the grass down carefully. The moon seemed at its largest as mid-summer was days away, and as it glowed in the sky, a shimmering light of white seemed to shine in a single beam to the edge of the island.

Rune stood in the dark with Gwynfor as she watched and smiled, as the fine line of light seemed to widen and touch the soft grass of the island. Gwynfor gave a mighty smile and gripped Rune's arm; he had seen the bridge of light to the crystal castle before. High up in the moon it looked like growing out of the light was a glorious castle that was built of shimmering crystal. It looked vast as it shone in and out of sight with the flickering of the bright light that pulsed down to the earth, as the bright light became more solid. Rune watched with delight and awe as she saw the legendary castle of crystal burning bright in the sky in front of the moon.

This was a realm few had encountered, as it was a realm that could only be entered by those of the line of the Fae of Moon. It had not been seen on the earth for almost a thousand years, as this was the realm of the goddess of the moon moulded by the goddess Tideguyde, when she first discovered the small fragment of hot rock in the time of the creation of all of the realms. Rune's eyes sparkled as she watched, Gwynfor gave her hand a squeeze as he saw the delight and wonder on her face. "Oh Gwynfor it is so beautiful."

"It was made by a spirit of extreme beauty who loved all things beautiful; she was the sister of Rhiannon, who was created in her likeness by Eve. You have the same qualities of her my dear Runestone, and so will your daughter for she will carry the true line of Fae on earth in human form."

The air seemed to fill with electric as the light touched the island and Rune felt the full power of the moon flow through her, it was immense and she felt the same kind of power as she did stood before Hearne. The small figures stepped on to the bridge, and it glowed in a bright intense light, they moved slowly as they started to make their way toward the island, the delegation from the line of the moon was ready to visit the mortal land for the first time in many generations, and Rune felt the wave of excitement grow in her.

The sleek blonde figure of Rhiannon led the group of two hundred of her guard down the bridge of light and off on to the land of Fae. Her deep blue feathered cloak flowed behind her, the slate grey eyes of the daughter of the moon shone brightly. The Violet Isle had high guests of honour for the coming of the new queen. They marched up the steep slope and Rune smiled as Rhiannon again opened her arms to welcome the line of her sister. "Rune my darling I am happy to see you here." She embraced her and held her close. "I have a few of my guards, you have no fear here child you will be safe."

"Oh Rhiannon, I am so happy to see you again." Rune slipped back and

Rhiannon turned to introduce her family. A tall man with the brightest violet eyes looked down at her; he looked powerful as his long blonde hair flowed down past his shoulders on to his cloak of the deepest blue, which bore the crest of a pale blue hooded bird. His face was filled with life and warmth, and his smile was with teeth as white as the moonlight. She needed no introduction as she realised how like her father Amethyst was.

"This is my son."

"RAYNE... Oh Rayne." They both turned as the voice screamed from the darkness across the field, the small figure in bright flowing white ran for all she was worth, and he turned and seeing her he gasped. Rune felt the tug at his heart and the conflict, as he wanted desperately to run to her. His voice was filled with emotion as he watched her running across the long stretch of grass crying out to him.

"Gwinne." Rune smiled at him as he looked back at her.

"Go to her, we can talk later, her need is more than mine." He gave Rune a smile and turned, and vaulting the wall, Rune watched him run across the large green field and sweep her into his arms. Gwinne wailed as her husband embraced her for the first time in almost fifteen years. He fell to his knees as he held her tight and kissed her. Rune watched with tears in her eyes as she saw the happy reunion; Rhiannon put her arm around Rune.

"I am happy she is here; he has missed her so much. He should have stayed and been with his children." Rune gave a chuckle.

"They are here also." Rhiannon, gasped.

"My grandchildren, they are here, where?"

"They are asleep in the cottage, if you want to see them, please go we have plenty of time." Rhiannon smiled back at Rune and gave a small laugh.

"No, let them see their father tonight, he deserves the time with them. I will wait another day."

Rayne wiped the tears from her happy smiling face and held her close. "I did not know, my mother said nothing. Oh my darling I have missed you so much." He lifted her up and kissed her again, she clung to him happy to feel his arms around her again.

"Oh my love, I have been so lonely without you." He held her face in his hands as he smiled and kissed her.

"I cannot tell you of the pain I have known being parted from you and my children. Oh Gwinne, I will never leave you again, I could not endure it."

"Come back to the house, I have a surprise for you." Gwinne's face filled with a wide happy grin.

Crystal lay sprawled out on the sofa; Amethyst lay across the chair, her long flowing blonde hair touching the floor. Both slept deeply unaware of the tear filled violet eyes that watched them. Rayne gasped at his daughter's and knelt quietly down between them. "Oh Gwinne, look at the beauty of my children." Gwinne watched with a heart filled with happiness as he leaned over Crystal and softly blew on her face, she wiped her hand across her face and mumbled.

"Oh don't daddy." He gasped and looked up at Gwinne.

"She remembers?" Gwinne gave a soft chuckle as he leaned over and softly blew her face again. "Criss my angel of the moon, it's time to wake up."

"Oh daddy not yet." She moved on the sofa as Gwinne held her hands to her mouth to suppress her giggles. He blew her again.

"Don't daddy." She opened her eyes and stared into the bright violet eyes of her father, "Daddy?" he nodded. Her eyes flicked to her mum and then back again. Tears filled her eyes as she leapt up and threw her arms around him "DADDY!"

"I am home Angel." He squeezed her tight as she wept on his shoulder;

Amethyst opened her eyes, and looked up at her father hugging her sister. It took a few seconds for her to understand what she was looking at, and soon the house filled with screams and wails as she dragged her father still holding Crystal down and hugged, and kissed and wept. It was not long before the whole house was up as Gwinne introduced her husband to Maddy and Mel, Una, Judy, Megan and Jaz. The kitchen was filled with happy excited talk and smiles; it was going to be a long night in the white cottage on Iona.

There was a cool wind on the moors as Rowan sat with Robbie and watched the sky light up with the flashes, from the combined efforts of the Night Strikers and the Bandits. Sensing the building up of troops, Robbie and Rowan had arranged to up the attacks. The Night Strikers now came in from the west and the bandits from the east. They used bigger explosives in hope of doing more damage and the yells and screams could be heard from the observation post. Robbie needed chaos and fear, and he hoped by building longer and heavier attacks, it would have the desired effect. He had no idea of knowing, but as his attacks took place and the line of the moon arrived on the isle of Iona, the Dark One had just sat up in her chair in Tintagel. The moment the bridge of light touched the island, their power surged across the earth and the Dark One noticed. She shot up from her chair by the fire where she had slumbered, a thin smile slid across her pale thin lips. "So, the time is almost upon us, I must prepare."

She swept down her room as the lights all flared up at the same moment, and she lifted the heavy black book and began to flick through her heavy pages. She muttered to herself as she hurriedly gathered her things into a large black bag; she needed to be at Dunnottar where she was closer and could move within moments to the spot. She sneered and laughed as she planned for the destruction of the flower girl, she knew her powers would fail at the moment of birth and she knew just how to swoop and attack her. The Dark One had planned this for a long time; she too had her ambitions to fulfil.

"Now we will see my little woodland flower, now we shall see who the smart one is. You have pushed your face into my affairs one too many times. I shall visit my crone and then when I see all that has befallen; I will take from you equal to what you have taken from me." She gave a high pitched wild laugh, as she felt a huge surge of joy pass through her. This had been the moment she had been waiting for, the windows blew open, and she lifted into the air and into the dark clouds, and blew out across the land and headed north for Dunnottar Island.

Markus sat with the Sage and looked up to the sky as the thunder rumbled, and the black clouds swept across the sky. Flashes of blue light bounced along the cliffs as she flew at speed across the town and turned inland heading north. "It looks my green friend like we may have some luck; she has left for a while."

The Sage nodded his head. "The new queen is coming to the Violet Isle, Runestone will be weak just after she is born, Le Fey will attack her and try to kill them both."

Markus looked shocked. "Can she do that?" The Sage looked into his bright eyes.

"She will try; there are other powers on this isle that will protect her. Runestone will be safe enough. We must do the job tomorrow; I have to free the old wizard he will be needed by Runestone." Markus patted his arm.

"Have no fear my friend, we will save him. I shall not let you fail your good lady."

The Sage smiled and nodded at his friend. He stared out across the sea and then down at the dimly lit town of Tintagel. Knowing she was not there helped, his greatest fear was she would recognise him, she would feel his presence and he knew that she would come at him. In her eyes, he was a traitor and her attack would be unrelenting. For now, the only problem to face was the guards and he could handle that.

The pressure felt like it was building, he knew Rune now more than anything needed to free up the old wizard, as her life depended on it. Pictures of Robbie with her flooded his mind, his brother needed him and whether or not he knew, it would be his brother that brought forth his protection. He got up off the grass and patted Markus on the shoulder. "Come we have a lot to prepare, time now is short."

Rhiannon stopped laughing and looked at Rune. Rune gave her a knowing look; Rhiannon gave a sigh. "You feel her too?" Rune nodded.

"I knew she would try; I am her greatest enemy; she will always use a time of weakness to attack." Rhiannon stretched her arms across the table and took Rune's in hers.

"You are now the Violetlines; she has no knowledge of what will happen when all the three powers are combined. Even I am not that sure Runestone. The green circle power has always faded for a time during birth, but you are not just green circle, you are Whiteline and White Circle also. No one truly knows what will happen until your time comes."

"I just want Robbie here. When I see he is safe I will relax and be happy. I am on sacred soil; if she attacks it will be her powers that fail."

"He will come have no fear."

Rune lay alone in her bed, as the sounds of the sea softly swayed her into an unrestful sleep. Outside around the Abbey, the guard of the line of the moon stood silently watching. Rhiannon looked out across the water in thought, she knew a time of great danger was upon her and her guards had been warned.

Morgan le Fey had taken the life of Eve, and she knew she would now attempt Rune's. This was the chance she had waited for, and with luck now she would settle the score. Isolde walked slowly across the grass and bowed as Rhiannon turned to look at her. "My Queen of the Silver Realm I am pleased to see you."

Rhiannon nodded her greeting. "I have come with the same purpose as yourself my dear child of the White Circle. Runestone is precious to all of us; the birth of this child will breathe life into the realm of Fae. The loss of your queen has left an uneven balance on our world."

"My Lord of the Isle is concerned that the Dark One has delved deeper into the Backlines' than any of us thought possible, he is afraid that sacred soil will no longer be a protection."

Rhiannon stared at the sea in thought for a moment and then turned to Isolde and smiled. "I feel the same as your high lord of this isle; it is why I have chosen to be present at this moment. Rest your heart my child of the White Circle, for I feel the fear in the hearts of your people. I will never again allow le Fey to take a queen of this realm. The new queen will have powers to match those of us who created this realm; never again will your people be driven from this land."

"Times seem darker now than ever before as our new queen comes, there is much uncertainty in the land, what do you see that gives you such hope for the future?" Rhiannon gave a little chuckle.

"It is true I have the power of foresight as is known to all. I have seen nothing in my mirrored waters that would help, but I feel the air around me and I know what I feel is of such power it has to be victorious. Do not underestimate the power of your line in the hooded man, I have walked with him and felt what he holds within himself." She lifted her arm to Isolde. "Young Robert of Loxley has a union with Runestone and the lines of white have now mixed with the white and green circles that are in its self a powerful combination, but they have something more between them that has created a powerful force not known to us. The Violetlines of power now command, and I do not think that Runestone fully understands that she is not a servant as her grandfather was, but she is the creator of this new power. The Violetlines are truly the new lines that will bring this world back to as it should be, she is still young and as she grows her understanding will grow with her. I think that our little raven of black has greatly misjudged Runestone."

Rhiannon turned to the Abbey and began to walk Isolde back. "It is almost dawn my child, it is very dark and yet soon the light will rise, and we will see the dawning of a new day. Fill your heart with cheer for within the next few days you shall have a queen again. White and silver will stand side by side with her, and soon the new council will form around her and a new dawning of awakening will begin. Our task now must be to guide the forces of Lord Robert and Runestone Violet line to their destiny." They walked quietly through the dark and into the dim lights of the abbey; Hornet stood with Jaz in the darkness and watched over the room of Runestone from the shadows. The guards of the line of the moon walked silently around the abbey, their keen night time eyes seeing everything. Gwinne curled up at the side of her husband, and Crystal and Amethyst slipped exhausted but happily into bed.

Out across the sea the horizon shimmered as a small boat chugged towards the island. The calm sea behind it shimmered with a faint white line that began to follow the little boat towards the island. Dawn was following and soon a new bright day would lift above the scenic isle of Iona and the new lines of the good people of Fae. Rune lay quietly as she slept her face pale and her long red hair hanging from the side of the pillow. Dreams of Robbie sent happy pictures through her mind, Filomena sat outside her door and smiled as she heard his name muttered as Rune dreamt.

Robbie and Rowan sat in the grass and heather, their hoods up and their cloaks wrapped warmly round them as they slept beside the lookout post. Jade and Smokes walked quietly as they watched through the darkness across the moors. The men on the front lines slept in groups taking it in turn to watch, all was silent through the darkness.

The pale light of dawn broke behind the black city, Robbie's eyes snapped open as the first explosive arrow flashed and shattered the silence; he was on his feet as his men jumped to their positions. The commanders barked their orders as they all loaded strikers and returned the fire. Claire jumped wide awake and ran down the path to the observation platform. Lord Loxley stood beside his general and directed the battle as he screamed down at the lower lines. Her flags shot into the air as the air rained fizzing arrows, Robbie gave his orders and she waved the messages rapidly. General Franklin had learned a few tricks from Scarlet, and now it seemed they would deploy the same tactics of explosive arrows. Rowan watched as more bowmen flooded past to the front lines. "It took them long enough to catch on, it will get bloody from now on."

Robbie nodded as he blinked his eyes awake. "This is the start my brother, I have expected this. It is now the time to start this war properly, gone are the days of testing the lines. Now we fight for Loxley."

"Don't you mean York?" He looked puzzled as he looked into Robbie's eyes. Robbie shook his head.

"This has never been about York that was just some petty ambition Mason has on the road. No my brother, this is the start of the defence of Loxley. We stand on the outer edge of a realm he will do anything to crush. York will amuse him as he passes." Rowan looked to the field where the fight raged from both front lines, as they showered each other in hope of finding a weakness. Loxley had the superior bowmen with greater range and they were inflicting damage, the woodsmen had their losses and the first of many stretchers came up the hill to the carts that would ship them back to York. The war of the Knox Empire verses the Woodland Realm had finally begun.

The lord of the realm of the woodsman watched from the ridge high above the front lines, his cloak was mud splattered and his face showed the growth of a day without a razor, and yet there was a fire in his eyes that burned brightly as he scanned his lines. He bellowed the orders of command down the line to his officers as he walked along.

"Watch that line, close that rank and shut them down. Claire tell Commander Wilkes to get out of bed and shut that bloody line down over there." The flags waved high as the authority of a father's son came in a moment of need. Robbie commanded with skill and authority, taking charge as the pressure built on his front lines. They held together, and took relief in the knowledge that high above them their lord watched for them.

Robbie walked back along the platform to Rowan and Smokes, Jade came up with a tray of drinks sent by Maggs, he lifted the cup of steaming coffee to his lips and enjoyed his first taste of warmth. He looked across the battlefield and then back to Rowan and Smokes. "It's time to get Scarlet's boards up here, do it tonight in the dark? I want us to be ready for the big surge, I have no intention of being caught out, I will fight these buggers to the last man to save Loxley." Rowan nodded and patted his arm as he lifted his cup; Robbie was preparing the tactical withdrawal that Scarlet had planned with Treen and Fuse. He knew that the whole of the black army would flood out, but he was ready for it.

Scarlet's boards were designed to fit on the posts that ran the whole length of the two-mile ridge. They were covered in heather and grass and when placed they would look like the ridge had increased in height. The idea was that the observation deck would be lifted to the top of the boards, and as dawn came up the view from the other side of the field, it would look the same. With a long row of catapults already in place, the bowman could hide low behind the boards in the shallow trenches already dug. As the front lines withdrew and the black forces came forward, long spiked wooden poles would be raised from the heather where they lay prepared. The whole of the ridge would have a collar of sharp spikes to impale the enemy as they raced up to them. From behind the boards, the bowman would rise and hit them with a heavy hail of arrows. It had been Scarlet's gamble that it would buy the woodland forces more time, to withdraw and prepare the lines of retreat. Cartloads of the bright violet exploding balls were now covered and ready to be shot into the air to bring massive devastation to the invading army.

She had prepared for over six months for this moment, and Robbie felt a little relief knowing she had paid attention to every detail, she was a true warrior queen and he felt her with him as he watched and prepared for the onslaught of Mason Knox. He was fearful for those miles away held safe within the stockade, and yet the sound of his father echoed in his head. "I might be afraid, but I won't let them buggers see it, or think for a moment I can't whip em."

CHAPTER FIFTEEN

RETURN OF THE GUARDIAN OF LINES

The old boat had anchored off the mainland, and bobbed up and down in the water, as Toby pulled the small rowboat up onto the slipway, and dry land out of the clear blue water. He lifted his bags and smiled with a rosy glow on his red round face. Mel slid her arms out from the two young teenagers, and they ran down the road and jumped into his happy open arms. She smiled as she watched him with his niece and nephew, as they chatted happy with him as he walked back. The captain of the old blue tug stood before her in his familiar thick black coat and his black skipper's hat wore slightly off line. He gave her a huge and happy smile. "Hello Mel love." She slid her arms round her oldest friend, as he brought his big heavy arms around her and squeezed her tight. It was a familiar feeling that she had not realised up until that moment, how much she had missed it.

"Oh Toby, I've missed you so much."

The captain of the small boat 'the Northwinds,' had run her supplies to her for many years to the island of Callanish. He knew all of the fastest routes, and had been her very important lifeline. At times; he had been her only source of conversation, and news of the world off the island of Lewis in the far north west of the Scottish Isles. When the time had come for her children to leave the island, as they had reached the age where they were maturing and Mel feared the curse of the island would take them, it had been Toby's old cottage in Kilmory where they had gone. Jasper and Sapphire had waited for their mother, and in return they had taken on the task of educating his orphan niece and nephew.

To Toby now, they were like family, and he loved them all dearly. As Mel slipped back from his arms he smiled with concern, he knew of the task that she had to do and he could see the worry in her slate grey eyes. "One more trip up the coast my love?"

She smiled at him. She knew he too was worried, but they had spoken so many times of it, he knew it was better not to mention it. Mel had insisted she ensure her sons place on the island, Toby had pleaded on many occasions for her to just leave and never return to the island. He could not see the point in living on such a small island when there was a country half-empty and land by the mile to live on.

Callanish was wild and rugged; it was a hard place to live, especially after the red death had wiped out all of the islanders.

He slid his arm around Mel as Will lifted his heavy canvass bag, and with Gaynor laughing and joking, the four of them set off toward the brother of his sea partner's house. Will and Gaynor had been staying there until Toby could find a new home. In secret he was waiting for Saff or Mel to find a place, he knew how much the teenagers loved them. It would be a quick breakfast and then the other members of the group would arrive ready to leave for Callanish and the long awaited task. Mel suddenly felt a lot safer knowing he would be taking them, in many ways he had been the one who had given her the confidence to face her life alone on the island, and face the future that was now looming in front of her.

Ben cleared his plate as the others all sat watching, still amazed someone so small could eat such large amounts. His eyes twinkled as he looked up and smiled, the Sage shook his head. "Well young Master Winters, I no longer see your bones, but if you carry eating the way you do, I feel you will grow as big as Markus here."

He collected the plates and washed them in the small amount of water they had, as the others prepared for their day of assault. Markus now wore the uniform of a captain of the guards and Martin a uniform of a general. Looking like the army members they had once been was their biggest hope of gaining entrance.

Martin felt uncomfortable wearing the clothes he wore for over twenty years. They all knew that without it they would not get into the city that was now built on the old town of Tintagel. It was an hour later when the group were ready to set off, the Sage swung his bag onto his shoulder and lifted his bow and quiver; he looked round the small circle of determined faces. "You all know what to do?" They all nodded and turned to look down on the walls looming a mile away. "Ok let's do it, may Hearne walk beside all of you." Martin patted his back.

"We will be fine my green friend, you will see." The Sage nodded as they began to walk down the hill out of the trees toward the road that would lead to the market outside of the city. Ben as ever asked a thousand and one questions, this time he chose to ask Markus. He had taken a little time getting use to the very tall dark skinned man, but now his shyness was wearing and Martin and the Sage laughed as he assaulted Markus with an endless supply of questions. "Where do you really come from?" Markus gave him a wide smile.

"Well, my friend that is a very long story, that starts back in the age of the nineteen fifties with my grandfather and father. They were born in Africa, which is a very long way from here in the south where it is very hot. They came here on a boat to work, as Africa was a very poor country. They lived in London and worked for the fine company known as British Railways. They worked on what then, was the old steam engines, and they shovelled the coal into the fires that made them run on the tracks."

"What's a steam engine?"

"Oh, now they were mighty fine machines that pulled people up and down the country, they were like rows upon rows of carts made of metal and wood which the people sat in."

"Why did people want to go up and down the country?" So it went on as they walked down the hill of wild and rough sedge scattered with corn cockle and thrift, and onto the road, and made their way slowly talking all the way down the long road to the market outside the walls of Tintagel City.

The group were assembled on the slipway as Mel walked beaming toward them with Toby; Gaynor spotted Jasper and ran with joy towards him. His face lit up with smiles as he lifted her into his arms. The others smiled as they watched the excitement of the young fourteen year old, as Mel introduced her friend.

"Everyone this is Toby, he is skipper of the Northwinds and my best friend in the world, he will be taking us." Rune gave a smile.

"It is very nice to meet finally, we have all heard a great deal about you Captain Toby." He gave his usual broad smile that lit his happy round face.

"Aye Mel can talk when you let her." He pulled her close as he laughed. "Use to talk me legs off when I visited." Everyone giggled as Mel beamed up at her friend.

It was to be two trips in the small rowboat to get them all on board, so Maddy, Una and Meg boarded first, Mel and Hornet stood on the slipway and watched as Toby pulled on the oars and rowed the small boat across to the bobbing boat. Rune looked at Mel and Hornet. "Remember to connect to each other and keep in the circle. Be clear and precise in every word you speak Mel, I have taken the precaution of preparing protection so as long as you all stay connected and touching you will be fine."

Mel nodded as Rune spoke, Hornet stood by her side looking a little nervous, Will winked at her and she smiled. Toby helped the others up on to the boat, and dropped back down and turned to row back. Rune walked with her arm around Hornet to the edge of the water. "Have no fear Judy; you have the power of the white in you. She will no longer recognise you when she feels you in amongst the others, Una has a great power of protection she will watch over you for me." Judy looked up at her.

"I do not like the idea of leaving you Rune. She will come for you; you have no idea of the hate she carries for you; I have seen her rage. You will be weak and she knows it." Rune pulled her into a hug.

"I have the protection of the sister of the moon and Isolde and Filomena of the lines of Fae. They hold a very powerful magic borne of the lines of the White

Circle, have no fear for me I will be safe. Help your sisters of the circle and work for the table of Runestone and I will see you soon." She leaned down and whispered in her ear. "I also feel that so will young Master Will here, I do believe he likes you."

Judy gave a shy giggle, as she looked back at the young seventeen-year old boy stood beside Jaz.

"He is quite cute." Rune smiled.

"He has not taken his eyes off you since he got here; I believe your powers are already at work my young apprentice." Rune gave her a big smile and kissed her head as she giggled. "Now go with Mel and enjoy the feel of those stones, which I can assure you, are a wonder to walk around."

Judy looked up at Rune. "I will see you soon, be careful." She hugged her tightly. "I love you Rune."

"I love you too, now go on." Judy climbed into the boat as Rune hugged Mel. "I will be with you my sweet sister have no fears." Mel nodded.

"I will see you soon. Take care Rune." Rune stood with Jasper and the two teenagers and waved as Toby pulled on the oars and rowed to the boat. She watched as they all climbed aboard, and then waving to them, they heard the engines fire, and the Northwinds chugged gently out of the bay, and down the inlet out into the sea heading north and the island of Lewis.

The sun shone as she slowly made her way down the main street of the small island town of Iona. The houses decorated with flowers stood warmed by the sun as she passed lost in thought. Rune pulled the old farm gate behind her and stepped into the field constantly grazed by the sheep and walked along the low granite wall. She smiled as she looked to the edge of the water where the rocks and soft white sand blended into the blue sea, and she remembered those three precious days she had spent alone with Robbie in the first week of November the previous year. It had been one of the happiest times of her life, and as she thought of them, she missed him more. He was miles away sat on the moors having fended off the first major attack of the day and preparing his troops for the next strike.

She stood by the corner of the wall and enjoyed the memories. The abbey stood behind her and the sun shone brightly and bounced off the waves, twinkling at her as she stared out to sea. The tug was a tiny speck on the horizon and she thought of Mel. The time had come and now Rune had to prepare as the Dark One was drawing power to herself in Dunnottar. It was going to be a difficult few days.

The market outside Tintagel was bustling. The air was filled with the noise of traders as they called out promoting their wares to the visitors from all over the region. Ben looked out from under his brown hooded cloak, and marvelled at the size of the market. It was five times bigger than that of Caernarfon, the wooden stalls lined the high walls, with large heavy woven canvass sheets, there were clothes and tools and foods of all kinds. People crowded and bunched and laughed, as they met up and spoke and the news of every area was brought to the ears of their friends.

The Sage was alert and watched everything. He was surprised at the many different kinds of people he saw. The farmers were easy to spot with their heavy wool coats, as were the traders in their many diverse forms of clothing of bright colours. He was surprised to see woodsmen, how could they support the will of Mason Knox?

The truth was that the whole of the south west of the country was shut off from the outside world, and none of them really knew what was going on far up north in York. Mason had always tried to keep his part of the country separate; here he was seen as the saviour of the people, his wall had prevented the red death from coming. The wind farms and small coal run power stations had to a degree kept all of the electricity running, the street lights no longer worked and there were very few cars now as the petrol had run out, but apart from that, most of the south west was preserved as it had been in the times of old modern man.

The only real changes to the life of old were the new concrete buildings that had sprawled across the rugged beauty of the wilds. New estates had sprung up everywhere as Mason populated his protected area. The southwest had become more like that of a small country separate from the rest of the nation. Everyone here lived their lives unaware of the control Mason and his empire held over them.

The market was set to the backdrop of grey walls. The high concrete walls were smooth and featureless and wound across the last of the green lands to the sea. They seemed unattractive and out of place as they loomed cold and harsh in a landscape of wild flowers and many coloured grasses. The Sage noticed the glint of the sun, as it reflected off the helmets and weapons of the guards high above, they looked downward watching everything that was happening in the market. The gates of the city were high and made of thick wood; they stood open under a large archway where a barrier was placed to restrict the flow of those who entered into the fortress. A long queue formed as the guards checked each individual, the scruffy attire of the Cutters Brigades was easily noticeable in the wings of the long tunnel like entrance that led inside the barracks. They leered at people who passed them in an intimidating fashion.

Martin skipped the queue and walked to a side entrance door. He wore the uniform of his station in the forces of the Knox army, and he was not going to stand in line. The sergeant on the gatehouse watched as they approached, he stepped out of his doorway and saluted.

"Good morning General." Martin saluted back as he approached in a businesslike manner.

"Good morning Sergeant Peters, it has been some time since we last spoke."

"It certainly has Sir, and if you don't mind me saying it's real good to see you are safe Sir."

Martin stopped with the Sage and Ben behind him. "I have a mystic and his young assistant to see the Lady of Cornwall."

The sergeant glanced at the Sage stood with arms folded and his hands up his sleeves. His hood was forward over his eyes and hiding the mask of white birch. Ben stood beside him in a long brown cloak, his head down and his hands together. "Are they safe enough, he has a bow?"

"I assume so Sergeant, he was her advisor in Dunnottar, we have travelled a long way to be here. How is the wife anyhow? I have only a short stay here but I will be back in a few weeks; tell her how much I have missed her extraordinary apple pies."

The Sergeant gave a large smile. "She is fine sir, and still running the kitchens with great efficiency. If you have time, I believe her special pie is on the menu today." Martin smiled and patted the Sergeant on the shoulder.

"I believe my good man if I can get these two settled quickly, I may just nip in before it all goes." The Sergeant gave a wide smile as Martin beckoned to the Sage and Ben, he walked off through the door and the Sergeant waved them through. Martin gasped a deep breath of relief as he walked down the long tunnel into the courtyard at the far end. The Cutters paid a lot of interest in the two hooded figures as they passed.

Markus came down the tunnel behind and noted the Cutters. He gave the man leaning on the wall a hard stare. "I hope you are behaving yourself Robson?" The Cutter jumped back as he looked into the dark eyes of the ex-captain of the guards, he had one too many memories of his encounters with Markus.

"What you doin back? I thought you had quit?" Markus smiled.

"Do any of us ever really leave an army? In times of need the best always get a recall? I will watch you if I return so think on?" Robson put his head down and spat on the floor, he scowled at the back of the old captain as he walked through the tunnel and into the sunlight.

"I will get him one day; you mark my words. I owe that one." The others nodded, but they knew of the reputation and were not in a rush to mess with Markus.

The walled city of Tintagel, which was mainly a fortress, was about two thirds of a mile across. It was built on three levels the highest of which was the main gate and tunnel, by which they had entered on the north side of the city. In the court yard of the city was a huge building of ten floors, this was the main garrison of the military, Ben looked around at the high stonewalls and the rows of windows running up and across the whole building, he had never seen so many floors stood on top of each other; it made him dizzy just looking up. The Sage tapped his shoulder as they crossed the yard and he hurried to catch up with Martin as they approached the low wall on the top level and looked out.

Looking down to the west was the building that they were interested in. The four-storey building of almost black glass like brick was the fortress of the Dark One, it ran out to the edge of the cliff. It backed on to the steep grey walls that fell to the back of the wild lands at the side of the market, and had four levels all marked with ornate arched leaded windows. The doorways were all intricately carved with runic letters and faces of strange beasts that Ben had never seen before; down the side of it was a long wide incline. The road was made of the same black glass like material, and had metal railings along the edge as it slipped down to the bottom of the hill and the wide flat open space that still contained the original town of Tintagel. Just past the town, endless, rows of small brick houses stretched right back to the large far wall on the south side of the city.

Here were the homes of those who worked for Mason Knox. The men of industry and the scientists all worked in the design offices and laboratories below the Dark One's quarters. This was the heart of the Knox Empire, here he brought together all the best of their fields to work under his leadership and help bring his dream alive. The Sage looked out across the pile of rubble that had once been the second fortress, if only Robbie had known at the time.

A huge area of the land had slipped into the sea as the mighty explosion had ripped through the top of the ancient mound creating a massive crater and dragging the black stone fortress and the old hotel into the sea. What was once a place of a king's birth, was now just a mound of sea washed rubble in a wide oblong, along the crumbled edges of the concrete Mason had poured all over it. The Sage leaned over to Martin as he stood at the top of the long road that led down to the lower entrance of the office building. "If the hooded man had just moved the explosives he would have wiped out all of the brains of Mason's operation in one go." Martin gave a smile.

"He almost got me; I was here at the time. No one ever believed this place would be attacked; we all thought we were safe here." They began to walk slowly down the footpath as Martin filled them in on the building they were going to enter. "The private door to her quarters is the last one, round the side out of sight is a small ledge, it is used for maintenance. It is high, and it is a long drop to the rocks so be careful." The Sage and Ben nodded. "I will move up to her floor and open the third window from the right, there are no windows below it as it is where the stairs are, I will drop the string, attach the rope and I will pull it up for you to climb."

They moved slowly down as the Sage watched from every angle to check who was and who was not watching. Martin checked his watch. "Any moment now it will be the shift change." As they approached the bottom door and loud horn wailed. Suddenly doors opened and people spilled out everywhere, the almost empty street was instantly full as the employees of Mason Knox came out of their offices for breaks, or headed into other offices for their daily work. Martin grabbed Ben's sleeve and pulled him quickly across the road, the Sage followed and they nipped down the narrow passage at the side of the building, and Martin went in through the door, and onto the stairs that made their way up to the high fourth floor and the apartments of the Dark One.

A small metal gate prevented the Sage and Ben getting on to the ledge. The Sage climbed up and grabbed Ben's hands, he gave a huge pull and Ben shot up in the air and over the other side where there was a two foot wide smooth ledge filled with chattering Seagulls. Ben lifted his leg to move the seagull and it turned snapping at him, he flinched and moved back.

The Sage slipped round him and smiled. "They make a good pie; I will get that one and you can bite him back." He sniggered as Ben stared at the large white bird with caution. The Sage slipped his bow off his shoulder and then with a rapid snap of his wrist, he hit the bird on the throat and it crumpled to the ledge. The Sage gave a big grin as he passed it to Ben. "There's Tea." Ben seemed a little put off as he gingerly took hold of the large dead bird. The Sage stood with his back to the shiny wall and opened his bag, he pulled out a long length of rope, twisted on the ledge and pulled the rope round Ben, who had leaned forward and seen just how high up they were. One hundred feet of cliff fell down to the white sand, where a small boat was drawn up and sat half tilted. The Sage tied the knot firmly; he leaned flat against the wall and steadied himself as he gasped for air.

"Ok are you ready for this?" Ben was pale but he nodded. "Alright my young friend, as soon as you are down push the boat as close to the water as you can. We will be coming fast and will need to get off that beach as quickly as possible." Ben nodded and gave a weak smile.

"I know." The Sage smiled and ruffled his hair.

"Ok over you go, and don't be scared I will not let you fall." Ben knelt down and carefully slipped off the ledge; he grabbed the dead bird and held it tightly close to the rope. The Sage took the weight on the rope and began to lower him down the edge of the rock face, Ben pushed his legs on to it as Markus had told him to, and slowly he descended the high wall of granite that made up the cliff. He felt a surge of relief as his feet touched the white sand, Ben dropped the bird and clutched at the rope as he pulled on the tight knot and undid it, the rope shot up as he turned, grabbing the large white bird, he scampered across the sand to the small rowboat. He threw the bird in and pushed with all his might the boat moved an inch, his feet slipped in the soft sand.

Martin looked round the corridor wall and smiled as he saw the frame of Markus leaning in the guardroom window; he moved to the window on the Dark One's private stairs and slipped back the catches of the two long arched leaded windows. Out of his pocket came the ball of string with the rock attached and he leaned out to see if the Sage was ready. Ben was far down below pushing on the boat; the Sage was on his hands and knees as he crawled along the thin ledge under the laboratory windows. Martin lowered the string quickly as he sporadically looked back checking he was still clear. The stone came down fast pulling the string behind it, and as the Sage stood up it hit him on the head. "Ouch" He looked up at Martin who mouthed sorry and smiled, the Sage tied the rope on the string and it shot back as Martin pulled quickly.

The rope came up through the window. He grabbed it quickly and he tied it to the stone pillar between both the open windows, he gave the rope a jerk and felt it go taught. The Sage shot up the wall on the rope as Martin watched the corridor. Markus kept his old guard friends talking about his chances of a return to service. The Sage came in through the window and sprang silently to the floor; he winked at Martin and looked up to where Markus was talking.

Without a moment to waste, he shot up the long corridor to the double doors of red stained wood. He checked he was still clear as he listened with his ear to the polished door, everything was silent inside as his heart beat rapidly in his chest, and he pulled on the handle of the door, it swung open and he slipped in. Martin held his breath as he constantly checked the stairs and long corridor to make sure all was clear.

The cold long room with the smouldering fire and two faded red chairs sent a cold tingle down his back. Glass jars still bubbled as they sent many shades of coloured liquid from one to the other; he walked slowly down the room alongside the long wooden highly polished table to the glass box containing the old wizard. He gasped. "Leenard?"

The Sage looked down on the older but distinct features of a man he had known most of his life, his eyes were closed as a golden mist swirled round the inside of the glass box. Quickly he took the four butterflies out of his pocket and placed them on each of the corners of the glass lid, they glowed a deep violet, and then the two above the head of Leenard began to slide slowly down the box towards the wizard's feet.

The Sage looked at the feet of the old wizard, where the glass was reverting to nature and pouring as sand into the bottom of the box as the top slid back. The Sage took out the golden violet flower and placed it on the centre of the old wizard's head, it began to glow a bright white and the wizard snapped his eyes open. The Sage jumped back with shock snapping his hand away from the old wizard quickly. "Run Boy!"

The Sage lifted his arms to balance as the floor and the building began to vibrate, he turned and began to run to the door, staggering as the floor shook more violently. Flashes of gold bounced from the walls to the centre of the room where the box lay on the long wooden table. He staggered sideways missing the handle and scrambled back toward the door, he gripped the door handle and pulled as an almighty flash filled the room and he felt himself lifted into the air and thrown through the door. The door slammed shut with a crash as he hit the wall and looked up panicked.

Ben heaved with all his might and the boat moved a few more inches, he panted and leaned back. "This is going to take all day." A violet hand touched the boat, and he jumped back in shock, his heart leapt in his chest as he looked into the kind smiling face of the violet lady of the woods.

"I feel young master you need a little more stew before you will be able to push this?" He grinned at Rune as she chuckled. "Shall we try together?" He gave her a nod and leaned on the boat, it glowed violet for a moment, and then ran down the beach and splashed into the water, Ben was almost dragged in with it but Rune gripped him and pulled him back with a smile. "Jump in and be ready, I must help your friends." Ben scrambled over the side and fell forward on to the floor of the boat. He pulled himself quickly to the seat, and grabbed one of the oars and slipped it into the bracket. He lifted the other and set it in place ready.

The clouds above Tintagel began to swirl and gather as Martin slipped out of the window on to the rope. The Sage slipped his bow over his shoulder and staggered as the floor shook violently. He scrambled to the window and pulled himself on to the ledge, Martin was flying down the cliff face as the Sage looked back towards Markus. Markus was running half staggering down the corridor; the guard ran out of his office and raised his crossbow and took aim at Markus.

The Sage was off the window, his bow slipped off his shoulder and shot round, as he loaded and fired. Markus suddenly looked frightened as he thought the Sage was going to shoot him; the arrow whipped past his shoulder and hit the guard lifting him off his feet. He smashed into the wall and slipped down a red line marking his route on the wall, Markus looked back and saw his old friend with the cross bow and realised he had just had a very narrow escape.

The Sage stood with his bow aimed down the corridor his hood up, as the second guard came out and Markus climbed out of the window. The guard saw the hooded figure, and screamed and ran back into the office; the Sage jumped onto the window, and grabbed the rope. His feet ran down the wall as the rope smoked in his gloved hands. Ten feet from the bottom, he let go and landed like a cat, he gave one last look to ensure they were still safe, and turned and scurried across the beach to the water where Martin sat in the boat and Ben helped Markus over the side and in.

The glass side panels exploded out of the case as the golden lightening bounced around the room. Bottles and potions exploded as the building shook more and more violently, clouds of shimmering colours rose into the air as the captive essences of many were released. Merlin stood up in one sweeping movement, and caught the golden violet as it fell; he stretched out his arms and leaned back his head as the roof exploded off the building, and blew into the sky shattering into millions of pieces that rained back on the walled city of Tintagel. The clouds swirled in the sky building up speed; they lit up with the bright electric blue lightening contained within them illuminating miles around. Then with a roar of thunder that sounded like a million cannons firing, a blinding white light flowed out from the clouds and down to the figure of the old wizard who screamed out a huge laugh of joy, and all of the windows in the building exploded out with huge force.

People screamed, chased by long shards of deadly slicing glass as they fled, and were thrown across the streets. Lights of every colour flashed out from the top of the roof and hit other buildings smashing the windows and throwing people already panicked across rooms. The power that plunged from the sky was enormous, as the Whitelines of Time flowed from high above the earth back down into their guardian.

Workers crawled on their hands and knees as the glass flew everywhere. Their faces and hands were cut and slashed as they wailed and they moaned, everywhere was filled with panic and the screaming of the terrified workers, as the high stonewalls held them captive and they could not easily flee. The long tunnel out to the market was filled with the trampled, as people tried to run to the entrance gate in their blind panic, and were stuck. Guards, soldiers and workers fought each other as the terror of death gripped them, while the earth below their feet shook violently, and they glimpsed the light of freedom ahead of the long tunnel of darkness.

The light funnelled down out of the sky and the old wizard held out his arms and basked as if in a gentle rainstorm, the lines on his old face softened and his beard receded, his eyes burned with bright violet light as his age left him and he felt the power grow inside him. The time of the Violetlines was upon him, and he felt the power of his granddaughter as she regenerated him. The light began to fill with flickers of lilac and then it powered down in the brightest of violet, Merlin was reborn in the power created by Runestone Sapphire the daughter of life, and he screamed with delight, as he felt stronger than he had in a thousand years.

The light stopped as quickly as it had begun the shuddering of the floor eased and the injured cried and moaned on the floor of the city. Merlin smiled as he looked around the smashed and devastated remains of the Dark One's home. He jumped off the table with a lightness he had not had for many years and he chuckled to himself as he walked round what was left of the smashed and shattered room. There on the floor in the corner he saw the long white carved staff he knew so well.

"Oh my, I wondered where I had left it." He walked to the corner and lovingly he lifted his staff of old, it felt good in his hands after all of these years. He walked as if on a stroll as he wandered around looking at the smashed jars and potions bottles, he came round what was left of her smashed table and walked up to the side of the glass case that had been his prison; there on the floor was a dusty circle. Merlin tapped with the end of his staff and the floor began to swirl slowly round as a table of power with a seven pointed red edged black star wound upwards out of the floor. His expression changed as he saw it, and his brow furrowed as he looked on the dark table of Morgan le Fey.

"I warned you I would not tolerate the Darklines Morgan?" Merlin smote the table with his staff, there was a huge flash of intense violet light, and it cracked down the centre and crumbled to the floor.

High in the tower of the castle at Dunnottar, the Dark One screamed in wild distress as she felt the pain of her table being torn from her world, she flew to the window with fear on her face and screamed across the ocean like a mother whose child had been stolen from her. Merlin turned and faced north as he smiled, the door at the end of the room opened and the violet figure walked in, he beamed with delight as he saw her. She ran down the room and he lifted her into his arms. "Runestone, my darling." She hugged him hard as he smiled with joy. "You have learned much my daughter of violet; your power is immense."

"I have missed you Grandfather; I was so afraid for you." He softly patted her back as he held her.

"This old badger does not leave easily my child. I was never going to let her hurt you."

"I am on Iona grandfather; my children will be born soon." He gave a happy chuckle and released her. Her bright eyes burned with delight as she looked at him.

"You look younger Grandfather." She curled her finger in his goatee and he gave a giggle. "I prefer this to the long beard; it makes you look dashing." She gave him a bright smile of love and his eyes seemed to soften as the love of his precious granddaughter showed on his wise face

"You must go and be with your Bowman, now is the time of family, fear not I will watch over the realm, I must speak with those who helped me and then I will visit my lord and master, for there will be much to do as the new queen comes. Go my darling and take my love with you." She gave him a huge smile, and reached up and kissed him on the cheek.

"I love you Grandfather."

"I love you too my precious Granddaughter." Rune faded and broke up as she slipped back to herself on the isle of Iona. Merlin walked across to the door and made his way out of the smashed and almost totally destroyed building. "What a mess, and to think my king was born here, Mason should be ashamed."

Martin and Markus pulled hard on the oars as the boat pulled away along the coast, the Sage looked back with a smile as he saw the devastation caused by the return of the old wizard. The boat swung inland three miles up the coast and they came up to the beach where the Sage jumped out and pulled on the rope to pull the boat onto the sand. He felt an enormous sense of relief and as Martin and Markus came up the beach, he took their hands with joy. Markus squeezed his hand hard. "I owe you a life my green friend."

"You owe me nothing, without you we could not have got this far, we are equals my dark friend." Markus gave a hearty laugh and pulled him into a vice like hug. "In all my years no one has ever had the courage to call me dark, I see my green friend we are truly equals on this land." He laughed a roaring laugh as he let go of the Sage and gave Martin a huge pat on the back. Happy and relieved the three of them made their way up through the tall matted grass of the dunes and up on to the lush green pastureland of northern Cornwall. Ben carried the huge bird on his back.

"Hey guys I am hungry." The Sage looked back and smiled.

"Why doesn't that surprise me?" Markus roared a hearty laugh.

As the sun headed west and began to fall toward the sea, the bright blue tug Northwinds, bounced and skipped across the waves towards Lewis. Mel leaned on the front of the cab with Toby as she saw what had been her home in the distance, she could not see the stones yet but she could feel the pull of them. For so many years, it had been her protection and she smiled to herself as she thought of walking within the circle again. Toby smiled. "You have missed them I can see." She lifted her cup and smiled as she drank.

"Believe it or not my friend, this is the place I call home. I love this land with its wild winds and constant rain, it is a hard place to live but I do love it." He lifted his arm around her shoulder and she slid up to him. "You have been a good friend to me Toby; I never would have made it without you, I owe you so much and yet you have never asked for anything." He turned and looked at her as she looked up and smiled.

"You know I love you?" She gave a quiet nod. "I am a man of the sea Mel; I do not have dry land below my feet. I will live and die on the water; if I had been any different I would have asked, you know?"

"I know Toby. I love you too, but I always knew it would never be more than just friends."

He gave a soft nod and then looked out to the island as it grew in the distance. "There has only ever been you Mel, I am sorry it could not have been more, but I know what I am like. I will never leave the sea, she will swallow me up and that's alright with me." Mel cuddled up against him.

"I am happy you have the thing in your life that gives you great joy, I have happiness in Loxley."

He gave a grin. "Aye, I could tell the moment I met you, I am happy for you my love, you deserve more than sitting in the stones alone grieving for a lost man."

"I was not too sure how you would feel." Her slate grey eyes met with his as he smiled.

"I don't cry when the cat spills the cream Mel love. I cannot give you what you will get from him, and you deserve it. I will be happy knowing you are cared for and still my greatest friend. I have many good memories of walking and talking with you in the stones. I stand in my cab in the dark as I make my way round this land for the millionth time, and I take comfort in the memory of a beautiful woman who gave me her love and friendship."

"Don't you get lonely and ache for someone to be close to you Toby?"

"Why would I when I have you?" Tears welled in her eyes.

"Oh Toby, you cannot spend the rest of your days alone. What will you do when I leave here? I will not be coming back."

"I know Mel love, but you see I have had twenty years of love and companionship with you, I have never been truly lonely. I now have all of that time to keep me; honestly, it is enough for me, I can live out the rest of my days knowing the most beautiful woman I have ever known once loved me. Tell me, what man could ask for more?" Toby pulled her close and held her tightly in his arms as the stones glistened with the red of the falling sun. The island was growing larger in front, as the small jetty came into view and the path leading up to the small cottage with the thatched heather roof. The engines gunned as they slowed, and the boat chugged softly towards the island. Mel and Toby stood together as they watched in the falling sunlight, the place that had bound them together for the very last time.

Robbie came through the blue window covered in mud and looking exhausted. Steph smiled at the door with Alice as he walked slowly up the glade towards them. Steph was packed and ready to go, Alice had little baby Jessie in a pouch on her chest as she waited with her bags. Rowan and Jade came out of the window followed by Saff and made their way across the grass. Steph leaned off the door as Robbie came up the steps. "You look exhausted." He smiled.

"It's been a rough day... Hey Alice... Hey, my little baby Jessie how are you?" He gave a smile at the little bright blue eyed girl, with bright rosy cheeks.

"She is teething it's not been her best day; the clove oil seems to be working now." Little Jessica gave a smile as he smiled at her and together, they all walked into the house, Steph had a hot meal waiting and all of them sat gratefully down at the table and tucked in. There were a lot of preparations, Rune knew how absent minded he could be and had already packed his bag, which sat by the door with Steph's. After the meal Robbie took Rowan and Jade to the office.

Rowan gave a sigh as Robbie went over the plans for withdrawal with him yet again. "Robbie please, I know the plans backwards, you have gone over them a thousand times already." Jade giggled at his side. "Look Robbie we are going home to wash and have one warm night in bed together." Jade's eyes twinkled. "I will see you in the morning before you go, if I have forgotten anything I am sure you will remind me."

Robbie relaxed a little and smiled. "I am sorry. I have so much on my mind at the moment, I cannot help it." Rowan gripped him by the shoulders.

"Listen to me my brother; you are one window away if we need you. You should be by the side of your wife, Rune needs you Robbie, and unbelievably you need her. This war will happen and we will win or fall whether you are there or not, we have planned for almost a year now, we are prepared so please go to your wife and relax a little. I will need you back fresh and bouncing with the joys of parenthood."

Robbie nodded. "Alright I hear you. Just keep yourselves safe till I get back and make you an uncle and aunt." Jade gave a loud giggle.

"I can't wait, tell Rune I love her." He gave her a happy nod as her eyes danced under her long shaggy fringe.

"I will auntie Pebbles have no fear."

Rowan and Jade left for their one night at home, and Robbie wandered around the office and then came down the stairs. Little Jessie was asleep in her basket crib on the chair and Steph and Alice sat out on the front in the seats and quietly talked with Saff. He wandered down to the table of Runestone below the house; the light was very dim as he walked round looking at the large white stone table with the twenty pointed sapphire blue star in the middle. It felt strange being here alone without Rune sat in her chair sweeping her hands across the surface. He walked to her seat and ran his fingers across the surface. Little violet flashes jumped from his hand to the table. The violet figure of Rune came up through the centre of the table. "Hi gorgeous."

He gave a huge smile to see her; he had missed her so much. "Hey beautiful, I am missing you and came down here to think of you." She came out of the table and pulled him close.

"I felt you touch the table. I knew it was you, because I felt great love for me." He rested his head on her shoulder and softly kissed her neck, she shuddered. "Ooh that is so weird; I just got goose bumps in Scotland." He giggled as he looked into her bright violet eyes.

"I will be with you first thing in the morning." She held him tight.

"Rhiannon thinks I will have her at mid-summer. They are a little late but she is not worried, she thinks Iona is waiting for a signal from Fae."

"Mid-summer is the day after tomorrow?"

"It would make her coming more powerful to be born on the day of the solstice."

"Will it protect you all more?" Rune looked into his eyes, she could see the worry and concerns that he carried, and felt the conflict in him as he worried about the war and Loxley and about his children and her.

"Robbie we will all be fine, please you are getting yourself too worked up. I have two of Fae's strongest fighters of evil and Rhiannon and Rayne to protect me. Please calm yourself."

"I love you Rune, how can you ask me that knowing that she is out there waiting for her chance to hurt you and my children? If she comes within a mile of that island I promise you, Destiny will have more than a few of her fingers." She gave a chuckle.

"You are funny at times. Oh, I love you Robbie, I cannot wait for the morning. You look so tired; you should get some sleep and then come to me first thing." She stretched up and kissed him softly. "I will see you in the morning, go to bed my love." He smiled as she waved and then shimmered away into nothing. Robbie stood in the dark feeling a little happier; he walked to the stairs and brushed the surface of the table, violet sparks jumped from his fingers. Rune sat alone in her bed on Iona and giggled.

It was a busy time as Maddy and Una helped Mel carry the bags up the steep steps to the top of the cliff. Jay and Hornet carried the food supplies, and Toby carried the drum of oil for the lamps. Mel was all giggles as she slid the old key in the lock and turned it. The old lock gave a resounding click, and the pale blue door swung open.

Inside was a small fireplace and white pot sink and a few cupboards. There were pictures drawn by Sapphire on the walls in neat little frames, and soft neatly embroidered cushions and shawls on the chairs. It was a small place with three small bedrooms and the shared kitchen and living room. It felt cosy and homely as Mel crouched and stacked wood on the fire. She flicked the flint lighter and the cotton caught fire and glowed vivid red. She pushed it into the pile of wood shavings and gave it a soft blow. Flames flickered out into the shavings and she slipped in some smaller pieces of wood. Within minutes, the fire cracked and snapped as the flames licked the larger logs and began to burn.

Toby refilled the oil lamps and placed the large half-filled drum outside by the door. The light burned bright as everyone settled in to their temporary accommodation. Toby pulled out his knife and stood by the sink as he cleaned the fresh fish, he had caught that afternoon. Within the hour, they were all sat enjoying the delights of fresh-poached fish, with boiled new potatoes, and fresh green peas. It felt like a feast as they all crammed around Mel's small wooden table, and talked. Toby opened a bottle of Joe's wine and they all drank a half of a glass; they knew how powerful it was and needed a very clear head for the following day. It was a happy affair as the three sisters and their company all laughed and joked with each other. It had been a long time since the three of them had spent such close time together, and it felt special to them. The sun had sunken low when Mel and Una walked out in the moonlight, together they quietly talked as without thinking Mel just took her usual route, she looked up and saw her stones all standing in rows like proud guards.

Una felt the power of protection within them. "Wow Mel, I had no idea. This is an impressive site; I can feel the power flowing through the earth." Una looked round the stones and down the avenues. She saw the significance of a circle that could follow the moon and the sun. The stars could be plotted and it was very obviously once used as a place of great worship. Her violet eyes flickered with the power of the place. "We will be fine here Mel, this place will fight the curse, have no fear when we gather, these stones will be working for us." She gave a smile and nodded.

"I love this place; I have spent many years sat here talking to Tor." She crouched in the very centre of the circle and saw the blue butterfly. "Look Una, Rune has been here." Una looked down and smiled.

"Leave that there; she wants to be with you when you do it." Mel smiled knowing that the Violetlines would protect her.

"I am glad to know she has been here; I will sleep better knowing Rune is watching."

Jay and Hornet shared a room and Una and Maddy shared one, Toby who had drunk the lion's share of the wine slept deeply on the couch, Mel curled in her bed, which felt so familiar and soon everyone was asleep. A long day's voyage in the sea air mixed with Joe's wine was a recipe for a good deep restful sleep. Safe and cosy, the night passed under the faithful watch of the tall stones, once again, they had become the guardians of Melanie Birch Rimmer Tor.

Markus and Ben were both asleep close to the fire. Martin sat and placed more wood into the yellow and orange flames. The Sage sat out in the trees watching across the wild fields, as the noise of the waves behind him crashed on to the beach in the distance. He saw the figure of the wizard wrapped in his long dark blue cloak as he walked through the grass toward him; the Sage stood and quietly walked through the long grass to meet with the old wizard.

Merlin gave a bow. "I am glad to see you young William. Your feet walk the line of white again, as I saw many years ago."

The Sage looked to the floor, and then back into the bright gleaming eyes of the wizard. "You saw and yet you said nothing to me."

Merlin gave a nod. "It was not my place to say anything; you were almost a man and had to choose your path Billy. The path you chose has brought you back in a circle and has brought the gifts you hold to the surface."

"It has cost me everything, a wife, a child, and a brother, if you knew, why did you not stop me to save your granddaughter and Robbie?" The old wizard thought for a moment.

"I have talked many times with the Green Lord on this Billy. Both of us knew that you would not harm either of them, for we all saw the conflict within you. The power of true love is a strong force and we knew that none more than Jessie had more than in her feelings to you. Your father used you as a tool to extract what he could for his greed, I still see the anger inside you that you carry for him, yet I also understand the need you felt to find out whom you are. We all look to our parents and peers to find our place in this realm; you have done well to come as far as you have alone."

"It's not very far is it? I am alone and cast out from the world I truly felt I belonged in. I ache to see a child I will never know, and yearn for the love of a woman who will love someone else. Why could you not have helped me? I would still be here now having been to your aid, but at least I would have a home and brother to go home to." He stared through the dark at Merlin who understood what he said.

"You would also be powerless."

"Why is that so important? You have these gifts; you know what it is like to wake in the night with pictures of confusion coursing through your head? I hardly understand most of them." Merlin nodded, as he did indeed know of the curse that could be the power of sight.

"Yet Billy you have already used these gifts for the good of others. You have prevented the death of your young companion, and you have ensured his murderer now has a chance of a better future. You have a great power brought up from the hidden depths inside you by the love of a brother with the power of the White Circle in his blade. Two lives have been spared for the good of others because you betrayed a brother. I have the power to help Robbie and Runestone and yet I was a prisoner. Billy two lives more will be spared because you helped free me, her table lies broken and by the time she can repair it the moment of Robbie and Rune's deaths will have passed. Tell me you would not do everything to protect them?"

"You know I would?" Merlin lifted a hand and stepped forward, he squeezed Billy's shoulder hard.

"They would have died; but today you gave them their life. I owe you my debt of thanks and that is why my young friend I am here. The ways in which the mystical powers of this land work is not always clear to see, but I know now I made the right choice when I chose to allow you to walk the path of destiny. No one can fully see the future; you and I are lucky to see the small flashes we do. Cast your doubts away and know that you still have a part to play and accept it Billy, for there may be a time when you have the things in this life that you desire. Walk the green path and learn like we all have, knowledge is the answer and courage is the question." Billy nodded as he looked into the kind and grateful eyes of a powerful wizard but also a grandfather.

"I miss him Len; I miss the closeness we had. I never felt fear because he was beside me, and I knew no matter what he would never leave me."

"He hasn't left you. He gave you your life when all called for your death. He did that because he loves his brother, have you any idea how powerful he has become? He truly is the lord hooded man; he could have flicked his wrist with that sword and ended your life. Believe me the fight inside him was vast, his strength showed when he chose not to take the easy route and granted you life. Honour his choice for he stayed at your side and protected you. You still have the brother of old, whether you believe it or not, he too has the same struggle inside him as you do."

"I want him to know I am sorry and to beg his forgiveness." Merlin smiled.

"That time may come; I cannot see that far ahead. He is still young like you are and wisdom will come with age. There may be a time when he will find it in his heart, the lines of time have not shown me. You must remember Billy that he was the one chosen as lord and many look to him to set the examples. What a man does in private may not always be the same as he can do in public, time will heal and time will tell. You must now follow your heart and find your path to the ways of your gifts, for they now will lead you."

Billy nodded and looked down as the turmoil swirled inside him, he looked back up and dared not ask but he needed to know. "Will my sister be safe? She is not like the others or me. Her heart has always been good, I cannot see her; she has been hidden from me." He gave a smile and patted his shoulder.

"So little time together and yet you found the thread that binds you? Be at peace my friend your brother and his wife protect her. They have great power, which will keep her safe; she is very special to Runestone. She carries the same love of her brother; your paths will meet again have no fear."

Billy smiled at the thought as the old wizard looked to the sky and then north. "My time here comes to its end; I must move on to the path of my own destiny. Take care my young friend and listen to your heart always, it beats with the pounding of a man of Loxley, good bye Billy, my granddaughter is watching have no fear." The Old wizard turned and began to walk back into the long grass.

"Len... Thank you." He lifted a hand in the air as he strolled away with his long staff pacing the land before him, the Sage turned and walked silently back into the trees.

Rune lay in her bed and smiled as her eyes faded back from violet to their normal bright blue, she snuggled under the blankets and thought of Robbie.

CHAPTER SIXTEEN

THE CIRCLE OF LIGHT AND VIOLET.

It was shortly before dawn when Robbie woke. The house was quiet and he wandered downstairs as he pulled together the last of his things. He lifted out his stock of fresh arrows and checked each one at the kitchen table, as he loaded his quiver and cleaned and sharpened his knives, although the dagger with the hooded Rune on the hilt was so well made that it kept its edge and seldom needed sharpening.

Once all his weapons and kit was ready he went back up to his room where he sat with a coffee, he brushed his hair and dressed in a fresh set of woodsman attire. His spare long green hooded cloak hung on the door and he smiled as he saw the crest of the able bowman on it. It felt strange at times when he looked at it and understood the meaning it all held for so many. It was a symbol he had grown up seeing, except the bowman's crest, had blue eyes and two crossed black arrows, his now carried the familiar symbol of red eyes and a white and black crossed arrow.

Robbie watched the glade of his beloved Mere as he finished his drink. The house felt strange and lonely without Rune and he was looking forward to seeing her. He felt the tension twist in his stomach, as much as he felt the excitement of having children he knew of the danger now of birth, if Rune lost her powers only for the briefest of moments, he knew that the Dark One would strike. He would face her he had no doubts, but he knew that she had old and dangerous powers. He gave a long sigh, the next couple of days would be a test of strength, and he would need every ounce of his courage to face her.

Alice moved in her room as she prepared Little Jessie who would be coming with her to Iona. It was hard to believe that such a small child required so many things, and Robbie chuckled at the size of the bag she had packed. No doubt, he would soon have the same, Steph wandered into the kitchen yawning, her hair stood on end, and she flopped into the chair as Robbie slid the cup across the table to her. "What time are we leaving?" She gave another huge yawn. "Sorry I was up late reading. It's my father and his bloody notes; it takes me two hours to work out five minutes' worth of reading."

"I am waiting for Rowan and Jade; they should be here soon. I told Jett and Rafe to be here on time, but you know those two, they are probably still tucked up in bed." Steph smiled.

"It has not been easy for Jett; I hope they keep an eye on her."

"Jett will be fine; she is a warrior like her mum. I know she can be flaky at times, but when push comes to shove, she has never let her friends down. I never worry about Jett; I always know she will be there at my side."

"Cheers Robbie that is cool to know." Jett smiled from the doorway. He gave her a smile as he crossed the kitchen and gave her a hug.

"How are you feeling now?" She gave him a squeeze.

"Sort of strange inside, but I will be fine now. Rafe is a good tonic, although I think I have worn him out a bit." She gave a little giggle; Jett still had black lines under her eyes, which carried an air of sadness. It was clear she was on the road back to herself, but she was noticeably quieter.

Rowan and Jade arrived smiling and looking happy, shortly after Saff had come down to the kitchen humming, the kitchen had filled and soon everyone was awake and talking happily. The sun rose over the glade of Robbie's Mere, and once Alice was ready, they all gathered on the grass. Saff opened the window and after hugs and best wishes, Rowan walked through with Jade closely followed by Rafe and Jett. Saff clicked her fingers and the window shimmered, a bright pulsating blue. Robbie led the way and they all stepped through on to the dirt track that led up to the white farm cottage on Iona. Gwinne smiled as she saw Robbie, it was a relief, as Rune had spent the last few days worried he would be caught up in the conflict and not get away. She walked down the track and gave him a hug.

"You are in the usual room in the abbey, everyone else is staying here. I am so happy to see you Robbie, Rune has really missed you, go on go to her." She kissed him on the cheek and he turned with his bag and walked across the field, as Gwinne hugged everyone else and showed them into the cottage. The guards of the moon snapped to attention as he walked toward the abbey, he gave a slight smile to himself, as he remembered the scenes of Caerleon; Rune was going to love this.

Rune lay quietly asleep; her long red hair was splayed across the sheets, as she lay on her side holding her tummy. Her face was pale and the freckles looked pale and dusty in the thin light, her eyes opened slowly and saw the two deep brown caring eyes looking at her from the pillow beside her. "Hey beautiful." She gave a large warm smile and her eyes glowed with happiness.

"Hi gorgeous."

He pulled her across as she snuggled round him, and he lay back and felt the joy of holding her close again. The heat radiated out of her, and she made happy little squeaks as she moved around him getting comfy. "I missed you. I hate sleeping alone." He smiled as he softly stroked her long red hair; he had missed her too, and lay back and soaked up the peace and quiet of the place

It was nice to be close to her and not have the sounds of soldiers or explosions going off in the background. It was silent except for the soft calming sound of the sea, as the tide came in and the seagulls called out to their mates. He closed his eyes and just drifted as he felt her breath on his shoulder, the past few weeks had been hard and he just wanted to try and forget the strains and pressures he had felt build inside him. Destiny would now play its part and he was ready to accept it, the bed gave a slight jolt, and Rune giggled. "Iona wants to see her Daddy."

The sun shone down in shafts, as the clouds blew across the sky carried down from the north on a soft breeze. The water lapped at the edges of the rocks as the sea pushed onto the washed white sands near the grass lined edge of the island. Gwinne walked with her arm around Rayne, and she carried a huge happy smile as she turned and he pulled her into his arms and softly kissed her.

Rhiannon smiled as she watched from the wall of the abbey, she had hardly spoken with her son since their arrival, and being reunited with his family, he had spent a great deal of time with them. Sapphire gave Rhiannon a warm smile, as she walked from the cottage towards the Queen of the moon. She gave a polite bow. "My Lady, I am pleased to see you here, we have all worried about the Lady Runestone. I am happy to see she has such good protection."

Rhiannon gave a smile. "I am pleased to be here and know that I have some roll to play in something of such importance. I am looking forward to the return of the Queen of Fae to the earth; we have been too long without this land blessed with the line of Fae."

Sapphire turned and looked out across the sea, she watched Rayne with Gwinne as he walked along the edge of the water. "You have a very kind and loving son, I am very happy to see him reunited with my aunt, she has missed him a great deal."

"It is nice to see him happy again; there is a little more love in this world which is a good thing. Love is a positive force for all of us; I believe you have found a little yourself my Lady Sapphire?"

Sapphire smiled and blushed a little. "I am very fortunate to have found someone who is very special; he is at York with Lord Rowan helping the defence of the city."

Rhiannon watched her son with happiness as she stood at the side of Sapphire. "I am sorry that Lord Rowan of Loxley is not here, I have heard a great deal about him, I was hoping I would have a chance to speak with him. He is very loyal to his lord and lady is he not?"

Sapphire was intrigued that Rhiannon would know so much of Robbie and his people; she was especially interested that she would ask of Rowan. "He is a very honourable man; he is Robbie's right hand, and we all have a great deal of respect for him. Lord Rowan and Lady Jade have been by his side since Robbie first set off against Mason Knox, he has become a great friend to Robbie."

"I know something of his line; his father was a very talented soldier; I have heard his mother was an exceptionally gifted teacher." Sapphire nodded unsure.

"We all know little of his past; we know he was sent to Robbie by the Lady Opal on the command of the Green Lord." She shrugged. "That is really all most of us know. He has proven himself to our lord many times over."

Rhiannon gave a soft smile and turned to Sapphire. "I am not casting doubt on your lord, have no fear I am very aware of the deeds of Lord Rowan, and pleased to know Lord Robert has a man of such high honour at the side of him." Sapphire smiled unsure of what exactly Rhiannon was trying to find out. Her eyes cast out to sea where she knew her mother and sisters would be preparing for their task. Rhiannon smiled, and turned and looked to the north, and the island of Lewis and the stones of Callanish. "The curse of that island will not stand the power of the Violetlines. The Dark One has never understood the power that is being made here, I feel your concern there is nothing to fear. I believe Runestone has placed a good protection there, it is good you have chosen to travel to them, the power of six will help."

Sapphire was amazed that Rhiannon could know so much. "I have more power than they have, I will not let my mother risk herself if I can protect her." Rhiannon raised her arm and gently patted her on the shoulder.

"There is much to do, but my eyes will also be your way should you need me, have no fear my Lady Sapphire, all of the sisters of power will stand together. I must prepare now as soon Rune's time will come." Rhiannon walked across the grass and headed into the Abbey. Sapphire sat down as the sun came out from behind the clouds, and rested her head on her knees as she watched the sea.

Two small hands came around her from behind and covered her eyes. "Guess who?"

Sapphire gave a giggle as the hands slipped back and the young teenager beamed with tears in her eyes. "Gaynor...? How did you get here?" Sapphire leapt up and swept in her into her arms. "Oh my darling I have missed you so much." She squeezed her hard as the young girl smiled happily at her.

"I have missed you too Saff, I am living here with my uncle's friend and his wife. It's alright, but I miss living with you and Jaz." Sapphire beamed with delight.

"Is Will here with you as well?" Gaynor nodded.

"He is in the village with Jaz, they are fishing. I got bored and came to look for you. Jaz says you are only here until later and I didn't want to miss you." She looked a little sad and Sapphire gave her a smile as she slipped a hand on to her.

"Come on back to the cottage, I do have to go later but we can spend the day together before I do. I will only be away for a few days and then I will be back." Gaynor gave a huge smile and slipped her arm round Saff's waist. They walked off together as Gaynor filled Saff in on everything that had happened since she had left on the boat with her mother.

Robbie sat with his back against the headboard, as Rune curled up on his lap. "Oh, this is nice."

Rune smiled and looked up at him from his chest, and her eyes twinkled. "It feels like ages since we were alone together like this, I have missed it." He stroked back her long red hair.

"I am sorry; I know this has been very hard on you. I miss you beside me, I know you are at the table watching, but it's not the same without you there."

"I wish we could get this over with and have done with it. Killing Mason has done nothing; she just brought him right back, which has really worried me Rob."

"Why?"

Rune's eyes shone bright sapphire blue as she looked up at him. "Rob when she brought Mordred back, she did not have the skill or power to put him back inside a body of his own. That is why she used the sword; Mason is back in his body."

He looked a little confused as he thought. "Are you saying she has somehow managed to learn more or acquire more power?"

"Both... She has grown a lot stronger than Dunnottar. I think she has learnt a lot more from her black book, you have to realise Rob she has been around for a long time." Rune looked worried, Robbie could sense her apprehension; he pulled his arms around her and held her tight.

"You will be safe Rune, I will be beside you at all times, and you have Rhiannon and the people of Fae to defend you. If she comes within a mile of the place, we will all protect you." She snuggled into him.

"I am a little frightened Rob. If I lose my power, I cannot defend Iona or Hal." Two tears ran from her cheeks and she gave a soft sniffle. Robbie pulled her tight as she looked down and her eyes shone with her tears. "These are our children Rob; she will try to kill them and I might not be able to stop her."

Robbie lowered his head as he held her in his arms and kissed her softly. "I am here and I promise you Rune, no one will harm our children. I will kill any who try and that includes her. Come on don't cry you will be safe and so will our children, I promise." She wiped her tears from her eyes and gave a sniffle,

"I am sorry, it's just without power it scares me to think of what she could do."

"The Lord Hearne and your grandfather are with us Rune; we have your mum, Gwinne, Rayne, and Crystal and Amethyst. All of them love you and will protect you, so please do not worry, you just concentrate on my two beautiful children." She gave a smile as she looked into his dark caring eyes.

"Don't leave me for a second."

He kissed her softy and held her close. "You are my whole world, where could I go? I love you Runestone Sapphire." She gave a little giggle and she snuggled in his arms feeling safe from the world. Robbie stared at the wall, Rune was as scared as he was, his mind drifted as he held her close, all he could do was stay close to her and if the Dark One came for her, he knew she would have a fight to get through him first.

Robbie and Rune lay together for most of the morning just holding each other close. Rune had dozed off for a while, and he sat and watched her sleep as he thought of the coming hours.

It was late evening when Sapphire walked across the long grass field towards the abbey as she laughed and talked to Gaynor. She had a woollen woven bag hanging on a long cord from her shoulder, she stopped at the stile as Gaynor climbed over and then she followed. Saff pointed to Robbie stood by the stone cross and she gave her a big hug. Gaynor scampered off across the grass and down the side of the long wall that led to the wooden gate and the road of the village.

Saff smiled as she came toward Robbie. He stood in his long tight green pants and his long flowing lace up top with the fluted sleeves; it rippled in the soft breeze. He gave her a smile as she approached. "You look ready to go?"

"I am. I just thought I would pop in and give Rune a hug and wish her my best."

"She will like that; she will be out in a second I left her dressing."

"You look a lot more relaxed Robbie; you needed a good rest and a lot of Rune." She gave him a beautiful smile, as her eyes twinkled. Sapphire suddenly looked a little serious. "You know I am only a moment away Robbie?"

He gave her a smile and nodded. "Thanks Saff, we should be fine, Rhiannon seems to have organised everything. It's nice to know though." Saff gave him a hug.

"I meant it Robbie; we must all look after each other more than ever now." He gave a little chuckle.

"Why do I feel you have become my guardian Angel?"

"I love you and Rune; I would never let anything hurt either of you. I feel a strong bond to you Robbie, we shared a hard time, I always felt it made us closer?" He gave her a squeeze.

"It did Saff; I will always be there for you too, so take care on that island." She stood back and her blue eyes shone bright.

"I will Robbie, keep yourself safe." She turned and smiled as Rune came out of the door; she walked across the grass and gave her a hug. "Oh, you are so lucky; I am so excited for you. I wish it was mine."

Rune smiled at her cousin. "Your time will come my sweet sister. You and Keith have much to look forward too, take care of yourself and let your mum know, she is not alone we are here and will help if needs be."

"I will, take care and I will see all of you soon." Sapphire turned and with a wave of her hand, the large blue pulsating orb appeared on the grass in front of her. She gave a wave to Robbie and stepped through, as Rune walked out in the warm sun and into his arms.

Robbie and Rune walked along the soft white sand where the tide had receded. The evening was warm and the clouds had blown away to the south, the sky was the brightest of blue and the last hours of the sun beat down on them. Rune seemed a lot happier, and a little more relaxed as she giggled at Robbie, as he fooled around at her side. She felt a burst of happiness growing inside of her, her body was starting to count down the time as Iona and Hal prepared to enter into the world. He smiled at her bright sapphire blue eyes as they danced. Rune seemed to have a radiance around her that she had not had when she left. Her cheeks were redder, and her skin seemed to glow as her long red and gold hair sparkled in the sunlight.

Holding her hand they walked slowly, Rune was holding two children inside and walking was no longer quite so easy. The evening seemed to slip by in moments of quiet happiness and as the sun began to slip slowly down in the sky they turned, and began to walk back toward the white cottage and past it to the abbey. Amethyst and Crystal, watched from the garden wall of the cottage, their bows rested against the wall just in case.

It was dark on the moors and Rowan sat in the cave as Jade took watch. He stretched his arms to try and pull out the aches. Blades came in with Todd and waved. Rowan gave a wave back as Harry and Woody appeared. Harry wandered down and slumped on the bed across from Rowan, Woody slumped on the bed at the side. Harry looked at Rowan. "Hey man we got like heavy problems dude." He looked worried; Rowan glanced as Rafe sat up with Jett a few beds down.

Rowan looked back at Harry.

"What have you seen Harry?" Harry gave a long sigh.

"Oh man, Knox is building up a huge army. It's like major heavy man. He has boats like totally coming from nowhere stacked with soldier dudes." Woody gave a long sigh.

"He has thousands General; we couldn't get that close; the place has guards all over it."

Rowan nodded. "We did expect this guys, Robbie thought Knox would ship men in from the south. Thanks guys, you did well." Harry shook his head and stood up.

"Oh dudes, it's goin to get like real unpeaceful." Rowan stood up and patted him on the back.

"We have planned for this Harry; get some sleep you look wasted." He walked up to the table where Treen stood looking at the map while Skip slept, her long red hair hung down as she studied the area of the map around the coast of

Scarborough. "It eez not an easy place to get too, we ave no way of firing at im across the water." She looked up at Rowan who stood opposite her and looked down at the map.

"Robbie knew this fight was coming, we should start to prepare the withdrawal plans of Scarlet's. Robbie always said this patch of ground was nothing more than a graveyard for Mason's troops. He has planned all along to withdraw and move into a better place for defence."

Treen shook her head. "We should not move so fast. Scarlet had many plans for Fatty Old Ear, just because he as gone does not mean us ave to give up this plans." Rowan nodded at her as Rafe walked up with his arm round a now black clad Jett. Jett gave another smile at Treen. She had rolled around with laughter when she had seen her dressed as her mother, Jett loved the idea of making General Walters think he had failed to kill Scarlet. Treen had been a little nervous and gasped with relief as Jett hugged her and thanked her.

Rafe looked at the table and the black city map. "It does not matter how many troops he has, look, he has to get out through a double gate; one I might add we have blown up twice already. He only has two hundred yards of empty black land and then it's the trees. Ox and his men have taken those guards out about fifty times, if you ask me, it makes more sense to push forward and attack him before he can get through those walls. We already have a front line that cuts off the south from those gates. Why do you not just move it forward? They are just sat waiting to be attacked, it makes more sense to move them and get them fighting in the trees."

Rowan watched as Rafe moved a row of green figures on the map up from the south of Filey to the tree line on the edge of the black walls. Rowan looked up at Treen.

"You worked closer with Scarlet than any of us, did she ever consider this?"

Treen nodded. "She wanted to do it from day first, but Robbie was not keen."

"That's day one darling." Skip sat up and rubbed his eyes. He gave a long stretch and stood up. "Robbie did not want to engage the enemy in striking distance of the walls because he knew they had cannons behind the walls, although we did look at blowing up parts of the harbour to prevent ships from docking. Scarlet thought that if we could find a way of sinking his ships in the harbour mouth it would make it impossible to get his troops in."

Rowan looked at Skip. "Is that possible?"

"Scarlet thought so; she worked for a long time on it with Treen." Rowan turned to her and she nodded.

"We made a plan with Fish, Amethyst and Blades with Myself to do it."

"Why you four, and not some of the others?"

"We all swim like the fishes." She gave a big smile. "It can only be got at by water, you ave to swim very long to do it."

Rowan gave a smile at Rafe and Jett. "I think we need to have a look at what Scarlet had in mind, show me everything she had planned Treen."

It was approaching dawn, and in the cave below the moors of York, Rowan looked at the plan of Scarlet with his team. On Callanish, everyone except Mel was asleep, she stood at her gate with her mind filled of thoughts of Dave Williams, and she missed him and knew that the coming day was going to be hard. They all knew that the Dark One could strike to prevent them from lifting her curse.

Fuse lay on a small bed at the back of the Village Hall in Loxley. He had worked until late looking at the plans for a wide scale attack, Penny Watson who had stayed back to work with him, had placed a blanket over him with a soft smile before she headed into the dark and her cottage.

Robbie lay in bed awake. Rune muttered in her sleep and moved around restless. He knew she was worried and her dreams were filled with the same worry.

At the top of the dark raven like tower at Dunnottar, the lights blazed in the mouth of the evil looking raven. The Dark One laughed and muttered to herself as she moved around her rooms. She sensed the time was near and now she laughed to herself as she planned her evil revenge on the house of Loxley.

The Sage sat in the garden of the small cottage just on the outside of the high walls of the south west of England. He watched as Martin helped Markus organise his family, they had intended to move away, as Markus had been seen in the city of Tintagel and they now knew that he was involved in the release of the old wizard. His wife Jemima was busy packing a few things and hiding others under the floor in the cellar. Ben was fast asleep on the sofa.

Merlin stood on the edge of Hearne's rock with the old lord and sensed the sky to see if he could feel the presence of the Dark One. His bright green eyes burned brightly in the darkness, he was worried about Rune, and the old lord of the woods could sense it in him. The first beam of light came over the horizon and the start of the summer solstice began on the cool island of Callanish. Dawn would now move south and light Iona and then the walled city of York, and Loxley on its way south to Devon.

Black clouds began to form above the castle at Dunnottar; they swirled in the sky as the windows in the mouth of the hideous stone raven opened. With a scream and wail of delight, the black streak of the Dark One, shot up into her clouds of black, and they blew inland heading west. Rune's eyes exploded with bright violet light and she sat up quickly making Robbie jump. Rhiannon turned round outside their window and touched Rayne's shoulder.

Robbie watched as Rune moved her head from side to side as if reading something. He had seen her do it a thousand times in the woods as she looked for the enemy. Her small warm hand slipped into his and he gave it a squeeze. "I am here Rune." Rune's eyes opened as she turned to him, the purple light streamed across his face.

"She is coming Rob." He felt the shiver like cold ice run down his spine. He slid his arm down to the floor at the side of the bed; and lifted the Sword of Destiny up and placed it against the headboard. He was ready to face her, and protect his wife and children. Isolde sat outside the room and she felt the Dark One coming, she stood up and walked to the door of the room two doors down from Robbie's. She quietly opened the door and saw Filomena sat in her chair; she was awake and had already felt her.

Rhiannon knocked quietly on the door and turned the handle; she peered in through the door and smiled as she saw Robbie and Rune sat in bed looking at her. Rune was curled round him, as he held her close, she gave Rhiannon a smile. Rhiannon lifted the tray off the chair by the door and carried it inside. "I thought a little breakfast might lift the spirits." Rune gave her a smile as she slipped out of Robbie's arms and sat back against the pillows.

"Oh, great I am starving." Rhiannon gave her a smile and winked at Robbie. She sat on the edge of the bed and slid the tray on to Rune's lap.

"We have all felt her Runestone. Promise me you will let us deal with this? I will not allow you outside if I know you will confront her, your children must not be put at risk. At the moment of birth your power will lessen, you must concentrate on the children and let me handle the defence of this island." Rune gave her a nod as she bit into her toast and honey; Rhiannon smiled and patted her leg. "Good... have your breakfast and then get up when you are ready." Robbie lifted his mug as she left the room and sipped it slowly as he watched Rune.

"You are going to do as she says, aren't you Rune?" He was not sure; maybe it was the way she looked; he knew her well enough to know when she was being evasive. She gave him a smile and leaned forward and kissed him, her lips were sticky with honey and she gave a giggle as he licked them.

They had all finished their breakfast and Una looked round at Meg and Maddy as they wiped the last of the pots. Her eyes flickered with violet flashes, "She is preparing I feel her. Get Mel, now is the time to go to the circle and get ready." Meg gave a sheepish nod and went into her room to get Judy. Maddy walked out of the door where Toby stood with Mel at the gate.

"Toby it is time for you to leave, the time is coming and you must be off this island." Mel kissed him on the cheek, he looked very worried.

"Be careful Mel love. I will be anchored off the coast just a mile upstream, send up a rocket if you need me." He gave her a big hug, as Maddy came back inside the cottage. All the others were now preparing for the lifting of the curse, they all looked nervous and Una gave a smile.

"We will be fine, Rune has left protection so have no fear, and we are sisters of the violet circle."

Maddy lifter her white bow. "I don't care what Rune thinks, this will be with me and if she comes within range, I will give her a reason to get hot under the collar. She took my mother; I still owe her."

It was an hour later when they set off up toward the tall stones of the great circle at Callanish. They came over the bluff and into view of the tall proud stones, the wind had dropped and the sun burned down on what was going to be a very hot day. The tall stones looked pale grey in the sun as they rose out of the floor, and as the group walked into the circle a strong sense of calm passed over the land. It was as if the stones knew of the task and wanted to calm the restless hearts of the group.

Mel felt the calmness of the stones wash over her; she had missed it and felt a little joy rise at being able to return. The group gathered and looked at Mel; she took a deep breath and smiled. "Ok, we must form a circle. Saff you stand here, now Maddy then Judy." She gave her a wink and she smiled nervously. "Una, I want you here, and Megan sweetheart you stand there. You now represent the star of our sisters, Saff you have the strongest power and will hold the place of Black. Maddy White Circle you hold the place of white, Judy you hold the place of knowledge, which is red. Una my protector you hold the place of violet and Jay my sweet you hold the place of green. I will be in the centre and stand by the butterfly of our centre of all circles."

She carefully lifted her battered old straw hat and bent to place it over the butterfly on the floor in the centre of the circle. It glowed violet for a moment, and she knew that Rune was with her; Mel gave a smile and breathed deeply. She placed the hat over the butterfly and stood up. "Alright everyone I want you to hold hands and stand at arm's length from each other. Please remember that our power is that of the circle, no matter what happens keep the circle together and do not let go of each other."

They all looked very nervous as they nodded to her. Una winked, Mel took another deep breath and swallowed hard; she raised her hands and turned slowly around the circle as her eyes began to flare with a bright blue light. "I look to the north, I praise the east, I bow to the south, and I welcome the west. Hear me as I join my sisters in the circle of the earth. Come join with me my sisters for I am the centre of the circle of these stones and I need your powers."

Una's eyes flickered first and violet light streamed out of her. Judy was next with bright white light flowing out of her eyes. Maddy's exploded with a soft pale blue light and Sapphire's streamed with a deep intense blue. Mel shook as it hit her and she felt the true power of her daughter.

Jasper sat quietly up on the rocks of the island of Iona, he thought of Megan and looked for her spirit, finding a living spirit was harder, and it took a lot of concentration. He found her and connected, she jumped as his voice quietly spoke in her mind. "Megan my sister, I need your faith and love of your friends to channel my power to the sisters of your circle, think of me and concentrate, and you will be safe and protected." She closed her eyes for a moment as Mel turned her eyes flowing with bright violet light. Meg opened her eyes and a deep burgundy light channelled out of her and connected with Mel. She felt Jasper and Megan mixed, together within her.

Mel looked up to the sky. "Hear me Runestone Sapphire, and centre of all circles, we are ready and prepared. We will seek the Violetlines and find our protection." All around the stones, bright violet light burst up from the ground, and shot into the sky. The sisters were now inside the stones, and protected in a tube of bright violet light that surrounded all of the circle of Callanish.

Rune sat on a chair by the Celtic cross and she turned to Robbie. "Mel is ready, be prepared."

High on the cliff tops ten miles south of Balnahard, a dark figure rose out of the rocks as her cloak of feathers fluttered in the wind. Her cold white face turned with a malicious smile and looked across the sea to the southwest. Iona was small in the distance as she gave an evil and cold chuckle to herself. "I am here my pretty little flower girl; we shall see now who has the true powers of the lines. You will bother me no more after this hour has passed."

Rune's eyes flickered as Robbie watched knowing she was watching her sisters.

The Dark one gave a giggle as she lifted her arms in the air, her dark cold black eyes burning with hate and malice. A violet hand gripped her shoulder and tugged hard. The Dark One spun round fast, and met the palm of Rune's hand. SLAP!

The slap connected and the ground vibrated, as a flash of blinding violet light exploded out of Rune's hand, her eyes burned with anger as she looked at the Dark One's shocked face.

"STAY AWAY FROM MY CHILDREN WITCH!"

Morgan le Fey stumbled back with shock, her feet slipping with the power of Rune's hand; her face had a large red burn on the side of it as she fell backwards off the high cliff. Screams of murderous rage rose up from the cliff as black feathers floated down from the air, and rested on the rock floor. She came back up like a thunderbolt spitting venom and hate, the cliff was empty and the violet figure had gone. Her rage shot into the air as she screamed with all her might, and the floor shook and rocks crashed into the sea.

Rhiannon turned on the grass. "RUNE NO!" Robbie snapped his head round to where Rune smiled and opened her eyes as the violet light faded. She smiled sweetly at Robbie.

"Rob darling can you help me?" She looked down at the chair where a puddle was forming on the floor dripping off the seat. His heart began to beat swiftly, he jumped back, and looked at her; the colour ran from his face.

"It's time...? Your waters...? Iona, Hal...? Rune it is time they are coming?" She gave him a huge smile.

"Yes Rob, it is time you met your daughter." Rhiannon rushed up the grass as Isolde came running out with Filomena, closely followed by Steph and Alice.

Rhiannon helped her up off the chair with Robbie.

"That was foolish Rune."

Rune smiled. "I am about to lose my powers, she knows I mean to fight her, I used my last moments to make her think twice. She will hesitate for a while before she comes, it will give all of you a little more time." Rune was taken to the prepared room.

Mel stood surrounded by her sisters as violet light swirled around the inside of the stone circle, her arms were stretched to the heavens and bright violet light flowed from her into the swirling light around her. "I call to me on the dawning of Life Circle Line, the lines of power. Bring forth the power of violet to my need in this hour, I stand before the trapped and the cursed of a bygone time, I link with the house of the lord from this line."

Lightening flashed in the sky above them, and a wind began to blow around the inside of the circle as the violet spinning wall became deeper and began to spin even faster. The colour of light in the eyes of the sisters all now became a soft purple colour, and flowed through Mel who was rigid holding her arms to the heavens and holding her head back as the light streamed out of her. She stepped forward and placed her feet on either side of the old battered straw hat, it lit up with a white light.

"Through me, through this possession of the past, bring forth the freedom so that the mantle may pass on." The ground shook and Judy squeaked a little, Maddy gave her hand a squeeze. There was a deep rumbling below them. Mel screamed into the sky as the ground trembled below her feet.

"LET THE LORD OF THESE STONES FROM THE TIME OF OLD. WALK FREE TO OTHER REALMS, AND PASS THE LINE FOR A SON TO HOLD."

A huge force burst up through the centre of the circle, and the old hat tore as white light exploded out of the ground and smothered Mel hiding her from the others. The ground shook violently and the sisters of the circle were thrown backwards on to the floor, Una screamed as her legs snapped open and met with Megan's and Judy's. She felt herself thrown back into the ground and fought to sit up, but the pressure pushed her flat to the floor. Mel rose ten feet into the air, and began to spin as she continued the incantation.

Maddy fought to move her arms, which seemed stuck to her sides. "I cannot move my arms."

Mel screamed from inside the white light. "DO NOT MOVE, YOU HAVE ALL CREATED A FIVE POINTED STAR." As Mel looked down, she could see the legs of all the sisters had met, and lay down on the ground with their arms pressed to their sides they looked like a star. She looked back up to the clouds, which were now starting to form, and swirl above her, the wind rushing into her ears was deafening.

"IN EARTH, ABOVE EARTH, BELOW SKY, HEAR MY CALL TO THE AID OF TOR." Lightening bounced down onto the tops of the stones, and Mel closed her eyes, as she flinched expecting to be hit. She opened her eyes and gasped with relief. "LIFT THE SINS OF THE PAST, SAVE THIS LAND FROM HER DECAY."

White light shot up each stone in the circle as the earth shook more violently and the white light streamed into the sky. The earth tore and a bolt of lightning exploded on top of the stones. Mel gasped as a white horse with a knight in gleaming armour burst out from the floor, and rode round the circle waving a shining sword. "Tor."

High on the cliff top the Dark One snapped her head to the North West and screamed "NOOOO!"

Her cloak opened and with a scream of anger, she burst into the sky and flew at great speed to the isle of Callanish. Mel gasped for breath as the power flowing through her was over powering, the colours of the star seemed to colour the earth around each of her sisters of the circle. She took a deep breath and spoke the last of her incantation as the knight rode his horse around the circle of protection.

Mel could barely hear as the wind thundered around her in the bright white and violet light, which was flowing from the stones and the earth. "Hearne give me courage I am afraid." Mel trembled as she looked up to the clouds and a bright violet butterfly fluttered up in front of her eyes and then landed on her shoulder. She smiled and whispered. "I love you Runestone."

She screamed into the air at the top of her voice as black seemed to spin into the clouds above her. "WELCOME LIFE, WELCOME CIRCLE, WELCOME LINE. BANISH THE DARKNESS, AND BRING FORTH THE VIOLET LINES."

The sky exploded as deep violet light shot down from the sky and hit Mel face on, her screams were drowned out as the whole island shook. The five sisters on the floor wailed as the power flowed through them into the ground, they were pressed tight against the floor, and could not move. Una fought as she felt the darkness and was helpless as she saw the Dark One come out of the sky like a huge bird and sweep through the air for Mel. The white horse reared up on its hind legs and the flash of the Sword of Courage in Tor's hand sliced through the air. The Dark One screamed as she recoiled from the blade and swept backwards as the light funnelled out of the sky at Mel.

Tor rode round the circle of the sisters and watched the sky, his horse almost glowing in the light as flashes of violet bounced from Mel to him. She shook held in the air as the Dark One screamed down at her, and made another sweep. Una fought with all her might but could not move.

Eagles screamed as they swept out of the sky, the largest led the charge and flew at the Dark One flashing their long talons as they made to slice her, and snatch her out of the air. The Dark One screamed with fear, as she shot through the air to avoid them. Flashes of blue and red lightening, shot out of her at the eagles, they swerved and dodged them, keeping to their chase of the evil old witch.

The light from the sky suddenly stopped and Mel fell to earth with a bump. Una shot up and grabbed her and pulled her into her arms, a ball of violet light exploded in the circle and Merlin walked out. He looked to the sky and the screaming Morgan le Fey as she swooped across the stones chased by the eagles; he gave a smile, and lifted his long white staff. A burst of white light erupted from the end of it and hit her as she flew past.

There was a horrendous scream, and black feathers dropped out of the sky. The air exploded in red light and Merlin waved his hand. White light flowed into the circle and the air above them seemed to ripple for a second, the light faded and the air above was blue and clear. Eagles hovered in a high circle flying in a ring of protection. Mel trembled in Una's arms; Una gave her a squeeze and looked at the others who all looked very shaken.

Maddy hugged Judy who was as white as a ghost and, Saff held Meg close. "We did it Mel sweetheart." She stroked the hair back from Mel's frightened face as Mel moved in her arms. She looked up at the shining figure sat high on his horse.

He dropped his shield to the floor and lifted his visor. Tears filled her eyes as she looked up at her husband as a young and gallant knight. Melanie Birch Tor rose from her sister's arms and looked into the eyes of a man she had loved as a young girl; he was the father of her children, and had spent all his life looking for her. In his final moments, the Dark One who had been after his sword had seized him. Tor had passed it on to his young nephew to protect it. The young Robert of Loxley had taken the sword to Hearne for its protection and it had been placed into the guardianship of the Duke of York. The passing of the sword had been the first task of the first hooded man and had begun a legacy that would run until the present day. The search for the heir to the kingdom had begun, and would last for over eight hundred years until the true king was revealed again. Filomena of Callanish had married Gwynfor Lyle Osborne, and her grandson had become the first hooded man and the first to hide a sword of power.

The Dark One had cursed Tor as he died and she imprisoned his soul within the stone circle preventing him from passing to the other realm. Her curse prevented a new lord from taking over the Isle of Callanish, which had once been a worship site for the pilgrims of Fae. Jasper had been forced to leave the island before he was eighteen, as he would have died the moment he became of age. The mantle of lord was prevented from passing on; it was the legacy of revenge of the Dark One.

Tor slipped off his heavy chain mail glove as Mel came to the side of his gleaming white horse. He wiped her eyes with his finger. "I have finally found you my love." She gasped a sob.

"I am sorry my darling, she took us and we could not get back to you. I love you husband." More tears rolled as he gently stroked her cheek.

"I have waited an eternity for this moment my precious Melanie, I knew we would meet once more on this earth, I never doubted it." He ran his finger down her nose as he had many times; she gave a giggle and sniffled. He smiled and lifted his hand. "Too long have you sat in these stones my rose of the land? I have to move to the other realm, and you have to live now. Do not throw your life away here alone my precious darling, you bring so much happiness. My time with you was short, and yet it was enough to fill my whole life with love." He slid the ring of Callanish from his finger. "My son will have my mantle and bear it with honour." He placed the bright golden ring in her hand. "Good bye my sweet love."

Mel wept, as he jerked his horse forward and rode round to Sapphire, and she burst into tears. "I love you daddy." He leant down on his horse and with powerful arms he lifted her into his arms. Sapphire hugged her father hard as she wept and he folded his large metal clad arms around her.

From under his chain mail, he pulled a golden chain out; it had on it a small golden Callanish eagle with eyes of Sapphires. "This belonged to my father; he was a proud and powerful man, who loved his granddaughter and gave this to me to pass to you when you were old enough. It has the same blue eyes as the granddaughter he loved so dearly. I looked at it many times in my life, as it helped me cope with the pain of not knowing where you were. I have told this a million times how much I love you, every moment you wear this my beautiful daughter, you will share a moment of my love for you."

He slid the weeping Sapphire from his horse and turned to Merlin. "My old friend protect my family, and tell my son I am proud of him." He raised his sword in salute, and then turning his horse, he faced the stones of the west and the dying sun. He nodded to Una and Maddy. "Fare thee well my sisters."

The horse reared up, and then shot at the long row of stones that led out from the circle into the west. The horse galloped at speed and then jumped into the air, and with a flash of violet, Tor rode out of this realm and into the next to be free to sit with his line in honour and watch from the peaceful realm.

Maddy lifted her bow from the floor and walked over to Sapphire, who gazed down at the golden eagle in her hand. She slid her hand round her waist. "Come on Saff my darling we all need a good cup of something strong. I think my legs will shake for a week I was so scared." Saff smiled.

"My dad really loved me Maddy."

Maddy gave her a squeeze. "He was quite a guy you know; we all thought he was the kindest man alive. Have I never told you of all the fun we had on the farm with him?" Saff smiled a big smile.

"No, you haven't I would love to hear about him."

"Oh Saff darling, he was the life and soul of the party, I remember when we all decided to have this huge celebration for his birthday, he was due back from the court and so we decorated the whole farm in lace and ribbons and we..." Saff giggled as she walked down the path with Maddy.

Merlin pulled Judy and Megan into each of his arms. "You did well my children, Runestone will be pleased." They looked very white but smiled as he led them out of the circle and onto the path.

Mel wiped her eyes and looked at Una. "I have freed him Una." Una pulled her sister close and hugged her.

"You surprised me Mel dear. You showed a great deal of bravery today, your love for Tor filled the air and helped the power of the violet. I am very proud of you."

"I was terrified, the power almost overcame me."

"It did not though, did it? I saw the butterfly; Rune was with us as I knew she would not leave you alone with her. I think we should go back to the cottage, and open the bottle of Joe's special recipe that I snuck up here with me." She gave a giggle. "How about a nip of something to restore my legs back to solids, they feel like jelly." Mel gave a giggle.

"Thanks Una, I could not have done this without you, I felt your protection." She smiled at her.

"You are my sister Melanie, and I love you." She kissed the tip of her nose.

"I love you too sister." She looked at the torn hat in Mel's hands.

"I think it is time for a new one, don't you?" Mel smiled and nodded.

The stones sat alone and silent as Mel and Una walked down the path away to the cottage. The air was warm and still, and the stones had witnessed yet another passing moment of power on the Isle. It would not be the last, and they were ready for the moment when others came to use the strength of their protections. For now, they stood like the guards of the realm and silently waited.

Rune lay back on the bed and gasped, as the others hurriedly prepared. Isolde turned to Robbie. "My Lord, I will call you when we are done."

Robbie frowned. "What...? I am not leaving." She looked surprised and blushed.

"But My Lord it is not heard of to have a man present at a birth." He moved to the side of Rune.

"Maybe not in your realm, but in mine I am Lord and I stay by my wife's side no matter what." Rune beamed up at him and he smiled at her. "I want to see her the moment she comes into this world." He took her hand and sat on the side of the bed. Rune gave him a smile and then gasped as she felt the contraction. Robbie's knuckles turned white. "Wow Rune, you are really strong when you want to be." He gasped through gritted teeth.

CHAPTER SEVENTEEN

NEW LIFE TO THE VIOLET ISLE

Robbie sat holding Rune's hand. On the other side of the bed, Steph watched nervously, she held Rune's other hand as Rune panted again, her contractions had been long and hard. Her face was red and her hair damp, both Robbie and Steph breathed easy for a moment, feeling the blood run back into their fingers, Steph gave a reassuring smile. "It's alright darling just breathe in rhythm."

Isolde looked up with soft hazel eyes. "It is almost time My Lady, our new queen will be with us soon." She gave Rune a warm smile.

Rune panted and looked up at Robbie. He sat on the side of the bed and faced her, as he wiped her face. Rune clenched his hand tight as the next contraction came. She screwed up her face as her eyes flared with violet; she felt the pains of new life. It eased and she gasped. "Oh god Rob, I will have to speak to my grandfather, we must make this easier for women." He chuckled as he wiped away her sweat, and Steph gave a soft giggle.

Jasper came smiling across the grass as Rayne watched the sky. The blue orb appeared and Saff stepped out and ran to him, she gave him a huge hug. "We are safe, Mum did it." He gave her a big hug.

The sky above the island of Iona began to grow darker. The sun seemed to fade as the moon crossed the line of the sun, and the whole of the sky was filled with a bright curtain of shimmering and waving light. The aurora seemed to fill all of the sky like a curtain that surrounded the island. Rayne smiled as he looked down at Saff and Jaz. "The Queen of Fae is almost with us, prepare Lord Jasper, your realm awaits you."

Sapphire waved her arm and the blue light of the shimmering orb pulsated on the grass. Jasper took a deep breath and waited ready for Rayne to give him the word.

Isolde smiled as Filomena looked over her shoulder. "It is time My Lady, her head is out I want you to push and bare down just one more time, she is ready to enter this realm."

Robbie took a firm hold of her hand and Rune gritted her teeth, and squeezing his hand with all her might, she pushed. "OOOOOOOOOH!!!" She held her breath as she pushed hard, and Robbie watched his whole hand turn white as he gritted his teeth. Rune's eyes flickered with pale violet light. She gasped for breath as she relaxed. Isolde smiled. "Please My Lady again."

Rune gasped as she pushed, and Robbie turned and looked down as he saw the small figure of his daughter move into the hands of Isolde. He turned with tears in his eyes. "Rune she is here, I can see her." Rune gasped a long hard breath and fell back on the pillow smiling at the look on Robbie's face. Steph wiped the tears from her eyes as she picked up the cloth and wiped the sweat from Rune's brow.

"I am a grandmother."

Isolde worked fast as she tied the cord and then cut it. She wiped the small child and passed her to Filomena. She turned with the small child, and cleaned her quickly and wrapped her in a bright white cloth.

Rayne patted Jasper on the shoulder, and he stepped forward into the blue light, as he walked into the circle, the sound of a baby's cries echoed in the abbey of Iona on the other side of the light. The new queen drew her first long breath of life, and came into the world of the hooded realm. The life of a queen named Violet Stone had begun.

Jasper stood in the circle and the air above him gave a rumble. The dark clouds that swirled above him parted, and the sun broke through and shone in a long bright shaft directly down on him. Merlin stood and gave a low bow. "Welcome My Lord Tor of Callanish." Jasper smiled and bowed back, Merlin gave him a huge smile and pulled him into a tight embrace.

Robbie looked down at the small face wrapped in white. His emotions were high as he looked at Iona, his first-born. Rune smiled as he leaned forward and Iona opened her eyes. Bright violet looked up at her parents for the very first time and Rune gave a laugh as her tears flowed down her cheeks. "Oh Robbie, she is beautiful." He beamed with delight, as he looked at Rune and then back at Iona.

"I have no words I am so happy." Steph blew her nose on her hankie and both Robbie and Rune gave a giggle. Steph looked on her granddaughter with tear filled eyes. Filomena came around by Robbie's side.

"We still have one more My Lord, and he does not want to wait, let her grandmother hold her while we bring your son into the world."

The moon began to move as the sky above Iona danced with multi coloured light. The whole of the Island shimmered with a bright radiance, and golden streaks of light crossed the sky like the passing of thousands of comets, and the first rays of light shone down from behind the moon to bring light again to the world of the Fae. The heavens seemed to fill with the sound of soft singing voices, as the sky became a happy chorus of the voices of what felt like the distant past. It was a sound that seemed to echo in Robbie's mind, and he thought of the sword and the singing he heard when he wielded it.

Robbie leaned over and kissed Rune softly. Steph beamed with delight as she held her granddaughter close, he smiled and his eyes showed the love that he felt for her, Rune's eyes flickered violet as he pulled away. "Now we bring the heir of my line and the son that will bind us together for all eternity. I love you Runestone."

She was tired and felt exhausted, but she beamed with delight as he took her hand in his. "I love you Robbie." Rune bore down hard as she pushed and he held her tight.

Jess came down the path at the side of the greenhouse from the orchard. She turned the corner as the huge blue ball appeared in the courtyard of the house; Saff stepped out and looked around. Beth came running out of the house as the bright happy eyes of Saff met with Jess; she gave her a huge beaming smile. "You have a new granddaughter to visit."

Beth squealed with delight, and flew at Saff, and almost dragged her to the floor. Tears filled the eyes of Jess as she dropped her basket and ran down the yard toward Saff, who struggled under the happy wailing of Beth. "Oh my, he and Runestone are a family, we have an heir to Loxley. Oh, our little Robbie has an even littler Robbie."

John came running out of the barn with his sword. "What's going on? What is it Beth baby?"

She wailed as she ran up the yard and leapt into his massive arms. "Oh John, they have done it."

John looked round confused, still holding his sword, as Beth wailed as she hung from his neck. He saw the look on Jess's face and he beamed a big smile as he dropped his sword and pulled Beth into a big hug. "Well bugger me, I am an uncle again." He roared a huge laugh and swung Beth in his arms. Saff pulled Jess into a big hug.

"His son is not here yet, but Iona has come to us. Come on Robbie wants you there." Her apron hit the yard floor as the blue pulsating orb disappeared. Beth wailed in tears as Rags and Lucy came out of the postal hut to see what was going on.

Isolde looked worried. "Please My Lady resist pushing a moment, he is not coming." She moved below the sheet as Rune panted and gasped, and tried to hold back from pushing. Robbie looked worried as he watched Isolde, who wore a definite look of concern. She looked up at him.

"Your son is stuck; you must tell her not to push." Robbie felt his heart pound, and turned to Rune. "Please hold on he is not ready yet." She saw the fear in his eyes as the door opened and Jess came in.

Jess looked across the room at Steph holding the first of her grandchildren and then down at Isolde, who was having distinct difficulty. She moved quickly to the bed. "He is caught on the cord; move over I have done this a thousand times." Isolde frowned a little, as Jess took over and moved down to Rune. Her eyes twinkled as she looked up at Rune, and she smiled a sweet and loving smile.

"Rune sweetheart, I need you to relax for me, Robbie help her?" She looked down under the sheet. Rune felt the discomfort as she tried to relax and avoid the instinct to push. Jess looked up and winked over the sheet. "Your son has tied himself in a knot, just relax and he will be fine." She gave a smile as she worked and Rune felt the confidence of the woman, she knew had delivered most of Loxley. Robbie felt the anxiety rising inside him as he watched his mother.

Rayne watched in wonder as the golden light flowed around the sky. Sapphire stood at his side with Gwinne as they watched the spirits of the Fae fly round above them in a bright golden circle. The sky was a deep violet blue, as the sun now beamed down and the moon passed over and out of sight. Rayne gasped as Gwinne slipped her arm round him. "Look how beautiful it is my love, this has not been seen here in over a thousand years, look in wonder as the line of Fae returns to earth. Saff swallowed deeply.

"I have never seen anything as beautiful." Her bright blue eyes sparkled as she watched the Fae gather ready to return and pay homage to their queen.

Jess looked over the sheet and gave a big smile. "He is ready for you now." Rune took hold of Robbie's hand and she pushed with all her might. Jess gave a squeak of delight. "Here he comes... another big push Rune sweetheart." Rune screwed up her face and gave a push with all her might, as she clung to Robbie's hand, her face turned a bright red with the effort. Robbie watched as his son slipped into the hands of his mother who squealed with delight.

Rune fell back on the pillows, her face bright red with damp hair, as she gasped for air. Robbie was still and silent as he held his breath. Jess worked quickly as she cut the cord, and passed the small child to Isolde with a beaming smile. The cries of his son bleated into the air and his eyes filled with tears, he turned to Rune who lay watching and crying and she swept forward into his arms.

"I have a son Rune."

Rune smiled from the shoulder of Robbie at Jess, as he hugged her and wept with joy. He slid back and he held her happy face in his hands, he kissed her and her eyes danced blue and sparkled with his delight. Jess lifted his son in her arms and smiled at Isolde. "Thank you. You have done my family proud."

Isolde smiled at Jess and nodded. Jess turned to Robbie and gave him a huge beaming smile. "My Lord of Loxley, congratulations you have a son." Rune burst into tears as she saw the love in the eyes of Robbie, as Jess carefully handed him his son. She leant forward and kissed Rune on the head

"Congratulations my daughter you truly are a family now. You have made me very happy."

Robbie held Halbert in his arms and turned to Rune, as Isolde finished off cleaning Rune. Halbert opened his eyes and looked up at her. He had the same bright sapphire blue eyes of his mother, and quite a head of hair for a newly born baby. Brown and red mixed with gold, flowed down to his neck and she laughed as he blinked in the daylight. "He will be strong like his daddy." She smiled at Robbie who was lost for words, Steph passed Iona over to Rune and she held her daughter for the first time. Jess stood next to Steph, and placed her arm on her shoulder, as they watched their two children sat together on the bed, with the two children of their own. Steph wiped her eyes and passed Jess a clean hankie. "Let's get some air and leave them for a moment."

The two happy grandparents stepped outside as Rune's eyes flickered lilac. Alice looked up holding little Jessie in her arms. "Well?"

Jess smiled. "You are now Auntie Alice to two very beautiful children." Alice chuckled and danced on the spot.

"Can I see them?" Steph gave her a big grin.

"Just give them a moment together."

Rayne gripped Gwinne's hand as he looked into the sky. The streak of black in the gold was instantly noticeable. Sapphires eyes burned bright blue. "She is coming."

Isolde and Filomena moved to the head of the bed and stood either side of Robbie and Rune. Rune's eyes flared bright violet, she was weak and tired and had no strength to move, but she felt the coming of the Dark One. Black clouds billowed into the sky above the island of Iona; they swirled around scattering the bright golden lights gathered in the air. Flashes of red and blue lightening shot from the clouds, and Rayne pushed Saff and Gwinne behind him as he stepped slowly back.

He waved his hand and a curtain of shimmering silver light appeared on the ground and rose up around the abbey, the dark cloud grew thicker and blacker as the light was sucked out of the sky over the island. The whole island of Iona was plunged into a dusk like darkness, the clouds swirled, and then from the centre, a thick swirling mass of dense black cloud, came down to the floor twenty yards in front of Rayne. He pushed Gwinne and Sapphire back further, and then stepped forward, Gwinne gasped. "No Rayne." He turned and his eyes burned vivid with violet light.

"I hold the power of the silver light; she will not pass me easily. Go to the doors and guard the children and their parents." Gwinne felt Saff's arm tug at her. She turned with fear in her eyes as Saff led her back to the abbey walls, and the wooden door that guarded the entrance to the abbey. Guards of the line of the moon formed a line across the grass to protect the abbey, as Rayne turned to the black column of cloud that had descended from the sky.

Morgan le Fey walked out of the cloud and stared into the violet eyes of the prince of the realm of the moon. She sighed. "Oh get out of my way moon boy, you and your soldiers are no match for me." She flicked her finger and the silver light around the abbey fizzed and sparked with blue flashes. It exploded in a haze of blinding blue light and was gone.

Rayne raised a hand and it glowed with a silvery light. "I am a guardian of the silver light you are on sacred ground and cannot enter here."

Morgan le Fey looked irritated. "Oh yes, yes, I know all the words boy. Do not waste your breath; it has no power over me." Her dark eyes glared at him from a white face that still bore the red mark of Rune's hand. Silver light erupted from Rayne's hand as she went to move forward, it hit her in the chest and she slid back several feet. The glint of evil walked past her eyes as she began to lose her patience. She raised a talon like black finger.

"You need to learn your craft boy. You need to know a superior power when you meet one, get out of my way, sacred ground or not, I will have the flower girl." She flicked her finger and Rayne rose into the air and shot backwards, sliding on the grass as he landed with a thump.

He wildly moved his arm and a flame of blinding white light flew at Le Fey. She spoke a quick incantation, and a red flame shot from her hand and engulfed the white light. She gave a satisfied smirk and stepped forward. Rayne jumped to his feet and lightening flashed out of his hands, he swiped his arm again and balls of fire erupted in the deepest violet.

Le Fey moved quickly casting her own spells as the light shot at her, she waved her arm and deflected it and then side stepped as the ball of fire only just missed her. It seemed to shake her and she scowled as she flicked her fingers. The air seemed to ripple as a wall of invisible force swept towards Rayne; it lifted him off his feet and threw him with huge force at Gwinne and Sapphire. The line of soldiers were tossed with huge force, and crashed into the walls, they moaned in pain as they slid down to the floor, some of them did not move.

Sapphire swept her arm across the front of Gwinne and a bright violet light appeared and caught Rayne as he crashed to the ground in front of them. They felt the ripple as it hit the stone and the walls shook. Rayne staggered to his feet defiant in the face of his enemy, he raised his arm and a long golden ring clad hand touched his. He stopped, as did the Dark One who gave a look of concern.

Rhiannon stepped forward her long golden hair flowing behind her as she walked calmly shimmering in the brightest of blue; her dark cloak of deep blue feathers flowed and rustled behind her. "You are not welcome here killer of my sister."

The eyes of Morgan le Fey widened slightly. "Rhiannon... The rules of your line prevent you from interfering in the lives of the earth." Rhiannon came to a standstill and looked into the eyes of a woman she hated.

"I am not on the earth le Fey, I stand on the realm of Fae, it is my realm to defend and I will have revenge for my sister. You wear a cloak you are not worthy enough to look at, I want it returned to the realm of my people." Rhiannon opened her palm and then closed it. A line of blue flame shot out of the sides of her hand as her staff of fire came forth as commanded. Le Fey looked worried as she looked at the goddess of the moon who shimmered with power as the blue radiance of the moon shone from within her. Her slate grey eyes burned with her power.

"The cloak is mine, I took it as a trophy of combat, it is no longer the property of Fae. It belongs to my realm of darkness now." Saff shuddered as the voice of Morgan le Fey fell cold to the floor, and slithered like a snake towards them.

The eyes of the Dark One began to burn with red fire, and her malice rose up in her as she prepared for combat. "I took your sister with ease, what makes you feel you can better a sister of twice your strength?"

She shot balls of fire out from under her black cloak, and Rhiannon was fast to sweep her bright burning blue staff and deflect them away as she twisted and parried the flames off the end of her staff. Le Fey swept her hand across in front of her and a wall of power shot towards Rhiannon. She swiped down hard with her staff and the wall sliced in front of her splitting before her and bouncing away to the sides of Rhiannon, where the walls of the fields exploded in small fragments.

Rhiannon swirled her staff in front of her, and a wheel of blue light shone before her, she pushed hard and it fired spinning towards the Dark One. Morgan le Fey waved her hands as the wheel of spinning light came fast, it hit her head on, and with a scream of anger, the dark figure lifted into the air and flew backwards squawking like an injured bird. She landed heavily and rolled on the grass screaming with rage.

Rhiannon smiled and swiped her staff of flame across her path as she walked forward, a ripple of blue light flowed out and lifted le Fey off the floor and threw her across the grass. "This is a protected realm witch, and you are not welcome." Morgan le Fey screamed in anger and pain, as she was hit with the blue light again and thrown back several yards.

She bounced to her feet, and curse after curse flew with rage at Rhiannon. The sleek shimmering figure gave a gasp as she swirled on the spot with her staff, and smashed each curse as it came at her; she swung round sweeping at one as the rage of the Dark One sent another in an onslaught of curses. Rhiannon gave a grunt as she pushed one away only to spin for another. She was caught on the arm and flames ignited; Rhiannon gave a scream of pain, and spun sending blinding flashes of blue light at le Fey as she was lifted into the air. Le Fey gave a howl as the light bounced all around her blowing her back to the floor. Rhiannon sat up her sleeve torn and blackened from where the curse had burned her. Saff watched in fear as she saw Rhiannon wince when she moved her arm, the curse had burned deep and it was hard for her to use it.

Robbie sat on the bed close to Rune, he held Halbert close and she cradled Iona in her arms. She was exhausted and felt very weak, her eyes flickered with a pale lilac as her powers failed, Destiny hung gleaming from his belt. The screams of the Dark One from outside echoed around the room, Rune looked up with fear in her eyes, it was enough and he slid Halbert over to her.

"Guard my children, I will return?" Rune trembled with fear.

"Robbie please... no... do not leave me." He pulled Destiny and it glowed with brilliance like he had never seen. He looked at his wrist, and then back at Rune. Robbie slid the white bangle off and slipped it on to her wrist where it glowed a bright shimmering blue.

"This is my task Rune, that witch will not take my children." He turned as Rune wailed and walked out of the door. Steph and Jess both pleaded with him as he walked down the corridor to the outer door.

The arm of Rhiannon hung limp as she spun the staff in one hand. Fire and lightening flowed out of it showering le Fey in a hail of spells. The Dark One screamed with anger and madness as she fired back as many curses hitting Rhiannon's and blasting them apart. One hit her hard in the chest, and she gasped at the pain at it lifted her into the air and launched her backwards over the wall in front of the white farm cottage. Rhiannon gasped for breath in pain.

Crystal and Amethyst ran up the corridor seeing Robbie head out with a wailing Jess and Alice behind him. Gwinne and Sapphire parted as Robbie came through with his sword. The arm of the Dark One came over the wall followed by her white enraged face with eyes of thin black evil malice; her anger had now peaked as she saw the struggling Rhiannon. Now was the time for the kill.

She raised a hand, and blasted a shot of white fire, Rhiannon saw it and knew she did not have the strength to fight it; she prepared for the impact and tried to summon the last of her strength. A white glowing blade swept in front of her, and the flame bounced up into the sky and exploded. She swooned as Robbie stepped passed, and she fell to the floor utterly spent, the pain of her arm engulfing her body.

Morgan le Fey beamed a large smile as she slithered over the wall and back to her feet. Robbie walked forward with determination in his heart. He loved Rune and his children, and if he had to, he would die to save them, the cool calmness of his destiny seemed to flow over him, as he walked toward her and his sword prepared.

She screamed with hideous laughter as she saw him. "What use are you wood boy?" He did not blink or falter and she felt a small twinge of fear. He was unafraid and carried the power of the White Circle. Behind him, ten yards back a line formed of Sapphire, Amethyst, Rayne, Gwinne, Crystal and Steph. Jess lifted the weakened Rhiannon and helped her back to the abbey where Alice waited.

Robbie came to a halt and his dark eyes stared at Morgan le Fey, she eyed the blade of Gwendolyn carefully. Robbie looked into her cold evil eyes. "My wife has warned you once, now I am telling you witch. Stay away from my family or you will pay the price, as your evil spawn of a son did."

She looked at him unsure of what to do, he had some power she felt it, but she knew he was no match for her. Her thin withered lips parted and screeched a horrible cold and evil laugh. "YOU... Who are you to tell me, the most powerful sorceress alive what to do? You are nothing go back to your trees your whole realm is mine, and as for my son, you were merely lucky you caught him by surprise, you will not have that advantage here boy."

Robbie waited for her laughter to die down and he spoke quietly and calmly. "I believe le Fey you have made a slight error." She looked stunned at the arrogance of him.

"What?"

"You are not the most powerful sorceress alive; I believe that would be my wife."

Laughter rained out of the sky as she looked at him in disbelief. "You are deluded boy, if she is so powerful where is she? Cowering under the bed with her children I suppose?"

Robbie did not move; he held the sword tightly in his hands ready for her. "She is here with me in my heart, it is all that I need to stop you le Fey." The love of Rune filled up inside him and he felt her warmth within him. Sat on the bed Rune's eyes glowed a bright vivid purple as the love he held for her flowed to her.

Le Fey screamed and flicked her wrists, a flash of light leapt out at Robbie.

Destiny came up and he hit the lightening, and it bounced back at le Fey and blew her over the wall. She screamed with hideous anger, and instantly shot back over the wall screaming curses and malice. Saff waved a hand across Robbie as he deflected each curse as his sword spun with skill. Flashes and explosions went off all around him as the curses fell to the floor deflected away by the force of the White Circle in his sword.

The anger of Morgan le Fey was at fever pitch as she blew a huge blast of power at him. His feet remained solid as he swung the blade of Gwendolyn and defended her realm of the Fae. Robbie stepped closer as he hit her curse, and he came to within striking distance of his blade, he swiped the blade round in a blur, and she screamed as the blade touched her and sliced into her side. The blast was huge as Robbie was lifted into the air, and shot over the others crashing to the earth with a heavy thump. The stars blasted into his eyes, and he moaned at the pain in his back.

The violet figure of Rune rose out of the floor as lines of coloured light swept through the air and down into the abbey. The power of her sisters had been called to her, and now Rune felt her strength growing inside her. Her eyes glowed a deep vivid purple with the anger that was boiling inside her, and the Dark One felt fear as she crawled up from the wall with the gash in her side. Rune spun round from Robbie and raised a finger. "I WARNED YOU WITCH!"

Violet light flowed out of Rune in the deepest of shades. Steph and Saff fell to the floor at it shot over their heads. It hit the Dark One head on, as she waved her hands to stop it, but her power was washed aside by the force of the Violetlines. There were terrified and blood curdling screams as Morgan le Fey was lifted, and thrown into the air over the roof of the farm cottage. She landed in the sea at the far end of the island, as Rune channelled all of her power at her with a scream of rage that had the others falling to their knees and covering their ears.

Black funnelled into the sky as the Dark One fled in fear. Rune lifted her finger and followed it as the line of light pulsated out of her and into the cloud where screams of pain and endless curses howled down from the sky. The hand of Sapphire grabbed the wrist of Rune. "Runestone my sweet sister, she has gone we are safe. Robbie is alright, you can stop now." Rune turned and looked into the blue smiling eyes of Sapphire, she lowered her hand and the light stopped.

"She was trying to hurt Robbie." Sapphire smiled at her.

"You beat her Runestone, Robbie is safe and she has gone. Go back to your children they need you." Rune smiled at her and then faded away. Steph helped Robbie to his feet. He looked around dazed; Steph looked at him as Jess came running up.

"ROBBIE, ARE YOU MAD, WHAT THE HELL WERE YOU DOING WITH THAT SWORD?"

He was shocked, Steph had never shouted at him before; he looked at his mum for support.

"ROBBIE, YOU HAVE A WIFE AND CHILDREN, WHAT THE HELL DO YOU THINK YOU WERE PLAYING AT?"

He fought for the words as both his parents looked at him demanding an answer. "I was saving my family from her." He pointed loosely towards the sky that now shone with thousands of tiny gold specks.

Jess snatched him into a big hug. "You are brave I will give you that, but you are also a FOOL" He jumped as she yelled down his ear.

"I am sorry mum, but Rune was in danger. I had to protect her." Steph gave a chuckle and pulled him off Jess and hugged him.

"I thought Harry was the insane one. I love what you did for my daughter Rob, but if you pull a stunt like that again, I promise I will kill you myself. You scared the living hell out of all of us." Jess gave a giggle.

Rune sat in bed breast feeding Halbert when he got into the room. He sat in the chair and Filomena gave him a huge smile as she lowered Iona into his arms. She looked up at him with bright violet eyes and lifted a small hand in the air, he pushed his finger to it and she gripped it. Her small hand looked so tiny hanging on to his finger. "She has the grip of her mother." Rune gave a giggle, as he looked at his other hand.

"She wants to shake hands and say hello to daddy. Are you happy Robbie?"
He looked up with wonder in his eyes and he gave a smile.

"I am ecstatic. I love you." She looked exhausted but she smiled the most beautiful smile, her bright eyes danced and he knew she could not be happier. He loved her with all his heart and now they were a true family, no one at that moment in time could have been as happy as he was.

The afternoon was spent in their room; Rune was exhausted and slept in the bed. Iona and Hal both having had a good feed were asleep in their woven wicker baskets. Robbie sat in bed drifting in and out of sleep as he kept waking to check his children were safe. He was tired and weary; the pressure of the past week had been heavy, and riddled with fears. As he sat against the bed, and drifted once more into sleep, he felt a little relief wash into him. The warmth of Rune safe by his side relaxed him and his eyes fluttered, he drifted and was gone into a deep restful sleep.

He woke, and opened his eyes and saw the caring eyes of Steph, she smiled. "I seem to make a habit of sitting and watching you two sleep." He gave a smile, as he looked at Rune who was curled round him still fast asleep. Steph looked in the baskets. "They are so beautiful Rob." Robbie leaned over and peered down at the sleeping figures.

"They seem as sleepy as their mum."

"You are lucky, Rune was never a problem, oh but Jade. She would never sleep; she was always awake and watching and trying everything to get out of her crib."

She leaned forward in her chair. "They will want to present them to the Isle at dusk, it will be important for the children to be accepted into the Isle of Fae"
Robbie nodded.

"I know, I don't mind that, I will hold them up to the sacred tree when we get back to Loxley. It is a tradition in my family that they are known to the realm of Loxley." She watched him as he spoke.

"Rob... it will be safe, won't it?"

"What you mean the Dark One?" Steph nodded. "I think we will be fine Steph; I cannot see her coming back to face Rune for a long time. She knows that she will have a fight on her hands.... How is Rhiannon?"

Steph gave a little nod and a smile. "A little bit of wounded pride and a bad burn, but the creepy twins are looking after her." She gave a slight giggle and looked at him. "You know what I mean, it's the Queen of Fae this and the Queen of Fae that, it was really starting to get on my nerves. It's your son and daughter." Robbie understood he had also felt a little irritated by it.

"It's not their fault really, is it? They have not had a queen for a thousand years so they are just a bit jumpy. Not like my mum at all, she just rolls up her sleeves and gets stuck right in... I am glad she was here; I was really starting to worry about Hal."

Steph smiled. "It's always good to have a real midwife on hand, and let's face it they do not come better trained than Jess, she has delivered most of the stockade over the past twenty years."

Robbie watched Hal as he slept curled in a ball like his mum did. "We have been lucky today Steph, I am not sure how Rune did what she did, but she came out with a lot of force. I am glad she did, that last blast, the Dark One really knocked me for six." Steph gave a happy look at her sleeping daughter.

"She was weak and then suddenly her strength returned, she channelled from her sisters on the island for extra power, but hell she hit the Dark One with some force, it blew her right off the island, I felt it pass me, there was a lot of power behind it." Robbie looked down at her.

"It always amazes me when it comes out of her. Look at her she is so frail and beautiful; you would not believe she had it in her. I really love her Steph; you have no idea how deep it goes; I would have died today to save her."

Steph patted his leg. "You faced the Dark One alone to protect her, which was enough to show all of us believe me? I still think you were mad but hell Robbie, I have a lot of respect for that." She stood and looked down on her grandchildren and smiled. "I will let them know you are awake, you both need to eat and get your strength back, I think Jess will want to bring it, she is itching to see them again." Steph gave a little wave as she crossed to the door, and quietly she slipped out passed Filomena who sat by the door.

Robbie sat for a while and watched his children, he leant over the basket and talked quietly to them of the wonders of Loxley, and how he was going to hold them up to the woodland realm, and present them to the woodland lord. Rune gave a little giggle and he turned. She looked much better now she was rested. "How long have you been awake?" She slid up by his side and kissed him.

"Long enough softy." He smiled as she cuddled round him.

"It is hard to believe they are actually here, we made them Rune, just you and me." She hugged him tight.

"I know it feels strange not having them inside me anymore." Her eyes seemed to sparkle brighter than ever, as she looked across at them. "They are the future Rob; they are part of the dream for the age of dreams." Robbie watched her as she smiled and he felt her happiness.

"We have to present them to the realm of Fae later." Rune looked up at him and caught his glance. "Don't you think this lot up here are just a tiny bit... You know... possessive over them?" She gave him a smile. Rune understood what he meant.

"It's just the occasion Rob, this is important to them that's all. Never forget these are our children, believe me no one will argue with me about it. You should talk to Gwynfor, he will understand you and maybe they will all relax a little. He is actually their leader until Iona is old enough." Robbie nodded he knew he would.

It was a little later when Jess brought them their meal. Rune gave her a huge hug and thanked her for taking over, Jess was over the moon, that she got to deliver the next of the line of Loxley; she sat on the bed and held Halbert whilst Rune and Robbie ate. Alice slipped in quietly very excited. Robbie let her hold Iona, and she wept bucket loads. She had more than a little bit of Beth in her than they all realised.

It was a few hours before the ceremony was to begin and each of the Specialists slipped quietly in. Crystal and Amethyst beamed with delight and Sapphire filled up when she saw them. Gwinne and Rayne were filled with excited happiness, as they watched from the chairs as they were fed by Rune. Rhiannon came last with her arm in a sling.

"I am so happy for you both, you have your heir My Lord, and the line of Loxley will continue. I am so happy; this is wonderful news for the world." She sat on the bed and looked serious for a moment. "I understand they are both now part of the line of Fae, so let me give you some good advice. Before and above everything they are your children, always remember that, I can recall many scowls at me for my way of raising my children. I ignored the lot of them and did what I thought was best, sometimes they can get a little bit carried away and lose sight of the fact they are still only children."

Robbie gave her a big smile. "I am a lord of my own realm as well, and I know how my children will be raised. They will be true Loxley above everything else." Rhiannon smiled; she patted his shoulder.

"It pleases me to hear that My Lord. We will gather in an hour and then after that all the fancy blabbering is over, alright mum and dad?" Rune smiled at Rhiannon.

"Thanks for today, you fought to protect my family. You are in my debt."

"There is no debt my dear Runestone; I fought for the future of this realm as we all do. I am looking at it in the four people before me."

It was when they were getting ready that Robbie started to giggle. Rune slipped on her dress and stood up. She had completely forgotten she no longer carried the huge large lump, and the violet dress hung from her like a tent. She giggled as she opened her bag and pulled out one of her other dresses. Robbie was surprised at how small she was again. She winked at him. "Never forget who I am." He gave her a smile as he pulled her in to his arms.

"You are Mrs Loxley, are you not My Lady?" She giggled in his arms as he kissed her softly.

Two chairs were placed at the front of the abbey, and Rune sat down with Robbie holding their children close. A blue pulsating orb opened before them and Maddy, Mel and Una came through filled with excitement. Judy ran across the grass with Megan, and Merlin with Jasper both walked up the long stretch of grass and bowed before the new Queen of Fae. Rune lifted her daughter to her grandfather. His eyes were filled with tears as he held her in his arms and he smiled at Rune. "She is very special; I feel the power inside her already."

Gwynfor gave a short bow and walked to the side of Robbie; he rested his hand on his shoulder and looked up to the darkening sky. The golden lights now almost filled the sky as they began to swirl and spiral down, Robbie and Rune sat nervously as the spiral approached them and began to swirl around them.

Soft voices sang in happy rhythm into the air, and Robbie gasped as he saw each golden light had a face that smiled with joy, they swirled past them sat holding their children, and flowed like water across the land. Each golden drop glowed brightly and then sank into the floor; it was beautiful to watch as all the others gathered in a line and watched the passing of the people of Fae. Gwynfor bent down to Robbie. "It is easier if they show themselves as their fairy spirits, if they all walked past in human form, your daughter would be an old woman before they all passed." He gave a deep chuckle and Rune gave a small giggle.

Iona was wide awake, and it seemed to Robbie that somehow, she understood what was going on. Her eyes seemed to move and follow the bright glowing swirls as they passed her. Her bright violet eyes shone like Rune's and he could see as they sat together how like her mother she was. The golden lights finally passed them and settled in the ground and Gwynfor stepped forward and spoke in a loud voice.

"I present to this honourable gathering the new Lord and Lady of Fae. Take to your hearts the Lord Halbert Thorn of Loxley and his sister and new ruler of this realm Lady Iona Violet of Fae and Loxley. Rejoice my people for a new world of the Fae is coming, on the day of her eighteenth year, she will return to take up her rightful place on this island, and until that time she will reside in the fair land of Loxley. All of you are charged with the duty to protect that realm, and if the lord of that realm calls, you are now charged with the duty of protection. Lord Robert of Loxley is of my line and yours, remember him."

Gwynfor spoke with surprising force considering he was so old. He gave Rune a cheeky wink as he turned to the golden land before him. "Welcome the Queen to her realm if you understand what has been said this night."

The golden haze of fairies shimmered on the floor and then in bright bursts of every colour they shot into the air and swirled in the sky like a thousand rainbows, glowing bright and lighting the whole island in a thousand different shades of every colour. Rune gasped as she watched, it was a spectacle of extreme beauty, as suddenly the whole sky turned violet as small parchments floated from the sky to the earth, each was the size of a snowflake and had words of welcome on it for the Queen of the Violet Isle.

It softly fluttered down and rested on everyone like a gentle violet snow, and Rune laughed with delight as it rested on her eyelids and in her hair. Robbie slipped his arm round her as it floated on to her and his children. Rune's eyes flickered violet as she watched the tribute of the people of Fae; Iona's also gave a flicker, which surprised Robbie a great deal.

Iona already had the power of her land building inside her. All of the floor was covered in a deep layer of violet, like a crisp snow on a fresh winter's morning, as the last of the flakes fell softly to earth. The colours in the air spiralled round, and softly faded as the new queen was given the official approval of the people of Fae.

Gwynfor crouched down between Robbie and Rune. "There is a powerful magic that has been bestowed on both of your children. She was born at the stroke of noon on midsummer's day. You must remain on the island until noon tomorrow, after that you may return to Loxley as the protection of her people will be complete." Robbie and Rune both nodded as everyone came forward to see the children again.

Rune bent down and took a large handful of the violet paper; she pulled a small cloth bag out of her pocket and filled it; Gwynfor smiled. Runestone knew her lore, she would sprinkle it around the glade of Robbie's Mere, which would make the glade a realm of the Fae. The protection of her people would follow Iona home to Loxley.

Rune looked at the grass below the paper and then pushed her finger down to it. A violet grew in the spot, she gave a smile as another appeared at its side. Slowly the clump spread in lines across the grass and Rhiannon looked at her feet and smiled. "It has been many years since the violet last grew here, it will again become the violet isle." Rune smiled as she stood up and looked at her.

"Wherever violets grow I find there is great happiness, when my daughter returns, she will always see the love of her mother." She smiled at Rhiannon who gave her a happy nod.

It was a long evening and soon Rune found it becoming a little tiring. Robbie slipped his arm round her waist as Steph and Jess stood side by side holding the children. "You look tired, let's call it a day." Rune nodded as Steph handed her Hal, Robbie made his excuses, and holding Iona in his arms they headed for their small room and some peace and quiet.

Robbie settled the children as Rune slid into bed; she would have a few hours before they needed feeding again and she slumped back exhausted. He pulled her close and spoke softly to her, but when he looked, she was already asleep in his arms. He settled back and closed his eyes, a happy contented feeling swept over him.

Earlier that day Treen had stood on the observation deck on the front lines, her eyes had glowed a deep orange colour and she had smiled. She looked out on the lines of the troops of the woodland army and shouted with all her might.

"Your lord as a son and a daughter, you ave an heir to your land." Bows raised and swords waved, as a huge roar of cheers went round the soldiers all dug in at the front. In the cave of the headquarters, Rafe hugged Rowan and Jett hugged Rafe and Jade screamed with delight hugging everyone. Maggs howled with delight as she jumped in Harry's arms and a party spirit echoed with joy at the coming of their lord's children. Rowan pulled Jade close and gave a huge happy hug.

"Well auntie Pebbles, we will have a celebration tomorrow." Jade's eyes glowed brightly with happiness as she giggled in Rowan's arms. It was a bright light in the darkness, which had been around all of them. Happiness flowed into their hearts and spirits, Harry found a bottle and poured everyone a measure, Rowan over looked it as he raised his glass before a crowd of happy smiling faces.

"To Halbert Thorn and Iona Violet of Loxley." They all toasted their new family members of Loxley with pride, and coughed as the liquor burned the insides of their throats.

Rune had been woken in the middle of the night to feed the children. Robbie had jumped awake when he felt the bed move as Rune sat back with Hal to feed him. Filomena smiled as she washed and cleaned Iona. Robbie had not realised that the two handmaidens of Fae were going to play an active role in the care of his children.

Filomena handed Iona to him with a smile, she said little, which he did not really mind, Isolde could at times be too talkative. He cradled Iona until Hal had been fed and then Rune swapped. He laid Hal gently back in his crib and talked to the bright blue eyes that danced up at him. When Iona had been fed, he laid her back and sat talking to both his children. He looked up and Rune was fast asleep again.

It was sometime before he had rocked them back to sleep and then he slid into bed and Rune instinctively curled around him. The sunlight was streaming when he opened his eyes to Rune's voice. The two children lay side by side on the bed and she was undoing the nappy of Hal. Robbie sat up and smiled; he slid out of bed and came up to Rune's side. She giggled as he looked for the pins to undo Iona's nappy. He was insistent he was going to do as much as he could; he opened the nappy and gasped with horror. Rune started to laugh as he recoiled with disgust. "Not quite a princess now, is she?" Rune giggled.

Robbie cleaned her down holding his breath, as Rune continued to giggle. "Wow that stinks, what the hell has she eaten?" Rune shook with laughter as she showed him how to fit the nappy and fasten it correctly. Iona made little gurgles as she laid back on the bed her bright violet eyes watching him all the time.

He lifted her up and breathed a long deep breath of relief. They had been fed and changed, and now both of them sat with the children while they ate their own breakfast. It was the start of a routine, which would last for years. Family life had entered its first day.

There was much to do now on the isle. Gwynfor and Rhiannon would organise as many of the people of Fae returned to their homeland. With the death of Gwendolyn, they had scattered all over other realms, and with the returning of their protective powers, they could finally come home. Rayne would accompany Robbie and Rune, which delighted Rune as it meant Gwinne would return with them.

Mel was delighted to see that she could have the teenagers for a while as Toby was heading south to see Wilbur, there was a great deal of excitement as Jess offered to put them up. Megan was happy; she had missed Ruby a great deal. Ruby had been her closest friend in Loxley, and she still felt the pain of not seeing her at home. Jess knew the company would help her.

Robbie was not at his happiest to know that Isolde and Filomena were to become a permanent addition to his family home, but as Rune had pointed out, she still had her realm of life, and with a war going on she would be needed.

It was almost early evening when the Specialists gathered and he watched as Rune hugged Gwynfor and Rhiannon. With his bag on his shoulder and Iona careful held in his arms, at the side of Jess he waited as Sapphire opened a window back into Loxley and the party stepped through and on to the Glade of Robbie's Mere at the front of the gate to his home.

It felt nice to be back and he gave a sigh of relief as the group trundled up the steps and into the house. Rune showed Isolde and Filomena the set up, and Robbie with Alice settled the children down in their room. For now, they would stay together and as they grew, they would have their own rooms. Somehow, Robbie knew the cribs would not be leaving his room for some time. It was all hands on deck as the group prepared; there would be a celebration in the Loxley household that night as the Specialists were relieved of their duties for a few hours. Robbie wanted Rowan and Jade by his side for the moment he had waited for.

The house was full with busy people as Rune looked out of her bedroom window with Jess. Robbie walked alone quietly down to his spot at the edge of the water in front of the wide mirror like mere. The evening sun reflected in shimmering lines against the reflection of the trees on the glass surface of the water. His hair blew softly in the gentle breeze as he slipped his hands in his pockets, and he looked out at the water. "Dad, I don't know if you can hear me, but I have my children. You have a Granddaughter and a Grandson. If you can hear me come to the Sacred Oak just after dusk, I really want you with me when I offer them to this realm."

Robbie stood silently watching the water as the pictures of his father passed through his mind. One memory was bright and clear in his thoughts as he remembered his father sat at the table beside him in Dunnottar. The voice of Robert Lox boomed in his mind as he saw the proud face of his father in that moment. "To my Pa it was the most important thing when it came to birth, I felt silly about it at first, but when I took you in my arms Robbie lad, and I showed you to the woods and all the spirits, I felt a pride and joy inside me like I had never known. I felt like you would become a woodsman of high value, and I was right."

He saw the moment as he asked his father to be at his side when he raised his own children up, and his father had turned with a smile of love and honour. "Of course Son, I would be proud."

Rune smiled as she watched and her hand took hold of Jess's. "He has told his Father. Robert will be by his side tonight."

CHAPTER EIGHTEEN.

TREE TO CELEBRATE, TREES TO CRUMBLE

The arrival of Jett and Jade was heard right across the glade. The clump of boots on the stairs grew louder, as Robbie looked across at Rune and smiled. "Well, that's the end of the silence." She gave a giggle as the door burst open and Jett and Jade with their mischievous faces stood smiling at the door.

Jade came nervously into the room and her eyes filled with tears, as Robbie lifted his son up. "Auntie Pebbles, Auntie Jett. I would like you to meet your future boss, Halbert Thorn Lord of Loxley."

Rune smiled at Jade as the tears rolled from her bright green eyes. She knew the pain Jade had felt thinking she had taken the life of Robbie's son. Rune took her gently by the hand. "This is my son Jade; he would like to feel his Aunties arms around him."

Jade looked up at her and gave a big sniffle, as she looked afraid. Rune smiled and took the small child out of Robbie's arms, and held him towards Jade.

Nervously she took hold of him and cradled him in her arms; she looked up with a huge smile. "He looks like you Robbie." He smiled as he came closer and slid his arm around her.

"You see the life in the future of this realm Jade, the past is over we all have a future."

She looked up at Robbie with a fierce look in her eyes. "I swear Robbie, on the life that I hold I will protect him at all costs, all my weapons and all my strength will protect him no matter what." She spoke with a fierce determination and Robbie smiled down at her.

"I am pleased to know that you will watch him from my side Jade, he will know a lady of high honour from this realm." She gave a smile and looked at Rune. Rune gave a nod and she smiled as Jett peered over Jade's shoulder.

"He is a hairy little bugger like his dad, isn't he?" Rune gave a giggle and turned to lift Iona. She held her out to Jett who looked quite scared. "Better not Rune, I err... Not really good at this baby stuff, I might drop her."

Rune gave a smile as she sat on the bed and patted it at the side of her. Jett sat down and looked at Iona, Rune slid her across and Jett looked terrified as Rune gently placed her into Jett's arms. She showed her how to hold Iona properly, and then stood up as Jett cradled the small child. Her face softened to a smile. "She is pretty like you Rune." She smiled her cheeky smile as Iona opened her eyes and looked up at her.

"Oh wow, Jade look how cool her eyes are?" Rune gave a giggle as Jade sat down beside her holding Hal. Robbie slipped his arm around Rune as he watched his children with their two aunts. Rowan and Rafe came in through the door quietly and looked down on the two largest mischief makers in the history of Loxley, sat with their niece and nephew in their arms.

Jade looked up at Rowan. "This is Halbert, he is my nephew." Rowan gave a huge grin, Jett giggled as Iona took hold of her finger, and she looked up at Rafe.

"Hey Wolfie look at that, she will have a great grip for a sword hilt." She beamed a huge smile. "I will teach both of them the best sword play ever, I can get her some boots like mine made." Rafe gave a laugh

"I think honey you should let her grow a little first." Rune giggled as he turned to her and gave her a big hug. He smiled at Robbie and pulled him into a hug. "I am so pleased for you both." He patted Robbie hard as he embraced him. Rowan squeezed Rune tight.

"This is the greatest gift I could know of for all of us, I am so delighted for you both." Rowan pulled Robbie into a hug with a beaming smile. "Congratulations Brother I am so happy for you." The two girls giggled as they sat side by side holding the small children and watched them both, pointing out which was doing what.

Later that evening, there was a long line of tables on the lawn, as the Specialists and family all gathered round to celebrate the birth of the children. Robbie sat by Rune at the end of the table, Jess sat by his side, and Steph and Pete sat at the side of Rune. Harry rose from his seat and tapped on the side of his glass and the noise level dropped as everyone looked up at him. He looked a little nervous.

"Whoa this is like totally vibe jangling." He looked at Robbie. "I am like... You know the main dude now in this family, cause I lost my bro." For a moment it looked like a wave of pain crossed his face and he gave a small smile. "I loved the dude you know? He was like totally there for me."

Jess gave a smile at Harry and squeezed Robbie's hand, as Harry looked round at everyone. "I love Robbie and Rune; they are like the most cosmic folk I know. I think you all should like totally raise your glasses and say hey dudes you are like radical and totally deserve this happy vibes thing."

Jade and Jett giggled as everyone raised their glasses and shouted. "Happy vibes dudes." Rune gave a giggle at the side of Robbie; she leaned forward and looked at Harry who beamed with affection next to the buck teeth gasping Maggs.

"We all love you very deeply Harry, and for a first speech as the head of the family I want to thank you for such heart felt words of love. I know the spirit of Robert is here with us and he would be proud of you."

Harry looked worried as his eyes darted left to right; he casually slipped his hand in his jacket, and pulled out his purple tinted glasses and slipped them on. He beamed with relief and nodded a big smile to everyone. "Hey it's cool."

The evening passed slowly and as dusk approached, Robbie got up with Rune as some of the guests made their way home. They all hugged them before leaving and the group lessoned. Jess held Iona in her arms beside Robbie and Rune. Steph carried Hal beside Pete with Rowan and Jade. Rafe with his arm round Jett walked with Harry, Maggs and Judy with Kate. John and Beth walked with Alice and Bear, as John thought of a moment in the snow earlier that year.

Happily talking they walked through the trees to the glade of the sacred oak, which stood quietly waiting surrounded by other old oak and beech. It was dark and the moon cast silver beams down through the gaps in the canopy of the trees, and gave a shimmering essence to the whole place. The happy group gathered in a circle around Robbie in front of the old tree that still had the wooden platform from his wedding around it. Rune's eyes danced as she felt the pride and joy inside Robbie.

He took Hal out of the arms of Steph as everyone quietened down. Rune took Iona and came up at his side; she smiled her white face radiant in the moonlight. Robbie stepped forward and looked at her, she gave a soft giggle. "Are you ready?" He nodded as they lifted their children up into the air in front of the sacred tree.

Robbie's voice boomed as loud as his father's did. "Hear me my lord of the woodland and all of creation. Hear me as lord of this land and hooded man. Hear me for I am a proud man of Loxley who offers you my praise for the birth of my son and my daughter. See the jewels of my line for they are the future of all of us. Take them into your realm and protect them, show your love to my son and heir, for this is Halbert Thorn Loxley. Show your love to my daughter the new Queen of the line of Fae, for she is Iona Violet Loxley. Hear me My Lord and let my father whom I love know he has a line to continue his blood."

He was tall and proud as he called into the blackness of the night. His voice bounced off the trees as the wind swirled round through the glade, the eyes of Rune flickered as the breeze lifted Robbie's hair, and the soft gentle words of the wind whispered in his ears as it passed. "Hearne."

Rune lowered her daughter into her arms, as the violet in her eyes glistened through her tears. She gave a bow as everyone knelt down on one knee and the sounds of creaking bark wove through the woods.

The tall frame of the man of the trees walked slowly toward them, and Rune beamed with delight as he came up to them both, as they knelt before him holding their children. His eyes shone like the fresh fruit of summer berries, and he looked down and the eyes of Iona flickered with soft lilac. Iona gave a happy squeak and Rune giggled.

"Grandfather of all creation, I am life." She rose slowly as the old lord smiled at her and lifted a long twig like finger to her face. His face showed a happiness Robbie had never seen, and he almost looked younger as the lines on his bark like skin seemed to lessen.

"I have a joy within me my dearest flower of my realm, which even I have not the words to describe. You hold a life before me to bless, and yet I feel that you have honoured me higher than any ever have. You hold two lives before me and show me the true meaning of hope." Rune rested her head on his hand as he spoke and she looked up into his soft kind eyes and smiled.

"I love you My Lord and grandfather, I have fought with my Robbie to save your realm, and my children will do the same. Our dreams and our lives and all of my line will protect you." Her tears fell as violets as Robbie watched the tenderness in the high lord of the wood as he spoke to his granddaughter of life.

"She has the power of her mother, and the softness and kindness of her great grandmother Opal." Hearne softly stroked the face of Iona, and her eyes flared in a bright violet light. He ran his hand around her face, and a small golden chain ran on to her neck. He smiled a kindly old smile and a tear fell from his eye, he caught it on the end of his long finger, and guided the tear to the small golden chain. As the tear touched the gold, it shone with bright violet light and a small violet flower appeared made from the stone of Sugilite. "Violet Stone of the Violet Isle filled with the power of the Violetlines. She will be her mother and will have the power to protect all things in this world. She is beautiful and very precious Runestone Sapphire; my woodland will never find two more wonder filled flowers than that of you and your daughter."

Rune gave a big sniffle as she looked with love into Hearne's eyes. "Thank you, Grandfather."

"I love you my child." Rune wept softly as the old man of the woods turned to face Robbie. He gave a bow.

"My Lord I am honoured by your words for my daughter." He gave a smile and raised his hand to Robbie's shoulder. "A life was taken and a life is returned my Bowman. You have an heir to the realm of these woodlands. I feel your pride and your joy and I am happy, as I too feel the same pride and joy. I see a young tree before me with the power of the sacred oak; he has the essence of the father that has led his people well." Hearne looked into the eyes of Halbert.

"The name of Bright Stone is well conceived I see, Robert means bright, and he is the son of Runestone, you show wisdom in the naming of your child. He carries the power of the Violetlines, and will be a woodsman of great skill. I have been honoured by your devotion to my line; I saw the power of a young tree match the power of darkness, you are a brave and courageous knight my young tree, you are worthy of a line of kings."

Hearne looked at the blue pendant of the bright stone that Gwynfor had given Robbie to tie on his neck. He touched it with his long fingernail and a thin ring of Sugilite appeared besides it on the tie.

"On the day of his eighteenth summer that will fit on his finger, it will mark him as the bright stone and next leader of the hooded realm. He too has the power of Violetlines, for he is the first male to come from my line, and so I too feel the pride of an heir as well my young bowman. You and my daughter of the woods honour me, rest and then move to your destiny, and bring back the dreams that will drive you through. The line of the king is coming."

Hearne stepped back and pulled Robbie and Rune shoulder to shoulder. Both of them held their children and he smiled at them. Hearne lifted a hand and his voice boomed out into the woodland. "Hear me for I am your creator. Hear my words and take heed, for here on this night before you all, I raise my hands and bless the lives of these four children who have the highest honour in my realm. Know that I have spoken this and protect them. The coming of the stones is now the way forward, follow them and keep them safe."

Hearne looked at them both and smiled. "There is one who will not enter my realm, as it is this time that has been waited upon. This is my gift to you Robert of Loxley for you need to heal for the fight that comes."

Hearne turned and faced the trees. "Walk to me child in the lost wood." The white mists rolled out from the trees as Hearne turned to Robbie. "You have but a short time use it well my son." The white swirling mist rolled back as Jess shot past Robbie and flew into the arms of Robert Lox. Hearne gave a smile as he looked back at Robbie.

"I fear my young tree this may be a little too funky for your uncle." Jade and Jett giggled at Harry passed out on the floor. Steph lifted Hal out of his arms and nodded.

"Go to your father Robbie."

Robbie looked back at Rune's eyes filled with tears; he lifted Iona out of her arms. "You show him my son." She nodded as her tears dripped from her face. Robbie and Rune walked side by side to the smiling face of Robert Lox. "I waited for you Rob Lad, I would not go in until I saw him, I gave you my word." Rune raised her son to Robert as Jess wept with her arms round him.

"Robert this is your grandson, Halbert Thorn Loxley." She sniffled as she swallowed back her tears. Robert slowly pulled his arm from round Jess, and his eyes glistened as he reached out and smiled, as he lifted Halbert into his arms. He looked across at Robbie and beamed.

"This is a true man of Loxley; I can feel it Rob lad. You done my boy proud Runestone." She smiled as she wiped her eyes.

"I love him Robert you know how much?" He nodded as he glanced down at

Jess. He lowered Halbert back into Rune's arms and turned to Robbie.

"This is my daughter Iona." Robert smiled as he lifted her into his arms.

"Aint she just perfect?" He looked at Robbie. "You watch this one she will be a looker, every bloody buck in the forest will be after her." Rune and Jess both gave a giggle as Robert smiled down at her. "My line has been truly blessed Rob lad; I will leave knowing you are all safe... Let me talk to John, our Harry aint much point he don't like us spooks."

Robbie gave a giggle as Jess pulled on Robert's arm, "Rob don't, Harry loves you and he has missed you."

Robbie took Iona back off his father as Robert strode down the glade; John threw his arms around his brother and wept as Robert patted his back. "Take good care of my family John, I love Harry but that nerve medicine of his jumbles his brains." John wept words of love into his brother's heavy shoulder.

John slid back and Robert patted his face. "Think on little brother, watch em all, you know what to do if they come at the walls?" John swallowed hard and nodded, Robert looked at the faces of Rowan and Rafe, stood with Jett and Jade. "Stay by his side and watch him for me." They all nodded and Robert winked at Rowan.

Hearne turned in the trees. "It is time Robert."

He nodded as he slipped his arm round Jess. "Let Robbie walk me back Jessie love, just remember what I said. All eternity." She smiled as her tears formed.

"I love you so much and I miss you Rob." He wiped the tears from her eyes.

"I know love, I miss you too, but I will wait there for you, take care of our boy and our grandkids, they need you more at the moment." She tried to smile as she nodded. He leaned over and gave her a soft kiss.

Robbie handed Iona back to Steph, and he walked slowly toward the trees with his father. Robert Lox spoke. "Steph was right, I would rather it was me you are needed, remember no matter how hard it looks, do not let them buggers think for a moment they are winning. Hold em as long as you can, do not retreat until you absolutely have to. You can win this if you are smart, keep hitting em in any way you can. I mean it Rob; keep the pressure up on them and you will save Loxley."

Robbie smiled, as he looked at the power of the man that was his father. "I will dad." Robert smiled and gripped his shoulders firmly.

"You are a fine man Robbie, I am so proud of you and what you have achieved, if ever in doubt look at the choices you have already made, you have the right instinct. Think of Rowan and Rafe, no general could ask for better at his side, look at the way you led them in and out of Tintagel, which took courage and skill of the mind. Look at Runestone Rob, just look at the woman you chose to be beside you. She is the best thing you ever thought of. You have the instinct use it." Robert gave his son a final hug. "I love you son, never forget that?"

Robbie held on tight, as he did not want him to leave yet. "I love you dad."

Robert patted him on the back and slowly slipped back out of his arms. He stepped back and smiled as the white swirled around him and drew back into the trees. Robbie stood and stared into the darkness of the woodland, the darkness seemed to sweep in and fill all the gaps between the trees, the silence hung in the still air, and his father was gone forever. Two slender white arms slipped round him from behind and he felt her headrest on his shoulder. "You OK?"

He slipped his hands on hers. "I will be." He slid round and faced her. Her hair shone golden and red with the moonlight behind it, her eyes shone bright sapphire blue with her concern and her love, her skin was soft, and pale and dusted with the lightest of pale freckles, she smiled and her cheekbones lifted to make her skin below her eyes flash with the softest of blue. "I love you Runestone. You are everything in my world and more, you know that don't you?" He lifted his hand and stroked the hair from the side of her face as she smiled back at him.

"I love you too Robert of Loxley." She giggled as he pulled her close and softly kissed her. Her eyes flickered with violet.

"Wow."

"Where are the children?"

"Mum and mum have them," she giggled, "You know what I mean?" She took his hand in hers.

"Let's go and tuck them in for the night." He gave her a smile, and arm in arm they came out of the trees and crossed the moonlit glade. They came into the house and up the stairs as the others all gathered in the kitchen. Robbie and Rune stood at the door of the children's bedroom, as Jess and Steph lovingly put the children in their cribs for the night, they smiled as they watched. Rowan came up the stairs and gave them both a smile as he looked at the grandparents putting their children to bed. He patted Robbie softly on the shoulder. "Jade and I are going to head off Robbie; we will see you in the morning."

Robbie walked to the garden gate as Jade and Rafe lifted their bags and followed with Jett. Robbie looked at four of his closest friends. "We will meet here in the morning; all the Specialists have been told to gather at lunch time. We will return to the moors and prepare for a second offensive." They nodded as they turned and walked to the trees.

It was dark and cool, as the heat of the day seemed to lift. Across Loxley, lights still burned in the Village Hall and the large wooden hotel. The house lights burned low at Lox Farm, and across the wide valley down to the reservoir was a sea of silent blackness. All seemed still and quiet as David Williams looked out across the high wall of the gate. In the woodland all around badgers looked for food, and the foxes slunk through the trees. A mouse squealed, as the silent wings of an owl lifted it up to the trees, the bright eyes of David Williams scanned the darkness.

The hooded and cloaked bowman carried his coffee, and he turned with a smile. "Oh thank Hearne, I need this." He took the cup and lifted it to his lips. "You can turn in for the night now bowman, we will be fine all is quiet."

The bowman looked from under the darkened hood, and David looked back wondering why he had not returned to his slumber. "Is everything alright bowmen? What is your name I cannot see your face?"

The hood moved as the bowman spoke. "Melanie." She slipped back the hood and her hair fell out across her shoulders. "I am home Davie."

She was swept off her feet as the tin cup clattered to the floor, and he pulled her into his arms. Her eyes glistened as he kissed her holding her tightly; she gave a soft giggle as he slowly released her. "I have done what was needed to be done; I would be yours if you want me."

His smile was wide and happy as he pulled her close. "Never leave me again Mel, stay here in Loxley as my wife." She lifted her hand to his face and softly stroked it.

"I love you Davie, yes I will stay here and make this my home. Yes, I will marry you."

David Williams held her close as Henry wiped a tear from his eye stood smiling a little way down from where he had brought Mel secretly up. Those soldiers on guard around all smiled as they looked out over the wall and watched the Vale of Loxley. Rune sat at her dressing table and stopped for a moment as the joy of Melanie swept round her sisters. She smiled to herself and looked in the mirror as she saw Robbie watching from the pillows. He gave her a grin and she smiled back him, Rune placed the silver hairbrush down and opened her draw to get a tie for her hair. Her face broke into another large smile as she pulled out the long folded letter with the seal of Lord Loxley on it. Her eyes danced, as she looked back at him. "Another one?" She gave him a happy giggle.

The following morning was busy at the postal office in Loxley. Judy had her small printer working in the night, and had created a special announcement leaflet, to bring the news of the births of the two children to Loxley. They were to be displayed in every area of the woodsman's world. Rags and Bobby were busy organising the distribution, as Lucy filled up the bags for the long queue of riders who were ready to leave. Just before noon, every rider sped through the gates and the message of the good news was now spreading in every direction.

The whole of the stockade seemed to have a lighter atmosphere, as the traders set up their stalls, and the people of the wooden town just inside the gates, all came out to shop and work in the fields or on the walls in defence. Rune sat in the nursery with Filomena as Isolde helped out downstairs with the arriving Specialists, it felt strange for Robbie who often found it hard having people working as servants. The two young women did not seem to mind a bit but he was uncomfortable with it. He sat at his desk later, as Filomena appeared with a drink.

"Lord Rowan of Loxley is here to see you My Lord."

Robbie put down his writing nib and looked up at her. "Filomena, would you sit down for a moment?" She looked a little surprised, as she sat quietly on the chair opposite him.

"Are you displeased with me My Lord?" Robbie looked at her with her long red hair and dark brown eyes, she looked nervous. Robbie thought for a moment and smiled.

"No I am not displeased with you or your sister." He gave himself a moment and looked back at her. "I understand that your people wish to protect my daughter, my wife was greatly weakened during her time of birth, and I am pleased that she has had your assistance with the children, she needs to recover her strength." He took a long breath, as he looked at her sat before him in her long yellow dress and golden slipper like shoes.

"I appreciate very much all you have done, but it concerns me that you feel you have to be a servant to everyone who comes here. In my home, myself, and my wife have always stood down on formality so that we can let everyone relax and feel at ease. I find it uncomfortable that you and your sister feel you have to act and speak like servants, we are simple people here who do not expect to be waited upon hand and foot."

She gave a small smile. "My Lord it is an honour to my sister and I to be here and help you. We requested this task for it gives us honour."

Robbie sat back in his seat. "So if I was to send you away from here you would be dishonoured?"

A frightened look crossed her face. "My Lord please do not say such things, it is our honour to be here. If we were to leave, we would not be able to return to our land such would be the shame of it."

Robbie felt trapped as he looked down at his papers for a moment. He looked back up at the worried face of Filomena. "I find this a difficult situation; I have never agreed with servants. I cannot send you away but this situation feels wrong to me, I feel we need to establish some new rules of my household in order for this to work and allow me the ease of it."

"My Lord we want only to help you and your wife with this task of raising the future queen of our realm. Please you must not concern yourself; I can assure you it is a task both of us chose freely."

He gave a long sigh. "Alright, I feel this is how this must be done. Firstly, I am Robbie and my wife is Runestone in this house, I will not accept any other title. In public and at engagements I recognise the title of lord, but not here. In the house you will be part of the family. This means that you can continue your roles, but I would wish that both of you take at least two days in each week off, so that you can pursue a life that is your own. You can arrange with your sister which days, that way my wife will have one of you to hand at all times. I wish it that you feel like one of us, and fit into the way in which we operate, it will create a much more relaxed and gentler atmosphere around the children. I do not wish my children to be raised expecting others to do everything for them; they will be raised to the standard of Loxley not Fae. You will of course instruct my daughter, as she gets older and prepare her for her role in the future. Nevertheless, I insist she is free to grow up as a normal child of this area would. This is the only acceptable arrangement I can live with; do you understand what it is that I am asking?"

She looked a little abashed as she considered his point of view. "I am in your household; I will abide by your rules My Lord."

"It's Robbie, Filomena."

She gave a smile and nodded. "Yes Robbie." He smiled at her.

"Alright, thank you for the coffee, it was nice of you to think of me up here when you are so busy."

Filomena gave him a bright smile. "I like being here very much, you have a very nice home."

He leaned back in his chair. "I'm pleased, you go and inform your sister of our new arrangement, and if you do not mind would you ask Rowan to come up here?" She got up out of the chair and smiled as she nodded.

"I will, thank you my.... Robbie."

He sat back in his chair and relaxed as he sipped his coffee, Rowan came up the stairs with a cup in his hand. "I see you have already corrupted the staff." He gave a smile "Thank Hearne, all this Lord Rowan this and that, it was driving me mad, I knew you would crack quickly." He gave a chuckle as he sat down in the chair. He leaned across the table. "I have never seen Rune look so happy my brother; I am happy for you."

Robbie gave a small laugh. "I think little Pebbles is equally as happy." Rowan nodded.

"It has given her a lot of joy to see you with an heir. I am pleased to see her so relieved, it hurt her deeply Robbie you mean a great deal to her."

"I know and I am happy for her." He sat up in his chair and looked at the plan on his table. "Tell me more of this idea of Scarlet's, for attacking his ships?"

The building of the black city along the edge of the moors from Scarborough up past Whitby had been a large project for Mason Knox. The long stretches of sand that had once been the attraction for many of the people in the times of old modern man, were now heavy harbour walls, as Mason had dredged out all along the sea front and built a large concrete harbour.

The harbour was a vast open square of towering stone that stretched right out into the sea. At the seaward end was a wide opening that allowed three of the huge ocean liners he was using to pass through at any one time. The harbour was a hive of activity as Mason was bringing his soldiers from the south up to Yorkshire to begin his large scale attack of York, followed by his eventual attack and destruction of Loxley.

Caerleon was still creating more problems as his convoys were attacked from within his walls, as they infiltrated the woodsmen of the large welsh army into the sprawling cities he had created in the south. Warwick had a programme of constant attack along the large wall running two miles east of the old M5 motorway. Fertilizer bombs were proving very useful, as the large walls were constantly blown up. Large areas of the walls had repair scars and in many of the remoter places, long sections of the walls were crumbled ruins as they were hit repeatedly. The walls of Newcastle and Sunderland found that they too were not so easy to escape the long hand of Loxley, as Ian of Carlisle sent men across the north of the country to pound the walls and make life as hard as possible for all the inhabitants of the city.

The concrete used was fast setting so it could be built in a rush, as large areas of land were cleared of woodsmen and then the land enclosed. Rune had paid a visit earlier in the year to the men up north and seen up close the soft crumbly concrete. During the last trip to Iona, she had noticed a stone built cottage that had been covered in cement and how the ivy had broken large areas of the cement off as it rooted through to the solid granite stone. It had been on her mind a lot, and as she sat with Steph looking through papers, she overheard Robbie and Rowan talking, as they considered the assault of the black city. She looked at Robbie and she smiled a warm and loving smile.

He gave her a smile and saw she wanted to ask him something; Rowan had noticed and stopped talking. He looked at her sat on the end of the long table; she leaned on the papers as she formed the question in her head. "What are you going to do when all the fertilizers run out?" Robbie looked at Rowan and then back to her.

"How do you mean Rune?" She looked at her mum who had been surprised by the question, and stopped shuffling through her papers. Rune looked at everyone who was now looking at her. "We do not have an unlimited supply; it just makes sense that eventually it will run out, and he will rebuild his walls and then you will be back to square one with no means of bringing his walls down." Rowan nodded as he looked across the table at Robbie who had slid back into his seat, and began to think about his options.

"It's a good point Robbie; we do not have the means to manufacture it, and Mason stores are deep in his city, when our supply runs out what then?" Robbie shrugged.

"I must admit I have not thought about it, the same goes for the dynamite. That is why Fuse and Meg are using the striker arrows; it uses less so our supplies will last longer." He looked at Rune and he knew she had something in mind. "What are you thinking Rune?"

She gave him a big smile; she loved the fact he was never afraid to ask her advice. She got up out of her chair and walked down the room toward them. "I just thought that we do actually have something that will never run out and will do long term damage." They both looked up at her and she gave then both a cheeky grin as she slipped down on to Robbie's lap. She gave a giggle as she kissed the end of his nose. He looked at her bright happy face.

"So what is it we have an endless supply of?" She gave a little giggle.

"Nature." Steph was way ahead of Robbie and Rowan as she smiled back at her daughter.

"That is brilliant sweetheart." Rowan looked at Steph as Robbie looked into Rune's bright sparkling blue eyes, he could see the mischief behind them.

"Just how exactly can we use nature to fight Mason Knox?" Steph gave a giggle.

"Oh Robbie, come on, how many woodlands have we walked through in the past year knowing that below our feet was the crumbled remains of a town or city? Just look out from the escarpment one of the biggest cities of the old modern age is buried below that endless sea of green you see. There is not one single trace of Old Sheffield left, it has gone forever."

Rune kissed him on the cheek. "Opal did that in just a week when she saw the evil on the edge of Loxley."

Robbie understood what she was saying but he was not convinced. "Rune I understand, but it has taken twenty seven years since the red death for most of the decay to set in. There are still many areas of this land, where cities still stand in ruins; nature will work over a long period. We are talking in weeks now before those cities spill out and we face one hell of a big army."

"Robbie, you forget who I am. I helped regrow an entire ancient woodland in a night. I turned the Scottish city into a garden in less than eight hours, there are many plants on my list of useful tools which I can grow fast, and they will help you destroy the walls."

"Like what?"

"Off the top of my head, Cherries and Ivy for starters." Steph gave a nod.

"I remember an old cherry at the farm in Avon, Pete's dad had it cut down. I was really angry about it and had a big scene with him, so he took me into the cellar and showed me part of the wall that had collapsed, and these huge roots had come through the wall. He had to cut it down because it was going to tear up the foundations and pull the cottage down." Rune smiled.

"They will cause lasting damage if planted close, and they spread fast sending up shoots from the roots, which will go under the walls and come up on the other side. They will look really beautiful in the spring; I should think that alone will annoy him. Rob I am life, with my will inside them they will not be easy to kill, and you will have the safety of less men attacking the walls, which will give you more men for defence."

Rowan sat back in his chair impressed. "I must admit Rune I love the idea. We use what we fight for, green life." Robbie was starting to understand her thinking and he nodded at Rowan.

"Ok Rune, how would we try this out to see if it works?"

She gave him a big happy smile. "The black city of Scarborough is preparing to attack us, so let's start there and see what trouble we can cause them." She kissed him and jumped up off his knee. "I think we should have a drink; the team will be here soon and the babies will need feeding."

Robbie chuckled as she skipped off down the stairs smiling. Robbie and Rowan followed her down the steps of the house and the Specialists looked up and smiled. Their leader and general looked relaxed and chatted happily, as they came out of the gate toward the fully tooled up team. All now wore green, except for Jett who was in her usual black. Crystal had on her green long poncho and a green cloak, over her white. Gwinne smiled at the side of Rayne. "We wondered if we could be of some use, we have a lot of experience in tactics, and thought we could do something useful." Robbie smiled at Gwinne who wore a powder blue cloak over her white long dress.

"I would certainly appreciate all the help I can get, especially knowing of Rayne's reputation in the field, I believe if I am right you put up quite a fight for the king in the past."

Rayne smiled at Robbie. "To know our king was inspiration Robbie, Arthur was no ordinary man."

"Welcome aboard, Skip and Treen left earlier but I think you will find them quite the tacticians, I feel you will work well with them." Rayne nodded and Robbie turned to the gathered group. Jade beamed at the side of Jett, Maggs smiled with delight in her many shades of green tie-dyed cloak.

"Good morrow my sweet Robbie, I see your aura is filled with joy and contentment, as is Rune's, we are all filled with the happiness of seeing your little bundles of joy."

Rowan smirked as Robbie gave her a smile. "Thanks Maggs, we are both delighted, and I am pleased to see my joy has also brought you such pleasure." Maggs gave a huge horsy gasp as her bangles rattled and she turned to Harry.

"Oh Chicken, he is such a darling." Harry nodded.

"Whoa chicken he is totally filled with happy vibes." Robbie moved into the centre of the group.

"We head to the moors and then we move into action as of this evening. We have work to do; Mason is now shipping in extra troops; we need to get busy and cause even more chaos if we are going to hold him at bay. I need all of you on your best game from now on. Jade, Jett, from now onwards you are off the leash. We are looking at the survival of Loxley, York must not fall."

Jett clenched her fist. "Yes." Her arm was still bandaged and had stitches in, but she was almost ready for more action. Jade gave a bright smile and winked at Saff.

It was a noisy group, which came through the window on to the moors. Explosions could be heard in the distance as the group walked up to the cave. Robbie looked up the long path to the platform that led up to the observation deck. The cover boards were now up with a long line of bowmen waiting behind them. Treen stood high up her long red hair blowing in the breeze, as she gave her commands to Claire stood at her side with her flags.

Rowan walked at his side and nodded to Treen dressed in red watching out across the field. "She has shown a great deal of skill Robbie, working with Scarlet has really rubbed off. I have been very impressed with her tactics; she has a lot of command up there."

Robbie gave a nod of agreement. "From what I have heard of Gwendolyn, I think we can say Treen has inherited much of her command skills."

Gwinne and Rayne went straight to work with Skip who filled them in on the current state of play, and the Specialists established themselves as they waited for their orders. Robbie and Rowan walked up to the observation platform. They climbed up the steps that had been built and walked along to Treen who looked out over the field. Behind the line of the black forces, it was instantly noticeable that there was a large increase of their troops. Catapult explosives were currently bombarding them, Treen gave her orders and Claire sent the signals. "Old Grey hair eez back, ow about telling im we ave missed his ugly face in the telescope." Claire smiled and waved her flags.

Treen turned to Robbie. "This frankly eez good, I ave to watch him careful." She smiled.

Rowan leaned over to Robbie and whispered, "She means General Franklin, he has taken over the command of the battle. Scarlet rated him quite highly." Robbie nodded and turned to the field.

"You have done very well Treen since we lost Scarlet. I am very pleased with the way you stepped up and helped fill the void. Scarlet would be proud of you."

Treen gave a slight smile. "I miss her Robbie; she was my friend." Robbie nodded.

"We all miss her; she was an exceptional commander of the battlefield. You have proven your skills beyond doubt, I am pleased to know I have you here at the side of Rowan; I will be taking the Specialists out for a few attacks, which I hope will take some of the pressure off you. We now start to fight for Loxley so we need to be on the ball." Treen gave a smile as she accepted the praise of Robbie, Claire beamed at him and he winked, she gave a giggle as Robbie patted Rowan shoulder.

"I have a garden to arrange for our old friends in the city, I will see you shortly."

Rowan nodded as Robbie headed down the steps and back to the cave.

It was late evening when the pale blue pulsating orb opened just two miles south of the black walled city. Rune had been experiencing some problems, as the draining of her powers had taken longer to return than she thought. Sapphire had gone back to Loxley to collect her and now as the window closed behind the group, Robbie instructed everyone.

Blades and Todd melted away to his right, as John with Fish went left, Rafe, Jett and Jade headed up front with Woody and Harry covering the rear with Maddy and Amethyst. Robbie looked at Rune as they sat in the trees waiting for the all clear from Jade. "You going to be alright?" She smiled in the low light.

"I just need a little more time, honestly Rob I am fine." He nodded a concerned look on his face.

"Just be careful, I will not risk you." She leaned over and kissed the side of his cheek.

"I will be fine; I just need a few more days rest to get use to the new routine, I am breast feeding two it takes a lot out of me."

He nodded. "I want you to rest more now we have help, let them take up some of the strain and get your strength back." She gave him a sweet smile.

The whistle came through the trees and Robbie signalled the group to move. The smells of the leaves and fresh honeysuckle filled his nostrils as he wove through the damp woodland with all its rich earthly smells, Rune felt his joy of the woodland and gave a smile as she followed behind him closely. They came to the edge of the trees and took a long defensive line as Robbie peered out with Rune. The gates were two hundred yards ahead of them across the black burned earth, he looked at her. "How do we do this?"

Rune gave a wink and slipped something out of her pocket, she passed it to Jade, and she gave a gasp of delight. "Oh wow, you kept it." Her eyes sparkled under her long curly blonde fringe as Jett peered across and smiled when she saw the catapult in Jade's hand.

"How cool is that, my mum banned me from having one after I smashed all the windows in the barracks." Rune lifted a bag of bright red cherries out from inside her cloak she passed them to Jade, Robbie watched not sure what Rune meant to do; he tapped her on the shoulder.

"We need trees near the gates, Rune they are over two hundred yards away."

She gave him a smile. "That is no ordinary catapult, Jade made it, believe me she is no ordinary shot." Rune turned back to Jade who had slipped one of the red fruits into the sling of the catapult, Rune leaned over and touched the fruit, two small green leaves sprouted out of it. "Ok Jade, hit the far gate and do not hang about, that will begin to grow very fast." Jade gave an evil little giggle and took aim.

The catapult gave a dull twang, and Robbie watched the gates. Jade loaded another, Rune touched it. "Right this side of the gates." She fired.

Robbie watched as on the far side of the gates as a tree shot up from the ground. The guards jumped back as it hurtled towards the top of the wall and the trunk filled out quickly. It touched the wall as the branches shot out forming a huge canopy over the top of the wall; two guards ran screaming as the long branches chased them across the top. Rune gave a little giggle; Robbie was amazed at the distance Jade could shoot with the catapult.

"Maybe you should put arrows in that." She gave a little giggle as she fired another. More trees shot up against the wall as Robbie leaned over. "What about putting a few on the road in front of the gates, with trees that wide, they won't get a single man through." Rune nodded and Jade took aim.

Soldiers were running around unsure of what to do, the sudden appearance of a tree was not something they were trained for, a group gathered on the road and looked at the two huge trees that now filled both sides of the gate. One clutched his face as the cherry hit him and Jade gave a little giggle.

There was a horrified scream as two trees shot up from the floor. Four soldiers were caught by surprise, and they shot up in the air caught in the branches of the trees, they sped into the air fast caught at the top of the rapidly expanding branches. Robbie gave a shudder as the wails were suddenly silenced and the soldiers were crushed between the thickening wood of the branches. Rune looked back at him. "That is the pressure applied, now for a little softening of the concrete."

She crouched down and touched the floor, four bright shiny heart shaped leaves shot out of the floor on a thin wiry stem. She smiled as she touched the ground and others popped up, Robbie watched as she gave a little giggle, and the plants seemed to sway in front of her. Rune's eyes turned a pale violet and Robbie jumped as the plants shot to six feet tall in a second. They stood menacing, as their tendrils seemed to stretch out looking to grab something, he gave Rune a nervous glance and Jett and Jade giggled.

Rune looked at the plants. "Go on babies, go and play." The ivy fell over on to the floor and Robbie watched as they shot across the open ground toward the city, where the cherry trees were still exploding out of the floor along the walls as the roots sent up side shoots. It was like unrolling a huge shining triangular carpet as the green spread out as it approached the city walls. Robbie watched with slight horror as the ivy hit the walls and shot up with enormous speed. It spread rapidly, and as it reached the top, any guard caught looking over was engulfed in leaves and screamed as the ivy bound round them fast crushing and squeezing them. He leaned over to Rune.

"What now?"

"We wait for a few moments." Robbie shuddered.

"Not hours?" She smiled sweetly.

"These are special, it will not take long."

Robbie turned back to where the walls had completely disappeared behind a curtain of green. Rune slipped her hand around his waist and pulled him close. Screams could be heard over the wall, which he presumed was some guard who thought a sword would do the trick. "You can be pretty scary Rune."

She gave a giggle as she leaned on his shoulder. "You are safe enough; I want more beautiful babies."

A blood curdling scream came from over the wall, and he cringed as his mind painted the pictures of death by penetrating ivy tendrils. "I better keep them coming then." Rune giggled.

The walls gave a soft groan, Robbie watched, as the concrete seemed to crack and rupture under the layer of green. Large sections slid inwards as the walls just crumbled, he looked into the city as he saw guards running away from the walls chased by the rampant ivy. The cherry trees were expanding and he could now see the damage done to the large wall as sections smashed to the floor leaving a wall of fat large trees. Rune seemed pleased. "They won't be coming out that way, it's a pity seaweed isn't as powerful."

Robbie gave a smile. "I wish we had thought of this earlier." Rune nodded a disappointed look.

"I should have realised at the cathedral, my grandfather did the same there."

The group moved back into the trees, Sapphire opened a window and they moved through to the moors, Robbie waited as she clicked her fingers and he stepped with Rune into the glade of Robbie's Mere.

He sat with the children while Rune fed them and he helped settle them for the night. They curled up in bed together and he watched her as she slid down on to his chest and closed her eyes. He knew she had once again used a lot of strength, which worried him. He lay back on the pillow and closed his eyes, her breathing whispered in his ears and he felt the tug of sleep as it gently pulled him into his dreams, where a little girl with violet eyes giggled at the side of a young boy with bright sapphire blue eyes.

CHAPTER NINETEEN

BOATS, AND GIRLS WITH NO SHAME

The captain of the guards wiped his brow and breathed a long slow sigh. Fires burned in a large circle round the green growth that had devastated the front walls of the city. He watched as his tired men stood back their face's black and sooty from the long nights work. They collapsed on the ground utterly exhausted from the fight with the deadly sea of green tendrils that grabbed those not paying attention, and dragged them screaming into the midst of rustling leaves. A young grime covered boy with a bucket and ladle walked up toward him, the coolness of the water running into his hot throat felt like a soft hand slowly stroking his neck, as the liquid extinguished his burning throat. He dropped his necktie on to the filled ladle and soaked it.

Captain Barrows nodded a smile to the young boy who moved on and he wiped his face of the clinging sweat and burnt dust, he looked up at the scene of chaos. The trees that Rune had brought to the walls of the city had grown rapidly; their huge mass had pushed onto the walls and moved them inwards. All that remained now was a long line of fat deep brown trunks, filled with the leaves and pale pink blossoms usually attributed to the spring.

The walls lay crumbled on the floor inside what had been the living quarters of the city. Most of the houses that had stood neatly in rows had been smashed down as the high walls toppled killing and crushing everything in their path. A fearsome wall of life now surrounded the black city, which was the result of their enemy. The Ivy had grown at an alarming speed running like wires of death, coated in the green shiny heart shaped leaves. It burrowed through the concrete and strangled the stone to a point where it simply crumbled and collapsed on the floor in huge piles of rubble.

Barrows had lost many men tonight. Running around in the dark it had been difficult to spot the deadly fine tendrils and they soon coiled rapidly around the legs of his men. It was a terrible thing to encounter watching as the plants grew rapidly, and penetrated his men strangling and devouring them as they screamed for help. He had been swift to think and pulled back his men away from the deadly attackers, gathering at the far end of the huge compound on the old market square. Captain Barrows had built long lines of fires across the compound in the path of the invading mass, pouring on oil and smashing down anything wooden, his men had finally after six long hours began to hold back the green carpet of death, which had crept toward them.

Fires raged as his men poured oil on to the ivy, which jumped and shot backwards with the heat of the flames, large areas of smouldering black stems and charred bodies littered the floor back to the remnants of the smoky walls of the city. Where the large gates had once stood, was a wide wall of trees, their trunks were so dense nothing would be able to weave past to get outside. Captain Barrow's felt like he had been caught in a prison, as his eyes ran along the long line of trunks that now replaced the high stonewalls. The city now looked more like the stockade at Loxley, the only difference being at Loxley the walls didn't try to kill you if you climbed them. The two large gates that led into the barracks compound stood behind him, they were open wide, and as the new troops woke, and headed out of their tents for breakfast, they found their progress slow as they all looked with disbelief in their eyes, at the scenes of utter chaos.

The burley sergeant came across the roadway holding his cap, and scratching his thick mass of soot filled tangled hair. His normal red fat face was streaked with black, and his eyes wore the look of a man who was exhausted. His collar was open and the sweat streaks ran down inside his shirt, he walked like a man whose legs felt heavier than the rest of him. The captain looked sideways at him and nodded.

"That will do Bill, the lads are buggered, pull them back and we can let some other lot clean up, we have done our bit here now." Bill nodded and turned, he walked back along the line of fires and shouted out his orders to the men who got up wearily from the floor and collected their discarded cloaks and weapons.

Slowly the troops, dragging their feet, walked silently back through the gates as a new line of clean fresh faced young soldiers came down the roadway and into the old market, Captain Barrows took one last look at the devastation and turning, he followed his men, and made his way to the commanders office to make his report.

It was June 24th, and the summer had now reached its height. Robbie had spent the last few hours at the gates with David Williams and Henry revising the plans for the protection of the stockade if it came under attack, and had decided to walk back up to the village. He came out of the gates of the compound with Fuse, and walked slowly up the dusty road toward the village, and the fourteen houses that formed the little shops, which gave Loxley the thriving small town status it now had. All down the road to his right there were long lines of the wooden houses, which accommodated most of the people that had been brought in for their protection. He stopped to view an area, which up until just over a year ago had been fields of turnips and sprouts, as well as a few wild meadow fields.

Behind him, the market ground was busy and on the long rows of the range, young woodsmen trained under the watchful eye of their instructors. Robbie watched as the carts passed and the people went about their daily business, his dark eyes cast a careful watch across the wooden town. "We have done well my friend." Fuse looked out across the stockade as he nodded to Robbie.

"Your father was very pleased with how many he could accommodate. Loxley has been transformed into quite a large town, most of the people are employed on the farm or in the army, and the others all have thriving little businesses. You have done very well indeed."

Robbie turned to walk back up the road. "How is everyone in the village doing?"

"Well to be honest Robbie, I don't think they have ever had it as good. Lady Judith seems happy with her books and printing, I know the Ashton family are all now working alongside Jess, and are now supervising many of the new staff. Joss and Maud are doing well with their candles, although I have asked them to consider taking on young new people to train in their skills, they do not appear to have done it yet."

Robbie nodded. "Yes, it is important we keep all the skills alive; I will talk to Joss; he can be a little old fashioned in his approach, Dad always liked him, thought him a reasonable man, what about the others?"

"Sue and Jake have a few young girls working for them, The Appleton's are doing very well with the livestock, your mother is happy as there has been a sharp increase in the herd this year. Agatha Patterdale is her usual gossiping self, although she has now hired three new staff. Reuben finally has taken on more. Alice and Anne have three staff, and Ian Hall is doing very well with all these new houses, he has five new staff learning furniture making."

They rounded the corner, and stepped on to the concrete road of the village, Robbie nodded to a passing couple and stopped and looked down the busy street between the two rows of cottages. He gave a smile as he looked to his favourite shop. Trinkets and Trousers with its little wooden shelter, which was filled with rails of neatly labelled clothes. Rune sat on the wall talking to her mother who he could just see sat in her usual chair by the door. Her long red hair spilled down the back of her pale lilac top and sparkled in the sunlight. Fuse gave a smile as he watched Robbie watching her.

"I believe that Lady Loxley now employs more than any other of the shops as they produce most of the clothing in the area?" Robbie smiled.

"It does seem to have become as big a family business as mums. Rune does have an unusually large family." He smiled. They walked down the street as Fuse looked at his notes, Robbie was happy that the stockade was running fine and everyone seemed to be getting along well. Rune gave a wave as he passed and he winked at her, her eyes sparkled and danced as Alice Kirk pulled his arm.

"Oh Robbie, I am so pleased to see you. Congratulations on the birth of your children, Runestone seems so happy, we are all delighted for you." She beamed up at him with her dark dancing eyes, and he had noticed the frown of Agatha Patterdale, who was more than a little put out about the fact Alice had got to him first.

"Thank you, Miss Kirk. We are both delighted and very happy." She gave him her usual big smile as she pushed a bag of freshly baked scones into his hand.

"I know how much you like these." Robbie gave her a big smile.

"You are very kind; give my best to your sister." They moved off as Alice scurried back into the shop and he nodded to Agatha as he passed. With the monthly inspection of the village affairs complete they walked back into the Village Hall, and the operations room, it was a busy hive of activity as usual. Rags gave a beaming smile as she came out with her bag on her shoulder.

"Big pile today Robbie, it's on ya desk as always, see ya." She skipped off out of the hall doors and headed off on her rounds. Robbie walked up to his office where Rowan worked on a pile of papers and looked up as he entered, everyone was busy, and Loxley was still growing fast.

Lucy wanted to learn how to shoot a bow, she was surrounded by the Bowmen and Specialists of Loxley, and Rags had been spending a lot of time when she was not in the postal service hut, practising on the range behind the barn with Maggs. Alice sat with her mum on the old wooden bench next to the compost heap. Baby Jessica was asleep in her basket between them. Alice smiled as Lucy kicked a stone and looked miserable. "What's up Lucy, nothing to do today?"

Lucy gave a small smile. "I want to learn to shoot, but Michelle and Maggs are too busy with the school and post, I wanted to borrow Michelle's bow, but she said no, it's not a toy."

Beth gave a warm happy smile. "Oh is that all? We thought that there was something really wrong, if it's a bow you need we have hundreds." Beth beamed a big smile at her. "You wait here my love, I am sure I have one of Alice's from when she was younger, I think you are bit small for a full size bow." Beth trotted off into the house with her usual big smile and Lucy walked slowly toward Alice.

Alice patted the seat next her, and Lucy came over with a smile. "So you want to follow the Loxley tradition and become a bow woman?" Lucy nodded.

"I deliver to this boys mum I really like; he is brilliant with a bow and he is only interested in girls who can shoot. I do want to be a Specialist one day as well." Alice gave a knowing smile.

"So, is this boy cute?" Lucy giggled and turned to Alice.

"Oh Alice, he is wonderful, and he can shoot better than most of the other lads, I really like him. He is very nice to me when I deliver when his mum is not in."

She seemed to go all bashful as she looked back at Alice her eyes twinkling, and her cheeks seemed to go a little pinker.

Alice gave a chuckle. "He sounds like a dish." Lucy beamed a big smile and nodded. "So Lucy, you will need to be the best if you are going to impress him. How would you like a few lessons with me?"

Lucy almost jumped off the seat. "Oh Alice would you? I would love you forever."

Alice laughed. "Ok then, I am still only on Specialist duty part time, so in the evenings when you have finished, I will take you on the range at the back for half an hour, and we will see what we can do. I could use the practice myself."

Lucy was over the moon and she giggled with excitement. "I can't wait to show Saucers how good I can shoot; I will practice really hard."

Alice gave a huge roar of laughter. "It is Saucers?" She gave a knowing nod, "Well you set the bar high my sweet I will say that much, he is good Lucy; we will have to really work hard to get you up to his level."

Lucy looked slightly confused. "Do you know him?"

Alice chuckled. "Why do you think he is called Saucers? The Specialists named him." Alice sat with Lucy and told her the story of the hooded man in the dark, and how it had been Robbie who had pinned him to the gatepost with an arrow. Lucy chuckled as Alice talked and explained how Robbie had given him the bow and told him to practice. She roared with laughter as Alice explained that Harry had given him the nickname because his eyes had gone so big when he met the Specialists. She tapped on Lucy's knee

"He may be good with a bow, but if you think about it Lucy, you have one of Rowan's wrist ties on your arm, and Rowan as you know thinks the world of you. You also I might add are good friends with all the Specialists. You are at ease around them because they see you as one of them. Jimmy has only met them once, I think Lucy if you think about it, you are in the best place on earth to beat every girl in this stockade." She winked at Lucy who beamed. "Let's put it this way, if you get good with a bow, you may find yourself as a Specialist long before Jimmy does."

Lucy seemed blown away, it had never occurred to her before, most of her friends were actually Specialists, and her own sister was one as well, she gave a big grin at Alice.

"All is fair in love and war my little apprentice bow woman." Alice gave her a shrewd smile as Beth appeared panting from the cellar steps.

"There we are, I knew I had one somewhere, it's a three quarter size, Alice was about your size when she used it, and Robert made it especially for her." Lucy beamed with delight as Beth handed it over.

"Oh Miss Lox, It is wonderful I am lost for words." Beth gave her a huge hug and smiled.

"I am glad you like it sweetheart, go on go off with Alice and give it a go." She winked at Alice who sat smiling.

Alice collected her bow and quiver and her cleaning kit, she took Lucy round on to the range and gave her the first of many lessons. She showed her how to clean and maintain the bow, and then how to sharpen and repair her arrows. Alice was thorough and made sure Lucy learned everything about Bowmanship before she took her first shot. Alice stood at her side and instructed her on her feet and balance and how to aim; she stepped back and allowed Lucy her first shot. Lucy hit the target, it was on the outer rim and she smiled. Alice gave her a nod. "Most people miss on their first shot, which is a good start. Right let's look on improving on that one."

Alice saw the concentration on Lucy's face, and in many ways, it reminded her of when she was younger trying to match the talent of her closest cousin. Robbie was always better, yet it had never stopped her trying to match him, Alice knew that today in Loxley she was seen as equal to Rune. Both of them were Able Bowmen, and they were second only to the hooded man, even Rowan found it hard at times to match Alice. In secret, the lessons continued as Alice now thought of training her own future Able Bowman.

It was mid afternoon as Robbie turned off the dirt track and on to the village street; he gave a smile as he saw the gathered group of women from the village at the gate of Steph's. Rune's horse and trap stood in the road waiting with Filomena beside it, as Rune stood with her mother holding the two wicker cribs. He heard the excited chatter as he got closer, and Rune looked up and noticed him. She gave him a broad smile and Alice and Anne Kirk turned and smiled. Anne beamed with delight as he drew level with the old ladies. "Oh Robbie, they are so beautiful, you must be so happy?" Rune's eyes danced with delight.

"We are both very happy indeed, thank you ladies." Everyone seemed to want to congratulate them both. Maude Baily, who seldom left her candle shop, was the most excited Robbie had ever seen her. Rueben Stein was all smiles and handshakes, and Sue and Jake Holmes gave him a huge hug each.

Robbie helped Rune into the trap next to Filomena, and Pete helped lift the two wicker baskets. Hal was fast asleep, which did surprise Robbie considering the hubbub of the crowd, Iona lay watching, her bright violet eyes seeing everything around her and he smiled as he lifted her gently up to Rune. The crowd gave loud goodbyes with lots of smiles and arm waving, as Robbie pulled the trap gently round to head back up the street. Alf smith came trundling out with a small paper wrapped package. "I thought this might be nice for the Lady Runestone." He smiled his fat red cheeked face. "It's a bit of good liver; it will help you build her up after the strains of the birth."

Rune leaned down and took the package off him. "That is so nice of you Alf, what a sweet thing to do, thank you... and Alf?" He nodded at Rune.

"Yes My Lady."

"You have known me since I was six years old. You have lived across the street all my life, I am Rune." Robbie smiled as Alf gave her a broad grin.

"Aye you are, I just didn't like being informal, I thought you might think me cheeky."

She gave a slight giggle. "You could never be cheeky Alf, you have always been nice to Jade and myself, I have not forgotten." Alf stepped back from the cart with a smile.

"Thanks miss... Err Rune. You take care of each other and those precious little ones." Robbie gave a smile.

"Thanks Alf." He nodded and jerked the horse on. Rune gave a wave as they trotted off up the street and most of the people nodded their heads to the passing cart containing the lord and his lady, Rune breathed a sigh of relief and sat back in the seat.

"Oh Rob I thought I was never going to get away, I could not get out of the gate." He gave a chuckle as the trap clattered up the path and through the gates of the farm and on to Orchards Road.

Jess waved from the orchard with Hanna, and Maggs gave a wave with her books from the schoolyard, as the cart turned into Sacred Wood Road, and headed down the long straight road towards the track on to Robbie's Mere and home. The children were settled and asleep, and Isolde sat reading in the nursery, the sun was high in the sky and the mere was its usual glass smooth. Robbie stood by the water enjoying the silence as two slender arms came round him from behind, he felt her head slide on to his shoulder and he leaned on to it. "Hey beautiful."

Her voice was soft. "Hi gorgeous."

He slid round and pulled her close as her head leaned on to his shoulder. "Oh Rob, this is nice." He kissed her on the top of her head.

"Fancy a walk in the trees?" She looked up and smiled.

"It would be nice to be alone together."

Hand in hand, they walked in the woodland under the dim light of the dense canopy of leaves, Rune felt calm as she felt the ease within him. They quietly talked as they moved through the shafts of light that broke through from the roof, and shot down to the earth bathing the ferns and Herb Robert with its masses of pink star like flowers. It was quiet and peaceful and she leaned against a tree and he faced her and kissed her. Her arms slid around him and pulled him close, it was soft and loving and her eyes gave a twinkle of violet. He smiled as he pulled his head back and looked at her. "Are you Ok now?" She gave a bright smile as her eyes danced.

"I am alone in your arms again; the world is perfect." She gave a soft giggle.

"That is not what I meant Rune. Are your powers recovering? I cannot say I am not worried, I am. She is still out there and you are still struggling."

"Please Rob I am fine, it is taking longer than expected that is all, I feel stronger every day." He gave a sigh as he looked at her bright blue eyes shining up at him. He lifted his hand and softly stroked her cheek.

"I will always worry about you while she is alive. To be honest I thought you would lose your power for just a day, it's now three and they have not come back as I thought they would. I am going to take Sapphire with us tonight as a precaution."

Rune looked down at the floor and took a breath; she looked back up at him. "You will not leave me here, will you?"

"No, I won't leave you, but I still want Saff there, I want you to save up your strength just in case. Have you spoken with Rhiannon?"

"Not since we left the island."

"You should talk with her Rune; she knows more about the powers of the lines than any. She must have some idea of what is happening to you, you are defenceless at the moment and the biggest target of the Dark One. If she feels you and she comes, I will have Saff bring you straight back here. I will not risk losing you." Rune nodded.

"Alright Robbie, I understand." She looked a little saddened and he pulled her back close and held her in his arms. She snuggled close to him and felt the strength and security of him.

"I love you Rune, I need to know you are safe."

"I know." She gave him a smile as she looked up into his dark concerned eyes. "Kiss me and hold me close, I have missed it." He gave a smile as he leaned forward and gently kissed her.

The birds chirped down from the high branches under the dappled shade as the two figures, one dressed all in sage green and the other in pale lilac, walked quietly and calmly between the old gnarled trunks of the ancient oak wood, which surrounded the edges of the mere. The Lady of the Woods and her protector slipped unseen passed by the woodland realm as they enjoyed their first real quiet time together in several weeks. High in the tallest of the oaks, a faint pale light sparkled; the land of the Fae was guarding the Violetlines.

Blades and Todd stood by the gate talking as the smiling Robbie and Rune walked slowly back up the wide grass plain of the glade. Both of them seemed calm and relaxed as Blades looked up and smiled. She gave Rune a big hug. "Hi Rune, it's been ages."

She smiled at Blades who seemed to be very relaxed and happy looking, she slipped her arm round Blades and they walked talking up the path; Blades gave a shy giggle at the door and looked back at Todd. Rune chuckled and pulled her in through the door, Robbie patted Todd on the back. "Good to see you Fox how are things? You have been with us for a while now, how are you settling in?" Todd nodded.

"Pretty good, I think I do Ok."

"It's good to hear Fox, come on in and have a drink, Saff will be a while longer with the others. Tell me something, Harry has mentioned you are good at making weapons." Robbie waffled on about improving his defences, and Fox nodded and thought as Robbie guided him up the steps and into the house in the direction of the kitchen. The glade of Robbie's Mere sat once again in sun filled silence, as the trees held their leaves still in the heat of late June. The pansy filled borders down either side of Rune's garden, sparkled with their blue and yellow faces and the violets popped open more flowers, the bright colours shone out into a blue empty sky, Nature was home in Loxley.

It was late afternoon and Lance Knox, who had grown a little taller, watched beside his father from the large glass window above the dock. The first of the large ships that had been sat outside the new dock for two days had now finally been pulled into the small port with the tugs, and the black vested soldiers bearing the emblem of a red dragon were finally starting to disembark. Lance watched dressed in black, his sleek blonde hair neatly groomed down his back. His bright blue eyes stared out across the dock, they had the same sparkle of his father, and he now carried the same cold air of a man of power.

Under the firm leadership of Dana, Lance had become a very different man, she had given him a daily spoon feeding of power, and now he had an arrogance to him that showed he was firmly in command. Mason was very proud of him, and even more proud of his wife who had taken control and maintained the Empire he had built up over the past twenty-ix years. He truly had a family of strengths that had given him the chance to realise his long awaited dreams, he knew of the age of dreams, and he was now convinced they belonged to him. It would be a little while longer but soon York would be crushed into the ground, and then he could turn his mind to the one task he had been waiting for. Now the time was coming to wipe Loxley off the map forever.

He lifted an arm to his son's shoulder. "It is our time now Lance. This is the moment I have waited for. It has been a long time coming, but you will see it has been worth the wait. Rimmer and his violet witches will beg at my feet before this is over, I will enjoy killing him." Lance let a thin smile cross his lips; it had a look of le Fey about it, he looked down on an Empire of soldiers, and felt the excitement of coming war bubble inside him. The Empire would be victorious, and he was now the only heir to the kingdom of stone.

Lance Knox could very easily be seen as the opposite of Robbie; it was something that Robbie and Rune had spoken of many times. At the age of almost seventeen, Robbie had been given the mantle of the hooded realm, he had struggled under the weight at first, but with the guidance of Steph and then Rune, he had found strength and moved forward slowly finding his feet. As he began to come to terms with his life and his destiny, he had faced Mason Knox and killed him; the irony was that at the moment he pulled his sword from the falling body of Knox, he created his own equal opposite. Like himself, Lance had found himself taking the mantle of the world of his father's people, he too had struggled to cope with the pressure of such a daunting task, it had been the power of a woman, which had helped him and guided him into the strong powerful leader he had now become.

Robbie was the highly respected and fair hand of power that guided the woodland world towards a dream of destiny. Lance was now the cold intimidating power of control that was building the world of stone towards the destiny of his father's dream. Both of them had started out feeling lost in very similar circumstances, now they had grown into the young men of power they were as leaders. The biggest difference now was that as people, they were very different indeed; Robbie was surrounded by love and respect, whereas Lance was surrounded by fear and terror.

Long lines of troops marched down the south side of the docks, as large wooden crates of supplies were unloaded down the north side. This was the biggest movement of soldiers and weapons Mason had ever undertaken. With his wife and son, he had planned it down to the last detail, and once his army was assembled and ready, he would sweep south to the walls of the start of his industrial city at Birmingham, and kill every woodsman that crossed his path. Britain was his for the taking and he knew it, he had superior numbers and superior weapons, now was the coming of the dragon, and Loxley would feel the heat that it breathed out as the earth before it turned black.

The sun was casting shadows across the shale and pebbles of the wide beach as the high edge loomed above it. The thick line of trees swayed in the warm breeze that lifted up off the sea, and swept up the slopes to them sat watching on the tops. The leaves parted and two bright blue shining eyes peeped out from under a sage green hood. "There are a lot Rob."

A second hood appeared at the side, and a hand with a silver bracelet of oak leaves appeared and gently pulled back on the branches. "Those out there do not worry me; it's the ones at the mouth of the docks we want." There was a flash of blue across pale cheeks, as she turned and looked north up the beach.

"That is a hell of a long swim, are you sure they can do this?" She turned and looked back under the hood, and the two bright eyes that watched her. They twinkled as he smiled and leaned forward. He kissed the end of her nose and she gave a quiet giggle.

"Trust me. I am the hooded man." The leaves closed together as she turned and watched him move back into the trees, she did trust him above all others, his faith and confidence inspired her. She gave a little smile and hurriedly followed.

Amethyst stood beside Treen in the centre of a cleared circle, she plaited her hair quickly as Treen who already had hers tied back lifted her top over her head. She folded it neatly and placed it on top of her folded cloak. She slipped her skirt off slowly revealing her long pale legs that were very shapely and toned up to her short tight fitting swimming shorts. Her pale orangey brown eyes twinkled as she smiled, Woody took a deep breath as he swallowed, and he trembled slightly as Treen placed her folded skirt on to the pile in his arms and gave a soft smile. "Thank you, Woody." He tried to avert his eyes, which had noticed the soft pale curves and lines of a woman who had a body that would fuel the fantasy of most men.

"Err... Yeah ... I mean, it's a pleasure. No... I mean you're welcome." He turned and faced the bronzed very scantily dressed white teethed goddess of Amethyst, her violet eyes danced.

"Hey Woody." Her smile could dazzle any man, and her figure, which was easily noted due to the very short and tight fitting clothing she wore, could probably kill most men. Woody took a very nervous step backward, he banged hard into the tree trunk and let out a squeal, as the broken off branch stabbed him in the back of the neck, Amethyst's expression changed to one of concern. "Oh Woody, sweetheart please be careful." She lifted a hand to pull him to safety, and he stepped back and squealed again as the branch stabbed harder into him.

Amethyst stepped close, and leaned round and softly rubbed the back of his neck.

"Oh that looks so red, here let me rub something on it." He nervously stepped sideways.

"No... I am err... fine, just a... you know.... bumpy thing." Treen gave a giggle as she rubbed the thick cream down her front and on to her toned arms; he gave another deep swallow, and turned and fled across the clearing to the safety of Ox and Bess his faithful dog.

Amethyst smiled as she turned to Treen. "I have no idea what it is, but I just want to mother him, he is so cute. It's like having my own little puppy."

"He eez a dithery dathery, I think he eez in need of a night with a good woman, she would pull im straight." Amethyst smiled.

"You think so? It's funny but I just cannot see him that way." Her violet eyes followed the nervous figure as he packed the clothes in the bags, and then carried them to the edge of the trees.

"It eez so obvious, look ow he walks?" She gave a little giggle. "He has never known a woman."

Amethyst gave a little chuckle. "It's such a shame, he is so sweet, maybe we should find him one."

"He would run like clackers. No, he will never ave a woman I think." Amethyst gave a laugh.

"You mean run like the clappers." Treen smiled.

"Your talk is so confused at times, I find it hard." She handed Amethyst the tub of cream to rub on to her skin so that the cold water would feel less, and bent down and began to rub her legs. Blades, was rubbing the cream into the back of Fish as Todd rubbed it into hers.

Robbie sat with Megan who was organising the explosives. The bunches of four sticks of dynamite had been covered in wax to make them waterproof, large magnets had been fixed to the back of them so they would just stick to the metal of the ships. Steph had provided some of her spare snap seal bags in which were wax covered matches, which could be struck on the rough metal of the ships and used to light the fuses. She smiled as Robbie crouched down in front of her.

"Everything set then?"

"I think so Robbie, it's not the best situation to use explosives but it's as good as we can do."

"You are a little wonder you know that? I mean it Jay; you have fitted in so well and really played your part. Lee would have been really proud of you." Megan looked up and gave a sad look.

"He was a really nice man, I miss him. Lee was kind to me and really helped me; I hope I could make him proud; I feel I owe him that."

"Believe me Jay, we are all proud of you." He patted her shoulder as he stood up. Wolf, Big John and Sting gave the all clear, as Harry and Fox, signalled from the beach. The trees parted as Ox followed by Treen, Amethyst and Blades headed down the path to the shingle beach. Fish, and Robbie grabbed the packs of explosives, and with Rune and Jay, they followed closely behind.

Earlier that day, Ox and his crew had pushed a large tree stump off the top of the high slope. It lay in the edge of the sea as the tide came in ready to be used as floating cover for the swimmers; Rune was going to provide a little extra natural assistance.

The four swimmers stood in a row against the wall of the rock out of the wind; Blades stretched, and shook her arms and legs to loosen up. They were almost ready as Robbie walked up toward them; Harry and Ox pushed the large tree stump into deeper water and placed the bags on the top of it, they stood waiting with the sea breaking across their legs as it crashed towards the beach.

Robbie smiled, as he looked at the four swimmers. "I want you to know, I really admire your bravery, this is not the easiest thing we have ever done." They all gave a slight laugh. "Take your time and watch out for each other, if we can block that harbour we have a chance at slowing him down, tonight you will save many lives if you succeed." They all nodded, and felt the pressure; a lot was riding on them being able to slow down the reinforcements to the cause of the black army. They all knew that very soon, the black city would empty and many woodsmen would die, Loxley was now closer to risk than ever before.

Robbie watched as they scampered across the stones into the water. The light was falling as they waded out to Harry and Ox and took up their places on the sides of the stump. Fish and Amethyst were going to guide it, with Blades and Treen taking up the rear, Rune was close to the water's edge, and watched as they guided the stump out to sea to move round in a wide arc. As they got out past the worst of the waves, she connected with Treen and Amethyst; Rune closed her eyes as the violet light flowed into them. The four swimmers kicked alongside holding on tight as they looked at the small dots of lights in the distance, the sea around them swirled and they tightened their grip.

Holding tightly the stump lurched forward, and began to move swiftly as if driven by a powerful current, seawater lapped over them as they moved along staying as close to the stump as possible. Robbie watched nervously as they moved slowly, fading in the water as they disappeared amongst the waves, all they could do now was to sit and wait.

They had been in the water for twenty minutes, as the lights of the docks grew brighter. Amethyst kicked hard below the ripping waves and peered over the top of the stump, she looked back at Blades who was smiling and seemed to be enjoying herself. "We need to slow down and drift as we prepare." She breathed hard her head up close to the stump, Blades nodded and stopped kicking her legs back as she drew closer to the stump and kicked down in the water, maintaining her upright position.

Amethyst winked and then slipped down under the water; she came back up at the side of Fish. He smiled. "Why I believe I found me a mermaid." She gave him a smile of bright white.

"We need to drift as we get ready." She looked back at Treen who nodded.

The opening to the dock was a lot wider than they had realised, it was wide enough for three large vessels to move through the gap. Four huge cruisers were lined up ready to move into place as the tug boats threw lines up to them, Fish watched as they prepared, he turned to the others who had all now gathered together on the darker side of the stump out of sight of the spotlights.

"They are taking them in two at a time; we will need to hit them together to block the gap." Treen and Blades nodded as he turned to Amethyst. "Do you think you can dive under one of those?"

She looked across at the huge vessel. "I have swum very deep in the sea, it's not a problem." He gave a smile and nodded, as he looked back at Treen and Blades. "Ok Amy and I will swim with you to the first one, you set the charges on yours, and we will swim underneath it and come up on the other side for the other one.

Set them and blow them, do not wait for us, just get the hell away as quickly as possible, light them as soon as the small boats start to pull them in, if we are lucky they will sink right in the mouth of the harbour."

Blades looked a little worried. "Fish if we blow that first one, how will you two get back?"

He gave her a smile. "We will set our charges and then head out to sea and come round; we will head for the log and meet you." Blades looked unsure but smiled and nodded.

"Be careful you two, those things have big propellers, they will drag you under and cut you in half."

Fish pulled a bag off the top of the log and handed it to her. "Relax we know what we are doing." Amethyst reached up and took her bag, as Fish handed one to Treen. "Alright let's stay close and head for the first one."

With the bags tied around their waists, they let go of the stump and kicked hard toward the side of the first huge ship. It rose like a mountain of rust out of the water, from the water level, it looked three times taller than the stockade wall at Loxley, and the air around it echoed with the deep resounding hum of the engines somewhere on the other side of the metal. It was now getting quite dark and each of them took long gasps and watched their course, as they swam towards the ship. The seawater bobbed in front of them and splashed in their eyes. Amethyst and Fish were fluid and forceful through the water, Amethyst had been raised always within easy reach of a lake and the sea and it showed. She swam with great power streaking through the waves like a dolphin; Treen who again had grown up off the coast of Morbihan in France, was no stranger to sea swimming. Blades had grown up swimming in the calmer waters of Dovestones, the old reservoir in Saddleworth. She was small but very agile and powerful; she cut through the water just behind Treen and swam with a smile enjoying the experience.

They came up in front of the wall of steel that was the hull of the ship; Blades watched the tug hand as he worked on the large thick rope. Side by side, they watched and then nodded, Fish whispered. "Ok set them and blow them as soon as those little boats start pulling. See you in a little while."

Fish and Amethyst took long breaths to fill their lungs with as much air as possible, and then with a thumb up, the two of them lowered out of sight into the water. Blades and Treen turned to face the side of the boat. Side by side, they kicked as they undid the bags around their waist and lifted out the wax-covered dynamite. The magnets clamped on the metal as they pushed them against the side, Treen gave a smile and lifted her eyebrows, Blades gave a smile and looked back checking all was clear on the small tug.

The lines were in place and the deck hand had gone. She felt down inside her swimming knickers for the small bag with the wax-coated matches, the sides of the boat were rough and very wet as the sea lapped up against the side of the boat.

Blades looked up for a dry bit; it was well out of reach for her. Treen tapped her shoulder and lifted a small plastic bag out of the water, it glinted silver through the plastic; she gave a smile as she showed Blades her dry metal nail file. "I love this, my grandma gave it to me, I ave used it much." Blades uncoiled the wax coated fuse and held them together, four large bundles of dynamite now stuck to the metal side just above their heads. Blade scratched some of the wax off as Treen carefully unrolled the plastic from her nail file. Holding it up at arm's reach above her head, she took the clump of matches off Blades and struck them on the nail file. Nothing happened. There was too much wax on the heads, she struck again and the bright light of the matches flooded the wall in front of them. Treen shoved it on to the fuses in Blades hand, and a loud fizzing began on the slow burning fuses set by Jay.

"Let's Bugger away." Blades smiled as Treen and herself kicked as hard as they could from the side of the boat and twisted, turning round and diving under the water. They stroked hard in the sea as they swam as fast as they could back in the direction of the stump. The engines of the tugboat roared, as it heaved hard on the rope and began to haul the large ship into the dock. It moved slowly in the water as the two small figures came up above the water and gasped as they headed away.

The large boats went deep into the blackness of the sea. Side by side, Fish and Amethyst kicked hard toward the murky bottom. It was almost total darkness and the violet of Amethysts eyes gleamed as Fish kept a watch on her. There was a forty foot gap below the bottom of the ship, and the thick muddy seaweed infested seabed. Amethyst clutched Fish tightly by the hand, as they found the bottom of the ship and swam under it. The underside was encrusted with barnacles and was sharp, violet eyes glowed to light their way through the murk, a loud chugging noise boomed in the dark underworld from the engines. Mud swirled up like a mist in front of them as they swam together, Fish watched the little white spots above him, which marked the lines of the hard razor sharp barnacles, his eyes scanned in the dark, burning with the salt as he looked for the edge so they could rise up again.

Rune sat quietly in the trees watching through the eyes of Amethyst. She sent violet light so she helped guide her in the darkness, Sapphire sat opposite her eyes closed, as she kept her mind connected with Treen, Robbie waited anxiously as he watched them both. His thoughts slipped to Rune as he looked at her, her face was pale in the moonlight, and the pale light seemed to radiate around her fiery red hair, she looked much paler than normal, and he was worried she was using too much of her strength. She smiled. "I am fine, think about something else, you are affecting my concentration." He smiled as his thoughts changed.

Rune opened one eye. "Rob I am connected to Amethyst; those are not pictures I want in my cousins head." He gave a giggle and turned away; she closed her eyes and smiled.

Fish came up above the water and took a long deep breath. He gasped the air into his lungs as Amethyst came up at his side smiling; she blew out the lungs of air and drew a long breath back. "So far so good."

Fish blinked with red eyes; the seawater was not the best of things for vision. He looked across as he regulated his breathing. "We better get a move on; the others should be ready by now." Amethyst nodded and kicked off the boat towards the other large vessel two hundred feet away. They swam quickly across the gap, as the first tug revved it engines and began to haul the first boat into the dock, Fish lifted the explosives out of his pouch, and pushed the magnetic side on to the boat just above the water line. Amethyst stuck hers on and moved toward him with the fuses.

Hurriedly he pulled them together and Amethyst pulled out the matches. She rubbed off some of the wax and she dragged them hard on her white teeth, the matches flared as she raised her eyebrows, and stuck them on the end of the fuses. The wax melted and then the fuse began to hiss, Fuse and Amethyst dived back into the water and began to swim for the gap at the back of the boat now being towed into dock, they swam fast along the centre of the lane between the two heading out to sea. The large liner moved slowly away as it was pulled inside the walls of the docks. Both of them gasped heavily as they came above the water to breathe in new air.

Treen stopped and began treading water as she scanned the surface for the old stump, Blades was forty feet away and had come up for a look round, and she swam towards Treen. "I cannot see the stump."

"It eez drifted, it could be anywhere." They scanned around as Sapphire searched to try and locate it; Rune sensed for it; the stump had drifted in the current along the dock wall. It was now very close to the ship that was just about to enter through the harbour walls.

Treen looked at Blades. "It eez too near the boat, we ave to head back to the beach." Blades nodded and looked across at the tall ship slowly passing in through the gap a thousand yards away.

"Let's get out of here before it blows, it cannot be much longer now." They turned and began to swim off towards the shore.

Wolfie and Jett watched as the whole horizon in the distance suddenly lit up. White light flashed out from the darkness, followed by a huge explosive bang. Jett blinked. "Let's get ready they will be heading our way."

She lifted her bow and got up. Wolfie, Jett, Harry and Ox scurried through the dark down to the small beach; a large pile of wood had been set ready for their beacon. Jett focused as she fixed on Treen, she connected with her and then got Treen to look at the shoreline. Jett could tell from the sight of high walls they still had some way to go. She waited as Wolfie and Harry set the fine tinder down ready to light.

The massive explosion echoed and vibrated through the water. The huge ship rose up to one side for a second, and then slipped back, they were ready for it as the huge wave lifted from the side of the listing vessel and headed back out to sea. Fish and Amethyst dived, the under current came through the water rapidly, as they headed as low as possible. Holding hands, they turned to face it as it swept below the high wave above them, it hit them and they felt it like a thousand hands, as it tried to pull them backwards. Both of them struck forward against the current, trying to break their way through as they headed back to the surface, they came up through the surface further out to sea than they expected.

Bells rang on the dockside as the huge vessel tilted and leaned over toward the dock wall. There was a huge hole in the side, and the sea was rushing in, and the ship was already starting to lean dangerously. Floodlights were sweeping in every direction, as small figures rushed up and down the harbour walls. High on the sides of the ship figures were appearing and clinging to the railings, as the vessel leaned over further. There was a deafening crunch as the boat leaned too far, and connected with the dock wall, the huge vessel ground into the concrete, and dragged and squealed, as the metal bit under huge force into the stone, and dragged it away with the side. Fish smiled and patted Amethyst who was relaying pictures back to Rune.

They were tired, it had already been a long swim and they needed to move before the other ship went up. Both of them turned and began to stroke back to the shore, the dark of night ran back again as the second ship exploded. The water vibrated with the force and they felt the waves of the sound pass quickly through the water.

Sapphire scanned the sea and found them, Jett gave the signal and the fire was lit. High above them Robbie, Megan and John took up cover with their bows, Woody gathered the clothing bags and prepared as he lit a small fire, and got the blankets ready. The bandits all around them in the woods heard the huge explosions and prepared as they watched the roads and shoreline.

The bright blue circle appeared on the water in front of Fish and Amethyst and they swam into it, the water seemed to swirl and then they were out again, just up in front Treen and Blades smiled, as they waited treading water, over to the south a little way off a bright bonfire lit up on the beach. With a sigh of relief, Fish turned and headed towards it, the others all fell in behind, and feeling the strain of the cold and long swim, they made their way slowly toward the light of the flames. Sapphire and Jett walked along the shale watching the water, Amethyst was the first to stand up and walk out of the sea, Saff gave her a huge hug and hurried her up the slope to the camp where Rune and Woody were waiting.

Rune gave her a hug as she wrapped the blanket round her. "Come quickly now we have hot drinks." Out of the water, she soon started to feel the numbness of her limbs, and began to shiver as she sat wrapped in her blanket by the fire. Treen walked into the clearing, and Woody lifted her a blanket and reached down for a hot cup.

"Ow I hate wet knickers!" Treen slid off her knickers, and top in front of the fire and lifted her blanket. Woody dropped the cup of hot coffee, scalded himself, and squealed, as he staggered backward from the stark naked Treen. Rune giggled as she jumped up and pulled the blanket round Treen quickly.

"Treen we tend to keep ourselves covered in company here."

She frowned. "Why, I ave a good body, do I not Woody?"

"I err... Oh dear... I err, what? Oh grief." He turned and flew out of the clearing; Amethyst chuckled as she looked at Rune who giggled.

"Poor Woody, you know he can be sensitive girls, that was wicked Treen." She smiled.

"It eez about time he saw a real woman." Rune looked back at the trees where he had disappeared.

"He was so embarrassed poor fellow, he has been sheltered, and he is not really use to female company." Treen looked up from the fire.

"That eez his problem, if I was not with Skippy I would take im in hand and give him the ropes." Rune shook her head as Fish walked into the clearing, he pointed back behind him.

"What's with Woody? He just ran past me and then fell off the cliff."

"WHAT? Is he alright?" Fish shrugged at Rune.

"He bounced, Harry caught him, and stopped him falling in the fire, I think he is fine. He needs to calm down a bit that one, jumpy little bugger at times, oh coffee, oh that is good I am freezing." Fish squatted by the fire as Rune looking worried placed a blanket over his shoulders.

Blades came into the camp with Harry and a very nervous looking, and somewhat bruised Woody. Rune walked through the trees to the edge of the high drop she stood in the moonlight and looked out across the shore toward the docks. Fire lit up the area in the distance, all they could do was hope it was enough to stop Mason Knox. The rest of the group were heading up the slope back to the camp, and she gave Robbie a smile as he came up toward her. He pulled her close and she rested her head on his shoulder. "Are you Ok?"

"I am fine, take me home and let's see the children." He gave her a smile and watched her bright blue eyes twinkle; he slipped his arm round her and they walked quietly into the trees.

CHAPTER TWENTY

THE CURSE OF THE VIOLET ISLE

Bright lights lit the walls, as men ran franticly along the dock. On the south wall of the dock entrance, the large vessel leaned down, its side twisted with the weight of the vessel pushing down on to the wall, which had now crumbled under the force being pushed on it. The ship leaned over, and men scrambled to the ladders and ropes being placed on it to get them off. Smoke funnelled up from the rear of the ship, as every window and crack provided its escape. It wafted in huge swirling clouds of thick black, choking the men who could not find their way through the dark suffocating fume.

Smaller boats littered the water, as men jumped off the large ship to escape. Wet figures were dragged out, and dumped gasping on the deck, the small boats filled quickly with cold shivering frightened faces. On the other side of the dock, the huge vessel burned quickly, panic touched everyone on the dockside as long hoses were dropped into the water and men franticly pumped and sprayed jets of seawater on to the burning ship packed with weapons and explosives.

The air was filled with shouting voices and ringing bells, the roar of the flames through the clouds of thick acrid black smoke, was deafening as the inferno took hold, and swept along the corridors deep inside the ship toward the holding bays. Men streamed on to the docks to help, as more large pumps on carts were heaved by a long row of men up through the chaos of the running men. It was a nightmare situation as the tugs now all out at sea; cast lines on to the burning vessel in hope of being able to tow it back out of the dock before it hit the bottom.

Their engines gunned wildly as they took the strain, and pulled hard on the rapidly tightening ropes. Men in the sea swam with desperation, as they tried to get clear of a ship they knew could soon explode. The large ship lurched in the water as the sterns of the tugs slipped low, under the strain they exerted as they pulled. Five small tug boats with long ropes screamed with wailing engines, as they tried to free the large vessel from the silt of the seabed, where it was now slowly starting to settle. The urgency and desperation of the moment was rising rapidly, as the flames grew brighter in the darkness. The captain of the small tug 'Adventurer' knew he was fighting a losing battle as he took the strain off his engine.

Mason Knox watched from the far end of the docks with his son. He carried a slight smile, as he knew once again; his opponent had used skillful tactics to blight his plans, Lance saw the smile of his father reflected on the large glass window, as he looked out at the scenes of desperation and panic. "You admire him, don't you?" It was a strange question to ask his father, but he sensed it and needed to know, Mason raised an arm around his son's shoulder.

"We are at war Lance. War is nothing to do with men or machines; war is the will of two leaders who pit their wits against each other in hope of driving victory. The woodchopper has proven to me he is a man of great resources. It's not admiration; it is respect for a worthy opponent."

Lance seemed confused. "How can you respect a man who has done that to us?" He felt anger and annoyance, and could not understand how his father could be so cool and calm about it.

"This is war son, we will try to destroy everything that matters to him, and he will do the same. If we walk into Loxley without a good fight, where will be the sport in that? No, he has proven to me that this will be a fight worthy of the moment. We will look back in years to come and feel greater pleasure, knowing our victory was won using skill. A man must be tested every day to know he truly is a man; I like the way the woodchopper tests me. You will understand the feeling of triumph when you look on his dead body, and know it was our mind and determination that brought about his end."

The window lit with the thousands of flashes that made up the bright ball that exploded out of the ship. The noise was so loud that the earth shook, and the fire emitted out from the ship and across the opening into the dock engulfing the other ship. Like a lethal hand sweeping down skittles, men were tossed into the sea, and thrown down the dock, their clothes igniting in the heat. The flame funnelled into the air lighting the whole of the coastline for miles around.

Lance moved back away from the window, and Mason held his arm tightly round his sons' shoulder as he pushed him back to the window. "Always stand firm and face what is thrown at you, never shy away Son, you are of the line of Knox, be the man I expect, tonight the woodchopper has been clever, and it has brought him limited success. He was lucky, but luck runs out, there is no place in my life for it, I force the advantage, I would never depend on something so wishful."

He turned from the window. "Come on Son, there is nothing here we can do until the fires are out. Go and see how your mother is settling in with your sister, we have a busy day tomorrow." The two black suited figures walked down the wooden steps that led from the office to the lower dock, the air was filled with the screams and moaning of dying men, as stretcher bearers ran up and down the sides of the long docks. The sky was orange from the bright flames that flickered, stroking the walls with the reflections of men moving cartloads of weapons. The soldier bowed as he opened the door, and the two men slipped into the long black car, he shut the door with a dull thump and signalled the vehicles in front. Mason and his son drove out of the docks in their long protective line of black cars, leaving the men of the army of the dragon and raven to fight the fires and bring back control of the docks.

Rune looked up from her table and rubbed her eyes. "It will slow him down, but it will not stop him Rob." Robbie watched the fires burn along the docks as the men fought hard to stop them from spreading.

"The more time I have to prepare the better, if I have to chip away at him bit by bit, then that will be fine by me. We have to hold him back Rune, he knows he has a bigger army, and he knows I know it, the longer I can prepare and disrupt him, the more chance Loxley has of survival." He looked across at her tired eyes and pale face, her eyes seemed dull and not the usual twinkling blue he was so use to.

"You have done too much today. Let's leave this, come on you need your sleep." Rune wearily rose from her seat and he smiled at her, he lifted her into his arms and she gave a long sigh as she rested against him. By the time they had reached the bedroom, she was fast asleep in his arms, Robbie lowered her gently onto the bed and slipped off her boots, he unclipped her belt and pulled her sword gently away from her, and pulled the covers up over her. He leaned over and kissed her gently on the head.

Sapphire dozed on the chair by the fire as Robbie came down the stairs, her long auburn hair hung from the side of the chair, and he gave a smile as he turned and headed for the kitchen. Filomena smiled as he walked in and she poured a second drink. "It all went well tonight I hear?" He nodded and gave a long sigh as he took the cup and slumped into the chair.

"We can only do so much, but it will slow their progress down."

She sat down at the table and looked at his worn face. "You carry a great deal of worry; can I be of service?" He looked up into her bright shining brown eyes.

"Rune is weak; she has not recovered from the birth, I have no understanding of her line; I thought that she would be fine now but I am very worried about her, she is in danger every moment she does not have her full power." Filomena nodded.

"It is strange to my sister and me. We have noticed how her vitality has been drained; we are of Fae and suffer only an hour or two of weakness, Runestone is the power of the green circle, she is life and yet she has lost power bringing it forth, I have no understanding of this, I think she should talk to the queen of the moon, her sister was the creator of that line, maybe she will know of what ails her."

Robbie sipped his drink as he thought, and he gave Filomena a smile. "Thanks, I think I will talk to Rhiannon, I need to get her recovered as soon as possible." She placed a hand on his shoulder as she stood up.

"Have no fear Robbie, she is protected here, Rune brought the prayers and wishes of my people here. The dark raven will not pass your fence, this place is also Fae." She made her way out of the kitchen and up the stairs to watch the children. Robbie lowered his head to his arms, he too felt very tired and his eyes felt heavy, his sleep was disturbed by his concern for Rune and he felt like he had not slept in weeks. He closed his eyes just for a moment to think.

"Robbie... Hey Robbie?" He opened his tired eyes and blinked. Two bright blue eyes set below a fringe of auburn hair watched him. She smiled. "Hi... It's dawn Robbie, you should be snuggled up with your wife, not sleeping on the table." He sat back in the chair as his senses came to him.

"What? Oh thanks Saff." He lifted his hands and rubbed his eyes. "I must have just dropped off"

She slid onto the seat next to him. "You have a lot on your mind, but you should at least try and make it up the stairs." She smiled at him as she brushed the hair back from his face. "Something is really bothering you isn't it?" He looked at the cup of cold coffee and then into the shining blues eyes of Sapphire.

"It's Rune." She looked puzzled.

"You two are Ok aren't you?" He gave a smile and nodded.

"It's nothing like that. I am worried at the loss of her powers; I know she is weaker than she is admitting, and I have no idea what it is, but I just know in my gut Saff that something is not right."

"Have you spoken to her?" He gave a long sigh.

"When I ask she just says she is fine, but she is sleeping more and more and using just a little power seems to completely wipe her out. It feels like when Opal was around and she had to share power. I do not know what, but something is wrong, I need to talk to someone who can help her."

"Like who?"

"I have wondered about Rhiannon; she has been around a long time and she does seem to know about these things." Sapphire nodded at him. She touched his arm with concern.

"Would you like me to go and see her? I can talk with her and find out if there is anything we can do to help. I can be there and back in a flash Robbie." He felt a sense of relief and gave her a smile.

"I would be really grateful if you could. I really am very worried about her." She smiled as she stood up.

"Go on get yourself upstairs to her and by the time you wake up, I will be back with news." She leant over and gave him a soft kiss on the cheek. "Rest your mind Robbie, we will get her back to full strength again."

Rune was fast asleep when he entered the bedroom, he ached as he undressed, and slipped into the bed beside her, she snuggled around him and made little whimpering noises in her sleep and he held her hand tight round his waist as he relaxed and closed his eyes. He was to return to the moors soon and the thought of the battle was too much to think about. He felt warm and relaxed with her head gently resting on his shoulder, his mind swirled and he drifted in the pale light of the morning.

His eyes opened with movement, Rune was slipping back into bed, and he slid his arm out to her. She cuddled up close as he folded his arm back round. "The children are fed, oh I feel so tired Rob." He stroked her hair back as she settled and held her close.

"You should not be this tired all the time Rune. Talk to Alice and see if she can give you something to help." She moved, as she got comfortable, her blue eyes looked up at him from a very pale face.

"I am feeding two very hungry babies Rob." She smiled. "I think at this rate they will grow as big as their daddy." He gave her a smile and kissed her.

"I still think you need building up more. You know we have a farm down the road, maybe we could feed them with some of the cow's milk to rest you a little."

"They will have my milk; it is better for them it has all the goodness and protection they will need to grow strong." He watched her white face as she closed her eyes and relaxed. It was minutes before she was sound asleep again.

It was late morning and Robbie was sat in the nursery alone with his children. Halbert slept deeply, but Iona was awake and looking up at him, she held the tip of his finger tightly and her eyes were bright as she watched him talking quietly to her. Iona had been very quiet for a new born child, it was easy to tell when Hal was hungry, he let the whole of the house know. Iona was different; she rarely made a noise, the only sounds he had ever heard were quiet little chuckles and squeaks, which he always thought were signs of her happiness and also her intelligence.

The violet eyes of Iona were deep and intense; when she had been born, they were very much like the eyes of Amethyst and Rayne. Over the days since her birth, they had intensified and now they were a deep bright violet, they were very like Rune's filled with a deepness that just told you there was a hidden power behind them. She gave a little squeak and he smiled; her head turned slightly and in the doorway stood the slender figure of Rhiannon. Iona had felt her presence; Robbie looked back down at her where she lay with a smile on her face, he looked back at Rhiannon. "She felt you arrive." Rhiannon smiled.

"Of course she did, she is the Queen of Fae, I am her equal to the realm of the moon, I shall always know where she is on the earth for we are connected to our people." He was surprised as he looked back at his daughter who now looked back at him.

"Rune was sixteen when her powers came to her; I thought it would be the same with Iona."

Rhiannon walked into the room, and gave a smile as she looked down at the small sleeping figure of Hal. "Robbie your daughter is of Fae; her mother is of the Green Circle. The line of Fae is born with its powers intact, your daughter is the leader of the fairy realm, and I might add is in a room that contains the five stones of violet of her ancestral home of the Violet Isle. I feel her power and she is as strong as her mother." Robbie looked up.

"Don't you mean as strong as her mother should be?" Rhiannon touched his shoulder and spoke quietly.

"Rune has power, it's just being blocked. We need to find out how."

"How do you mean being blocked?" Rhiannon sat down beside him.

"Many years ago the Dark One placed a curse on the isle of Callanish. We are still unsure how she did it, but Rune soon worked out that the Violetlines carried the power of four immense powers." Robbie frowned.

"Four... I thought it was three." She gave a chuckle.

"So did all of us, but Rune has discovered a fourth, and it is a power more potent than any of the other three. This is what has bonded the three together and formed the Violetlines of power; have you really no idea of what she has discovered?"

He shook his head as he thought. "I only know of life circle line; I have never heard her give a name to another." Rhiannon patted his knee.

"You gave it her, through you Rune has blended the most powerful force known to any of us."

Robbie was still confused. "How could I give her power; I am mortal and have none of my own."

"I would give you a long and strong argument if I had the time. Robbie inside you is the most powerful force on earth, you have some of the White Circle within you, and you are not entirely powerless. From the moment you first saw Runestone, you and her have been building a power of huge force, and when you finally came together, it was your love for her that built it up, and her powers came to her earlier than any of us had expected. Have you not seen that all of her relatives have gained their powers after they were eighteen years old? Rune was powerful before she was seventeen, the reason for that is you."

He was bewildered as he looked at the smiling face of Rhiannon as she nodded. "I might also add that a young cousin of hers, also found a great love of her cousin's future husband, and in a loving act of kindness and friendship you also brought her powers forward earlier than any expected. Little Ruby loved you deeply as I know you did her, you have a gift inside you Robbie, and it has worked to the greater good of all of your wife's line. Even Sapphire grows stronger than we expected around you."

"So if everyone is growing stronger, why is Rune growing weaker?"

Rhiannon gave a laugh. "I am talking off on tangents again. As I was saying the Isle of Callanish carried a curse that if the true lord to the land was to walk upon it he would grow weaker by the day, and eventually he would die. It was a powerful curse that each of us, in turn have tried to lift. All of us have failed, Rune realised that it would take the power of the Violetlines to break the curse. So shortly before the birth of her children she let the Violetlines flow free of her and to Melanie, who needed her help on Callanish. Rune was right and the power of violet broke the curse."

Robbie thought for a moment. "So she no longer has the power of the Violetlines?"

Rhiannon shrugged. "I think she does, but I also think the Dark One followed them back to the island of Iona, and in some way found it possible to trap those powers on the island. When Rune confronted her and blew her off the island, she was screaming all sorts of curses from the air at her, I think one of them was designed to contain Rune's power there."

He nodded as it did make strange sorts of sense to him. "So, if Rune returns to Iona she will grow stronger?"

"I think she will, but I also think that until we find out about this curse, she will only have power on Iona."

"Rune will have to live there until she can find a way to break the curse." She patted his leg and stood up.

"I will look at her and see what I can find out, but if I am right, then yes Robbie, Rune will have to leave here until she can find a way to free herself by lifting the curse. With her powers intact I am sure she will be able to find a way."

"What we need to do is kill the Dark One and then all our troubles will be over, if anything happens to Rune, I swear I will tear her apart feather by black bloody feather." Robbie followed Rhiannon down the corridor and into the bedroom.

Rune lay asleep; her hair spread fiery red on the white pillows beside her. Her face was now so white it looked almost blue. Rhiannon hurried round the bed and sat down. She held her hand up above Rune's heart and it shimmered slightly, slowly she moved it down across her stomach and down to her legs, she placed her other hand on Rune's forehead. She looked up with a worried look on her face. "We have not much time bring me the violet stones." Fear touched the inside of his heart as he realised that something was very wrong. He ran down the corridor and into the nursery, Isolde was seeing to the children, Robbie dropped to his knees and pulled a cloth bag out from under the bed of Iona.

"Prepare the children, my wife is in danger, we are going back to Iona." He turned and flew out of the room with the bag before Isolde could even answer. Rhiannon took the stones and lay one down the centre of Rune's chest; she slipped one under her neck and one on her stomach. The fourth was slid under her knees and the last against the soles of her feet.

The five bright violet elongated stones began to glow as Rhiannon hurriedly whispered in a language Robbie knew, but did not understand. Rune's body became surrounded with violet light that pulsated on the bed. He felt panic inside him as he watched Rhiannon. "She is going to live isn't she?" His voice held an air of desperation.

Rhiannon looked up and smiled. "She will not die she still has the power of the Green Circle, she may sleep for a while. The Dark One has been clever; one of the curses she used on the island against Rune contained the curse of the age of sleep. We need Merlin and we need to get her to Iona."

Robbie ran down the stairs to where Sapphire stood waiting. "I need you to tell Steph to contact Merlin and to meet us at Iona, then tell her to get here as fast as she can, we are leaving shortly Rune is at risk here." His hands shook as Sapphire nodded and her eyes began to flicker blue. He spun round and shot back up the stairs, his heart was beating furiously as the panic and pain at just the thought of losing her flowed through him.

It was just ten minutes later when a cart from the farm came hurtling into the glade. Steph, Smokes and Judy jumped off and ran up the path and into the house. The two teenagers off the island sat in the back with Jay. They dropped off the back and picked up their bags, Mel and Una rode on to the glade at high speed; they dropped from the horses and rushed to the gate. Smokes swept out of the house with Saff, Rune hung limp in his arms as she opened a window and they both shot through it, the window closed behind them. Una looked panicked as Steph came out with a large packed bag in her hands. Mel looked at her frightened face. "What is going on Steph?"

Tears filled her eyes. "She is in danger; I have to get her and the children to Iona. The Dark One has done something and we are not sure what." Mel pulled her close as Steph burst into tears and wept on her shoulder, Una hurried into the house. Mel held Steph close and hugged her as she trembled in her arms.

The group reappeared, Robbie carried Iona in her wicker basket and Isolde carried Halbert. Judy carried the bags of the children, and Rhiannon followed with Rune's sword and another bag. The bright blue orb reappeared and Sapphire came through, her bright blue eyes looked straight into Robbie's.

"She is safe in the Abbey; her dad is waiting with her." He nodded and breathed a small sigh of relief. The group gathered and then stepped through into the yard of the abbey on Iona. Robbie hurried with the crib as he pushed open the door, and hurried to the small brown door at the end of the passage, this was the room they had always had together when they stayed.

He pushed the door open to see Smokes on his knees by the bed holding her hand, she lay silent and still the violet stones placed as Rhiannon had placed them in their home. Robbie settled down the crib and walked around the bed; he sat down and softly stroked the hair from her face. Rune lay still her face whiter than ever, and he realised the full and true meaning of the word fear as he felt it inside him.

Isolde came in with the other crib and set it down. She looked over to Rune and Robbie where he sat with his head hung low as he held on to her hand. Rhiannon came in through the door. "Take the children next door, she must not be disturbed, I have called for a wet nurse, see the children are cared for." Isolde nodded and lifted the crib back up, Filomena came in and lifted Iona up in her crib, as she carried her out of the room Iona began to cry, it was a strange feeling to hear her first cries and Robbie looked back at the door.

He stood up and walked into the corridor where Filomena shushed Iona quietly as she moved to the room next door. Robbie walked up and looked down at the tears in his daughter's eyes. Small violets sprung up in the side of the crib, she had the powers of Rune. He stopped Filomena and lifted Iona out of the crib where she cried in his arms. He turned and walked back to the room of her mother, Filomena followed, as Robbie stepped back into the room everyone looked up and Iona stopped crying. They watched as he stepped back out of the room and his daughter burst into tears.

Rhiannon had spotted it and was up on her feet, Robbie looked to Rhiannon. "She is connected to Rune, it must be similar to the connection Opal had with her. Iona shares her mother's power." Rhiannon looked at Filomena.

"She must stay by her mother's side. Tell your sister to take care of the boy; you care for this one here." Filomena nodded and went to inform her sister; Rhiannon lifted Iona out of Robbie's arm. "Well my queen, you are full of little surprises."

Jade stood up on the observation platform, as Rowan looked at her. "Jade how can you go to her; she is hundreds of miles away and we have no window until Sapphire gets here." Jade was white with fear.

"I have to find a way Rowan, she needs me, maybe I can ride to Loxley and use her table, I know it will help me." Rowan grabbed her arm and pulled her toward him, Jade pulled back "NO ROWAN!" Her eyes flared green as she flung her arm back. A bright green line appeared in the air in front of her, Rowan jumped back as it burned brightly. Jett peered from behind Rowan.

"Wow that's freaky, don't piss her off any more." Jade looked at the bright line in the air and moved closer. It was thin and very bright as she peered at it closely. Jett came up at her side.

"What did you do?" Jade shrugged.

"I don't know, I just knew I had to get to Rune, I was thinking of her in Iona when I lost my temper. It jumped out of my hand." Jett leaned closer.

"Touch it."

"Why me?" Jett shrugged.

"I figure you made it, it won't hurt you. It could throttle me if it is some sort of weapon." It did make a strange sort of sense, everyone watched as Jade lifted her hand, Rowan swallowed deeply.

"Are you sure it is safe, you were angry when you made it?" Jade hesitated and looked at Jett who now eyed it with wide curious dark eyes.

"Rowan has a point; I was a little pissed off." Jett shook her head.

"You made it using your magic, it will not harm you."

"Are you sure?" She nodded back at Jade.

"Pretty much... yeah."

Jade lifted her hand again, and pointing a finger, she slowly pushed it towards the line of green light. Her finger touched it and the green line widened like the doors of an elevator opening. Bright green light flooded out and she jumped back in surprise. Jett beamed at her.

"Oh wow, you opened a doorway." Jade seemed surprised.

"How?" Jett shrugged.

"You are the sister of our centre, maybe you have some of her other powers."

"Or the powers of her children." Rowan looked at the shocked look on Jade's face. He realised she had suddenly understood, she had one of the lives meant for Rune's children. Rune had said all her children would carry some of the Violetlines, Jade leaned forward and pushed her hand into the green light. It went right through and she jumped back. Jett giggled.

"Hey girl this is so cool." Jett pushed her face through, and smiled at the guard. "Hey sexy this wouldn't be Iona, would it? We seem to be lost."

The guard looked very worried as he looked at Jett's head suspended in midair surrounded by green light; he gave a rather shaky nod. She smiled at him.

"Cool." Her head disappeared, and he jumped back a little more. Jade stepped through and looked round; Jett's head came back through. "Hey girl, don't forget if you need me flash back." She winked at the guard and giggled, her head disappeared and the door closed behind Jade. She looked up at the guard who surveyed her suspiciously. Jade was armed to the teeth; she smiled sweetly as her eyes danced below her fringe.

"I am looking for Lord Loxley; my name is Lady Jade Opal. I am his sister; do you know where I can find him?" The guard gave a short bow and she smiled, he pointed to the Abbey behind him.

"I believe he is in there My Lady." She gave her usual large beaming smile.

"Thanks, that is sweet of you." He smiled at her as she walked past and headed for the abbey.

Iona had settled in the basket and Robbie now sat and watched Rune. The violet stones glowed brighter surrounding her with violet light. Steph and Smokes sat nervously in two chairs, Rhiannon leaned over and examined Rune, as Sapphire stood by her side, the door opened and Jade came in. She saw the worried look on Robbie's face and rushed to him. Jade threw her arms round him and he smiled as he held her. She looked down at her sister as Steph gasped. "Jade how did you get here?"

She looked at her mum and then Sapphire. "I can do the door thing. The only problem is I did it by accident and got here, I have no idea how I will get back." She gave a giggle. "I am just glad I got here, I was worried about Rune and thought of her and you Robbie, it brought me here. It freaked Rowan out."

He smiled at her bright eyes below her curly white fringe, and he gave her a hug. "It's nice to see you Pebbles, thanks she loves you and she will be happy to know you are with her." Jade smiled.

"I love you both."

The door opened and Merlin strode in, he looked round the room. "Everyone leave, Robbie you stay." He crossed the room as everyone got up looking a little surprised; he looked at Rhiannon and then sat on the bed beside Rune, and stared down at her. He lifted his hand and it shone with white light, he waved it slowly over her body and Iona gave a little squeak. Merlin turned and smiled. "Good girl"

Robbie and Rhiannon both looked at him confused. Robbie looked at the wizard who looked a lot like he had as Leenard, only a little younger.

"Why is my daughter a good girl?" The old wizard gave a big smile and took Robbie's hand in his.

"My dear Lord, your daughter is gifted beyond all time, she is but a few days old and already she holds on to her mother to protect her." The words bounced around inside his head before he finally made sense.

"Iona is protecting Rune, how?"

"The Violetlines are very powerful; your daughter has been born with her gifts. At this moment Runestone lies in the realm of endless sleep, she has suffered a curse from the Dark One. It was probably cast during their fight, and has taken time to act as Rune needed to reach a certain level of weakness before it could pull her away for a sleep of a thousand years." Robbie looked at the crib.

"But the age of sleep is over, this is the age of dreams." The old wizard gave a hearty laugh.

"Exactly my point my young lord, I am so glad you are keeping up. Right your daughter has a good hold, all we need to do is enter the realm and find her, she will be wandering around in there somewhere looking for a way out."

Rhiannon looked anxious. "I hope you are not thinking of going in there, she will feel you straight away and come looking, she will know Rune is awake and try to find and kill her." The wizard looked up and nodded.

"Good point, well it will have to be young Robbie here then. We will need a window maker as well; I think Sapphire will suffice." Robbie looked up at Rhiannon.

"Jade can make windows, and she has the Violetlines inside her. She has a life destined for one of my children." Rhiannon nodded.

"I see your point Robbie, but Jade has not had the practice, you will need to find Rune and get out fast." He understood but still felt it should be Jade.

"Rune will be with us; she will help Jade." Merlin nodded.

"The bond and the power of family will be strong; they are of the line of Opal and she was the one who got all of us out before. I trust her blood more than anything else; her love runs in it for those children. Take Jade and good luck. Leave me now with her and I will prepare. Go and get ready we will call you soon." He looked up at Rhiannon. "I don't suppose you brought a table?" Rhiannon smiled.

"I never leave home without one, you know me too well my old friend." She gave a soft chuckle.

Robbie walked down the corridor; he took Jade and Sapphire by the arm. "Go outside and teach Jade how to open and close her windows, we do not have much time. Jade you will be coming with me."

"Why where are we going?" Robbie stopped and looked at her.

"Rune needs you Jade; you have some of the Violetlines inside you. Both of us are going to travel to this realm of eternal sleep and find her, she is in there somewhere and she is alone and awake. If we cannot get her out, we will lose her forever." Steph looked horrified.

"Robbie that realm trapped Opal and my father for seven hundred years." Her face was white and filled with fear as he looked up to her.

"They only had the Whitelines and Green Circle; we have the power of four, and Destiny, I don't care how long it takes I am not coming back without her." His voice softened. "I cannot live here alone without her Steph." Robbie turned to Judy and Jay; they stood at the side of Sapphire. "Please guard my children for me." Jay nodded and Saff gave him a smile, Judy took his hand in hers as she looked at him.

"We all love you both; I will let nothing come close to your children, not even my grandmother. Find her Robbie and bring her home."

Sapphire took Jade outside to practice, and Judy and Jay took up their guard duty on the two rooms. Robbie prepared his weapons, he cleaned Destiny and his bow, he filled one quiver with strikers and one with new arrows. He slung Rune's sword down his back between the two quivers and slipped an extra silver dagger down inside his right boot. He pulled his cloak round to one side and lifted the lilac silk scarf of Rune's off the bed. He smiled as he looked at it; he slipped it round his neck and tucked it inside his tunic behind the laces, slipping on his fingerless sage green leather gloves, he was ready.

He felt nervous; a knock came to the door, it opened and Rhiannon walked in. she looked at his weapons and smiled. "Wear this on your right wrist; it will guide you to her." Rhiannon tied a thin braid of Rune's golden and red hair around his wrist. "It is something of hers, and there is the smallest fragment of Iona's woven into it. The protection of them will be with you, take care and good luck. Come to the main hall in ten minutes, we should be ready by then."

Jade was armed to the teeth, as was Robbie, as they walked down the corridor towards the main hall. Sapphire followed behind them, Jade looked up at Robbie from under her long curly fringe. "You nervous?"

"A little." She smiled.

"Good...me too." He lifted his arm on to her shoulder.

"Thanks Pebbles how are the windows?"

"Don't ask that's why I am nervous." He looked down and gave a little chuckle.

"Look on the bright side, you can fade away if it gets hairy, if they cannot see you, they cannot attack you."

"Who is going to attack us?" He gave it a moment of thought.

"I am not sure, call it a gut feeling."

"Oh cheers, now I am not nervous."

"That's a good thing, isn't it?"

"Not really, now I am scared stupid." Robbie started to laugh.

"Oh Pebbles, I am so glad you will be with me." Jade suddenly stopped.

"Oh God." He looked at her.

"What is it?" She looked really scared.

"Robbie, I need to go back a minute."

"Why what's up?" She looked at him with a really worried look.

"What if I pee myself? I have not brought clean knickers." Sapphire burst into laughter, she gave Jade a big hug.

"You are priceless, go on I have a few spare pairs. I will run back and get them for you, go with Robbie and get ready." Sapphire giggled as she ran back down the corridor, and Robbie put his arm round Jade and headed for the doors at the bottom of the corridor.

The main hall had in the past, been used for dining when the abbey had been full. Now the red death had wiped out all of the islanders and most of the monks the few that met for meals shared a small room in the back. The tables that once formed the long lines of the eating hall were now folded neatly against the sidewalls, and in the middle of the room was a huge gleaming crystal table, Jade gave a gasp as she saw it. The table was at least three times bigger than that of Rune's, it was bright white and shimmered with shining silver flecks. In the centre was a huge five-pointed star of shining silver platinum, on which was a golden symbol of the moon.

Rune lay on the table her head at the point of the uppermost point of the star, in the position of the sword of truth, Una lay in the next point on what Robbie knew as Justice. The crib of Iona was on knowledge, and the crib of Halbert was on courage. Steph lay calmly on Honour. Robbie walked round the table to Merlin.

"Why are you using my children? Is this safe for them?" Merlin smiled.

"Have no fear; they are on sacred ground in the protection of a very powerful table. Una is also a guardian of protection as you have seen by her violet eyes; your children and my daughter are all linked to Runestone by blood. The blood of the last person to escape the realm of endless sleep, Opal lives in these people and she had the power needed to escape. All of this is to help Rune recover her powers when you find her." Robbie nodded and turned.

He looked down on Rune's pale face, as she lay covered in the cloak of Rhiannon. Her skin was white and her freckles seemed deeper, her eyelashes sparkled in the light as he leaned over and stroked her soft white cheeks. "Hold on my darling, I am coming to get you." He leaned forward and kissed her softly. Her lips flashed violet as they met with his and her body jumped; he stepped back at the shock he had felt.

Rhiannon came up and looked at Rune. "Do it again." He looked a little worried as everyone looked round. Robbie leaned over her face.

"I love you Runestone Sapphire." He softly touched her lips and Rune jumped on the table. Iona gave a little happy squeal of laughter, and Rhiannon gave a huge smile.

"You made contact; she knows you are coming." He felt the bright burst of a small violet inside him, hope was a small light in his heart, the door burst open and Saff came panting into the room. She handed two pairs of pale blue lace French knickers to Jade. "Hope these will be OK?"

Jade eyes danced. "Wow Saff these are see through and pretty sexy." Sapphire turned a little pink as she gave a soft smile at Robbie.

"Keith sort of likes me in them; Rune makes them especially for me." Jade gave a big grin.

"Keith is a bit of a wild man, you naughty girl Saff." She went a little redder.

"I like to please him."

"You're not kidding; I could do with some of these in red for Rowan." She gave Saff a wink and slipped them into her side pocket.

Merlin came round the table and nodded at Sapphire. "Right, you two, Sapphire will open the window when Rhiannon begins the incantation. Wait for my signal and when I say so go through, we will try to lift the curse of the Isle from this side, while you find Runestone. Saff will stay connected to you Jade so listen to what she tells you as I instruct her. As soon as you find Rune you must head north to the well of hidden secrets, with luck and the right incantations we should get you all back safe."

Robbie swallowed and took a deep breath as he nodded. Jade slipped her hand into his and he looked down at her. "I love you and Rune, Robbie." He gave her hand a squeeze.

"We both love you too, don't worry we will find her." She smiled and nodded.

Rhiannon raised her hands in the air and nodded to Sapphire. Saff stood in front of Robbie and Jade and waved her hand, as Rhiannon began to chant. The bright blue orb appeared in front of her, and glowed a deep sapphire blue, as the voice of Rhiannon rose into the air, the table of the moon began to glow with a bright silvery essence. It intensified as the light swirled into the air in a fast spinning column, her voice echoed round the room with power.

"Hear me powers of the line of the moon. Obey your queen and bring your lines to her aid, I call on the silver lines of my line and the powers of the past realms; I am Tideguyde reborn and summon you. Hear me my sisters of the moon, and send forth your line as we seek a bridge to the realm of darkness and sleep. I call to the day to hide my travellers as you do my realm, and I command the night to light their way. I am Rhiannon the carrier of souls to the lost realm, and I am Vivian the guardian of the water filled realm, hear me and obey me."

The floor shook a little and Jade swallowed hard and squeezed Robbie's hand. He gave it a little squeeze back, and thought of how he would do that with Rune. White light filled the room as Rhiannon commanded her powers, and it swirled out of the air and down on to the table. Robbie looked back but could not see Rune, as the whole table was filled with white light. He caught his breath as he saw violet stream up out of Iona's basket, and the power of the Violetlines joined with that of the moon.

Rhiannon stumbled on her words for a second as she watched; Merlin gave a satisfied smile, as violet flashed in the bright cloud that now swirled above the table. There was a flash of silver and the mass shot sideways. Robbie ducked with Jade as it shot over their head into the blue pulsating orb.

Merlin shouted across the room. "NOW, GO BOY AND FOLLOW IT."

Holding on tightly to Jade's hand Robbie ran into the white light, Jade squealed as their legs shot from under them, and they spun into the air at high speed. They were in a long white and silver tube, and they spun faster and faster as they shot quicker than a bullet down the long line of white. "Oh God I think I am going to be sick." Wailed Jade, hanging on to Robbie for dear life.

"Close your eyes it's not as bad" He yelled back to Jade as he felt the contents of his own stomach swirling inside him. He held out his right hand and grabbed Jade; he pulled her close, as his legs seemed to whip round with enormous force. Jade dragged herself close to him and hung on for all she was worth, he wrapped his arms round her as she buried her face in his neck, and they both spun out of control down the tunnel of light.

It felt like an eternity and his head reeled with the motion, Jade trembled slightly close to him and he opened his eyes to see where they were, Robbie looked round at a dark forest of tall trees and high grasses, his head spun and he slid out a hand to steady himself. "We are here."

Jade lifted her head and swayed slightly. "Where?" She stood up staggered sideways and fell over. Robbie lay on the grass as Jade giggled.

"Oh God I am dizzy."

"I think we'd better stay still until it passes. I think my head and stomach still think they are in the tube." He looked up at the world that was spinning around him. "I am glad it's woodland that will help us."

Rhiannon looked at Merlin as the shimmering swirled around her table. "They are there; all we can do now is hope and put our trust in the power of the hooded man." Merlin nodded as he stroked Rune's hair in the swirling light.

"Hold on my darling Robbie is coming for you."

CHAPTER TWENTY~ONE

THE HIDDEN REALM OF SLEEP

Rune sat bolt upright on the grassy bank next to the crystal clear pool. "Robbie?"

She looked round at the strange and unfamiliar place, she had felt him and now she could not feel him at all, she leaned over the edge of the bank and gazed into the water, her throat felt dry and hot. Rune lowered her face to the water, and an almost glass like shape rose from the water and formed into Robbie's face. His voice felt millions of miles away as he softly spoke.

"I love you Runestone Sapphire." The water came up and touched her lips, her eyes blazed in bright violet.

"I love you Robbie." The water dropped and splashed covering her face in tingling cold water; she caught her breath and sat back up. Rune looked round at the dark woodland; she had no idea where she was, or if it was dawn or dusk. She suddenly felt very cold and alone and without Robbie nearby, she felt afraid. She pulled her cloak round her and slid her knees up to her chest, Rune was beginning to realise she was somewhere trapped and in trouble, this was not Loxley and she tried to remember what she had been doing before she fell asleep.

Her mind felt cloudy and she tried hard to focus and concentrate, what was the last thing she did? It pounded round in her dull mind, a tear rolled from her cheek and dropped to the grass where a violet sprung up. She whispered to herself. "Violet."

Two violet eyes opened in her thoughts, as she looked down and saw her daughter Iona feeding. She smiled to herself. "I fed my babies." The pictures flooded into her mind, as she remembered feeding her two children and then feeling exhausted she made her way into her room and took off her robe.

The pictures of Robbie sliding his hand to her and pulling her close played in her head. She had got into bed and then curled round him and snuggled down that was the last thing she remembered; something had happened but what? She could not recall anything else. Rune looked round the woodland, which seemed to stretch for miles in every direction; the crystal pool seemed to be in the centre of a large open clearing, around were mighty oaks and beech trees. Tall grasses she did not know grew high and thick, bramble crept everywhere, it looked like no wood she had ever been through. She closed her eyes and thought for a moment as she gathered her powers.

"Hear me my sisters, for I am Runestone and the centre of your circle."

A soft quiet voice spoke back to her. *"They cannot hear you mummy; you are lost to them."*

Her heart leapt as a voice she had heard twice before came to her. *"Iona darling, is that you?"*

"I am here Mummy." A small warm hand touched hers, and Rune opened her eyes. They filled with tears as she smiled at the small figure in front of her. Iona looked about five years old and had long wavy brown hair with gold and red streaks through it. Her bright violet eyes sparkled with love and compassion, Rune pulled her close and held her tight as she wept with Joy.

"Oh my sweet, I thought I was lost forever."

"Daddy is coming." Rune released her and wiped her tears as she smiled at Iona.

"Where am I sweetheart?" Iona smiled.

"You are in my realm being watched by granddaddy Whiteline. The dark lady sent you here and Daddy is coming to get you with Auntie Pebbles. I like her." Rune gave a giggle. She lifted her hand and stroked the face of her daughter.

"Your Aunt Jade is crazy at times, but she will love you forever." Rune looked round at the woodland, which all looked pretty much the same. "Do you know which way Daddy will come sweetheart?" Iona pointed south.

"He will come down the tube to down there somewhere." Rune stood up and brushed the grass off her cloak. She took her daughters hand and smiled.

"I am glad you are with me, come on if we head toward him, we will meet up quicker." Holding her mother's hand she walked with her into the thick trees, Rune felt a joy inside her as she looked down at the bright violet eyes of her daughter. "How are you doing this, when you are only days old?"

"I am using your power, we are connected and have been since I was born, Granny Opal knew about this and made sure you had someone with you." Rune thought about her grandmother in all white, she had told her so many times of the joys she had seen for Rune in her life, especially with her children.

"Your granny was clever." Iona gave a giggle.

"She made me clever to help you; I won't be this clever when I am really five." Rune smiled.

"Oh I don't know, you have your Daddy's genes, his mum is the cleverest woman I know, your granny Jess helps everyone with all sorts of things, and she grows so many different kinds of plants it makes my head spin."

"Granny Jess is nice, so is Granny Steph. I want to be like both of them." Rune gave a happy chuckle as they followed the path into the trees under the dim light of the canopy of dense leaves. The long path seemed to bend and weave for miles in front of them; Rune looked as far ahead as possible through the trees. She stopped and looked behind her; the path seemed to flow back for miles.

"How long have we been walking?" Iona looked up the track behind her.

"Not long, I think about ten minutes." Rune was not sure, she felt like time had little meaning here. She turned and looked ahead where she hoped Robbie would come from.

"I can see for miles and yet I cannot see where the pool was. I am sure we should still be able to see it; this does not feel like any wood I have been in. I hope your dad finds us soon; this place is giving me the creeps. What did you say it was called again?"

"Granddaddy Whiteline calls it the Hidden Realm of Sleep, he lived here once before."

Rune's heart almost froze, as she suddenly realised where she was, she dropped to her knees. "Iona sweetheart you have to find your Daddy and stop him. He cannot come here; this is the realm where the age of sleep took place, you must find him and tell him to leave me here, I will find a way out." Her eyes filled with tears. "Go back and stop him Iona, I could be here for a thousand years, he has to save Loxley and protect you."

Iona smiled and touched her mother's nose; Rune gave a smile as she wiped a tear from her eye. "Daddy knows mummy, he is here already and coming for you. Granddaddy Whiteline told him how to get out, when he gets you out you will have your powers again in my world. It's all right mummy the dark lady doesn't know he is here; she cannot see in here. That is why Granny Opal sent me to you; she talks to me and tells me what to do." Rune looked into the violet eyes of her daughter, and just for a split second, she thought she saw a soft kind pair of familiar eyes.

"Grandmother?" Rune gave a smile and nodded at Iona. "Now I understand my darling, all right we will carry on until we find your daddy." Iona gave a big smile.

"I love my daddy he is brave." Rune laughed and pulled her close and hugged her.

"You Daddy is the nicest man in the world, and we both love him. He is brave, kind, and fair with everyone, and he loves you and your brother so much. Come on let's go and find your big brave daddy."

Rune stood up and gave a long sigh, she took a deep breath, and then with a bright smile she started again through the trees heading south on the path that just never seemed to end. Iona skipped along holding her hand tightly.

Robbie sat up as his head cleared. He took out his compass and watched it spin wildly round. "Great this place has no magnetic north." He looked up at the trees and tried to work out if there was any light above them. He would need sunlight or stars to plot a direction; he looked at the compass again and saw the thin braid of her hair on his wrist. He thought of her lost and alone in this wilderness. "Where are you my darling?" The compass stopped spinning and pointed north; he looked up at Jade and smiled. She gave him a shrug.

"What?"

"This is the hidden realm of sleep; here dreams come true if you really desire them. I really want to find Rune, as soon as I asked her where she was the compass started to work, it's pretty cool."

Jade looked round at the thick dense trees and brambles. "I don't know about dreams; this place looks like it could be a nightmare." She stood up and looked around. "I suppose we should make tracks, the sooner we get going the quicker we will find my sis."

Robbie stood up, and picked up his bow, Jade grabbed hers, and looking at his compass he pointed, she nodded and they moved off into the trees. Robbie was the best woodsman in the country and Jade was not far off him, he felt a strong sense of urgency and both of them moved with agility and speed, they swept past the trees, and wove around through the dense patches of tall grass heading north at all times. It was at least an hour, when they came up the side of a long path. Jade peered out at it.

"It looks like it runs for miles in a straight line, it's well used look how low the grass is?"

Robbie stepped out and looked both ways. "It's clear for miles, whatever uses it will be seen long before it reaches us it heads our way Pebbles, we will be twice as fast on this road. What do you think; do you want to risk it?"

She stepped out on to the track. "If it helps us find Rune faster then I am up for it, we can hide in the bushes if we need to." Robbie nodded.

"Ok let's do it." Together they set off at a fast pace down the long road, which Robbie hoped would bring him to Rune, the trees and bushes on either side were thick and dense, and he just hoped that there was nothing in there hiding or watching him. He felt Jade was feeling the same as he watched her eyes dart from side to side. They had been running for some time when he began to slow a little, Jade slowed with him as he looked behind him and then turned to face forward. The road looked the same both front and back, and he looked over at Jade. "You ever had that dream where you are running and no matter how long you run for, you just see more and more road in front of you?"

Her breathing was a little fast and she nodded. "Yeah why?"

He gave her a grin. "Does this road look familiar?" Jade stopped and stood still, she looked behind her and then turned and looked up in front. She breathed in new air as she gasped

"It is sort of the same, it's just in my dream I don't have two dozen black clad riders in the distance."

Robbie looked up. "I think we better get off the path and see who the company is, I am not keen to run into that many unfriendly people." Robbie and Jade scurried off the path and slipped into the trees, like true woodsmen they melted away without a trace.

Iona turned and looked behind her. "We need to hide mummy." Rune looked back and saw the riders in the distance. She felt a pang of fear, it was enough to warn her, and she picked up Iona and slipped into the trees. She wove her way in some distance, and found a fork in a tree where she could watch through the leaves without being seen. She kept Iona close to her.

The riders slowed as they came level with the part of the track where Rune had left. She felt nervous as she watched the large man clad in black leather look round across the tops of the low bushes. His face was covered in a black leather mask, and his eyes burned red behind it. Rune felt a cold shiver run down her spine. Iona took her hand in hers, she whispered up to Rune. "Granny Opal says they are the nightmares. She says stay still and if he takes off his helmet do not look at him."

The cold feeling he gave her was enough, she was not about to move, and she held her breath. He looked up and down the woodland and then looked across to the other side. His head turned slowly as he scanned the whole woodland, he looked back again across the side that Rune was on, and then waved his hand. The troop of horses moved off slowly, Rune let out her breath and took a new long one.

A green hand patted her shoulder; Rune squealed as she shot round and looked at the figure with a green hood and a white face. "God Billy you scared the hell out of me." Her heart pounded in her chest, as she took another a deep breath and looked back up at the sage clad figure of Billy. "What the bloody hell are you doing here?"

He gave a giggle. "I am a Mystic Rune, this is now my territory." He smiled. "I was sleeping and you walked into my thoughts, being the curious type I am, I thought I would wander in and have a look. Good job as well, I have a bow and you have no weapons, if you had messed with those boys you really would be in trouble." He looked down at Iona and smiled. "Hi sweet pea, you look like your old man."

Iona smiled. "I know you, you are Jessie's daddy." Rune gave a smile as she saw the surprise on his face. He looked up at Rune.

"Just like her dad, he always had that way of saying something that left me stumped." Rune giggled.

"We are lost Billy can you help us?"

"Where are you trying to get to?"

"Robbie is in here somewhere trying to find me. I got caught with a curse by the Dark One, you know the one."

"Ar, my dear old grandmother." Rune nodded.

"Well I got sent here, and Robbie has come after me with Jade. My grandfather is on Iona trying to help us." The Sage nodded and thought for a moment.

"He is about to encounter a nightmare; I think it may be advisable if you wait here by the path and I will have a quick wander down and see if I can help. I take it he has no idea about me?"

Rune smiled. "I gave you my word, he will not hear from me." He nodded. "What about young hood here?"

"I keep lots of secrets." Her violet eyes twinkled and he smiled.

"You are so like him, it's scary." Iona giggled. "Ok Rune, stay close and I will help him find you. I have not much time as it's almost dawn in our realm, although somewhere in here is my little helper, she will find him quicker. We have to be out when the cock crows." He gave Iona a wink, and she smiled.

"I like Sandling's, they are funny." He gave a grin.

"Not mine, she is pretty depressed at the moment, like I don't have enough on my plate, and I have to cheer up her as well."

Robbie sat with Jade as the horses slowed a little way up in front. He rose slightly out of the leaves to get a better view. One of the riders slid down from his horse and walked into the trees, there was a terrified scream and then the sound of trampled undergrowth. Something was running straight toward them. Robbie braced as the wide eyed figure burst out of the trees and hit him. As soon as she saw his face, she closed her eyes and screwed up her face, there was a loud pop and she disappeared, Jade looked really surprised.

The dark clad figure walked out of the trees and looked at Jade and then Robbie. Jade gave him a smile. "Cute suit, what did you come as?"

His red eyes glared through the mask. "I am your worst nightmare." His voice was deep and sinister as his arm lifted up, and slipped up the helmet, Jade wet herself as she saw the face of the Dark One laughing at her with a cold malicious voice. Destiny gleamed as it came round and swiped at the head, the Dark One's laughing head exploded as it hit the floor, and turned into a rotting face filled with maggots. Jade stared at it with horror.

Robbie grabbed her shoulder and tugged. "Get with the plot Jade, we got trouble." With destiny gleaming, he ran towards the path, the bushes were moving rapidly to his right as the others had dismounted and were coming at them through the grass and trees. Robbie looked back at Jade as he still clung to her shoulder, and was almost dragging her. "You alright?" She nodded and looked back behind her.

"I peed myself Robbie."

"Not to worry you got kinky knickers." Jade gave a giggle and hurried to his side.

"What do we do Robbie there is a lot of them?"

He looked back and saw them appearing through the trees. "I want to get on the path where I can see them come at me, I think the bow to start and then sword if needs be. If any of them go to lift their mask, shoot em in the eye, it will keep their masks on, I am not keen to see more of the Dark One."

"Me neither I only have two pairs of clean knickers." Jade gave a giggle as they burst out of the long grass and on to the path, Robbie veered off and ran past the horses, he slipped his bow off his arm as he slowed and turned ready to shoot. The black leather clad figures came round the side of the horses, Robbie and Jade were swift and their arrows hit hard knocking them to the floor. Jade hit them all in the eye just to make sure. The others came round and Robbie fired at the first one, there were ten of them and they all went to raise their masks, he fired and reloaded as quickly as he could. Jade shook a little as her arrow released, she hit the man and fumbled her bow.

There were three raising their masks, and Robbie took the first, he loaded quickly as an arrow shot past his shoulder and hit the next man, Robbie fired and then looked back. He saw the sage green hooded figure and nodded. He turned and fired at the next one, as Jade released taking out another. He began to walk backward reloading as he moved, he expected some to stay hidden, and come out and surprise him from the sides. Jade moved her bow up and aiming at his side, the trees parted and before the figure could step out two arrows whipped into him and threw him back into the bushes. Their pace slowed, as they got further away, Robbie looked at Jade. "Did we get all of them?"

She nodded. "I think so. Oh, bugger Robbie I hope so." Robbie looked back.

"Where did that hooded guy go?"

"What hooded guy?" Robbie was sure he was now at the point where the man in sage green had stood, he looked at the ground, but there were no footprints.

"There was a man in a green hood stood about here; he shot one of them for us."

"I didn't see anyone; mind you I got a bit rattled at that one lifting his mask. I did fumble a bit. God Robbie that frightened me." He patted her shoulder.

"You did fine, he was scary, or she was scary I am not sure which. I wonder what the hell they are."

"He told us, our worst nightmares. He got that one right; the Dark One scares me more than anything."

They still walked backward as Robbie watched the path, the horses moved uneasily beside the piled up bodies, his eyes scanned the edges of the trees and shrubs but all now seemed still, he turned and looked up the path behind him. The dim light seemed to intensify through the trees ahead; he gave a long sigh, turned round, and stopped. "Where did they go?" Jade turned and looked down the path, it was clear for miles. There was no sign of a horse, or body, they had all simply vanished. Jade shuddered.

"I hate this place Robbie, but let's get off the path so I can change my knickers, I hate wet legs more."

Robbie gave a giggle. "Ok let's slip in here so I can watch the road, stay close to my side, I have no wish to lose you in all this undergrowth." They moved into the edge of the trees and Robbie watched as Jade stood behind him with her back to him. She slipped off her boots and dropped her pants. Slipping off her knickers she quickly pulled on her clean pair. She looked down at them.

"Oh wow Saff is more kinky than I figured, I would show you but It would embarrass me, and possibly upset Rowan. Oh wow he is so gonna love these." Robbie chuckled from the trees as she tied her cloak round her waist and slung her pants over her shoulder to dry. She slipped on her boots and picked up her bow.

A pair of violet eyes watched from the other side of the road, Robbie had not noticed at first, but he saw them move, he whispered back to Jade. "We have company." The eyes blinked and a small pale hand slipped out of the trees and waved.

"Oh look Robbie it's a kid." He gave a smile and waved back. The little face moved forward and smiled. "You know Robbie she almost looks like Rune." His eyes filled with tears.

"She is, well at least half of her is." Jade looked down, and saw the tears in his eyes, and suddenly it hit her. The pictures from Rune's table came to mind when she saw Robbie with the little girl in the cave. He went down on one knee as the tiny figure rushed out across the path and into his arms.

"Hey princess, how did you get here?"

"I came to help you find mummy, daddy." Jade gasped and stood helpless as she watched the tenderness of Robbie with his daughter.

"Oh Iona, my princess, you are brave, just like your mummy." He pulled her close and hugged her as he looked up into Rune's tear filled eyes.

"Rune." Jade swept across the path and leapt into her arms; Rune smiled at him as she hugged Jade. Iona pulled at his hand and he stood up and walked across the path to her. Jade stepped back as he dragged her into his arms and kissed her. Jade knelt down and looked at Iona.

"Hey I'm your Auntie Jade, but everyone calls me Pebbles."

"Hi, I'm Iona Violet." Jade giggled.

"I know. Give me a hug I have been dying to meet you." She pulled Iona into a hug and smiled up at Rune and Robbie. He held her face and kissed her.

"Hey beautiful I missed you." Rune wept and slid back into his arms.

"Robbie, you have put yourself at risk, we could be trapped here for years."

"Maybe, but at least I won't be alone; I got my three favourite women for company." Robbie looked down at the small figure of Iona and smiled. She looked up with violet eyes at him and he felt a huge wave of happiness inside him. Rune slipped her arm round his waist as she felt the happy feeling that was growing inside him.

"So, what do we do now?" Rune watched as he crouched down at Iona's side, and took out his compass. He held it in his hand and looked down the path.

"Now we head north to the Well of Hidden Secrets. That my little princess is where we can find a way out." Iona leaned over and watched the compass spinning round fast.

"Daddy, I think it is broken." He gave a smile, and whispered.

"Not really, you have to think very hard about where you want to go and make it your heart's desire."

Robbie thought about getting out through the well, and being home and free on Iona. The compass spun fast and then slowed to point the way. Robbie looked across into the trees, he raised his finger and Iona looked down the line at the dense woodland. She gave a big smile and looked at him. "That's very clever Daddy." Rune chuckled as she watched his smile. Robbie kissed the end of Iona's nose.

"We have to be very clever if we are going to get out of here." She nodded and smiled at him.

"Daddy I have to go back now, Granny Opal says now you have found mummy I have to use the fairy power and go back so mummy can have her power back. Will you hurry home?"

The thought of so suddenly having to let her go, felt painful. He stroked her hair from her small white face that was so like Rune's and he nodded. "We will be as quick as we can princess." He pulled her into a hug and held her tight. Rune knelt down and Iona turned.

"Be careful mummy and look after Daddy." Rune's eyes glistened as he held her daughter so very tightly.

"I love you sweetheart; we will be as fast as we can." Iona gave her mum a kiss on the cheek and then jumped back into Robbie's arms. She kissed him on the cheek and gave him a big smile, her bright violet eyes shone like dark sapphires.

"Bye daddy."

"Good bye princess see you soon." He reluctantly let her slip out of his arms as Iona turned and looked at the smiling Jade.

"I will see you soon Auntie Pebbles." Jade gave a giggle and lifted her into her arms.

"I will be back to look after you always my sweet little niece, and don't worry I will look after your mum and dad." She hugged her hard and lowered her to the floor. Iona ran a few paces and turned to face them as Rune slipped her arm round Robbie. She lifted a small hand and waved; they all smiled and waved back. Iona spun on the spot and with a little pop; she became a small speck of bright violet light. It hovered above the floor for a second and with a tiny flash, it shot into the trees and was gone. Jade gasped.

"She is a fairy." Rune looked at her as she pulled Robbie close.

"She is their queen." She looked at Robbie. "Are you alright?" He nodded as he looked back to where Iona had stood.

"I didn't want her to go." Rune slid close to him and held him.

"This is the hidden realm of sleep Rob. It is here that all our dreams live; you have seen just a small part of yours. Be happy knowing what you have to come."

"She is so like you Rune; she is so beautiful." Rune kissed him on the cheek.

"I think she is very like her daddy; she is clever and kind." He smiled at her and her eyes shone with happiness and life. "I love you Robbie; you make me happier than I ever thought I could be."

He kissed her softly. "I love you too Runestone."

"Yeah right, now we have established what just about everyone in the world knows already, can we go? You two make me miss Rowan." Rune gave a giggle as she slipped out of Robbie's arms.

"Sorry sis." Robbie looked at the trees and checked his compass bearing, and then shouldering his bow he moved off with Rune at his side. Within moments the path was quiet again and the hooded man with his two companions slipped through the trees heading north in hope of finding the well of hidden secrets.

Iona gave a little squeak from her basket and opened her eyes. Rhiannon looked down and smiled at the violet eyes that looked up at her. "She has returned, which can only mean Robbie has found her." Steph gave a gasp of relief as Una pulled her close. Sapphire watched Rhiannon as she moved round the table, which now had Rune lay alone on it.

"What do we do now?" Rhiannon gave a long sigh.

"We have to wait until we know they have found the well. In the meantime, we have to hope that Merlin can lift the curse on this Isle to allow her back here. If he cannot lift it, only Robbie and Jade can return." She looked anxious as she softly stroked Rune's hair. Sapphire looked round at the others.

"I am a centre; if we need the Violetlines can I not channel them?" Rhiannon gave her a smile as she walked towards her.

"Sapphire it is not that simple. You are strong in the Whitelines and White Circle, for they are the lines of your house, Rune also is the power of the Green Circle and she has the power of love she feels for Robbie. Those are the four ingredients of the Violetlines; her love is so strong it has created a new line of power."

"I love him too." Her voice was soft and filled with emotion. Rhiannon smiled at Sapphire, she put her arm round her and walked down the long hallway away from the table.

"Sapphire, I feel your feelings for Robbie, I see the power you hold inside you. You are very strong in the powers of Fae, but you must understand, and I mean you no disrespect for what you feel. The power of love that Rune feels is vast, you have to understand that. It is a force no one ever saw coming, and it is that huge force which has bound together the other three powers. Her love for him is stronger than all of the other powers, Rune is the Violetlines." Sapphire nodded and Rhiannon put her arms around her.

"Oh my poor child, you hide such a wonderful thing. You must find a way to channel it to the good of everyone, for there is nothing more wonderful than the feeling of loving another." Sapphire rested her head on Rhiannon shoulder.

"I know I can never show it, but I cannot help how I feel, I do truly love him and try so hard to hide it." Rhiannon stroked her hair down her back.

"You have the love of another; use what you feel for Robbie to aid him as his friend. He treasures your friendship and there is a strong bond made between you in the cave. Be happy with your woodsman, and live your life around all of them, help Robbie with his cause and use your love of him to the advantage of others. There is not just you who feels such a strong bond of love for him, there are others my child who feel the same way."

"Melissa?" Rhiannon smiled.

"I feel there was just a hint of a bitter note there my sweet child. Melissa has suffered a great deal alone, her feelings are no less worthy than yours, I feel you may have more in common with your future sister than you realise. Try to understand her by understanding yourself; you both have parts to play in helping him before all of this is over."

Sapphire nodded. "I know what you are saying is right."

"But it still has its pains, I understand. I have lived a long time my sweet child, I have wisdom beyond my years and have seen many things. I will always be here if you need me." Rhiannon kissed her on the head and she smiled at Sapphire. "Maybe you should try to help Merlin; they will all need our help before this is over." Sapphire smiled at Rhiannon and nodded.

Jade collapsed on an old stump and gasped. "The floor looks flat but it feels like walking up hill."

Rune wiped her face, as she looked round at the trees of the endless wood. "We have been walking for hours, how big is this place?" Robbie flicked the damp hair out of his eyes and looked back at the compass.

"We are definitely heading the right way. I just wish I knew if it was day or night, there is no sense of time here." He sat down on the grass and rested his legs, Rune touched a small twig on the ground and it sprouted leaves, Jade gave a giggle as it flowered in clusters of white, which faded quickly, and began to swell into large red round apples. She broke one off and handed it to Jade.

"That is pretty cool sis, great I am starving." She took a large bite and chewed happily as Rune handed one to Robbie. He had not realised how hungry he was until he started to chew, he looked up at the canopy high above him.

"You know it might not be a bad idea to climb up and look out. It might give us a better idea of distance." Rune looked up.

"These trees are a lot bigger than in Loxley, and that is a long climb Rob."

"It could help us see if we are going the right way Rune, I could climb up there if you and Robbie want to watch down here." Jade leaned right back as she looked up at the high canopy. Rune gave a shudder.

"To be honest we might all be better up there for the night, this place gives me the shivers at times." Robbie looked at her; he could feel a little apprehension in her.

"Are you sensing danger?" She looked around the empty wood.

"I am not sure; I have felt many things in here. There is little life here, is it me or for a huge empty woodland like this don't you think there should be birds and animals all over the place?"

Jade watched the branches in the trees. "It does seem sort of odd, maybe this realm is empty."

Rune shook her head. "All of the realms as far as I know of have life, this one has life I can feel it a long way off. No there is a reason there is no life here, I am just not sure what." Robbie stood up and discarded his apple core.

"That is it then, we climb into the tree and get as high as we can, then I will climb up to the top and have a good look round. We can then decide what the best thing to do is." Rune and Jade both looked up at him and nodded. Robbie walked round the tree and looked at the lower branches. Rune came up at his side.

"That first branch is pretty high up, how will you reach it?" He gave a frown as he looked up.

"Normally I would throw a rope over, but I don't have one." Rune gave a smile.

"I do." She knelt down and touched the floor; two small leaves appeared on the ground.

"That isn't ivy is it?" Robbie gave a concerned look. "It's just I have seen what your ivy can do."

Rune gave a giggle and stood up; she kissed him on the end of the nose. "It's a vine and quite safe... You are funny at times." He smiled a smile of relief. Rune stood back as new leaves appeared and then the vine shot up the side of the tree, the green leaves exploded out as the vine climbed higher and higher into the tree. Robbie took hold of the thick wooden stem, it was very solid and he pulled himself up on it. He was surprised at the toughness of it, and soon he found himself climbing fast. Rune followed as Jade had suddenly become a little self conscious.

"I borrowed a pair of knickers off Saff, I err... am not sure my sister should see so much of me, I like the idea of just Rowan knowing what's inside them." Rune gave a giggle.

"Jade we are sisters, we have bathed together many times, you have a beautiful body don't be embarrassed about it."

"Yeah, you always did the comfy with your body thing well, I never quite got the hang of it."

Rune climbed up behind Robbie, and Jade waited until he had got to the first large branch and helped Rune on to it. Jade scampered up the tree as fast as she could, and they began to climb higher. It took quite some time before the floor was a dizzying height below them.

The trees were much bigger than was first noted. In the centre of four sprawling branches that reached high into the canopy, was quite a wide area where they could all sit in safety, the vine had shot right up to the very top of the tree and Jade sat with her back to a large branch and picked a fat bunch of black succulent grapes off the vine. "Oh I love grapes."

Robbie climbed higher as Rune sat with Jade and picked off the grapes. Jade's pants were now dry and she slid them on with a giggle. Robbie wiped the sweat off his face on the lilac scarf as he finally saw the top of the tree. He made the last ten feet and pushed his head and shoulders through the leaves as he stood on two wide branches. He looked round the vast forest, which seemed to stretch for miles. To the north, the forest rose higher and higher covering the sides of a mountain. That explained the uphill climb they were already quite a way up. He turned round slowly and looked to the south; somehow, he was not surprised at what he saw.

In the distance out of the vast sprawling trees of the woodland rose a high piece of dark rock. It formed a plateau on which stood a huge dark and imposing castle of black stone. He realised he had seen it twice now, the first time he had seen it he was in a dream at the barrow when he fought to save his woodland and the Green Lord. The last time he had seen it, he had seen just the top section of the castle and that was now sitting on the island of Dunnottar.

The cold seemed to swirl around him as he realised that somehow the hidden realm of sleep was under the control of The Dark One. He knew without having to question, this was where she had established her seat of power. Suddenly everything made sense; he looked at Rune and Jade far below him, they were in more danger than he had thought, they would have to move fast and get out of this realm, Rune was sat right in the lap of the Dark One, and in more danger than anyone realised.

The light was dim as clouds came out of the castle and blocked most of the light. Robbie could see from the distance that the sun still shone over the mountain, it must have been late afternoon, which meant they still had at least six hours before dusk. He had a sneaking feeling that come the night time the woodland would not be as quiet as the day. Those nightmare figures must have disappeared because dawn had come up, he was beginning to see how this realm worked, during the day would be relatively safe.

He slid back down through the leaves and climbed down to the bowl in the tree where Rune and Jade sat eating the grapes; Rune gave a smile and passed him a bunch. "So what did you see?" Robbie hesitated and Jade looked at him.

"I will need more dry knickers won't I?" He gave a slight nod.

"Let's just say a lot of questions about many things are about to be answered, I think we should move and move fast. We can talk on our feet, the mountain that I think has the well is north and we are on track, it is still a long way off and it is all up hill. To the south there is a very big black castle, and the top of it has been copied at Dunnottar." Jade swallowed her grapes hard, Rune looked nervous.

"She brought me here to kill me." Robbie touched the side of her cheek.

"She thinks you are alone here. You are in the woods with the hooded man, she will not find you easily, and if she does, I still have a few surprises for her, now I am glad Iona is not with us."

It was a fast climb down, and soon they were on the floor side by side heading north as quick as they could. Robbie wound through the trees with great skill, Rune always at his shoulder with Jade just two feet behind. Rune was putting two and two together.

"This is the age of dreams. She knew her time would end and the others would come back, so she made this her domain. Through the age of sleep, she has controlled man by controlling their dreams, if they did not do as she wanted, she used their nightmares to defeat them." Robbie glanced across at her as he swept through the long grass.

"You have to admit, it is a clever way to control so many. Her powers must have been limited, controlling here is a lot easier than being in our realm and trying to control everything. From here she can tap into the mind of anyone she wanted, and model the world to her own design."

Rune could now understand the one thing that had always bothered her. She had never understood why it had taken her so long to come out and show herself. Morgan le Fey could have ruled the world while all the other powers were trapped, and yet she had not. "There is something she must need Rob to take full control, we have something she needs and we are not aware of it, if she had all of this power that she boasts about, she would have taken over and set herself up as supreme ruler. What have we got that she wants?"

He looked back to see if Jade was listening and slowed a little to a walk, the sweat was running down his face. "That is the easy part; she wants what we ourselves are looking for." Jade shrugged.

"Which is?"

"A king Pebbles." It hit Rune out of nowhere.

"Of course, oh god Rob why did I not see it? Her powers are strong, but they would be unparalleled if she was to take the life of a king in the sacred rights of life and death. She still does not know the incantation of life, Gwendolyn and Opal never revealed that most guarded of secrets, she knows the incantation of death, she was going to use it to kill Hearne. To take control of every realm she must use the words of death to take the life of a ruler of high power. There isn't a greater ruling line of power than Arthur's." The blocks fell into place as Rune worked it all out in her mind; Jade was also working it out.

"Rune you are the force of life, Opal escaped, she will have to kill you as she says the incantation for her to draw away your powers. That is what she did to Gwendolyn, but she was White Circle not green." The fear swept quickly across her face. "Rune I am scared."

Rune gave a smile and pulled her sister into her arms. "Come on now I am not dead yet, I have you and Robbie with me, we will escape this place as Opal and our grandfather did. We have the Violetlines Jade, it was a power sent to us to balance the darkness she has created; we will not be without weapons ourselves." Jade trembled in her arms, as Rune looked at Robbie. It was a sobering moment of truth; he pulled both of them close and hugged them.

"We have the love we hold between us to light this dark place, and we have the ways of woodland to keep us safe. We will use all of our skills and find a way through. Be brave little Pebbles we are not finished yet."

She lifted her head and looked into his bright dark eyes. "I will be fine; I will not let you down." Robbie gave her a smile.

"I have never thought for a moment you would." She smiled as he leaned down and kissed the top of her head. "Let's make a move we still have a few hours before dusk." She nodded.

Hot and tired they set off again into the trees, Robbie now felt a greater sense of urgency, he needed to find shelter and water for the night and some other form of food. The night would be her time and he needed to ensure that Rune was protected at all costs. His mind whirled as he moved silently and quickly, he had been told so many times not to underestimate the Dark One and he always thought he made sure not too. The truth was, she like her son had plotted for much longer and like a spider she had woven her webs of secrecy around everything.

His only consolation was that now the truth had been uncovered, he faced a war on two fronts. Not only had he to face Mason on the battlefield, he now had to face the Dark One on a field where dreams became nightmares in the minds of men. He was not sure but somehow, he felt that he had to get Rune to safety and then return to defeat the Dark One on her own turf, his dream of dying trees in Loxley wood now seemed more relevant. He had to find a way to destroy her power in this realm, the age of dreams was no longer about fighting for an ideal; it was about the fight to control the hidden realm of dreams.

He looked across at Rune who he knew was trying to read his thoughts; she

Nodded. "I know, the age of dreams has changed, you must not lose hope Rob, your dream still lives in this realm. We will have to find it and make it stronger than anything she has."

"She knew long before we did that is why she came here. From here she can destroy the root of our dreams and stamp out anything that is not to her wishes. She has men in black who find you and turn all your dreams and hopes into nightmares. That is how she thinks she will win I now need another army. This is just getting harder by the day."

"Do not lose hope, if you do she will capture your dreams and kill them, as long as we have hope we have a chance to defeat her. Hold on to your dreams for they are mine, and my love of all things, I am what you fight to save Robbie, please never give up on me." He saw the tears in her eyes as they moved through the trees.

"I will never give up on you Runestone; my life is bound to you. I will find a way I promise." He looked through the trees and wove past them, his eyes fixed on the north as the woodland now rose more steeply. Ahead was a clearing and he slowed a little to make sure it was empty, he signalled back to Jade, and they came to a halt.

Robbie walked forward to the edge of the trees. There was a large wide area lit by the sun that was covered with soft mossy short grass. In the centre was a stone plinth on which a small fire crackled, steam rose from the bubbling ingredients of a large cauldron. He looked round the trees cautiously, but there was no sign of anyone. A voice came out of the trees to his left and he saw a glint of blue on white.

"Have no fear this place is hidden and protected." It was a voice from the past and he strained to see into the dense undergrowth, the trees moved a little, and Robbie felt the breeze as Rune and Jade both rushed past him. "Grandmother."

CHAPTER TWENTY TWO

SIMPLE SYMBOLISM AND MAGIC

The light through the stained glass windows flowed down to the floor in shafts of blazing colour. Large areas of the dim simple church were illuminated, and the age worn old pews, looked bright from the polish that had been applied the previous day. The air was still and silent, and the bright cut flowers that now festooned the small church, released their scent and the whole of the place smelt with the charm of their sweet perfume. The altar was dressed in green and the carved stone cross, engraved with the runes of an age long since passed, stood proud in the centre.

The church was dressed for a wedding, and the darkened shape of the black dressed father knelt by the altar rail in silent prayer. He felt the joy of acceptance and the love of his parish, and he was a very different man who smiled with more ease, and arose every morning to face the wonder and delight of the new day in Derbyshire. Light flooded in from the back of the church as the door opened, and a figure in all black swept in. The light was snuffed away as he closed the door, and he walked slowly up the aisle admiring the high quality of the small country church. He nodded to the altar as he waited for the father to finish his prayer.

Father Warren stood up and bowed, he turned and was surprised as he looked into the eyes of Bishop John Stevens, he gave a nod. "My Lord Bishop I am honoured and somewhat surprised to see you."

Bishop Stevens gave a warm smile. "I am delighted to be able to visit, I did request we could meet and talk again." He looked around the church with a fond smile. "Oh, this brings back memories. I too began as a father in such a country church as this one, I have very happy memories of those times."

Father Warren gave a warm smile. "This place has been a tonic to me My Lord; I had forgotten the wonder of parish life in the Black City. Here I have found a passion for life and the teaching of the word of our lord."

Bishop Stevens gestured to the front pews. "Could we sit and talk a while, I have nowhere near as much time as I want, but I would be very grateful to seek your opinion on important matters."

Father Warren was surprised, and he nodded. "My Lord I am sorry, yes of course your time is very valuable, although I fail to see how I could offer advice on matters that would be important to the church."

The bishop sat down and crossed his legs, he seemed to relax in the surroundings and enjoy the peace. "You do not mind if I call you Peter? Sometimes the formality of the church goes a little too far, and I like yourself, believe in the simple approach, call me John."

"You can address me as you like, I am here to serve the church My Lord... Err John. I will of course help in any way possible."

John Stevens leaned back and smiled, the lines on his face were gentle, and his expression one of calm kindness. "Peter, I have been offered the place of archbishop, I am not sure if you are aware of the sudden demise of our last candidate Bishop Holmes. It appears he and the council of eleven had a disagreement with some of the Cutters he employed, and they were killed in the evening of the last May Day parade."

Father Warren looked nervous. "I am not sorry to hear it, but I will state clearly to you My Lord Bishop in the name of my lord and protector, I have no knowledge of this deed." He gave a smile.

"I am not here to investigate the murder of those who would use the church as cover for gain. I am aware of what the truth may be; a red feather does not fool the eyes of the old as quickly as the young. I believe the lord works in ways that are not always clear to us, but with time we usually work it out. I am here to ask you about certain things divulged to me by the Lady Sapphire."

Once again Father Warren was surprised. "Lady Sapphire? What has Sapphire said that has such relevance to the church?"

John Steven moved to get comfortable in his seat. "I am not sure you are aware of this, but I had a long conversation with both the Lady Sapphire and the Lady Loxley." Warren seemed surprised at the mention of Rune's name.

"I was not aware; I played no part in the rescue of Sapphire, for I was concerned that harm would be done on sacred ground." Stevens gave a smile.

"No harm came to any, well not lasting, I must admit that Brother Argus is a little more nimble in his approach to life, but no blood was spilt." Warren gave a smile.

"Lady Sapphire did inform me of his encounter with Runestone." The bishop gave a rye chuckle.

"She is a convincing woman, there is no doubt of that." He chuckled again. "The reason I have made the journey to meet with you, is to ask your advice on the claim made by both Sapphire and Runestone that there is an heir of true decent from Arthur to this present day. I believe that they intend to bring forth this heir and place him on the throne."

Father Warren nodded seriously. "I have read the books of Geoffrey of Almesbury; I have translated one of them, in it, he speaks of a meeting with a woman in white, who told that the line of the king was not broken. She instructed him to look for the bowman, for he will be the herald of new days. There are some that say that Robert of Loxley is that bowman."

Stevens sat back and nodded. "I remember some talk of that text when I was in college; my tutor at the time dismissed it as being related to the story of King Richard the Lionheart and Robin Hood." Father Warren nodded.

"To be honest I would have thought the same except that in the books I translated from the old text, Geoffrey also mentioned a text in the form of a prophecy made by Rhiannon."

"I thought she was a myth from the old Celtic folklore." Warren gave a big smile.

"I would not let her hear you say that if I were you, she was here just a few days ago, I saw her when I visited the Lady Runestone who was ill." Stevens looked confounded.

"Surely you jest?" Father Warren shook his head.

"You must believe me when I tell you that Runestone is a very mighty power, and much of the things I have studied over my life on the teachings of Column Cille and his unshakeable belief in the Celt line of old have come true before my eyes. John you must understand that no matter what has happened in the past two thousand years, the beliefs of the old Celts have survived. They have survived because a great deal of those core stories is indeed quite true. Everyone thought Arthur was only myth until Mason Knox came forth with proof he had lived."

"Knox was proven a fraud by that Rimmer fellow, in fact I was in the cathedral when his daughter waved the papers that proved he was a fraud. I must admit it was a great relief to me, I was completely against the crowning of the vile and sadistic man in the first place." Father Warren gave a reassuring nod.

"It was true that Knox was not the heir to Arthur, but only in so much as they know who the real heir is... well I am sure that they do not know exactly who he is, but they have the documents that will state who he is and where he is, but that is beside the point. Rhiannon was my point, and I have wondered. Rhiannon made a prophecy almost a thousand years ago just after the death of Arthur, she made it quite clear that a snake with wings and legs would try to take over the country; she was most specific about gathering with the daughters of the woods. She then stated the bowman would lead them and forge a world anew."

The old bishop thought very deeply about the words of Father Warren, he stroked his chin as he thought and then looked back up at the Father. "The sisters of the woods would be Rune and her many female cousins like Sapphire? The bowman would obviously be the new hooded man, which we know is Robert of Loxley. I must admit I have seen far too many black vests to not recognise a snake with wings and legs, and young Robert has already challenged Knox and prevented his crowning. I think that shows clearly he is serious about his claim to an heir, he certainly was very convincing in the cathedral."

"I can assure you John, at Loxley their belief in this cause is total, why do you think the army of Mason Knox marches to war against him? Knox knows he is right and wants to kill the heir to clear the way again for himself to take the crown. I would strongly advise you take the time at some point to visit Loxley and its lord and lady, this is no game they are playing, they really mean it."

Bishop John Stevens could see in the eyes of the younger Father that he was convinced, and knew the truth when he saw it. Father Warren's sincerity had been proven beyond doubt when he defended with passion and commitment the Lady Sapphire. Now John Steven saw again the same values in his belief in the people he served as the spiritual leader of a community.

"Thank you Peter, as archbishop, I will have to evaluate the position of any who come forward with a claim to the throne. You have been of great assistance to me and I will not forget this. I believe I will arrange a visit to Loxley in the near future and consult with their lord and his wife. If they really do have the proof that this heir exists and can find him, I will back them in placing him on the throne. The church will follow my lead as I instruct them." He got up from the pew and gave a warm smile to Father Warren.

"I would appreciate it if you could send me copies of these texts so that I may study them deeper, as the good lady in violet reminded me; I still have much to learn." He smiled as he shook the hand of Father Warren. "You must come to dine with me at the cathedral in Lincoln. I shall be there until August twenty first."

Father Warren shook his hand and gave a bright smile. "I would very much love to, I have heard wonderful things about the cathedral, it would be a visit to cherish."

"I will have my understudy Simon give you the tour, it is remarkable how much he knows about the place, you will be enthralled... I will say goodbye my dear colleague and leave you in the very capable hands of our lord, until we meet my friend farewell."

Father Warren stood at the door of his church as he watched the carriage draw away. He felt a great relief in knowing that it would be John Stevens, who would lead the church into the future. Hope flooded into him, the witch trials were gone, and the church was turning to love and compassion, he smiled as he looked up at the figure of his lord hanging on the cross. "Thank you, my lord, of all I have asked that is the most precious to me. I am in your debt."

"**R**owan... Why are you shouting at me? There is not a single person in here who does not love all of them, I agree with you I want to be by their side just as much as you do but it is just not that simple."

Sapphire's eyes burned bright blue with her anger. The Specialists watched as their general walked up and down the cave, he was angry, and he was scared Jade was in another realm surrounded by danger with Robbie and Rune, he felt frustrated and shouted it out. Sapphire who was already upset took no time at screaming back at him. Rowan looked at her with tears in her eyes and softened.

"I am sorry Sapphire; I am not angry with you. I tell him over, and over he must be protected, and he just refuses to listen. He is now in a realm god knows where, and he needs the people who can protect him, but we are all here. He drives me insane at times." Saff gave a smile and wiped her eyes.

"Merlin says there is nothing we can do till he finds Rune and she brings them out. They thought he had met with Rune just before I left. Rowan, Jade has the Violetlines in her; she has powers no one knows about, she will be safe with Robbie and Rune, the only question now is what do we all do while we wait?"

Rowan leaned on the table and looked at the Specialists. "Iona is not as safe as we thought it was, I want a team there as soon as possible, and I want that island sealed and protected, if they find their way out, I want every one of you to put your lives on the line to protect him. Maddy, Blades, Fox, Jaz, Amethyst, Crystal, Fish, John and Hawk to lead, go with Saff and make sure nothing moves on that island without my approval. Melissa you are the nurse here, can you cope unsupervised on Iona?"

Melissa nodded and smiled at Jaz. "If Alice thinks I will be fine I will do everything I can to help."

Alice nodded at Rowan. "She has enough skill to cope with it if anyone gets hurt." Rowan nodded.

"Alright Melissa you are in, everyone pack your kit and be ready to leave in fifteen, Hawk a word before you go, Rafe you too." Rowan moved to the desk where Bear sat. Bear patted his arm, and Rowan nodded, he opened the drawer and took something out, he walked back to the table as Hawk and Rafe both stood waiting. He threw the commander bars across the table in front of Keith.

"I need Rafe here, but I need authority on that island. You have earned those the hard way, congratulations Commander Sherman; I want to know the moment they arrive back. I do not care how you do it, but I want my wife here in less than five minutes of her arrival on that island. Tie her up if you have to, just get her back to me, do you understand?" Hawk smiled.

"Yes, General Loxley." Rowan smiled.

"Thank you, Commander. Ok go and get ready." Rafe beamed a smile at Rowan.

"Did you see his face? I bet five bits as soon as he gets outside, he dances."

Rowan nodded. "No way, he will drag Saff into his arms and kiss her; it will be Saff that screams. Five bits, you are on." Jett walked up to the table.

"He will kiss Saff and punch the air, and then he will become a commander and lead them off with pride. You two are suckers I will enjoy taking your money." Jett slapped five brass bits down on the table. Rafe beamed at her, and placed his neatly stacked beside hers. Rowan shook his head.

"It's a done deal I just got richer." He placed his beside the others and watched, as the Specialists got ready.

Saff stood outside waiting as the team prepared to leave, they gathered outside as Hawk came up to Rowan. He shook his hand as Rafe patted him on the back. Keith walked out into the sunlight and Rowan, Jett and Rafe hurried to the door and peeped.

Keith looked at Sapphire who beamed with delight; he slipped his arm round her and kissed her softly. Jett tittered; as Keith stepped back, he punched the air and then turned to the group. "Ok Saff open the window, right let's move out and prepare for our lords return." The group moved off through the open window. Jett gave a whoop.

"You guys are such suckers." She beamed as Bear laughed and she slid the money off the table. "Candy from a baby." Her eyes twinkled as she smiled at the two of them. Rowan and Rafe looked down heartedly at each other.

The Specialists came out on Iona just outside the abbey. The captain of the guard walked down toward them; the blue clad bird insignia shone brightly in the moonlight. Keith who knew the island was talking to the team as the captain walked up. He turned round and the commander's bars gave the captain a start and she saluted.

"Commander, I was not aware of any of the woodland forces being deployed here."

"We are the close protection unit of Lord Loxley, we are part of his Specialists and we are here under the orders of General Rowan of Loxley. Our orders are to help reinforce the island and place close protection to Lord Loxley on his arrival back from the other realm. I take it there is no objection Captain?" Saff gave a smile.

"None whatsoever Commander, we were just not aware and you surprised us. We already know the Lady Sapphire and one or two of your party, the extra help will be greatly appreciated. I will inform the lady of the moon of your arrival and find you all adequate quarters."

Keith nodded. "Thank you, Captain, we would be very appreciative." She turned and walked away, as Keith gave his orders and the group began their movements into position. Merlin stood with Smokes and watched the Specialists move out.

"I wonder what Rowan is up to?" Smokes gave him a sly look.

"Rowan is doing his job, when Robbie gets back, he will have a few extra eyes on him." Merlin gave a small frown.

"Rowan expects trouble; he thinks she will strike again."

"Rowan is no fool dad; I think we should let him get on with it. If he expects trouble then some will come, this is just the landing party it would not surprise me if there were not more being prepared."

Merlin stood and watched as Keith placed his men and women with skill. Every aspect of the abbey was covered from air and sea invasion. All day he felt the Dark One stirring on the west coast and he knew that she had something more in mind. The curse could still not be lifted, which meant she would know the moment Rune arrived back. Rune would be caught in the curse of the Isle and drained of her powers. Morgan le Fey had been very clever in the way she had come to the island, what had been seen as an attack, had just been a ruse to lay the curse down at her feet. He needed to act and fast.

The Castle at Dunnottar had been quiet since the violent storms the day before midsummer. Angus and Grace now stationed in the large warehouse below the steps to the surface of the city had received very few reports of activities. It had felt like the quiet moments after the hooded men had left, and Gracie remembered the conversations she had spoken with her aunt.

The pictures of Rose came into her mind as they sat high above the castle on the rooftops. Rose had slipped the Celtic cross she wore over her long black silver streaked hair and handed it to her. "You are the last in my family Grace; I am way too old for bairns."

"You are thirty nine Aunt, you could still have one." Rose took her hands in hers she looked very serious.

"Grace I love you. You are my brother's daughter, but I have watched you grow into the beautiful young woman you are today, and I love you as if you were my child. Listen carefully to what I say. Lord Robert has done a great thing here, but call me superstitious, I do not care, I know she will come back, she had something planned for here and I am not sure what, I just know that whatever it is it will be fouler and more evil than before. Promise me you will run like hell into the trees if she comes back, get as far away as you can, because I think, something terrible is going to happen here. Promise me Grace on the life of your father, and swear on the oldest heirloom of my house."

Grace felt frightened, as she looked into the fear filled watery blue eyes of her Aunt. "Aunt Rose you are starting to frighten me."

"Good, because it seems to me that fear has kept me alive all these years, and if it keeps you alive, and through all of this I will die happy. Grace use the fear as your strength, sometimes it is better to retreat and muster your forces before turning and going back in. The one thing, Lord Robert did confirm to me, is to use the skills of my people carefully as the hooded man did. He watched and created his own opportunity using stealth and skill, his Specialists do not make themselves targets, which is why they can do what they do. You must learn these tactics if you are to lead when I am gone."

"But Aunt Rose you are not leaving us." Rose smiled at her.

"Grace my child; we have broken down her home. She will come and she will look for me, I am the leader and she knows who I am, do you not see it was I, who stood on the bridge and gave the orders; I was the one she was coming for when Rune appeared and fought her back into the castle. Grace my sweet and wonderful child; as much as I love you, I know I will not last a moment longer than her arrival. I gave you the job of protecting and watching Lord Robert to show the others my faith in you, your time of leadership will come sooner than you think, you must prepare."

Grace pulled Rose into her arms. "But I don't want you to leave me, I love you." Rose held her tight and kissed the top of her head.

"I will always be with you in the cross you wear; it is the symbol of my family, and the pride I have served my people with. Never forget you one day will be the heir of this land and the new queen of Scotland, and I will be there watching you can have no doubts."

The woodsman in green walked up. "Excuse me My Lady, but Lord Forbes is looking for you, he has received reports of strange noises coming from the castle. He asked me if you would meet him at the observation point." Rose nodded to the soldier and then released Grace.

"Go down to the cave and find your dad for me." Grace nodded as Rose kissed her on the cheek.

Grace sat at her desk and looked down as her eyes filled with tears. Rose had known that her father was in the deep cutting, and had sent her to the cave to protect her. By the time Grace had got to the surface again, it was raining hard and she had watched from the observation platform as Rune had lifted her aunt's dead body and sent it to the other realm. Rose had saved her life as she had lost her own, and passed the legacy of future leader on to her.

How she had known, Grace never knew, she just knew that the woman who was her aunt and her hero, had also been the only woman she had known as a mother. The pain was still hard to bear after all of the time, but her words that day had never left her. Grace now knew something evil was coming, and she knew that the only way to survive was to empty the city. Her aunt's last word of retreat and regroup sounded in her head, her father disagreed with her, but she was adamant that her force of seventy women would pull into the trees, and she had now convinced the old Scot he should do the same. A force of over two thousand now camped five miles up in the ancient forest, and she felt now was the time for her to leave. Something was coming back to Dunnottar that no mortal man could fight.

"Grandmother." Rune and Jade squealed with delight, as the white robed woman stepped out from the trees and hugged her grandchildren. Robbie leant against the tree with a smile on his face, and watched the happy tearful faces of Rune and Jade. It was several minutes before Opal could get a word in as Jade told her everything that had happened. He shouldered his bow and walked to the fire where the smell of fresh coffee was nectar to his nose. He sat down and poured a cup as he waited for the two sisters to guide their grandmother back to the fire. Opal had her hood down, and looked a little younger than she had last time, although her hair was snow white and glistened in the sun. Robbie stood up and bowed.

"My Lady of the Woods I am very pleased we can meet again." Opal gave a little chuckle.

"I am afraid my bowman, I am no longer the lady of the woodland realm, that is the title of your wife, here I am simply Opal, but to you I should be Grandmother for you have married into my line and are now family." She smiled and took his hand. "You have brought joy to my heart with your gifts of life to my granddaughter. Your son and your daughter honour you and all of us my dearest Bowman."

"I am a man of many treasures My Lady." Opal looked at her granddaughters.

"Come sit and eat we are all safe here, none of the creatures of the night can enter here, we are veiled to all on this sacred site." Opal seemed so happy as she ladled out the hot stew, and passed it round. None of them had realised how hungry they were and broke large pieces of bread and dipped them in the stew as they ate. Robbie sat and listened to the excited talk of Jade as she talked about her wedding to Rowan, and the castle of Dunnottar, and when she mentioned the birth of Iona she smiled at Rune.

Opal placed her hand on Rune's. "Did I not tell you of the joy to come in your life?" Rune's eyes twinkled as she looked across at Robbie.

"My children are beautiful grandmother; I have never been happier than the moment I first saw them in their father's arms." Opal looked at Robbie and saw the love in his eyes as he watched Rune.

"My children you are so blessed, and that brings me to this point in which we sit, for here is very sacred and also no one beyond the edges of this grass can hear our voices." Jade looked up at Opal.

"Why is this place sacred?"

She smiled. "Believe it or not but below you sunken into the floor is a circle of stone. It was used to hold a large wooden disc of black and white, for once it was the heart of the country and sat in the halls of Camelot."

Robbie thought he heard her wrong. "We sit above the round table of Arthur?"

"The round table was made of wood my bowman. When Arthur was taken to Avalon, it was taken apart in secret and transported to a sacred place to be preserved for all time. The table was laid on a huge circle of stone, which was blessed by many before the table was placed on top of it. The round table was many things, it was a table of power, and a table of gatherings for it could seat one hundred and fifty men in one sitting, however it was also an altar. The consecrated stone below it gave it such status and it was a place where worship could be practiced. When the wooden table was removed the stone below it was brought here by Eve and Hearne, who as you know are my mother and father."

Rune turned to Opal. "This site saved you in the age of sleep." Opal smiled.

"You are clever my child, I have the gift of sight so I knew of this place and the deeds of the Dark One. She thought she was being so clever when she caught us; she brought me to a realm I already knew as I like all mystics had travelled the realm many times. I found Merlin who had been very badly hurt and I brought him here to heal. She cannot see into this site, as it is for the purposes of good, the stone below still holds the powers of the round table. I fear I was not quick enough to aid Gwendolyn; she fought long and hard and suffered terribly in the castle. It was here we recovered and found our strength before we could try and find a way out. She guarded all of the usual entrances and exits, and we could not penetrate them. Here we lived together and fought side by side." Opal gave a little chuckle. "He was very dashing; he was bold and brave and a very clever wizard." Jade gave a giggle.

"What granddad?" Rune chuckled; Opal gave a fond smile.

"Oh girls, back then he was so beautiful, I was young and pretty and I fell so deeply in love with him, I had no idea he was feeling the same. A little I feel like you and Runestone my bowman." Rune gave him a smile as he nodded.

"What then grandma?" Jade was filled with excitement, as she wanted to know more. Opal looked down and pushed a finger onto Jade's nose.

"Then my little wood nymph, he told me how he felt."

"Cool." Rune giggled at the bright wide eyes of Jade.

"It was in that moment the power between us joined as one and the Whiteline blended with the Green Circle. I felt it straight away, and I knew we had to find a way out. Merlin had learned of the well of hidden secrets, and we talked about it. He told of the old stone well that you use to travel to the land of the Fae, we searched for it for a long time, you see at first, I did not want to stray too far from here, I knew we were safe here. Merlin was clever and he took up some of the grass and made a Taliesin of the clay, as long as we wore them we travelled unseen by any in this realm. It was an act of genius that took us up into the mountains and to the old stone well. Using the incantation of the circle and line we travelled to the island of violets and we escaped."

"Wow that is a really cool story Grandma." Robbie gave a laugh.

"Only now the Dark One knows it is a way out and she put a curse at the other end to kill Rune if she comes out that way."

"That my dear bowman is correct, you will have to find a way to lift the curse before Rune can travel back, and without it her powers will be stripped and channelled into the Dark One." Rune looked at Robbie and her face dropped.

"So we are still trapped here?" Opal nodded.

"Not necessarily, Leenard is working as you speak to lift the curse; he was reborn by you Rune, into the Violetlines. Unfortunately, he has not worked that out yet and he is still using the commands of the Whitelines, he always was a forgetful old buzzard." Robbie and Rune both started giggling.

Robbie watched Opal for a moment and she looked up as if expecting him to talk. He marvelled at the intense blue of her eyes, which were so like Rune's. "There is something else you might be able to help me understand." She smiled at him.

"I know what it is that you ask, why build a castle on an island when you have one safe and protected here?"

Rune smiled as she saw the surprise on his face. "It makes no sense to build a smaller replica of the one she has here. She can slip between realms, so why bother; if she needs to hide no one can get to her here."

"Think my bowman what has she here but not up there?" Robbie frowned at the question.

"She has nothing here she cannot already use in our realm; she has controlled our realm with it throughout the age of sleep." Opal smiled again.

"Do you think that is a weakness?"

"How? As soon as men sleep, she can fill them with dread." It suddenly hit him, all day he tried to puzzle it out and now the moment of inspiration came. Opal nodded and Jade and Rune both looked at them confused. Rune leaned over to Robbie.

"What is it?" Robbie looked up as the brilliance of the idea came to him.

"We have under estimated her Rune, in the past she has only been able to control men during the time that they sleep. She needs total control both day and night. The reason this land is so empty is because she has created a passage from here to Dunnottar. The Dark One will let those black nightmare men out in the daylight; it will give her total control of every mortal in the land."

"You have come far since last we met bowman. You carry the wisdom of a lord, and you think like a man of power. Your destruction of Dunnottar was not complete, because you did not know of the passage. She has rebuilt it bigger and stronger, although the line of the rose still makes it hard for her."

"I can destroy it again grandma, but what can I do to prevent her from rebuilding it?"

"There is a protection known of old by millions my granddaughter, how do we stop any spirits when we cleanse a home?"

"I use salt and water." Jade smiled. Opal gave a chuckle.

"So do I my little green eyed nymph." Rune's eyes sparkled.

"Sea water... I have to completely remove the island, and the sea will cover the spot. Salt and water will provide a protection and prevent any spirit from passing up. I cannot believe it is that simple."

"Sometimes my dear children we look too hard, and forget the simple things.

Was it not the simplicity of stealth that has gained you the greatest advantage? It is no coincidence that a woodsman was chosen for these tasks; within the simple life are the solutions to most things." Opal closed her hand and then opened it, and a white daisy floated to the floor.

"There is nothing simpler than a flower, and yet in times gone by it has been used to bring love, and help ease the pains of death. It is the symbol of many countries and a thing worn to remember sacrifice. Many problems of the old modern ways were linked to the simplest of flowers. I know how you love your violets Rune, but I have always loved the vibrancy of a daisy." Opal stood up and looked at them all. "The day slips away my children, rest now so you can rise refreshed. There is a long day still ahead of you, sleep peacefully knowing you are protected." Robbie stood up, and walked to Opal as she turned to walk to the trees.

"If I may there is one more question." Opal turned to face him and nodded. "If you were imprisoned for all of those years here, why have you returned to this realm?"

"Very simply My Bowman, I know this realm better than any; I have explored every area and aspect of it, I am a mystic and I know other mystics who wish to travel here, they are your guides in the other realm. I can protect them here and so I chose to do so. My dear bowman I spent seven hundred years trapped here with my husband, odd as it sounds like your mere is to you, this is to me. I fell in love in this spot to a man I still love dearly, this is my home." Robbie smiled at her. He understood the importance of Robbie's Mere to Rune and him, he too felt like it would always be the only place he could think of as home. Opal winked and slipped up her hood. He watched as she walked into the trees to do her work for the night.

Jade settled by the fire and Rune slipped a blanket round her. Robbie sat with a drink as he thought of everything he had learned that day; Rune slid on to his knees and faced him. She smiled a happy glowing smile; her eyes were bright sapphire blue and they sparkled. He lifted his hand and stroked her soft white face; she leaned on to his hand and closed her eyes. Rune gave a contented sigh.

"Jade will have to travel back alone and tell Merlin to use the power of the Violetlines. I will not leave you here alone." She opened her eyes and looked at him.

"You know you cannot remain here for long, don't you? I am here in essence I can remain here like this forever, but you have come here whole; if you stay you will die."

"Then I will stay and my spirit will stay with you, I will not leave you Rune and I will not debate it with you."

"But Robbie they need you. How can you desert them at their time of greatest need? You must leave when the time comes."

"My realm has an heir and a fine man to teach him, you are more important to the woodland realm than I am. Without you Rune, there will be no new life, and my realm will die. I will remain here to protect you; my place is beside you, the priority changed when my son was born. I will fight her here if that is what it takes to save Loxley." Rune leant forward and put her arms around him.

"I want you to live; I want to grow old beside you."

"So do I, but if the choice comes, you know now the decision is made and is out of your hands, you have no control over life here, this is a spirit world. You cannot change anything."

The darkness was falling over the island of Iona. Merlin stood by the sea and watched the stars, he felt a fear inside him he had not felt before, and he seemed to feel old and useless. Steph slipped her arm round him and looked out to the sea. The breeze lifted her hair on her shoulders as she leaned against her father. He lifted his arm and pulled her close. "I have missed you my little moonstone." She gave a chuckle.

"I have missed you too dad."

"She is alone out there, and I fear for her."

"Robbie is with her dad; she will not be alone."

"Oh moonstone, I have made such silly mistakes, and now I find I am so angry with myself. Time has taken its toll on me; I feel my age and stupidity."

"You will work it out. In all of her life, you have never once let her down, I know you will remember? I know the pressure you put yourself under to show her how much you love her."

"Two of the most precious people in my world are there because I sent them. If I had been here, she would not have placed the curse, and Runestone would be at home safe with her sister."

"I have great faith in those three. One way or another they have been bound together for as long as I can remember. I was never sure which one he would marry; I just knew he would marry one of them. They both love him equally and I think he too loves them the same. They have their own circle of power there believe me."

Merlin dropped his arm from Steph and looked at her with wide eyes open. "Moonstone my angel you are brilliant."

Steph looked shocked as her father filled with wild happiness and joy. "DAD... what the hell are you going on about?" Merlin almost danced he laughed so much, he ran up and down the edge of the beach searching the sand as Steph watched looking at him as if he had gone mad.

"Aha!" Merlin picked up a stick and ran chuckling up the beach back to his daughter. "Brilliant, absolutely brilliant, I always knew you know? Oh, you would have made such a wonderful wizard. Still, I have you all to myself and I love you my precious and wonderfully gifted Moonstone."

Steph could barely keep up he spoke so fast, "Dad please calm down you are losing me."

His eyes blazed with bright green, as he chuckled and handed her the stick, he grabbed her hand, and pulled her onto the white sand. "You will see... Brilliant, I am so stupid, you are brilliant. Have I said that before, well believe me, you are outstanding." Steph started to laugh.

"You have not changed; you still can be as crazy as you were when I was a girl." Merlin pointed to the sand as he shook with excitement.

"Draw the symbol, the new one that Rune created for her daughter. Come on draw it for me here." Steph tittered as she leant forward and drew the first letter 'L' it swept into the top of the 'C' on an angle, and then she drew the 'L' coming out of the bottom of the 'C'. Merlin jumped with excitement.

"Look at it, what do you see?" Steph knew the symbol by heart; Robbie has scribbled it on every spare piece of paper he owned at the house.

"Dad it's line circle life. It is the equation of the Violetlines and the new runic symbol of Iona. Everyone here knows it." He clapped his hands together excitedly and raised a pointed finger as he danced on the spot.

"Yes... Yes, but what do you see?" Steph looked down at the symbol she had drawn.

"Well Rune has always liked a curly 'L' so I suppose they do look a little like love hearts..." Her voice dropped as she looked at the symbol. She looked back at her father who beamed with delight. "Oh my god... She has a circle flanked by two hearts, which is Robbie with two women who love him." She stared back down as Merlin positively exploded with joy. He took the stick and drew two circles with a curly 'L' between them.

"I was Whiteline, who was in love with two women. White Circle and Green Circle. See the heart, between the two circles? This was during the age of sleep I was torn when Gwendolyn came back for a while because I thought in a way I had betrayed her. She understood, she was a very loving woman, but it acted as a negative equation." He looked at Steph to make sure she was following.

"Moonstone my angel, look what she has done? Rune has reversed it, and that is what has made the Violetlines a positive force of such power. She has used the equation to name her daughter, who is the result of such power."

Steph was staggered but completely understood, her father had taught her pure math's as a child and she marvelled at the brilliance. "Dad the equations of math's and magic are the same."

Merlin leapt into the air and raised his hands, "She is a genius; she is the symbol reader, my beautiful and wonderful Runestone."

Steph laughed with excitement at her father as he danced wildly on the beach. He came running back up to her. "She understood that Robbie was a close friend of her sister, he could not marry her, because it would ruin a wonderful friendship. She knew that Jade loved Robbie, but she also knew he could not marry her. With Jade as his friend no other woman would go near him, because let's face it sweet as she is, she can be a little bit scary." Steph laughed at her father.

"Dad slow down you are starting to talk as fast as Jade." His eyes burned with green life, as he took several large breaths and calmed himself.

"Oh Moonstone my angel, you have such a gifted daughter. Rune always knew he would marry her. She worked out the mathematical equation and solved the riddle of magical theory. With Jade protecting her and Robbie, she knew he would fall in love with her, she knew she would bring the line and the two circles together. She is brilliant."

"She did know dad, I must admit in all of the years she sat by that window, she knew one day he would come to the door and ask her out. I use to admire her so much for it, her faith in the magic was absolute and it worked. Rune predicted her own destiny at the age of nine." Steph hugged her panting father.

"My word I have not been this excited since Newton finally understood what the hell I was talking about." He took deep long breaths and folded his arms around his daughter. "Amazing man clever as a whip at times, bloody stupid at others. I hit him right on the head with an apple I got so angry, and then puff, his mind finally got it. It only took four years to convince him." Steph beamed up at her dad.

"You do know that symbol could also represent Rune and Iona." He smiled.

"I think that is why she chose it, the day she was married the game changed. Every father knows how much his daughter loves him." She smiled.

"I do love you dad." He pulled her close.

"I love you too Moonstone."

Merlin and Steph walked smiling up the long grassy slope towards the Abbey, they talked quietly and smiled. Steph had not felt this close to him in a long time, she had missed him a great deal, he had lived next door for so long and recently he had been permanently away. She felt whole again in the arms of the man she admired and respected above all others. She loved her dad dearly.

As the moon rose high in the sky, Merlin stood by the table where Rune lay asleep. Iona and Hal were in small cribs at the side of the table wrapped up snug and warm. Isolde sat and smiled as the old wizard stroked the long red and gold hair of his granddaughter. He pushed his head down to hers and kissed her softly on the forehead.

"I love you Runestone." A flash of violet flickered in her eyes. He smiled and rested his head to hers. "I am here my sweet child; I will not fail you."

Rune sat bolt upright in the glade and Robbie jumped, her eyes exploded with violet.

"Grandfather is that you?"

"I am here my darling, I have seen the equation of Iona and I now understand."

"Grandfather you have the Violetlines inside you, I put them there in Tintagel."

"You are very clever; I would never have thought of reversing the equation."

"Violet is rebirth, a reversal from death to life, I have always loved the symbol of death. I never realised it was because I was life. Your negative became my positive. Does that make sense?"

"Oh Runestone, it is an act of genius, I am so proud of what you have achieved alone. Get to the well and I will guide you through safely."

"I am with Robbie and Jade and we are safe. Granddad Opal is with me; she is the guardian of the realm. I am sat in the circle of the stone table; she is here because for her it is home."

Merlin closed his eyes as two tears filled them. "Tell her I love her and miss her."

"I will granddad. I love you too."

"I will see you soon Runestone, I will know when you reach the well."

He raised his head and the connection broke. He wiped the tears softly from her face and swallowed hard. "Goodnight my precious angel." Isolde bowed her head as she saw the special moment between a grandfather and his granddaughter. The air was filled with his love and his sorrow, and she showed him the respect of it.

Robbie looked up at Rune as her eyes cleared of violet. She smiled at him. "Grandfather knows, he will break the curse and we can go home, then you can make love to me all night."

"Rune shut up... I am here wearing really kinky knickers and Rowan's not here." Robbie gave a giggle as Jade turned round and smiled.

"Hey you couldn't make me some in red, could you?" Rune started to laugh.

"Why don't you like blue, Saff does?"

"Yeah, but that's Saff, I want mine hot for my hot man." She gave a little giggle. "I want to drive him wild; he is so hot when he's wild." Robbie coughed.

"That is my General Jade, you are putting pictures in my mind that should really not be there." She gave a wild giggle and rolled over. Rune pulled him close and snuggled into him.

"You can be pretty wild when you want to."

"Hey beautiful I am the hooded man." She leaned over him and kissed him slowly. "Oh wow."

"Oh Guys please, I am really missing him." Rune giggled as she looked down at him, she kissed his nose and curled round him under the blanket.

"It's alright she will be asleep in a while."

"No I won't."

CHAPTER TWENTY THREE

THE FIGHT FOR SECRETS AND DREAMS

As dawn rose, Mason Knox stood beside his son and wife, high on the balcony of the Black Palace. Before him was a sea of black vested fighters bearing the crests of a red dragon and red raven. The combined forces of his army now numbered one hundred thousand. Behind the palace and the next high wall, line after line of troops stood in the drizzle waiting for the address of their leader.

He looked down with pride. "See Son, he blew up a couple of boats, and yet every man is landed and here for us to order into war. Remember, it is not the moment that matters, but the outcome of the man who controls his time well. We lost a few, but today the woodsmen will lose many." He patted his son warmly on the shoulder as Lance looked out at the assembled mass and smiled.

There was no mistaking the power that Knox held over the country. He had worked night and day for over twenty years for this one final moment of history. He gave a slight smile of satisfaction, as he raised his arm, and the assembled mass of troops roared up to him in a mass salute. The noise was deafening, and could be heard outside the city, where Saff crouched quietly with Ox.

"How long has it been like this?" She looked nervously back at Ox.

He shook his head in worry. "All morning, I think this is the big one, it takes a hell of a lot of men to make a noise that loud."

Saff lifted the telescope to the top of the wall and scanned along it. Where the top floor of the Black Palace rose higher than the wall, she saw the black clad figures of Knox, his wife and Lance. Mason stepped up to the microphone and she lowered the scope. "It looks like old snaky is going to give a speech." The speakers were switched on and squealed for a moment. Harry leaned over.

"Hey the dude is too close to the mike, if he leaned back it wouldn't squeal like that man."

Saff rolled her eyes. "Hang on Harry I will let him know."

"Whoa girl that is not like an option, you go over there and you're like totally karmic toast."

Ox gave a chuckle and looked at Saff who smiled. Mason Knox took the mike.

"Citizens of the free world, we gather today with one single purpose in mind."

"Yeah man like we know, we been totally livin it for over a year."

"Harry keep it down we need to hear this."

"Oh like sorry dudet."

"Today we will march out of here and face the biggest threat to our way of life known to date. We fight for our freedom to build this land a new, a land in which all of us can fulfil our true potential as members of society. We need the engineering and technology of the old world to return, so that we can start a new future with a better way of life for everyone."

"Yeah right, better for him and shit for the rest of us, I totally hated the hassling politicians of the old ways."

"HARRY!"

"Oops sorry Dudet."

"The woodland realm wants to stop you and push you into the sea, they want to destroy all the work we have done to rebuild a nation, they will have you starve for most of the year and freeze in the winter. Your children will be uneducated godless heathens, and your lives will be one of endless toil and struggle."

"Yeah, and like factory work is like totally party time."

"Right Harry, I mean it, one more peep and I will bring Jasper here with a few of his oldest friends, and I aint talking human."

"Hey peace chicken, I don't need your hassling unfunky vibes."

"This land is yours for the taking, and under my command all of you will share in its bounty. Today we start the end of the trees and the pests they contain; we strike for York and then Loxley, go my soldiers of glory and take back what is rightfully yours. Raise your weapons and destroy the men of the woods and let's clean this country we hold close to our hearts forever."

The roar from the soldiers was deafening, as all those before, and behind the black palace roared their praises into the air. Sapphire stood up. "Ok I have heard enough; I have to warn Rowan." Saff slid a dragonfly clasp out of her hair and gave it to Ox. "Take this and if you have trouble squeeze it, and it will take you back to Loxley and safety." She waved her hand and the blue light appeared in front of her. "Come on Harry we are off." Saff slipped quickly through and was followed by Harry, the light faded away and Ox signalled the withdrawal to his men.

The drums had beat on the moors for most of the night, Rowan sensed something coming as he stood beside Treen. "It will not be much longer now." She turned with pale brown eyes.

"We are ready General. We ave time yet." He nodded

"I hope so Robbie is counting on us." Treen looked down her long scope.

"We ave held them here for four months, if we fall back to the woods we will hold longer."

Sapphire ran down the path toward the observation platform. She hurried up the steps and gasped for breath as she faced Rowan. "It's starting, Mason is addressing his troops, he said today begins the end of the woodland realm. I am not sure how he intends to get them through the blocked gates, but it sounds like he has one hell of an army heading our way."

"He will blow the walls, that eez what I would do. He will ave no use for an empty city."

Rowan nodded in agreement. "We are as ready as we could ever be. Scarlet is with us remember that, these are her plans; let's make them work for her."

Rowan slid down the steps and headed for the headquarters in the cave, Sapphire ran down at his side. "Go back to Iona and fill everyone in, if Robbie arrives let him know our plans as soon as he gets there. Warn him he may also have a fight." Sapphire nodded.

"I will see you soon, good luck." The blue light appeared and she shot through, it was gone again in seconds.

Rowan came into the operations room of the headquarters. "Listen up everyone, the big one is coming. Skip, I want this Opp's room down and out of here in two hours. Go back to York we are moving house. All strikers, I want you up top behind the boards now, your commanders are waiting. Specialists hold back here, Night Strikers you help move all this to York. Let's get moving; time is not on our side. Commander Rafe, Commander Jett Amber, a word outside please." There was instant movement as the plans put in place by Scarlet finally went into operation.

Treen stood up on the platform next to Claire, she smiled at her. "We are good friends Yes?"

Claire smiled. "I have enjoyed working with you Treen, yes we are friends." She smiled

"You are scared a little?" Claire nodded.

"I am a little bit."

"This eez good, I am terrified." Claire gave a giggle. "You ave a man for you?"

"Not really, I spend a lot of time here."

"Oh that eez not good, I must find you big hunky like my Skippy." Clair gave a giggle.

The large boom of an explosion echoed in the distance, Treen lifted her scope and looked in the direction of the Black City where a column of smoke rose into the air. "He eez so predictable, alright Claire ave your flags ready we play Scarlet style for a while."

Claire nervously unrolled her flags and stood up front next to Treen ready to send her signals, Treen watched carefully down the scope.

Rowan looked at Rafe and Jett. "I know they are your men out there at the front, and I know how loyal you are to them, but I have another favour to ask of you. I want you both to leave this field and go to Iona." Rafe looked uncertain.

"Rowan you need us here, those men will do anything we ask them they trust us."

"Rafe I know how loyal you are to those men, but I believe the moment Robbie returns to Iona she will attack it, Merlin now believes the same. Keith can handle the Specialists, I have two hundred strikers prepared and ready to go at a moment's notice, I want you and Jett to lead one hundred each. Robbie is walking into a trap and the Dark One thinks she has the upper hand. I need leaders who can inspire in difficult conditions. The reports from Dunnottar are the same as they were before the army of the dead came out, I know I am not wrong on this and I need to know I have people up there that I trust. I have to be here or I would be there by his side."

Jett nodded and gripped his shoulder. "Ok Rowan we will go. We love him as well; I promise I will keep all of them safe." Rowan gave a long gasp.

"I really am frightened for him; I hate that bloody woman. I will settle with her before all of this is over." Rafe gave a smile.

"I bet you ten it's me." Rowan laughed, Jett turned and looked up at Rafe.

"Beginner, I bet you ten I finish her." Rowan pulled Jett into a hug

"Take care of each other." Rafe patted his back.

"I will be back for my winnings General." Rowan gave him a warm embrace.

"I hope you earn it, I will enjoy taking it." Rafe laughed.

"Keep safe my friend, we will all meet soon."

The army of Mason Knox began its march to the battlefield, as the woodsmen prepared for their last battle on the moors. Boards were up and ready, and along the front lines, the first of many rows of long wooden spikes rose up out of the heather. Bowmen now lined the top of the ridge with stinger arrows. Behind the ridge, catapults were wound up into their firing positions, and the first of many highly explosive bombs were loaded and ready to fire. Rowan stood flanked by Treen and Rayne. Claire waved her flags as the orders were given and the code for today was red. All the commanders tore up the blue book that had been their coded orders for the past three months. Scarlet's new codes would ensure that the enemy did not understand the orders.

Treen gave a grin as she turned to Clair. "This will be fun. Send the order skirts up and the boobies out."

Rayne turned and gave a strange look at Treen. Rowan gave a giggle. "Scarlet had a strange sense of humour." Rayne nodded and smiled. On the battlefield, the orders were given and the boards lifted up and the bows came over the tops ready to fire. Rowan tittered. "It does actually make a strange sort of sense."

The time passed slowly as the sound of drums echoed across the field. The small group up on the platform watched as the army of Mason Knox trudged in the distance toward them. Behind the scenes the Headquarters was almost clear as the Specialists stood with two hundred strikers waiting for their orders. Skip and Gwinne were already in carts heading for York as they passed the lines of woodsmen who now formed the protected long lines of retreat.

In the circle of trees that now grew tall and dense around the city of York, twenty thousand woodsmen now took to their final positions. Carts trailed in long lines as new hospitals needed to be set up by the walls of York. Over in Winsford in the House of Good Hope, Alley prepared to receive wounded men. Long rows of canopies had been set up outside, and the nuns rushed around getting their final preparations in order. A whole floor of the tall accommodation block was now empty and lined with long rows of beds. The older girls and boys of the convent had been given white aprons, as they were to help as extra nurses and stretcher bearers. Alley and her staff had spent several months training them.

At Loxley Fuse ran the Village Hall as Jess and Beth took time out from the farm to organise extra staff at the barracks. A whole floor there was ready to act as an emergency hospital. Melissa prepared space on Iona in the abbey. Young Gaynor helped her and her brother Will moved beds from empty rooms with Jasper, to give them enough if they were needed. The whole of the woodsman world was on high alert, and the clock ticked slowly by, as resolve strengthened and the search for hidden courage began. Treen lowered her telescope, she turned to Rowan.

"They ave arrived, ow we beat them I ave no ideas, but we will. I ave been honoured to stand with you, I love all of you." Rowan nodded.

"You have been my inspiration Treen thank you; I have known great honour to stand beside a leader of such high calibre. Now we fight for Loxley." Rowan stepped off the platform and walked down the ranks of his waiting soldiers. His voice rose high as he began to address the woodland forces.

"Loxley stands proud behind you, it holds your mother's and wives and children, out there is an army that wants to destroy them. Your Lord of Loxley stands to stop them. Who stands with him?"

Bows rose into the air, as the troops roared at Rowan, and he smiled at the faces of thousands who loved their lord as he did. He lifted his bow in salute. "We fight with Robert of Loxley and defend the realm of the hooded man." He walked back up to the platform as the soldiers shouted, and shook their weapons above their heads, and Rowan looked across at Claire. "Send the orders." The flags shot up as the heavy beat of drums pounded louder in rhythm with the marching feet of the massive army of Mason Knox.

Rowan turned and faced the army that flowed like a sea of black on to the battlefield behind the already assembled lines of the Knox front line. The green lush colours of the heather on the moors had gone, and like thousands of ants, the dots of black swarmed over everything, Rowan watched and swallowed deeply. "Hearne protect us."

The roar of the enemy came as their front line dropped their barriers and they swarmed towards the lines of the woodsmen. "Brace yourselves, FIRE!"

Rowan gave the order and Claire signalled as Treen screamed out her commands. Now was the time of the test of the hooded realm, as arrows fizzed into the air? Rowan watched as the enemy hit the first lines of impaling poles. The catapults launched their first long line of high explosives; they whizzed overhead, and landed deep in the ranks of the black army. The ground shook with the might of the violet bombs.

Rune hugged Opal tightly. "Goodbye Grandmother, I will watch for you in my dreams." Opal smiled and kissed her.

"I will be there if you need me." Jade flung her arms round her grandmother.

"I hate saying goodbye." She squeezed Jade tightly.

"Then don't my cheeky little nymph. I will see you again when you sleep." Jade gave a quiet laugh.

"I hope so, I will be looking." Opal looked up at Robbie.

"My granddaughter is happier than I have ever seen her; she waited a long time for your love. I am so proud of you Robert." She pulled him close and gave him a big squeeze. "I know you worry, but it always looks darkest before the dawn. Have no fear; I am watching your children." She let go and looked him right in the eyes and smiled. "Go and be my bowman."

"Goodbye Grandmother, and thank you for all of the help and guidance you have given me. I owe you a great debt of thanks."

"It is paid, seeing the happiness of my children is more than you will ever know. Take care and the Green Lord will protect you." He gave her a nod and walked into the trees with Rune and Jade. It was early morning and they had a long walk ahead of them up to the high plateau where the Well of Hidden Secrets was waiting.

Robbie moved along through the trees with a lighter heart. Meeting Opal had certainly brought a lot of happiness to Rune and Jade, who walked in front of him chatting happily. Rune seemed filled with fun, and smiled and giggled with her sister. It was a relief, since the birth she had seemed to be so withdrawn and quiet, now he saw the Rune he knew and loved, as she looked back at him with dazzling bright blue eyes, and smiled a loving smile.

As they pressed on through the morning sunlight, the terrain was gradually getting steeper and the trees were starting to thin out. Opal had told him to look for a stream and follow it to its top; there he would find the well. The thought of being able to get there, and finally get Rune out to safety lifted his spirits. The news that Merlin would be able to lift the curse of the Violet Isle off the island had lifted a great weight off his shoulders. For a moment, he had considered staying here in this realm of constant dappled light, and dark clad figures that stalked the trees, Robbie's mind made a short jolt as he thought. 'For what?' He had never thought to actually ask.

What was it that the dark nightmares had been looking for in an empty realm? They were patrolling for something, had they known that Rune and Iona were there? He moved his pace up and caught up with Rune. He looked at her as he walked between her and Jade. She smiled at him.

"Hi gorgeous." She slipped her arm round his waist.

"Hey beautiful." She giggled. "Rune you know those dark figures?" Jade shuddered.

"Do you have to talk about the Darkmares Robbie? They give me the creeps."

"The Dark what?"

"Darkmares... you know dressed in black with masks that hide your worst fears and nightmares... The Darkmares." Jade looked around the trees cautiously.

Robbie smiled it was quite a good description. "Yeah... these Darkmares, I have been thinking and it just sort of came to me, what do you think they are looking for? They could not have known we were there that quickly, so what else were they looking for? I have seen no life at all in these woodlands."

Rune shrugged as she looked across at Jade. "To be honest Rob I have not really thought about it, we have been at war so long I guess I am just used now to seeing patrols. I suppose they must have been looking for something?" It was obvious that just one form of life in these woods was enough for Jade; she was not keen to explore the possibility of others. Robbie watched Rune's face; he could see she was thinking.

"It might sound mad but do you think they have an enemy?" That had been his thoughts exactly.

"I have wondered Rune. What if this realm has something they are keen to kill? They looked like they had confidence; I mean they wasted no time coming into the trees to look for us. Do you think these woods contain something the Dark One fears?" Rune slowed her pace as Robbie started to really make a lot of sense.

"You know you could be on to something; the problem is if there was life here, I would feel it."

"But Rune there isn't life here, you said so last night, this is a spirit realm. Any life here would soon die, Opal and Merlin only survived because they had the protection of the circle, and they are in a way part spirit. I am thinking there is some sort of spirit here that she must fear, why else would she hunt it?"

She stopped and looked at him. "If this was an empty realm, there would be no need for guards, and grandmother was quick to point out how safe we would be in the circle. She knew there were things out there that hunted at night; you know Robbie, I just never questioned her. I was so happy to see her that I did not stop to think for one minute, you are right. This is a realm that she has control over, but there must be something that is resisting her or frightens her, why else would you hunt?"

"Food." Jade looked up and shrugged. "It's why we hunt." Rune gave a nod.

"But we have seen nothing to catch or trap, there aren't even any birds."

"No offence Rune but with the Darkmares about, I would hide as well." Rune gave a giggle.

"It's a good point Sis." She looked back at Robbie. "The thing is spirits tend to feed on other things."

Jade gave another violent shudder. "You are going to mention karma chompers aren't you?"

Robbie sniggered and Rune gave a burst of laughter. "Oh Jade, you should not listen to Harry and his wild thoughts, spirits tend to feed on other types of spirit."

"See... Karma Chompers, I knew it." Robbie pulled her into a hug.

"Pebbles, I thought you didn't believe in all that cosmic vibes stuff? These guys want spirits to feed on."

"I didn't believe in anything Harry said until I came here. Robbie these things attack with no weapons, that thing took off its mask and its face was hers. I knew it was going to try to kill me, what else could it do without any weapons? It had to suck out my spirit, didn't it? So, Harry is almost right, his spirit is his karma, and one of those things would eat it. Call me as mad as him, but to me that's a Karma Chomper."

Rune gave him a weak smile. "She makes sense."

Robbie rubbed his eyes. "Ok, let's just say that at some point we are going to get out of here." They both nodded at him. "Whose karma is going to get chomped then?" Robbie looked round at the empty woodland, there was no sight or sound of anything spirit or living. "You see what I mean? There is nothing at all here, so who are these Darkmares hunting?"

Jade looked up at him her face was pale. "Robbie who cares, I want to get out of here as quickly as possible. Please can we just go?" He gave a sigh and nodded.

Jade moved off in front and Rune took his hand. "Why is it so important Robbie?"

"You are both missing the point Rune. We may have a chance to find out something about the Dark One that could help us. Mason wants to destroy us because we oppose him, those who don't he enslaves. Honestly Rune where do you think he learned that from?"

She gave him a sideways glance and watched Jade just up ahead. "Rob, I understand you, and I can see that you have a point, but you are forgetting we have a war already and children to protect. Oh, and not forgetting we still have a king to find. I just think that whatever it is she is hunting does not have the power to face her. If it did, we would have seen some sign."

He gave a long sigh. "I suppose so, if I see anything though I will try and contact it. I cannot miss an opportunity to talk to something that opposes her."

"Alright Rob, if we do come across anything that might help, we will investigate.

But for now, let's just find that stream; I want to get back to my babies." He gave her hand a squeeze and smiled.

"Come on then." The three of them made their way through the gradually thinning trees of the strange empty woodland. The trees here were younger and a lot smaller. They were thick and bushy and spread in a wide band of dense foliage up toward the foot of a large rock. The floor was covered in thousands of different types of grasses that grew in all different hues, and formed a thick quilt of bright colour below the trees. Robbie parted the foliage as he moved soundlessly through the thick growth. He kept low with his bow firmly grasped in his hand; Jade and Rune followed his lead as he wove them through the wood of small trees toward the sound of running water.

The trees began to thin out as they reached the outer edges of the woodland, and soon there was just a long wide band of grasses, with the occasional small sapling, that struggled to heave itself up out of the long tufts of grass. At the edge of the grassland, was a shallow dip in which fresh water bounced and chattered across the dark grey stone of the stream bed.

Rune was relieved as she sat at the edge of the bank and leaned over. She scooped the water up in her hands and drank, it was ice cold and she patted her red face with it. Jade lay down on the grass and leaned over as she drank her fill; she pushed her hot face into the water and felt the instant relief. Her head came up dripping as she gasped, her fringe hung wet in thick wet strands across her forehead as the water ran down her hot red face. Rune wiped her neck with a silk hankie she soaked in the water, and Robbie looked round at the rock and the woodland they had come from.

From the base of the rock, he could now see across the tops of the vast woodland. Robbie was surprised at how far they had come. The large black castle in the middle of the wood now looked tiny it was so far away. Rune came up to his side and looked back. "She doesn't really build to blend in, does she?"

He gave a smile. "As long as she is there and we are here I am happy, it's not much further now hopefully." He turned and looked at the rugged climb upwards. "I think we should not waste time, everything in this realm seems to take longer than expected." She leaned over his shoulder and kissed his cheek.

"We will just be a minute."

Robbie took a long drink as Rune dampened her cloth, and then looking north, they began to climb. The path was steep with rough rocks, and their feet slid as they slowly wove their way upwards. The daylight seemed brighter here as the clouds of dark seemed to fade above them. A little sun filtered through the clouds, the sun showing as a white ball behind them, it was warm work and soon all of them felt the heat as they sweated. It was well over an hour and they were very high on the edge of the slippery path, as it began to weave inwards to the top of the rock. Robbie looked up at the top that was coming closer as they wound round the face of the rock. His hand was on the wall as he leaned inwards and he stepped over a loose part of the stone, and leaned back on the wall to guide Rune. He felt the wall slip and he fell backwards; Rune gave a squeak and quickly stepped up to the spot where Robbie had disappeared.

The rock seemed solid but she felt the power radiating from it, she stepped forward and walked into the dimly lit cave. Jade shot through behind her looking panicked. Robbie sat up on the floor and looked around in the gloom. Jade's eyes widened. "Oh wow, how cool is that?"

Rune walked across the cave to the centre where a bright gleaming wall, surrounded a well of gold. She ran her fingers softly across the top of the wall as she looked over and into the deep dark murky depths. She smiled as she looked up at Robbie. "Can we go home now?"

Robbie walked over towards her as Jade scurried across and leaned right over and looked down the well; two red eyes looked up from the bottom. Robbie grabbed the back of Jade's hood and heaved her backwards. She sprawled back on to the floor with a scream; Rune staggered back as Robbie pushed her and drew Destiny out. The blade shone white as he planted his feet square and waited.

"Robbie what the hell are you doing?" Rune looked really angry and Jade looked startled, he stepped back and prepared, as he lifted his left arm and pointed to a small archway in the rock face.

"Opal said an old stone well, this most certainly isn't stone. Go that way NOW!" A white withered hand with long black fingernails slipped over the edge of the golden wall. Robbie swallowed deeply as he swung back, and moved round the well so his back covered the arch, Jade shrieked and fled as Rune followed her. Robbie stepped back a pace. "Come on le Fey let's end this."

The air was thick and black with arrows. Rowan wiped the grime from his face as yet another violet bomb exploded in a long line tossing bodies, heather and dirt into the air, which showered down on him. "Treen prepare to pull the front ones back?" His shout was at the top of his voice but she hardly heard him above the noise. She nodded and gave the message to the white faced frightened looking Claire. The flags shot into the air as she signalled to the other flag girls down the line. The first defence of long sharp wooden poles had held fast. Mason had been clever enough to send the remaining army of the dead first. Unable to die they writhed unsure of why they were not moving forward, the long rough shafts of pine and beech wood driven through them by the hoard behind. The front line picked off the troops as they tried to climb over the impaled army of the dead, and now after three hours of fighting the pile of the dead had formed a hill which the army behind was now starting to climb. The front line pulled back to their next defensive positions, and another long line of poles came up to waist height ready for the second wave.

The scenes before Rayne and Treen were one of horror. The battlefield was littered with thousands of moaning wounded and dead, as the generals pushed more black clad fighters on the field. They swarmed forward trampling their comrades to death. Along the top of the two mile long ridge, the bowmen of the woodsman world lifted their bows over the wall of defence. Gates opened all along the ridge as the tired and exhausted and frightened soldiers of the front line rushed backwards through the gaps to safety.

The gates closed and the second long lines of poles were set. Rowan knew this was the last line of defence on the moors. Behind the traps were being set ready for the retreat, large barrels of moonshine and oil were placed every five feet along the top of the ridge. Their withdrawal would be behind a wall of fire, and now the time had come to test the resolve of the bowmen.

Alone on the wall without swords men, they waited for the dam of death five hundred yards in front of them to break, and the black masses swarm over. Treen lifted her bow ready, Rowan and Rayne stood by her side with Claire, and they were the highest targets now, as the lines on the bowmen ran level with their feet. Rowan had to hold for at least another three hours to give the men behind the chance to fall back and prepare. The arrows sprayed through the air like hornets, as the next long volley of violet bombs lifted into the air. Rowan looked back at the carts which were now starting to empty, the bombs which had been used initially by Ox and his bandits on the city, had become a bit of a pet project with Scarlet, and now Rowan saw the cleverness of her.

The constant bombardment of the long line of bombs, had created a deepening ravine in the battlefield. The men swarmed over the side and down, and then scrambled up the damp moist peat. It slowed them down and took the pressure off the front line. Each time the violet bombs landed in the same spot, the ravine widened and deepened. Everything in the ravine was instantly wiped out, as it was blown into fragments. Rowan ducked as more fragments showered out of the sky, Treen turned with a red streaked face. "I ate this, If I had known I would ave left my hair blonde, it would be red now anyhow." She sighted her bow and fired as a man climbed up on top of the pile. It hit him head on and threw him backwards into the masses.

Rayne wiped his face. "We are holding well, how much more time do they need for Robbie?"

Rowan shook his head. "I have no idea; Rafe is still down there with his men so I presume at the moment they are fine. We need to hold them here for as long as possible. The rear defences are almost ready, the more time they have the better."

"You certainly know how to keep a guy busy here in the north." Rayne gave a smile at Rowan who laughed.

"Welcome to York, it's wet and wild, you will love it." He patted Rayne on the back and looked down the long line, which was just holding under the pressure.

Robbie watched the vile figure slither up and on to the top of the golden well, Jade shot through the archway as Rune followed, she looked back for Robbie who had held up his sword, Rune gave a gasp. She turned and ran back to him and gripped his shoulder. "That's not le Fey, it's Zandra."

The figure slid off the wall and stood up. The hair was long and black; her arms were thin and wispy, as her flesh seemed thin and transparent, her clothes were dirty and torn revealing her body, which was emaciated and almost skeletal. Rune gripped his shoulder as he stepped back, looking into the black eyes of the dead. The blue lips seemed to vibrate as she gasped her long drawn breaths, which rattled inside what was the emptiness within. Robbie swallowed as he looked at her and took another step back; Rune's small hand still on his shoulder. "I did that to her Rune. She is here because of me, what the hell has le Fey done to her?"

He watched as the retched figure took an unstable step toward him, her head swung in a soft rhythm from side to side, swinging the lank long hair across her white starved body, Robbie felt repulsed by her.

"The Dark One uses everything Rob, even her own. She has reanimated her to guard this place and trap the unwelcome. It was not your fault, you aimed for Mason." He felt her hand squeeze his shoulder tight, he found his blade swinging in rhythm with her head, as he watched her creep slowly forwards.

"She spent a lifetime with Mason, she has suffered enough. This is no life for Judy's mum." He lifted the blade and she stopped. Zandra stared through dead eyes at him, he was not sure if she even knew who she was, but in his heart he felt her pain. He had shot and she had taken the arrow for her husband, he had thought of it many times. Every time he saw Judy, he knew he had made one mistake and taken an innocent life. This was the mother of the little girl who had grown so much in his care. How could he tell her of this? Rune felt the struggle inside him.

"End it Rob, give her peace." Rune let go of his shoulder as Zandra watched with evil eyes, her fingers twitching. Robbie drew a long breath and breathed out slowly, he moved with lightning speed and Destiny glinted high in the air, Zandra flicked her head to look and smiled. All of his power came down the blade that took her head clean off. Rune waved a hand, and from inside the well faint golden speckles lifted into the air. They shone brightly as they spiraled into the air towards the ceiling of the cave; they sparkled as they touched the roof of the cave and faded away. "She is where the Dark One will never touch her again. She is at peace now Rob." He nodded as he watched the remains of her body dissolve on the floor, Rune pulled on his hand. "Come on Rob we have to catch up with Jade."

Jade ran up the long flight of stone steps, she shot through the archway in the wall and skidded as her feet slipped on the shiny floor, with her arms swinging wildly, her feet shot over the edge of the huge round hole in the floor, and with a squeal she dropped.

Rune ran up the steps followed by Robbie to catch up with Jade, she came out at the top through the archway and her boots slid on the smooth floor. She twisted round her heels sliding over the edge as she faced the sliding Robbie. Her arms flailed as he stopped just in front of her, as he lifted his hand, Rune snatched and gripped the laces of his shirt. He looked down as she fell backwards, and watched his laces extend to the tug. "Shit!"

Rune gave a scream, as he was dragged head first over the edge. His eyes seemed to fall forwards, but his body felt like it had been dragged backwards, as together they fell into the darkness, Rune snatched at him and he caught her hand and pulled her towards him. She moaned as they spun and twisted at a horrendous speed, and then fell or climbed into the darkness. All his senses reeled, and all he could do was hold onto Rune as they swept down into the well of hidden secrets.

Jade hit the floor with a bump and moaned, she opened her eyes. Her hands shot out as she tried to grip the floor, or ceiling, she was not sure which. Below her or above her a woman in white walked round an old stone well. "Grandma are you upside down or am I?"

Opal walked to below her and clicked her fingers; Jade felt a strange feeling in her stomach, and then sat up on the floor at the side of Opal. "That was too freaky for me, where am I?"

Opal smiled. "All in good time my darling; let's wait for your sister and Robbie." Jade giggled as Rune shot out of the well with Robbie and hit the ceiling. Robbie moaned as Rune landed on top of him. He lay flat as Rune lifted her head and looked at the floor, or ceiling. She gave a giggle and kissed him.

"That was a nice soft landing." He moaned on his back.

"Speak for yourself." She giggled as she rolled off him and gasped. Rune lay back fast and gripped the ceiling as Jade laughed up at her.

"Kinda freaky isn't it?"

Opal gave a smile and clicked her fingers. Robbie and Rune disappeared and then sat up at the side of Jade. She jumped as she looked at Rune who gave her a smile. "What is this place?" Robbie sat up and stretched his arm.

Opal walked round the room and raised her arms. Bright blue bubbles appeared around the ceiling in their millions, she gave a big bright smile. "This is the realm of the hidden secrets. Here is the heart of the age of dreams." The bubbles swirled in the air and Jade gave a loud giggle.

"Oh wow." The air was filled with the dancing little bubbles that all shone with light. Opal walked over and offered her hand to Rune and Jade. They both stood up and lifted their heads back to look at the bright beautiful bubbles that fell from the ceiling. Jade giggled as one floated down to her, she lifted her finger to poke it and Opal grabbed it.

"Jade don't spoil it for him." She caught the bubble gently and then placed it into the palm of her hand. Jade lifted it up and looked inside; her eyes sparkled as she saw a little boy run into the arms of his father.

"Oh Grandma, this is so cool."

Opal smiled as she bent down and looked. "That is his dream; he wants his daddy to come home safe from the war." Jade looked up.

"Will it come true?" Opal smiled at her.

"Not if you pop it." Jade's eyes sparkled as she looked at the little bubble filled with moving figures.

"He looks really happy; he should get his dream." She looked up at Rune and carefully lifted her hand. "Look how happy he is Rune." She gave a warm smile as she watched the little figure of a small boy hug his father. Robbie walked round looking at all the bubbles. "This is what she is after." He turned to Opal. "Le Fey wants these. That is what her Darkmares are doing up there, they are hunting the dreams of people and destroying them."

Opal gave a nod. "You are most correct again My Lord. Every dream is a hidden secret wish, and only those who really wish for something to happen know it. The Dark One breathes hate and pain, misery is her preferred tool."

Robbie sat on the edge of the stone well. "She knows of my dream for this land. She thinks if she can destroy all the dreams, then eventually she will come to mine and crush it. So you go out each night and collect them up and bring them here to safety." Opal smiled at him.

"You are clever My Bowman, you are quite correct, I am the guardian of the hidden well and the age of dreams. I gather and protect, and when the time is right, the dreams flow up into the well, and travel into the night to the person who's dream is about to come true."

"Oh Grandma, that is such a beautiful thing to do. Are my dreams here?" Rune's eyes gave a sparkle as she looked at Robbie. Opal gave a soft giggle.

"Your dreams are here my child floating around with the others." Rune looked up and gave a giggle.

"Is Robbie's dream here, the one she is looking for?" Opal looked at her granddaughter and her eyes twinkled brightly.

"His dream is safe, oh yes his dream is very safe, she will not find it." Robbie looked back at the millions of bubbles bobbing around and floating to the floor and back up again.

"What about Mason's? It will be his or mine that succeeds, is his in here?"

Robbie looked back down at Opal, Rune watched as their eyes met and she gave him a shrewd look.

"His dream is safe, although it is not here My Bowman." She knew already what lay in his thoughts. "I have seen it; it hangs round the neck of his mother." Rune gasped.

"His mother has it, how can we smash a dream if it is round her foul neck?"

"That my dear granddaughter is why it is round her neck. Mason is clever, but she is much cleverer. The Dark One knows that it will come to no harm in her keep, it is her strength and her weakness." Robbie nodded.

"She thinks she is invincible, so therefore no one can harm her sons dream. It gives her the false confidence that he will win." Opal nodded and smiled.

"You truly do think like a leader of men, you already know much. You paid more attention than most people realise."

"I listen and I read. I have thoughts of what my future holds." Opal gave him a look of understanding and she nodded to him. Rune saw the respect for him in her grandmother's eyes. She turned to him and looked at him. Her eyes were questioning and he smiled and winked at her. Her eyes gave a twinkle as she smiled.

"Do I have any dreams here grandma?" Jade turned slowly, her head held back she looked up; she wobbled and almost fell over. Opal pulled her forward and smiled at her happy bright face.

"I have seen some of the dreams that will come to you my sweet little wood nymph." Jade gave a giggle.

"Are they wonderful?" Her grandmothers faced softened.

"Oh my darling, they are glorious, you have such moments of wonder to come in your life. I have seen great happiness for you and your woodsman." Jade's eyes danced with delight.

"Honestly grandma?" Opal gave a smile and kissed her. She pulled her close and hugged her tightly.

"Honestly Jade Opal. You have much happiness to come." Rune watched and smiled as she sat on the side of the well and took Robbie's hand.

"We still have a chance Rob." He lifted her hand and kissed it. He pulled it over his shoulder and slipped his arm round her waist pulling her closer.

"We have always had a chance Rune, it's always been slim, but it is a chance none the less. We have to fight and believe we can do it, just like we did that day we left Loxley in a small group, we had huge odds stacked against us, but we still pushed hard and got through. You have to believe Rune."

Rune turned and looked into his dark eyes; they seemed a little older and carried the weight of the pressure that constantly weighed on him. She smiled and his eyes twinkled. "I believe in you. I hope you know that, I know that you will find a way to guide all of us. I love you Robbie."

He pulled her close and kissed her. "Then my dreams have already come true Runestone Sapphire." She gave a soft giggle as she leaned her forehead to his and she looked deeply into his eyes.

"I want to go home and see my babies."

"Me too." He kissed the end of her nose. Opal and Jade both watched and smiled at them.

Iona opened her eyes and gave a happy little squeak; Merlin smiled and looked across the table to Steph. "It is time; talk to her she is waiting." Steph smiled and pushed her head down to the sleeping Rune.

"Hear me Runestone Sapphire, centre and daughter."

"I hear you mother, oh mother, I am so happy to hear you, I want to come home."

"Runestone sweetheart be patient, your grandfather is here to lift the curse, and as soon as it is done you will know. Look for the blue light and it will be time."

"All right we will wait, but hurry, I want to be with my children."

"They are safe and here beside you my darling."

"We are ready."

Robbie watched as her eyes burned bright violet, Opal took his hand and pulled him away from the well. "Wait here by my side My Bowman, you too Runestone." Rune stood up and moved to Robbie's shoulder, she slipped her hand into his and he gave it a quick squeeze. Opal watched the well. "When the blue light comes waste no time, it will not last for long. Step into it and you will be taken back to the Isle of Fae. Remember my children I love you and will watch over your dreams." Jade gave a smile.

"We all love you too grandma. I will watch for you in every dream I have." Opal smiled.

"Then I will take the time to visit you often."

"I still have my marble."

"Good you will need it again one day. You still all have much to do, just remember to keep your dreams alive, and you will always find a way through."

The burst of light that shot out of the well made all of them jump, as it shot to the roof in a bright dazzling blue. "Go my children quickly." Robbie and Rune holding hands ran at the low wall and leapt into the light, Jade was a second behind them and it flashed bright purple and shot back down the well. Opal stood alone in the hidden realm of dreams, she put her hand in her pocket, and pulled out a small bright blue bubble. She held it up and looked at it and smiled. "Oh young Robbie, you have such a lot to do, this will be yours eventually." Opal opened her hand and it floated up to the ceiling and mixed in with all the others that bobbed around the bright ceiling. She gave a chuckle. "Jade Opal you will never change, even your own children will be happy little wood nymphs." She drew the second bubble out from inside her robe and let it float to the ceiling. "Dream well my children."

CHAPTER TWENTY FOUR

THE FIGHT ON TWO FRONTS

The boards along the top of the ridge were riddled with arrows. Rowan, Treen and Rayne now commanded from the ground. The observation platform looked like a tree in the winter it had so many arrows stuck out of it. They had now reached the final stages, and everything was prepared for the big retreat. The last of the violet bombs were lifted on to the catapults and prepared. These would not be fired, in the dying moments of the retreat, the fuses would be lit to give the bowmen time to withdraw as they exploded and blew up everything they were leaving behind.

Several long lines of sharp poles waited to be lifted as the retreat was made, and the brave woodsmen who had volunteered for the duty stood silently waiting for their general to give the order. Jett stood nervously at the side of Rafe, behind them, the long lines of the bowmen with strikers stood patiently; the Specialists were tooled up and ready to go, as they watched the small figures up by the platform giving their orders over the noise of the explosions.

Merlin raised his hands over the table of the Silver Star and began to talk. Steph watched her daughter nervously, as she lay motionless in the centre covered with Rhiannon's dark blue-feathered cloak. Rhiannon stood quietly at the table beside Saff, who was waiting for her orders from Robbie. The faint blue light began to swirl on the table of light. Merlin lifted his head to the ceiling. "I call to me a servant of the White and Violetlines, the forces bound in line circle and life. Bring forth the Violetlines to aid the cause of your creator. Heed me and draw your power to lift the curse of this sacred isle."

Light flickered in Rune's eyes, and small sparks of violet flashed up to the ceiling. From under the cloak, deep violet light seeped out and spiraled like ink dropping into swirling water. It ran round the table and mixed with the silver and pale blue light, and as it span faster, it started to rise above the table, and Rune disappeared below it. Merlin held his arms out across the large table. "Let your Lady of Violet walk free from this land. Draw in the darkness and devour it. Bathe her in violet and draw her back to the land of her father's." A pulse of white light shot out of the table and everyone jumped. It rose like a column of white marble, and it shone brighter than fresh snow and glistened, as silvery specks seemed to pop and crackle within it. It began to spin round and pick up speed. Merlin pushed his hand into the light and shook with the force of it.

"In earth, above earth, below sky, hear my call to the forces of nature." He shook harder as he fought to control the huge power that flooded into him and through him. "DEPART DARKNESS... GO BACK TO THE NIGHT... ARISE VIOLETS.... BRING BACK VIOLET LIFE."

Rhiannon watched with concern as she saw Merlin struggle to stay in control, his eyes glowed a bright shade of violet as he shook in front of the table; violet swirled up from the base of the column of light, and mixed quickly into the silvery white light. The floor of the room began to shake and vibrate, Steph gripped the back of the chair and Isolde and Filomena held on to the cribs on their stands. Sapphire looked worried as Rhiannon lifted an arm to her shoulder to steady her. Dust began to fall from the ceiling.

The column exploded in blue light and Merlin was thrown across the room, Smokes grabbed him and lifted him off the floor, he looked back to the table where Rune stood in her long white robe, her hair flowing up into the air all around her and her eyes burning with bright violet light. Her arms were out stretched and she tilted back her head and cried into the ceiling, as her gown flapped with the speed of the flowing power around her.

"I am one with this world, I am life and love. I am the stone on which you are written, return to me what is mine and obey me." Iona gave a huge squeal of happiness and Rune turned and smiled, her eyes now burning with intense violet light. "Daughter of Eve, to daughter of line, creator of violet flow to Violetline." She screamed with wild laughter and power, as Robbie rose out of the table with Jade.

Steph clasped her hands to her mouth with the joy of seeing them. Rune bathed in the bright violet light, looked up to the ceiling. "I am one. I am your mistress lift from this land and welcome all new life." The table exploded with millions of bright violet sparks that shot all over the room, as everyone dived for the floor their hands over their heads to protect themselves. Steph looked up and smiled as Jade swung her legs on the edge of the table.

"Hi mum." She gave a cheeky smile, and rolled her eyes. "Rune is getting a little bit dramatic don't you think?"

Steph gave a giggle as she sat up, and Jade slipped off the table and dropped to her knees. Steph pulled her into a big hug, Rune sat smiling on the table wrapped in a violet feathered cloak hugging and kissing Robbie. Rhiannon lifted her head above the table and smiled. "You dyed my cloak." Rune looked down at it and then back at Rhiannon.

"I think violet is so much nicer." She gave a smile "It will match with your eyes so much better now." Rhiannon gave a giggle.

"Welcome back, we missed you." Rune coiled out from Robbie and slid across the table to hug Rhiannon. Iona gave a squeak and Rune smiled as she slipped off the table and went to her. The bright violet eyes shone up at her as she lifted her out of the crib.

"Hey beautiful, I missed you." She pulled her close and held her in her arms; she looked down into the other crib where Halbert watched with bright sapphire blue eyes. "Hi gorgeous, I missed you too."

Steph slid her arms round Rune from behind and rested her head on her daughter's shoulder; she kissed Rune on the cheek. "Hi sweetheart, see they are both safe and well."

Rune looked at her. "Thanks Mum." She turned to Isolde who sat smiling and watching. "Thank you, Isolde. You kept them safe; I am in your debt."

Robbie lifted Halbert up and looked at him. "Hey little man, I hope you kept our realm safe while I was gone." Robbie held him close and turned to Rune; he looked down at his daughter in her arms. "Hey princess." Iona watched her daddy with bright eyes.

Merlin gave a long deep breath. "That was quite funky, if you will pardon the phrase; it appears Harry does have the odd useful word." Smokes gave a smile and patted his back.

Robbie looked across at Sapphire. "Tell me." She smiled.

"I hate being Rowan's bearer of bad tidings. Robbie Mason has unleashed everything, Rowan has no choice but to pull back, he is being battered by thousands." Robbie nodded. "He is also worried there may be an attack here, he has already sent a forward guard of Specialists who are all over the island. He has Rafe and Jett ready with reinforcements. I have to report back to him as soon as I have told you and he wants Jade to go straight back with me."

"How soon does he expect an attack here?" Saff shrugged.

"He thinks the moment you arrive back." Robbie nodded and turned to Isolde.

"Take my wife and children back to Loxley and keep them safe." Rune looked defiantly at him.

"Robbie, you need me here, I can fight these things and her if she comes." He turned to her and looked at her.

"Rune I have just got you back, I cannot risk losing you again." She passed Iona over to Filomena and took his hand. She looked at him with bright blue determined eyes.

"Now listen to me Robert of Loxley. You made me a promise on my birthday. Send the children to safety I am not leaving your side. I am fully restored to power now and you need me, so give me my sword and I will meet you outside in a little while. I cannot fight in this can I?" She looked down at the long flowing baggy white robe.

Isolde gave a little laugh and turned her back; Rune smiled as he reluctantly undid her sword and handed it over. It was pointless to argue with her and he knew it, he looked at Saff who smirked. "Come on let's go and see what is happening."

Robbie came out of the Abbey on to the grass with Saff. Melissa smiled just outside the door in her nursing apron; Robbie nodded a little surprised to see her. Blades stood with Maddy watching the sky, she turned to Robbie and smiled. She pointed to the black clouds rolling in from the east. "Not too sure what they are yet Robbie, but there is a lot of em." Robbie looked at the sky where the dark cloud was rolling towards the island at great pace.

"We call them Darkmares, they are particularly nasty, let everyone know if they lift their masks not to look at their faces, just cut the buggers heads off or shoot them in the head. Believe me you do not want to know what they look like. If Harry gets here do not mention the word uncosmic monster, because I think for once the mad fool has got a point." Maddy looked stunned.

"You are kidding Robbie?"

"I wish I was Maddy, those things up there terrify Pebbles. Now that frightens me... Saff get back to Rowan and let him know I have my hands full, tell him I will be with him as soon as I can, if he needs help tell him to squeeze his pendant, Rune will come,"

"Right Gov." She smiled as she waved her hand and Jade came running out of the door, she saw the sky and gave a worried look, Maddy noted it and looked back. The blue flashed and they were gone.

Jade came out of the light into the Specialists, she saw Harry and smiled.

"Listen guys there are these uncosmic monsters attacking Robbie." Harry looked at her with a fixed stare.

"They have masks on, so shoot them in the head." She walked right up to the wide eyed and nervous looking Harry. "If they lift their masks and you see them. They suck your karma out of your eyes." Harry stepped back and whimpered. Jade pulled her damp knickers out of her pocket. "Harry I was so scared I peed myself, they almost ate all my vibes, Robbie saved me just in time, they are really scary."

Jade turned and smiled at everyone who now witnessed the true unravelling of Harry, she ran down the path giggling into the mayhem and leapt into Rowan's arms.

Harry grabbed Rafe's arm. "Hey man, like do you think Rowan needs like extra help? Some of us could like mosey on over there and totally make a difference." Rafe smiled and patted Harry's arm.

"No Harry, Rowan is a proud man, it would just hurt his feelings; I think we need to help Robbie with the uncosmic monsters. You are a very sweet man to offer your aid to him though; I wonder what they taste like these uncosmic monster things." Alice and Bear tittered as Rowan holding Jade gave the signal. Rafe turned to the assembled group.

"Get ready my howling fools, we move out to fight the uncosmic monsters of a dark world, shoot for the head and don't look at their faces. If you have blue glasses, you are fine, because they cannot see blue. Black and purple are dangerous colours so do not wear them, it makes them more angry." Jett and Alice shook with laughter as Harry whipped off his purple glasses and panicked. He looked down at his black pants and shirt and screamed. The window opened and the group moved into it.

The sky above the island turned black as Rune ran out to Robbie's side. The soldiers of the line of the moon knelt on the grass up against the wall, with their quivers in front of them and their bows rose ready. The Specialists were placed all around the walls of the fields their bows up ready. Blades stood in the middle of the grass with her two gleaming swords held out at her sides. Fox and Jay were either side knelt down with their bows raised. Fox had the samurai sword sheathed on his back ready.

The sky swirled as Robbie walked out with his bow and loaded a striker. He held the lighting stick as it smouldered like a cigarette in his mouth. Rune stood at his side flanked by Maddy and Crystal. The sky got blacker as they turned and swooped over the sea. Robbie raised his bow and lit the arrow. "HERE THEY COME!"

His arrow was fast and followed by Rune's. The snarling Darkmares had swords in one hand and held their masks with the other. Robbie's arrow hit the first one over the sea and he screamed and then lit up and blew into a thousand pieces. Rune's hit next and he blew apart scattering those either side of him. They came across the island like a plague of locust, and the arrows leapt into the air. Black bodies hit the floor, and screamed and writhed in agony, before exploding into thick black smoke. It was a scary thing to witness a few feet in front of you. Robbie held his ground as they skimmed above his head; they crossed the island and turned in the air. Robbie turned round to face them coming from the west, and raised his bow. "STAY SHARP, THEY WILL BE LOWER THIS TIME."

He took aim as they swooped at him. "Get ready to duck." Rune nodded as she sighted her arrow. They released with pace at the oncoming mass, as they screamed terror down at the land below them. The arrow from Maddy's bow exploded in flames across the grass like a missile, it shot into the midst of the Darkmares and exploded engulfing a huge mass in bright orange flames. They screamed and squealed as they shot over the heads of the crouching group, and splashed hissing into the sea on the other side of the island.

The blue window opened, and the Specialists came running out followed by the striker forces. Harry turned to see thousands of black screaming beings flying at him across the sea. Harry screamed even louder, and hit the floor with the rest of the group, as they whistled past swinging their swords. Heads of bowmen rolled across in front of Harry's wide eyes.

He clutched his pendant in his teeth, and muttered his prayers under his breath, a black unmasked body thumped to the ground in front of Harry, a white tipped arrow sticking out of a torn and slashed face; it gurgled as the red eyes looked at him and turned green. "Harry?" Its voice drained out of its throat and exploded into smoke.

"Oh whoa, it's the green evils and there are like millions of them, they come for me and Robbie, we done bad uncosmic things, my vibes is gonna like totally split with their sucking of my eyes. Oh man this aint happenin, it's not cosmic." He pushed his face into the floor and screamed as another landed dead on his back, and exploded into smoke. He shook from head to foot afraid to look until he heard the familiar screams of his daughter. "Oh.... Baby girl."

He looked up to see Blades spin into the air, she leapt at least ten feet and as she spun like the queen of the ballet, her blades came slicing round like a shredder. Bodies fell out of the air like rain as she landed with the grace of a cat her blades glinting red on gold. Robbie watched with awe. "Hell, she is something special Rune." Rune nodded lost for words at first.

"Scarlet admired her; there is nothing else to say."

Harry saw his precious daughter, and he woke from his fear. She was the most valuable thing in his life, and he jumped from the floor and ran towards her. Keith screamed from the edge of the wall. "They are coming in to land." Robbie dropped his bow by his foot and stood up. Destiny gleamed as Harry's blades slid out next to his daughter and the Specialists rose to fight.

The Sword of Knowledge ignited in Rune's hand as she moved to Robbie's side, Crystal, and Maddy lifted their bows, as Sting and Wolfie joined the ranks with their swords. The Darkmares hit the floor and came fast with their swords in the air; they tugged at their masks and revealed their hideous faces that brought instant torment to some of the fighters. Harry wailed across the field as the green evils headed towards him.

Robbie stepped into the face of a dying Rune, and with anger, he sliced off the head. In his mind, he knew they would not win him, and he cut up fast as he sliced hard through the slashed face of Iona. Everyone he faced as he ignored the grotesque features, as he pictured the Dark One, he forced his mind to bend to his will, and cut and sliced the woman who wanted to kill his wife a thousand times. No one had ever seen him fight with such power; there was no nightmare in her control which could defeat him. He knew his dream was safe, he was not going to die and he was going to win, for the first time since he had taken on the mantle of hooded man, Robbie knew and accepted his destiny fully. The doubts were replaced with courage and a determination to force her into a corner and kill her.

By his side with the sword of burning knowledge, Rune clenched her teeth as her eyes burned violet, and she sliced and cut her way through. She too was fixed on Robbie's thoughts, and saw how he overcame the nightmares of his eyes, to defeat the Dark One's men. She felt his power of mind and power of his spirit; Rune could feel all the doubt leaving him as he waded into the thick of the fight. Almost in a second something inside him had flicked on like a light switch, and the boy of eighteen who had faced so much pain and anguish in the past two years stepped forward as a true man of his father's line. In the back of his mind, two sets of eyes burned brightly, one blue and one violet, and she realised that Robbie's dream was his family.

To live in the wood with the woman he loved, and the children were all he wanted and all he desired. It was so simple to see, and yet the Dark One and her brood threatened to take it away. Rune felt the surge of power of it in him, as he focused his mind on the good in his life and defeated his enemy. The hooded man faced an army on two fronts of overwhelming power, and yet she knew as she fought beside him, they could not win; the power of his dream of a life was so overpowering it could match the Violetlines. He staggered into the seawater and stopped as he gasped for breath; he turned around and looked back at the trail of dead that was exploding into smoke. He was covered in blood and fragments of bone; he looked to his side and smiled. "Hey beautiful, I am tired." She smiled at him as he looked back up at the others fighting. "Two seconds and then we go back in." Robbie breathed hard and caught his breath as Jett and Rafe gasped by his side.

He looked up at Rune, and winked. "I know how to kill le Fey." He swiped his sword in the water to clean it, and stood up. "People this land belongs to my daughter, and is sacred to Loxley, let's throw these vile bastards off it." He lifted his sword, and walked out of the water toward the masses of black that still fought with his men.

Harry fought back to back with Blades, their swords swirling in tandem, doing more damage than a combined harvester, nothing got near without being shredded. Harry squealed and chanted each time a mask lifted off the face of a Darkmare. Maggs dragged out the injured with Melissa to the walls of the abbey, where they helped Alice tend to their wounds. Jay covered them with Judy and Steph as Smokes and Big John defended with swords. Keith and Saff now stood high on a wall with Fish and Mel, as they fired volley after volley into the faces of the oncoming Darkmares.

Bear stood by Jasper with large swords, Bear also swung his axe and they worked like a steamroller pounding and mincing the Darkmares into the floor. Amethyst and Woody stood together, and as Woody pounded the Darkmares with his shepherds crook, he smacked them into the crashing blows of Amethysts close quarters sword. Una prowled with Crystal who looked for tight groups, she fired her silver arrows and froze large groups at once. They were not sure if it killed them, they just knew it stopped them.

Large groups of flames would suddenly ignite as Maddy hit one and took out twenty. Bowmen huddled in groups and fired strikers into the large numbers that tried to swarm into the sky; they would lift into the air only to explode into millions of pieces. The guards of the silver line were deadly as they hit everything they aimed at. Robbie was quite impressed as he stopped to wipe his face of sweat.

How many they faced no one really knew. The fight lasted for three hours and they hardly stopped once, their enemy knew no fear as the Dark One drove them on. It was a fight to the last man, as some of the bowmen had collapsed in corners having faced the horror of their own nightmares, Sting danced and screamed as she fought towards Blades and the last groups of the Darkmares, Blades swung with tired arms and still was deadly accurate, as she sliced her way to her best friend.

They met with a force of devastation like two twisters merging as one, and they spun together at the final mass, which tore off their masks and saw Sting and Blades faces. It was a long final whoop and a scream, from the lower end of the field that marked the end of the fight. Everyone slumped on to the grass, and gasped with relief. They were hot and sweaty and exhausted. Blades put her arm round Jett and they walked back across the field with an exhausted look on their blood splattered face's

Robbie sat down in the shade next to Rune, against the cool wall of the Abbey. He slipped off his empty quiver and dropped it on the floor, and unclipped his cloak. He hung his head down between his legs as he breathed hard, Rune rubbed his shoulder and he moaned with relief, he sat back and leaned on the wall. As he looked at her she smiled at his dirty face and touched the tip of his nose. "You know Mrs Loxley, I really do love you." She gave a giggle.

"Go get your own water I am as tired as you are." He started to laugh.

"You know my sweet; I do believe that you do know stuff." Rune giggled at him.

"I know you are everything to me."

"All right I will get the water." Rune laughed as he got up moaning, and walked over toward Maggs who held a dozen bottles of lemon grass cooler, which Crystal had cooled. "Maggs you are a true wonder."

"Oh Robbie, sweetheart, you are so lovely, here you go my darling." He took the two bottles and bowed, she gave a horsey laugh as her teeth dropped down her lip, and he walked back to Rune and passed her a cold drink. He loosened the laces of his shirt and pulled it out of his trousers. He flopped back down beside Rune and lifted the cool drink to his lips.

"I wonder what she will throw at us next?" He wiped the damp hair out of his face.

"I am not sure Rob, the dragons died out before they ever really got established so we are safe there." Robbie looked at her.

"I thought dragons were just a myth, did they really exist?" Rune took a large gulp and then smiled.

"Don't be silly, I am just having some fun. They got too well established; poor George had a hell of a job sorting them out." She started to laugh at his stunned face and leaned over and kissed him. "You are funny at times."

Amethyst and Blades dropped their weapons and ran past them. They headed down the slope and ran splashing into the sea; Robbie looked at Rune and gave a big smile. "Oh no not again... Rob I mean it I will use magic... Robbie put me down... Rob no." Rune screamed in his arms as he headed to the water, with an almighty splash she squealed. He came up out of the water and pulled her close, she giggled in his arms as he kissed her.

Very few made it past the poles, which were now piled high with the dead. The battle for York had raged all day and everyone was hot and feeling the strain. Rowan felt the tempo drop and knew now was the time. As the forces of the dark army struggled to move forward, the barrels were pushed over and the moonshine and oil mix flowed towards them.

The last line of bowmen fired one huge volley of arrows taking out most of those who had struggled to the tops of the mounds of the dead and stepped back loading wadded arrows. The fuses of the violet bombs were lit, and as the army of the woodsmen pulled back, the flaming arrows hit the rise of the hill that had been the outpost of the woodsmen army for eight months. The flames roared into the air in a two mile line of fire, and Rowan called everyone back to York. The men piled into the carts, which moved at high speed out of the headquarters, and on to the ten mile road back to York. Rowan sat with Jade on the last cart and watched as the horizon burned. The explosions lifted into the air and all traces of the woodsmen camp was obliterated.

Mason Knox had won nothing; he was lord of a land of flattened heather and dead black clad soldiers. Hundreds of thousands had raged across the moors and got caught in lack of space. The meticulous planning of Scarlet had proven she was without doubt the best. Her bombs and her spikes and her ability to judge the enemy had won the day.

The realm of the woodsmen had paid a high price, the cost of life was high and the wounded was higher than any expected as the House of Good Hope filled quickly. The barracks at Loxley was full, and an army of nurses at York treated the walking wounded. It had been a hard and long bloody day for the realm of the woodsmen; no area of the country controlled now by Robbie was unaffected.

Rowan felt pride at the power and resolve of such a highly outnumbered group, the war for York and Loxley now faced phase two. They would head into the trees and fight a war that they knew gave them the upper hand. The might of stone would come face to face with the power of nature, this was going to be a long war and Rowan bowed his head exhausted. He would have some time of rest, as he knew that the black army would not understand the withdrawal.

The road to York was paved with surprises, and it would be at least a week before they hit the trees. A week in which everyone could rest, the troops of the front line all now moved to the back and fresh eyes and arms would guard the woodland Rune had created round York. Jade cuddled round Rowan as he slid into her arms and enjoyed the feeling of her close again; she was all he needed for recovery.

Treen sat and smiled as she thought of Skip in the safety of York, and although tired and exhausted she was looking forward to some time off. Rowan opened one eye and looked up at her. "You did a wonderful job up there today Treen." He turned and looked at Claire with her dirty face and tattered flag. "You too Claire, both of you was extremely brave, I was proud to fight beside you."

Claire looked down embarrassed, and Treen lifted an arm and pulled her close. "I think we should ave a hot bath and then ow about a big party?" Everyone looked up exhausted, as she gave a big smile. "I ave never been really drunk, it eez tradition is it no?" Rowan began to giggle as the others all laughed at her bright smiling face covered in mud, blood and bits of heather.

Jade looked round at everyone in the cart. "Hey I am up for it." Rowan closed his eyes; the cart trundled on down the long road towards the trees, and the new forest of York. Bowmen saluted the front line troops as they passed; most of them were already asleep.

Rune walked with her grandfather along the long green grassy slope as the sun sunk slowly over the island of Iona. The guards all watched in pairs quietly situated round the abbey. He rested his arm on her shoulder as she told him of her time in the hidden realm with Opal. His tired old eyes seemed saddened as he thought of his wife. "We knew back then she was interested in the realm, Opal bless her, she was right. You have done well Runestone; you have many of her qualities, and you have shown greater wisdom than even I thought possible."

Rune gave a slight smile at the compliment form her grandfather. "I will have to go after her. If she is in that realm I will have to go in there again and stop her." Merlin seemed to ponder the point.

"I am not sure that you will to be honest... The castle at Dunnottar is her passage between realms, maybe that would be the best way to defeat her. Simply lock her in, and hide the keys." He gave a small chuckle.

"But won't she just find another way out?"

"I think she will, but that for the moment is not the point." Merlin stopped and looked up at the old abbey; he gave the point some consideration and then looked down into the bright blue eyes of his granddaughter. "Runestone my child, Robbie needs a little more time, he has come so far and yet there is still some difficult road ahead of him. Put le Fey in her prison and you will hinder her son, and that will give you the time you need to find the king."

"Grandfather why can you not just tell him where to look? Mum has spent weeks now decoding the diaries; they all run to a dead end." Merlin took a long breath and shook his head.

"The simple truth my dear child is I have no idea where to look. I was not part of their protection; I was never really meant to know. You see I was the first to suffer when Morgan le Fey attacked, she could not risk being caught by me and so she set a trap. I was imprisoned already when Arthur returned to Guinevere. None of us saw that night coming, it was Sian who understood the full meaning of what had happened, and after Arthur died, it was Sian who took her to safety. I stumbled on to the documents whilst looking for something completely different. I know all the names, dates and places of birth, what I do not know is where any of them were hidden, all I know is that any who were involved were all sworn to secrecy, never to reveal the knowledge until they were given a sign. I am sorry; I was working at Oxford and hidden from the green and spirit realm. I had no contact not even with Opal. I was forced to hide and in doing so I worked side by side with the man who is now your enemy."

Rune felt yet more frustration; she had thought that her grandfather had known of the king's identity, and her heart sunk. "I don't suppose you know what this sign is?"

"I haven't a clue." She breathed a sigh.

"We seem to be moving along really well, and then everything slips back to the king and we see we are no nearer."

"I think you are nearer than you think, when you fill a bottle with water at what point does it become full? Sometimes my dearest granddaughter it looks full, but you need just one more drop." He smiled at her. "I think we need to find that drop." She smiled up at her grandfather and he turned and pulled her into a warm embrace. "You need to rest, go to Robbie and your children. I still have many tasks of my own to attend to, and I need some time alone to think. You have shown me some brilliance of mind today, and I need now to look at many past matters. Sometimes Runestone my child we look at things but we do not see them." He gave her a kiss on the head and released her. "Go on go to Robbie."

Rune ran across the grass as her grandfather watched, he felt a great happiness for her and he turned and looked at the sea. "Now where was I? Oh yes Mason."

Rune closed the door quietly, and smiled at her two children wrapped up snug in their cribs. She quietly slipped off her dress and crossed to the bed where Robbie lay fast asleep. Gently she lifted the covers and slipped in beside him, she snuggled close and he moved almost out of instinct as he slid his arm round her and pulled her close. Rune snuggled up with her head on his shoulder and watched him sleep. She smiled and softly stroked back his long brown hair, he gave a grunt in his sleep and she tried to stifle her giggles.

Merlin sat alone and remembered his life as the historian Leenard Rimmer, there had been so many occasions where he had sat with his friend and fellow researcher Mason. How had it all come to this? Mason had always been a little hard, but in most things, he had been good natured and quick to laugh. The pictures of his young friend with bright blue eyes, curly short blonde hair, flowed through his mind. There had been so many times when both of them had found some relevant document in the archives of a church or University, and Mason had laughingly slapped him on the back in excitement.

The time of the small church at Edwinstowe in 1979 came into his mind. Leenard looked up from the book and gave a smile. "You know what this proves don't you my young friend? Mason leaned over, and looked at the entry in the book he gave a smile.

"My god Leen, you have done it." He sat with a bump, his eyes bright blue as he smiled. "You have found the missing piece of your puzzle after all these years, you deserve it my friend, this must be worth at least one book."

Leenard leant back and rubbed his eyes. "I always knew the myth had to have some truth; little did I know that all of it is true. Oh, Mason finally my search is over. Robert of Loxley was real, and this proves he married Marion." Mason leaned forward and slapped his knee.

"Well my good friend, you owe me a pint, we will need copies of course, and then we can head off back to Oxford, and put every document together and, you can write that book at last. I am delighted, right I will have a chat with the old vicar and see if we can borrow the book to copy, I will meet you at the car."

He walked with a smile up the stairs and out of the old vault, Leenard smiled as he slipped a piece of his note paper into the old red leather bound register of marriages and then began to lift the other books on to the shelf. A thin piece of parchment fluttered out of the back and on to the floor. He placed the book on the shelf and stooped down to lift the sheet. The Celtic text was instantly recognisable.

Be warned lords of the realm that in days to come the land will burn red and your people will die.

Then will the snake grow legs and wings, and come forth to you with offers and treaties, and he will covert his true plan to unseat you. Your people will start to die again.

He will poison the land and rid the world of the green one, and in doing so destroy everything.

Gather the swords of the heirs of this land, and bring them to the daughters of the woods, for there is the only hope of saving what is important, and the true swords man of your land will fight again to restore the balance of power.

Look for the bowman for he will lead them together and forge anew a world that will be truly for earth and man.

Heed my words for if you stray away from them the world is doomed.

Leenard read it twice, and then looked at the bottom of the text, Tp. Rhiannon GOA 516 was written in faint ink. He stared at the paper and thought; he had seen those initials before, he thought deeply and then without thinking he slipped it into his bag.

Mason was leaning against the black Ford smoking a cigarette, when Leenard came out of the old church. He opened the car door and leaned over the window. "Come on we can be back at the digs in time for the pubs opening. This is worthy of celebration." He smiled at Mason and walked round to the passenger door; he saw the sheet of paper on the seat and threw his bag on to the back seat.

"What's this?" Mason smiled as he puffed on his cigarette.

"It is a copy my old friend, it seems like you are not alone in your quest. Some fellow called Moore's was up here a few months back with his son. The vicar had a few extra copies made as he was not even aware that the virtuous Maid Marion was married here." He gave a big grin as he shifted the gear stick, and the car trundled down the grit track and out on to the road.

Leenard knew the initials and it bothered him, his mind kept flowing back to them as they drove through the tree lined roads of Sherwood, and headed south back to the large Hotel..

"Do you remember anyone from about 516 with the initials GOA?" Mason gave a chuckle.

"Only that old fraud Geoffrey of Almesbury, why?"

"It's nothing really just some text I read recently, and I could not remember the initials."

"To be honest old man, I wouldn't let that bother you; he was that old monk who wrote about Arthur. He reckoned he was really Sir Percival and he met a woman in white at the lakeside after the king had been carried off to Avalon. You must remember it; she told him Arthur had a son who would one day have an heir who will come back and be crowned the true king of England. Throw these Germans we have now out he will." He gave a laugh as he looked across at Leenard. "I laughed when his papers came to light and caused havoc at the time, you must remember it?" Leenard thought back.

"He was the one who made the prediction that a bowman would lead the way of a new world. Hey, you never know it could be your bowman, maybe Robin Hood will come back and we will find the king. I keep telling you old man, I am the king of the Briton's. When you go to Loxley you will have to tell them I have been waiting for years for them."

Mason laughed as he drew another cigarette out of his packet, and drove down the long lane lined with trees. Leenard sat back in his seat and thought about the name Rhiannon. It was a name he knew well, how had he missed such an important piece of his jigsaw, and how much more about Arthur did Mason know? He had always shared his facts with Mason, and yet he felt this parchment should be kept secret, he looked at the smiling face beside him, puffing away as the car bumped down the lane. Suddenly Leenard felt a cold tingle run down his spine.

Mason had used a curious turn of phrase, Leenard did remember the event it was in 1939. Mason did look about mid forties, but what five year old would remember such an isolated event in the scholastic world. It brought a strange sensation he had not felt in a very long time to his heart, Leenard suddenly felt very suspicious of his friend and fellow researcher from Oxford.

The sea swept up the bank and Merlin came out of his thoughts. It was very dark and the seagulls had quietened down for the night. The guards stood vigilant as he walked slowly back to the Abbey, it appeared now that Mason had known about the bowman a lot sooner than he had realised. Being veiled for so long had been a mistake, Merlin now realised why Mason had got such a foothold. Merlin should have revealed himself a lot sooner, he would have to return to Caerleon and consult the books again, as there was something he had missed or forgotten, a talk with a friend on route might not be that bad an idea; there was a king to find now. Merlin walked into the Abbey and decided that a night's rest first might just clear his thoughts, the force of the Violetlines had been very powerful and he felt tired and weary. "Oh age can be such a curse."

Robbie sat up and scratched his head; he blinked his eyes as Alice smiled sat feeding Iona out of a bottle. He stared at her. "Why isn't Rune breast feeding?" Alice smiled.

"She is, I sent a breast pump with Melissa so that the children could be fed while Rune was asleep."

He was not altogether sure what that entailed, he was just glad it was Rune's milk in the bottle. He looked down at her fast asleep beside him, then lay flat on the pillow and stretched. "Oh Hearne I ache."

"I could give you a massage later if you want." Alice giggled. "Or maybe Rune could?" He smiled at Alice as she placed Iona on her shoulder, and gently patted her back. "It's nice to see her back again, we were all worried for a while." He stroked the long red hair down her white back.

"She is lucky that we found her, none of us would have got back otherwise." Alice lay Iona in her crib and gently tucked her in.

"Oh Rob, she is so beautiful, Ok they are clean and fed, it's still early, you should try and get a little more sleep, it could be a busy day." He yawned and nodded as Alice slipped out of the door. He lay down and kissed Rune's back, she moved a little as he kissed up to her shoulder. A faint happy moan came from under her hair as she moved softly on the bed. He smiled and moved down her shoulder on to her neck, Rune made happy little whimpers and then rolled over. He stroked back her hair as she blinked in the pale light. "Hey beautiful." She smiled

"Hi gorgeous." He winked.

"The children are fed and asleep and it's very early." She gave a giggle as she lifted her arms up round his neck and pulled him down into a kiss.

"I feel very awake Rob."

"Good." She gave a happy giggle.

The Sage stood on the edge of the circle deep within the hidden realm; he gave a bow to Opal. "I must return My Lady, dawn is almost upon us." She nodded as she walked across to him. Opal linked his arm as she turned into the trees.

"You must now work hard my Green One, remember what I have said. His realm of stone is propped up on just a few blocks of loyalty. Spread the word of the green realm and bring the truth to the realm of concrete and stone. The hooded man needs everyone now to play their part, the south is sealed and no one can get inside, you and your friends are all that the hooded man has in there. Merlin will find you and help you; he will travel south to the seat of my family, then on to his home."

The Sage nodded to her as he walked into the trees. "I will do all I can to help." She smiled at him.

"You have done well my green friend. My father always had faith in you, I am sorry I did not see it back then. It is a long road you have travelled to find the fine path of truth, take my blessing and go with speed. Look to the coming of the lights and you will know the time is near, dreams of freedom are numerous in this realm and they will soon start to drift into yours."

The Sage bowed and ran into the trees with his small companion, as he did so he faded from sight and was gone back to the realm of the hooded man. His eyes opened and he smiled as Ben stared at him.

"What's it like?" He gave a chuckle.

"Well my young apprentice, it feels like sleeping on a cloud. You close your eyes and you walk in a forest filled with light. The pictures come and you do your best to understand them." Ben smiled.

"It sounds nice." The Sage sat up by the fire, and poured a hot coffee into his cup.

"It can be, sometimes you see things that you want and you know you cannot have them, which can be hard. Other times you see bad things that will happen; when I come back, I try to prevent them. It is a good feeling knowing you have stopped a wrongdoing. All we can do in this world Ben is to try and cut out the bad things and replace them with good."

Markus opened his eyes and smiled at the scene of the Sage trying to answer a question and provide an education. He had spent only a short time with the small group of friends, and yet he had learned a great deal and felt more alive than ever before. He closed his eyes and listened to the endless questions of Ben.

CHAPTER TWENTY FIVE

HIDDEN DRAGONS

Breakfast was at the white cottage as Mel and Steph, cooked everyone a hearty breakfast of fried eggs sausages and tomatoes. Robbie and Rune had small pouches on, in which their children hung in front of them as they walked hand in hand towards the cottage. Harry smiled as he sat on the wall with his plate next to Fish, eating and keeping watch. He waved as Maggs came out with two huge mugs of coffee; she placed them on the wall next to Harry and Fish, and gave a big bucked teeth smile as Robbie and Rune came through the gate into the cottage yard.

"Good morrow my chickens, Oh are they not just the most beautiful and most cosmic children ever, how groovy." Rune beamed as Maggs looked down on the children in their snug little pouches. "Oh Rune darling you must let me make them little clothes to wear, I just get all herbal and cosmic making little things." Rune gave a smile.

"That would be really sweet of you Maggs thank you." Robbie gave a stifled titter as he saw the look on Rune's face. He knew she could just picture his children in matching tie dyed clothes. Maggs turned towards the door. "Come along my sweets we have plenty of food and you both will need all your strength, raising children can really sap your vibes." Rune giggled as Robbie nudged her.

"Come chicken, our vibes is wilted."

"Robbie shush!" She giggled as they headed to the door.

The plates were piled high as the group sat round in the crowded kitchen chatting happily, in the living room through the open door, Blades and Judy giggled with Will, Gaynor and Jay, as they ate their breakfasts on the comfy chairs. Steph lifted Hal off Rune and held him in her arms, and Una cradled Iona. Robbie felt a surge of happiness as he sat with a full plate. He felt starving and tucked in, Rune smiled as she looked at the room filled with her family and friends, Steph sat beside Rune as everyone admired the children. She spoke quietly to her daughter and Robbie looked up. "Have you chosen God Parents yet?"

Although the Earth Faith tradition did not really follow any Christian beliefs, one aspect of the ways of old modern man, was to have a small ceremony a week after a birth, and place two life guardians and three God Parents to each child. This made clear to the whole community who would have responsibility in the case of the death of an entire family. One or two in the room heard and everyone looked at Rune; she lowered her fork and looked round the room. "We did want everyone together when we made the announcement." She looked at Robbie who looked up at everyone. Mel smiled.

"It's alright Rune if you don't want to say yet, we know Rowan and Jade will be Guardians." Rune looked at Robbie who smiled. She looked round at everyone and gave an excited smile. "If we tell, you must promise us that you will not breathe a word until we can tell the others who are missing, it would not be fair and it would spoil the surprise."

Everyone nodded excitedly. "We promise." Rune gave a giggle.

"Alright then yes, we would like Rowan and Jade to be the guardians of Halbert. We would like you Una to be one of his God Mothers." Una's eyes filled with tears and Mel pulled her into a hug. Rune lifted her hand and squeezed Una's. "You have been so important to us Una, the heir to the hooded realm needs a protector." She smiled as she wept.

"Oh Rune, Robbie, you have no idea how much it means, I love you both so much." Robbie smiled and nodded at her.

"It is why we know you will be there if anything happens to us." Robbie looked across the table. "I would like it very much if you would also be a god mother to my son Sapphire." She stood in the corner and looked white; her blue eyes shone as Keith pulled her close.

"I... would ...feel honoured Robbie, Rune. I don't know what to say." He smiled as Rune beamed at her.

"Say yes." Sapphire filled up.

"Yes I would love to." Everyone gave a giggle; Rune looked up at every one.

"We are going to ask Brandon to be Hal's godfather." Everyone shook their heads in approval, and Rune grinned as she looked across at Bear and Alice. "Will you two be god parents to Iona?" Alice squealed with delight and hugged Bear; he sat with a huge proud face and small tears in his eyes.

"I would be honoured and proud My Lord and Lady." Everyone giggled, Rune got up out of her seat and walked through into the other room, and everyone watched as she knelt down and looked at Judy. "Robbie and I would be honoured if you too would be a god parent to our daughter Judy."

Judy looked quietly down as her eyes filled with tears. "I cannot believe you would ask me." Rune smiled and took her hands in hers.

"Robbie and I see a very kind and loving person, who has a very big heart filled with the most beautiful love. Why would we not want that person to guide and protect our very special daughter?"

Her tears fell on the floor as she wept. "But I am his daughter, my name is Knox." Rune pulled Judy into a hug, as she wept on Rune's shoulder, she held her close.

"You are not a Knox; I see only the qualities of a Hargreaves. I see the love of a woman called Zandra, I am Runestone centre of all circles and the bringer of life, and do you honestly think I cannot see beauty in a person? I am the most powerful sorceress alive, and I am asking a friend that I love to watch over my daughter if the need arises."

Judy looked up from the shoulder of Rune and everyone smiled and nodded at her. Rune released her and looked into her eyes. "Will you do this for Robbie and me Judy?" Judy gave a sniffle and nodded.

"It would be the greatest honour I have ever had." Rune smiled and kissed her wet cheek.

"No more tears now, we all love you here Judy, you are one of us." Every one nodded at her and she smiled.

"I love my life with all of you." Robbie smiled and winked at her, she gave a little giggle. Blades pulled her over into a hug. Jett looked round as Rune walked into the kitchen.

"So, who are the guardians of Iona? Rowan and Jade?" Robbie gave a grin and gave a laugh.

"Who do you think?" Rune smiled at Jett. Jett looked at Robbie and then Rune and she gave a big smile.

"Oh don't tease, no one in their right mind would ask me." Rune looked at Robbie and smiled.

"Told you she would not believe you." She looked back at Jett and up at Rafe. "I think a Sting and a Wolfman would be ideal to protect the Queen of Fae." Rafe smiled, he was lost for words as Jett stared up at him. He looked at Robbie.

"My Lord honours me deeply, I am lost for words." Jett giggled

"No way Wolfie they are having us on." He nodded slowly to her and she looked back at the beaming Rune who nodded her head. Jett's voice went very high and squeaky as she realised and looked at Robbie.

"You know I would die to protect her don't you?" He smiled; she looked at Rune "If you really mean it I would you know?" Rune opened her arms and Jett fell to her knees and threw her arms round Rune.

"We know you would do anything to keep her safe my wild cousin. I will be happy knowing that my daughter will have the best protection ever from two of our top Specialists." Jett held her tight and hid her tears in Rune's shoulder. Robbie raised a hand and shook Rafe's.

"Congratulations Commander." Everyone patted his back as he beamed with delight.

"I feel I should howl." Jett giggled in Rune's shoulder.

It was a very happy group, which sat in the sun as they waited for Robbie who sat with Gwynfor by the Abbey wall. "I would love to be able to spend more time with you; there are so many things I want to talk to you about. Will you not come back to Loxley for a while and stay with me?"

Gwynfor patted Robbie on the knee. "There is still much to do here my young Robert, but I promise I will spend the feast of Samhain with you and help celebrate that lovely wife of yours birthday." He smiled. Robbie gave him a hug.

"I will really look forward to that." The old man smiled up at Robbie as he bowed to the old Celt, and turned and walked toward his smiling team. Rune hugged Rhiannon and then her grandfather. "Take care of yourself and help Philip; he will be lost without Scarlet. Please do not stay away too long this time, I miss you." He held her tight.

"I will be around, you will see. Look after your children my precious Runestone Sapphire. You know what to do if you need me." Sapphire opened her window and Isolde and Filomena carried the children through into Loxley followed by Alice and Steph. The window closed as Rune's violet arch opened and she took Robbie by the hand and walked through into the large rooms at York.

Rowan pulled Robbie into a close hug, as Brett and Sebastian hugged Bear. Rowan stood back and smiled a huge smile. "I am happy to see you both safe." Rune pulled him into a hug.

Brandon was lost for words as Treen chuckled with delight when Robbie and Rune asked him to be a godparent to their son. It was clear to see the deep impact it had on him, and Robbie gave him a huge hug. "I have so many things I want to thank you for Skip; you are truly a good friend." Treen just exploded with excitement and hugged both of them and then Rune.

Jade went very quiet, and then burst into tears as Robbie held her in his arms. He knew how much it would mean to her to be the guardian of his son, and he talked quietly, of how special it would be to him and Rune as she wept in his arms.

Sebastian was filled with joy, and sorry he had missed the children. He congratulated Rune and Robbie, and insisted that he open several bottles of champagne to toast the children. Everyone was handed the finest cigars made from the leaves that Joe grew, and rolled by the last tobacconist in Britain, which so happened to have a little shop in York. Rune and Jade screamed with laughter, as Rowan and Robbie turned green, and coughed and choked, slapping each other on the back.

There was a large meal prepared and everyone sat down in happy spirits and ate together. The wine flowed and the food was very tasty, Sebastian assured everyone the days of bland food at York were over, Rune giggled.

It was mid afternoon as Lord Loxley and General Loxley, walked along the north wall of the city of York. They stood above the north gate and looked past the rows of tents to the tree line of the woodland that would be their last defence of the city. "We have paid a high price Rowan; we have a lot of badly wounded men." Rowan patted his shoulder.

"We always knew casualties would be high if he sent out a large force." Robbie looked out at the line of green.

"We have the trees above our heads now, which will help. It has taken a lot of courage this year my brother. The men of the woodland realm have fought hard battles, it will not get easier."

"They fight for a man of true honour Robbie; you should have seen them when I told them they fought for Loxley and their lord. I have never seen such pride in the faces of men. You have the force of half this country behind you, have faith in them."

Robbie stood and looked at his friend. "I am tired Rowan; I feel such exhaustion it has been hard these past months." Rowan smiled and gripped his shoulders.

"We are all tired and have a few days to rest... We are prepared and have the very best of Loxley here to command, let them take the strain and go home and rest. We will be fine Robbie, you will see."

Robbie gave a long sigh and patted his friend on the shoulder as he smiled. "I am glad you are back at my side Rowan, I missed you." He gave a smile.

"I am glad to hear it; maybe next time you decide to slip off, you will remember that." Robbie chuckled and nodded; he knew it was an argument he would never win. Rune stood with Jade as they watched their two husbands up on the ramparts, they could see the love and closeness that was the bond between them. Rune smiled as she watched Robbie laugh with Rowan, as they came down the steps and crossed the old roadway towards them.

The group all assembled and with Rune's window shimmering they all trooped back into the Farm at Loxley. They all made their way for their time off to their homes and Jess pulled the cart round and drove Robbie and Rune back to the mere. They dropped off Jade and Rowan, and swung the cart on to the old track through the woods and up to the front gate of the wooden house. It was nice to be home again and have the quietness of the woods. Jess and Rune went up to the nursery and Robbie walked into his bedroom. He slipped into bed and lay back as the year took its toll, his eyes closed and he was asleep in minutes as the worry and long nights finally caught up with him. Phase two of a long war would be planned and organised, and the search for a king would continue. That would come soon enough, for the moment he would just sleep.

Robbie slept for most of the following day. Rune got up, and fed the children and left him to sleep. It was late afternoon when he came down the stairs in his shirt and thin green trousers. He sat out under the canopy on the chairs as he watched the heavy rain and relaxed in the fresh warm air of late June sipping his coffee, Rune and Steph worked on the papers upstairs in the office. Steph looked up as Rune read a parchment, and then scribbled the translation down on her pad; she smiled to herself at the speed at which she translated them. Steph had spent hours copying each sheet carefully into a translated text. Rune looked up at her mum. "I think I have something important here. Steph stopped writing and looked at her.

"What is it darling?" Rune gave a smile.

"This is a letter written in old Celtic; only the paper is quite modern, it's a letter from Sian to a Peter Pendragon. It is dated June first 1964, it is congratulating him on the birth of his grandson Richard."

Steph suddenly looked excited. "What else does it say? I have been looking for a link to him for over a month."

Rune looked down and read the old Celtic. "Oh wow."

"What Rune?"

"Oh yeah that explains a lot."

"Rune will you stop bloody reading it to yourself and let me hear what the bloody thing says." Rune looked up at her mum and smiled.

"Sorry... Mum, Richard Pendragon was the son of William Peter Pendragon who was born in 1936. He married a woman called Petra in Feb 1963. They had a son Richard on June first 1964, the day Sian wrote this letter."

Steph stood up her face white. "Please tell me they had children?"

Rune gave a giggle. "It doesn't say so, but what it does say is the reason he has been unable to find his children, is because Sian and a few of her friends took them into hiding, as an unknown source has been asking a lot of questions about their family line."

Steph nodded. "I have read something else like that; through the fifties and sixties someone was trying to trace them."

"Yeah mum, but that is not the good bit, she also says that in order to hide them from everyone they have christened and registered their son in their mother's maiden name. You know what that means?"

Steph slumped back in her chair with a bump. "Oh no I have to dig through all of this lot again to find a marriage to someone who is not called Pendragon." Rune smiled.

"At least we are closer; we just jumped from 1936 to 1964. Now we know that within at least 30 years of that date we have another generation of Pendragon's." Rune sifted through the pile of untranslated documents, as Steph started to look for marriage dates. She lifted the sheets and looked at them and threw them to one side, as she lifted another and started to read. "This looks interesting, it mentions Petra and her son and his wife, and she is pregnant." Steph beamed a smile.

"A male heir that will be another generation, what is the date." Steph grabbed her pencil and looked back at Rune.

"It's a bit faint but it looks like September 1998." Steph scribbled on her paper and smiled at Rune.

"Darling I love you. That was three years before I was born, you do realise if that son had a child he would have been born after 2012." Rune thought for a moment.

"So that could mean that the heir could be anything up to twenty seven years old." Steph nodded.

"As long as his bum is young enough to fit the throne of England I do not care."

"Oh God Mum." Steph stopped smiling and looked at Rune who was reading an old piece of Celtic text. Rune looked up and had gone a little pale; she stared quietly at her daughter. Rune looked down at the paper and then back again.

"Mum this is a letter from Rhiannon to Opal. It says here that Gwendolyn made two sets of talismans to protect the line of Pendragon. There are two silver lions with diamond eyes, and two golden Pendragon's." She looked at the parchment and then back at her. "Mum, Robbie has one of them." Steph stared at her daughter's stunned face.

Markus moved close to the table as the two grey clad workers smiled nervous smiles at the Sage, as he slid into the corner by the wall opposite them across the table. Markus put down the three large tankards of ale and leaned in to them. "Ok here he is, now tell him what you told me."

Both men looked very nervous, a man in green with a white mask did rather stand out a bit, and for a few seconds everyone in the alehouse looked at them. The man opposite the Sage had a long face with dark scruffy short hair. "We are woodsmen, or at least we were, until the wall came round and they pulled up all the trees." The Sage nodded.

"That is useful to know." The man looked very nervous as he spoke quietly.

"We have to be careful; you know what it is like? Everyone talks in these places and you get picked up and tortured." The Sage nodded.

"I understand what it is like. It is the same in every stone town in this country; you know why I am here so all you have to do is tell me if you can help me. I am sure my large friend here has given you some idea of our quest."

The long faced man leaned even closer. "They call me Pat and this ere is Wilcox. We both still run the local Fellowship of Bowmen." The Sage smiled as he extended his hand.

"It is nice to meet men loyal to Loxley so far south, gents we can help each other I think."

Pat gave a smile. "I hope so Mr Sage because we are sick of the way we get pushed around. We want to get out of here and go back to the trees.”

The Sage looked round as two men walked past, and then looked back at Pat. “I am not interested in getting out of here and going back to the trees. Lord Loxley wants everyone to bring the trees back here within the walls. How would you like to see green here instead of grey?”

Pat looked back and seemed confused. “How the hell can you put the trees back here?”

The Sage gave a knowing smile. “All you need my friend is the right sort of dream, you will be surprised at what you can achieve.” Pat looked at his friend Wilcox and then back at the Sage.

“It all sounds very nice like, but I am not sure you quite understand us. We want to leave here not stay.” The Sage leaned over the table so that he was almost nose to nose.

“Listen to me my friends, leaving is not the answer. There is no longer anywhere left to go; Knox has sealed off most of the country, there is only a small proportion of this country left that is green, and the truth is soon we will not all fit into it. In less than a year most of this country has gone under his slash and burn machines, no my friends leaving is not the answer.”

Pat seemed quite startled as he looked at the Sage and Markus. “Then what is?” Markus leaned forward and looked at the two men.

“We have to stay and fight from the inside. We have to gather together every man and women who is trapped, and use the way of the woodsmen to fight from within. It can be done my friends if you gather together, we can prove it and we can help you.”

Wilcox took a large swig of his ale and looked at Pat. “I reckon they are right, with a bit of back up and some guidance we could fight to get our land back, and put it to the way it should be, I hate what he has gone done to it.” Markus smiled and the Sage held out his hand.

“Gather your people my friend, and I will show you the way to fight Mason Knox.” Wilcox took the hand of the Sage and gave a big smile as he squeezed it. He lifted his pint pot.

“Here is to a bit of trouble, and the hooded man.”

It was almost the evening in Loxley, and the Specialists were relaxing making the most of their time off. In the small bookshop Blades and Todd curled up together next to Jay, Will and Gaynor as they all chatted happily with Rags and Judy. Across the street, Commander Rafe was still in bed with Jett Amber, as they held each other close and talked whilst enjoying the delights of cheese on toast, cooked by Jett.

Harry and Maggs enjoyed a quiet and restful day in the garden. Maggs tended the herb plot whilst Harry and Woody tinkered with an old bike. Alice and Bear walked in the orchard with Jess and Beth, and down by the gates Sapphire sat with Jaz and her mother as they all talked and laughed, as David kept watch over the wall. Fish took Amethyst to White Rock Mere, which was a large hidden lake in Loxley Wood, which Joe had told him about. It was raining hard but they sat in the cave there and had a picnic.

Maddy sat with Una outside the little shop of Trinkets and Trousers, under the wooden roof, and laughed and joked with Smokes and Crystal. Jade curled in Rowan's lap under her porch and listened to the tree of chimes, as Rowan rocked them in their swinging seat. Skip and Treen went for a walk in the rain under her bright orange parasol, and Treen laughed and giggled as Skip talked and joked. It was a time of rest before the next big push.

Rune quietly slipped out on to the porch with a long blue shawl round her shoulders, and smiled as Robbie sat with his feet on the rail asleep. She gently slid on to his lap and curled on to him, and laid her head on his shoulder and cuddled close. His arm came round her and he opened one eye, she smiled and gave a soft giggle.

The rain eased off as the evening started and the sky cleared to a bright blue, the late afternoon sun came out and Robbie relaxed with Rune in his arms and watched the mere reflect the sun and the trees. He watched as the water turned red and yellow, then green, blue and violet. He leaned forward in his chair and Rune disturbed as he looked at the sky. "Wow that is beautiful."

Rune looked up and blinked. The sky above Loxley shone with a thousand different shades of colours, which flowed like rippling curtains of colour and mixed with each other in the sky. Rune slipped off his lap and holding his hand, they walked smiling to the gate and looked up at the sky, as the bands of colours streaked and rippled across all of Loxley. "Oh Robbie isn't it beautiful." Her eyes danced as she looked up, and her face filled with happiness. It was a remarkable sight that lasted for over an hour.

There was a loud scream from inside the house, as Steph bounded down the stairs with her arms filled with paper, she burst out on the porch and looked up at the sky. "Oh wow that is amazing." Her arm flopped to her side holding the papers.

Rune giggled and slid close to Robbie.

"The age of dreams is truly here." She pulled him close and kissed him as Steph stood looking up at the sky in wonder. Robbie looked down at her bright sapphire blue sparkling eyes and smiled as her white cheekbones lifted, and the little flashes of blue seemed to decorate them.

"I love you Runestone, you are my life." She held him tight as she felt the joy inside him and rested her head on his shoulder. She smiled as she saw her mum staring up at the sky.

"What have you found mum?" Steph looked down at her.

"What... oh yeah... Oh god Robbie, Rune, look at this." Rune giggled as her mum came back to excited life again and Steph waved the papers in the air.

"William Peter Pendragon had a son. Richard Pendragon, he had a son and a daughter and from what I can gather, they had children. Rose had a son who is about eighteen to nineteen and Arnold who is the line apparent had a son who is sixteen or seventeen. I am still looking for the birth dates, and of course their names. I have him, I need a few more details but that cannot be too far off." She gave a huge smile at them stood watching from the gate. "I have the king. We almost know who the heir of this land is."

Robbie smiled as he ran up the path and lifted Steph into the air, she screamed with delight as he spun her round, and Rune howled with laughter at the shock on her mother's face. Robbie pulled her into a hug. "That is news I really needed, thanks Steph." She glowed with excitement.

"I realise it's a bit thin on detail, but we are almost there Robbie, I just know I will know shortly. Oh Rob, this is so exciting if we can just find him and seat him we can all have our lives back." He gave her a kiss on the cheek, as Rune slipped her arms round both of them.

It was a tonic to all of them as they watched the sky and laughed and joked. Rune was all giggles when she slipped into bed beside him. He yawned and she looked at him shocked. "How can you be tired you have slept for almost a whole day?" He smiled at her.

"Who says I am tired?" His eyes twinkled as she slid across the bed and lay close to him. Rune gave a soft giggle as he lifted her and pulled her up to him. "Come here beautiful eyes." She rolled over and he looked down on her as she giggled. He kissed her softly and pulled up the blanket. "Remember the night with Harry passed out at your mums?" She gave another giggle.

"Oh yes indeed." He kissed her.

"Wasn't it wonderful?" Rune smiled as he looked down at her

"I thought it was." He smiled.

"I wrote you a letter about it."

"I have never read that."

"I know it was very naughty, I had to get rid of it." She started to laugh.

"What did it say?"

"It's easier to show you." Rune screamed with laughter as he tickled her under the covers and pulled the sheet right over their heads.

On the edge of Hearne's Rock, the tall figure of the Green Lord watched the last of the fading colour fade away in the sky, he smiled to himself as he turned to head back to his cave home. "It was done just in time, they are lucky, the age starts in earnest tonight, and dreams will rule with the new Violetlines, now will be the test of everything, and especially my young sapling." He silently shook his head. "How much more they have to learn; this will not be easy." He entered the coolness of his cave to rest.

Robbie felt very light hearted as he made his way into the village the following day. He dropped Rune off with the children at the farm and headed on foot to the Village Hall. It was its usual hive of activity as Treen and Skip worked with Fuse on the new lay out of all the troops. Mason had not moved forward, he had set up his new camp at the old cave of the woodsmen forces, and looked at his options for the attack of York. Things had changed a lot as his scouts soon found out when they walked into traps or ambushes.

Robbie's delay tactics seemed to be working as the enemy slowed as they tried to get through a land of thick scrub that was riddled with all kinds of traps. They now had the chance to fine tune the defences for the woodland round York, and the borders of Loxley. It was a long busy morning and just after midday, Rune turned up with a new pram that John had made. The Village Hall stopped, as everybody gathered round to see the new children, all the women smiled and complimented Rune on how beautiful her children were as they crowded round her.

The afternoon was spent walking round Loxley as Robbie pushed the pram, and Rune linked his arm and smiled, as everyone stopped to give his or her respects to the children. They came down by the barracks as Alley came out of the door; she waved with a big smile. Robbie had not seen her for a while and he smiled as he waved back. Alley stood in her tight brown leather pants and her flowing lemon top with fluted sleeves and slipped on her black wide brimmed hat. Her dazzling green eyes shone under her long white curly fringe as she saw the pram and squealed with delight. She ran towards them.

"Oh, let me have a look, I have been dying to see them." She peered inside the pram and gasped. "Oh Robbie, oh Rune you are so lucky, are you walking back to the village? I am off to see Jade and Jett; they are trying out the new recruits on the training fields." Alley walked between Robbie and Rune, as they made their way to the footpath, that led behind the barracks toward the field and the Village Hall. Alley talked happily making up for the time since she had last seen them.

"The Convent is doing so well now; Carla seems to have found a whole other lease of life. It has helped having the soldiers around, those who are healing fast have been helping out, and done so many odd jobs about the place you would not recognise it." Rune smiled.

"I must admit Alley you do seem really happy."

"Oh Rune, it is so wonderful. The kids are such a joy to be around, and Sister Carla and the staff are so nice with me. It has been nice being able to pop back here to see mum and Treen, and I really miss Jade and Jett, but when I am here to check on the hospital I always try and see them."

They walked along the fence of the training field and Jett and Jade waved, as they put the new recruits through their paces, Blades was in the thick with Rafe giving tips and advice as they separated out the new groups. One of the new recruits waved to Alley, and she smiled and waved back.

Jett walked down the line, and they all began to fight with their swords, and Rune and Robbie turned and walked on to the grass. Robbie watched the young boy with a silver sword as he fought, he was talented and Robbie was quite impressed with his skill for such a young boy. Alley watched as she saw Robbie admire his skill. "Your little friend has some talent with a blade." She smiled.

"He has done well for his age."

Robbie walked down the field and looked at him, the duelling partners stopped, and he pointed to the boy, the boy looked and Robbie beckoned to him. The boy came running toward him as Rune and Alley caught up with him. The boy gave a bow to Robbie who looked at his sword. "You fight well with a blade; I was greatly impressed." The boy nodded gasping slightly.

"Thank you, My Lord."

"That is a very fine blade you use; may I see it?"

The boy lifted his blade hilt first, and Robbie took it and held it up in his hand. It was a blade of high quality; he turned it slowly in his hand. "This was made by a gifted hand."

"Thank you, My Lord, it was my father's." He looked at Alley and smiled, she gave a happy smile.

Robbie handed him his blade back. "This will serve you well in combat."

"Thank you, My Lord." He bowed again to Robbie and turned. Robbie lifted a hand to his shoulder.

"Wait a moment." The teenage boy turned round and Robbie looked at the slightly unbuttoned shirt. He leaned forward and lifted the golden chain from his neck. The Golden Pendragon glinted in the sunlight as Robbie turned back to Alley. Rune gave a gasp as she saw it, and Robbie looked into the eyes of Alley, who now looked very nervous.

"Robbie I was going to see you today in private."

"You knew?"

The coming of the golden age, with a golden crown is upon you.

When the Bowman stands in a ring of trees with the white rose.

You will know the age of dreams is now upon you.

Good deeds from honourable men should be well received.

For within those deeds, lie the real truth.

Look to the north and the curtain of lights.

For it is at that time the king shall be known.

Cross the water and recover from the men of green.

The last standard of a king known from days of old,

In the moment of great glory, Avalon will return to this fair realm.

(The prophecy of Opal Green Circle)

More Author's
From
Violet Circle Publishing

Mike Beale. (Children's Book)

Crumble's Adventures.
ISBN: 978-1-910299-06-7
Digital ISBN: 978-1-910299-08-1

Colin Smith (Play)

Heaven knows I'm Miserable Now
ISBN: 978-1-910299-16-6
Digital ISBN: 978-1-910299-23-4

Ted Morgan. (Poetry and verse)

Wordsmith's Wanderings.
ISBN: 978-1-910299-04-3
Digital ISBN: 978-1-910299-09-8
Peregrinations of the Wordsmith
ISBN: 978-1-910299-18-0
Digital ISBN: 978-1-910299-21-0
Silhouette Soldiers
ISBN: 978-1-910299-19-7
Digital ISBN: 978-1-910299-22-7
A Menu of Memories
Digital ISBN: 978-1-910299-32-6
Digital ISBN: 978-1-910299-33-3

Robin John Morgan. (Fiction/Fantasy/Slice of Life)

Heirs to the Kingdom.

Book One, The Bowman of Loxley.
ISBN: 978-1-910299-00-5
Digital ISBN: 978-1-910299-10-4
Book Two, The Lost Sword of Carnac.
ISBN: 978-1-910299-01-2
Digital ISBN: 978-1-910299-11-1
Book Three, The Darkness of Dunnottar.
ISBN: 978-1-910299-02-9
Digital ISBN: 978-1-910299-12-8
Book Four, Queen of the Violet Isle.
ISBN: 978-1-910299-03-6
Digital ISBN: 978-1-910299-13-5
Book Five, Crystals of the Mirrored Waters.
ISBN: 978-1-910299-05-0
Digital ISBN: 978-1-910299-14-2
Book Six, Last Arrow of the Woodland Realm.
ISBN: 978-1-910299-07-4
Digital ISBN: 978-1-910299-15-9
Book Seven, Bridge Of Sequana.
ISBN: 978-1-910299-17-3
Digital ISBN: 978-1-910299-20-3
Book Eight, The Circle of Darkness.
ISBN: 978-1-910299-26-5
Digital ISBN: 978-1-910299-29-6

The Curio Chronicles.

Part One, Abigail's Summer.
ISBN: 978-1-910299-27-2
Part Two, Curio's Summer.
ISBN: 978-1-910299-34-0
Digital ISBN: 978-1-910299-35-7
Part Three, Curio's Christmas.
ISBN: 978-1-910299-38-8
Digital ISBN: 978-1-910299-39-5

Other Works.

Rise Of The Raven
ISBN: 978-1-910299-30-2
Digital ISBN: 978-1-910299-31-9
The Countess Of Darkness
ISBN: 978-1-910299-40-1
Digital ISBN: 978-1-910299-41-8

Han's Cottage.
ISBN: 978-1-910299-36-4
Digital ISBN: 978-1-910299-37-1

Find out more about our authors and their books at
www.violetcirclepublishing.co.uk